THE COLLECTED GHOST STORIES E. F. BENSON

THE COLLECTED GHOST STORIES OF E. F. BENSON

Edited by Richard Dalby

CARROLL & GRAF PUBLISHERS
New York

Carroll & Graf Publishers
An imprint of Avalon Publishing Group, Inc.
161 William Street
New York
NY 10038 2607
www.carrollandgraf.com

First published in the UK by Robinson Publishing

First Carroll & Graf edition 2001

ISBN 0-7867-0980-4

Printed and bound in the EU

Library of Congress Cataloging-in-Publication Data is available on file.

Contents

Foreword

I first came to E.F. Benson's ghost stories when I was around six years old, and beginning to pick about and choose my own reading-matter from our family's vast and miscellaneous houseful of books. *Spook Stories*, the collection I read, came out in 1928, and was the property of my brother John, who had actually played chess with the old boy when we lived in Mermaid Street, Rye, and Benson was up at the top of the hill in Lamb House.

I had already read *Ghost Stories of an Antiquary* by M.R. James, and nearly died of delicious terror at "Oh Whistle and I'll Come to You". Searching for more fodder of a similar kind – children of that age seem to be infinitely tough and infinitely masochistic – I was immediately attracted by the picture of a corpse dangling from a gallows on the front cover of *Spook Stories*, and rather disappointed to discover that this corpse never actually figured in the text. (In his autobiographical work, *Final Edition*, Benson tells the story of Breads, who in 1742 murdered the brother-in-law of James Lamb, then Mayor of Rye. Breads was tried and hanged, and his body exposed on the road from Rye to Winchelsea. Later the bones were transferred to the Town Hall, "where they stand today", Benson reported in *Final Edition*. Perhaps this grisly relic gave rise to the cover design of *Spook Stories*?)

I must acknowledge that as a six-year-old I found these stories tamer, less imbued with sheer terror, than those of M.R. James. Benson does not have at command the icy, creaky damp dark, the ancient malevolent mystery of his predecessor. Nonetheless, there was something very likable about the collection, and, up to age twelve, I read the dozen in *Spook Stories* over a good many times.

One of the features that attracted me, a rather lonely child, was the manner in which Benson, in these stories, depicts a comfortable, definite, and instantly recognisable world, inhabited by cheerful, middle-aged professional men, who were not at all unlike my stepfather, Martin Armstrong, and his circle of literary and journalistic friends. In fact their circles must have overlapped. Martin was fifteen years younger than Benson, had followed him to Cambridge, then on to the life of letters in London. Both men had feet firmly planted in the Victorian era, when manners were important, and certain subjects were not mentioned.

The heroes of Benson's ghost stories mostly come in pairs, the narrator and his friend Hugh (or Jack or Fred or Frank or Philip); they are for ever renting summer holiday houses in very agreeable and familiar coastal regions of the British Isles. The houses sound perfectly delightful – positively archetypal – with lavender hedges and rose garden and flagged walks and lime alleys. Fred brings along a parlour-maid and Frank a house-maid, and, as soon as they are settled in, the heroes bustle off to play golf and swim and do something called 'loafing' which nobody seems to practise any more. After a while there is some slightly unnerving occurrence, then another, rather worse; events build up to a climax, which often takes place in a thunderstorm, and then, by means of confrontation, exposure, atonement, or reconciliation, everything settles down, the old crime is ventilated, disinfected, and laid to rest. Benson's ghost stories, most of them, are tidy and predictable. Most of them, too, relate to events in the past which are not connected with the heroes and narrators, who are merely spectators, bystanders, who merely chance to trigger off a recurrence on the astral plane of some bygone crime or calamity; they are witnesses, but not directly involved. – It is almost as if Benson is reassuring himself that life can always be tidied up in the end; though an exception, 'Pirates', that touching tale, in complete contrast to the other stories, suggests in the writer an unappeasable longing for the lost past, the safety and security of childhood and family life, and the original Edenlike family home. All those desirable houses in his stories, on the surface so welcoming and comfortable, in reality infected by some sinister haunt, appear to represent the vanished state of infancy, the sequestrated womb.

In fact Benson's cheerful and comfortable world is a great deal less cheerful, on a closer look, than it seems at first sight.

'Unattached and middle-aged persons' – the phrase he often uses to describe the narrators of his ghost stories – this phrase may be a pointer. Unattached, Benson certainly was; he never married, or contracted any close or long-term relationship with members of either sex. Unattached to people his heroes may be, but for houses they have a positively Freudian passion. In several of the stories, the lust to possess a particular house forms the fulcrum of the plot (as in 'Bagnell Terrace') and the unassuaged anger and revengefulness of the dispossessed owner is often what creates the haunt. 'Reconciliation' and 'Naboth's Vineyard' are two of his most successful stories, especially the latter, which has a really blood-curdling climax:

'His body was pressed against the wall at the head of the bed, and the face was a mask of agonised horror and fruitless entreaty. But the eyes were already glazed in death, and before Francis could reach the bed the body had toppled over and lay inert and lifeless. Even as he looked, he heard a limping step go down the passage outside.'

And here we are given an interesting sidelight: Benson's more alarming spectres tend to limp. The angry ghost of 'Naboth's Vineyard' limps; so does the terrifying unseen whistler in 'A Tale of an Empty House'. The dread-inspiring headmaster in Benson's semi-autobiographical novel of school days, *David Blaize*, also limps; he was modelled on Benson's own headmaster, Waterfield, and also, I suspect, on Benson's father, the equally terrifying Edward White Benson, first headmaster of Wellington College and subsequently Archbishop of Canterbury. Arthur Benson, brother of E.F., once wrote 'I hate Papa' on a piece of paper and buried it in the garden. A father capable of arousing this kind of suppressed resentment and fear in his children seems a fertile source for the grim material of ghost stories.

Women very rarely feature as the central figures in Benson's ghost stories. When they do, their role is both potent and ominous.

Consider Mrs. Amworth. She has a vital and voluminous presence and a loud jolly laugh. She nods and smiles and floats about on the outside of second-storey windows. She is always cheery and enthusiastic about village affairs; she is a particularly nasty vampire, preferring to prey on adolescent boys. Or consider the two ladies in the story called 'The Sanctuary', Mrs. Ray and Judith. Judith is a precociously oncoming girl, who strolls with her arm round the neck of a teenage boy she has only just met, and lends him a salacious French novel. She and her mother are in the habit of celebrating the Black Mass. Or consider the portrait of Mrs. Stone, in 'The Room in the Tower': 'A dreadful exuberance and vitality shone through the envelope of flesh, an exuberance wholly malign, a vitality that foamed and frothed with unimaginable evil . . . The whole face was instinct with some secret and appalling mirth; the hands, clasped together on the knee, seemed shaking with suppressed and nameless glee . . .' (One wonders why, when something is nameless, it is always so much nastier?) Or consider Mrs. Labson, in 'The Corner House', a woman who has nagged her wretched husband to the point of breakdown, and then murdered him: 'My breath caught in my throat as I looked at that appalling countenance. It was fat and bloated beyond belief, the eyes were but slits above her cheeks, and the lines of her mouth were invisible . . . her face was flushed with some purplish hue that seemed nearly black . . . I felt that I had looked on something hellish.' Or consider the sister, Alice Faraday, in 'The Bath-Chair', who housekeeps for her brother and is bullied by him: 'There was glee and gusto in her voice' (she is talking about her brother's increasing lameness) 'And how slovenly and uncouth she was, with that lock of grey hair loose across her forehead and her uncared-for hands. Dr. Inglis . . . wondered if she was quite right in the head.' And what happens in that story? Alice, who detests her brother, conspires *with the limping ghost of their father*, dead already, to perpetrate a kind of supernatural murder; the brother is ultimately found lying dead in the father's wheelchair. Suppressed sibling rivalry is plainly evident here, as well as a strong patricidal wish. In fact when Benson's characters do step off the sidelines, stop merely observing, and take part in the action, they engage in the most ferocious kind of family warfare.

At age six I found *Spook Stories* comfortable and not too frightening. Re-reading them many years later, my impression was quite the reverse.

One of the most potent features that emerged, on this later reading, is the underlying fear and dislike of women – some women, at all events, the large, bossy, dynamic, interfering, knowing kind of woman. Benson must have been acquainted with some fearful examples of this type; or, at least, he must have known *one*. Perhaps, like Mrs. Amworth, she preyed on adolescent boys.

I think it no accident that the story called 'The Face', which I have always found the most frightening of Benson's *oeuvre*, falls outside the usual pattern. For a start, there is no explanation for what happens in it, and no solution. The central character, or victim, is a woman – as I have said, a rarity in a Benson story. There are women villainesses, but no heroines. The doom that lies in wait for Hester Ward, the recurring dream, the portrait she sees of her dream-attacker, the coastal resort she flees to, which turns out to be the landscape of her dream – all this builds up to a dreadful inevitability, made infinitely more sinister because it completely lacks Benson's usual tidy explanation. The story carries a particular impact, too, because Hester, the main character, is wholly inoffensive, not at all one of Benson's female harpies; the reader is told nothing about her save that she has a husband and two children and has hitherto led a blameless life. Why should she be singled out for this grim fate? What motivates such apparently random malignity from the past? Benson's other ghosts are not capricious; they all have their springs of action clearly laid out.

To me it seems possible that Benson unloaded into this story a pile of unexpressed animus against the whole female tribe, using Hester, the almost anonymous, featureless woman, as his target.

We know that Benson was not overtly homosexual; judging by what evidence we have, he seems to have led a celibate life. His feelings for members of the male sex, of which he made no secret, all seem to have been kept rigidly within bounds. He was a devoted son to a rather odd mother who, hideously browbeaten by her formidable husband while he was alive, after his death changed her name from Minnie to Ben, and spent her latter years cohabiting with a female friend – which must have put a certain strain, at least, on the feelings of her son. He was a caring brother to a sister who, in her forties, had a fit of matricidal mania, attacked her mother, and had to be kept under restraint thereafter. And he maintained good and friendly relations with his neurotic and difficult brothers. We can see, indeed, that Benson was a thoroughly nice, kindly man, who took his responsibilities with great seriousness; he was probably too nice for his own good. About his partially autobiographical character David Blaize he comments, when the subject of sex is raised: 'The whole matter was vague and repugnant to him, and he did not want to hear or know more.'

But if you turn your back on sex, it does not vanish away, simply assumes more and more importance in your subconscious mind. It seems probable that this is what happened to Benson.

In his ghost stories we find him pursued by those two shapes of menace, the bossy, jolly woman, and the limping man. We may identify the jolly woman with all that active essence of womanhood which he has so firmly expelled from his own life; the archetypal woman is always attempting to batter her way back into a central position.

And what of the limping man? Superficially, as I have suggested, he appears to be a combination of father and headmaster. Did Archbishop Benson limp? His son suffered from severe arthritis, so it seems genetically possible. But peel off yet another layer, and I believe the lame man is revealed as the writer himself. At the end of his life – long after he wrote 'Naboth' or 'Tale of an Empty House' – Benson was obliged to walk with the aid of two sticks; this must have been a particularly penitential affliction for a man who had thrown himself into so many different kinds of sport – golf, squash, tennis, swimming, skiing – with so much enthusiasm; it must have seemed like unfair and savage retribution. Retribution for what? For those suppressed feelings that he, like David Blaize, had never allowed himself to indulge?

The sister, in the Bath-Chair story, says, '"It was as if this sort of double of himself showed what was going to happen to him!" There was glee and gusto in her voice.'

Benson must certainly have read Henry James's ghost story 'The Jolly Corner', in which the hero, returning to his childhood home in New York, is confronted with a hideous apparition of himself, but maimed, lacking two fingers of one hand, 'evil, odious, blatant, vulgar'; and several other writers around that time, Edith Wharton, Oscar Wilde, Sheridan le Fanu, had used a similar theme, a man's gruesome vision of what he might or would become.

Benson's limping phantom embodies the same threat as the James story: that what, ultimately, haunts us, what frightens us most of all, is the doppelganger, the obverse side of our own selves.

Joan Aiken

Introduction

During the last fifty years, before the recent very successful revival of his "Mapp and Lucia" novels, E.F. Benson (1867–1940) was known mainly through his superb horror and "spook" stories. More than his hundred other books, it was always these tales that kept his name before the public gaze through their appearance in numerous anthologies. The bulk of his ghost stories have never been reprinted, and all four of his rare collections have been out of print since the war. Their revival is long overdue.

Benson was always interested in psychic phenomena and ghosts, and later described some of his own strange encounters in his autobiography *Final Edition* (1940). On one hot bright summer day, he and the Vicar of Rye both saw the ghostly apparition of a man in black at the bottom of his garden. 'Ghost stories', he wrote, 'are a branch of literature at which I have often tried my hand. By a selection of disturbing details it is not very difficult to induce in the reader an uneasy frame of mind which, carefully worked up, paves the way for terror. The narrator, I think, must succeed in frightening himself before he can hope to frighten his readers and, as a matter of fact, this man in black had not occasioned me the slightest qualms. However, I worked myself up and wrote my ghost story, describing how there developed an atmosphere of horror in my secret garden, how when I took Taffy there he cowered whining at my heels, how at night a faint stale luminance hovered over the enclosing walls, and so led up, after due preparation, for the appearance of the spectre . . .' A visit to the archives at the local Town Hall provided a gruesome explanation to the haunting.

Benson was well acquainted with that other great master of the genre, M.R. James, for nearly fifty years. He was a member of the Chitchat Society, a Cambridge literary society which had for its object 'the promotion of rational conversation' and met on Saturday evenings, and was present at the historic meeting on 28 October 1893 when James read his first two ghost stories, 'Canon Alberic's Scrapbook' and 'Lost Hearts'. Of the ten club members who avidly listened to these horrific tales, Benson was the only one destined to follow the lead of the incomparable Dr. James. The two writers always agreed that the most successful ghosts and elementals in supernatural fiction should be malevolent and terrifying.

In June 1895 Benson displayed his keen interest in the supernatural when he analysed the notorious case of the 'Clonmel Witch Burning' which had taken place in Ireland only three months previously. A young Irish woman had been tortured to death by her husband, family and friends in order to 'forcibly eject an evil spirit that had taken possession of her body'. Realising that the murderers' pagan beliefs were identical to those of primitive tribes worldwide, he urged that the hideous crime ought to be called manslaughter rather than murder. Soon after Benson's article was published in the prestigious *Nineteenth Century* magazine, the Crown Prosecutor did indeed withdraw the charge of murder, and replaced it with manslaughter.

Benson began his productive career as a writer of ghost stories half way through the Edwardian era, in magazines such as the *Pall Mall* and the *Illustrated London News*, and over the next three decades he penned at least two a year, with an even more prolific rate in the 1920s.

The Christmas number of the *Windsor Magazine*, 1911, contained Benson's 'How Fear Departed from the Long Gallery', illustrated by Fred Pegram. The ghosts in this story are a pair of young children, murdered in the seventeenth century, who haunt a country house. To set eyes on them means almost certain death, but a sympathetic woman who sees them defuses their fatal qualities with her compassion, and they no longer have the power to harm. This was Benson's own personal favourite from all the short tales he ever wrote, and it later appeared as the lead title in the Faber anthology *My Best Story* (1933).

The Room in the Tower, Benson's first collection of supernatural tales, was published in 1912 by Mills and Boon, who had a good reputation for quality horror fiction including Leroux's *The Phantom of the Opera*, published the previous year.

The title story is a fine dreamlike tale of vampirism. Other memorable stories include 'Caterpillars', with its zodiacal pun (a relentless tide of huge, writhing caterpillars with crablike pincers instead of suckers, force their way into a painter's bedroom, after which the painter contracts cancer), and 'The Bus-Conductor', which contains the memorable line "Just room for one inside, sir". This was later turned into an episode of the classic British movie *Dead of Night*. In his preface Benson 'fervently wishes his readers a few uncomfortable moments.'

After the first World War, Benson was a frequent contributor to one of the most attractive monthlies of the 1920s and early 1930s,

Hutchinson's Magazine, which proudly declared 'Another Spook Story by E.F. Benson' on its covers many times over fifteen years. These were often illustrated by the popular artist Edmund Blampied. Hutchinsons published the best of these stories in three collections, *Visible and Invisible* (1923), *Spook Stories* (1928) and *More Spook Stories* (1934).

His stories are extremely varied in content, ranging from the horror of vampires, homicidal ghosts and monstrous spectral worms and slugs (in the classic 'Negotium Perambulans' and 'And No Bird Sings') to the satire of humorous tales which poke fun at charlatan mediums and fake seances ('Spinach' and 'Mr. Tilly's Seance').

There is a very noticeable autobiographical thread running through nearly all the ghost stories. Most are narrated by an unnamed bachelor whom one may assume to be Benson himself. The narrator is often to be found on a long working holiday where he can finish writing manuscripts undisturbed. Switzerland and winter sports are a favourite theme. In one of his most horrific tales, 'The Horror-Horn' is found high in the Alps, where the narrator discovers a naked, excessively hairy prehistoric woman slowly dismembering a live chamois, and he is then pursued down the icy slopes by this blood-crazed creature. (Benson plumbed deep into his psyche for this story, which was written around the same time as his *Winter Sports in Switzerland*!) Egypt, the Italian Riviera, Sussex (specifically Rye, where he lived), and other favourite Benson haunts, consistently recur throught the tales.

'Pirates', one of Benson's very best ghost stories, is both heavily autobiographical and extremely subtle. The sole survivor of five children revisits the Cornish country house near Truro in which he grew up, buys and restores it – then dies there, imagining himself back in his childhood, surrounded by his siblings. The title of this story refers to the game that Benson used to play as a child with the entire family in the garden of his father's house near Truro. (His father, Edward White Benson, was Bishop of Truro, 1877–83, before becoming the Archbishop of Canterbury.)

Benson was often called upon to read his horror stories to select gatherings (like the boys at Wellington College, his former school) and to old friends like Lord Halifax, an inveterate collector of spooky tales. In *Final Edition*, Benson recalled that the elderly Viscount was getting rather deaf, and sat close, with his hand up to his ear; and, if the story was fulfilling its aim, he became more and more uncomfortable and entranced. "It's too frightful", he said. "Go on, go on. I can't bear it!"

Roald Dahl was always an admirer of Benson's ghost stories, and included 'In the Tube' in his own 1983 anthology, where he recalled that (in the 1950s) he had been commissioned to write a series of television screenplays entitled 'Ghost Time', with Benson's controversial tale 'The Hanging of Alfred Wadham' set as the pilot to launch the series. The story involves the delicate subject of Roman Catholicism, and the inability of a priest to break the secrecy rule of the confessional. The priest cannot save the wrong man being hanged for murder, and the ghost of Alfred Wadham (the hanged man) returns to wreak vengeance on the wretched priest. This was too "strong" for 1950s TV audiences (especially in America), so the entire series was dropped.

In my first anthology, *The Sorceress in Stained Glass*, I stated: 'E.F. Benson certainly deserves to follow in the footsteps of M.R. James and have his four magnificent collections of ghost stories brought out in an omnibus volume'. This is now realised in the present volume, a worthy companion and successor to *The Collected Ghost Stories of M.R. James*.

In addition to the 54 stories from *The Room in the Tower* (1912), *Visible and Invisible* (1923), *Spook Stories* (1928) and *More Spook Stories* (1934), E.F. Benson's seminal essay on 'The Clonmel Witch-Burning' and primitive beliefs in elementals, ghosts and the supernatural, is reprinted here for the first time since 1895.

Richard Dalby

These stories have been written in the hopes of giving some pleasant qualms to their reader, so that, if by chance, anyone may be occupying in their perusal a leisure half-hour before he goes to bed when the night and house are still, he may perhaps cast an occasional glance into the corners and dark places of the room where he sits, to make sure that nothing unusual lurks in the shadow. For this is the avowed object of ghost-stories and such tales as deal with the dim unseen forces which occasionally and perturbingly make themselves manifest. The author therefore fervently wishes his readers a few uncomfortable moments.

E. F. Benson

The Room in the Tower

It is probable that everybody who is at all a constant dreamer has had at least one experience of an event or a sequence of circumstances which have come to his mind in sleep being subsequently realised in the material world. But, in my opinion, so far from this being a strange thing, it would be far odder if this fulfilment did not occasionally happen, since our dreams are, as a rule, concerned with people whom we know and places with which we are familiar, such as might very naturally occur in the awake and daylit world. True, these dreams are often broken into by some absurd and fantastic incident, which puts them out of court in regard to their subsequent fulfilment, but on the mere calculation of chances, it does not appear in the least unlikely that a dream imagined by anyone who dreams constantly should occasionally come true. Not long ago, for instance, I experienced such a fulfilment of a dream which seems to me in no way remarkable and to have no kind of psychical significance. The manner of it was as follows.

A certain friend of mine, living abroad, is amiable enough to write to me about once in a fortnight. Thus, when fourteen days or thereabouts have elapsed since I last heard from him, my mind, probably, either consciously or subconsciously, is expectant of a letter from him. One night last week I dreamed that as I was going upstairs to dress for dinner I heard, as I often heard, the sound of the postman's knock on my front door, and diverted my direction downstairs instead. There, among other correspondence, was a letter from him. Thereafter the fantastic entered, for on opening it I found inside the ace of diamonds, and scribbled across it in his well-known hand-writing, "I am sending you this for safe custody, as you know it is running an unreasonable risk to keep aces in Italy." The next evening I was just preparing to go upstairs to dress when I heard the postman's knock, and did precisely as I had done in my dream. There, among other letters, was one from my friend. Only it did not contain the ace of diamonds. Had it done so, I should have attached more weight to the matter, which, as it stands, seems to me a perfectly ordinary coincidence. No doubt I consciously or subconsciously expected a letter from him, and this suggested to me my dream. Similarly, the fact that my friend had not written to me for a fortnight suggested to him that he should do so. But occasionally it is not so easy to find such an explanation, and for the following story I can find no explanation at all. It came out of the dark, and into the dark it has gone again.

All my life I have been a habitual dreamer: the nights are few, that is to say, when I do not find on awaking in the morning that some mental experience has been mine, and sometimes, all night long, apparently, a series of the most dazzling adventures befall me. Almost without exception these adventures are pleasant, though often merely trivial. It is of an exception that I am going to speak.

It was when I was about sixteen that a certain dream first came to me, and this is how it befell. It opened with my being set down at the door of a big red-brick house, where, I understood, I was going to stay. The servant who opened the door told me that tea was going on in the garden, and led me through a low dark-panelled hall, with a large open fireplace, on to a cheerful green lawn set round with flower beds. There were grouped about the tea-table a small party of people, but they were all strangers to me except one, who was a school-fellow called Jack Stone, clearly the son of the house, and he introduced me to his mother and father and a couple of sisters. I was, I remember, somewhat astonished to find myself here, for the boy in question was scarcely known to me, and I rather disliked what I knew of him: moreover, he had left school nearly a year before. The afternoon was very hot, and an intolerable oppression reigned. On the far side of the lawn ran a red-brick wall, with an iron gate in its centre, outside which stood a walnut tree. We sat in the shadow of the house opposite a row of long windows, inside which I could see a table with cloth laid, glimmering with glass and silver. This garden front of the house was very long, and at one end of it stood a tower of three stories, which looked to me much older than the rest of the building.

Before long, Mrs. Stone, who, like the rest of the party, had sat in absolute silence, said to me, "Jack will show you your room: I have given you the room in the tower."

Quite inexplicably my heart sank at her words. I felt as if I had known that I should have the room in the tower, and that it contained something dreadful and significant. Jack instantly got up, and I understood that I had to follow him. In silence we passed through the hall, and mounted a great oak staircase with many corners, and arrived at a small landing with two doors set in it. He pushed one of these open for me to enter, and without coming in himself, closed it behind me. Then I knew that my conjecture had been right: there was something awful in the room, and with the terror of nightmare growing swiftly and enveloping me, I awoke in a spasm of terror.

Now that dream or variations on it occurred to me intermittently for fifteen years. Most often it came in exactly this form, the arrival, the tea laid out on the lawn, the deadly silence succeeded by that one deadly sentence, the mounting with Jack Stone up to the room in the tower where horror dwelt, and it always came to a close in the nightmare of terror at that which was in the room, though I never saw what it was. At other times I experienced variations on this same theme. Occasionally, for instance, we would be sitting at dinner in the dining-room, into the windows of which I had looked on the first night when the dream of this house visited me, but wherever we were, there was the same silence, the same sense of dreadful oppression and foreboding. And the silence I knew would always be broken by Mrs. Stone saying to me, "Jack will show you your room: I have given you the room in the tower." Upon which (this was invariable) I had to follow him up the oak staircase with many corners, and enter the place that I dreaded more and more each time that I visited it in sleep. Or, again, I would find myself playing cards still in silence in a drawing-room lit with immense chandeliers, that gave a blinding illumination. What the game was I have no idea; what I remember, with a sense of miserable anticipation, was that soon Mrs. Stone would get up and say to me, "Jack will show you your room: I have given you the room in the tower." This drawing-room where we played cards was next to the dining-room, and, as I have said, was always brilliantly illuminated, whereas the rest of the house was full of dusk and shadows. And yet, how often, in spite of those bouquets of lights, have I not pored over the cards that were dealed me, scarcely able for some reason to see them. Their designs, too, were strange: there were no red suits, but all were black, and among them there were certain cards which were black all over. I hated and dreaded those.

As this dream continued to recur, I got to know the greater part of the house. There was a smoking-room beyond the drawing-room, at the end of a passage with a green baize door. It was always very dark there, and as often as I went there I passed somebody whom I could not see in the doorway coming out. Curious developments, too, took place in the characters that peopled the dream as might happen to living persons. Mrs. Stone, for instance, who, when I first saw her, had been black haired, became grey, and instead of rising briskly, as she had done when she said, "Jack will show you your room: I have given you the room in the tower," got up very feebly, as if the strength was leaving her limbs. Jack also grew up, and became a rather ill-looking young man, with a brown moustache, while one of the sisters ceased to appear, and I understood she was married.

Then it so happened that I was not visited by this dream for six months or more, and I began to hope, in such inexplicable dread did I hold it, that it had passed away for good. But one night after this interval I again found myself being shown out on to the lawn for tea, and Mrs. Stone was not there, while the others were all dressed in black. At once I guessed the reason, and my heart leaped at the thought that perhaps this time I should not have to sleep in the room in the tower, and though we usually all sat in silence, on this occasion the sense of relief made me talk and laugh as I had never yet done. But even then matters were not altogether comfortable, for no one else spoke, but they all looked secretly at each other. And soon the foolish stream of my talk ran dry, and gradually an apprehension worse than anything I had previously known gained on me as the light slowly faded.

Suddenly a voice which I knew well broke the stillness, the voice of Mrs. Stone, saying, "Jack will show you your room: I have given you the room in the tower." It seemed to come from near the gate in the red-brick wall that bounded the lawn, and looking up, I saw that the grass outside was sown thick with gravestones. A curious greyish light shone from them, and I could read the lettering on the grave nearest me, and it was, "In evil memory of Julia Stone." And as usual Jack got up, and again I followed him through the hall and up the staircase with many corners. On this occasion it was darker than usual, and when I passed into the room in the tower I could only just see the furniture, the position of which was already familiar to me. Also there was a dreadful odour of decay in the room, and I woke screaming.

The dream, with such variations and developments as I have mentioned, went on at intervals for fifteen years. Sometimes I would dream it two or three nights in succession; once, as I have said, there was an intermission of six months, but taking a reasonable average, I should say that I dreamed it quite as often as once in a month. It had, as is plain, something of nightmare about it, since it always ended in the same appalling terror, which so far from getting less, seemed to me to gather fresh fear every time that I experienced it. There was, too, a strange and dreadful consistency about it. The characters in it, as I have mentioned, got regularly older, death and marriage visited this silent family, and I never in the dream, after Mrs. Stone had died, set eyes on her again. But it was always her voice that told me that the room in the tower was prepared for me, and whether we had tea out on the lawn, or the scene was laid in one of the rooms overlooking it, I could always see her gravestone standing just outside the iron gate. It was the same, too, with the married daughter; usually she was not present, but once or twice she returned again, in company with a man, whom I took to be her husband. He, too, like the rest of them, was always silent. But, owing to the constant repetition of the dream, I had ceased to attach, in my walking hours, any significance to it. I never met Jack Stone again during all those years, nor did I ever see a house that resembled this dark house of my dream. And then something happened.

I had been in London in this year, up till the end of July, and during the first week in August went down to stay with a friend in a house he had taken for the summer months, in the Ashdown Forest district of Sussex. I left London early, for John Clinton was to meet me at Forest Row Station, and we were going to spend the day golfing, and go to his house in the evening. He had his motor with him, and we set off, about five of the afternoon, after a thoroughly delightful day, for the drive, the distance being some ten miles. As it was still so early we did not have tea at the club house, but waited till we should get home. As we drove, the weather, which up till then had been, though hot, deliciously fresh, seemed to me to alter in quality, and become very stagnant and oppressive, and I felt that indefinable sense of ominous apprehension that I am accustomed to before thunder. John, however, did not share my views, attributing my loss of lightness to the fact that I had lost both my matches. Events proved, however, that I was right, though I do not think that the thunderstorm that broke that night was the sole cause of my depression.

Our way lay through deep high-banked lanes, and before we had gone very far I fell asleep, and was only awakened by the stopping of the motor. And with a sudden thrill, partly of fear but chiefly of curiosity, I found myself standing in the doorway of my house of dream. We went, I half wondering whether or not I was dreaming still, through a low oak-panelled hall, and out on to the lawn, where tea was laid in the shadow of the house. It was set in flower beds, a red-brick wall, with a gate in it, bounded one side, and out beyond that was a space of rough grass with a walnut tree. The façade of the house was very long, and at one end stood a three-storied tower, markedly older than the rest.

Here for the moment all resemblance to the repeated dream ceased. There was no silent and somehow terrible family, but a large assembly of exceedingly cheerful persons, all of whom were known to me. And in spite of the horror with which the dream itself had always filled me, I felt nothing of it now that the scene of it was thus reproduced before me. But I felt the intensest curiosity as to what was going to happen.

Tea pursued its cheerful course, and before long Mrs. Clinton got up. And at that moment I think I knew what she was going to say. She spoke to me, and what she said was:

"Jack will show you your room: I have given you the room in the tower."

At that, for half a second, the horror of the dream took hold of me again. But it quickly passed, and again I felt nothing more than the most intense curiosity. It was not very long before it was amply satisfied.

John turned to me.

"Right up at the top of the house," he said, "but I think you'll be comfortable. We're absolutely full up. Would you like to go and see it now? By Jove, I believe that you are right, and that we are going to have a thunderstorm. How dark it has become."

I got up and followed him. We passed through the hall, and up the perfectly familiar staircase. Then he opened the door, and I went in. And at that moment sheer unreasoning terror again possessed me. I did not know for certain what I feared: I simply feared. Then like a sudden recollection, when one remembers a name which has long escaped the memory, I knew what I feared. I feared Mrs. Stone, whose grave with the sinister inscription, "In evil memory," I had so often seen in my dream, just beyond the lawn which lay below my window. And then once more the fear passed so completely that I wondered what there was to fear, and I found myself, sober and quiet and sane, in the room in the tower, the name of which I had so often heard in my dreams, and the scene of which was so familiar.

I looked round it with a certain sense of proprietorship, and found that nothing had been changed from the dreaming nights in which I knew it so well. Just to the left of the door was the bed, lengthways along the wall, with the head of it in the angle. In a line with it was the fireplace and a small bookcase; opposite the door the outer wall was pierced by two lattice-paned windows, between which stood the dressing-table, while ranged along the fourth wall was the washing-stand and a big cupboard. My luggage had already been unpacked, for the furniture of dressing and undressing lay orderly on the washstand and toilet-table, while my dinner clothes were spread out on the coverlet of the bed. And then, with a sudden start of unexplained dismay, I saw that there were two rather conspicuous objects which I had not seen before in my dreams: one a life-sized oil-painting of Mrs. Stone, the other a black-and-white sketch of Jack Stone, representing him as he had appeared to me only a week before in the last of the series of these repeated dreams, a rather secret and evil-looking man of about thirty. His picture hung between the windows, looking straight across the room to the other portrait, which hung at the side of the bed. At that I looked next, and as I looked I felt once more the horror of nightmare seize me.

It represented Mrs. Stone as I had seen her last in my dreams: old and withered and white haired. But in spite of the evident feebleness of body, a dreadful exuberance and vitality shone through the envelope of flesh, an exuberance wholly malign, a vitality that foamed and frothed with unimaginable evil. Evil beamed from the narrow, leering eyes; it laughed in the demon-like mouth. The whole face was instinct with some secret and appalling mirth; the hands, clasped together on the knee, seemed shaking with suppressed and nameless glee. Then I saw also that it was signed in the left-hand bottom corner, and wondering who the artist could be, I looked more closely, and read the inscription, "Julia Stone by Julia Stone."

There came a tap at the door, and John Clinton entered.

"Got everything you want?" he asked.

"Rather more than I want," said I, pointing to the picture.

He laughed.

"Hard-featured old lady," he said. "By herself, too, I remember. Anyhow, she can't have flattered herself much."

"But don't you see?" said I. "It's scarcely a human face at all. It's the face of some witch, of some devil."

He looked at it more closely.

"Yes; it isn't very pleasant," he said. "Scarcely a bedside manner, eh? Yes; I can imagine getting the nightmare if I went to sleep with that close by my bed. I'll have it taken down if you like."

"I really wish you would," I said.

He rang the bell, and with the help of a servant we detached the picture and carried it out on to the landing, and put it with its face to the wall.

"By Jove, the old lady is a weight," said John, mopping his forehead. "I wonder if she had something on her mind."

The extraordinary weight of the picture had struck me too. I was about to reply, when I caught sight of my own hand. There was blood on it, in considerable quantities, covering the whole palm.

"I've cut myself somehow," said I.

John gave a little startled exclamation.

"Why, I have too," he said.

Simultaneously the footman took out his handkerchief and wiped his hand with it. I saw that there was blood also on his handkerchief.

John and I went back into the tower room and washed the blood off; but neither on his hand nor on mine was there the slightest trace of a scratch or cut. It seemed to me that, having ascertained this, we both, by a sort of tacit consent, did not allude to it again. Something in my case had dimly occurred to me that I did not wish to think about. It was but a conjecture, but I fancied that I knew the same thing had occurred to him.

The heat and the oppression of the air, for the storm we had expected was still undischarged, increased very much after dinner, and for some time most of the party, among whom were John Clinton and myself, sat outside on the path bounding the lawn, where we had had tea. The night was absolutely dark, and no twinkle of star or moon ray could penetrate the pall of cloud that overset the sky. By degrees our assembly thinned, the women went up to bed, men dispersed to the smoking or billiard room, and by eleven o'clock my host and I were the only two left. All the evening I thought that he had something on his mind, and as soon as we were alone he spoke.

"The man who helped us with the picture had blood on his hand, too, did you notice?" he said. "I asked him just now if he had cut himself, and he said he supposed he had, but that he could find no mark of it. Now where did that blood come from?"

By dint of telling myself that I was not going to think about it, I had succeeded in not doing so, and I did not want, especially just at bedtime, to be reminded of it.

"I don't know," said I, "and I don't really care so long as the picture of Mrs. Julia Stone is not by my bed."

He got up.

"But it's odd," he said. "Ha! Now you'll see another odd thing."

A dog of his, an Irish terrier by breed, had come out of the house as we talked. The door behind us into the hall was open, and a bright oblong of light shone across the lawn to the iron gate which led on to the rough grass outside, where the walnut tree stood. I saw that the dog had all his hackles up, bristling with rage and fright; his lips were curled back from his teeth, as if he were ready to spring at something, and he was growling to himself. He took not the slightest notice of his master or me, but stiffly and tensely walked across the grass to the iron gate. There he stood for a moment, looking through the bars and still growling. Then of a sudden his courage seemed to desert him: he gave one long howl, and scuttled back to the house with a curious crouching sort of movement.

"He does that half-a-dozen times a day," said John. "He sees something which he both hates and fears."

I walked to the gate and looked over it. Something was moving on the grass outside, and soon a sound which I could not instantly identify came to my ears. Then I remember what it was: it was the purring of a cat. I lit a match, and saw the purrer, a big blue Persian, walking round and round in a little circle just outside the gate, stepping high and ecstatically, with tail carried aloft like a banner. Its eyes were bright and shining, and every now and then it put its head down and sniffed at the grass.

I laughed.

"The end of that mystery, I am afraid," I said. "Here's a large cat having Walpurgis night all alone."

"Yes, that's Darius," said John. "He spends half the day and all night there. But that's not the end of the dog mystery, for Toby and he are the best of friends, but the beginning of the cat mystery. What's the cat doing there? And why is Darius pleased, while Toby is terror-stricken?"

At that moment I remembered the rather horrible detail of my dreams when I saw through the gate, just where the cat was now, the white tombstone with the sinister inscription. But before I could answer the rain began, as suddenly and heavily as if a tap had been turned on, and simultaneously the big cat squeezed through the bars of the gate, and came leaping across the lawn to the house for shelter. Then it sat in the doorway, looking out eagerly into the dark. It spat and struck at John with its paw, as he pushed it in, in order to close the door.

Somehow, with the portrait of Julia Stone in the passage outside, the room in the tower had absolutely no alarm for me, and as I went to bed, feeling very sleepy and heavy, I had nothing more than interest for the curious incident about our bleeding hands, and the conduct of the cat and dog. The last thing I looked at before I put out my light was the square empty space by my bed where the portrait had been. Here the paper was of its original full tint of dark red: over the rest of the walls it had faded. Then I blew out my candle and instantly fell asleep.

My awaking was equally instantaneous, and I sat bolt upright in bed under the impression that some bright light had been flashed in my face, though it was now absolutely pitch dark. I knew exactly where I was, in the room which I had dreaded in dreams, but no horror that I ever felt when asleep approached the fear that now invaded and froze my brain. Immediately after a peal of thunder crackled just above the house, but the probability that it was only a flash of lightning which awoke me gave no reassurance to my galloping heart. Something I knew was in the room with me, and instinctively I put out my right hand, which was nearest the wall, to keep it away. And my hand touched the edge of a picture-frame hanging close to me.

I sprang out of bed, upsetting the small table that stood by it, and I heard my watch, candle, and matches clatter on to the floor. But for the moment there was no need of light, for a blinding flash leaped out of the clouds, and showed me that by my bed again hung the picture of Mrs. Stone. And instantly the room went into blackness again. But in that flash I saw another thing also, namely a figure that leaned over the end of my bed, watching me. It was dressed in some close-clinging white garment, spotted and stained with mould, and the face was that of the portrait.

Overhead the thunder cracked and roared, and when it ceased and the deathly stillness succeeded, I heard the rustle of movement coming nearer me, and, more horrible yet, perceived an odour of corruption and decay. And then a hand was laid on the side of my neck, and close beside my ear I heard quick-taken, eager breathing. Yet I knew that this thing, though it could be perceived by touch, by smell, by eye and by ear, was still not of this earth, but something that had passed out of the body and had power to make itself manifest. Then a voice, already familiar to me, spoke.

"I knew you would come to the room in the tower," it said. "I have been long waiting for you. At last you have come. To-night I shall feast; before long we will feast together."

And the quick breathing came closer to me; I could feel it on my neck.

At that the terror, which I think had paralysed me for the moment, gave way to the wild instinct of self-preservation. I hit wildly with both arms, kicking out at the same moment, and heard a little animal-squeal, and something soft dropped with a thud beside me. I took a couple of steps forward, nearly tripping up over whatever it was that lay there, and by the merest good-luck found the handle of the door. In another second I ran out on the landing, and had banged the door behind me. Almost at the same moment I heard a door open somewhere below, and John Clinton, candle in hand, came running upstairs.

"What is it?" he said. "I slept just below you, and heard a noise as if – Good heavens, there's blood on your shoulder."

I stood there, so he told me afterwards, swaying from side to side, white as a sheet, with the mark on my shoulder as if a hand covered with blood had been laid there.

"It's in there," I said, pointing. "She, you know. The portrait is in there, too, hanging up on the place we took it from."

At that he laughed.

"My dear fellow, this is mere nightmare," he said.

He pushed by me, and opened the door, I standing there simply inert with terror, unable to stop him, unable to move.

"Phew! What an awful smell!" he said.

Then there was silence; he had passed out of my sight behind the open door. Next moment he came out again, as white as myself, and instantly shut it.

"Yes, the portrait's there," he said, "and on the floor is a thing – a thing spotted with earth, like what they bury people in. Come away, quick, come away."

How I got downstairs I hardly know. An awful shuddering and nausea of the spirit rather than of the flesh had seized me, and more than once he had to place my feet upon the steps, while every now and then he cast glances of terror and apprehension up the stairs. But in time we came to his dressing-room on the floor below, and there I told him what I have here described.

The sequel can be made short; indeed, some of my readers have perhaps already guessed what it was, if they remember that inexplicable affair of the churchyard at West Fawley, some eight years ago, where an attempt was made three times to bury the body of a certain woman who had committed suicide. On each occasion the coffin was found in the course of a few days again protruding from the ground. After the third attempt, in order that the thing should not be talked about, the body was buried elsewhere in unconsecrated ground. Where it was buried was just outside the iron gate of the garden belonging to the house where this woman had lived. She had committed suicide in a room at the top of the tower in that house. Her name was Julia Stone.

Subsequently the body was again secretly dug up, and the coffin was found to be full of blood.

The Dust-Cloud

The big French windows were open on to the lawn, and, dinner being over, two or three of the party who were staying for the week at the end of August with the Combe-Martins had strolled out on to the terrace to look at the sea, over which the moon, large and low, was just rising and tracing a path of pale gold from horizon to shore, while others, less lunar of inclination, had gone in search of bridge or billiards. Coffee had come round immediately after dessert, and the end of dinner, according to the delectable custom of the house, was as informal as the end of breakfast. Every one, that is to say, remained or went away, smoked, drank port or abstained, according to his personal tastes. Thus, on this particular evening it so happened that Harry Combe-Martin and I were very soon left alone in the dining-room, because we were talking unmitigated motor "shop," and the rest of the party (small wonder) were bored with it, and had left us. The shop was home-shop, so to speak, for it was almost entirely concerned with the manifold perfections of the new six-cylinder Napier which my host in a moment of extravagance, which he did not in the least regret, had just purchased; in which, too, he proposed to take me over to lunch at a friend's house near Hunstanton on the following day. He observed with legitimate pride that an early start would not be necessary, as the distance was only eighty miles and there were no police traps.

"Queer things these big motors are," he said, relapsing into generalities as we rose to go. "Often I can scarcely believe that my new car is merely a machine. It seems to me to possess an independent life of its own. It is really much more like a thoroughbred with a wonderfully fine mouth."

"And the moods of a thoroughbred?" I asked.

"No; it's got an excellent temper, I'm glad to say. It doesn't mind being checked, or even stopped, when it's going its best. Some of these big cars can't stand that. They get sulky – I assure you it is literally true – if they are checked too often."

He paused on his way to ring the bell. "Guy Elphinstone's car, for instance," he said: "it was a bad-tempered brute, a violent, vicious beast of a car."

"What make?" I asked.

"Twenty-five horse-power Amédée. They are a fretful strain of car; too thin, not enough bone – and bone is very good for the nerves. The brute liked running over a chicken or a rabbit, though perhaps it was less the car's ill-temper than Guy's, poor chap. Well, he paid for it – he paid to the uttermost farthing. Did you know him?"

"No; but surely I have heard the name. Ah, yes, he ran over a child, did he not?"

"Yes," said Harry, "and then smashed up against his own park gates."

"Killed, wasn't he?"

"Oh, yes, killed instantly, and the car just a heap of splinters. There's an old story about it, I'm told, in the village: rather in your line."

"Ghosts?" I asked.

"Yes, the ghost of his motor-car. Seems almost too up-to-date, doesn't it?"

"And what's the story?" I demanded.

"Why, just this. His place was outside the village of Bircham, ten miles out from Norwich; and there's a long straight bit of road there – that's where he ran over the child – and a couple of hundred yards further on, a rather awkward turn into the park gates. Well, a month or two ago, soon after the accident, one old gaffer in the village swore he had seen a motor there coming full tilt along the road, but without a sound, and it disappeared at the lodge gates of the park, which were shut. Soon after another said he had heard a motor whirl by him at the same place, followed by a hideous scream, but he saw nothing."

"The scream is rather horrible," said I.

"Ah, I see what you mean! I only thought of his syren. Guy had a syren on his exhaust, same as I have. His had a dreadful frightened sort of wail, and always made me feel creepy."

"And is that all the story?" I asked: "that one old man thought he saw a noiseless motor, and another thought he heard an invisible one?"

Harry flicked the ash off his cigarette into the grate. "Oh dear no!" he said. "Half a dozen of them have seen something or heard something. It is quite a heavily authenticated yarn."

"Yes, and talked over and edited in the public-house," I said.

"Well, not a man of them will go there after dark. Also the lodge-keeper gave notice a week or two after the accident. He said he was always hearing a motor stop and hoot outside the lodge, and he was kept running out at all hours of the night to see what it was."

"And what was it?"

"It wasn't anything. Simply nothing there. He thought it rather uncanny, anyhow, and threw up a good post. Besides, his wife was always hearing a child scream, and while her man toddled out to the gate she would go and see whether the kids were all right. And the kids themselves—"

"Ah, what of them?" I asked.

"They kept coming to their mother, asking who the little girl was who walked up and down the road and would not speak to them or play with them."

"It's a many-sided story," I said. "All the witnesses seem to have heard and seen different things."

"Yes, that is just what to my mind makes the yarn so good," he said. "Personally I don't take much stock in spooks at all. But given that there are such things as spooks, and given that the death of the child and the death of Guy have caused spooks to play about there, it seems to me a very good point that different people should be aware of different phenomena. One hears the car, another sees it, one hears the child scream, another sees the child. How does that strike you?"

This, I am bound to say, was a new view to me, and the more I thought of it the more reasonable it appeared. For the vast majority of mankind have all those occult senses by which is perceived the spiritual world (which, I hold, is thick and populous around us), sealed up, as it were; in other words, the majority of mankind never hear or see a ghost at all. Is it not, then, very probable that of the remainder – those, in fact, to whom occult experiences have happened or can happen – few should have every sense unsealed, but that some should have the unsealed ear, others the unsealed eye – that some should be clairaudient, others clairvoyant?

"Yes, it strikes me as reasonable," I said. "Can't you take me over there?"

"Certainly! If you will stop till Friday I'll take you over on Thursday. The others all go that day, so that we can get there after dark."

I shook my head. "I can't stop till Friday, I'm afraid," I said. "I must leave on Thursday. But how about to-morrow? Can't we take it on the way to or from Hunstanton?"

"No; it's thirty miles out of our way. Besides, to be at Bircham after dark means that we shouldn't get back here till midnight. And as host to my guests—"

"Ah! things are only heard and seen after dark, are they?" I asked. "That makes it so much less interesting. It is like a séance where all lights are put out."

"Well, the accident happened at night," he said. "I don't know the rules, but that may have some bearing on it, I should think."

I had one question more in the back of my mind, but I did not like to ask it. At least, I wanted information on this subject without appearing to ask for it.

"Neither do I know the rules of motors," I said; "and I don't understand you when you say that Guy Elphinstone's machine was an irritable, cross-grained brute, that liked running over chickens and rabbits. But I think you subsequently said that the irritability may have been the irritability of its owner. Did he mind being checked?"

"It made him blind-mad if it happened often," said Harry. "I shall never forget a drive I had with him once: there were hay-carts and perambulators every hundred yards. It was perfectly ghastly; it was like being with a madman. And when we got inside his gate, his dog came running out to meet him. He did not go an inch out of his course: it was worse than that – he went for it, just grinding his teeth with rage. I never drove with him again."

He stopped a moment, guessing what might be in my mind. "I say, you mustn't think – you mustn't think—" he began.

"No, of course not," said I.

Harry Combe-Martin's house stood close to the weather-eaten, sandy cliffs of the Suffolk shore, which are being incessantly gnawed away by the hunger of the insatiable sea. Fathoms deep below it, and now many hundred yards out, lies what was once the second port in England; but now of the ancient town of Dunwich, and of its seven great churches, nothing remains but one, and that ruinous and already half destroyed by the falling cliff and the encroachments of the sea. Foot by foot, it too is disappearing, and of the graveyard which surrounded it more than half is gone, so that from the face of the sandy cliff on which it stands there stick out like straws in glass, as Dante says, the bones of those who were once committed there to the kindly and stable earth.

Whether it was the remembrance of this rather grim spectacle as I had seen it that afternoon, or whether Harry's story had caused some trouble in my brain, or whether it was merely that the keen bracing air of this place, to one who had just come from the sleepy languor of the Norfolk Broads, kept me sleepless, I do not know; but, anyhow, the moment I put out my light that night and got into bed, I felt that all the footlights and gas-jets in the internal theatre of my mind sprang into flame, and that I was very vividly and alertly awake. It was in vain that I counted a hundred forwards and a hundred backwards, that I pictured to myself a flock of visionary sheep coming singly through a gap in an imaginary hedge, and tried to number their monotonous and uniform countenances, that I played noughts and crosses with myself, that I marked out scores of double lawn-tennis courts, – for with each repetition of these supposedly soporific exercises I only became more intensely wakeful. It was not in remote hope of sleep that I continued to repeat these weary performances long after their inefficacy was proved to the hilt, but because I was strangely unwilling in this timeless hour of the night to think about those protruding relics of humanity; also I quite distinctly did not desire to think about that subject with regard to which I had, a few hours ago, promised Harry that I would not make it the subject of reflection. For these reasons I continued during the black hours to practise these narcotic exercises of the mind, knowing well that if I paused on the tedious treadmill my thoughts, like some released spring, would fly back to rather gruesome subjects. I kept my mind, in fact, talking loud to itself, so that it should not hear what other voices were saying.

Then by degrees these absurd mental occupations became impossible; my mind simply refused to occupy itself with them any longer; and next moment I was thinking intently and eagerly, not about the bones protruding from the gnawed section of sandcliff, but about the subject I had said I would not dwell upon. And like a flash it came upon me why Harry had bidden me not think about it. Surely in order that I should not come to the same conclusion as he had come to.

Now the whole question of "haunt" – haunted spots, haunted houses, and so forth – has always seemed to me to be utterly unsolved, and to be neither proved nor disproved to a satisfactory degree. From the earliest times, certainly from the earliest known Egyptian records, there has been a belief that the scene of a crime is often revisited, sometimes by the spirit of him who has committed it – seeking rest, we must suppose, and finding none; sometimes, and more inexplicably, by the spirit of his victim, crying perhaps, like the blood of Abel, for vengeance. And though the stories of these village gossips in the alehouse about noiseless visions and invisible noises were all as yet unsifted and unreliable, yet I could not help wondering if they (such as they were) pointed to something authentic and to be classed under this head of appearances. But more striking than the yarns of the gaffers seemed to me the questions of the lodge-keeper's children. How should children have imagined the figure of a child that would not speak to them or play with them? Perhaps it was a real child, a sulky child. Yes – perhaps. But perhaps not. Then after this preliminary skirmish I found myself settling down to the question that I had said I would not think about; in other words, the possible origin of these phenomena interested me more than the phenomena themselves. For what exactly had Guy Elphinstone, that savage driver, done? Had or had not the death of the child been entirely an accident, a thing (given he drove a motor at all) outside his own control? Or had he, irritated beyond endurance at the checks and delays of the day, not pulled up when it was just possible he might have, but had run over the child as he would have run over a rabbit or a hen, or even his own dog? And what, in any case, poor wretched brute, must have been his thoughts in that terrible instant that intervened between the child's death and his own, when a moment later he smashed into the closed gates of his own lodge? Was remorse his – bitter, despairing contrition? That could hardly have been so; or else surely, knowing only for certain that he had knocked a child down, he would have stopped; he would have done his best, whatever that might be, to repair the irreparable harm. But he had not stopped: he had gone on, it seemed, at full speed, for on the collision the car had been smashed into matchwood and steel shavings. Again, with double force, had this dreadful thing been a complete accident, he would have stopped. So then – most terrible question of all – had he, after making murder, rushed on to what proved to be his own death, filled with some hellish glee at what he had done? Indeed, as in the church-yard on the cliff, bones of the buried stuck starkly out into the night.

The pale tired light of earliest morning had turned the window-blinds into glimmering squares before I slept; and when I woke, the servant who called me was already rattling them briskly up on their rollers, and letting the calm serenity of the August day stream into the room. Through the open windows poured in sunlight and sea-wind, the scent of flowers and the song of birds; and each and all were wonderfully reassuring, banishing the hooded forms that had haunted the night, and I thought of the disquietude of the dark hours as a traveller may think of the billows and tempests of the ocean over which he has safely journeyed, unable, now that they belong to the limbo of the past, to recall his qualms and tossings with any vivid uneasiness. Not without a feeling of relief, too, did I dwell on the knowledge that I was definitely not going to visit this equivocal spot. Our drive to-day, as Harry had said, would not take us within thirty miles of it, and to-morrow I but went to the station and away. Though a thorough-paced seeker after truth might, no doubt, have regretted that the laws of time and space did not permit him to visit Bircham after the sinister dark had fallen, and test whether for him there was visible or audible truth in the tales of the village gossips, I was conscious of no such regret. Bircham and its fables had given me a very bad night, and I was perfectly aware that I did not in the least want to go near it, though yesterday I had quite truthfully said I should like to do so. In this brightness, too, of sun and seawind I felt none of the *malaise* at my waking moments which a sleepless night usually gives me; I felt particularly well, particularly pleased to be alive, and also, as

I have said, particularly content not to be going to Bircham. I was quite satisfied to leave my curiosity unsatisfied.

The motor came round about eleven, and we started at once, Harry and Mrs. Morrison, a cousin of his, sitting behind in the big back seat, large enough to hold a comfortable three, and I on the left of the driver, in a sort of trance – I am not ashamed to confess it – of expectancy and delight. For this was in the early days of motors, when there was still the sense of romance and adventure round them. I did not want to drive, any more than Harry wanted to; for driving, so I hold, is too absorbing; it takes the attention in too firm a grip: the mania of the true motorist is not consciously enjoyed. For the passion for motors is a taste – I had almost said a gift – as distinct and as keenly individual as the passion for music or mathematics. Those who use motors most (merely as a means of getting rapidly from one place to another) are often entirely without it, while those whom adverse circumstances (over which they have no control) compel to use them least may have it to a supreme degree. To those who have it, analysis of their passion is perhaps superfluous; to those who have it not, explanation is almost unintelligible. Pace, however, and the control of pace, and above all the sensuous consciousness of pace, is at the root of it; and pleasure in pace is common to most people, whether it be in the form of a galloping horse, or the pace of the skate hissing over smooth ice, or the pace of a free-wheel bicycle humming down-hill, or, more impersonally, the pace of the smashed ball at lawn-tennis, the driven ball at golf, or the low boundary hit at cricket. But the sensuous consciousness of pace, as I have said, is needful: one might experience it seated in front of the engine of an express train, though not in a wadded, shut-windowed carriage, where the wind of movement is not felt. Then add to this rapture of the rush through riven air the knowledge that huge relentless force is controlled by a little lever, and directed by a little wheel on which the hands of the driver seem to lie so negligently. A great untamed devil has there his bridle, and he answers to it, as Harry had said, like a horse with a fine mouth. He has hunger and thirst, too, unslakeable, and greedily he laps of his soup of petrol which turns to fire in his mouth; electricity, the force that rends clouds asunder, and causes towers to totter, is the spoon with which he feeds himself; and as he eats he races onward, and the road opens like torn linen in front of him. Yet how obedient, how amenable is he! – for with a touch on his snaffle his speed is redoubled, or melts into thin air, so that before you know you have touched the rein he has exchanged his swallow-flight for a mere saunter through the lanes. But he ever loves to run; and knowing this, you will bid him lift up his voice and tell those who are in his path that he is coming, so that he will not need the touch that checks. Hoarse and jovial is his voice, hooting to the wayfarer; and if his hooting be not heard he has a great guttural falsetto scream that leaps from octave to octave, and echoes from the hedges that are passing in blurred lines of hanging green. And, as you go, the romantic isolation of divers in deep seas is yours; masked and hooded companions may be near you also, in their driving-dress for this plunge through the swift tides of air; but you, like them, are alone and isolated, conscious only of the ripped riband of road, the two great lantern-eyes of the wonderful monster that look through drooped eyelids by day, but gleam with fire by night, the two ear-laps of splash-boards, and the long lean bonnet in front which is the skull and brain-case of that swift, untiring energy that feeds on fire, and whirls its two tons of weight up hill and down dale, as if some new law as ever-lasting as gravity, and like gravity making it go ever swifter, was its sole control.

For the first hour the essence of these joys, any description of which compared to the real thing is but as a stagnant pond compared to the bright rushing of a mountain stream, was mine. A straight switchback road lay in front of us, and the monster plunged silently down hill, and said below his breath, "Ha-ha – ha-ha – ha-ha," as, without diminution of speed, he breasted the opposing slope. In my control were his great vocal chords (for in those days hooter and syren were on the driver's left, and lay convenient to the hand of him who occupied the box-seat), and it rejoiced me to let him hoot to a pony-cart, three hundred yards ahead, with a hand on his falsetto scream if his ordinary tones of conversation were unheard or disregarded. Then came a road crossing ours at right angles, and the dear monster seemed to say, "Yes, yes, – see how obedient and careful I am. I stroll with my hands in my pockets." Then again a puppy from a farmhouse staggered warlike into the road, and the monster said, "Poor little chap! get home to your mother, or I'll talk to you in earnest." The poor little chap did not take the hint, so the monster slackened speed and just said "Whoof!" Then it chuckled to itself as the puppy scuttled into the hedge, seriously alarmed; and next moment our self-made wind screeched and whistled round us again.

Napoleon, I believe, said that the power of an army lay in its feet: that is true also of the monster. There was a loud bang, and in thirty seconds we were at a standstill. The monster's off fore-foot troubled it, and the chauffeur said, "Yes, sir – burst."

So the burst boot was taken off and a new one put on, a boot that had never been on foot before. The foot in question was held up on a jack during this operation, and the new boot laced up with a pump. This took exactly twenty-five minutes. Then the monster got his spoon going again, and said, "Let me run: oh, let me run!"

And for fifteen miles on a straight and empty road it ran. I timed the miles, but shall not produce their chronology for the benefit of a forsworn constabulary.

But there were no more dithyrambics that morning. We should have reached Hunstanton in time for lunch. Instead, we waited to repair our fourth puncture at 1.45 p.m., twenty-five miles short of our destination. This fourth puncture was caused by a spicule of flint three-quarters of an inch long – sharp, it is true, but weighing perhaps two pennyweights, while we weighed two tons. It seemed an impertinence. So we lunched at a wayside inn, and during lunch the pundits held a consultation, of which the upshot was this:

We had no more boots for our monster, for his off fore-foot had burst once, and punctured once (thus necessitating two socks and one boot). Similarly, but more so, his off hind-foot had burst twice (thus necessitating two boots and two socks). Now, there was no certain shoemaker's shop at Hunstanton, as far as we knew, but there was a regular universal store at King's Lynn, which was about equidistant.

And, so said the chauffeur, there was something wrong with the monster's spoon (ignition), and he didn't rightly know what, and therefore it seemed the prudent part not to go to Hunstanton (lunch, a thing of the preterite, having been the object), but to the well-supplied King's Lynn. And we all breathed a pious hope that we might get there.

Whizz: hoot: purr! The last boot held, the spoon went busily to the monster's mouth, and we just flowed into King's Lynn. The return journey, so I vaguely gathered, would be made by other roads; but personally, intoxicated with air and movement, I neither asked nor desired to know what those roads would be. This one small but rather salient fact is necessary to record here, that as we waited at King's Lynn, and as we buzzed homewards afterwards, no thought of Bircham entered my head at all. The subsequent hallucination, if hallucination it was, was not, as far as I know, self-suggested. That we had gone out of our way for the sake of the garage, I knew, and that was all. Harry also told me that he did not know where our road would take us.

The rest that follows is the baldest possible narrative of what actually occurred. But it seems to me, a humble student of the occult, to be curious.

While we waited we had tea in an hotel looking on to a big empty square of houses, and after tea we waited a very long time for our monster to pick us up. Then the telephone from the garage inquired for "the gentleman on the motor," and since Harry had strolled out to get a local evening paper with news of the last Test Match, I applied ear and mouth to that elusive instrument. What I heard was not encouraging: the ignition had gone very wrong indeed, and "perhaps" in an hour we should be able to start. It was then about half-past six, and we were just seventy-eight miles from Dunwich.

Harry came back soon after this, and I told him what the message from the garage had been. What he said was this: "Then we shan't get back till long after dinner. We might just as well have camped out to see your ghost."

As I have already said, no notion of Bircham was in my mind, and I mention this as evidence that, even if it had been, Harry's remark would have implied that we were not going through Bircham.

The hour lengthened itself into an hour and a half. Then the monster, quite well again, came hooting round the corner, and we got in.

"Whack her up, Jack," said Harry to the chauffeur. "The roads will be empty. You had better light up at once."

The monster, with its eyes agleam, was whacked up, and never in my life have I been carried so cautiously and yet so swiftly. Jack never took a risk or the possibility of a risk, but when the road was clear and open he let the monster run just as fast as it was able. Its eyes made day of the road fifty yards ahead, and the romance of night was fairyland round us. Hares started from the roadside, and raced in front of us for a hundred yards, then just wheeled in time to avoid the ear-flaps of the great triumphant brute that carried us. Moths flitted across, struck sometimes by the lenses of its eyes, and the miles peeled over our shoulders. When it occurred we were going top-speed. And this was It – quite unsensational, but to us quite inexplicable unless my midnight imaginings happened to be true.

As I have said, I was in command of the hooter and of the syren. We were flying along on a straight down-grade, as fast as ever we could go, for the engines were working, though the decline was considerable. Then quite suddenly I saw in front of us a thick cloud of dust, and knew instinctively and on the instant, without thought or reasoning, what that must mean. Evidently something going very fast (or else so large a cloud could not have been raised) was in front of us, and going in the same direction as ourselves. Had it been something on the road coming to meet us, we should of course have seen the vehicle first and run into the dust-cloud afterwards. Had it, again, been something of low speed – a horse and dog-cart, for instance – no such dust could have been raised. But, as it was, I knew at once that there was a motor travelling swiftly just ahead of us, also that it was not going as fast as we were, or we should have run into its dust much more gradually. But we went into it as into a suddenly lowered curtain.

Then I shouted to Jack. "Slow down, and put on the brake," I shrieked. "There's something just ahead of us."

As I spoke I wrought a wild concerto on the hooter, and with my right hand groped for the syren, but did not find it. Simultaneously I heard a wild, frightened shriek, just as if I had sounded the syren myself. Jack had felt for it too, and our hands fingered each other. Then we entered the dust-cloud.

We slowed down with extraordinary rapidity, and still peering ahead we went dead-slow through it. I had not put on my goggles after leaving King's Lynn, and the dust stung and smarted in my eyes. It was not, therefore, a belt of fog, but real road-dust. And at the moment we crept through it I felt Harry's hands on my shoulder.

"There's something just ahead," he said. "Look! don't you see the tail light?"

As a matter of fact, I did not; and, still going very slow, we came out of that dust-cloud. The broad empty road stretched in front of us; a hedge was on each side, and there was no turning either to right or left. Only, on the right, was a lodge, and gates which were closed. The lodge had no lights in any window.

Then we came to a standstill; the air was dead-calm, not a leaf in the hedgerow trees was moving, not a grain of dust was lifted from the road. But behind, the dust-cloud still hung in the air, and stopped dead-short at the closed lodge-gates. We had moved very slowly for the last hundred yards: it was difficult to suppose that it was of our making. Then Jack spoke, with a curious crack in his voice.

"It must have been a motor, sir," he said. "But where is it?"

I had no reply to this, and from behind another voice, Harry's voice, spoke. For the moment I did not recognise it, for it was strained and faltering.

"Did you open the syren?" he asked. "It didn't sound like our syren. It sounded like, like—"

"I didn't open the syren," said I.

Then we went on again. Soon we came to scattered lights in houses by the wayside.

"What's this place?" I asked Jack.

"Bircham, sir," said he.

GAVON'S EVE

It is only the largest kind of ordnance map that records the existence of the village of Gavon, in the shire of Sutherland, and it is perhaps surprising that any map on whatever scale should mark so small and huddled a group of huts, set on a bare, bleak headland between moor and sea, and, so one would have thought, of no import at all to any who did not happen to live there. But the river Gavon, on the right bank of which stand this half-dozen of chimneyless and wind-swept habitations, is a geographical fact of far greater interest to outsiders, for the salmon there are heavy fish, the mouth of the river is clear of nets, and all the way up to Gavon Loch, some six miles inland, the coffee-coloured water lies in pool after deep pool, which verge, if the river is in order and the angler moderately sanguine, on a fishing probability amounting almost to a certainty. In any case, during the first fortnight of September last I had no blank day on those delectable waters, and up till the 15th of that month there was no day on which some one at the lodge in which I was stopping did not land a fish out of the famous Picts' pool. But after the 15th that pool was not fished again. The reason why is here set forward.

The river at this point, after some hundred yards of rapid, makes a sudden turn round a rocky angle, and plunges madly into the pool itself. Very deep water lies at the head of it, but deeper still further down on the east side, where a portion of the stream flicks back again in a swift dark backwater towards the top of the pool again. It is fishable only from the western bank, for to the east, above this backwater, a great wall of black and basaltic rock, heaved up no doubt by some fault in strata, rises sheer from the river to the height of some sixty feet. It is in fact nearly precipitous on both sides, heavily serrated at the top, and of so curious a thinness, that at about the middle of it where a fissure breaks its topmost edge, and some twenty feet from the top, there exists a long hole, a sort of lancet window, one would say, right through the rock, so that a slit of daylight can be seen through it. Since, therefore, no one would care to cast his line standing perched on that razor-edged eminence, the pool must needs be fished from the western bank. A decent fly, however, will cover it all.

It is on the western bank that there stand the remains of that which gave its title to the pool, namely, the ruins of a Pict castle, built out of rough and scarcely hewn masonry, unmortared but on a certain large and impressive scale, and in a very well-preserved condition considering its extreme antiquity. It is circular in shape and measures some twenty yards of diameter in its internal span. A staircase of large blocks with a rise of at least a foot leads up to the main gate, and opposite this on the side towards the river is another smaller postern through which down a rather hazardously steep slope a scrambling path, where progress demands both caution and activity, conducts to the head of the pool which lies immediately beneath it. A gate-chamber still roofed over exists in the solid wall: inside there are foundation indications of three rooms, and in the centre of all a very deep hole, probably a well. Finally, just outside the postern leading to the river is a small artificially levelled platform, some twenty feet across, as if made to support some super-incumbent edifice. Certain stone slabs and blocks are dispersed over it.

Brora, the post-town of Gavon, lies some six miles to the south-west, and from it a track over the moor leads to the rapids immediately above the Picts' pool, across which by somewhat extravagant striding from boulder to boulder a man can pass dry-foot when the river is low, and make his way up a steep path to the north of the basaltic rock, and so to the village. But this transit demands a steady head, and at the best is a somewhat giddy passage. Otherwise the road between it and Brora lies in a long detour higher up the moor, passing by the gates of Gavon Lodge, where I was stopping. For some vague and ill-defined reason the pool itself and the Picts' Castle had an uneasy reputation on the countryside, and several times trudging back from a day's fishing I have known my gillie take a longish circuit, though heavy with fish, rather than make this short cut in the dusk by the castle. On the first occasion when Sandy, a strapping yellow-bearded viking of twenty-five, did this he gave as a reason that the ground round about the castle was "mossy," though as a God-fearing man he must have known he lied. But on another occasion he was more frank, and said that the Picts' pool was "no canny" after sunset. I am now inclined to agree with him, though, when he lied about it, I think it was because as a God-fearing man he feared the devil also.

It was on the evening of September 14 that I was walking back with my host, Hugh Graham, from the forest beyond the lodge. It had been a day unseasonably hot for the time of year, and the hills were blanketed with soft, furry clouds. Sandy, the gillie of whom I have spoken, was behind with the ponies, and, idly enough, I told

Hugh about his strange distaste for the Picts' pool after sunset. He listened, frowning a little.

"That's curious," he said. "I know there is some dim local superstition about the place, but last year certainly Sandy used to laugh at it. I remember asking him what ailed the place, and he said he thought nothing about the rubbish folk talked. But this year you say he avoids it."

"On several occasions with me he has done so."

Hugh smoked a while in silence, striding noiselessly over the dusky fragrant heather.

"Poor chap," he said, "I don't know what to do about him. He's becoming useless."

"Drink?" I asked.

"Yes, drink in a secondary manner. But trouble led to drink, and trouble, I am afraid, is leading him to worse than drink."

"The only thing worse than drink is the devil," I remarked.

"Precisely. That's where he is going. He goes there often."

"What on earth do you mean?" I asked.

"Well, it's rather curious," said Hugh. "You know I dabble a bit in folklore and local superstition, and I believe I am on the track of something odder than odd. Just wait a moment."

We stood there in the gathering dusk till the ponies laboured up the hillside to us, Sandy with his six feet of lithe strength strolling easily beside them up the steep brae, as if his long day's trudging had but served to half awaken his dormant powers of limb.

"Going to see Mistress Macpherson again tonight?" asked Hugh.

"Aye, puir body," said Sandy. "She's auld, and she's lone."

"Very kind of you, Sandy," said Hugh, and we walked on.

"What then?" I asked when the ponies had fallen behind again.

"Why, superstition lingers here," said Hugh, "and it's supposed she's a witch. To be quite candid with you, the thing interests me a good deal. Supposing you asked me, on oath, whether I believed in witches, I should say 'No.' But if you asked me again, on oath, whether I suspected I believed in them, I should, I think, say 'Yes.' And the fifteenth of this month – to-morrow – is Gavon's Eve."

"And what in Heaven's name is that?" I asked. "And who is Gavon? And what's the trouble?"

"Well, Gavon is the person, I suppose, not saint, who is what we should call the eponymous hero of this district. And the trouble is Sandy's trouble. Rather a long story. But there's a long mile in front of us yet, if you care to be told."

During that mile I heard. Sandy had been engaged a year ago to a girl of Gavon who was in service at Inverness. In March last he had gone, without giving notice, to see her, and as he walked up the street in which her mistress's house stood, had met her suddenly face to face, in company with a man whose clipped speech betrayed him English, whose manner a kind of gentleman. He had a flourish of his hat for Sandy, pleasure to see him, and scarcely any need of explanation as to how he came to be walking with Catrine. It was the most natural thing possible, for a city like Inverness boasted its innocent urbanities, and a girl could stroll with a man. And for the time, since also Catrine was so frankly pleased to see him, Sandy was satisfied. But after his return to Gavon, suspicion, fungus-like, grew rank in his mind, with the result that a month ago he had, with infinite pains and blottings, written a letter to Catrine, urging her return and immediate marriage. Thereafter it was known that she had left Inverness; it was known that she had arrived by train at Brora. From Brora she had started to walked across the moor by the path leading just above the Picts' Castle, crossing the rapids to Gavon, leaving her box to be sent by the carrier. But at Gavon she had never arrived. Also it was said that, although it was hot afternoon, she wore a big cloak.

By this time we had come to the lodge, the lights of which showed dim and blurred through the thick hill-mists that had streamed sullenly down from the higher ground.

"And the rest," said Hugh, "which is as fantastic as this is sober fact, I will tell you later."

Now, a fruit-bearing determination to go to bed is, to my mind, as difficult to ripen as a fruit-bearing determination to get up, and in spite of our long day, I was glad when Hugh (the rest of the men having yawned themselves out of the smoking-room) came back from the hospitable dispensing of bedroom candlesticks with a briskness that denoted that, as far as he was concerned, the distressing determination was not imminent.

"As regards Sandy," I suggested.

"Ah, I also was thinking of that," he said. "Well, Catrine Gordon left Brora, and never arrived here. That is fact. Now for what remains. Have you any remembrance of a woman always alone walking about the moor by the loch? I think I once called your attention to her."

"Yes, I remember," I said. "Not Catrine, surely; a very old woman, awful to look at. Moustache, whiskers, and muttering to herself. Always looking at the ground, too."

"Yes, that is she – not Catrine. Catrine! My word, a May morning! But the other – it is Mrs. Macpherson, reputed witch. Well, Sandy trudges there, a mile and more away, every night to see her. You know Sandy: Adonis of the north. Now, can you account by any natural explanation for that fact? That he goes off after a long day to see an old hag in the hills?"

"It would seem unlikely," said I.

"Unlikely! Well, yes, unlikely."

Hugh got up from his chair and crossed the room to where a bookcase of rather fusty-looking volumes stood between windows. He took a small morocco-backed book from a top shelf.

"Superstitions of Sutherlandshire," he said, as he handed it to me. "Turn to page 128, and read."

"September 15 appears to have been the date of what we may call this devil festival. On the night of that day the powers of darkness held pre-eminent dominion, and over-rode for any who were abroad that night and invoked their aid, the protective Providence of Almighty God. Witches, therefore, above all, were peculiarly potent. On this night any witch could entice to herself the heart and the love of any young man who consulted her on matters of philtre or love charm, with the result that on any night in succeeding years of the same date, he, though he was lawfully affianced and wedded, would for that night be hers. If, however, he should call on the name of God through any sudden grace of the Spirit, her charm would be of no avail. On this night, too, all witches had the power by certain dreadful incantations and indescribable profanities, to raise from the dead those who had committed suicide."

"Top of the next page," said Hugh. "Leave out this next paragraph; it does not bear on this last."

"Near a small village in this country," I read, "called Gavon, the moon at midnight is said to shine through a certain gap or fissure in a wall of rock close beside the river on to the ruins of a Pict castle, so that the light of its beams falls on to a large flat stone erected there near the gate, and supposed by some to be an ancient and pagan altar. At that moment, so the superstition still lingers in the countryside, the evil and malignant spirits which hold sway on Gavon's Eve, are at the zenith of their powers, and those who invoke their aid at this moment and in this place, will, though with infinite peril to their immortal souls, get all that they desire of them."

The paragraph on the subject ended here, and I shut the book.

"Well?" I asked.

"Under favourable circumstances two and two make four," said Hugh.

"And four means—"

"This. Sandy is certainly in consultation with a woman who is supposed to be a witch, whose path no crofter will cross after nightfall. He wants to learn, at whatever cost, poor devil, what happened to Catrine. Thus I think it more than possible that to-morrow, at midnight, there will be folk by the Picts' pool. There is another curious thing. I was fishing yesterday, and just opposite the river gate of the castle, someone has set up a great flat stone, which has been dragged (for I noticed the crushed grass) from the débris at the bottom of the slope."

"You mean that the old hag is going to try to raise the body of Catrine, if she is dead?"

"Yes, and I mean to see myself what happens. Come too."

The next day Hugh and I fished down the river from the lodge, taking with us not Sandy, but another gillie, and ate our lunch on the slope of the Picts' Castle after landing a couple of fish there. Even as Hugh had said, a great flat slab of stone had been dragged on to the platform outside the river gate of the castle, where it rested on certain rude supports, which, now that it was in place, seemed certainly designed to receive it. It was also exactly opposite that lancet window in the basaltic rock across the pool, so that if the moon at midnight did shine through it, the light would fall on the stone. This, then, was the almost certain scene of the incantations.

Below the platform, as I have said, the ground fell rapidly away to the level of the pool, which owing to rain on the hills was running very high, and, streaked with lines of greyish bubbles, poured down in amazing and ear-filling volume. But directly underneath the steep escarpment of rock on the far side of the pool it lay foamless and black, a still backwater of great depth. Above the altar-like erection again the ground rose up seven rough-hewn steps to the gate itself, on each side of which, to the height of about four feet, ran the circular wall of the castle. Inside again were the remains of partition walls between the three chambers, and it was in the one nearest to the river gate that we determined to conceal ourselves that night. From there, should the witch and Sandy keep tryst at the altar, any sound of movement would reach us, and through the aperture of the gate itself we could see, concealed in the shadow of the wall, whatever took place at the altar or down below at the pool. The lodge, finally, was but a short ten minutes away, if one went in the direct line, so that by starting at a quarter to twelve that night, we could enter the Picts' Castle by the gate away from the river, thus not betraying our presence to those who might be waiting for the moment when the moon should shine through the lancet window in the wall of rock on to the altar in front of the river gate.

Night fell very still and windless, and when not long before midnight we let ourselves silently out of the lodge, though to the east the sky was clear, a black continent of cloud was creeping up from the west, and had now nearly reached the zenith. Out of the remote fringes of it occasional lightning winked, and the growl of very distant thunder sounded drowsily at long intervals after. But it seemed to me as if another storm hung over our heads, ready every moment to burst, for the oppression in the air was of a far heavier quality than so distant a disturbance could have accounted for.

To the east, however, the sky was still luminously clear; the curiously hard edges of the western cloud were star-embroidered, and by the dove-coloured light in the east it was evident that the moonrise over the moor was imminent. And though I did not in my heart believe that our expedition would end in anything but yawns, I was conscious of an extreme tension and rawness of nerves, which I set down to the thunder-charged air.

For noiselessness of footstep we had both put on india-rubber-soled shoes, and all the way down to the pool we heard nothing but the distant thunder and our own padded tread. Very silently and cautiously we ascended the steps of the gate away from the river, and keeping close to the wall inside, sidled round to the river gate and peered out. For the first moment I could see nothing, so black lay the shadow of the rock-wall opposite across the pool, but by degrees I made out the lumps and line of the glimmering foam which streaked the water. High as the river was running this morning it was infinitely more voluminous and turbulent now, and the sound of it filled and bewildered the ear with its sonorous roaring. Only under the very base of the rock opposite it ran quite black and unflecked by foam: there lay the deep still surface of the backwater. Then suddenly I saw something black move in the dimness in front of me, and against the grey foam rose up first the head, then the shoulders, and finally the whole figure of a woman coming towards us up the bank. Behind her walked another, a man, and the two came to where the altar of stone had been newly erected and stood there side by side silhouetted against the churned white of the stream. Hugh had seen too, and touched me on the arm to call my attention. So far then he was right: there was no mistaking the stalwart proportions of Sandy.

Suddenly across the gloom shot a tiny spear of light, and momentarily as we watched, it grew larger and longer, till a tall beam, as from some window cut in the rock opposite, was shed on the bank below us. It moved slowly, imperceptibly to the left till it struck full between the two black figures standing there, and shone with a curious bluish gleam on the flat stone in front of them. Then the roar of the river was suddenly overscored by a dreadful screaming voice, the voice of a woman, and from her side her arms shot up and out as if in invocation of some power.

At first I could catch none of the words, but soon from repetition they began to convey an intelligible message to my brain, and I was listening as in paralytic horror of nightmare to a bellowing of the most hideous and un-nameable profanity. What I heard I cannot bring myself to record; suffice it to say that Satan was invoked by every adoring and reverent name, that cursing and unspeakable malediction was poured forth on Him whom we hold most holy. Then the yelling voice ceased as suddenly as it had began, and for a moment there was silence again, but for the reverberating river.

Then once more that horror of sound was uplifted.

"So, Catrine Gordon," it cried, "I bid ye in the name of my master and yours to rise from where ye lie. Up with ye – up!"

Once more there was silence; then I heard Hugh at my elbow draw a quick sobbing breath, and his finger pointed unsteadily to the dead black water below the rock. And I too looked and saw.

Right under the rock there appeared a pale subaqueous light, which waved and quivered in the stream. At first it was very small and dim, but as we looked it seemed to swim upwards from remote depths and grew larger till I suppose the space of some square yard was illuminated by it. Then the surface of the water was broken, and a head, the head of a girl, dead-white and with long, flowing hair, appeared above the stream. Her eyes were shut, the corners of her mouth drooped as in sleep, and the moving water stood in a frill round her neck. Higher and higher rose the figure out of the tide, till at last it stood, luminous in itself, so it appeared, up to the middle. The head was bent down over the breast, and the hands clasped together. As it emerged from the water it seemed to get nearer, and was by now half-way across the pool, moving quietly and steadily against the great flood of the hurrying river.

Then I heard a man's voice crying out in a sort of strangled agony.

"Catrine!" it cried; "Catrine! In God's name; in God's name!"

In two strides Sandy had rushed down the steep bank, and hurled himself out into that mad swirl of waters. For one moment I saw his arms flung up into the sky, the next he had altogether gone. And on the utterance of that name the unholy vision had vanished too, while simultaneously there burst in front of us a light so blinding, followed by a crack of thunder so appalling to the senses, that I know I just hid my face in my hands. At once, as if the flood-gates of the sky had been opened, the deluge was on us, not like rain, but like one sheet of solid water, so that we cowered under it. Any hope or attempt to rescue Sandy was out of the question; to dive into that whirlpool of mad water meant instant death, and even had it been possible for any swimmer to live there, in the blackness of the night there was absolutely no chance of finding him. Besides, even if it had been possible to save him, I doubt whether I was sufficiently master of my flesh and blood as to endure to plunge where that apparition had risen.

Then, as we lay there, another horror filled and possessed my mind. Somewhere close to us in the darkness was that woman whose yelling voice just now had made my blood run ice-cold, while it brought the streaming sweat to my forehead. At that moment I turned to Hugh.

"I cannot stop here," I said. "I must run, run right away. Where is She?"

"Did you not see?" he asked.

"No. What happened?"

"The lightning struck the stone within a few inches of where she was standing. We – we must go and look for her."

I followed him down the slope, shaking as if I had the palsy, and groping with my hands on the ground in front of me, in deadly terror of encountering something human. The thunder-clouds had in the last few minutes spread over the moon, so that no ray from the window in the rock guided our search. But up and down the bank from the stone that lay shattered there to the edge of the pool we groped and stumbled, but found nothing. At length we gave it up: it seemed morally certain that she, too, had rolled down the bank after the lightning stroke, and lay somewhere deep in the pool from which she had called the dead.

None fished the pool next day, but men with drag-nets came from Brora. Right under the rock in the backwater lay two bodies, close together, Sandy and the dead girl. Of the other they found nothing.

It would seem, then, that Catrine Gordon, in answer to Sandy's letter, left Inverness in heavy trouble. What happened afterwards can only be conjectured, but it seems likely she took the short cut to Gavon, meaning to cross the river on the boulders above the Picts' pool. But whether she slipped accidentally in her passage, and so was drawn down by the hungry water, or whether unable to face the future, she had thrown herself into the pool, we can only guess. In any case they sleep together now in the bleak, wind-swept graveyard at Brora, in obedience to the inscrutable designs of God.

THE CONFESSION OF CHARLES LINKWORTH

Dr. Teesdale had occasion to attend the condemned man once or twice during the week before his execution, and found him, as is often the case, when his last hope of life has vanished, quiet and perfectly resigned to his fate, and not seeming to look forward with any dread to the morning that each hour that passed brought nearer and nearer. The bitterness of death appeared to be over for him: it was done with when he was told that his appeal was refused. But for those days while hope was not yet quite abandoned, the wretched man had drunk of death daily. In all his experience the doctor had never seen a man so wildly and passionately tenacious of life, nor one so strongly knit to this material world by the sheer animal lust of living. Then the news that hope could no longer be entertained was told him, and his spirit passed out of the grip of that agony of torture and suspense, and accepted the inevitable with indifference. Yet the change was so extraordinary that it seemed to the doctor rather that the news had completely stunned his powers of feeling, and he was below the numbed surface, still knit into material things as strongly as ever. He had fainted when the result was told him, and Dr. Teesdale had been called in to attend him. But the fit was but transient, and he came out of it into full consciousness of what had happened.

The murder had been a deed of peculiar horror, and there was nothing of sympathy in the mind of the public towards the perpetrator. Charles Linkworth, who now lay under capital sentence, was the keeper of a small stationery store in Sheffield, and there lived with him his wife and mother. The latter was the victim of his atrocious crime; the motive of it being to get possession of the sum of five hundred pounds, which was this woman's property. Linkworth, as came out at the trial, was in debt to the extent of a hundred pounds at the time, and during his wife's absence from home on a visit to relations, he strangled his mother, and during the night buried the body in the small back-garden of his house. On his wife's return, he had a sufficiently plausible tale to account for the elder Mrs. Linkworth's disappearance, for there had been constant jarrings and bickerings between him and his mother for the last year or two, and she had more than once threatened to withdraw herself and the eight shillings a week which she contributed to household expenses, and purchase an annuity with her money. It was true, also, that during the younger Mrs. Linkworth's absence from home, mother and son had had a violent quarrel arising originally from some trivial point in household management, and that in consequence of this, she had actually drawn her money out of the bank, intending to leave Sheffield next day and settle in London, where she had friends. That evening she told him this, and during the night he killed her.

His next step, before his wife's return, was logical and sound. He packed up all his mother's possessions and took them to the station, from which he saw them despatched to town by passenger train, and in the evening he asked several friends in to supper, and told them of his mother's departure. He did not (logically also, and in accordance with what they probably already knew) feign regret, but said that he and she had never got on well together, and that the cause of peace and quietness was furthered by her going. He told the same story to his wife on her return, identical in every detail, adding, however, that the quarrel had been a violent one, and that his mother had not even left him her address. This again was wisely thought of: it would prevent his wife from writing to her. She appeared to accept his story completely: indeed there was nothing strange or suspicious about it.

For a while he behaved with the composure and astuteness which most criminals possess up to a certain point, the lack of which, after that, is generally the cause of their detection. He did not, for instance, immediately pay off his debts, but took into his house a young man as lodger, who occupied his mother's room, and he dismissed the assistant in his shop, and did the entire serving himself. This gave the impression of economy, and at the same time he openly spoke of the great improvement in his trade, and not till a month had passed did he cash any of the bank-notes which he had found in a locked drawer in his mother's room. Then he changed two notes of fifty pounds and paid off his creditors.

At that point his astuteness and composure failed him. He opened a deposit account at a local bank with four more fifty-pound notes, instead of being patient, and increasing his balance at the savings bank pound by pound, and he got uneasy about that which he had buried deep enough for security in the back garden. Thinking to render himself safer in this regard, he ordered a cartload of slag and stone fragments, and with the help of his lodger employed the summer evenings when work was over in building a sort of rockery over the spot. Then came the chance circumstance which really set match to this dangerous train. There was a fire in the lost luggage office at King's Cross Station (from which he ought to have claimed his mother's property) and one of the two boxes was partially burned. The company was liable for compensation, and his mother's name on her linen, and a letter with the Sheffield address on it, led to the arrival of a purely official and formal notice, stating that the company were prepared to consider claims. It was directed to Mrs. Linkworth's and Charles Linkworth's wife received and read it.

It seemed a sufficiently harmless document, but it was endorsed with his death-warrant. For he could give no explanation at all of the fact of the boxes still lying at King's Cross Station, beyond suggesting that some accident had happened to his mother. Clearly he had to put the matter in the hands of the police, with a view to tracing her movements, and if it proved that she was dead, claiming her property, which she had already drawn out of the bank. Such at least was the course urged on him by his wife and lodger, in whose presence the communication from the railway officials was read out, and it was impossible to refuse to take it. Then the silent, uncreaking machinery of justice, characteristic of England, began to move forward. Quiet men lounged about Smith Street, visited banks, observed the supposed increase in trade, and from a house near by looked into the garden where ferns were already flourishing on the rockery. Then came the arrest and the trial, which did not last very long, and on a certain Saturday night the verdict. Smart women in large hats had made the court bright with colour, and in all the crowd there was not one who felt any sympathy with the young athletic-looking man who was condemned. Many of the audience were elderly and respectable mothers, and the crime had been an outrage on motherhood, and they listened to the unfolding of the flawless evidence with strong approval. They thrilled a little when the judge put on the awful and ludicrous little black cap, and spoke the sentence appointed by God.

Linkworth went to pay the penalty for the atrocious deed, which no one who had heard the evidence could possibly doubt that he had done with the same indifference as had marked his entire demeanour since he knew his appeal had failed. The prison chaplain who had attended him had done his utmost to get him to confess, but his efforts had been quite ineffectual, and to the last he asserted, though without protestation, his innocence. On a bright September morning, when the sun shone warm on the terrible little procession that crossed the prison yard to the shed where was erected the apparatus of death, justice was done, and Dr. Teesdale was satisfied that life was immediately extinct. He had been present on the scaffold, had watched the bolt drawn, and the hooded and pinioned figure drop into the pit. He had heard the chunk and creak of the rope as the sudden weight came on to it, and looking down he had seen the queer twitchings of the hanged body. They had lasted but a second or two; the execution had been perfectly satisfactory.

An hour later he made the post-mortem examination, and found that his view had been correct: the vertebrae of the spine had been broken at the neck, and death must have been absolutely instantaneous. It was hardly necessary even to make that little piece of dissection that proved this, but for the sake of form he did so. And at that moment he had a very curious and vivid mental impression that the spirit of the dead man was close beside him, as if it still dwelt in the broken habitation of its body. But there was no question at all that the body was dead: it had been dead an hour. Then followed another little circumstance that at the first seemed insignificant though curious also. One of the warders entered, and asked if the rope which had been used an hour ago, and was the hangman's perquisite, had by mistake been brought into the mortuary with the body. But there was no trace of it, and it seemed to have vanished altogether, though it was a singular thing to be lost: it was not here; it was not on the scaffold. And though the disappearance was of no particular moment it was quite inexplicable.

Dr. Teesdale was a bachelor and a man of independent means, and lived in a tall-windowed and commodious house in Bedford Square, where a plain cook of surpassing excellence looked after his food, and her husband his person. There was no need for him to practise a profession at all, and he performed his work at the prison for the sake of the study of the minds of criminals. Most crime – the transgression, that is, of the rule of conduct which the human race has framed for the sake of its own preservation – he held to be either the result of some abnormality of the brain or of starvation. Crimes of theft, for instance, he would by no means refer to one head; often it is true they were the result of actual want, but more often dictated by some obscure disease of the brain. In marked cases it was labelled as kleptomania, but he was convinced there were many others which did not fall directly under the dictation of physical need. More especially was this the case where the crime in question involved also some deed of violence, and he mentally placed underneath this heading, as he went home that evening, the criminal at whose last moments he had been present that morning. The crime had been abominable, the need of money not so very pressing, and the very abomination and unnaturalness of the murder inclined him to consider the murderer as lunatic rather than criminal. He had been, as far as was known, a man of quiet and kindly disposition, a good husband, a sociable neighbour. And then he had committed a crime, just one, which put him outside all pales. So monstrous a deed, whether perpetrated by a sane man or a mad one, was intolerable; there was no use for the doer of it on this planet at all. But somehow the doctor felt that he would have been more at one with the execution of justice, if the dead man had confessed. It was morally certain that he was guilty, but he wished that when there was no longer any hope for him he had endorsed the verdict himself.

He dined alone that evening, and after dinner sat in his study which adjoined the dining-room, and feeling disinclined to read, sat in his great red chair opposite the fireplace, and let his mind graze where it would. At once almost, it went back to the curious sensation he had experienced that morning, of feeling that the spirit of Linkworth was present in the mortuary, though life had been extinct for an hour. It was not the first time, especially in cases of sudden death, that he had felt a similar conviction, though perhaps it had never been quite so unmistakable as it had been to-day. Yet the feeling, to his mind, was quite probably formed on a natural and psychical truth. The spirit – it may be remarked that he was a believer in the doctrine of future life, and the non-extinction of the soul with the death of the body – was very likely unable or unwilling to quit at once and altogether the earthly habitation, very likely it lingered there, earth-bound, for a while. In his leisure hours Dr. Teesdale was a considerable student of the occult, for like most advanced and proficient physicians, he clearly recognised how narrow was the boundary of separation between soul and body, how tremendous the influence of the intangible was over material things, and it presented no difficulty to his mind that a disembodied spirit should be able to communicate directly with those who still were bounded by the finite and material.

His meditations, which were beginning to group themselves into definite sequence, were interrupted at this moment. On his desk near at hand stood his telephone, and the bell rang, not with its usual metallic insistence, but very faintly, as if the current was weak, or the mechanism impaired. However, it certainly was ringing, and he got up and took the combined ear and mouth-piece off its hook.

"Yes, yes," he said, "who is it?"

There was a whisper in reply almost inaudible, and quite unintelligible.

"I can't hear you," he said.

Again the whisper sounded, but with no greater distinctness. Then it ceased altogether.

He stood there, for some half minute or so, waiting for it to be renewed, but beyond the usual chuckling and croaking, which showed, however, that he was in communication with some other instrument, there was silence. Then he replaced the receiver, rang up the Exchange, and gave his number.

"Can you tell me what number rang me up just now?" he asked.

There was a short pause, then it was given him. It was the number of the prison, where he was doctor.

"Put me on to it, please," he said.

This was done.

"You rang me up just now," he said down the tube. "Yes; I am Doctor Teesdale. What is it? I could not hear what you said."

The voice came back quite clear and intelligible.

"Some mistake, sir," it said. "We haven't rung you up."

"But the Exchange tells me you did, three minutes ago."

"Mistake at the Exchange, sir," said the voice.

"Very odd. Well, good-night. Warder Draycott, isn't it?"

"Yes, sir; good-night, sir."

Dr. Teesdale went back to his big arm-chair, still less inclined to read. He let his thoughts wander on for a while, without giving them definite direction, but ever and again his mind kept coming back to that strange little incident of the telephone. Often and often he had been rung up by some mistake, often and often he had been put on to the wrong number by the Exchange, but there was something in this very subdued ringing of the telephone bell, and the unintelligible whisperings at the other end that suggested a very curious train of reflection to his mind, and soon he found himself pacing up and down his room, with his thoughts eagerly feeding on a most unusual pasture.

"But it's impossible," he said, aloud.

He went down as usual to the prison next morning, and once again he was strangely beset with the feeling that there was some unseen presence there. He had before now had some odd psychical experiences, and knew that he was a "sensitive" – one, that is, who is capable, under certain circumstances, of receiving supernormal impressions, and of having glimpses of the unseen world that lies about us. And this morning the presence of which he was conscious was that of the man who had been executed yesterday morning. It was local, and he felt it most strongly in the little prison yard, and as he passed the door of the condemned cell. So strong was it there that he would not have been surprised if the figure of the man had been visible to him, and as he passed through the door at the end of the passage, he turned round, actually expecting to see it. All the time, too, he was aware of a profound horror at his heart; this unseen presence strangely disturbed him. And the poor soul, he felt, wanted something done for it. Not for a moment did he doubt that this impression of his was objective, it was no imaginative phantom of his own invention that made itself so real. The spirit of Linkworth was there.

He passed into the infirmary, and for a couple of hours busied himself with his work. But all the time he was aware that the same invisible presence was near him, though its force was manifestly less here than in those places which had been more intimately associated with the man. Finally, before he left, in order to test his theory he looked into the execution shed. But next moment with a face suddenly stricken pale, he came out again, closing the door hastily. At the top of the steps stood a figure hooded and pinioned, but hazy of outline and only faintly visible. But it was visible, there was no mistake about it.

Dr. Teesdale was a man of good nerve, and he recovered himself almost immediately, ashamed of his temporary panic. The terror that had blanched his face was chiefly the effect of startled nerves, not of terrified heart, and yet deeply interested as he was in psychical phenomena, he could not command himself sufficiently to go back there. Or rather he commanded himself, but his muscles refused to act on the message. If this poor earth-bound spirit had any communication to make to him, he certainly much preferred that it should be made at a distance. As far as he could understand, its range was circumscribed. It haunted the prison yard, the condemned cell, the execution shed, it was more faintly felt in the infirmary. Then a further point suggested itself to his mind, and he went back to his room and sent for Warder Draycott, who had answered him on the telephone last night.

"You are quite sure," he asked, "that nobody rang me up last night, just before I rang you up?"

There was a certain hesitation in the man's manner which the doctor noticed.

"I don't see how it could be possible, sir," he said. "I had been sitting close by the telephone for half an hour before, and again before that. I must have seen him, if anyone had been to the instrument."

"And you *saw* no one?" said the doctor with a slight emphasis.

The man became more markedly ill at ease.

"No, sir, I *saw* no one," he said, with the same emphasis.

Dr. Teesdale looked away from him.

"But you had perhaps the impression that there was some one there?" he asked, carelessly, as if it was a point of no interest.

Clearly Warder Draycott had something on his mind, which he found it hard to speak of.

"Well, sir, if you put it like that," he began. "But you would tell me I was half asleep, or had eaten something that disagreed with me at my supper."

The doctor dropped his careless manner.

"I should do nothing of the kind," he said, "any more than you would tell me that I had dropped asleep last night, when I heard my telephone bell ring. Mind you, Draycott, it did not ring as usual, I could only just hear it ringing, though it was close to me. And I could only hear a whisper when I put my ear to it. But when you spoke I heard you quite distinctly. Now I believe there was something – somebody – at this end of the telephone. You were here, and though you saw no one, you, too, felt there was someone there.

The man nodded.

"I'm not a nervous man, sir," he said, "and I don't deal in fancies. But there was something there. It was hovering about the instrument, and it wasn't the wind, because there wasn't a breath of wind stirring, and the night was warm. And I shut the window to make certain. But it went about the room, sir, for an hour or more. It rustled the leaves of the telephone book, and it ruffled my hair when it came close to me. And it was bitter cold, sir."

The doctor looked him straight in the face.

"Did it remind you of what had been done yesterday morning?" he asked suddenly.

Again the man hesitated.

"Yes, sir," he said at length. "Convict Charles Linkworth."

Dr. Teesdale nodded reassuringly.

"That's it," he said. "Now, are you on duty to-night?"

"Yes, sir, I wish I wasn't."

"I know how you feel, I have felt exactly the same myself. Now whatever this is, it seems to want to communicate with me. By the way, did you have any disturbance in the prison last night?"

"Yes, sir, there was half a dozen men who had the nightmare. Yelling and screaming they were, and quiet men too, usually. It happens sometimes the night after an execution. I've known it before, though nothing like what it was last night."

"I see. Now, if this – this thing you can't see wants to get at the telephone again to-night, give it every chance. It will probably come about the same time. I can't tell you why, but that usually happens. So unless you must, don't be in this room where the telephone is, just for an hour to give it plenty of time between half-past nine and half-past ten. I will be ready for it at the other end. Supposing I am rung up, I will, when it has finished, ring you up to make sure that I was not being called in – in the usual way."

"And there is nothing to be afraid of, sir!" asked the man.

Dr. Teesdale remembered his own moment of terror this morning, but he spoke quite sincerely.

"I am sure there is nothing to be afraid of," he said, reassuringly.

Dr. Teesdale had a dinner engagement that night, which he broke, and was sitting alone in his study by half past-nine. In the present state of human ignorance as to the law which governs the movements of spirits severed from the body, he could not tell the warder why it was that their visits are so often periodic, timed to punctuality according to our scheme of hours, but in scenes of tabulated instances of the appearance of *revenants*, especially if the soul was in sore need of help, as might be the case here, he found that they came at the same hour of day or night. As a rule, too, their power of making themselves seen or heard or felt grew greater for some little while after death, subsequently growing weaker as they became less earth-bound, or often after that ceasing altogether, and he was prepared to-night for a less indistinct impression. The spirit apparently for the early hours of its disembodiment is weak, like a moth newly broken out from its chrysalis – and then suddenly the telephone bell rang, not so faintly as the night before, but still not with its ordinary imperative tone.

Dr. Teesdale instantly got up, put the receiver to his ear. And what he heard was heartbroken sobbing, strong spasms that seemed to tear the weeper.

He waited for a little before speaking, himself cold with some nameless fear, and yet profoundly moved to help, if he was able.

"Yes, yes," he said at length, hearing his own voice tremble. "I am Dr. Teesdale. What can I do for you? And who are you?" he added, though he felt that it was a needless question.

Slowly the sobbing died down, the whispers took its place, still broken by crying.

"I want to tell, sir – I want to tell – I must tell."

"Yes, tell me, what is it?" said the doctor.

"No, not you – another gentleman, who used to come to see me. Will you speak to him what I say to you? – I can't make him hear me or see me."

"Who are you?" asked Dr. Teesdale suddenly.

"Charles Linkworth. I thought you knew. I am very miserable. I can't leave the prison – and it is cold. Will you send for the other gentleman?"

"Do you mean the chaplain?" asked Dr. Teesdale.

"Yes, the chaplain. He read the service when I went across the yard yesterday. I shan't be so miserable when I have told."

The doctor hesitated a moment. This was a strange story that he would have to tell Mr. Dawkins, the prison chaplain, that at the other end of the telephone was the spirit of the man executed yesterday. And yet he soberly believed that it was so, that this unhappy spirit was in misery and wanted to "tell." There was no need to ask what he wanted to tell.

"Yes, I will ask him to come here," he said at length.

"Thank you, sir, a thousand times. You will make him come, won't you?"

The voice was growing fainter.

"It must be to-morrow night," it said. "I can't speak longer now. I have to go to see – oh, my God, my God."

The sobs broke out afresh, sounding fainter and fainter. But it was in a frenzy of terrified interest that Dr. Teesdale spoke.

"To see what?" he cried. "Tell me what you are doing, what is happening to you?"

"I can't tell you; I mayn't tell you," said the voice very faint. "That is part—" and it died away altogether.

Dr. Teesdale waited a little, but there was no further sound of any kind, except the chuckling and croaking of the instrument. He put the receiver on to its hook again, and then became aware for the first time that his forehead was streaming with some cold dew of horror. His ears sang; his heart beat very quick and faint, and he sat down to recover himself. Once or twice he asked himself if it was possible that some terrible joke was being played on him, but he knew that could not be so; he felt perfectly sure that he had been speaking with a soul in torment of contrition for the terrible and irremediable act it had committed. It was no delusion of his senses, either; here in this comfortable room of his in Bedford Square, with London cheerfully roaring round him, he had spoken with the spirit of Charles Linkworth.

But he had no time (nor indeed inclination, for somehow his soul sat shuddering within him) to indulge in meditation. First of all he rang up the prison.

"Warder Draycott?" he asked.

There was a perceptible tremor in the man's voice as he answered.

"Yes, sir. Is it Dr. Teesdale?"

"Yes. Has anything happened here with you?"

Twice it seemed that the man tried to speak and could not. At the third attempt the words came

"Yes, sir. He has been here. I saw him go into the room where the telephone is."

"Ah! Did you speak to him?"

"No, sir: I sweated and prayed. And there's half a dozen men as have been screaming in their sleep to-night. But it's quiet again now. I think he has gone into the execution shed."

"Yes. Well, I think there will be no more disturbance now. By the way, please give me Mr. Dawkins's home address.

This was given him, and Dr. Teesdale proceeded to write to the chaplain, asking him to dine with him on the following night. But suddenly he found that he could not write at his accustomed desk, with the telephone standing close to him, and he went upstairs to the drawing-room which he seldom used, except when he entertained his friends. There he recaptured the serenity of his nerves, and could control his hand. The note simply asked Mr. Dawkins to dine with him next night, when he wished to tell him a very strange history and ask his help. "Even if you have any other engagement," he concluded, "I seriously request you to give it up. To-night, I did the same. I should bitterly have regretted it if I had not."

Next night accordingly, the two sat at their dinner in the doctor's dining-room, and when they were left to their cigarettes and coffee the doctor spoke.

"You must not think me mad, my dear Dawkins," he said, "when you hear what I have got to tell you."

Mr. Dawkins laughed.

"I will certainly promise not to do that," he said.

"Good. Last night and the night before, a little later in the evening than this, I spoke through the telephone with the spirit of the man we saw executed two days ago. Charles Linkworth."

The chaplain did not laugh. He pushed back his chair, looking annoyed.

"Teesdale," he said, "is it to tell me this – I don't want to be rude – but this bogey-tale that you have brought me here this evening?"

"Yes. You have not heard half of it. He asked me last night to get hold of you. He wants to tell you something. We can guess, I think, what it is."

Dawkins got up.

"Please let me hear no more of it," he said. "The dead do not return. In what state or under what condition they exist has not been revealed to us. But they have done with all material things."

"But I must tell you more," said the doctor. "Two nights ago I was rung up, but very faintly, and could only hear whispers. I instantly inquired where the call came from and was told it came from the prison. I rang up the prison, and Warder Draycott told me that nobody had rung me up. He, too, was conscious of a presence."

"I think that man drinks," said Dawkins, sharply.

The doctor paused a moment.

"My dear fellow, you should not say that sort of thing," he said. "He is one of the steadiest men we have got. And if he drinks, why not I also?"

The chaplain sat down again.

"You must forgive me," he said, "but I can't go into this. These are dangerous matters to meddle with. Besides, how do you know it is not a hoax?"

"Played by whom?" asked the doctor. "Hark!"

The telephone bell suddenly rang. It was clearly audible to the doctor.

"Don't you hear it?" he said.

"Hear what?"

"The telephone bell ringing."

"I hear no bell," said the chaplain, rather angrily. "There is no bell ringing."

The doctor did not answer, but went through into his study, and turned on the lights. Then he took the receiver and mouthpiece off its hook.

"Yes?" he said, in a voice that trembled. "Who is it? Yes: Mr. Dawkins is here. I will try and get him to speak to you."

He went back into the other room.

"Dawkins," he said, "there is a soul in agony. I pray you to listen. For God's sake come and listen."

The chaplain hesitated a moment.

"As you will," he said.

He took up the receiver and put it to his ear.

"I am Mr. Dawkins," he said.

He waited.

"I can hear nothing whatever," he said at length. "Ah, there was something there. The faintest whisper."

"Ah, try to hear, try to hear!" said the doctor.

Again the chaplain listened. Suddenly he laid the instrument down, frowning.

"Something – somebody said, 'I killed her, I confess it. I want to be forgiven.' It's a hoax, my dear Teesdale. Somebody knowing your spiritualistic leanings is playing a very grim joke on you. I *can't* believe it."

Dr. Teesdale took up the receiver.

"I am Dr. Teesdale," he said. "Can you give Mr. Dawkins some sign that it is you?"

Then he laid it down again.

"He says he thinks he can," he said. "We must wait."

The evening was again very warm, and the window into the paved yard at the back of the house was open. For five minutes or so the two men stood in silence, waiting, and nothing happened. Then the chaplain spoke.

"I think that is sufficiently conclusive," he said.

Even as he spoke a very cold draught of air suddenly blew into the room, making the papers on the desk rustle. Dr. Teesdale went to the window and closed it.

"Did you feel that?" he asked.

"Yes, a breath of air. Chilly."

Once again in the closed room it stirred again.

"And did you feel that?" asked the doctor.

The chaplain nodded. He felt his heart hammering in his throat suddenly.

"Defend us from all peril and danger of this coming night," he exclaimed.

"Something is coming!" said the doctor.

As he spoke it came. In the centre of the room not three yards away from them stood the figure of a man with his head bent over on to his shoulder, so that the face was not visible. Then he took his head in both his hands and raised it like a weight, and looked them in the face. The eyes and tongue protruded, a livid mark was round the neck. Then there came a sharp rattle on the boards of the floor, and the figure was no longer there. But on the floor there lay a new rope.

For a long while neither spoke. The sweat poured off the doctor's face, and the chaplain's white lips whispered prayers. Then by a huge effort the doctor pulled himself together. He pointed at the rope.

"It has been missing since the execution," he said.

Then again the telephone bell rang. This time the chaplain needed no prompting. He went to it at once and the ringing ceased. For a while he listened in silence.

"Charles Linkworth," he said at length, "in the sight of God, in whose presence you stand, are you truly sorry for your sin?"

Some answer inaudible to the doctor came, and the chaplain closed his eyes. And Dr. Teesdale knelt as he heard the words of the Absolution.

At the close there was silence again.

"I can hear nothing more," said the chaplain, replacing the receiver.

Presently the doctor's man-servant came in with the tray of spirits and syphon. Dr. Teesdale pointed without looking to where the apparition had been.

"Take the rope that is there and burn it, Parker," he said.

There was a moment's silence.

"There is no rope, sir," said Parker.

At Abdul Ali's Grave

Luxor, as most of those who have been there will allow, is a place of notable charm, and boasts many attractions for the traveller, chief among which he will reckon an excellent hotel containing a billiard-room, a garden fit for the gods to sit in, any quantity of visitors, at least a weekly dance on board a tourist steamer, quail shooting, a climate as of Avilion, and a number of stupendously ancient monuments for those archæologically inclined. But to certain others, few indeed in number, but almost fanatically convinced of their own orthodoxy, the charm of Luxor, like some sleeping beauty, only wakes when these things cease, when the hotel has grown empty and the billard-marker "has gone for a long rest" to Cairo, when the decimated quail and the decimating tourist have fled northwards, and the Theban plain, Danæ to a tropical sun, is a gridiron across which no man would willingly make a journey by day, not even if Queen Hatasoo herself should signify that she would give him audience on the terraces of Deir-el-Bahari. A suspicion however that the fanatic few were right, for in other respects they were men of estimable opinions, induced me to examine their convictions for myself, and thus it came about that two years ago, certain days toward the beginning of June saw me still there, a confirmed convert.

Much tobacco and the length of summer days had assisted us to the analysis of the charm of which summer in the south is possessed, and Weston – one of the earliest of the elect – and myself had discussed it at some length, and though we reserved as the principal ingredient a nameless something which baffled the chemist, and must be felt to be understood, we were easily able to detect certain other drugs of sight and sound, which we were agreed contributed to the whole. A few of them are here subjoined.

The waking in the warm darkness just before dawn to find that the desire for stopping in bed fails with the awakening.

The silent start across the Nile in the still air with our horses, who, like us, stand and sniff at the incredible sweetness of the coming morning without apparently finding it less wonderful in repetition.

The moment infinitesimal in duration but infinite in sensation, just before the sun rises, when the grey shrouded river is struck suddenly out of darkness, and becomes a sheet of green bronze.

The rose flush, rapid as a change of colour in some chemical combination, which shoots across the sky from east to west, followed immediately by the sunlight which catches the peaks of the western hills, and flows down like some luminous liquid.

The stir and whisper which goes through the world: a breeze springs up; a lark soars, and sings; the boatman shouts "Yallah, Yallah"; the horses toss their heads.

The subsequent ride.

The subsequent breakfast on our return.

The subsequent absence of anything to do.

At sunset the ride into the desert thick with the scent of warm barren sand, which smells like nothing else in the world, for it smells of nothing at all.

The blaze of the tropical night.

Camel's milk.

Converse with the fellahin, who are the most charming and least accountable people on the face of the earth except when tourists are about, and when in consequence there is no thought but backsheesh.

Lastly, and with this we are concerned, the possibility of odd experiences.

The beginning of the things which make this tale occurred four days ago, when Abdul Ali, the oldest man in the village, died suddenly, full of days and riches. Both, some thought, had probably been somewhat exaggerated, but his relations affirmed without variation that he had as many years as he had English pounds, and that each was a hundred. The apt roundness of these numbers was incontestable, the thing was too neat not to be true, and before he had been dead for twenty-four hours it was a matter of orthodoxy. But with regard to his relations, that which turned their bereavement, which must soon have occurred, into a source of blank dismay instead of pious resignation, was that not one of these English pounds, not even their less satisfactory equivalent in notes, which, out of the tourist season, are looked upon at Luxor as a not very dependable variety of Philosopher's stone, though certainly capable of producing gold under favourable circumstances, could be found. Abdul Ali with his hundred years was dead, his century of sovereigns – they might as well have been an annuity – were dead with him, and his son Mohamed, who had previously enjoyed a sort of brevet rank in anticipation of the event, was considered to be throwing far more dust in the air than the genuine affection even of a chief mourner wholly justified.

Abdul, it is to be feared, was not a man of stereotyped respectability; though full of years and riches, he enjoyed no great reputation for honour. He drank wine whenever he could get it, he ate food during the days of Ramadan, scornful of the fact, when his appetite desired it, he was supposed to have the evil eye, and in his last moments he was attended by the notorious Achmet, who is well known here to be practised in Black Magic, and has been suspected of the much meaner crime of robbing the bodies of those lately dead. For in Egypt, while to despoil the bodies of ancient kings and priests is a privilege for which advanced and learned societies vie with each other, to rob the corpses of your contemporaries is considered the deed of a dog. Mohamed, who soon exchanged the throwing of dust in the air for the more natural mode of expressing chagrin, which is to gnaw the nails, told us in confidence that he suspected Achmet of having ascertained the secret of where his father's money was, but it appeared that Achmet had as blank a face as anybody when his patient, who was striving to make some communication to him, went out into the great silence, and the suspicion that he knew where the money was gave way, in the minds, of those who were competent to form an estimate of his character, to a but dubious regret that he had just failed to learn that very important fact.

So Abdul died and was buried, and we all went to the funeral feast, at which we ate more roast meat than one naturally cares about at five in the afternoon on a June day, in consequence of which Weston and I, not requiring dinner, stopped at home after our return from the ride into the desert, and talked to Mohamed, Abdul's son, and Hussein, Abdul's youngest grandson, a boy of about twenty, who is also our valet, cook and housemaid, and they together woefully narrated of the money that had been and was not, and told us scandalous tales about Achmet concerning his weakness for cemeteries. They drank coffee and smoked, for though Hussein was our servant, we had been that day the guests of his father, and shortly after they had gone, up came Machmout.

Machmout, who says he thinks he is twelve, but does not know for certain, is kitchen-maid, groom and gardener, and has to an extraordinary degree some occult power resembling clairvoyance. Weston, who is a member of the Society for Psychical Research, and the tragedy of whose life has been the detection of the fraudulent medium Mrs. Blunt, says that it is all thought-reading, and has made notes of many of Machmout's performances, which may subsequently turn out to be of interest. Thought-reading, however, does not seem to me to fully explain the experience which followed

Abdul's funeral, and with Machmout I have to put it down to White Magic, which should be a very inclusive term, or to Pure Coincidence, which is even more inclusive, and will cover all the inexplicable phenomena of the world, taken singly. Machmout's method of unloosing the forces of White Magic is simple, being the ink-mirror known by name to many, and it is as follows.

A little black ink is poured into the palm of Machmout's hand, or, as ink has been at a premium lately owing to the last post-boat from Cairo which contained stationery for us having stuck on a sand-bank, a small piece of black American cloth about an inch in diameter is found to be a perfect substitute. Upon this he gazes. After five or ten minutes his shrewd monkey-like expression is struck from his face, his eyes, wide open, remain fixed on the cloth, a complete rigidity sets in over his muscles, and he tells us of the curious things he sees. In whatever position he is, in that position he remains without the deflection of a hair's breadth until the ink is washed off or the cloth removed. Then he looks up and says "Khalás," which means, "It is finished."

We only engaged Machmout's services as second general domestic a fortnight ago, but the first evening he was with us he came upstairs when he had finished his work, and said, "I will show you White Magic; give me ink," and proceeded to describe the front hall of our house in London, saying that there were two horses at the door, and that a man and woman soon came out, gave the horses each a piece of bread and mounted. The thing was so probable that by the next mail I wrote asking my mother to write down exactly what she was doing and where at half-past five (English time) on the evening of June 12. At the corresponding time in Egypt Machmout was describing speaking to us of a "sitt" (lady) having tea in a room which he described with some minuteness, and I am waiting anxiously for her letter. The explanation which Weston gives us of all these phenomena is that a certain picture of people I know is present in my mind, though I may not be aware of it, – present to my subliminal self, I think, he says, – and that I give an unspoken suggestion to the hypnotised Machmout. My explanation is that there isn't any explanation, for no suggestion on my part would make my brother go out and ride at the moment when Machmout says he is so doing (if indeed we find that Machmout's visions are chronologically correct). Consequently I prefer the open mind and am prepared to believe anything. Weston, however, does not speak quite so calmly or scientifically about Machmout's last performance, and since it took place he has almost entirely ceased to urge me to become a member of the Society for Psychical Research, in order that I may no longer be hidebound by vain superstitions.

Machmout will not exercise these powers if his own folk are

present, for he says that when he is in this state, if a man who knew Black Magic was in the room, or knew that he was practising White Magic, he could get the spirit who presides over the Black Magic to kill the spirit of White Magic, for the Black Magic is the more potent, and the two are foes. And as the spirit of White Magic is on occasions a powerful friend – he had before now befriended Machmout in a manner which I consider incredible – Machmout is very desirous that he should abide long with him. But Englishmen it appears do not know the Black Magic, so with us he is safe. The spirit of Black Magic, to speak to whom it is death, Machmout saw once "between heaven and earth, and night and day," so he phrases it, on the Karnak road. He may be known, he told us, by the fact that he is of paler skin than his people, that he has two long teeth, one in each corner of his mouth, and that his eyes, which are white all over, are as big as the eyes of a horse.

Machmout squatted himself comfortably in the corner, and I gave him the piece of black American cloth. As some minutes must elapse before he gets into the hypnotic state in which the visions begin, I strolled out on to the balcony for coolness. It was the hottest night we had yet had, and though the sun had set three hours, the thermometer still registered close on 100°. Above, the sky seemed veiled with grey, where it should have been dark velvety blue, and a fitful puffing wind from the south threatened three days of the sandy intolerable khamseen. A little way up the street to the left was a small café in front of which were glowing and waning little glowworm specks of light from the water pipes of Arabs sitting out there in the dark. From inside came the click of brass castanets in the hands of some dancing-girl, sounding sharp and precise against the wailing bagpipe music of the strings and pipes which accompany these movements which Arabs love and Europeans think so unpleasing. Eastwards the sky was paler and luminous, for the moon was imminently rising, and even as I looked the red rim of the enormous disc cut the line of the desert, and on the instant, with a curious aptness, one of the Arabs outside the café broke out into that wonderful chant—

"I cannot sleep for longing for thee, O full moon.
Far is thy throne over Mecca, slip down, O beloved, to me."

Immediately afterwards I heard the piping monotone of Machmout's voice begin, and in a moment or two I went inside.

We have found that the experiments gave the quickest result by contact, a fact which confirmed Weston in his explanation of them by thought transference of some elaborate kind, which I confess I cannot understand. He was writing at a table in the window when I came in, but looked up.

"Take his hand," he said; "at present he is quite incoherent."

"Do you explain that?" I asked.

"It is closely analogous, so Myers thinks, to talking in sleep. He has been saying something about a tomb. Do make a suggestion, and see if he gives it right. He is remarkably sensitive, and he responds quicker to you than to me. Probably Abdul's funeral suggested the tomb!"

A sudden thought struck me.

"Hush!" I said, "I want to listen."

Machmout's head was thrown a little back, and he held the hand in which was the piece of cloth rather above his face. As usual he was talking very slowly, and in a high staccato voice, absolutely unlike his usual tones.

"On one side of the grave," he pipes, "is a tamarisk tree, and the green beetles make *fantasia* about it. On the other side is a mud wall. There are many other graves about, but they are all asleep. This is *the* grave, because it is awake, and it moist and not sandy."

"I thought so," said Weston. "It is Abdul's grave he is talking about."

"There is a red moon sitting on the desert," continued Machmout, "and it is now. There is the puffing of khamseen, and much dust coming. The moon is red with dust, and because it is low."

"Still sensitive to external conditions," said Weston. "That is rather curious. Pinch him, will you?"

I pinched Machmout; he did not pay the slightest attention.

"In the last house of the street, and in the doorway stands a man. Ah! ah!" cried the boy suddenly, "it is the Black Magic he knows. Don't let him come. He is going out of the house," he shrieked, "he is coming – no, he is going the other way towards the moon and the grave. He has the Black Magic with him, which can raise the dead, and he has a murdering knife, and a spade. I cannot see his face, for the Black Magic is between it and my eyes."

Weston had got up, and, like me, was hanging on Machmout's words.

"We will go there," he said. "Here is an opportunity of testing it. Listen a moment."

"He is walking, walking, walking," piped Machmout, "still walking to the moon and the grave. The moon sits no longer on the desert, but has sprung up a little way."

I pointed out of the window.

"That at any rate is true," I said.

Weston took the cloth out of Machmout's hand, and the piping ceased. In a moment he stretched himself, and rubbed his eyes.

"Khalás," he said.

"Yes, it is Khalás."

"Did I tell you of the sitt in England?" he asked.

"Yes, oh, yes," I answered; "thank you, little Machmout. The White Magic was very good to-night. Get you to bed."

Machmout trotted obediently out of the room, and Weston closed the door after him.

"We must be quick," he said. "It is worth while going and giving the thing a chance, though I wish he had seen something less gruesome. The odd thing is that he was not at the funeral, and yet he describes the grave accurately. What do you make of it?"

"I make that the White Magic has shown Machmout that somebody with black magic is going to Abdul's grave, perhaps to rob it," I answered resolutely.

"What are we to do when we get there?" asked Weston.

"See the Black Magic at work. Personally I am in a blue funk. So are you."

"There is no such thing as Black Magic," said Weston. "Ah, I have it. Give me that orange."

Weston rapidly skinned it, and cut from the rind two circles as big as a five shilling piece, and two long, white fangs of skin. The first he fixed in his eyes, the two latter in the corners of his mouth.

"The Spirit of Black Magic?" I asked.

"The same."

He took up a long black burnous and wrapped it round him. Even in the bright lamp light, the spirit of black magic was a sufficiently terrific personage.

"I don't believe in black magic," he said, "but others do. If it is necessary to put a stop to – to anything that is going on, we will hoist the man on his own petard. Come along. Whom do you suspect it is – I mean, of course, who was the person you were thinking of when your thoughts were transferred to Machmout."

"What Machmout said," I answered, "suggested Achmet to me."

Weston indulged in a laugh of scientific incredulity, and we set off.

The moon, as the boy had told us, was just clear of the horizon, and as it rose higher, its colour at first red and sombre, like the blaze of some distant conflagration, paled to a tawny yellow. The hot wind from the south, blowing no longer fitfully but with a steadily increasing violence, was thick with sand, and of an incredibly scorching heat, and the tops of the palm trees in the garden of the deserted hotel on the right were lashing themselves to and fro with a harsh rattle of dry leaves. The cemetery lay on the outskirts of the village, and, as long as our way lay between the mud walls of the huddling street, the wind came to us only as the heat from behind closed furnace doors. Every now and then with a whisper and whistle rising into a great buffeting flap, a sudden whirlwind of dust would scour some twenty yards along the road, and then break like a shore-quenched wave against one or other of the mud walls or throw itself heavily against a house and fall in a shower of sand. But once free of obstructions we were opposed to the full heat and blast of the wind which blew full in our teeth. It was the first summer khamseen of the year, and for the moment I wished I had gone north with the tourist and the quail and the billiard marker, for khamseen fetches the marrow out of the bones, and turns the body to blotting paper. We passed no one in the street, and the only sound we heard, except the wind, was the howling of moonstruck dogs.

The cemetery is surrounded by a tall mud-built wall, and sheltering for a few moments under this we discussed our movements. The row of tamarisks close to which the tomb lay went down the centre of the graveyard, and by skirting the wall outside and climbing softly over where they approached it, the fury of the wind might help us to get near the grave without being seen, if anyone happened to be there. We had just decided on this, and were moving on to put the scheme into execution, when the wind dropped for a moment, and in the silence we could hear the chump of the spade being driven into the earth, and what gave me a sudden thrill of intimate horror, the cry of the carrion-feeding hawk from the dusky sky just overhead.

Two minutes later we were creeping up in the shade of the tamarisks, to where Abdul had been buried. The great green beetles which live on the trees were flying about blindly, and once or twice one dashed into my face with a whirr of mail-clad wings. When we were within some twenty yards of the grave we stopped for a moment, and, looking cautiously out from our shelter of tamarisks, saw the figure of a man already waist deep in the earth, digging out the newly turned grave. Weston, who was standing behind me, had adjusted the characteristics of the spirit of Black Magic so as to be ready for emergencies, and turning round suddenly, and finding myself unawares face to face with that realistic impersonation, though my nerves are not precariously strong, I could have found it within me to shriek aloud. But that unsympathetic man of iron only shook with suppressed laughter, and, holding the eyes in his hand, motioned me forward again without speaking to where the trees grew thicker. There we stood not a dozen yards away from the grave.

We waited, I suppose, for some ten minutes, while the man, whom we saw to be Achmet, toiled on at his impious task. He was entirely naked, and his brown skin glistened with the dews of exertion in the moonlight. At times he chattered in a cold uncanny manner to himself, and once or twice he stopped for breath. Then he began scraping the earth away with his hands, and soon afterwards searched in his clothes, which were lying near, for a piece of rope, with which he stepped into the grave, and in a moment reappeared again with both ends in his hands. Then, standing astride the grave, he pulled strongly, and one end of the coffin appeared above the ground. He chipped a piece of the lid away to make sure that he had the right end, and then, setting it upright, wrenched off the top with his knife, and there faced us, leaning against the coffin lid, the small shrivelled figure of the dead Abdul, swathed like a baby in white.

I was just about to motion the spirit of Black Magic to make his appearance, when Machmout's words came into my head: "He had with him the Black Magic which can raise the dead," and sudden overwhelming curiosity, which froze disgust and horror into chill unfeeling things, came over me.

"Wait," I whispered to Weston, "he will use the Black Magic."

Again the wind dropped for a moment, and again, in the silence that came with it, I heard the chiding of the hawk overhead, this time nearer, and thought I heard more birds than one.

Achmet meantime had taken the covering from off the face, and had undone the swathing band, which at the moment after death is bound round the chin to close the jaw, and in Arab burial is always left there, and from where we stood I could see that the jaw dropped when the bandage was untied, as if, though the wind blew towards us with a ghastly scent of mortality on it, the muscles were not even now set, though the man had been dead sixty hours. But still a rank and burning curiosity to see what this unclean ghoul would do next stifled all other feelings in my mind. He seemed not to notice, or, at any rate, to disregard that mouth gaping awry, and moved about nimbly in the moonlight.

He took from a pocket of his clothes, which were lying near, two small black objects, which now are safely embedded in the mud at the bottom of the Nile, and rubbed them briskly together. By degrees they grew luminous with a sickly yellow pallor of light, and from his hands went up a wavy, phosphorescent flame. One of these cubes he placed in the open mouth of the corpse, the other in his own, and, taking the dead man closely in his arms as though he would indeed dance with death, he breathed long breaths from his mouth into that dead cavern which was pressed to his. Suddenly he started back with a quick-drawn breath of wonder and perhaps of horror, and stood for a space as if irresolute, for the cube which the dead man held instead of lying loosely in the jaw was pressed tight between clenched teeth. After a moment of irresolution he stepped back quickly to his clothes again, and took up from near them the knife with which he had stripped off the coffin lid, and holding this in one hand behind his back, with the other he took out the cube from the dead man's mouth, though with a visible exhibition of force, and spoke.

"Abdul," he said, "I am your friend, and I swear I will give your money to Mohamed, if you will tell me where it is."

Certain I am that the lips of the dead moved, and the eyelids fluttered for a moment like the wings of a wounded bird, but at that sight the horror so grew on me that I was physically incapable of stifling the cry that rose to my lips, and Achmet turned round. Next moment the complete Spirit of Black Magic glided out of the shade of the trees, and stood before him. The wretched man stood for a moment without stirring, then, turning with shaking knees to flee, he stepped back and fell into the grave he had just opened.

Weston turned on me angrily, dropping the eyes and the teeth of the Afrit.

"You spoiled it all," he cried. "It would perhaps have been the most interesting . . ." and his eye lighted on the dead Abdul, who peered open-eyed from the coffin, then swayed, tottered, and fell forward, face downwards on the ground close to him. For one moment he lay there, and then the body rolled slowly on to its back without visible cause of movement, and lay staring into the sky. The face was covered with dust, but with the dust was mingled fresh blood. A nail had caught the cloth that wound him, underneath which, as usual, were the clothes in which he had died, for the Arabs do not wash their dead, and it had torn a great rent through them all, leaving the right shoulder bare.

Weston strove to speak once, but failed. Then:

"I will go and inform the police," he said, "if you will stop here, and see that Achmet does not get out."

But this I altogether refused to do, and, after covering the body with the coffin to protect it from the hawks, we secured Achmet's arms with the rope he had already used that night, and took him off to Luxor.

Next morning Mohamed came to see us.

"I thought Achmet knew where the money was," he said exultantly.

"Where was it?"

"In a little purse tied round the shoulder. The dog had already begun stripping it. See" – and he brought it out of his pocket— "it is all there in those English notes, five pounds each, and there are twenty of them."

Our conclusion was slightly different, for even Weston will allow that Achmet *hoped* to learn from dead lips the secret of the treasure, and then to kill the man anew and bury him. But that is pure conjecture.

The only other point of interest lies in the two black cubes which we picked up, and found to be graven with curious characters. These I put one evening into Machmout's hand, when he was exhibiting to us his curious powers of "thought transference." The effect was that he screamed aloud, crying out that the Black Magic had come, and though I did not feel certain about that, I thought they would be safer in mid-Nile. Weston grumbled a little, and said that he had wanted to take them to the British Museum, but that I feel sure was an afterthought.

The Shootings of Achnaleish

The dining-room windows, both front and back, the one looking into Oakley Street, the other into a small back-yard with three sooty shrubs in it (known as the garden), were all open, so that the table stood in mid-stream of such air as there was. But in spite of this the heat was stifling, since, for once in a way, July had remembered that it was the duty of good little summers to be hot. Hot in consequence it had been: heat reverberated from the house-walls, it rose through the boot from the paving-stones, it poured down from a large superheated sun that walked the sky all day long in a benignant and golden manner. Dinner was over, but the small party of four who had eaten it still lingered.

Mabel Armytage – it was she who had laid down the duty of good little summers – spoke first.

"Oh, Jim, it sounds too heavenly," she said. "It makes me feel cool to think of it. Just fancy, in a fortnight's time we shall all four of us be there, in our own shooting-lodge—"

"Farm-house," said Jim.

"Well, I didn't suppose it was Balmoral, with our own coffee-coloured salmon river roaring down to join the waters of our own loch."

Jim lit a cigarette.

"Mabel, you mustn't think of shooting-lodges and salmon rivers and lochs," he said. "It's a farm-house, rather a big one, though I'm sure we shall find it hard enough to fit in. The salmon river you speak of is a big burn, no more, though it appears that salmon have been caught there. But when I saw it, it would have required as much cleverness on the part of a salmon to fit into it as it will require on our parts to fit into our farm-house. And the loch is a tarn."

Mabel snatched the "Guide to Highland Shootings" out of my hand with a rudeness that even a sister should not show her elder brother, and pointed a withering finger at her husband.

"'Achnaleish,'" she declaimed, "'is situated in one of the grandest and most remote parts of Sutherlandshire. To be let from August 12 till the end of October, the lodge with shooting and fishing belonging. Proprietor supplies two keepers, fishing-gillie, boat on loch, and dogs. Tenant should secure about 500 head of grouse, and 500 head of mixed game, including partridge, black-game, woodcock, snipe, roe deer; also rabbits in very large number, especially by ferreting. Large baskets of brown trout can be taken from the loch, and whenever the water is high sea-trout and occasional salmon. Lodge contains' – I can't go on; it's too hot, and you know the rest. Rent only £350!"

Jim listened patiently.

"Well?" he said. "What then?"

Mabel rose with dignity.

"It *is* a shooting-lodge with a salmon river and a loch, just as I have said. Come, Madge, let's go out. It is too hot to sit in the house."

"You'll be calling Buxton 'the major-domo' next," remarked Jim, as his wife passed him.

I had picked up the "Guide to Highland Shootings" again which my sister had so unceremoniously plucked from me, and idly compared the rent and attractions of Achnaleish with other places that were to let.

"Seems cheap, too," I said. "Why, here's another place, just the same sort of size and bag, for which they ask £500; here's another at £550."

Jim helped himself to coffee.

"Yes, it does seem cheap," he said. "But, of course, it's very remote; it took me a good three hours from Lairg, and I don't suppose I was driving very noticeably below the legal limit. But it's cheap, as you say."

Now, Madge (who is my wife) has her prejudices. One of them – an extremely expensive one – is that anything cheap has always some hidden and subtle drawback, which you discover when it is too late. And the drawback to cheap houses is drains or offices – the presence, so to speak, of the former, and the absence of the latter. So I hazarded these.

"No, the drains are all right," said Jim, "because I got the certificate of the inspector, and as for offices, really I think the servants' parts are better than ours. No – why it's so cheap, I can't imagine."

"Perhaps the bag is overstated," I suggested.

Jim again shook his head.

"No, that's the funny thing about it," he said. "The bag, I am sure, is understated. At least, I walked over the moor for a couple of hours, and the whole place is simply crawling with hares. Why, you could shoot five hundred hares alone on it."

"Hares?" I asked. "That's rather queer, so far up, isn't it?"

Jim laughed.

"So I thought. And the hares are queer, too; big beasts, very dark in colour. Let's join the others outside. Jove! what a hot night!"

Even as Mabel had said, that day fortnight found us all four, the four who had stifled and sweltered in Chelsea, flying through the cool and invigorating winds of the North. The road was in admirable condition, and I should not wonder if for the second time Jim's big Napier went not noticeably below the legal limit. The servants had gone straight up, starting the same day as we, while we had got out at Perth, motored to Inverness, and were now, on the second day, nearing our goal. Never have I seen so depopulated a road. I do not suppose there was a man to a mile of it.

We had left Lairg about five that afternoon expecting to arrive at Achnaleish by eight, but one disaster after another overtook us. Now it was the engine, and now a tyre that delayed us, till finally we stopped some eight miles short of our destination, to light up, for with evening had come a huge wrack of cloud out of the West, so that we were cheated of the clear post-sunset twilight of the North. Then on again, till, with a little dancing of the car over a bridge, Jim said:

"That's the bridge of our salmon river; so look out for the turning up to the lodge. It is to the right, and only a narrow track. You can send her along, Sefton," he called to the chauffeur; "we shan't meet a soul."

I was sitting in front, finding the speed and the darkness extraordinarily exhilarating. A bright circle of light was cast by our lamps, fading into darkness in front, while at the sides, cut off by the casing of the lamps, the transition into blackness was sharp and sudden. Every now and then, across this circle of illumination some wild thing would pass: now a bird, with hurried flutter of wings when it saw the speed of the luminous monster, would just save itself from being knocked over; now a rabbit feeding by the side of the road would dash on to it and then bounce back again; but more frequently it would be a hare that sprang up from its feeding and raced in front of us. They seemed dazed and scared by the light, unable to wheel into the darkness again, until time and again I thought we must run over one, so narrowly, in giving a sort of desperate sideways leap, did it miss our wheels. Then it seemed that one started up almost from under us, and I saw, to my surprise, it was enormous in size, and in colour apparently quite black. For some hundred yards it raced in front of us, fascinated by the bright light pursuing it, then, like the rest, it dashed for the darkness. But it was too late, and with a horrid jolt we ran over it. At once Sefton slowed down and stopped, for Jim's rule is to go back always and make sure that any poor run-over is dead. So, when we stopped, the chauffeur jumped down and ran back.

"What was it?" Jim asked me, as we waited.

"A hare."

Sefton came running back.

"Yes, sir, quite dead," he said. "I picked it up, sir."

"What for!"

"Thought you might like to see it, sir. It's the biggest hare I ever see, and it's quite black."

It was immediately after this that we came to the track up to the house, and in a few minutes we were within doors. There we found that if "shooting-lodge" was a term unsuitable, so also was "farm-house," so roomy, excellently proportioned, and well furnished was our dwelling, while the contentment that beamed from Buxton's face was sufficient testimonial for the offices. In the hall, too, with its big open fireplace, were a couple of big solemn bookcases, full of serious works, such as some educated minister might have left, and, coming down dressed for dinner before the others, I dipped into the shelves. Then – something must long have been vaguely simmering in my brain, for I pounced on the book as soon as I saw it – I came upon Elwes's "Folklore of the North-West Highlands," and looked out "Hare" in the index. Then I read:

"Nor is it only witches that are believed to have the power of changing themselves into animals . . . Men and women on whom no suspicion of the sort lies are thought to be able to do this, and to don the bodies of certain animals, notably hares . . . Such, according to local superstition, are easily distinguishable by their size and colour, which approaches jet black."

I was up and out early next morning, prey to the vivid desire that attacks many folk in new places – namely, to look on the fresh country and the new horizons – and, on going out, certainly the surprise was great. For I had imagined an utterly lonely and solitary habitation; instead, scarce half a mile away, down the steep brae-side at the top of which stood our commodious farmhouse, ran a typically Scotch village street, the hamlet no doubt of Achnaleish. So steep was this hill-side that the village was really remote; if it was half a mile away in crow-flying measurement, it must have been a couple of hundred yards below us. But its existence was the odd thing to me:

there were some four dozen houses, at the least, while we had not seen half that number since leaving Lairg. A mile away, perhaps, lay the shining shield of the western sea; to the other side, away from the village, I had no difficulty in recognising the river and the loch. The house, in fact, was set on a hog's back; from all sides it must needs be climbed to. But, as is the custom of the Scots, no house, however small, should be without its due brightness of flowers, and the walls of this were purple with clematis and orange with tropæolum. It all looked very placid and serene and home-like.

I continued my tour of exploration, and came back rather late for breakfast. A slight check in the day's arrangements had occurred, for the head keeper, Maclaren, had not come up, and the second, Sandie Ross, reported that the reason for this had been the sudden death of his mother the evening before. She was not known to be ill, but just as she was going to bed she had thrown up her arms, screamed suddenly as if with fright, and was found to be dead. Sandie, who repeated this news to me after breakfast, was just a slow, polite Scotchman, rather shy, rather awkward. Just as he finished – we were standing about outside the back-door – there came up from the stables the smart, very English-looking Sefton. In one hand he carried the black hare.

He touched his hat to me as he went in.

"Just to show it to Mr. Armytage, sir," he said. "She's as black as a boot."

He turned into the door, but not before Sandie Ross had seen what he carried, and the slow, polite Scotchman was instantly turned into some furtive, frightened-looking man.

"And where might it be that you found that, sir?" he asked.

Now, the black-hare superstition had already begun to intrigue me.

"Why does that interest you?" I asked.

The slow Scotch look was resumed with an effort.

"It'll no interest me," he said. "I just asked. There are unco many black hares in Achnaleish."

Then his curiosity got the better of him.

"She'd have been nigh to where the road passes by and on to Achnaleish?" he asked.

"The hare? Yes, we found her on the road there."

Sandie turned away.

"She aye sat there," he said.

There were a number of little plantations climbing up the steep hill-side from Achnaleish to the moor above, and we had a pleasant slack sort of morning shooting there, walking through and round them with a nondescript tribe of beaters, among whom the serious Buxton figured. We had fair enough sport, but of the hares which

Jim had seen in such profusion none that morning came to the gun, till at last, just before lunch, there came out of the apex of one of these plantations, some thirty yards from where Jim was standing, a very large, dark-coloured hare. For one moment I saw him hesitate – for he holds the correct view about long or doubtful shots at hares – then he put up his gun to fire. Sandie, who had walked round outside, after giving the beaters their instructions, was at this moment close to him, and with incredible quickness rushed upon him and with his stick struck up the barrels of the gun before he could fire.

"Black hare!" he cried. "Ye'd shoot a black hare? There's no shooting of hares at all in Achnaleish, and mark that."

Never have I seen so sudden and extraordinary a change in a man's face: it was as if he had just prevented some blackguard of the street from murdering his wife.

"An' the sickness about an' all," he added indignantly. "When the puir folk escape from their peching fevered bodies an hour or two, to the caller muirs."

Then he seemed to recover himself.

"I ask your pardon, sir," he said to Jim. "I was upset with ane thing an' anither, an' the black hare ye found deid last night – eh, I'm blatherin' again. But there's no a hare shot on Achnaleish, that's sure."

Jim was still looking in mere speechless astonishment at Sandie when I came up. And, though shooting is dear to me, so too is folk-lore.

"But we've taken the shooting of Achnaleish, Sandie," I said. "There was nothing there about not shooting hares."

Sandie suddenly boiled up again for a minute.

"An' mebbe there was nothing there about shooting the bairns and the weemen!" he cried.

I looked round, and saw that by now the beaters had all come through the wood: of them Buxton and Jim's valet, who was also among them, stood apart: all the rest were standing round us two with gleaming eyes and open mouths, hanging on the debate, and forced, so I imagined, from their imperfect knowledge of English to attend closely in order to catch the drift of what went on. Every now and then a murmur of Gaelic passed between them, and this somehow I found peculiarly disconcerting.

"But what have the hares to do with the children or women of Achnaleish?" I asked.

There was no reply to this beyond the reiterated sentence: "There's na shooting of hares in Achnaleish whatever," and then Sandie turned to Jim.

"That's the end of the bit wood, sir," he said. "We've been a'roound."

Certainly the beat had been very satisfactory. A roe had fallen to Jim (one ought also to have fallen to me, but remained, if not standing, at any rate running away). We had a dozen of black-game, four pigeons, six brace of grouse (these were, of course, but outliers, as we had not gone on to the moor proper at all), some thirty rabbits, and four couple of woodcock. This, it must be understood, was just from the fringe of plantations about the house, but this was all we meant to do to-day, making only a morning of it, since our ladies had expressly desired first lessons in the art of angling in the afternoon, so that they too could be busy. Excellently too had Sandie worked the beat, leaving us now, after going, as he said, all round, a couple of hundred yards only from the house, at a few minutes to two.

So, after a little private signalling from Jim to me, he spoke to Sandie, dropping the hare-question altogether.

"Well, the beat has gone excellently," he said, "and this afternoon we'll be fishing. Please settle with the beaters every evening, and tell me what you have paid out. Good morning to you all."

We walked back to the house, but the moment we had turned a hum of confabulation began behind us, and, looking back, I saw Sandie and all the beaters in close whispering conclave. Then Jim spoke.

"More in your line than mine," he said; "I prefer shooting a hare to routing out some cock-and-bull story as to why I shouldn't. What does it all mean?"

I mentioned what I had found in Elwes last night.

"Then do they think it was we who killed the old lady on the road, and that I was going to kill somebody else this morning?" he asked. "How does one know that they won't say that rabbits are their aunts, and woodcock their uncles, and grouse their children? I never heard such rot, and to-morrow we'll have a hare drive. Blow the grouse! We'll settle this hare-question first."

Jim by this time was in the frame of mind typical of the English when their rights are threatened. He had the shooting of Achnaleish, on which were hares, sir, hares. And if he chose to shoot hares, neither papal bull nor royal charter could stop him.

"Then there'll be a row," said I, and Jim sniffed scornfully.

At lunch Sandie's remark about the "sickness," which I had forgotten till that moment, was explained.

"Fancy that horrible influenza getting here," said Madge. "Mabel and I went down to the village this morning, and, oh, Ted, you can get all sorts of things, from mackintoshes to peppermints, at the most heavenly shop, and there was a child there looking awfully ill and feverish. So we inquired: it was the 'sickness' – that was all they knew. But, from what the woman said, it's clearly influenza. Sudden fever, and all the rest of it."

"Bad type?" I asked.

"Yes; there have been several deaths already among the old people from pneumonia following it."

Now, I hope that as an Englishman I too have a notion of my rights, and attempt anyhow to enforce them, as a general rule, if they are wantonly threatened. But if a mad bull wishes to prevent my going across a certain field, I do not insist on my rights, but go round instead, since I see no reasonable hope of convincing the bull that according to the constitution of my country I may walk in this field unmolested. And that afternoon, as Madge and I drifted about the loch, while I was not employed in disentangling her flies from each other or her hair or my coat, I pondered over our position with regard to the hares and men of Achnaleish, and thought that the question of the bull and the field represented our standpoint pretty accurately. Jim *had* the shooting of Achnaleish, and that undoubtedly included the right to shoot hares: so too he might have the right to walk over a field in which was a mad bull. But it seemed to me not more futile to argue with the bull than to hope to convince these folk of Achnaleish that the hares were – as was assuredly the case – only hares, and not the embodiments of their friends and relations. For that, beyond all doubt, was their belief, and it would take, not half an hour's talk, but perhaps a couple of generations of education to kill that belief, or even to reduce it to the level of a superstition. At present it was no superstition – the terror and incredulous horror on Sandie's face when Jim raised his gun to fire at the hare told me that – it was a belief as sober and commonplace as our own belief that the hares were not incarnations of living folk in Achnaleish. Also, virulent influenza was raging in the place, and Jim proposed to have a hare-drive to-morrow! What would happen?

That evening Jim raved about it in the smoking-room.

"But, good gracious, man, what can they *do*?" he cried. "What's the use of an old gaffer from Achnaleish saying I've shot his grand-daughter and, when he is asked to produce the corpse, telling the jury that we've eaten it, but that he has got the skin as evidence? What skin? A hare-skin! Oh, folklore is all very well in its way, a nice subject for discussion when topics are scarce, but don't tell me it can enter into practical life. What can they do?"

"They can shoot us," I remarked.

"The canny, God-fearing Scotchmen shoot us for shooting hares?" he asked.

"Well, it's a possibility. However, I don't think you'll have much of a hare-drive in any case."

"Why not?"

"Because you won't get a single native beater, and you won't get a keeper to come either. You'll have to go with Buxton and your man."

"Then I'll discharge Sandie," snapped Jim.

"That would be a pity: he knows his work."

Jim got up.

"Well, his work to-morrow will be to drive hares for you and me," said Jim. "Or do you funk?"

"I funk," I replied.

The scene next morning was extremely short. Jim and I went out before breakfast, and found Sandie at the back door, silent and respectful. In the yard were a dozen young Highlanders, who had beaten for us the day before.

"Morning, Sandie," said Jim shortly. "We'll drive hares to-day. We ought to get a lot in those narrow gorges up above. Get a dozen beaters more, can you?"

"There will be na hare-drive here," said Sandie quietly.

"I have given you your orders," said Jim.

Sandie turned to the group of beaters outside and spoke half a dozen words in Gaelic. Next moment the yard was empty, and they were all running down the hillside towards Achnaleish. One stood on the skyline a moment, waving his arms, making some signal, as I supposed, to the village below. Then Sandie turned again.

"An' whaur are your beaters, sir?" he asked.

For the moment I was afraid Jim was going to strike him. But he controlled himself.

"You are discharged," he said.

The hare-drive, therefore, since there were neither beaters nor keeper – Maclaren, the head-keeper, having been given this "day-off" to bury his mother – was clearly out of the question, and Jim, still blustering rather, but a good bit taken aback at the sudden disciplined defection of the beaters, was in betting humour that they would all return by to-morrow morning. Meanwhile the post which should have arrived before now had not come, though Mabel from her bedroom window had seen the post-cart on its way up the drive a quarter of an hour ago. At that a sudden idea struck me, and I ran to the edge of the hog's back on which the house was set. It was even as I thought: the post-cart was just striking the high-road below, going away from the house and back to the village, without having left our letters.

I went back to the dining-room. Everything apparently was going wrong this morning: the bread was stale, the milk was not fresh, and the bell was rung for Buxton. Quite so: neither milkman nor baker had called.

From the point of view of folk-lore this was admirable.

"There's another cock-and-bull story called 'taboo,'" I said. "It means that nobody will supply you with anything."

"My dear fellow, a little knowledge is a dangerous thing," said Jim, helping himself to marmalade.

I laughed.

"You are irritated," I said, "because you are beginning to be afraid that there is something in it."

"Yes, that's quite true," he said. "But who could have supposed there was anything in it? Ah, dash it! there *can't* be. A hare is a hare."

"Except when it is your first cousin," said I.

"Then I shall go out and shoot first cousins by myself," he said.

That, I am glad to say, in the light of what followed, we dissuaded him from doing, and instead he went off with Madge down the burn. And I, I may confess, occupied myself the whole morning, ensconced in a thick piece of scrub on the edge of the steep brae above Achnaleish, in watching through a field-glass what went on there. One could see as from a balloon almost: the street with its houses was spread like a map below.

First, then, there was a funeral – the funeral, I suppose, of the mother of Maclaren, attended, I should say, by the whole village. But after that there was no dispersal of the folk to their work: it was as if it was the Sabbath; they hung about the street talking. Now one group would break up, but it would only go to swell another, and no one went either to his house or to the fields. Then, shortly before lunch, another idea occurred to me, and I ran down the hill-side, appearing suddenly in the street, to put it to the test. Sandie was there, but he turned his back square on me, as did everybody else, and as I approached any group talk fell dead. But a certain movement seemed to be going on; where they stood and talked before, they now moved and were silent. Soon I saw what that meant. None would remain in the street with me: every man was going to his house.

The end house of the street was clearly the "heavenly shop" we had been told of yesterday. The door was open and a small child was looking round it as I approached, for my plan was to go in, order something, and try to get into conversation. But, while I was still a yard or two off, I saw through the glass of the door a man inside come quickly up and pull the child roughly away, banging the door and locking it. I knocked and rang, but there was no response: only from inside came the crying of the child.

The street which had been so busy and populous was now completely empty; it might have been the street of some long-deserted place, but that thin smoke curled here and there above the houses. It was as silent, too, as the grave, but, for all that, I knew it was watching. From every house, I felt sure, I was being watched by eyes of mistrust and hate, yet no sign of living being could I see. There was to me something rather eerie about this: to know one is watched by invisible eyes is never, I suppose, quite a comfortable sensation; to know that those eyes are all hostile does not increase the sense of security. So I just climbed back up the hillside again, and from my thicket above the brae again I peered down. Once more the street was full.

Now, all this made me uneasy: the taboo had been started, and – since not a soul had been near us since Sandie gave the word, whatever it was, that morning – was in excellent working order. Then what was the purport of these meetings and colloquies? What else threatened? The afternoon told me.

It was about two o'clock when these meetings finally broke up, and at once the whole village left the street for the hill-sides, much as if they were all returning to work. The only odd thing indeed was that no one remained behind: women and children alike went out, all in little parties of two and three. Some of these I watched rather idly, for I had formed the hasty conclusion that they were all going back to their usual employments, and saw that here a woman and girl were cutting dead bracken and heather. That was reasonable enough, and I turned my glass on others. Group after group I examined; all were doing the same thing, cutting fuel . . . fuel.

Then vaguely, with a sense of impossibility, a thought flashed across me; again it flashed, more vividly. This time I left my hiding-place with considerable alacrity and went to find Jim down by the burn. I told him exactly what I had seen and what I believed it meant, and I fancy that his belief in the possibility of folk-lore entering the domain of practical life was very considerably quickened. In any case, it was not a quarter of an hour afterwards that the chauffeur and I were going, precisely as fast as the Napier was able, along the road to Lairg. We had not told the women what my conjecture was, because we believed that, making the dispositions we were making, there was no cause for alarm-sounding. One private signal only existed between Jim within the house that night and me outside. If my conjecture proved to be correct, he was to place a light in the window of my room, which I should see returning after dark from Lairg. My ostensible reason for going was to get some local fishing-flies.

As we flowed – there is no other word for the movement of these big cars but that – over the road to Lairg, I ran over everything in my mind. I felt no doubt whatever that all the brushwood and kindling I had seen being gathered in was to be piled after nightfall round our walls and set on fire. This certainly would not be done till after dark; indeed, we both felt sure that it would not be done till it was supposed that we were all abed. It remained to see whether the police at Lairg agreed with my conjecture, and it was to ascertain this that I was now flowing there.

I told my story to the chief constable as soon as I got there, omitting nothing and, I think, exaggerating nothing. His face got graver and graver as I proceeded.

"Yes, sir, you did right to come," he said. "The folk at Achnaleish are the dourest and the most savage in all Scotland. You'll have to give up this hare-hunting, though, whatever," he added.

He rang up his telephone.

"I'll get five men," he said, "and I'll be with you in ten minutes."

Our plan of campaign was simple. We were to leave the car well out of sight of Achnaleish, and – supposing the signal was in my window – steal up from all sides to command the house from every direction. It would not be difficult to make our way unseen through the plantations that ran up close to the house, and hidden at their margins we could see whether the brushwood and heather were piled up round the lodge. There we should wait to see if anybody attempted to fire it. That somebody, whenever he showed his light, would be instantly covered by a rifle and challenged.

It was about ten when we dismounted and stalked our way up to the house. The light burned in my window; all else was quiet. Personally, I was unarmed, and so, when I had planted the men in places of advantageous concealment round the house, my work was over. Then I returned to Sergeant Duncan, the chief constable, at the corner of the hedge by the garden, and waited.

How long we waited I do not know, but it seemed as if æons slipped by over us. Now and then an owl would hoot, now and then a rabbit ran out from cover and nibbled the short sweet grass of the lawn. The night was thickly overcast with clouds, and the house seemed no more than a black dot, with slits of light where windows were lit within. By and by even these slits of illumination were extinguished, and other lights appeared in the top story. After a while they, too, vanished; no sign of life appeared on the quiet house. Then suddenly the end came: I heard a foot grate on the gravel; I saw the gleam of a lantern, and heard Duncan's voice.

"Man," he shouted, "if you move hand or foot I fire. My rifle-bead is dead on you."

Then I blew the whistle; the others ran up, and in less than a minute it was all over. The man we closed in on was Maclaren.

"They killed my mither with that hell-carriage," he said, "as she juist sat on the road, puir body, who had niver hurt them."

And that seemed to him an excellent reason for attempting to burn us all to death.

But it took time to get into the house: their preparations had been singularly workmanlike, for every window and door on the ground floor was wired up.

Now, we had Achnaleish for two months, but we had no wish to be burned or otherwise murdered. What we wanted was not a prosecution of our head-keeper, but peace, the necessaries of life, and beaters. For that we were willing to shoot no hares, and release Maclaren. An hour's conclave next morning settled these things; the ensuing two months were most enjoyable, and relations were the friendliest.

But if anybody wants to test how far what Jim still calls cock-and-bull stories can enter into practical life, I should suggest to him to go a-shooting hares at Achnaleish.

How Fear Departed from the Long Gallery

Church-Peveril is a house so beset and frequented by spectres, both visible and audible, that none of the family which it shelters under its acre and a half of green copper roofs takes psychical phenomena with any seriousness. For to the Peverils the appearance of a ghost is a matter of hardly greater significance than is the appearance of the post to those who live in more ordinary houses. It arrives, that is to say, practically every day, it knocks (or makes other noises), it is observed coming up the drive (or in other places). I myself, when staying there, have seen the present Mrs. Peveril, who is rather short-sighted, peer into the dusk, while we were taking our coffee on the terrace after dinner, and say to her daughter:

"My dear, was not that the Blue Lady who has just gone into the shrubbery. I hope she won't frighten Flo. Whistle for Flo, dear."

(Flo, it may be remarked, is the youngest and most precious of many dachshunds.)

Blanche Peveril gave a cursory whistle, and crunched the sugar left unmelted at the bottom of her coffee-cup between her very white teeth.

"Oh, darling, Flo isn't so silly as to mind," she said. "Poor blue

Aunt Barbara is such a bore! Whenever I meet her she always looks as if she wanted to speak to me, but when I say, 'What is it, Aunt Barbara?' she never utters, but only points somewhere towards the house, which is so vague. I believe there was something she wanted to confess about two hundred years ago, but she has forgotten what it is."

Here Flo gave two or three short pleased barks, and came out of the shrubbery wagging her tail, and capering round what appeared to me to be a perfectly empty space on the lawn.

"There! Flo has made friends with her," said Mrs. Peveril. "I wonder why she dresses in that very stupid shade of blue."

From this it may be gathered that even with regard to psychical phenomena there is some truth in the proverb that speaks of familiarity. But the Peverils do not exactly treat their ghosts with contempt, since most of that delightful family never despised anybody except such people as avowedly did not care for hunting or shooting, or golf or skating. And as all of their ghosts are of their family, it seems reasonable to suppose that they all, even the poor Blue Lady, excelled at one time in field-sports. So far, then, they harbour no such unkindness or contempt, but only pity. Of one Peveril, indeed, who broke his neck in vainly attempting to ride up the main staircase on a thoroughbred mare after some monstrous and violent deed in the back-garden, they are very fond, and Blanche comes downstairs in the morning with an eye unusually bright when she can announce that Master Anthony was "very loud" last night. He (apart from the fact of his having been so foul a ruffian) was a tremendous fellow across country, and they like these indications of the continuance of his superb vitality. In fact, it is supposed to be a compliment, when you go to stay at Church-Peveril, to be assigned a bedroom which is frequented by defunct members of the family. It means that you are worthy to look on the august and villainous dead, and you will find yourself shown into some vaulted or tapestried chamber, without benefit of electric light, and are told that great-great-grandmamma Bridget occasionally has vague business by the fireplace, but it is better not to talk to her, and that you will hear Master Anthony "awfully well" if he attempts the front staircase any time before morning. There you are left for your night's repose, and, having quakingly undressed, begin reluctantly to put out your candles. It is draughty in these great chambers, and the solemn tapestry swings and bellows and subsides, and the firelight dances on the forms of huntsmen and warriors and stern pursuits. Then you climb into your bed, a bed so huge that you feel as if the desert of Sahara was spread for you, and pray, like the mariners who sailed with St. Paul, for day. And, all the time, you are aware that Freddy and

Harry and Blanche and possibly even Mrs. Peveril are quite capable of dressing up and making disquieting tappings outside your door, so that when you open it some inconjecturable horror fronts you. For myself, I stick steadily to the assertion that I have an obscure valvular disease of the heart, and so sleep undisturbed in the new wing of the house where Aunt Barbara, and great-great-grandmamma Bridget and Master Anthony never penetrate. I forget the details of great-great-grandmamma Bridget, but she certainly cut the throat of some distant relation before she disembowelled herself with the axe that had been used at Agincourt. Before that she had led a very sultry life, crammed with amazing incident.

But there is one ghost at Church-Peveril at which the family never laugh, in which they feel no friendly and amused interest, and of which they only speak just as much as is necessary for the safety of their guests. More properly it should be described as two ghosts, for the "haunt" in question is that of two very young children, who were twins. These, not without reason, the family take very seriously indeed. The story of them, as told me by Mrs. Peveril, is as follows:

In the year 1602, the same being the last of Queen Elizabeth's reign, a certain Dick Peveril was greatly in favour at Court. He was brother to Master Joseph Peveril, then owner of the family house and lands, who two years previously, at the respectable age of seventy-four, became father of twin boys, first-born of his progeny. It is known that the royal and ancient virgin had said to handsome Dick, who was nearly forty years his brother's junior, "'Tis pity that you are not master of Church-Peveril," and these words probably suggested to him a sinister design. Be that as it may, handsome Dick, who very adequately sustained the family reputation for wickedness, set off to ride down to Yorkshire, and found that, very conveniently, his brother Joseph had just been seized with an apoplexy, which appeared to be the result of a continued spell of hot weather combined with the necessity of quenching his thirst with an augmented amount of sack, and had actually died while handsome Dick, with God knows what thoughts in his mind, was journeying northwards. Thus it came about that he arrived at Church-Peveril just in time for his brother's funeral. It was with great propriety that he attended the obsequies, and returned to spend a sympathetic day or two of mourning with his widowed sister-in-law, who was but a faint-hearted dame, little fit to be mated with such hawks as these. On the second night of his stay, he did that which the Peverils regret to this day. He entered the room where the twins slept with their nurse, and quietly strangled the latter as she slept. Then he took the twins and put them into the fire which warms the long gallery. The weather, which up to the day of Joseph's death had been so hot, had changed suddenly to bitter cold, and the fire was heaped high with burning logs and was exultant with flame. In the core of this conflagration he struck out a cremation-chamber, and into that he threw the two children, stamping them down with his riding-boots. They could just walk, but they could not walk out of that ardent place. It is said that he laughed as he added more logs. Thus he became master of Church-Peveril.

The crime was never brought home to him, but he lived no longer than a year in the enjoyment of his blood-stained inheritance. When he lay a-dying he made his confession to the priest who attended him, but his spirit struggled forth from its fleshly coil before Absolution could be given him. On that very night there began in Church-Peveril the haunting which to this day is but seldom spoken of by the family, and then only in low tones and with serious mien. For only an hour or two after handsome Dick's death, one of the servants passing the door of the long gallery heard from within peals of the loud laughter so jovial and yet so sinister which he had thought would never be heard in the house again. In a moment of that cold courage which is so nearly akin to mortal terror he opened the door and entered, expecting to see he knew not what manifestation of him who lay dead in the room below. Instead he saw two little white-robed figures toddling towards him hand in hand across the moon-lit floor.

The watchers in the room below ran upstairs startled by the crash of his fallen body, and found him lying in the grip of some dread convulsion. Just before morning he regained consciousness and told his tale. Then pointing with trembling and ash-grey finger towards the door, he screamed aloud, and so fell back dead.

During the next fifty years this strange and terrible legend of the twin-babies became fixed and consolidated. Their appearance, luckily for those who inhabit the house, was exceedingly rare, and during these years they seem to have been seen four or five times only. On each occasion they appeared at night, between sunset and sunrise, always in the same long gallery, and always as two toddling children scarcely able to walk. And on each occasion the luckless individual who saw them died either speedily or terribly, or with both speed and terror, after the accursed vision had appeared to him. Sometimes he might live for a few months: he was lucky if he died, as did the servant who first saw them, in a few hours. Vastly more awful was the fate of a certain Mrs. Canning, who had the ill-luck to see them in the middle of the next century, or to be quite accurate, in the year 1760. By this time the hours and the place of their appearance were well known, and, as up till a year ago, visitors were warned not to go between sunset and sunrise into the long gallery.

But Mrs. Canning, a brilliantly clever and beautiful woman, admirer also and friend of the notorious sceptic M. Voltaire, wilfully went and sat night after night, in spite of all protestations, in the haunted place. For four evenings she saw nothing, but on the fifth she had her will, for the door in the middle of the gallery opened, and there came toddling towards her the ill-omened innocent little pair. It seemed that even then she was not frightened, but she thought good, poor wretch, to mock at them, telling them it was time for them to get back into the fire. They gave no word in answer, but turned away from her crying and sobbing. Immediately after they disappeared from her vision and she rustled downstairs to where the family and guests in the house were waiting for her, with the triumphant announcement that she has seen them both, and must needs write to M. Voltaire, saying that she had spoken to spirits made manifest. It would make him laugh. But when some months later the whole news reached him he did not laught at all.

Mrs. Canning was one of the great beauties of her day, and in the year 1760 she was at the height and zenith of her blossoming. The chief beauty, if it is possible to single out one point where all was so exquisite, lay in the dazzling colour and incomparable brilliance of her complexion. She was now just thirty years of age, but, in spite of the excesses of her life, retained the snow and roses of girlhood, and she courted the bright light of day which other women shunned, for it but showed to great advantage the splendour of her skin. In consequence she was very considerably dismayed one morning, about a fortnight after her strange experience in the long gallery, to observe on her left cheek, an inch or two below her turquoise-coloured eyes, a little greyish patch of skin, about as big as a threepenny piece. It was in vain that she applied her accustomed washes and unguents: vain, too, were the arts of her *fardeuse* and of her medical adviser. For a week she kept herself secluded, martyring herself with solitude and unaccustomed physics, and for result at the end of the week she had no amelioration to comfort herself with: instead this woeful grey patch had doubled itself in size. Thereafter the nameless disease, whatever it was, developed in new and terrible ways. From the centre of the discoloured place there sprouted forth little lichen-like tendrils of greenish-grey, and another patch appeared on her lower lip. This, too, soon vegetated, and one morning, on opening her eyes to the horror of a new day, she found that her vision was strangely blurred. She sprang to her looking-glass, and what she saw caused her to shriek aloud with horror. From under her upper eye-lid a fresh growth had sprung up, mushroom-like, in the night, and its filaments extended downwards, screening the pupil of her eye. Soon after, her tongue and throat were attacked: the air passages became obstructed, and death by suffocation was merciful after such suffering.

More terrible yet was the case of a certain Colonel Blantyre who fired at the children with his revolver. What he went through is not to be recorded here.

It is this haunting, then, that the Peverils take quite seriously, and every guest on his arrival in the house is told that the long gallery must not be entered after nightfall on any pretext whatever. By day, however, it is a delightful room and intrinsically merits description, apart from the fact that the due understanding of its geography is necessary for the account that here follows. It is full eighty feet in length, and is lit by a row of six tall windows looking over the gardens at the back of the house. A door communicates with the landing at the top of the main staircase, and about half-way down the gallery in the wall facing the windows is another door communicating with the back staircase and servants' quarters, and thus the gallery forms a constant place of passage for them in going to the rooms on the first landing. It was through this door that the baby-figures came when they appeared to Mrs. Canning, and on several other occasions they have been known to make their entry here, for the room out of which handsome Dick took them lies just beyond at the top of the back stairs. Further on again in the gallery is the fireplace into which he thrust them, and at the far end a large bow-window looks straight down the avenue. Above this fireplace there hangs with grim significance a portrait of handsome Dick, in the insolent beauty of early manhood, attributed to Holbein, and a dozen other portraits of great merit face the windows. During the day this is the most frequented sitting-room in the house, for its other visitors never appear there then, nor does it then ever resound with the harsh jovial laugh of handsome Dick, which sometimes, after dark has fallen, is heard by passers-by on the landing outside. But Blanche does not grow bright-eyed when she hears it: she shuts her ears and hastens to put a greater distance between her and the sound of that atrocious mirth.

But during the day the long gallery is frequented by many occupants, and much laughter in no wise sinister or saturnine resounds there. When summer lies hot over the land, those occupants lounge in the deep window seats, and when winter spreads his icy fingers and blows shrilly between his frozen palms, congregate round the fireplace at the far end, and perch, in companies of cheerful chatterers, upon sofa and chair, and chair-back and floor. Often have I sat there on long August evenings up till dressing-time, but never have I been there when anyone has seemed disposed to linger over-late without hearing the warning: "It is close on sunset: shall we go?" Later on in the shorter autumn days they often have tea laid there, and sometimes it has happened that, even while merriment was most uproarious, Mrs. Peveril has suddenly looked out of the window and said, "My dears, it is getting so late: let us finish our nonsense downstairs in the hall." And then for a moment a curious hush always falls on loquacious family and guests alike, and as if some bad news had just been known, we all make our silent way out of the place. But the spirits of the Peverils (of the living ones, that is to say) are the most mercurial imaginable, and the blight which the thought of handsome Dick and his doings casts over them passes away again with amazing rapidity.

A typical party, large, young, and peculiarly cheerful, was staying at Church-Peveril shortly after Christmas last year, and as usual on December 31, Mrs. Peveril was giving her annual New Year's Eve ball. The house was quite full, and she had commandeered as well the greater part of the Peveril Arms to provide sleeping-quarters for the overflow from the house. For some days past a black and windless frost had stopped all hunting, but it is an ill windlessness that blows no good (if so mixed a metaphor may be forgiven), and the lake below the house had for the last day or two been covered with an adequate and admirable sheet of ice. Everyone in the house had been occupied all the morning of that day in performing swift and violent manoeuvres on the elusive surface, and as soon as lunch was over we all, with one exception, hurried out again. This one exception was Madge Dalrymple, who had had the misfortune to fall rather badly earlier in the day, but hoped, by resting her injured knee, instead of joining the skaters again, to be able to dance that evening. The hope, it is true, was the most sanguine sort, for she could but hobble ignobly back to the house, but with the breezy optimism which characterises the Peverils (she is Blanche's first cousin), she remarked that it would be but tepid enjoyment that she could, in her present state, derive from further skating, and thus she sacrificed little, but might gain much.

Accordingly, after a rapid cup of coffee which was served in the long gallery, we left Madge comfortably reclined on the big sofa at right-angles to the fireplace, with an attractive book to beguile the tedium till tea. Being of the family, she knew all about handsome Dick and the babies, and the fate of Mrs. Canning and Colonel Blantyre, but as we went out I heard Blanche say to her, "Don't run it too fine, dear," and Madge had replied, "No; I'll go away well before sunset." And so we left her alone in the long gallery.

Madge read her attractive book for some minutes, but failing to get absorbed in it, put it down and limped across to the window. Though it was still but little after two, it was but a dim and uncertain light that entered, for the crystalline brightness of the morning had given place to a veiled obscurity produced by flocks of thick clouds which were coming sluggishly up from the north-east. Already the whole sky was overcast with them, and occasionally a few snow-flakes fluttered waveringly down past the long windows. From the darkness and bitter cold of the afternoon, it seemed to her that there was like to be a heavy snowfall before long, and these outward signs were echoed inwardly in her by that muffled drowsiness of the brain, which to those who are sensitive to the pressures and lightness of weather portends storm. Madge was peculiarly the prey of such external influences: to her a brisk morning gave an ineffable brightness and briskness of spirit, and correspondingly the approach of heavy weather produced a somnolence in sensation that both drowsed and depressed her.

It was in such mood as this that she limped back again to the sofa beside the log-fire. The whole house was comfortably heated by water-pipes, and though the fire of logs and peat, an adorable mixture, had been allowed to burn low, the room was very warm. Idly she watched the dwindling flames, not opening her book again, but lying on the sofa with face towards the fireplace, intending drowsily and not immediately to go to her own room and spend the hours, until the return of the skaters made gaiety in the house again, in writing one or two neglected letters. Still drowsily she began thinking over what she had to communicate: one letter several days overdue should go to her mother, who was immensely interested in the psychical affairs of the family. She would tell her how Master Anthony had been prodigiously active on the staircase a night or two ago, and how the Blue Lady, regardless of the severity of the weather, had been seen by Mrs. Peveril that morning, strolling about. It was rather interesting: the Blue Lady had gone down the laurel walk and had been seen by her to enter the stables, where, at the moment, Freddy Peveril was inspecting the frost-bound hunters. Identically then, a sudden panic had spread through the stables, and the horses had whinnied and kicked, and shied, and sweated. Of the fatal twins nothing had been seen for many years past, but, as her mother knew, the Peverils never used the long gallery after dark.

Then for a moment she sat up, remembering that she was in the long gallery now. But it was still but a little after half-past two, and if she went to her room in half an hour, she would have ample time to write this and another letter before tea. Till then she would read her book. But she found she had left it on the window-sill, and it seemed scarcely worth while to get it. She felt exceedingly drowsy.

The sofa where she lay had been lately recovered, in a greyish green shade of velvet, somewhat the colour of lichen. It was of very thick soft texture, and she luxuriously stretched her arms out, one on each side of her body, and pressed her fingers into the nap. How horrible that story of Mrs. Canning was: the growth on her face was of the colour of lichen. And then without further transition or blurring of thought Madge fell asleep.

She dreamed. She dreamed that she awoke and found herself exactly where she had gone to sleep, and in exactly the same attitude. The flames from the logs had burned up again, and leaped on the walls, fitfully illuminating the picture of handsome Dick above the fireplace. In her dream she knew exactly what she had done to-day, and for what reason she was lying here now instead of being out with the rest of the skaters. She remembered also (still dreaming), that she was going to write a letter or two before tea, and prepared to get up in order to go to her room. As she half-rose she caught sight of her own arms lying out on each side of her on the grey velvet sofa. But she could not see where her hands ended, and where the grey velvet began: her fingers seemed to have melted into the stuff. She could see her wrists quite clearly, and a blue vein on the backs of her hands, and here and there a knuckle. Then, in her dream, she remembered the last thought which had been in her mind before she fell asleep, namely the growth of the lichen-coloured vegetation on the face and the eyes and the throat of Mrs. Canning. At that thought the strangling terror of real nightmare began: she knew that she was being transformed into this grey stuff, and she was absolutely unable to move. Soon the grey would spread up her arms, and over her feet; when they came in from skating they would find here nothing but a huge misshapen cushion of lichen-coloured velvet, and that would be she. The horror grew more acute, and then by a violent effort she shook herself free of the clutches of this very evil dream, and she awoke.

For a minute or two she lay there, conscious only of the tremendous relief at finding herself awake. She felt again with her fingers the pleasant touch of the velvet, and drew them backwards and forwards, assuring herself that she was not, as her dream had suggested, melting into greyness and softness. But she was still, in spite of the violence of her awakening, very sleepy, and lay there till, looking down, she was aware that she could not see her hands at all. It was very nearly dark.

At that moment a sudden flicker of flame came from the dying fire, and a flare of burning gas from the peat flooded the room. The portrait of handsome Dick looked evilly down on her, and her hands were visible again. And then a panic worse than the panic of her dreams seized her. Daylight had altogether faded, and she knew that she was alone in the dark in the terrible gallery. This panic was of the nature of nightmare, for she felt unable to move for terror. But it was worse than nightmare because she knew she was awake.

And then the full cause of this frozen fear dawned on her; she knew with the certainty of absolute conviction that she was about to see the twin-babies.

She felt a sudden moisture break out on her face, and within her mouth her tongue and throat went suddenly dry, and she felt her tongue grate along the inner surface of her teeth. All power of movement had slipped from her limbs, leaving them dead and inert, and she stared with wide eyes into the blackness. The spurt of flame from the peat had burned itself out again, and darkness encompassed her.

Then on the wall opposite her, facing the windows, there grew a faint light of dusky crimson. For a moment she thought it but heralded the approach of the awful vision, then hope revived in her heart, and she remembered that thick clouds had overcast the sky before she went to sleep, and guessed that this light came from the sun not yet quite sunk and set. This sudden revival of hope gave her the necessary stimulus, and she sprang off the sofa where she lay. She looked out of the window and saw the dull glow on the horizon. But before she could take a step forward it was obscured again. A tiny sparkle of light came from the hearth which did no more than illuminate the tiles of the fireplace, and snow falling heavily tapped at the window panes. There was neither light nor sound except these.

But the courage that had come to her, giving her the power of movement, had not quite deserted her, and she began feeling her way down the gallery. And then she found that she was lost. She stumbled against a chair, and, recovering herself, stumbled against another. Then a table barred her way, and, turning swiftly aside, she found herself up against the back of a sofa. Once more she turned and saw the dim gleam of the firelight on the side opposite to that on which she expected it. In her blind gropings she must have reversed her direction. But which way was she to go now. She seemed blocked in by furniture. And all the time insistent and imminent was the fact that the two innocent terrible ghosts were about to appear to her.

Then she began to pray. "Lighten our darkness, O Lord," she said to herself. But she could not remember how the prayer continued, and she had sore need of it. There was something about the perils of the night. All this time she felt about her with groping, fluttering hands. The fire-glimmer which should have been on her left was on her right again; therefore she must turn herself round again. "Lighten our darkness," she whispered, and then aloud she repeated, "Lighten our darkness."

She stumbled up against a screen, and could not remember the existence of any such screen. Hastily she felt beside it with blind hands, and touched something soft and velvety. Was it the sofa on which she had lain? If so, where was the head of it. It had a head and a back and feet – it was like a person, all covered with grey lichen. Then she lost her head completely. All that remained to her was to pray; she was lost, lost in this awful place, where no one came in the dark except the babies that cried. And she heard her voice rising from whisper to speech, and speech to scream. She shrieked out the holy words, she yelled them as if blaspheming as she groped among tables and chairs and the pleasant things of ordinary life which had become so terrible.

Then came a sudden and an awful answer to her screamed prayer. Once more a pocket of inflammable gas in the peat on the hearth was reached by the smouldering embers, and the room started into light. She saw the evil eyes of handsome Dick, she saw the little ghostly snow-flakes falling thickly outside. And she saw where she was, just opposite the door through which the terrible twins made their entrance. Then the flame went out again, and left her in blackness once more. But she had gained something, for she had her geography now. The centre of the room was bare of furniture, and one swift dart would take her to the door of the landing above the main staircase and into safety. In that gleam she had been able to see the handle of the door, bright-brassed, luminous like a star. She would go straight for it; it was but a matter of a few seconds now.

She took a long breath, partly of relief, partly to satisfy the demands of her galloping heart. But the breath was only half-taken when she was stricken once more into the immobility of nightmare.

There came a little whisper, it was no more than that, from the door opposite which she stood, and through which the twin-babies entered. It was not quite dark outside it, for she could see that the door was opening. And there stood in the opening two little white figures, side by side. They came towards her slowly, shufflingly. She could not see face or form at all distinctly, but the two little white figures were advancing. She knew them to be the ghosts of terror, innocent of the awful doom they were bound to bring, even as she was innocent. With the inconceivable rapidity of thought, she made up her mind what to do. She had not hurt them or laughed at them, and they, they were but babies when the wicked and bloody deed had sent them to their burning death. Surely the spirits of these children would not be inaccessible to the cry of one who was of the same blood as they, who had committed no fault that merited the doom they brought. If she entreated them they might have mercy, they might forebear to bring the curse on her, they might allow her to pass out of the place without blight, without the sentence of death, or the shadow of things worse than death upon her.

It was but for the space of a moment that she hesitated, then she sank down on to her knees, and stretched out her hands towards them.

"Oh, my dears," she said, "I only fell asleep. I have done no more wrong than that—"

She paused a moment, and her tender girl's heart thought no more of herself, but only of them, those little innocent spirits on whom so awful a doom was laid, that they should bring death where other children bring laughter, and doom for delight. But all those who had seen them before had dreaded and feared them, or had mocked at them.

Then, as the enlightenment of pity dawned on her, her fear fell from her like the wrinkled sheath that holds the sweet folded buds of Spring.

"Dears, I am so sorry for you," she said. "It is not your fault that you must bring me what you must bring, but I am not afraid any longer. I am only sorry for you. God bless you, you poor darlings."

She raised her head and looked at them. Though it was so dark, she could now see their faces, though all was dim and wavering, like the light of pale flames shaken by a draught. But the faces were not miserable or fierce – they smiled at her with shy little baby smiles. And as she looked they grew faint, fading slowly away like wreaths of vapour in frosty air.

Madge did not at once move when they had vanished, for instead of fear there was wrapped round her a wonderful sense of peace, so happy and serene that she would not willingly stir, and so perhaps disturb it. But before long she got up, and feeling her way, but without any sense of nightmare pressing her on, or frenzy of fear to spur her, she went out of the long gallery, to find Blanche just coming upstairs whistling and swinging her skates.

"How's the leg, dear," she asked. "You're not limping any more."

Till that moment Madge had not thought of it.

"I think it must be all right," she said; "I had forgotten it, anyhow. Blanche, dear, you won't be frightened for me, will you, but – but I have seen the twins."

For a moment Blanche's face whitened with terror.

"What?" she said in a whisper.

"Yes, I saw them just now. But they were kind, they smiled at me, and I was so sorry for them. And somehow I am sure I have nothing to fear."

It seems that Madge was right, for nothing untoward has come to her. Something, her attitude to them, we must suppose, her pity, her sympathy, touched and dissolved and annihilated the curse. Indeed, I was at Church-Peveril only last week, arriving there after dark. Just as I passed the gallery door, Blanche came out.

"Ah, there you are," she said: "I've just been seeing the twins. They looked too sweet and stopped nearly ten minutes. Let us have tea at once."

Caterpillars

I saw a month or two ago in an Italian paper that the Villa Cascana, in which I once stayed, had been pulled down, and that a manufactory of some sort was in process of erection on its site. There is therefore no longer any reason for refraining from writing of those things which I myself saw (or imagined I saw) in a certain room and on a certain landing of the villa in question, nor from mentioning the circumstances which followed, which may or may not (according to the opinion of the reader) throw some light on or be somehow connected with this experience.

The Villa Cascana was in all ways but one a perfectly delightful house, yet, if it were standing now, nothing in the world – I use the phrase in its literal sense – would induce me to set foot in it again, for I believe it to have been haunted in a very terrible and practical manner. Most ghosts, when all is said and done, do not do much harm; they may perhaps terrify, but the person whom they visit usually gets over their visitation. They may on the other hand be entirely friendly and beneficent. But the appearances in the Villa Cascana were not beneficent, and had they made their "visit" in a very slightly different manner, I do not suppose I should have got over it any more than Arthur Inglis did.

The house stood on an ilex-clad hill not far from Sestri di Levante on the Italian Riviera, looking out over the iridescent blues of that enchanted sea, while behind it rose the pale green chestnut woods that climb up the hillsides till they give place to the pines that, black in contrast with them, crown the slopes. All round it the garden in the luxuriance of mid-spring bloomed and was fragrant, and the scent of magnolia and rose, borne on the salt freshness of the winds from the sea, flowed like a stream through the cool vaulted rooms.

On the ground floor a broad pillared *loggia* ran round three sides of the house, the top of which formed a balcony for certain rooms of the first floor. The main staircase, broad and of grey marble steps, led up from the hall to the landing outside these rooms, which were three in number, namely, two big sitting-rooms and a bedroom arranged *en suite*. The latter was unoccupied, the sitting-rooms were in use. From these the main staircase was continued to the second floor, where were situated certain bedrooms, one of which I occupied, while from the other side of the first-floor landing some half-dozen steps led to another suite of rooms, where, at the time I am speaking of, Arthur Inglis, the artist, had his bedroom and studio. Thus the landing outside my bedroom at the top of the house commanded both the landing of the first floor and also the steps that led to Inglis' rooms. Jim Stanley and his wife, finally (whose guest I was), occupied rooms in another wing of the house, where also were the servants' quarters.

I arrived just in time for lunch on a brilliant noon of mid-May. The garden was shouting with colour and fragrance, and not less delightful after my broiling walk up from the *marina*, should have been the coming from the reverberating heat and blaze of the day into the marble coolness of the villa. Only (the reader has my bare word for this, and nothing more), the moment I set foot in the house I felt that something was wrong. This feeling, I may say, was quite vague, though very strong, and I remember that when I saw letters waiting for me on the table in the hall I felt certain that the explanation was here: I was convinced that there was bad news of some sort for me. Yet when I opened them I found no such explanation of my premonition: my correspondents all reeked of prosperity. Yet this clear miscarriage of a presentiment did not dissipate my uneasiness. In that cool fragrant house there was something wrong.

I am at pains to mention this because to the general view it may explain that though I am as a rule so excellent a sleeper that the extinction of my light on getting into bed is apparently contemporaneous with being called on the following morning, I slept very badly on my first night in the Villa Cascana. It may also explain the fact that when I did sleep (if it was indeed in sleep that I saw what I thought I saw) I dreamed in a very vivid and original manner, original, that is to say, in the sense that something that, as far as I knew, had never previously entered into my consciousness, usurped it then. But since, in addition to this evil premonition, certain words and events occurring during the rest of the day might have suggested something of what I thought happened that night, it will be well to relate them.

After lunch, then, I went round the house with Mrs. Stanley, and during our tour she referred, it is true, to the unoccupied bedroom on the first floor, which opened out of the room where we had lunched.

"We left that unoccupied," she said, "because Jim and I have a charming bedroom and dressing-room, as you saw, in the wing, and if we used it ourselves we should have to turn the dining-room into a dressing-room and have our meals downstairs. As it is, however, we have our little flat there, Arthur Inglis has his little flat in the other passage; and I remembered (aren't I extraordinary?) that you once said that the higher up you were in a house the better you were pleased. So I put you at the top of the house, instead of giving you that room."

It is true, that a doubt, vague as my uneasy premonition, crossed my mind at this. I did not see why Mrs. Stanley should have explained all this, if there had not been more to explain. I allow, therefore, that the thought that there was something to explain about the unoccupied bedroom was momentarily present to my mind.

The second thing that may have borne on my dream was this.

At dinner the conversation turned for a moment on ghosts. Inglis, with the certainty of conviction, expressed his belief that anybody who could possibly believe in the existence of supernatural phenomena was unworthy of the name of an ass. The subject instantly dropped. As far as I can recollect, nothing else occurred or was said that could bear on what follows.

We all went to bed rather early, and personally I yawned my way upstairs, feeling hideously sleepy. My room was rather hot, and I threw all the windows wide, and from without poured in the white light of the moon, and the love-song of many nightingales. I undressed quickly, and got into bed, but though I had felt so sleepy before, I now felt extremely wide-awake. But I was quite content to be awake: I did not toss or turn, I felt perfectly happy listening to the song and seeing the light. Then, it is possible, I may have gone to sleep, and what follows may have been a dream. I thought, anyhow, that after a time the nightingales ceased singing and the moon sank. I thought also that if, for some unexplained reason, I was going to lie awake all night, I might as well read, and I remembered that I had left a book in which I was interested in the dining-room on the first floor. So I got out of bed, lit a candle, and went downstairs. I went into the room, saw on a side-table the book I had come to look for, and then, simultaneously, saw that the door into the unoccupied bedroom was open. A curious grey light, not of dawn nor of moonshine, came out of it, and I looked in. The bed stood just opposite the door, a big four-poster, hung with tapestry at the head. Then I saw that the greyish light of the bedroom came from the bed, or rather from what was on the bed. For it was covered with great caterpillars, a foot or more in length, which crawled over it. They were faintly luminous, and it was the light from them that showed me the room. Instead of the sucker-feet of ordinary caterpillars they had rows of pincers like crabs, and they moved by grasping what they lay on with their pincers, and then sliding their bodies forward. In colour these dreadful insects were yellowish-grey, and they were covered with irregular lumps and swellings. There must have been hundreds of them, for they formed a sort of writhing, crawling pyramid on the bed. Occasionally one fell off on to the floor, with a soft fleshy thud, and though the floor was of hard concrete, it yielded to the pincerfeet as if it had been putty, and, crawling back, the caterpillar would mount on to the bed again, to rejoin its fearful companions. They appeared to have no faces, so to speak, but at one end of them there was a mouth that opened sideways in respiration.

Then, as I looked, it seemed to me as if they all suddenly became conscious of my presence. All the mouths, at any rate, were turned in my direction, and next moment they began dropping off the bed with those soft fleshy thuds on to the floor, and wriggling towards me. For one second a paralysis as of a dream was on me, but the next I was running upstairs again to my room, and I remember feeling the cold of the marble steps on my bare feet. I rushed into my bedroom, and slammed the door behind me, and then – I was certainly wide-awake now – I found myself standing by my bed with the sweat of terror pouring from me. The noise of the banged door still rang in my ears. But, as would have been more usual, if this had been mere nightmare, the terror that had been mine when I saw those foul beasts crawling about the bed or dropping softly on to the floor did not cease then. Awake, now, if dreaming before, I did not at all recover from the horror of dream: it did not seem to me that I had dreamed. And until dawn, I sat or stood, not daring to lie down, thinking that every rustle or movement that I heard was the approach of the caterpillars. To them and the claws that bit into the cement the wood of the door was child's play: steel would not keep them out.

But with the sweet and noble return of day the horror vanished: the whisper of wind became benignant again: the nameless fear, whatever it was, was smoothed out and terrified me no longer. Dawn broke, hueless at first; then it grew dovecoloured, then the flaming pageant of light spread over the sky.

The admirable rule of the house was that everybody had breakfast where and when he pleased, and in consequence it was not till lunch-time that I met any of the other members of our party, since I had breakfast on my balcony, and wrote letters and other things till lunch. In fact, I got down to that meal rather late, after the other three had begun. Between my knife and fork there was a small pill-box of cardboard, and as I sat down Inglis spoke.

"Do look at that," he said, "since you are interested in natural history. I found it crawling on my counterpane last night, and I don't know what it is."

I think that before I opened the pill-box I expected something of the sort which I found in it. Inside it, anyhow, was a small caterpillar, greyish-yellow in colour, with curious bumps and excrescences on its rings. It was extremely active, and hurried round the box, this way and that. Its feet were unlike the feet of any caterpillar I ever saw: they were like the pincers of a crab. I looked, and shut the lid down again.

"No, I don't know it," I said, "but it looks rather unwholesome. What are you going to do with it?"

"Oh, I shall keep it," said Inglis. "It has begun to spin: I want to see what sort of a moth it turns into."

I opened the box again, and saw that these hurrying movements were indeed the beginning of the spinning of the web of its cocoon. Then Inglis spoke again.

"It has got funny feet, too," he said. "They are like crabs' pincers. What's the Latin for crab? Oh, yes, Cancer. So in case it is unique, let's christen it: 'Cancer Inglisensis.'"

Then something happened in my brain, some momentary piecing together of all that I had seen or dreamed. Something in his words seemed to me to throw light on it all, and my own intense horror at the experience of the night before linked itself on to what he had just said. In effect, I took the box and threw it, caterpillar and all, out of the window. There was a gravel path just outside, and beyond it, a fountain playing into a basin. The box fell on to the middle of this.

Inglis laughed.

"So the students of the occult don't like solid facts," he said. "My poor caterpillar!"

The talk went off again at once on to other subjects, and I have only given in detail, as they happened, these trivialities in order to be sure myself that I have recorded everything that could have borne on occult subjects or on the subject of caterpillars. But at the moment when I threw the pill-box into the fountain, I lost my head: my only excuse is that, as is probably plain, the tenant of it was, in miniature, exactly what I had seen crowded on to the bed in the unoccupied room. And though this translation of those phantoms into flesh and blood – or whatever it is that caterpillars are made of – ought perhaps to have relieved the horror of the night, as a matter of fact it did nothing of the kind. It only made the crawling pyramid that covered the bed in the unoccupied room more hideously real.

After lunch we spent a lazy hour or two strolling about the garden or sitting in the *loggia*, and it must have been about four o'clock when Stanley and I started off to bathe, down the path that led by the fountain into which I had thrown the pill-box. The water was shallow and clear, and at the bottom of it I saw its white remains. The water had disintegrated the cardboard, and it had become no more than a few strips and shreds of sodden paper. The centre of the fountain was a marble Italian Cupid which squirted the water out of a wine-skin held under its arm. And crawling up its leg was the caterpillar. Strange and scarcely credible as it seemed, it must have survived the falling-to-bits of its prison, and made it's way to shore, and there it was, out of arm's reach, weaving and waving this way and that as it evolved its cocoon.

Then, as I looked at it, it seemed to me again that, like the caterpillar I had seen last night, it saw me, and breaking out of the threads that surrounded it, it crawled down the marble leg of the Cupid and began swimming like a snake across the water of the fountain towards me. It came with extraordinary speed (the fact of a caterpillar being able to swim was new to me), and in another moment was crawling up the marble lip of the basin. Just then Inglis joined us.

"Why, if it isn't old 'Cancer Inglisensis' again," he said, catching sight of the beast. "What a tearing hurry it is in!"

We were standing side by side on the path, and when the caterpillar had advanced to within about a yard of us, it stopped, and began waving again as if in doubt as to the direction in which it should go. Then it appeared to make up its mind, and crawled on to Inglis' shoe.

"It likes me best," he said, "but I don't really know that I like it. And as it won't drown I think perhaps—"

He shook it off his shoe on to the gravel path and trod on it.

All afternoon the air got heavier and heavier with the Sirocco that was without doubt coming up from the south, and that night again I went up to bed feeling very sleepy; but below my drowsiness, so to speak, there was the consciousness, stronger than before, that there was something wrong in the house, that something dangerous was close at hand. But I fell asleep at once, and – how long after I do not know – either woke or dreamed I awoke, feeling that I must get up at once, *or I should be too late*. Then (dreaming or awake) I lay and fought this fear, telling myself that I was but the prey of my own nerves disordered by Sirocco or what not, and at the same time quite clearly knowing in another part of my mind, so to speak, that every moment's delay added to the danger. At last this second feeling became irresistible, and I put on coat and trousers and went out of my room on to the landing. And then I saw that I had already delayed too long, and that I was now too late.

The whole of the landing of the first floor below was invisible under the swarm of caterpillars that crawled there. The folding doors into the sitting-room from which opened the bedroom where I had seen them last night were shut, but they were squeezing through the cracks of it and dropping one by one through the keyhole, elongating themselves into mere string as they passed, and growing fat and lumpy again on emerging. Some, as if exploring, were nosing about the steps into the passage at the end of which were Inglis' rooms, others were crawling on the lowest steps of the staircase that led up to where I stood. The landing, however, was completely covered with them: I was cut off. And of the frozen horror that seized me when I saw that I can give no idea in words.

Then at last a general movement began to take place, and they grew thicker on the steps that led to Inglis' room. Gradually, like some hideous tide of flesh, they advanced along the passage, and I saw the foremost, visible by the pale grey luminousness that came from them, reach his door. Again and again I tried to shout and warn him, in terror all the time that they would turn at the sound of my voice and mount my stair instead, but for all my efforts I felt that no sound came from my throat. They crawled along the hinge-crack of his door, passing through as they had done before, and still I stood there, making impotent efforts to shout to him, to bid him escape while there was time.

At last the passage was completely empty: they had all gone, and at that moment I was conscious for the first time of the cold of the marble landing on which I stood barefooted. The dawn was just beginning to break in the Eastern sky.

Six months after I met Mrs. Stanley in a country house in England. We talked on many subjects and at last she said:

"I don't think I have seen you since I got that dreadful news about Arthur Inglis a month ago."

"I haven't heard," said I.

"No? He has got cancer. They don't even advise an operation, for there is no hope of a cure: he is riddled with it, the doctors say."

Now during all these six months I do not think a day had passed on which I had not had in my mind the dreams (or whatever you like to call them) which I had seen in the Villa Cascana.

"It is awful, is it not?" she continued, "and I feel I can't help feeling, that he may have—"

"Caught it at the villa?" I asked.

She looked at me in blank surprise.

"Why did you say that?" she asked. "How did you know?"

Then she told me. In the unoccupied bedroom a year before there had been a fatal case of cancer. She had, of course, taken the best advice and had been told that the utmost dictates of prudence would be obeyed so long as she did not put anybody to sleep in the room, which had also been thoroughly disinfected and newly white-washed and painted. But—

The Cat

Many people will doubtless, remember that exhibition at the Royal Academy, not so many seasons ago which came to be known as Alingham's year, when Dick Alingham vaulted, with one bound, as it were, out of the crowd of strugglers and seated himself with admirably certain poise on the very topmost pinnacle of contemporary fame. He exhibited three portraits, each a masterpiece, which killed every picture within range. But since that year nobody cared anything for pictures whether in or out of range except those three, it did not signify so greatly. The phenomenon of his appearance was as sudden as that of the meteor, coming from nowhere and sliding large and luminous across the remote and star-sown sky, as inexplicable as the bursting of a spring on some dust-ridden rocky hillside. Some fairy godmother, one might conjecture, had bethought herself of her forgotten godson, and with a wave of her wand bestowed on him this transcendent gift. But, as the Irish say, she held her wand in her left hand, for her gift had another side to it. Or perhaps, again, Jim Merwick is right, and the theory he propounds in his monograph, "On certain obscure lesions of the nerve centres," says the final word on the subject.

Dick Alingham himself, as was indeed natural, was delighted with his fairy godmother or his obscure lesion (whichever was responsible), and (the monograph spoken of above was written after Dick's death) confessed frankly to his friend Merwick, who was still struggling through the crowd of rising young medical practitioners, that it was all quite as inexplicable to himself as it was to anyone else.

"All I know about it," he said, "is that last autumn I went through two months of mental depression so hideous that I thought again and again that I must go off my head. For hours daily, I sat here, waiting for something to crack, which as far as I am concerned would end everything. Yes, there was a cause; you know it."

He paused a moment and poured into his glass a fairly liberal allowance of whisky, filled it half up from a syphon, and lit a cigarette. The cause, indeed, had no need to be enlarged on, for Merwick quite well remembered how the girl Dick had been engaged to threw him over with an abruptness that was almost superb, when a more eligible suitor made his appearance. The latter was certainly very eligible indeed with his good looks, his title, and his million of money, and Lady Madingley – ex-future Mrs. Alingham – was perfectly content with what she had done. She was one of those blonde, lithe, silken girls, who, happily for the peace of men's minds, are rather rare, and who remind one of some humanised yet celestial and bestial cat.

"I needn't speak of the cause," Dick continued, "but, as I say, for those two months I soberly thought that the only end to it would be madness. Then one evening when I was sitting here alone – I was always sitting alone – something did snap in my head. I know I wondered, without caring at all, whether this was the madness which I had been expecting, or whether (which would be preferable) some more fatal breakage had happened. And even while I wondered, I was aware that I was not depressed or unhappy any longer."

He paused for so long in a smiling retrospect that Merwick indicated to him that he had a listener.

"Well?" he said.

"It was well indeed. I haven't been unhappy since. I have been riotously happy instead. Some divine doctor, I suppose, just wiped off that stain on my brain that hurt so. Heavens, how it hurt! Have a drink, by the way?"

"No, thanks," said Merwick. "But what has all this got to do with your painting?"

"Why, everything. For I had hardly realised the fact that I was happy again, when I was aware that everything looked different. The colours of all I saw were twice as vivid as they had been, shape and outline were intensified too. The whole visible world had been dusty and blurred before, and seen in a half-light. But now the lights were turned up, and there was a new heaven and a new earth. And in the same flash, I knew that I could paint things as I saw them. Which," he concluded, "I have done."

There was something rather sublime about this, and Merwick laughed.

"I wish something would snap in my brain, if it kindles the

perceptions in that way," said he, "but it is just possible that the snapping of things in one's brain does not always produce just that effect."

"That is possible. Also, as I gather, things don't snap unless you have gone through some such hideous period as I have been through. And I tell you frankly that I wouldn't go through that again even to ensure a snap that would make me see things like Titian."

"What did the snapping feel like?" asked Merwick.

Dick considered a moment.

"Do you know when a parcel comes, tied up with string, and you can't find a knife," he said, "and therefore you burn the string through, holding it taut? Well, it was like that: quite painless, only something got weaker and weaker, and then parted, softly without effort. Not very lucid, I'm afraid, but it was just like that. It had been burning a couple of months, you see."

He turned away and hunted among the letters and papers which littered his writing-table till he found an envelope with a coronet on it. He chuckled to himself as he took it up.

"Commend me to Lady Madingley," he said, "for a brazen impudence in comparison with which brass is softer than putty. She wrote to me yesterday, asking me if I would finish the portrait I had begun of her last year, and let her have it at my own price."

"Then I think you have had a lucky escape," remarked Merwick. "I suppose you didn't even answer her."

"Oh, yes, I did: why not? I said the price would be two thousand pounds, and I was ready to go on at once. She has agreed, and sent me a cheque for a thousand this evening."

Merwick stared at him in blank astonishment. "Are you mad?" he asked.

"I hope not, though one can never be sure about little points like that. Even doctors like you don't know exactly what constitutes madness."

Merwick got up.

"But is it possible that you don't see what a terrible risk you run?" he asked. "To see her again, to be with her like that, having to look at her – I saw her this afternoon, by the way, hardly human – may not that so easily revive again all that you felt before? It is too dangerous: much too dangerous."

Dick shook his head.

"There is not the slightest risk," he said; "everything within me is utterly and absolutely indifferent to her. I don't even hate her: if I hated her there might be a possibility of my again loving her. As it is, the thought of her does not arouse in me any emotion of any kind. And really such stupendous calmness deserves to be rewarded. I respect colossal things like that."

He finished his whisky as he spoke, and instantly poured himself out another glass.

"That's the fourth," said his friend.

"Is it? I never count. It shows a sordid attention to uninteresting detail. Funnily enough, too, alcohol does not have the smallest effect on me now."

"Why drink then?"

"Because if I give it up this entrancing vividness of colour and clarity of outline is a little diminished.

"Can't be good for you," said the doctor. Dick laughed.

"My dear fellow, look at me carefully," he said, "and then if you can conscientiously declare that I show any signs of indulging in stimulants, I'll give them up altogether."

Certainly it would have been hard to find a point in which Dick did not present the appearance of perfect health. He had paused, and stood still a moment, his glass in one hand, the whisky-bottle in the other, black against the front of his shirt, and not a tremor of unsteadiness was there. His face of wholesome sun-burnt hue was neither puffy nor emaciated, but firm of flesh and of a wonderful clearness of skin. Clear too was his eye, with eyelids neither baggy nor puckered; he looked indeed a model of condition, hard and fit, as if he was in training for some athletic event. Lithe and active too was his figure, his movements were quick and precise, and even Merwick, with his doctor's eye trained to detect any symptom, however slight, in which the drinker must betray himself, was bound to confess that no such was here present. His appearance contradicted it authoritatively, so also did his manner; he met the eye of the man he was talking to without sideway glances; he showed no signs, however small, of any disorder of the nerves. Yet Dick was altogether an abnormal fellow; the history he had just been recounting was abnormal, those weeks of depression, followed by the sudden snap in his brain which had apparently removed, as a wet cloth removes a stain, all the memory of his love and of the cruel bitterness that resulted from it. Abnormal too was his sudden leap into high artistic achievement from a past of very mediocre performance. Why should there then not be a similar abnormality here?

"Yes, I confess you show no sign of taking excessive stimulant," said Merwick, "but if I attended you professionally – ah, I'm not touting – I should make you give up all stimulant, and go to bed for a month."

"Why in the name of goodness?" asked Dick.

"Because, theoretically, it must be the best thing you could do. You had a shock, how severe, the misery of those weeks of depression tells you. Well, common sense says, 'Go slow after a shock; recoup.' Instead of which you go very fast indeed and produce. I grant it seems to suit you; you also became suddenly capable of feats which – oh, it's sheer nonsense, man."

"What's sheer nonsense?"

"You are. Professionally, I detest you, because you appear to be an exception to a theory that I am sure must be right. Therefore I have got to explain you away, and at present I can't."

"What's the theory?" asked Dick.

"Well, the treatment of shock first of all. And secondly, that in order to do good work, one ought to eat and drink very little and sleep a lot. How long do you sleep, by the way?"

Dick considered.

"Oh, I go to bed about three usually," he said; "I suppose I sleep for about four hours."

"And live on whisky, and eat like a Strasburg goose, and are prepared to run a race to-morrow. Go away, or at least I will. Perhaps you'll break down, though. That would satisfy me. But even if you don't, it still remains quite interesting."

Merwick found it more than quite interesting in fact, and when he got home that night he searched in his shelves for a certain dusky volume in which he turned up a chapter called "Shock." The book was a treatise on obscure diseases and abnormal conditions of the nervous system. He had often read it before, for in his profession he was a special student of the rare and curious. And the following paragraph which had interested him much before, interested him more than ever this evening.

"The nervous system also can act in a way that must always even to the most advanced student be totally unexpected. Cases are known, and well-authenticated ones, when a paralytic person has jumped out of bed on the cry of 'Fire.' Cases too are known when a great shock, which produces depression so profound as to amount to lethargy, is followed by abnormal activity, and the calling into use of powers which were previously unknown to exist, or at any rate existed in a quite ordinary degree. Such a hyper-sensitised state, especially since the desire for sleep or rest is very often much diminished, demands much stimulant in the way of food and alcohol. It would appear also that the patient suffering from this rare form of the after-consequences of shock has sooner or later some sudden and complete break-down. It is impossible, however, to conjecture what form this will take. The digestion, however, may become suddenly atrophied, delirium tremens may, without warning, supervene, or he may go completely off his head . . ."

But the weeks passed on, the July suns made London reel in a haze of heat, and yet Alingham remained busy, brilliant, and altogether exceptional. Merwick, unknown to him, was watching him closely, and at present was completely puzzled. He held Dick to his word that if he could detect the slightest sign of over-indulgence in stimulant, he would cut it off altogether, but he could see absolutely none. Lady Madingley meantime had given him several sittings, and in this connection again Merwick was utterly mistaken in the view he had expressed to Dick as to the risks he ran. For, strangely enough, the two had become great friends. Yet Dick was quite right, all emotion with regard to her on his part was dead, it might have been a piece of still-life that he was painting, instead of a woman he had wildly worshipped.

One morning in mid-July she had been sitting to him in his studio, and contrary to custom he had been rather silent, biting the ends of his brushes, frowning at his canvas, frowning too at her. Suddenly he gave a little impatient exclamation.

"It's so like you," he said, "but it just isn't you. There's a lot of difference! I can't help making you look as if you were listening to a hymn, one of those in four sharps, don't you know, written by an organist, probably after eating muffins. And that's not characteristic of you!"

She laughed.

"You must be rather ingenious to put all that in," she said.

"I am."

"Where do I show it all?"

Dick sighed.

"Oh, in your eyes of course," he said. "You show everything by your eyes, you know. It is entirely characteristic of you. You are a throw-back; don't you remember we settled that ever so long ago, to the brute creation, who likewise show everything by their eyes."

"Oh-h. I should have thought that dogs growled at you, and cats scratched."

"Those are practical measures, but short of that you and animals use their eyes only, whereas people use their mouths and foreheads and other things. A pleased dog, an expectant dog, a hungry dog, a jealous dog, a disappointed dog – one gathers all that from a dog's eyes. Their mouths are comparatively immobile, and a cat's is even more so."

"You have often told me that I belong to the genus cat," said Lady Madingley, with complete composure.

"By Jove, yes," said he. "Perhaps looking at the eyes of a cat would help me to see what I miss. Many thanks for the hint."

He put down his palette and went to a side table on which stood bottles and ice and syphons.

"No drink of any kind on this Sahara of a morning?" he asked.

"No, thanks. Now when will you give me the final sitting? You said you only wanted one more."

Dick helped himself."

"Well, I go down to the country with this," he said, "to put in the background I told you of. With luck it will take me three days' hard painting, without luck a week or more. Oh, my mouth waters at the thought of the background. So shall we say to-morrow week?"

Lady Madingley made a note of this in a minute gold and jewelled memorandum book.

"And I am to be prepared to see cat's eyes painted there instead of my own when I see it next?" she asked, passing by the canvas.

Dick laughed.

"Oh, you will hardly notice the difference," he said. "How odd it is that I always have detested cats so – they make me feel actually faint, although you always reminded me of a cat."

"You must ask your friend Mr. Merwick about these metaphysical mysteries," said she.

The background to the picture was at present only indicated by a few vague splashes close to the side of the head of brilliant purple and brilliant green, and the artist's mouth might well water at the thought of the few days painting that lay before him. For behind the figure in the long panel-shaped canvas was to be painted a green trellis, over which, almost hiding the woodwork, there was to sprawl a great purple clematis in full flaunting glory of varnished leaf and starry flower. At the top would be just a strip of pale summer sky, at her feet just a strip of grey-green grass, but all the rest of the background, greatly daring, would be this diaper of green and purple. For the purpose of putting this in, he was going down to a small cottage of his near Godalming, where he had built in the garden a sort of outdoor studio, an erection betwixt a room and a mere shelter, with the side to the north entirely open, and flanked by this green trellis which was now one immense constellation of purple stars. Framed in this, he well knew how the strange pale beauty of his sitter would glow on the canvas, how she would start out of the background, she and her huge grey hat, and shining grey dress, and yellow hair and ivory white skin and pale eyes, now blue, now grey, now green. This was indeed a thing to look forward to, for there is probably no such unadulterated rapture known to men as creation, and it was small wonder that Dick's mood, as he travelled down to Godalming, was buoyant and effervescent. For he was going, so to speak, to realise his creation: every purple star of clematis, every green leaf and piece of trellis-work that he put in, would cause what he had painted to live and shine, just as it is the layers of dusk that fall over the sky at evening which make the stars to sparkle there, jewel-like. His scheme was assured, he had hung his constellation – the figure of Lady Madingley – in the sky: and now he had to surround it with the green and purple night, so that it might shine.

His garden was but a circumscribed plot, but walls of old brick circumscribed it, and he had dealt with the space at his command with a certain originality. At no time had his grass plot (you could scarcely call it "lawn") been spacious; now the outdoor studio, twenty-five feet by thirty, took up the greater part of it. He had a solid wooden wall on one side and two trellis walls to the south and east, which creepers were beginning to clothe and which were faced internally by hangings of Syrian and Oriental work. Here in the summer he passed the greater part of the day, painting or idling, and living an outdoor existence. The floor, which had once been grass, which had withered completely under the roof, was covered with Persian rugs; a writing-table and a dining-table were there, a bookcase full of familiar friends and a half-dozen of basket chairs. One corner, too, was frankly given up to the affairs of the garden, and a mowing machine, a hose for watering, shears, and spade stood there. For like many excitable persons, Dick found that in gardening, that incessant process of plannings and designings to suit the likings of plants, and make them gorgeous in colour and high of growth, there was a wonderful calm haven of refuge for the brain that had been tossing on emotional seas. Plants, too, were receptive, so responsive to kindness; thought given to them was never thought wasted, and to come back now after a month's absence in London was to be assured of fresh surprise and pleasure in each foot of garden-bed. And here, with how regal a generosity was the purple clematis to repay him for the care lavished on it. Every flower would show its practical gratitude by standing model for the background of his picture.

The evening was very warm, warm not with any sultry premonition of thunder, but with the clear, clean heat of summer, and he dined alone in his shelter, with the after-flames of the sunset for his lamp. These slowly faded into a sky of velvet blue, but he lingered long over his coffee, looking northwards across the garden towards the row of trees that screened him from the house beyond. These were acacias, most graceful and feminine of all green things that grow, summer-plumaged now, yet still fresh of leaf. Below them ran a little raised terrace of turf and nearer the beds of the beloved garden; clumps of sweet-peas made an inimitable fragrance, and the rose-beds were pink with *Baroness Rothschild* and *La France*, and copper-coloured with *Beauté inconstante*, and the *Richardson* rose. Then, nearer at hand, was the green trellis foaming with purple.

He was sitting there, hardly looking, but unconsciously drinking in this great festival of colour, when his eye was arrested by a dark slinking form that appeared among the roses, and suddenly turned two shining luminous orbs on him. At this he started up, but his movement caused no perturbation in the animal, which continued with back arched for stroking, and poker-like tail, to advance towards him, purring. As it came closer Dick felt that shuddering faintness, which often affected him in the presence of cats, come over him, and he stamped and clapped his hands. At this it turned tail quickly: a sort of dark shadow streaked the garden-wall for a moment, and it vanished. But its appearance had spoiled for him the sweet spell of the evening, and he went indoors.

The next morning was pellucid summer: a faint north wind blew, and a sun worthy to illumine the isles of Greece flooded the sky. Dick's dreamless and (for him) long sleep had banished from his mind that rather disquieting incident of the cat, and he set up his canvas facing the trellis-work and purple clematis with a huge sense of imminent ecstasy. Also the garden, which at present he had only seen in the magic of sunset, was gloriously rewarding, and glowed with colour, and though life – this was present to his mind for the first time for months – in the shape of Lady Madingley had not been very propitious, yet a man, he argued to himself, must be a very poor hand at living if, with a passion for plants and a passion for art, he cannot fashion a life that shall be full of content. So breakfast being finished, and his model ready and glowing with beauty, he quickly sketched in the broad lines of flowers and foliage and began to paint.

Purple and green, green and purple: was there ever such a feast for the eye? Gourmet-like and greedy as well, he was utterly absorbed in it. He was right too: as soon as he put on the first brush of colour he knew he was right. It was just those divine and violent colours which would cause his figure to step out from the picture, it was just that pale strip of sky above which would focus her again, it was just that strip of grey-green grass below her feet that would prevent her, so it seemed, from actually leaving the canvas. And with swift eager sweeps of the brush which never paused and never hurried, he lost himself in his work.

He stopped at length with a sense of breathlessness, feeling too as if he had been suddenly called back from some immense distance off. He must have been working some three hours, for his man was already laying the table for lunch, yet it seemed to him that the morning had gone by in one flash. The progress he had made was extraordinary, and he looked long at his picture. Then his eye wandered from the brightness of the canvas to the brightness of the garden-beds. There, just in front of the bed of sweet-peas, not two yards from him, stood a very large grey cat, watching him.

Now the presence of a cat was a thing that usually produced

in Dick a feeling of deadly faintness, yet, at this moment, as he looked at the cat and the cat at him, he was conscious of no such feeling, and put down the absence of it, in so far as he consciously thought about it, to the fact that he was in the open air, not in the atmosphere of a closed room. Yet, last night out here, the cat had made him feel faint. But he hardly gave a thought to this, for what filled his mind was that he saw in the rather friendly interested look of the beast that expression in the eye which had so baffled him in his portrait of Lady Madingley. So, slowly, and without any sudden movement that might startle the cat, he reached out his hand for the palette he had just put down, and in a corner of the canvas not yet painted over, recorded in half a dozen swift intuitive touches, what he wanted. Even in the broad sunlight where the animal stood, its eyes looked as if they were internally smouldering as well as being lit from without: it was just so that Lady Madingley looked. He would have to lay colour very thinly over white . . .

For five minutes or so he painted them with quiet eager strokes, drawing the colour thinly over the background of white, and then looked long at that sketch of the eye to see if he had got what he wanted. Then he looked back at the cat which had stood so charmingly for him. But there was no cat there. That, however, since he detested them, and this one had served his purpose, was no matter for regret, and he merely wondered a little at the suddenness of its disappearance. But the legacy it had left on the canvas could not vanish thus, it was his own, a possession, an achievement. Truly this was to be a portrait which would altogether out-distance all he had ever done before. A woman, real, alive, wearing her soul in her eyes, should stand there, and summer riot round her.

An extraordinary clearness of vision was his all day, and towards sunset an empty whisky-bottle. But this evening he was conscious for the first time of two feelings, one physical, one mental, altogether strange to him: the first an impression that he had drunk as much as was good for him, the second a sort of echo in his mind of those tortures he had undergone in the autumn, when he had been tossed aside by the girl, to whom he had given his soul, like a soiled glove. Neither was at all acutely felt, but both were present to him.

The evening altogether belied the brilliance of the day, and about six o'clock thick clouds had driven up over the sky, and the clear heat of summer had given place to a heat no less intense, but full of the menace of storm. A few big hot drops, too, of rain warned him further, and he pulled his easel into shelter, and gave orders that he would dine indoors. As was usual with him when he was at work, he shunned the distracting influence of any companionship, and he dined alone. Dinner finished, he went into his sitting-room prepared to enjoy his solitary evening. His servant had brought him in the tray, and till he went to bed he would be undisturbed. Outside the storm was moving nearer, the reverberation of the thunder, though not yet close, kept up a continual growl: any moment it might move up and burst above in riot of fire and sound.

Dick read a book for a while, but his thoughts wandered. The poignancy of his trouble last autumn, which he thought had passed away from him for ever, grew suddenly and strangely more acute, also his head was heavy, perhaps with the storm, but possibly with what he had drunk. So, intending to go to bed and sleep off his disquietude, he closed his book, and went across to the window to close that also. But, half-way towards it, he stopped. There on the sofa below it sat a large grey cat with yellow gleaming eyes. In its mouth it held a young thrush, still alive.

Then horror woke in him: his feeling of sick-faintness was there, and he loathed and was terrified at this dreadful feline glee in the torture of its prey, a glee so great that it preferred the postponement of its meal to a shortening of the other. More than all, the resemblance of the eyes of this cat to those of his portrait suddenly struck him as something hellish. For one moment this all held him bound, as if with paralysis, the next his physical shuddering could be withstood no longer, and he threw the glass he carried at the cat, missing it. For one second the animal paused there glaring at him with an intense and dreadful hostility, then it made one spring of it out of the open window. Dick shut it with a bang that startled himself, and then searched on the sofa and the floor for the bird which he thought the cat had dropped. Once or twice he thought he heard it feebly fluttering, but this must have been an illusion, for he could not find it.

All this was rather shaky business, so before going to bed he steadied himself, as his unspoken phrase ran, with a final drink. Outside the thunder had ceased, but the rain beat hissing on to the grass. Then another sound mingled with it the mewing of a cat, not the long drawn screeches and cries that are usual, but the plaintive calls of the beast that wants to be admitted into its own home. The blind was down, but after a while he could not resist peeping out. There on the window-sill was seated the large grey cat. Though it was raining heavily its fur seemed dry, for it was standing stiffly away from its body. But when it saw him it spat at him, scratching angrily at the glass, and vanished.

Lady Madingley . . . heavens, how he had loved her! And, infernally as she had treated him, how passionately he wanted her now! Was all his trouble, then, to begin over again? Had that nightmare dawned anew on him? It was the cat's fault: the eyes of the cat had done it. Yet just now all his desire was blurred by this dullness of brain that was as unaccountable as the re-awakening of his desire. For months now he had drunk far more than he had drunk to-day, yet evening had seen him clear-headed, acute, master of himself, and revelling in the liberty that had come to him, and in the cool joy of creative vision. But to-night he stumbled and groped across the room.

The neutral-coloured light of dawn awoke him, and he got up at once, feeling still very drowsy, but in answer to some silent imperative call. The storm had altogether passed away, and a jewel of a morning star hung in a pale heaven. His room looked strangely unfamiliar to him, his own sensations were unfamiliar, there was a vagueness about things, a barrier between him and the world. One desire alone possessed him, to finish the portrait. All else, so he felt, he left to chance, or whatever laws regulate the world, those laws which choose that a certain thrush shall be caught by a certain cat, and choose one scapegoat out of a thousand, and let the rest go free.

Two hours later his servant called him, and found him gone from his room. So as the morning was so fair, he went out to lay breakfast in the shelter. The portrait was there, it had been dragged back into position by the clematis, but it was covered with strange scratches, as if the claws of some enraged animal or the nails perhaps of a man had furiously attacked it. Dick Alingham was there, too, lying very still in front of the disfigured canvas. Claws, also, or nails had attacked him, his throat was horribly mangled by them. But his hands were covered with paint, the nails of his fingers too were choked with it.

The Bus-Conductor

My friend, Hugh Grainger, and I had just returned from a two days' visit in the country, where we had been staying in a house of sinister repute which was supposed to be haunted by ghosts of a peculiarly fearsome and truculent sort. The house itself was all that such a house should be, Jacobean and oak-panelled, with long dark passages and high vaulted rooms. It stood, also, very remote, and was encompassed by a wood of sombre pines that muttered and whispered in the dark, and all the time that we were there a south-westerly gale with torrents of scolding rain had prevailed, so that by day and night weird voices moaned and fluted in the chimneys, a company of uneasy spirits held colloquy among the trees, and sudden tattoos and tappings beckoned from the window-panes. But in spite of these surroundings, which were sufficient in themselves, one would almost say, to spontaneously generate occult phenomena, nothing of any description had occurred. I am bound to add, also, that my own state of mind was peculiarly well adapted to receive or even to invent the sights and sounds we had gone to seek, for I was, I confess, during the whole time that we were there, in a state of abject apprehension, and lay awake both nights through hours of terrified unrest, afraid of the dark, yet more afraid of what a lighted candle might show me.

Hugh Grainger, on the evening after our return to town, had dined with me, and after dinner our conversation, as was natural, soon came back to these entrancing topics.

"But why you go ghost-seeking I cannot imagine," he said, "because your teeth were chattering and your eyes starting out of your head all the time you were there, from sheer fright. Or do you like being frightened?"

Hugh, though generally intelligent, is dense in certain ways; this is one of them.

"Why, of course, I like being frightened," I said. "I want to be made to creep and creep and creep. Fear is the most absorbing and luxurious of emotions. One forgets all else if one is afraid."

"Well, the fact that neither of us saw anything," he said, "confirms what I have always believed."

"And what have you always believed?"

"That these phenomena are purely objective, not subjective, and that one's state of mind has nothing to do with the perception that perceives them, nor have circumstances or surroundings anything to do with them either. Look at Osburton. It has had the reputation of being a haunted house for years, and it certainly has all the accessories of one. Look at yourself, too, with all your nerves on edge, afraid to look round or light a candle for fear of seeing something! Surely there was the right man in the right place then, if ghosts are subjective."

He got up and lit a cigarette, and looking at him – Hugh is about six feet high, and as broad as he is long – I felt a retort on my lips, for I could not help my mind going back to a certain period in his life, when, from some cause which, as far as I knew, he had never told anybody, he had become a mere quivering mass of disordered nerves. Oddly enough, at the same moment and for the first time, he began to speak of it himself.

"You may reply that it was not worth my while to go either," he said, "because I was so clearly the wrong man in the wrong place. But I wasn't. You for all your apprehensions and expectancy have never seen a ghost. But I have, though I am the last person in the world you would have thought likely to do so, and, though my nerves are steady enough again now, it knocked me all to bits."

He sat down again in his chair.

"No doubt you remember my going to bits," he said, "and since I believe that I am sound again now, I should rather like to tell you about it. But before I couldn't; I couldn't speak of it at all to anybody. Yet there ought to have been nothing frightening about it; what I saw was certainly a most useful and friendly ghost. But it came from the shaded side of things; it looked suddenly out of the night and the mystery with which life is surrounded."

"I want first to tell you quite shortly my theory about ghost-seeing," he continued, "and I can explain it best by a simile, an image. Imagine then that you and I and everybody in the world are like people whose eye is directly opposite a little tiny hole in a sheet of cardboard which is continually shifting and revolving and moving about. Back to back with that sheet of cardboard is another, which also, by laws of its own, is in perpetual but independent motion. In it too there is another hole, and when, fortuitously it would seem, these two holes, the one through which we are always looking, and the other in the spiritual plane, come opposite one another, we see through, and then only do the sights and sounds of the spiritual world become visible or audible to us. With most people these holes never come opposite each other during their life. But at the hour of death they do, and then they remain stationary. That, I fancy, is how we 'pass over.'

"Now, in some natures, these holes are comparatively large, and are constantly coming into opposition. Clairvoyants, mediums are like that. But, as far as I knew, I had no clairvoyant or mediumistic powers at all. I therefore am the sort of person who long ago made up his mind that he never would see a ghost. It was, so to speak, an incalculable chance that my minute spy-hole should come into opposition with the other. But it did: and it knocked me out of time."

I had heard some such theory before, and though Hugh put it rather picturesquely, there was nothing in the least convincing or practical about it. It might be so, or again it might not.

"I hope your ghost was more original than your theory," said I, in order to bring him to the point.

"Yes, I think it was. You shall judge."

I put on more coal and poked up the fire. Hugh has got, so I have always considered, a great talent for telling stories, and that sense of drama which is so necessary for the narrator. Indeed, before now, I have suggested to him that he should take this up as a profession, sit by the fountain in Piccadilly Circus, when times are, as usual, bad, and tell stories to the passers-by in the street, Arabian fashion, for reward. The most part of mankind, I am aware, do not like long stories, but to the few, among whom I number myself, who really like to listen to lengthy accounts of experiences, Hugh is an ideal narrator. I do not care for his theories, or for his similes, but when it comes to facts, to things that happened, I like him to be lengthy.

"Go on, please, and slowly," I said. "Brevity may be the soul of wit, but it is the ruin of story-telling. I want to hear when and where and how it all was, and what you had for lunch and where you had dined and what—

Hugh began:

"It was the 24th of June, just eighteen months ago," he said. "I had let my flat, you may remember, and came up from the country to stay with you for a week. We had dined alone here—"

I could not help interrupting.

"Did you see the ghost here?" I asked. "In this square little box of a house in a modern street?"

"I was in the house when I saw it."

I hugged myself in silence.

"We had dined alone here in Graeme Street," he said, "and after dinner I went out to some party, and you stopped at home. At dinner your man did not wait, and when I asked where he was, you told me he was ill, and, I thought, changed the subject rather abruptly.

You gave me your latch-key when I went out, and on coming back, I found you had gone to bed. There were, however, several letters for me, which required answers. I wrote them there and then, and posted them at the pillar-box opposite. So I suppose it was rather late when I went upstairs.

"You had put me in the front room, on the third floor, overlooking the street, a room which I thought you generally occupied yourself. It was a very hot night, and though there had been a moon when I started to my party, on my return the whole sky was cloud-covered, and it both looked and felt as if we might have a thunderstorm before morning. I was feeling very sleepy and heavy, and it was not till after I had got into bed that I noticed by the shadows of the window-frames on the blind that only one of the windows was open. But it did not seem worth while to get out of bed in order to open it, though I felt rather airless and uncomfortable, and I went to sleep.

"What time it was when I awoke I do not know, but it was certainly not yet dawn, and I never remember being conscious of such an extraordinary stillness as prevailed. There was no sound either of foot-passengers or wheeled traffic; the music of life appeared to be absolutely mute. But now, instead of being sleepy and heavy, I felt, though I must have slept an hour or two at most, since it was not yet dawn, perfectly fresh and wide-awake, and the effort which had seemed not worth making before, that of getting out of bed and opening the other window, was quite easy now and I pulled up the blind, threw it wide open, and leaned out, for somehow I parched and pined for air. Even outside the oppression was very noticeable, and though, as you know, I am not easily given to feel the mental effects of climate, I was aware of an awful creepiness coming over me. I tried to analyse it away, but without success; the past day had been pleasant, I looked forward to another pleasant day to-morrow, and yet I was full of some nameless apprehension. I felt, too, dreadfully lonely in this stillness before the dawn.

"Then I heard suddenly and not very far away the sound of some approaching vehicle; I could distinguish the tread of two horses walking at a slow foot's pace. They were, though not yet visible, coming up the street, and yet this indication of life did not abate that dreadful sense of loneliness which I have spoken of. Also in some dim unformulated way that which was coming seemed to me to have something to do with the cause of my oppression.

"Then the vehicle came into sight. At first I could not distinguish what it was. Then I saw that the horses were black and had long tails, and that what they dragged was made of glass, but had a black frame. It was a hearse. Empty.

"It was moving up this side of the street. It stopped at your door.

"Then the obvious solution struck me. You had said at dinner that your man was ill, and you were, I thought, unwilling to speak more about his illness. No doubt, so I imagined now, he was dead, and for some reason, perhaps because you did not want me to know anything about it, you were having the body removed at night. This, I must tell you, passed through my mind quite instantaneously, and it did not occur to me how unlikely it really was, before the next thing happened.

"I was still leaning out of the window, and I remember also wondering, yet only momentarily, how odd it was that I saw things – or rather the one thing I was looking at – so very distinctly. Of course, there was a moon behind the clouds, but it was curious how every detail of the hearse and the horses was visible. There was only one man, the driver, with it, and the street was otherwise absolutely empty. It was at him I was looking now. I could see every detail of his clothes, but from where I was, so high above him, I could not see his face. He had on grey trousers, brown boots, a black coat buttoned all the way up, and a straw hat. Over his shoulder there was a strap, which seemed to support some sort of little bag. He looked exactly like – well, from my description what did he look exactly like?"

"Why – a bus-conductor," I said instantly.

"So I thought, and even while I was thinking this, he looked up at me. He had a rather long thin face, and on his left cheek there was a mole with a growth of dark hair on it. All this was as distinct as if it had been noonday, and as if I was within a yard of him. But – so instantaneous was all that takes so long in the telling – I had not time to think it strange that the driver of a hearse should be so unfunereally dressed.

"Then he touched his hat to me, and jerked his thumb over his shoulder.

"'Just room for one inside, sir,' he said.

"There was something so odious, so coarse, so unfeeling about this that I instantly drew my head in, pulled the blind down again, and then, for what reason I do not know, turned on the electric light in order to see what time it was. The hands of my watch pointed to half-past eleven.

"It was then for the first time, I think, that a doubt crossed my mind as to the nature of what I had just seen. But I put out the light again, got into bed, and began to think. We had dined; I had gone to a party, I had come back and written letters, had gone to bed and had slept. So how could it be half-past eleven? . . . Or – *what* half-past eleven was it?

"Then another easy solution struck me; my watch must have stopped. But it had not; I could hear it ticking.

"There was stillness and silence again. I expected every moment to hear muffled footsteps on the stairs, footsteps moving slowly and smally under the weight of a heavy burden, but from inside the house there was no sound whatever. Outside, too, there was the same dead silence, while the hearse waited at the door. And the minutes ticked on and ticked on, and at length I began to see a difference in the light in the room, and knew that the dawn was beginning to break outside. But how had it happened, then, that if the corpse was to be removed at night it had not gone, and that the hearse still waited, when morning was already coming?

"Presently I got out of bed again, and with the sense of strong physical shrinking I went to the window and pulled back the blind. The dawn was coming fast; the whole street was lit by that silver hueless light of morning. But there was no hearse there.

"Once again I looked at my watch. It was just a quarter-past four. But I would swear that not half an hour had passed since it had told me that it was half-past eleven.

"Then a curious double sense, as if I was living in the present and at the same moment had been living in some other time, came over me. It was dawn on June 25th, and the street, as natural, was empty. But a little while ago the driver of a hearse had spoken to me, and it was half-past eleven. What was that driver, to what plane did he belong? And again *what* half-past eleven was it that I had seen recorded on the dial of my watch?

"And then I told myself that the whole thing had been a dream. But if you ask me whether I believed what I told myself, I must confess that I did not.

"Your man did not appear at breakfast next morning, nor did I see him again before I left that afternoon. I think if I had, I should have told you about all this, but it was still possible, you see, that what I had seen was a real hearse, driven by a real driver, for all the ghastly gaiety of the face that had looked up to mine, and the levity of his pointing hand. I might possibly have fallen asleep soon after seeing him, and slumbered through the removal of the body and the departure of the hearse. So I did not speak of it to you."

There was something wonderfully straight-forward and prosaic in all this; here were no Jacobean houses oak-panelled and surrounded by weeping pine-trees, and somehow the very absence of suitable surroundings made the story more impressive. But for a moment a doubt assailed me.

"Don't tell me it was all a dream," I said.

"I don't know whether it was or not. I can only say that I believe myself to have been wide awake. In any case the rest of the story is – odd."

"I went out of town again that afternoon," he continued, "and

I may say that I don't think that even for a moment did I get the haunting sense of what I had seen or dreamed that night out of my mind. It was present to me always as some vision unfulfilled. It was as if some clock had struck the four quarters, and I was still waiting to hear what the hour would be.

"Exactly a month afterwards I was in London again, but only for the day. I arrived at Victoria about eleven, and took the underground to Sloane Square in order to see if you were in town and would give me lunch. It was a baking hot morning, and I intended to take a bus from the King's Road as far as Graeme Street. There was one standing at the corner just as I came out of the station, but I saw that the top was full, and the inside appeared to be full also. Just as I came up to it the conductor, who, I suppose, had been inside, collecting fares or what not, came out on to the step within a few feet of me. He wore grey trousers, brown boots, a black coat buttoned, a straw hat, and over his shoulder was a strap on which hung his little machine for punching tickets. I saw his face, too; it was the face of the driver of the hearse, with a mole on the left cheek. Then he spoke to me, jerking his thumb over his shoulder.

"'Just room for one inside, sir,' he said.

"At that a sort of panic-terror took possession of me, and I knew I gesticulated wildly with my arms, and cried, 'No, no!' But at that moment I was living not in the hour that was then passing, but in that hour which had passed a month ago, when I leaned from the window of your bedroom here just before the dawn broke. At this moment too I knew that my spy-hole had been opposite the spy-hole into the spiritual world. What I had seen there had some significance, now being fulfilled, beyond the significance of the trivial happenings of to-day and to-morrow. The Powers of which we know so little were visibly working before me. And I stood there on the pavement shaking and trembling.

"I was opposite the post-office at the corner, and just as the bus started my eye fell on the clock in the window there. I need not tell you what the time was.

"Perhaps I need not tell you the rest, for you probably conjecture it, since you will not have forgotten what happened at the corner of Sloane Square at the end of July, the summer before last. The bus pulled out from the pavement into the street in order to get round a van that was standing in front of it. At the moment there came down the King's Road a big motor going at a hideously dangerous pace. It crashed full into the bus, burrowing into it as a gimlet burrows into a board."

He paused.

"And that's my story," he said.

The Man Who Went Too Far

The little village of St. Faith's nestles in a hollow of wooded hill up on the north bank of the river Fawn in the country of Hampshire, huddling close round its grey Norman church as if for spiritual protection against the fays and fairies, the trolls and "little people," who might be supposed still to linger in the vast empty spaces of the New Forest, and to come after dusk and do their doubtful businesses. Once outside the hamlet you may walk in any direction (so long as you avoid the high road which leads to Brockenhurst) for the length of a summer afternoon without seeing sign of human habitation, or possibly even catching sight of another human being. Shaggy wild ponies may stop their feeding for a moment as you pass, the white scuts of rabbits will vanish into their burrows, a brown viper perhaps will glide from your path into a clump of heather, and unseen birds will chuckle in the bushes, but it may easily happen that for a long day you will see nothing human. But you will not feel in the least lonely; in summer, at any rate, the sunlight will be gay with butterflies, and the air thick with all those woodland sounds which like instruments in an orchestra combine to play the great symphony of the yearly festival of June. Winds whisper in the birches, and sigh among the firs; bees are busy with their redolent labour among the heather, a myriad birds chirp in the green temples of the forest trees, and the voice of the river prattling over stony places, bubbling into pools, chuckling and gulping round corners, gives you the sense that many presences and companions are near at hand.

Yet, oddly enough, though one would have thought that these benign and cheerful influences of wholesome air and spaciousness of forest were very healthful comrades for a man, in so far as Nature can really influence this wonderful human genus which has in these centuries learned to defy her most violent storms in its well-established houses, to bridle her torrents and make them light its streets, to tunnel her mountains and plough her seas, the inhabitants of St. Faith's will not willingly venture into the forest after dark. For in spite of the silence and loneliness of the hooded night it seems that a man is not sure in what company he may suddenly find himself, and though it is difficult to get from these villagers any very clear story of occult appearances, the feeling is widespread. One story indeed I have heard with some definiteness, the tale of a monstrous goat that has been seen to skip with hellish glee about the woods and shady places, and this perhaps is connected with the story which I have here attempted to piece together. It too is well-known to them; for all remember the young artist who died here not long ago, a young man, or so he struck the beholder, of great personal beauty, with something about him that made men's faces to smile and brighten when they looked on him. His ghost they will tell you "walks" constantly by the stream and through the woods which he loved so, and in especial it haunts a certain house, the last of the village, where he lived, and its garden in which he was done to death. For my part I am inclined to think that the terror of the Forest dates chiefly from that day. So, such as the story is, I have set it forth in connected form. It is based partly on the accounts of the villagers, but mainly on that of Darcy, a friend of mine and a friend of the man with whom these events were chiefly concerned.

The day had been one of untarnished midsummer splendour, and as the sun drew near to its setting, the glory of the evening grew every moment more crystalline, more miraculous. Westward from St. Faith's the beechwood which stretched for some miles toward the heathery upland beyond already cast its veil of clear shadow over the red roofs of the village, but the spire of the grey church, over-topping all, still pointed a flaming orange finger into the sky. The river Fawn, which runs below, lay in sheets of sky-reflected blue, and wound its dreamy devious course round the edge of this wood, where a rough two-planked bridge crossed from the bottom of the garden of the last house in the village, and communicated by means of a little wicker gate with the wood itself. Then once out of the shadow of the wood the stream lay in flaming pools of the molten crimson of the sunset, and lost itself in the haze of woodland distances.

This house at the end of the village stood outside the shadow, and the lawn which sloped down to the river was still flecked with sunlight. Garden-beds of dazzling colour lined its gravel walks, and down the middle of it ran a brick pergola, half-hidden in clusters of rambler-rose and purple with starry clematis. At the bottom end of it, between two of its pillars, was slung a hammock containing a shirtsleeved figure.

The house itself lay somewhat remote from the rest of the village, and a footpath leading across two fields, now tall and fragrant with hay, was its only communication with the high road. It was low-built, only two stories in height, and like the garden, its walls were a mass of flowering roses. A narrow stone terrace ran along the garden front, over which was stretched an awning, and on the terrace a young silent-footed man-servant was busied with the laying of the table for dinner. He was neat-handed and quick with his job, and having finished it he went back into the house, and reappeared again with a large rough bath-towel on his arm. With this he went to the hammock in the pergola.

"Nearly eight, sir," he said.

"Has Mr. Darcy come yet?" asked a voice from the hammock.

"No, sir."

"If I'm not back when he comes, tell him that I'm just having a bathe before dinner."

The servant went back to the house, and after a moment or two Frank Halton struggled to a sitting posture, and slipped out on to the grass. He was of medium height and rather slender in build, but the supple ease and grace of his movements gave the impression of great physical strength: even his descent from the hammock was not an awkward performance. His face and hands were of very dark complexion, either from constant exposure to wind and sun, or, as his black hair and dark eyes tended to show, from some strain of southern blood. His head was small, his face of an exquisite beauty of modelling, while the smoothness of its contour would have led you to believe that he was a beardless lad still in his teens. But something, some look which living and experience alone can give, seemed to contradict that, and finding yourself completely puzzled as to his age, you would next moment probably cease to think about that, and only look at this glorious specimen of young manhood with wondering satisfaction.

He was dressed as became the season and the heat, and wore only a shirt open at the neck, and a pair of flannel trousers. His head, covered very thickly with a somewhat rebellious crop of short curly hair, was bare as he strolled across the lawn to the bathing-place that lay below. Then for a moment there was silence, then the sound of splashed and divided waters, and presently after, a great shout of ecstatic joy, as he swam up-stream with the foamed water standing in a frill round his neck. Then after some five minutes of limb-stretching struggle with the flood, he turned over on his back, and with arms thrown wide, floated down-stream, ripple-cradled and inert. His eyes were shut, and between half-parted lips he talked gently to himself.

"I am one with it," he said to himself, "the river and I, I and the river. The coolness and splash of it is I, and the water-herbs that wave in it are I also. And my strength and my limbs are not mine but the river's. It is all one, all one, dear Fawn."

A quarter of an hour later he appeared again at the bottom of the lawn, dressed as before, his wet hair already drying into its crisp short curls again. There he paused a moment, looking back at the stream with the smile with which men look on the face of a friend, then turned towards the house. Simultaneously his servant came to the door leading on to the terrace, followed by a man who appeared to be some half-way through the fourth decade of his years. Frank and he saw each other across the bushes and garden-beds, and each quickening his step, they met suddenly face to face round an angle of the garden walk, in the fragrance of syringa.

"My dear Darcy," cried Frank, "I am charmed to see you."

But the other stared at him in amazement.

"Frank!" he exclaimed.

"Yes, that is my name," he said, laughing; "what is the matter?"

Darcy took his hand.

"What have you done to yourself?" he asked.

"You are a boy again."

"Ah, I have a lot to tell you," said Frank.

"Lots that you will hardly believe, but I shall convince you—"

He broke off suddenly, and held up his hand.

"Hush, there is my nightingale," he said.

The smile of recognition and welcome with which he had greeted his friend faded from his face, and a look of rapt wonder took its place, as of a lover listening to the voice of his beloved. His mouth parted slightly, showing the white line of teeth, and his eyes looked out and out till they seemed to Darcy to be focussed on things beyond the vision of man. Then something perhaps startled the bird, for the song ceased.

"Yes, lots to tell you," he said. "Really I am delighted to see you. But you look rather white and pulled down; no wonder after that fever. And there is to be no nonsense about this visit. It is June now, you stop here till you are fit to begin work again. Two months at least."

"Ah, I can't trespass quite to that extent."

Frank took his arm and walked him down the grass.

"Trespass? Who talks of trespass? I shall tell you quite openly when I am tired of you, but you know when we had the studio together, we used not to bore each other. However, it is ill talking of going away on the moment of your arrival. Just a stroll to the river, and then it will be dinner-time."

Darcy took out his cigarette case, and offered it to the other.

Frank laughed.

"No, not for me. Dear me, I suppose I used to smoke once. How very odd!"

"Given it up?"

"I don't know. I suppose I must have. Anyhow I don't do it now. I would as soon think of eating meat."

"Another victim on the smoking altar of vegetarianism?"

"Victim?" asked Frank. "Do I strike you as such?"

He paused on the margin of the stream and whistled softly. Next moment a moor-hen made its splashing flight across the river, and ran up the bank. Frank took it very gently in his hands and stroked its head, as the creature lay against his shirt.

"And is the house among the reeds still secure?" he half-crooned to it. "And is the missus quite well, and are the neighbours flourishing? There, dear, home with you," and he flung it into the air.

"That bird's very tame," said Darcy, slightly bewildered.

"It is rather," said Frank, following its flight.

During dinner Frank chiefly occupied himself in bringing himself up-to-date in the movements and achievements of this old friend whom he had not seen for six years. Those six years, it now appeared, had been full of incident and success for Darcy; he had made a name for himself as a portrait painter which bade fair to outlast the vogue of a couple of seasons, and his leisure time had been brief. Then some four months previously he had been through a severe attack of typhoid, the result of which as concerns this story was that he had come down to this sequestered place to recruit.

"Yes, you've got on," said Frank at the end. "I always knew you would. A.R.A. with more in prospect. Money? You roll in it, I suppose, and, O Darcy, how much happiness have you had all these years? That is the only imperishable possession. And how much have you learned? Oh, I don't mean in Art. Even I could have done well in that."

Darcy laughed.

"Done well? My dear fellow, all I have learned in these six years you knew, so to speak, in your cradle. Your old pictures fetch huge prices. Do you never paint now?"

Frank shook his head.

"No, I'm too busy," he said.

"Doing what? Please tell me. That is what everyone is for ever asking me."

"Doing? I suppose you would say I do nothing."

Darcy glanced up at the brilliant young face opposite him.

"It seems to suit you, that way of being busy," he said. "Now, it's your turn. Do you read? Do you study? I remember you saying that it would do us all – all us artists, I mean – a great deal of good if we would study any one human face carefully for a year, without recording a line. Have you been doing that?"

Frank shook his head again.

"I mean exactly what I say," he said. "I have been *doing* nothing. And I have never been so occupied. Look at me; have I not done something to myself to begin with?"

"You are two years younger than I," said Darcy, "at least you used to be. You therefore are thirty-five. But had I never seen you before I should say you were just twenty. But was it worth while to spend six years of greatly-occupied life in order to look twenty? Seems rather like a woman of fashion."

Frank laughed boisterously.

"First time I've ever been compared to that particular bird of prey," he said. "No, that has not been my occupation – in fact I am only very rarely conscious that one effect of my occupation has been that. Of course, it must have been if one comes to think of it. It is not very important. Quite true my body has become young. But that is very little; I have become young."

Darcy pushed back his chair and sat sideways to the table looking at the other.

"Has that been your occupation then?" he asked.

"Yes, that anyhow is one aspect of it. Think what youth means! It is the capacity for growth, mind, body, spirit, all grow, all get stronger, all have a fuller, firmer life every day. That is something, considering that every day that passes after the ordinary man reaches the full-blown flower of his strength, weakens his hold on life. A man reaches his prime, and remains, we say, in his prime for ten years, or perhaps twenty. But after his primest prime is reached, he slowly, insensibly weakens. These are the signs of age in you, in your body, in your art probably, in your mind. You are less electric than you were. But I, when I reach my prime – I am nearing it – ah, you shall see."

The stars had begun to appear in the blue velvet of the sky, and to the east the horizon seen above the black silhouette of the village was growing dovecoloured with the approach of moon-rise. White moths hovered dimly over the garden-beds, and the footsteps of night tip-toed through the bushes. Suddenly Frank rose.

"Ah, it is the supreme moment," he said softly. Now more than at any other time the current of life, the eternal imperishable current runs so close to me that I am almost enveloped in it. Be silent a minute."

He advanced to the edge of the terrace and looked out, standing stretched with arms outspread. Darcy heard him draw a long breath into his lungs, and after many seconds expel it again. Six or eight times he did this, then turned back into the lamplight.

It will sound to you quite mad, I expect," he said, "but if you want to hear the soberest truth I have ever spoken and shall ever speak, I will tell you about myself. But come into the garden if it is not damp for you. I have never told anyone yet, but I shall like to tell you. It is long, in fact, since I have even tried to classify what I have learned."

They wandered into the fragrant dimness of the pergola, and sat down. Then Frank began:

"Years ago, do you remember," he said, "we used often to talk about the decay of joy in the world. Many impulses, we settled, had contributed to this decay, some of which were good in themselves, others that were quite completely bad. Among the good things, I put what we may call certain Christian virtues, renunciation, resignation, sympathy with suffering, and the desire to relieve sufferers. But out of those things spring very bad ones, useless renunciation, asceticism for its own sake, mortification of the flesh with nothing to follow, no corresponding gain that is, and that awful and terrible disease which devastated England some centuries ago, and from which by heredity of spirit we suffer now, Puritanism. That was a dreadful plague, the brutes held and taught that joy and laughter and merriment were evil: it was a doctrine the most profane and wicked. Why, what is the commonest crime one sees? A sullen face. That is the truth of the matter.

"Now all my life I have believed that we are intended to be happy, that joy is of all gifts the most divine. And when I left London, abandoned my career, such as it was, I did so because I intended to devote my life to the cultivation of joy, and, by continuous and unsparing effort, to be happy. Among people, and in constant intercourse with others, I did not find it possible; there were too many distractions in towns and work-rooms, and also too much suffering. So I took one step backwards or forwards, as you may choose to put it, and went straight to Nature, to trees, birds, animals, to all those things which quite clearly pursue one aim only, which blindly follow the great native instinct to be happy without any care at all for morality, or human law or divine law. I wanted, you understand, to get all joy first-hand and unadulterated, and I think it scarcely exists among men; it is obsolete."

Darcy turned in his chair.

"Ah, but what makes birds and animals happy?" he asked. "Food, food and mating."

Frank laughed gently in the stillness.

"Do not think I became a sensualist," he said. "I did not make that mistake. For the sensualist carries his miseries pick-a-back, and round his feet is wound the shroud that shall soon enwrap him. I may be mad, it is true, but I am not so stupid anyhow as to have tried that. No, what is it that makes puppies play with their own tails, that sends cats on their prowling ecstatic errands at night?"

He paused a moment.

"So I went to Nature," he said. "I sat down here in this New Forest, sat down fair and square, and looked. That was my first difficulty, to sit here quiet without being bored, to wait without being impatient, to be receptive and very alert, though for a long time nothing particular happened. The change in fact was slow in those early stages."

"Nothing happened?" asked Darcy, rather impatiently, with the sturdy revolt against any new idea which to the English mind is synonymous with nonsense. "Why, what in the world *should* happen?"

Now Frank as he had known him was the most generous but most quick-tempered of mortal men; in other words his anger would flare to a prodigious beacon, under almost no provocation, only to be quenched again under a gust of no less impulsive kindliness. Thus the moment Darcy had spoken, an apology for his hasty question was half-way up his tongue. But there was no need for it to have travelled even so far, for Frank laughed again with kindly, genuine mirth.

"Oh, how I should have resented that a few years ago," he said. "Thank goodness that resentment is one of the things I have got rid of. I certainly wish that you should believe my story – in fact, you are going to – but that you at this moment should imply that you do not does not concern me."

"Ah, your solitary sojournings have made you inhuman," said Darcy, still very English.

"No, human," said Frank. "Rather more human, at least rather less of an ape."

"Well, that was my first quest," he continued, after a moment, "the deliberate and unswerving pursuit of joy, and my method, the eager contemplation of Nature. As far as motive went, I daresay it was purely selfish, but as far as effect goes, it seems to me about the best thing one can do for one's follow-creatures, for happiness is more infectious than small-pox. So, as I said, I sat down and waited; I looked at happy things, zealously avoided the sight of anything unhappy, and by degrees a little trickle of the happiness of this blissful world began to filter into me. The trickle grew more abundant, and now, my dear fellow, if I could for a moment divert from me into you one half of the torrent of joy that pours through me day and night, you would throw the world, art, everything aside, and just live, exist. When a man's body dies, it passes into trees and flowers. Well, that is what I have been trying to do with my soul before death."

The servant had brought into the pergola a table with syphons and spirits, and had set a lamp upon it. As Frank spoke he leaned forward towards the other, and Darcy for all his matter-of-fact common sense could have sworn that his companion's face shone, was luminous in itself. His dark brown eyes glowed from within, the unconscious smile of a child irradiated and transformed his face. Darcy felt suddenly excited, exhilarated.

"Go on," he said. "Go on. I can feel you are somehow telling me sober truth. I daresay you are mad; but I don't see that matters."

Frank laughed again.

"Mad?" he said. "Yes, certainly, if you wish. But I prefer to call it sane. However, nothing matters less than what anybody chooses to call things. God never labels his gifts; He just puts them into our hands; just as he put animals in the garden of Eden, for Adam to name if he felt disposed."

"So by the continual observance and study of things that were happy," continued he, "I got happiness, I got joy. But seeking it, as I did, from Nature, I got much more which I did not seek, but stumbled upon originally by accident. It is difficult to explain, but I will try.

"About three years ago I was sitting one morning in a place I will show you to-morrow. It is down by the river brink, very green, dappled with shade and sun, and the river passes there through some little clumps of reeds. Well, as I sat there, doing nothing, but just looking and listening, I heard the sound quite distinctly of some flute-like instrument playing a strange unending melody. I thought at first it was some musical yokel on the highway and did not pay much attention. But before long the strangeness and indescribable beauty of the tune struck me. It never repeated itself, but it never came to an end, phrase after phrase ran its sweet course, it worked gradually and inevitably up to a climax, and having attained it, it went on; another climax was reached and another and another. Then with a sudden gasp of wonder I localised where it came from. It came from the reeds and from the sky and from the trees. It was everywhere, it was the sound of life. It was, my dear Darcy, as the Greeks would have said, it was Pan playing on his pipes, the voice of Nature. It was the life-melody, the world-melody."

Darcy was far too interested to interrupt, though there was a question he would have liked to ask, and Frank went on:

"Well, for the moment I was terrified, terrified with the impotent horror of nightmare, and I stopped my ears and just ran from the place and got back to the house panting, trembling, literally in a panic. Unknowingly, for at that time I only pursued joy, I had begun, since I drew my joy from Nature, to get in touch with Nature. Nature, force, God, call it what you will, had drawn across my face a little gossamer web of essential life. I saw that when I emerged from my terror, and I went very humbly back to where I had heard the Pan-pipes. But it was nearly six months before I heard them again."

"Why was that?" asked Darcy.

"Surely because I had revolted, rebelled, and worst of all been frightened. For I believe that just as there is nothing in the world which so injures one's body as fear, so there is nothing that so much shuts up the soul. I was afraid, you see, of the one thing in the world which has real existence. No wonder its manifestation was withdrawn."

"And after six months?"

"After six months one blessed morning I heard the piping again. I wasn't afraid that time. And since then it has grown louder, it has become more constant. I now hear it often, and I can put myself into such an attitude towards Nature that the pipes will almost certainly sound. And never yet have they played the same tune, it is always something new, something fuller, richer, more complete than before."

"What do you mean by 'such an attitude towards Nature'?" asked Darcy.

"I can't explain that; but by translating it into a bodily attitude it is this."

Frank sat up for a moment quite straight in his chair, then slowly sunk back with arms outspread and head drooped.

"That;" he said, "an effortless attitude, but open, resting, receptive. It is just that which you must do with your soul."

Then he sat up again.

"One word more," he said, "and I will bore you no further. Nor unless you ask me questions shall I talk about it again. You will find me, in fact, quite sane in my mode of life. Birds and beasts you will see behaving somewhat intimately to me, like that moor-hen, but that is all. I will walk with you, ride with you, play golf with you, and talk with you on any subject you like. But I wanted you on the threshold to know what has happened to me. And one thing more will happen."

He paused again, and a slight look of fear crossed his eyes.

"There will be a final revelation," he said, "a complete and blinding stroke which will throw open to me, once and for all, the full knowledge, the full realisation and comprehension that I am one, just as you are, with life. In reality there is no 'me,' no 'you,' no 'it.' Everything is part of the one and only thing which is life. I know that that is so, but the realisation of it is not yet mine. But it will be, and on that day, so I take it, I shall see Pan. It may mean death, the death of my body, that is, but I don't care. It may mean immortal, eternal life lived here and now and for ever. Then having gained that, ah, my dear Darcy, I shall preach such a gospel of joy, showing myself as the living proof of the truth, that Puritanism, the dismal religion of sour faces, shall vanish like a breath of smoke, and be dispersed and disappear in the sunlit air. But first the full knowledge must be mine."

Darcy watched his face narrowly.

"You are afraid of that moment," he said. Frank smiled at him.

"Quite true; you are quick to have seen that. But when it comes I hope I shall not be afraid."

For some little time there was silence; then Darcy rose.

"You have bewitched me, you extraordinary boy," he said. "You have been telling me a fairy-story, and I find myself saying, 'Promise me it is true.'"

"I promise you that," said the other.

"And I know I shan't sleep," added Darcy.

Frank looked at him with a sort of mild wonder as if he scarcely understood.

"Well, what does that matter?" he said.

"I assure you it does. I am wretched unless I sleep."

"Of course I can make you sleep if I want," said Frank in a rather bored voice.

"Well, do."

"Very good: go to bed. I'll come upstairs in ten minutes."

Frank busied himself for a little after the other had gone, moving the table back under the awning of the verandah and quenching the lamp. Then he went with his quick silent tread upstairs and into Darcy's room. The latter was already in bed, but very wide-eyed and wakeful, and Frank with an amused smile of indulgence, as for a fretful child, sat down on the edge of the bed.

"Look at me," he said, and Darcy looked.

"The birds are sleeping in the brake," said Frank softly, "and the winds are asleep. The sea sleeps, and the tides are but the heaving of its breast. The stars swing slow, rocked in the great cradle of the Heavens, and—"

He stopped suddenly, gently blew out Darcy's candle, and left him sleeping.

Morning brought to Darcy a flood of hard common sense, as clear and crisp as the sunshine that filled his room. Slowly as he woke he gathered together the broken threads of the memories of the evening which had ended, so he told himself, in a trick of common hypnotism. That accounted for it all; the whole strange talk he had had was under a spell of suggestion from the extraordinary vivid boy who had once been a man; all his own excitement, his acceptance of the incredible had been merely the effect of a stronger, more potent will imposed on his own. How strong that will was, he guessed from his own instantaneous obedience to Frank's suggestion of sleep. And armed with impenetrable common sense he came down to breakfast. Frank had already begun, and was consuming a large plateful of porridge and milk with the most prosaic and healthy appetite.

"Slept well?" he asked.

"Yes, of course. Where did you learn hypnotism?"

"By the side of the river."

"You talked an amazing quantity of nonsense last night," remarked Darcy, in a voice prickly with reason.

"Rather. I felt quite giddy. Look, I remembered to order a dreadful daily paper for you. You can read about money markets or politics or cricket matches."

Darcy looked at him closely. In the morning light Frank looked even fresher, younger, more vital than he had done the night before, and the sight of him somehow dinted Darcy's armour of common sense.

"You are the most extraordinary fellow I ever saw," he said. "I want to ask you some more questions."

"Ask away," said Frank.

For the next day or two Darcy plied his friend with many questions, objections and criticisms on the theory of life, and gradually got out of him a coherent and complete account of his experience. In brief, then, Frank believed that "by lying naked," as he put it, to the force which controls the passage of the stars, the breaking of a wave, the budding of a tree, the love of a youth and maiden, he had succeeded in a way hitherto undreamed of in possessing himself of the essential principle of life. Day by day, so he thought, he was getting nearer to, and in closer union with, the great power itself which caused all life to be, the spirit of nature, of force, or the spirit of God. For himself, he confessed to what others would call paganism; it was sufficient for him that there existed a principle of life. He did not worship it, he did not pray to it, he did not praise it. Some of it existed in all human beings, just as it existed in trees and animals; to realise and make living to himself the fact that it was all one, was his sole aim and object.

Here perhaps Darcy would put in a word of warning.

"Take care," he said. "To see Pan meant death, did it not."

Frank's eyebrows would rise at this.

"What does that matter?" he said. "True, the Greeks were always right, and they said so, but there is another possibility. For the nearer I get to it, the more living, the more vital and young I become."

"What then do you expect the final revelation will do for you?"

"I have told you," said he. "It will make me immortal."

But it was not so much from speech and argument that Darcy grew to grasp his friend's conception, as from the ordinary conduct of his life. They were passing, for instance, one morning down the village street, when an old woman, very bent and decrepit, but with an extraordinary cheerfulness of face, hobbled out from her cottage. Frank instantly stopped when he saw her.

"You old darling! How goes it all?" he said.

But she did not answer, her dim old eyes were riveted on his face; she seemed to drink in like a thirsty creature the beautiful radiance which shone there. Suddenly she put her two withered old hands on his shoulders.

"You're just the sunshine itself," she said, and he kissed her and passed on.

But scarcely a hundred yards further a strange contradiction of such tenderness occurred. A child running along the path towards them fell on its face and set up a dismal cry of fright and pain. A look of horror came into Frank's eyes, and, putting his fingers in his ears, he fled at full speed down the street, and did not pause till he was out of hearing. Darcy, having ascertained that the child was not really hurt, followed him in bewilderment.

"Are you without pity then?" he asked. Frank shook his head impatiently.

"Can't you see?" he asked. "Can't you understand that that sort of thing, pain, anger, anything unlovely, throws me back, retards the coming of the great hour! Perhaps when it comes I shall be able to piece that side of life on to the other, on to the true religion of joy. At present I can't."

"But the old woman. Was she not ugly?"

Frank's radiance gradually returned.

"Ah, no. She was like me. She longed for joy, and knew it when she saw it, the old darling."

Another question suggested itself.

"Then what about Christianity?" asked Darcy.

"I can't accept it. I can't believe in any creed of which the central doctrine is that God who is Joy should have had to suffer. Perhaps it was so; in some inscrutable way I believe it may have been so, but I don't understand how it was possible. So I leave it alone; my affair is joy."

They had come to the weir above the village, and the thunder of riotous cool water was heavy in the air. Trees dipped into the translucent stream with slender trailing branches, and the meadow where they stood was starred with midsummer blossomings. Larks shot up carolling into the crystal dome of blue, and a thousand voices of June sang round them. Frank, bare-headed as was his wont, with his coat slung over his arm and his shirt sleeves rolled up above the elbow, stood there like some beautiful wild animal with eyes half-shut and mouth half-open, drinking in the scented warmth of the air. Then suddenly he flung himself face downwards on the grass at the edge of the stream, burying his face in the daisies and cowslips, and lay stretched there in wide-armed ecstasy, with his long fingers pressing and stroking the dewy herbs of the field. Never before had Darcy seen him thus fully possessed by his idea; his caressing fingers, his half-buried face pressed close to the grass, even the clothed lines of his figure were instinct with a vitality that somehow was different from that of other men. And some faint glow from it reached Darcy, some thrill, some vibration from that charged recumbent body passed to him, and for a moment he understood as he had not understood before, despite his persistent questions and the candid answers they received, how real, and how realised by Frank, his idea was.

Then suddenly the muscles in Frank's neck became stiff and alert, and he half-raised his head.

"The Pan-pipes, the Pan-pipes," he whispered. "Close, oh, so close."

Very slowly, as if a sudden movement might interrupt the melody, he raised himself and leaned on the elbow of his bent arm. His eyes opened wider, the lower lids drooped as if he focussed his eyes on something very far away, and the smile on his face broadened and quivered like sunlight on still water, till the exultance of its happiness was scarcely human. So he remained motionless and rapt for some minutes, then the look of listening died from his face, and he bowed his head satisfied.

"Ah, that was good," he said. "How is it possible you did not hear? Oh, you poor fellow! Did you really hear nothing?"

A week of this outdoor and stimulating life did wonders in restoring to Darcy the vigour and health which his weeks of fever had filched from him, and as his normal activity and higher pressure of vitality returned, he seemed to himself to fall even more under the spell which the miracle of Frank's youth cast over him. Twenty times a day he found himself saying to himself suddenly at the end of some ten minutes' silent resistance to the absurdity of Frank's idea: "But it isn't possible; it can't be possible," and from the fact of his having to assure himself so frequently of this, he knew that he was struggling and arguing with a conclusion which already had taken root in his mind. For in any case a visible living miracle confronted him, since it was equally impossible that this youth, this boy, trembling on the verge of manhood, was thirty-five. Yet such was the fact.

July was ushered in by a couple of days of blustering and fretful rain, and Darcy, unwilling to risk a chill, kept to the house. But to Frank this weeping change of weather seemed to have no bearing on the behaviour of man, and he spent his days exactly as he did under the suns of June, lying in his hammock, stretched on the dripping grass, or making huge rambling excursions into the forest, the birds hopping from tree to tree after him, to return in the evening, drenched and soaked, but with the same unquenchable flame of joy burning within him.

"Catch cold?" he would ask; "I've forgotten how to do it, I think I suppose it makes one's body more sensible always to sleep out-of-doors. People who live indoors always remind me of something peeled and skinless."

"Do you mean to say you slept out-of-doors last night in that deluge?" asked Darcy. "And where, may I ask?"

Frank thought a moment.

"I slept in the hammock till nearly dawn," he said. "For I remember the light blinked in the east when I awoke. Then I went – where did I go – oh, yes, to the meadow where the Pan-pipes sounded so close a week ago. You were with me, do you remember? But I always have a rug if it is wet."

And he went whistling upstairs.

Somehow that little touch, his obvious effort to recall where he had slept, brought strangely home to Darcy the wonderful romance of which he was the still half-incredulous beholder. Sleep till close on dawn in a hammock, then the tramp – or probably scamper – underneath the windy and weeping heavens to the remote and lonely meadow by the weir! The picture of other such nights rose before him; Frank sleeping perhaps by the bathing-place under the filtered twilight of the stars, or the white blaze of moon-shine, a stir and awakening at some dead hour, perhaps a space of silent wide-eyed thought, and then awandering through the hushed woods to some other dormitory, alone with his happiness, alone with the joy and the life that suffused and enveloped him, without other thought or desire or aim except the hourly and never-ceasing communion with the joy of nature.

They were in the middle of dinner that night, talking on indifferent subjects, when Darcy suddenly broke off in the middle of a sentence.

"I've got it," he said. "At last I've got it."

"Congratulate you," said Frank. "But what?"

"The radical unsoundness of your idea. It is this: 'All Nature from highest to lowest is full, crammed full of suffering; every living organism in Nature preys on another, yet in your aim to get close to, to be one with Nature, you leave suffering altogether out; you run away from it, you refuse to recognise it. And you are waiting, you say, for the final revelation."

Frank's brow clouded slightly.

"Well," he asked, rather wearily.

"Cannot you guess then when the final revelation will be? In joy you are supreme, I grant you that; I did not know a man could be so master of it. You have learned perhaps practically all that Nature can teach. And if, as you think, the final revelation is coming to you, it will be the revelation of horror, suffering, death, pain in all its hideous forms. Suffering does exist: you hate it and fear it."

Frank held up his hand.

"Stop; let me think," he said.

There was silence for a long minute.

"That never struck me," he said at length. "It is possible that what you suggest is true. Does the sight of Pan mean that, do you think? Is it that Nature, take it altogether, suffers horribly, suffers to a hideous inconceivable extent? Shall I be shown all the suffering?"

He got up and came round to where Darcy sat.

"If it is so, so be it," he said. "Because, my dear fellow, I am near, so splendidly near to the final revelation. To-day the pipes have sounded almost without pause. I have even heard the rustle in the bushes, I believe, of Pan's coming. I have seen, yes, I saw to-day, the bushes pushed aside as if by a hand, and piece of a face, not human, peered through. But I was not frightened, at least I did not run away this time."

He took a turn up to the window and back again.

"Yes, there is suffering all through," he said, "and I have left it all out of my search. Perhaps, as you say, the revelation will be that. And in that case, it will be good-bye. I have gone on one line. I shall have gone too far along one road, without having explored the other. But I can't go back now. I wouldn't if I could; not a step would I retrace! In any case, whatever the revelation is, it will be God. I'm sure of that."

The rainy weather soon passed, and with the return of the sun Darcy again joined Frank in long rambling days. It grew extraordinarily hotter, and with the fresh bursting of life, after the rain, Frank's vitality seemed to blaze higher and higher. Then, as is the habit of the English weather, one evening clouds began to bank themselves up in the west, the sun went down in a glare of coppery thunder-rack, and the whole earth broiling under an unspeakable oppression and sultriness paused and panted for the storm. After sunset the remote fires of lightning began to wink and flicker on the horizon, but when bed-time came the storm seemed to have moved no nearer, though a very low unceasing noise of thunder was audible. Weary and oppressed by the stress of the day, Darcy fell at once into a heavy uncomforting sleep.

He woke suddenly into full consciousness, with the din of some appalling explosion of thunder in his ears, and sat up in bed with racing heart. Then for a moment, as he recovered himself from the panic-land which lies between sleeping and waking, there was silence, except for the steady hissing of rain on the shrubs outside his window. But suddenly that silence was shattered and shredded into fragments by a scream from somewhere close at hand outside in the black garden, a scream of supreme and despairing terror. Again and once again it shrilled up, and then a babble of awful words was interjected. A quivering sobbing voice that he knew said:

"My God, oh, my God; oh, Christ!"

And then followed a little mocking, bleating laugh. Then was silence again; only the rain hissed on the shrubs.

All this was but the affair of a moment, and without pause either to put on clothes or light a candle, Darcy was already fumbling at his door-handle. Even as he opened it he met a terror-stricken face outside, that of the man-servant who carried a light.

"Did you hear?" he asked.

The man's face was bleached to a dull shining whiteness.

"Yes, sir," he said. "It was the master's voice."

Together they hurried down the stairs and through the dining-room where an orderly table for breakfast had already been laid, and out on to the terrace. The rain for the moment had been utterly stayed, as if the tap of the heavens had been turned off, and under the lowering black sky, not quite dark, since the moon rode somewhere serene behind the conglomerated thunder-clouds, Darcy stumbled into the garden, followed by the servant with the candle. The monstrous leaping shadow of himself was cast before him on the lawn; lost and wandering odours of rose and lily and damp earth were thick about him, but more pungent was some sharp and acrid smell that suddenly reminded him of a certain châlet in which he had once taken refuge in the Alps. In the blackness of the hazy light from the sky, and the vague tossing of the candle behind him, he saw that the hammock in which Frank so often lay was tenanted. A gleam of white shirt was there, as if a man were sitting up in it, but across that there was an obscure dark shadow, and as he approached the acrid odour grew more intense.

He was now only some few yards away, when suddenly the black shadow seemed to jump into the air, then came down with tappings of hard hoofs on the brick path that ran down the pergola, and with frolicsome skippings galloped off into the bushes. When that was gone Darcy could see quite clearly that a shirted figure sat up in the hammock. For one moment, from sheer terror of the unseen, he hung on his step, and the servant joining him they walked together to the hammock.

It was Frank. He was in shirt and trousers only, and he sat up with braced arms. For one half-second he stared at them, his face a mask of horrible contorted terror. His upper lip was drawn back so that the gums of the teeth appeared, and his eyes were focussed not on the two who approached him, but on something quite close to him; his nostrils were widely expanded, as if he panted for breath, and terror incarnate and repulsion and deathly anguish ruled dreadful lines on his smooth cheeks and forehead. Then even as they looked the body sank backwards, and the ropes of the hammock wheezed and strained.

Darcy lifted him out and carried him indoors. Once he thought there was a faint convulsive stir of the limbs that lay with so dead a weight in his arms, but when they got inside, there was no trace of life. But the look of supreme terror and agony of fear had gone from his face, a boy tired with play but still smiling in his sleep was the burden he laid on the floor. His eyes had closed, and the beautiful mouth lay in smiling curves, even as when a few mornings ago, in the meadow by the weir, it had quivered to the music of the unheard melody of Pan's pipes. Then they looked further.

Frank had come back from his bathe before dinner that night in his usual costume of shirt and trousers only. He had not dressed, and during dinner, so Darcy remembered, he had rolled up the sleeves of his shirt to above the elbow. Later, as they sat and talked after dinner on the close sultriness of the evening, he had unbuttoned the front of his shirt to let what little breath of wind there was play on his skin. The sleeves were rolled up now, the front of the shirt was unbuttoned, and on his arms and on the brown skin of his chest were strange discolorations which grew momently more clear and defined, till they saw that the marks were pointed prints, as if caused by the hoofs of some monstrous goat that had leaped and stamped upon him.

Between the Lights

The day had been one unceasing fall of snow from sunrise until the gradual withdrawal of the vague white light outside indicated that the sun had set again. But as usual at this hospitable and delightful house of Everard Chandler where I often spent Christmas, and was spending it now, there had been no lack of entertainment, and the hours had passed with a rapidity that had surprised us. A short billiard tournament had filled up the time between breakfast and lunch, with Badminton and the morning papers for those who were temporarily not engaged, while afterwards, the interval till tea-time had been occupied by the majority of the party in a huge game of hide-and-seek all over the house, barring the billiard-room, which was sanctuary for any who desired peace. But few had done that; the enchantment of Christmas, I must suppose, had, like some spell, made children of us again, and it was with palsied terror and trembling misgivings that we had tip-toed up and down the dim passages, from any corner of which some wild screaming form might dart out on us. Then, wearied with exercise and emotion, we had assembled again for tea in the hall, a room of shadows and panels on which the light from the wide open fireplace, where there burned a divine mixture of peat and logs, flickered and grew bright again on the walls. Then, as was proper, ghost-stories, for the narration of which the electric light was put out, so that the listeners might conjecture anything they pleased to be lurking in the corners, succeeded, and we vied with each other in blood, bones, skeletons, armour and shrieks. I had, just given my contribution, and was reflecting with some complacency that probably the worst was now known, when Everard, who had not yet administered to the horror of his guests, spoke. He was sitting opposite me in the full blaze of the fire, looking, after the illness he had gone through during the autumn, still rather pale and delicate. All the same he had been among the boldest and best in the exploration of dark places that afternoon, and the look on his face now rather startled me.

"No, I don't mind that sort of thing," he said. "The paraphernalia of ghosts has become somehow rather hackneyed, and when I hear of screams and skeletons I feel I am on familiar ground, and can at least hide my head under the bed-clothes."

"Ah, but the bed-clothes were twitched away by my skeleton," said I, in self-defence.

"I know, but I don't even mind that. Why, there are seven, eight skeletons in this room now, covered with blood and skin and other horrors. No, the nightmares of one's childhood were the really frightening things, because they were vague. There was the true atmosphere of horror about them because one didn't know what one feared. Now if one could recapture that—"

Mrs. Chandler got quickly out of her seat.

"Oh, Everard," she said, "surely you don't wish to recapture it again. I should have thought once was enough."

This was enchanting. A chorus of invitation asked him to proceed: the real true ghost-story first-hand, which was what seemed to be indicated, was too precious a thing to lose.

Everard laughed. "No, dear, I don't want to recapture it again at all," he said to his wife. Then to us: "But really the – well, the nightmare perhaps, to which I was referring, is of the vaguest and most unsatisfactory kind. It has no apparatus about it at all. You will probably all say that it was nothing, and wonder why I was frightened. But I was; it frightened me out of my wits. And I only just saw something, without being able to swear what it was, and heard something which might have been a falling stone."

"Anyhow, tell us about the falling stone," said I.

There was a stir of movement about the circle round the fire, and the movement was not of purely physical order. It was as if – this is only what I personally felt – it was as if the childish gaiety of the hours we had passed that day was suddenly withdrawn; we had jested on certain subjects, we had played hide-and-seek with all the power of earnestness that was in us. But now – so it seemed to me – there was going to be real hide-and-seek, real terrors were going to lurk in dark corners, or if not real terrors, terrors so convincing as to assume the garb of reality, were going to pounce on us. And Mrs. Chandler's exclamation as she sat down again, "Oh, Everard, won't it excite you?" tended in any case to excite us. The room still remained in dubious darkness except for the sudden lights disclosed on the walls by the leaping flames on the hearth, and there was wide field for conjecture as to what might lurk in the dim corners. Everard, moreover, who had been sitting in bright light before, was banished by the extinction of some flaming log into the shadows. A voice alone spoke to us, as he sat back in his low chair, a voice rather slow but very distinct.

"Last year," he said, "on the twenty-fourth of December, we were down here, as usual, Amy and I, for Christmas. Several of you who are here now were here then. Three or four of you at least."

I was one of these, but like the others kept silence, for the identification, so it seemed to me, was not asked for. And he went on again without a pause.

"Those of you who were here then," he said, "and are here now, will remember how very warm it was this day year. You will remember, too, that we played croquet that day on the lawn. It was perhaps a little cold for croquet, and we played it rather in order to be able to say – with sound evidence to back the statement – that we had done so."

Then he turned and addressed the whole little circle.

"We played ties of half-games," he said, "just as we have played billiards to-day, and it was certainly as warm on the lawn then as it was in the billiard-room this morning directly after breakfast, while to-day I should not wonder if there was three feet of snow outside. More, probably; listen."

A sudden draught fluted in the chimney, and the fire flared up as the current of air caught it. The wind also drove the snow against the windows, and as he said, "Listen," we heard a soft scurry of the falling flakes against the panes, like the soft tread of many little people who stepped lightly, but with the persistence of multitudes who were flocking to some rendezvous. Hundreds of little feet seemed to be gathering outside; only the glass kept them out. And of the eight skeletons present four or five, anyhow, turned and looked at the windows. These were small-paned, with leaden bars. On the leaden bars little heaps of snow had accumulated, but there was nothing else to be seen.

"Yes, last Christmas Eve was very warm and sunny," went on Everard. "We had had no frost that autumn, and a temerarious dahlia was still in flower. I have always thought that it must have been mad."

He paused a moment.

"And I wonder if I were not mad too," he added.

No one interrupted him; there was something arresting, I must suppose, in what he was saying; it chimed in anyhow with the hide-and-seek, with the suggestions of the lonely snow. Mrs. Chandler had sat down again, but I heard her stir in her chair. But never was there a gay party so reduced as we had been in the last five minutes. Instead of laughing at ourselves for playing silly games, we were all taking a serious game seriously.

"Anyhow, I was sitting out," he said to me, "while you and my wife played your half-game of croquet. Then it struck me that it was not so warm as I had supposed, because quite suddenly I shivered. And shivering I looked up. But I did not see you and her playing croquet at all. I saw something which had no relation to you and her – at least I hope not."

Now the angler lands his fish, the stalker kills his stag, and the speaker holds his audience. And as the fish is gaffed, and as the stag is shot, so were we held. There was no getting away till he had finished with us.

"You all know the croquet lawn," he said, "and how it is bounded all round by a flower border with a brick wall behind it, through which, you will remember, there is only one gate. Well, I looked up and saw that the lawn – I could for one moment see it was still a lawn – was shrinking, and the walls closing in upon it. As they closed in too, they grew higher, and simultaneously the light began to fade and be sucked from the sky, till it grew quite dark overhead and only a glimmer of light came in through the gate.

"There was, as I told you, a dahlia in flower that day, and as this dreadful darkness and bewilderment came over me, I remember that my eyes sought it in a kind of despair, holding on, as it were, to any familiar object. But it was no longer a dahlia, and for the red of its petals I saw only the red of some feeble firelight. And at that moment the hallucination was complete. I was no longer sitting on the lawn watching croquet, but I was in a low-roofed room, something like a cattle-shed, but round. Close above my head, though I was sitting down, ran rafters from wall to wall. It was nearly dark, but a little light came in from the door opposite to me, which seemed to lead into a passage that communicated with the exterior of the place. Little, however, of the wholesome air came into this dreadful den; the atmosphere was oppressive and foul beyond all telling, it was as if for years it had been the place of some human menagerie, and for those years had been uncleaned and unsweetened by the winds of heaven. Yet that oppressiveness was nothing to the awful horror of the place from the view of the spirit. Some dreadful atmosphere of crime and abomination dwelt heavy in it, its denizens, whoever they were, were scarce human, so it seemed to me, and though men and women, were akin more to the beasts of the field. And in addition there was present to me some sense of the weight of years; I had been taken and thrust down into some epoch of dim antiquity."

He paused a moment, and the fire on the hearth leaped up for a second and then died down again. But in that gleam I saw that all faces were turned to Everard, and that all wore some look of dreadful expectancy. Certainly I felt it myself, and waited in a sort of shrinking horror for what was coming.

"As I told you," he continued, "where there had been that unseasonable dahlia, there now burned a dim firelight, and my eyes were drawn there. Shapes were gathered round it; what they were I could not at first see. Then perhaps my eyes got more accustomed to the dusk, or the fire burned better, for I perceived that they were of human form, but very small, for when one rose with a horrible chattering, to his feet, his head was still some inches off the low roof. He was dressed in a sort of shirt that came to his knees, but his arms were bare and covered with hair. Then the gesticulation and chattering increased, and I knew that they were talking about me, for they kept pointing in my direction. At that my horror suddenly deepened, for I became aware that I was powerless and could not move hand or foot; a helpless, nightmare impotence had possession of me. I could not lift a finger or turn my head. And in the paralysis of that fear I tried to scream, but not a sound could I utter.

"All this I suppose took place with the instantaneousness of a dream, for at once, and without transition, the whole thing had vanished, and I was back on the lawn again, while the stroke for which my wife was aiming was still unplayed. But my face was dripping with perspiration, and I was trembling all over.

"Now you may all say that I had fallen asleep, and had a sudden nightmare. That may be so; but I was conscious of no sense of sleepiness before, and I was conscious of none afterwards. It was as if someone had held a book before me, whisked the pages open for a second and closed them again."

Somebody, I don't know who, got up from his chair with a sudden movement that made me start, and turned on the electric light. I do not mind confessing that I was rather glad of this.

Everard laughed.

"Really I feel like Hamlet in the play-scene," he said, "and as if there was a guilty uncle present. Shall I go on?"

I don't think anyone replied, and he went on.

"Well, let us say for the moment that it was not a dream exactly, but a hallucination. Whichever it was, in any case it haunted me; for months, I think, it was never quite out of my mind, but lingered somewhere in the dusk of consciousness, sometimes sleeping quietly, so to speak, but sometimes stirring in its sleep. It was no good my telling myself that I was disquieting myself in vain, for it was as if something had actually entered into my very soul, as if some seed of horror had been planted there. And as the weeks went on the seed began to sprout, so that I could no longer even tell myself that that vision had been a moment's disorderment only. I can't say that it actually affected my health. I did not, as far as I know, sleep or eat insufficiently, but morning after morning I used to wake, not gradually and through pleasant dozings into full consciousness, but with absolute suddenness, and find myself plunged in an abyss of despair. Often too, eating or drinking, I used to pause and wonder if it was worth while.

"Eventually, I told two people about my trouble, hoping that perhaps the mere communication would help matters, hoping also, but very distantly, that though I could not believe at present that digestion or the obscurities of the nervous system were at fault, a doctor by some simple dose might convince me of it. In other words I told my wife, who laughed at me, and my doctor, who laughed also, and assured me that my health was quite unnecessarily robust. At the same time he suggested that change of air and scene does wonders for the delusions that exist merely in the imagination. He also told me, in answer to a direct question, that he would stake his reputation on the certainty that I was not going mad.

"Well, we went up to London as usual for the season, and though nothing whatever occurred to remind me in any way of that single moment on Christmas Eve, the reminding was seen to all right, the moment itself took care of that, for instead of fading as is the way of sleeping or waking dreams, it grew every day more vivid, and ate, so to speak, like some corrosive acid into my mind, etching itself there. And to London succeeded Scotland.

"I took last year for the first time a small forest up in Sutherland, called Glen Callan, very remote and wild, but affording excellent stalking. It was not far from the sea, and the gillies used always to warn me to carry a compass on the hill, because sea-mists were liable to come up with frightful rapidity, and there was always a danger of being caught by one, and of having perhaps to wait hours till it cleared again. This at first I always used to do, but, as everyone knows, any precaution that one takes which continues to be unjustified gets gradually relaxed, and at the end of a few weeks, since the weather had been uniformly clear, it was natural that, as often as not, my compass remained at home.

"One day the stalk took me on to a part of my ground that I had seldom been on before, a very high table-land on the limit of my forest, which went down very steeply on one side to a loch that lay below it, and on the other, by gentler gradations, to the river that came from the loch, six miles below which stood the lodge. The wind had necessitated our climbing up – or so my stalker had insisted – not by the easier way, but up the crags from the loch. I had argued the point with him for it seemed to me that it was impossible that the deer could get our scent if we went by the more natural path, but he still held to his opinion; and therefore, since after all this was his part of the job, I yielded. A dreadful climb we had of it, over big boulders with deep holes in between, masked by clumps of heather, so that a wary eye and a prodding stick were necessary for each step if one wished to avoid broken bones. Adders also literally swarmed in the heather; we must have seen a dozen at least on our way up, and adders are a beast for which I have no manner of use. But a couple of hours saw us to the top, only to find that the stalker had been utterly at fault, and that the deer must quite infallibly have got wind of us, if they had remained in the place where we last saw them. That, when we could spy the ground again, we saw had happened; in any case they had gone. The man insisted the wind had changed, a palpably stupid excuse, and I wondered at that moment what other reason he had – for reason I felt sure there must be – for not wishing to take what would clearly now have been a better route. But this piece of bad management did not spoil our luck, for within an hour we had spied more deer, and about two o'clock I got a shot, killing a heavy stag. Then sitting on the heather I ate lunch, and enjoyed a well-earned bask and smoke in the sun. The pony meantime had been saddled with the stag, and was plodding homewards.

"The morning had been extraordinarily warm, with a little wind blowing off the sea, which lay a few miles off sparkling beneath a blue haze, and all morning in spite of our abominable climb I had had an extreme sense of peace, so much so that several times I had probed my mind, so to speak, to find if the horror still lingered there. But I could scarcely get any response from it. Never since Christmas had I been so free of fear, and it was with a great sense of repose, both physical and spiritual, that I lay looking up into the blue sky, watching my smoke-whorls curl slowly away into nothingness. But I was not allowed to take my ease long, for Sandy came and begged that I would move. The weather had changed, he said, the wind had shifted again, and he wanted me to be off this high ground and on the path again as soon as possible, because it looked to him as if a sea-mist would presently come up.

"'And yon's a bad place to get down in the mist,' he added, nodding towards the crags we had come up.

"I looked at the man in amazement, for to our right lay a gentle slope down on to the river, and there was now no possible reason for again tackling those hideous rocks up which we had climbed this morning. More than ever I was sure he had some secret reason for not wishing to go the obvious way. But about one thing he was certainly right, the mist was coming up from the sea, and I felt in my pocket for the compass, and found I had forgotten to bring it.

"Then there followed a curious scene which lost us time that we could really ill afford to waste, I insisting on going down by the way that common sense directed, he imploring me to take his word for it that the crags were the better way. Eventually, I marched off to the easier descent, and told him not to argue any more but follow. What annoyed me about him was that he would only give the most senseless reasons for preferring the crags. There were mossy places, he said, on the way I wished to go, a thing patently false, since the summer had been one spell of unbroken weather; or it was longer, also obviously untrue; or there were so many vipers about. But seeing that none of these arguments produced any effect, at last he desisted, and came after me in silence.

"We were not yet half down when the mist was upon us, shooting up from the valley like the broken water of a wave, and in three minutes we were enveloped in a cloud of fog so thick that we could barely see a dozen yards in front of us. It was therefore another cause for self-congratulation that we were not now, as we should otherwise have been, precariously clambering on the face of those crags up which we had come with such difficulty in the morning, and as I rather prided myself on my powers of generalship in the matter of direction, I continued leading, feeling sure that before long we should strike the track by the river. More than all, the absolute freedom from fear elated me; since Christmas I had not known the instinctive joy of that; I felt like a schoolboy home for the holidays. But the mist grew thicker and thicker, and whether it was that real rain-clouds had formed above it, or that it was of an extraordinary density itself, I got wetter in the next hour than I have ever been before or since. The wet seemed to penetrate the skin, and chill the very bones. And still there was no sign of the track for which I was making. Behind me, muttering to himself, followed the stalker, but his arguments and protestations were dumb, and it seemed as if he kept close to me, as if afraid.

"Now there are many unpleasant companions in this world; I would not, for instance, care to be on the hill with a drunkard or a maniac, but worse than either, I think, is a frightened man, because his trouble is infectious, and, insensibly, I began to be afraid of being frightened too. From that it is but a short step to fear. Other perplexities too beset us. At one time we seemed to be walking on flat ground, at another I felt sure we were climbing again, whereas all the time we ought to have been descending, unless we had missed the way very badly indeed. Also, for the month was October, it was beginning to get dark, and it was with a sense of relief that I remembered that the full moon would rise soon after sunset. But it had grown very much colder, and soon, instead of rain, we found we were walking through a steady fall of snow.

"Things were pretty bad, but then for the moment they seemed to mend, for, far away to the left, I suddenly heard the brawling of the river. It should, it is true, have been straight in front of me and we were perhaps a mile out of our way, but this was better than the blind wandering of the last hour, and turning to the left, I walked towards it. But before I had gone a hundred yards, I heard a sudden choked cry behind me, and just saw Sandy's form flying as if in terror of pursuit, into the mists. I called to him, but got no reply, and heard only the spurned stones of his running. What had frightened him I had no idea, but certainly with his disappearance, the infection of his fear disappeared also, and I went on, I may almost say, with gaiety. On the moment, however, I saw a sudden well-defined blackness in front of me, and before I knew what I was doing I was half stumbling, half walking up a very steep grass slope.

"During the last few minutes the wind had got up, and the driving snow was peculiarly uncomfortable, but there had been a certain consolation in thinking that the wind would soon disperse these mists, and I had nothing more than a moonlight walk home. But as I paused on this slope, I became aware of two things, one, that the blackness in front of me was very close, the other that, whatever it was, it sheltered me from the snow. So I climbed on a dozen yards into its friendly shelter, for it seemed to me to be friendly.

"A wall some twelve feet high crowned the slope, and exactly where I struck it there was a hole in it, or door rather, through which a little light appeared. Wondering at this I pushed on, bending down, for the passage was very low, and in a dozen yards came out on the other side. Just as I did this the sky suddenly grew lighter, the wind, I suppose, having dispersed the mists, and the moon, though not yet visible through the flying skirts of cloud, made sufficient illumination.

"I was in a circular enclosure, and above me there projected from the walls some four feet from the ground, broken stones which must have been intended to support a floor. Then simultaneously two things occurred.

"The whole of my nine months' terror came back to me, for I saw that the vision in the garden was fulfilled, and at the same moment I saw stealing towards me a little figure as of a man, but only about three foot six in height. That my eyes told me; my ears told me that he stumbled on a stone; my nostrils told me that the air I breathed was of an overpowering foulness, and my soul told me that it was sick unto death. I think I tried to scream, but could not; I know I tried to move and could not. And it crept closer.

"Then I suppose the terror which held me spellbound so spurred me that I must move, for next moment I heard a cry break from my lips, and was stumbling through the passage. I made one leap of it down the grass slope, and ran as I hope never to have to run again. What direction I took I did not pause to consider, so long as I put distance between me and that place. Luck, however, favoured me, and before long I struck the track by the river, and an hour afterwards reached the lodge.

"Next day I developed a chill, and as you know pneumonia laid me on my back for six weeks.

"Well, that is my story, and there are many explanations. You may say that I fell asleep on the lawn, and was reminded of that by finding myself, under discouraging circumstances, in an old Picts' castle, where a sheep or a goat that, like myself, had taken shelter from the storm, was moving about. Yes, there are hundreds of ways in which you may explain it. But the coincidence was an odd one, and those who believe in second sight might find an instance of their hobby in it."

"And that is all?" I asked.

"Yes, it was nearly too much for me. I think the dressing-bell has sounded."

Outside the Door

The rest of the small party staying with my friend Geoffrey Aldwych in the charming old house which he had lately bought at a little village north of Sheringham on the Norfolk coast had drifted away soon after dinner to bridge and billiards, and Mrs. Aldwych and myself had for the time been left alone in the drawing-room, seated one on each side of a small round table which we had very patiently and unsuccessfully been trying to turn. But such pressure, psychical or physical, as we had put upon it, though of the friendliest and most encouraging nature, had not overcome in the smallest degree the very slight inertia which so small an object might have been supposed to possess, and it had remained as fixed as the most constant of the stars. No tremor even had passed through its slight and spindle-like legs. In consequence we had, after a really considerable period of patient endeavour, left it to its wooden repose, and proceeded to theorise about psychical matters instead, with no stupid table to contradict in practice all our ideas on the subject.

This I had added with a certain bitterness born of failure, for if we could not move so insignificant an object, we might as well give up all idea of moving anything. But hardly were the words out of my mouth when there came from the abandoned table a single peremptory rap, loud and rather startling.

"What's that?" I asked.

"Only a rap," said she. "I thought something would happen before long."

"And do you really think that is a spirit rapping?" I asked.

"Oh dear no. I don't think it has anything whatever to do with spirits."

"More perhaps with the very dry weather we have been having. Furniture often cracks like that in the summer."

Now this, in point of fact, was not quite the case. Neither in summer nor in winter have I ever heard furniture crack as the table had cracked, for the sound, whatever it was, did not at all resemble the husky creak of contracting wood. It was a loud sharp crack like the smart concussion of one hard object with another.

"No, I don't think it had much to do with dry weather either," said she, smiling. "I think, if you wish to know, that it was the direct result of our attempt to turn the table. Does that sound nonsense?"

"At present, yes," said I, "though I have no doubt that if you tried you could make it sound sense. There is, I notice, a certain plausibility about you and your theories—"

"Now you are being merely personal," she observed.

"For the good motive, to goad you into explanations and enlargements. Please go on."

"Let us stroll outside, then," said she, "and sit in the garden, if you are sure you prefer my plausibilities to bridge. It is deliciously warm, and—"

"And the darkness will be more suitable for the propagation of psychical phenomena. As at séances," said I.

"Oh, there is nothing psychical about my plausibilities," said she. "The phenomena I mean are purely physical, according to my theory."

So we wandered out into the transparent half light of multitudinous stars. The last crimson feather of sunset, which had hovered long in the West, had been blown away with the breath of the night wind, and the moon, which would presently rise, had not yet cut the dim horizon of the sea, which lay very quiet, breathing gently in its sleep with stir of whispering ripples. Across the dark velvet of the close-cropped lawn, which stretched seawards from the house, blew a little breeze full of the savour of salt and the freshness of night, with, every now and then, a hint so subtly conveyed as to be scarcely perceptible of its travel across the sleeping fragrance of drowsy garden-beds, over which the white moths hovered seeking their night-honey. The house itself, with its two battlemented towers of Elizabethan times, gleamed with many windows, and we passed out of sight of it, and into the shadow of a box-hedge, clipped into shapes and monstrous fantasies, and found chairs by the striped tent at the top of the sheltered bowling-alley.

"And this is all very plausible," said I. "Theories, if you please, at length, and, if possible, a full length illustration also."

"By which you mean a ghost-story, or something to that effect?"

"Precisely: and, without presuming to dictate, if possible, first-hand."

"Oddly enough, I can supply that also," said she. "So first I will tell you my general theory, and follow it by a story that seems to bear it out. It happened to me, and it happened here."

"I am sure it will fill the bill," said I.

She paused a moment while I lit a cigarette, and then began in her very clear, pleasant voice. She has the most lucid voice I know, and to me sitting there in the deep-dyed dusk, the words seemed the very incarnation of clarity, for they dropped into the still quiet of the darkness, undisturbed by impressions conveyed to other senses.

"We are only just beginning to conjecture," she said, "how inextricable is the interweaving between mind, soul, life – call it what you will – and the purely material part of the created world. That such interweaving existed has, of course, been known for centuries; doctors, for instance, knew that a cheerful optimistic spirit on the part of their patients conduced towards recovery; that fear, the mere emotion, had a definite effect on the beat of the heart, that anger produced chemical changes in the blood, that anxiety led to indigestion, that under the influence of strong passion a man can do things which in his normal state he is physically incapable of performing. Here we have mind, in a simple and familiar manner, producing changes and effects in tissue, in that which is purely material. By an extension of this – though, indeed, it is scarcely an extension – we may expect to find that mind can have an effect, not only on what we call living tissue, but on dead things, on pieces of wood or stone. At least it is hard to see why that should not be so."

"Table-turning, for instance?" I asked.

"That is one instance of how some force, out of that innumerable cohort of obscure mysterious forces with which we human beings are garrisoned, can pass, as it is constantly doing, into material things. The laws of its passing we do not know; sometimes we wish it to pass and it does not. Just now, for instance, when you and I tried to turn the table, there was some impediment in the path, though I put down that rap which followed as an effect of our efforts. But nothing seems more natural to my mind than that these forces should be transmissible to inanimate things. Of the manner of its passing we know next to nothing, any more than we know the manner of the actual process by which fear accelerates the beating of the heart, but as surely as a Marconi message leaps along the air by no visible or tangible bridge, so through some subtle gateway of the body these forces can march from the citadel of the spirit into material forms, whether that material is a living part of ourselves or that which we choose to call inanimate nature."

She paused a moment.

"Under certain circumstances," she went on, "it seems that the force which has passed from us into inanimate things can manifest its presence there. The force that passes into a table can show itself in movements or in noises coming from the table. The table has been charged with physical energy. Often and often I have seen a table or a chair move apparently of its own accord, but only when some outpouring of force, animal magnetism – call it what you will – has been received by it. A parallel phenomenon to my mind is exhibited in what we know as haunted houses, houses in which, as a rule, some crime or act of extreme emotion or passion has been committed, and in which some echo or re-enactment of the deed is periodically made visible or audible. A murder has been committed, let us say, and the room where it took place is haunted. The figure of the murdered, or less commonly of the murderer, is seen there by sensitives, and cries are heard, or steps run to and fro. The atmosphere has somehow been charged with the scene, and the scene in whole or part repeats itself, though under what laws we do not know, just as a phonograph will repeat, when properly handled, what has been said into it."

"This is all theory," I remarked.

"But it appears to me to cover a curious set of facts, which is all we ask of a theory. Otherwise, we must frankly state our disbelief in haunted houses altogether, or suppose that the spirit of the murdered, poor, wretch, is bound under certain circumstances to re-enact the horror of its body's tragedy. It was not enough that its body was killed there, its soul has to be dragged back and live through it all again with such vividness that its anguish becomes visible or audible to the eyes or ears of the sensitive. That to me is unthinkable, whereas my theory is not. Do I make it at all clear?"

"It is clear enough," said I, "but I want support for it, the full-sized illustration."

"I promised you that, a ghost-story of my own experience."

Mrs. Aldwych paused again, and then began the story which was to illustrate her theory.

"It is just a year," she said, "since Jack bought this house from old Mrs. Denison. We had both heard, both he and I, that it was supposed to be haunted, but neither of us knew any particulars of the haunt whatever. A month ago I heard what I believe to have been the ghost, and, when Mrs. Denison was staying with us last week, I asked her exactly what it was, and found it tallied completely with my experience. I will tell you my experience first, and give her account of the haunt afterwards.

"A month ago Jack was away for a few days and I remained here alone. One Sunday evening I, in my usual health and spirits, as far as I am aware, both of which are serenely excellent, went up to bed about eleven. My room is on the first floor, just at the foot of the staircase that leads to the floor above. There are four more rooms on my passage, all of which that night were empty, and at the far end of it a door leads into the landing at the top of the front staircase. On the other side of that, as you know, are more bedrooms, all of which that night were also unoccupied; I, in fact, was the only sleeper on the first floor.

"The head of my bed is close behind my door, and there is an electric light over it. This is controlled by a switch at the bed-head, and another switch there turns on a light in the passage just outside my room. That was Jack's plan: if by chance you want to leave your room when the house is dark, you can light up the passage before you go out, and not grope blindly for a switch outside.

"Usually I sleep solidly: it is very rarely indeed that I wake, when once I have gone to sleep, before I am called. But that night I woke, which was rare; what was rarer was that I woke in a state of shuddering and unaccountable terror; I tried to localise my panic, to run it to earth and reason it away, but without any success. Terror of something I could not guess at stared me in the face, white, shaking terror. So, as there was no use in lying quaking in the dark, I lit my lamp, and, with the view of composing this strange disorder of my fear, began to read again in the book I had brought up with me. The volume happened to be 'The Green Carnation,' a work one would have thought to be full of tonic to twittering nerves. But it failed of success, even as my reasoning had done, and after reading a few pages, and finding that the heart-hammer in my throat grew no quieter, and that the grip of terror was in no way relaxed, I put out my light and lay down again. I looked at my watch, however, before doing this, and remember that the time was ten minutes to two.

"Still matters did not mend: terror, that was slowly becoming a little more definite, terror of some dark and violent deed that was momently drawing nearer to me held me in its vice. Something was coming, the advent of which was perceived by the sub-conscious sense, and was already conveyed to my conscious mind. And then the clock struck two jingling chimes, and the stable-clock outside clanged the hour more sonorously.

"I still lay there, abject and palpitating. Then I heard a sound just outside my room on the stairs that lead, as I have said, to the second story, a sound which was perfectly commonplace and unmistakable. Feet feeling their way in the dark were coming downstairs to my passage: I could hear also the groping hand slip and slide along the bannisters. The footfalls came along the few yards of passage between the bottom of the stairs and my door, and then against my door itself came the brush of drapery, and on the panels the blind groping of fingers. The handle rattled as they passed over it, and my terror nearly rose to screaming point.

"Then a sensible hope struck me. The midnight wanderer might be one of the servants, ill or in want of something, and yet – why the shuffling feet and the groping hand? But on the instant of the dawning of that hope (for I knew that it was of the step and that which was moving in the dark passage of which I was afraid) I turned on both the light at my bed-head, and the light of the passage outside, and, opening the door, looked out. The passage was quite bright from end to end, but it was perfectly empty. Yet as I looked, seeing nothing of the walker, I still heard. Down the bright boards I heard the shuffle growing fainter as it receded, until, judging by the ear, it turned into the gallery at the end and died away. And with it there died also all my sense of terror. It was It of which I had been afraid: now It and my terror had passed. And I went back to bed and slept till morning."

Again Mrs. Aldwych paused, and I was silent. Somehow it was in the extreme simplicity of her experience that the horror lay. She went on almost immediately.

"Now for the sequel," she said, "of what I choose to call the explanation. Mrs. Denison, as I told you, came down to stay with us not long ago, and I mentioned that we had heard, though only vaguely, that the house was supposed to be haunted, and asked for an account of it. This is what she told me:

"'In the year 1610 the heiress to the property was a girl Helen Denison, who was engaged to be married to young Lord Southern. In case therefore of her having children, the property would pass away from Denisons. In case of her death, childless, it would pass to her first cousin. A week before the marriage took place, he and a brother of his entered the house, riding here from thirty miles away, after dark, and made their way to her room on the second story. There they gagged her and attempted to kill her, but she escaped from them, groped her way along this passage, and into the room at the end of the gallery. They followed her there, and killed her. The facts were known by the younger brother turning king's evidence.'

"Now Mrs. Denison told me that the ghost had never been seen, but that it was occasionally heard coming downstairs or going along the passage. She told me that it was never heard except between the hours of two and three in the morning, the hour during which the murder took place."

"And since then have you heard it again?" I asked.

"Yes, more than once. But it has never frightened me again. I feared, as we all do, what was unknown."

"I feel that I should fear the known, if I knew it was that," said I.

"I don't think you would for long. Whatever theory you adopt about it, the sounds of the steps and the groping hand, I cannot see that there is anything to shock or frighten one. My own theory you know—"

"Please apply it to what you heard," I asked.

"Simply enough. The poor girl felt her way along this passage in the despair of her agonised terror, hearing no doubt the soft footsteps of her murderers gaining on her, as she groped along her lost way. The waves of that terrible brainstorm raging within her, impressed themselves in some subtle yet physical manner on the place. It would only be by those people whom we call sensitives that the wrinkles, so to speak, made by those breaking waves on the sands would be perceived, and by them not always. But they are there, even as when a Marconi apparatus is working the waves are there, though they can only be perceived by a receiver that is in tune. If you believe in brain-waves at all, the explanation is not so difficult."

"Then the brain-wave is permanent?"

"Every wave of whatever kind leaves its mark, does it not? If you disbelieve the whole thing, shall I give you a room on the route of that poor murdered harmless walker?"

I got up.

"I am very comfortable, thanks, where I am," I said.

The Terror by Night

The transference of emotion is a phenomenon so common, so constantly witnessed, that mankind in general have long ceased to be conscious of its existence, as a thing worth our wonder or consideration, regarding it as being as natural and commonplace as the transference of things that act by the ascertained laws of matter. Nobody, for instance, is surprised, if when the room is too hot, the opening of a window causes the cold fresh air of outside to be transferred into the room, and in the same way no one is surprised when into the same room, perhaps, which we will imagine as being peopled with dull and gloomy persons, there enters some one of fresh and sunny mind, who instantly brings into the stuffy mental atmosphere a change analogous to that of the opened windows. Exactly how this infection is conveyed we do not know; considering the wireless wonders (that act by material laws) which are already beginning to lose their wonder now that we have our newspaper brought as a matter of course every morning in mid-Atlantic, it would not perhaps be rash to conjecture that in some subtle and occult way the transference of emotion is in reality material too. Certainly (to take another instance) the sight of definitely material things, like writing on a page, conveys emotion apparently direct to our minds, as when our pleasure or pity is stirred by a book, and it is therefore possible that mind may act on mind by means as material as that.

Occasionally, however, we come across phenomena which, though they may easily be as material as any of these things, are rarer, and therefore more astounding. Some people call them ghosts, some conjuring tricks, and some nonsense. It seems simpler to group them under the head of transferred emotions, and they may appeal to any of the senses. Some ghosts are seen, some heard, some felt, and though I know of no instance of a ghost being tasted, yet it will seem in the following pages that these occult phenomena may appeal at any rate to the senses that perceive heat, cold, or smell. For, to take the analogy of wireless telegraphy, we are all of us probably "receivers" to some extent, and catch now and then a message or part of a message that the eternal waves of emotion are ceaselessly shouting aloud to those who have ears to hear, and materialising themselves for those who have eyes to see. Not being, as a rule, perfectly tuned, we grasp but pieces and fragments of such messages, a few coherent words it may be, or a few words which seem to have no sense. The following story, however, to my mind, is interesting, because it shows how different pieces of what no doubt was one message were received and recorded by several different people simultaneously. Ten years have elapsed since the events recorded took place, but they were written down at the time.

Jack Lorimer and I were very old friends before he married, and his marriage to a first cousin of mine did not make, as so often happens, a slackening in our intimacy. Within a few months after, it was found out that his wife had consumption, and, without any loss of time, she was sent off to Davos, with her sister to look after her. The disease had evidently been detected at a very early stage, and there was excellent ground for hoping that with proper care and strict regime she would be cured by the life-giving frosts of that wonderful valley.

The two had gone out in the November of which I am speaking, and Jack and I joined them for a month at Christmas, and found that week after week she was steadily and quickly gaining ground. We had to be back in town by the end of January, but it was settled that Ida should remain out with her sister for a week or two more. They both, I remember, came down to the station to see us off, and I am not likely to forget the last words that passed:

"Oh, don't look so woebegone, Jack," his wife had said; "you'll see me again before long."

Then the fussy little mountain engine squeaked, as a puppy squeaks when its toe is trodden on, and we puffed our way up the pass.

London was in its usual desperate February plight when we got back, full of fogs and still-born frosts that seemed to produce a cold far more bitter than the piercing temperature of those sunny altitudes from which we had come. We both, I think, felt rather lonely, and even before we had got to our journey's end we had settled that for the present it was ridiculous that we should keep open two houses when one would suffice, and would also be far more cheerful for us both. So, as we both lived in almost identical houses in the same street in Chelsea, we decided to "toss," live in the house which the coin indicated (heads mine, tails his), share expenses, attempt to let the other house, and, if successful, share the proceeds. A French five-franc piece of the Second Empire told us it was "heads."

We had been back some ten days, receiving every day the most excellent accounts from Davos, when, first on him, then on me, there descended, like some tropical storm, a feeling of indefinable fear. Very possibly this sense of apprehension (for there is nothing in the world so virulently infectious) reached me through him: on the other hand both these attacks of vague foreboding may have come from the same source. But it is true that it did not attack me till he spoke of it, so the possibility perhaps inclines to my having caught it from him. He spoke of it first, I remember, one evening when we had met for a good-night talk, after having come back from separate houses where we had dined.

"I have felt most awfully down all day," he said; "and just after receiving this splendid account from Daisy, I can't think what is the matter."

He poured himself out some whisky and soda as he spoke.

"Oh, touch of liver," I said. "I shouldn't drink that if I were you. Give it me instead."

"I was never better in my life," he said.

I was opening letters, as we talked, and came across one from the house agent, which, with trembling eagerness, I read.

"Hurrah," I cried, "offer of five gu^as^ – why can't he write it in proper English – five guineas a week till Easter for number 31. We shall roll in guineas!"

"Oh, but I can't stop here till Easter," he said.

"I don't see why not. Nor by the way does Daisy. I heard from her this morning, and she told me to persuade you to stop. That's to say, if you like. It really is more cheerful for you here. I forgot, you were telling me something."

The glorious news about the weekly guineas did not cheer him up in the least.

"Thanks awfully. Of course I'll stop."

He moved up and down the room once or twice.

"No, it's not me that is wrong," he said, "it's It, whatever It is. The terror by night."

"Which you are commanded not to be afraid of," I remarked.

"I know; it's easy commanding. I'm frightened: something's coming."

"Five guineas a week are coming," I said. "I shan't sit up and be infected by your fears. All that matters, Davos, is going as well as it can. What was the last report? Incredibly better. Take that to bed with you."

The infection – if infection it was – did not take hold of me then, for I remember going to sleep feeling quite cheerful, but I awoke in some dark still house and It, the terror by night, had come while I slept. Fear and misgiving, blind, unreasonable, and paralysing, had taken and gripped me. What was it? Just as by an aneroid we can foretell the approach of storm, so by this sinking of the spirit, unlike anything I had ever felt before, I felt sure that disaster of some sort was presaged.

Jack saw it at once when we met at breakfast next morning, in the brown haggard light of a foggy day, not dark enough for candles, but dismal beyond all telling.

"So it has come to you too," he said.

And I had not even the fighting-power left to tell him that I was merely slightly unwell. Besides, never in my life had I felt better.

All next day, all the day after that fear lay like a black cloak over my mind; I did not know what I dreaded, but it was something very acute, something that was very near. It was coming nearer every moment, spreading like a pall of clouds over the sky; but on the third day, after miserably cowering under it, I suppose some sort of courage came back to me: either this was pure imagination, some trick of disordered nerves or what not, in which case we were both "disquieting ourselves in vain," or from the immeasurable waves of emotion that beat upon the minds of men, something within both of us had caught a current, a pressure. In either case it was infinitely better to try, however ineffectively, to stand up against it. For these two days I had neither worked nor played; I had only shrunk and shuddered; I planned for myself a busy day, with diversion for us both in the evening.

"We will dine early," I said, "and go to the 'Man from Blankley's.' I have already asked Philip to come, and he is coming, and I have telephoned for tickets. Dinner at seven."

Philip, I may remark, is an old friend of ours, neighbour in this street, and by profession a much-respected doctor.

Jack laid down his paper.

"Yes, I expect you're right," he said. "It's no use doing nothing, it doesn't help things. Did you sleep well?"

"Yes, beautifully," I said rather snappishly, for I was all on edge with the added burden of an almost sleepless night.

"I wish I had," said he.

This would not do at all.

"We have got to play up!" I said. "Here are we two strong and stalwart persons, with as much cause for satisfaction with life as any you can mention, letting ourselves behave like worms. Our fear may be over things imaginary or over things that are real, but it is the fact of being afraid that is so despicable. There is nothing in the world to fear except fear. You know that as well as I do. Now let's read our papers with interest. Which do you back, Mr. Druce, or the Duke of Portland, or the Times Book Club?"

That day, therefore, passed very busily for me; and there were enough events moving in front of that black background, which I was conscious was there all the time, to enable me to keep my eyes away from it, and I was detained rather late at the office, and had to drive back to Chelsea, in order to be in time to dress for dinner instead of walking back as I had intended.

Then the message, which for these three days had been twittering in our minds, the receivers, just making them quiver and rattle, came through.

I found Jack already dressed, since it was within a minute or two of seven when I got in, and sitting in the drawing-room. The day had been warm and muggy, but when I looked in on the way up to my room, it seemed to me to have grown suddenly and bitterly cold, not with the dampness of English frost, but with the clear and stinging exhilaration of such days as we had recently spent in Switzerland. Fire was laid in the grate but not lit, and I went down on my knees on the hearth-rug to light it.

"Why, it's freezing in here," I said. "What donkeys servants are! It never occurs to them that you want fires in cold weather, and no fires in hot weather."

"Oh, for heaven's sake don't light the fire," said he, "it's the warmest muggiest evening I ever remember."

I stared at him in astonishment. My hands were shaking with the cold. He saw this.

"Why, you are shivering!" he said. "Have you caught a chill? But as to the room being cold let us look at the thermometer."

There was one on the writing-table.

"Sixty-five," he said.

There was no disputing that, nor did I want to, for at that moment it suddenly struck us, dimly and distantly, that It was "coming through." I felt it like some curious internal vibration.

"Hot or cold, I must go and dress," I said.

Still shivering, but feeling as if I was breathing some rarefied exhilarating air, I went up to my room. My clothes were already laid out, but, by an oversight, no hot water had been brought up, and I rang for my man. He came up almost at once, but he looked scared, or, to my already-startled senses, he appeared so.

"What's the matter?" I said.

"Nothing, sir," he said, and he could hardly articulate the words. "I thought you rang."

"Yes. Hot water. But what's the matter?"

He shifted from one foot to the other.

"I thought I saw a lady on the stairs," he said, "coming up close behind me. And the front door bell hadn't rung that I heard."

"Where did you think you saw her?" I asked.

"On the stairs. Then on the landing outside the drawing-room door, sir," he said. "She stood there as if she didn't know whether to go in or not."

"One – one of the servants," I said. But again I felt that It was coming through.

"No, sir. It was none of the servants," he said.

"Who was it then?"

"Couldn't see distinctly, sir, it was dim-like. But I thought it was Mrs. Lorimer."

"Oh, go and get me some hot water," I said.

But he lingered; he was quite clearly frightened.

At this moment the front-door bell rang. It was just seven, and already Philip had come with brutal punctuality while I was not yet half dressed.

"That's Dr. Enderly," I said. "Perhaps if he is on the stairs you may be able to pass the place where you saw the lady."

Then quite suddenly there rang through the house a scream, so terrible, so appalling in its agony and supreme terror, that I simply stood still and shuddered, unable to move. Then by an effort so violent that I felt as if something must break, I recalled the power of motion, and ran downstairs, my man at my heels, to meet Philip who was running up from the ground floor. He had heard it too.

"What's the matter?" he said. "What was that?"

Together we went into the drawing-room. Jack was lying in front of the fireplace, with the chair in which he had been sitting a few minutes before overturned. Philip went straight to him and bent over him, tearing open his white shirt.

"Open all the windows," he said, "the place reeks."

We flung open the windows, and there poured in so it seemed to me, a stream of hot air into the bitter cold. Eventually Philip got up.

"He is dead," he said. "Keep the windows open. The place is still thick with chloroform."

Gradually to my sense the room got warmer, to Philip's the drug-laden atmosphere dispersed. But neither my servant nor I had smelt anything at all.

A couple of hours later there came a telegram from Davos for me. It was to tell me to break the news of Daisy's death to Jack, and was sent by her sister. She supposed he would come out immediately. But he had been gone two hours now.

I left for Davos next day, and learned what had happened. Daisy had been suffering for three days from a little abscess which had to be opened, and, though the operation was of the slightest, she had been so nervous about it that the doctor gave her chloroform. She made a good recovery from the anæsthetic, but an hour later had a sudden attack of syncope, and had died that night at a few minutes before eight, by Central European time, corresponding to seven in English time. She had insisted that Jack should be told nothing about this little operation till it was over, since the matter was quite unconnected with her general health, and she did not wish to cause him needless anxiety.

And there the story ends. To my servant there came the sight of a woman outside the drawing-room door, where Jack was, hesitating about her entrance, at the moment when Daisy's soul hovered between the two worlds; to me there came – I do not think it is fanciful to suppose this – the keen exhilarating cold of Davos; to Philip there came the fumes of chloroform. And to Jack, I must suppose, came his wife. So he joined her.

The Other Bed

I had gone out to Switzerland just before Christmas, expecting, from experience, a month of divinely renovating weather, of skating all day in brilliant sun, and basking in the hot frost of that windless atmosphere. Occasionally, as I knew, there might be a snowfall, which would last perhaps for forty-eight hours at the outside, and would be succeeded by another ten days of cloudless perfection, cold even to zero at night, but irradiated all day long by the unflecked splendour of the sun.

Instead the climatic conditions were horrible. Day after day a gale screamed through this upland valley that should have been so windless and serene, bringing with it a tornado of sleet that changed to snow by night. For ten days there was no abatement of it, and evening after evening, as I consulted my barometer, feeling sure that the black finger would show that we were coming to the end of these abominations, I found that it had sunk a little lower yet, till it stayed, like a homing pigeon, on the S of storm. I mention these things in depreciation of the story that follows, in order that the intelligent reader may say at once, if he wishes, that all that occurred was merely a result of the malaise of nerves and digestion that perhaps arose from those storm-bound and disturbing conditions. And now to go back to the beginning again.

I had written to engage a room at the Hôtel Beau Site, and had been agreeably surprised on arrival to find that for the modest sum of twelve francs a day I was allotted a room on the first floor with two beds in it. Otherwise the hotel was quite full. Fearing to be billeted in a twenty-two franc room, by mistake, I instantly confirmed my arrangements at the bureau. There was no mistake: I had ordered a twelve-franc room and had been given one. The very civil clerk hoped that I was satisfied with it, for otherwise there was nothing vacant. I hastened to say that I was more than satisfied, fearing the fate of Esau.

I arrived about three in the afternoon of a cloudless and glorious day, the last of the series. I hurried down to the rink, having had the prudence to put skates in the forefront of my luggage, and spent a divine but struggling hour or two, coming up to the hotel about sunset. I had letters to write, and after ordering tea to be sent up to my gorgeous apartment, No. 23, on the first floor, I went straight up there.

The door was ajar and – I feel certain I should not even remember this now except in the light of what followed – just as I got close to it, I heard some faint movement inside the room and instinctively knew that my servant was there unpacking. Next moment I was in the room myself, and it was empty. The unpacking had been finished, and everything was neat, orderly, and comfortable. My barometer was on the table, and I observed with dismay that it had gone down nearly half an inch. I did not give another thought to the movement I thought I had heard from outside.

Certainly I had a delightful room for my twelve francs a day. There were, as I have said, two beds in it, on one of which were already laid out my dress-clothes, while night-things were disposed on the other. There were two windows, between which stood a large washing-stand, with plenty of room on it; a sofa with its back to the light stood conveniently near the pipes of central heating, there were a couple of good arm-chairs, a writing table, and, rarest of luxuries, another table, so that every time one had breakfast it was not necessary to pile up a drift of books and papers to make room for the tray. My window looked east, and sunset still flamed on the western faces of the virgin snows, while above, in spite of the dejected barometer, the sky was bare of clouds, and a thin slip of pale crescent moon was swung high among the stars that still burned dimly in these first moments of their kindling. Tea came up for me without delay, and, as I ate, I regarded my surroundings with extreme complacency.

Then, quite suddenly and without cause, I saw that the disposition of the beds would never do; I could not possibly sleep in the bed that my servant had chosen for me, and without pause I jumped up, transferred my dress clothes to the other bed, and put my night things where they had been. It was done breathlessly almost, and not till then did I ask myself why I had done it. I found I had not the slightest idea. I had merely felt that I could not sleep in the other bed. But having made the change I felt perfectly content.

My letters took me an hour or so to finish, and I had yawned and blinked considerably over the last one or two, in part from their inherent dullness, in part from quite natural sleepiness. For I had been in the train for twenty-four hours, and was fresh to these bracing airs which so conduce to appetite, activity, and sleep, and as there was still an hour before I need dress, I lay down on my sofa with a book for excuse, but the intention to slumber as reason. And consciousness ceased as if a tap had been turned off.

Then – I dreamed. I dreamed that my servant came very quietly into the room, to tell me no doubt that it was time to dress. I supposed there were a few minutes to spare yet, and that he saw I was dozing, for, instead of rousing me, he moved quietly about the room, setting things in order. The light appeared to me to be very dim, for I could not see him with any distinctness, indeed, I only knew it was he because it could not be any body else. Then he paused by my washing-stand, which had a shelf for brushes and razors above it, and I saw him take a razor from its case and begin stropping it; the light was strongly reflected on the blade of the razor. He tried the edge once or twice on his thumb-nail, and then to my horror I saw him trying it on his throat. Instantaneously one of those deafening dream-crashes awoke me, and I saw the door half open, and my servant in the very act of coming in. No doubt the opening of the door had constituted the crash.

I had joined a previously-arrived party of five, all of us old friends, and accustomed to see each other often; and at dinner, and afterwards in intervals of bridge, the conversation roamed agreeably over a variety of topics, rocking-turns and the prospects of weather (a thing of vast importance in Switzerland, and not a commonplace subject) and the performances at the opera, and under what circumstances as revealed in dummy's hand, is it justifiable for a player to refuse to return his partner's original lead in no trumps. Then over whisky and soda and the repeated "last cigarette," it veered back via the Zantzigs to thought transference and the transference of emotion. Here one of the party, Harry Lambert, put forward the much discussed explanation of haunted houses based on this principle. He put it very concisely.

"Everything that happens," he said, "whether it is a step we take, or a thought that crosses our mind, makes some change in its immediate material world. Now the most violent and concentrated emotion we can imagine is the emotion that leads a man to take so extreme a step as killing himself or somebody else. I can easily imagine such a deed so eating into the material scene, the room or the haunted heath, where it happens, that its mark lasts an enormous time. The air rings with the cry of the slain and still drips with his blood. It is not everybody who will perceive it, but sensitives will. By the way, I am sure that man who waits on us at dinner is a sensitive."

It was already late, and I rose.

"Let us hurry him to the scene of a crime," I said. "For myself I shall hurry to the scene of sleep."

Outside the threatening promise of the barometer was already finding fulfilment, and a cold ugly wind was complaining among the pines, and hooting round the peaks, and snow had begun to fall. The night was thickly overcast, and it seemed as if uneasy presences were going to and fro in the darkness. But there was no use in ill augury, and certainly if we were to be house-bound for a few days I was lucky in having so commodious a lodging. I had plenty to occupy myself with indoors, though I should vastly have preferred to be engaged outside, and in the immediate present how good it was to lie free in a proper bed after a cramped night in the train.

I was half-undressed when there came a tap at my door, and the waiter who had served us at dinner came in carrying a bottle of whisky. He was a tall young fellow, and though I had not noticed him at dinner, I saw at once now, as he stood in the glare of the electric light, what Harry had meant when he said he was sure he was a sensitive. There is no mistaking that look: it is exhibited in a peculiar "inlooking" of the eye. Those eyes, one knows, see further than the surface . . .

"The bottle of whisky for monsieur," he said putting it down on the table.

"But I ordered no whisky," said I.

He looked puzzled.

"Number twenty-three?" he said.

Then he glanced at the other bed.

"Ah, for the other gentleman, without doubt," he said.

"But there is no other gentleman," said I.

"I am alone here."

He took up the bottle again.

"Pardon, monsieur," he said. "There must be a mistake. I am new here; I only came today. But I thought—"

"Yes?" said I.

"I thought that number twenty-three had ordered a bottle of whisky," he repeated. "Goodnight, monsieur, and pardon."

I got into bed, extinguished the light, and feeling very sleepy and heavy with the oppression, no doubt, of the snow that was coming, expected to fall asleep at once. Instead my mind would not quite go to roost, but kept sleepily stumbling about among the little events of the day, as some tired pedestrian in the dark stumbles over stones instead of lifting his feet. And as I got sleepier it seemed to me that my mind kept moving in a tiny little circle. At one moment it drowsily recollected how I had thought I had heard movement inside my room, at the next it remembered my dream of some figure going stealthily about and stropping a razor, at a third it wondered why this Swiss waiter with the eyes of a "sensitive" thought that number twenty-three had ordered a bottle of whisky. But at the time I made no guess as to any coherence between these little isolated facts; I only dwelt on them with drowsy persistence. Then a fourth fact came to join the sleepy circle, and I wondered why I had felt a repugnance against using the other bed. But there was no explanation of this forthcoming, either, and the outlines of thought grew more blurred and hazy, until I lost consciousness altogether.

Next morning began the series of awful days, sleet and snow falling relentlessly with gusts of chilly wind, making any out-of-door amusement next to impossible. The snow was too soft for tobogganning, it balled on the skis, and as for the rink it was but a series of pools of slushy snow. This in itself, of course, was quite enough to account for any ordinary depression and heaviness of spirit, but all the time I felt there was something more than that to which I owed the utter blackness that hung over those days. I was beset too by fear that at first was only vague, but which gradually became more definite, until it resolved itself into a fear of number twenty-three and in particular a terror of the other bed. I had no notion why or how I was afraid of it, the thing was perfectly causeless, but the shape and the outline of it grew slowly clearer, as detail after detail of ordinary life, each minute and trivial in itself, carved and moulded this fear, till it became definite. Yet the whole thing was so causeless and childish that I could speak to no one of it; I could but assure myself that it was all a figment of nerves disordered by this unseemly weather.

However, as to the details, there were plenty of them. Once I woke up from strangling nightmare, unable at first to move, but in a panic of terror, believing that I was sleeping in the other bed. More than once, too, awaking before I was called, and getting out of bed to look at the aspect of the morning, I saw with a sense of dreadful misgiving that the bed-clothes on the other bed were strangely disarranged, as if some one had slept there, and smoothed them down afterwards, but not so well as not to give notice of the occupation. So one night I laid a trap, so to speak, for the intruder of which the real object was to calm my own nervousness (for I still told myself that I was frightened of nothing), and tucked in the sheet very carefully, laying the pillow on the top of it. But in the morning it seemed as if my interference had not been to the taste of the occupant, for there was more impatient disorder than usual in the bed-clothes, and on the pillow was an indentation, round and rather deep, such as we may see any morning in our own beds. Yet by day these things did not frighten me, but it was when I went to bed at night that I quaked at the thought of further developments.

It happened also from time to time that I wanted something brought me, or wanted my servant. On three or four of these occasions my bell was answered by the "Sensitive," as we called him, but the Sensitive, I noticed, never came into the room. He would open the door a chink to receive my order and on returning would again open it a chink to say that my boots, or whatever it was, were at the door. Once I made him come in, but I saw him cross himself as, with a face of icy terror, he stepped into the room, and the sight somehow did not reassure me. Twice also he came up in the evening, when I had not rung at all, even as he came up the first night, and opened the door a chink to say that my bottle of whisky was outside. But the poor fellow was in a state of such bewilderment when I went out and told him that I had not ordered whisky, that I did not press for an explanation. He begged my pardon profusely; he thought a bottle of whisky had been ordered for number twenty-three. It was his mistake, entirely – I should not be charged for it; it must have been the other gentleman. Pardon again; he remembered there was no other gentleman, the other bed was unoccupied.

It was on the night when this happened for the second time that I definitely began to wish that I too was quite certain that the other bed was unoccupied. The ten days of snow and sleet were at an end, and to-night the moon once more, grown from a mere slip to a shining shield, swung serenely among the stars. But though at dinner everyone exhibited an extraordinary change of spirit, with the rising of the barometer and the discharge of this huge snow-fall, the intolerable gloom which had been mine so long but deepened and blackened. The fear was to me now like some statue, nearly finished, modelled by the carving hands of these details, and though it still stood below its moistened sheet, any moment, I felt, the sheet might be twitched away, and I be confronted with it. Twice that evening I had started to go to the bureau, to ask to have a bed made up for me, anywhere, in the billiard-room or the smoking-room, since the hotel was full, but the intolerable childishness of the proceeding revolted me. What was I afraid of? A dream of my own, a mere nightmare? Some fortuitous disarrangement of bed linen? The fact that a Swiss waiter made mistakes about bottles of whisky? It was an impossible cowardice.

But equally impossible that night were billiards or bridge, or any form of diversion. My only salvation seemed to lie in downright hard work, and soon after dinner I went to my room (in order to make my first real counter-move against fear) and sat down solidly to several hours of proof-correcting, a menial and monotonous employment, but one which is necessary, and engages the entire attention. But first I looked thoroughly round the room, to reassure myself, and found all modern and solid; a bright paper of daisies on the wall, a floor parquetted, the hot-water pipes chuckling to themselves in the corner, my bed-clothes turned down for the night, the other bed—

The electric light was burning brightly, and there seemed to me to be a curious stain, as of a shadow, on the lower part of the pillow and the top of the sheet, definite and suggestive, and for a moment I stood there again throttled by a nameless terror. Then taking my courage in my hands I went closer and looked at it. Then I touched it; the sheet, where the stain or shadow was, seemed damp to the hand, so also was the pillow. And then I remembered; I had thrown some wet clothes on the bed before dinner. No doubt that was the reason. And fortified by this extremely simple dissipation of my fear, I sat down and began on my proofs. But my fear had been this, that the stain had not in that first moment looked like the mere greyness of water-moistened linen.

From below, at first came the sound of music, for they were dancing to-night, but I grew absorbed in my work, and only recorded the fact that after a time there was no more music. Steps went along the passages, and I heard the buzz of conversation on landings, and the closing of doors till by degrees the silence became noticeable. The loneliness of night had come.

It was after the silence had become lonely that I made the first pause in my work, and by the watch on my table saw that it was already past midnight. But I had little more to do; another half-hour would see the end of the business, but there were certain notes I had to make for future reference, and my stock of paper was already exhausted. However, I had bought some in the village that afternoon, and it was in the bureau downstairs, where I had left it, when I came in and had subsequently forgotten to bring it upstairs. It would be the work of a minute only to get it.

The electric light had brightened considerably during the last hour, owing no doubt to many burners being put out in the hotel, and as I left the room I saw again the stain on the pillow and sheet of the other bed. I had really forgotten all about it for the last hour, and its presence there came as an unwelcome surprise. Then I remembered the explanation of it, which had struck me before, and for purposes of self-reassurement I again touched it. It was still damp, but— Had

I got chilly with my work? For it was warm to the hand. Warm, and surely rather sticky. It did not seem like the touch of the water-damp. And at the same moment I knew I was not alone in the room. There was something there, something silent as yet, and as yet invisible. But it was there.

Now for the consolation of persons who are inclined to be fearful, I may say at once that I am in no way brave, but that terror which, God knows, was real enough, was yet so interesting, that interest overruled it. I stood for a moment by the other bed, and, half-consciously only, wiped the hand that had felt the stain, for the touch of it, though all the time I told myself that it was but the touch of the melted snow on the coat I had put there, was unpleasant and unclean. More than that I did not feel, because in the presence of the unknown and the perhaps awful, the sense of curiosity, one of the strongest instincts we have, came to the fore. So, rather eager to get back to my room again, I ran downstairs to get the packet of paper. There was still a light in the bureau, and the Sensitive, on night-duty, I suppose, was sitting there dozing. My entrance did not disturb him, for I had on noiseless felt slippers, and seeing at once the package I was in search of, I took it, and left him still unawakened. That was somehow of a fortifying nature. The Sensitive anyhow could sleep in his hard chair; the occupant of the unoccupied bed was not calling to him to-night.

I closed my door quietly, as one does at night when the house is silent, and sat down at once to open my packet of paper and finish my work. It was wrapped up in an old news-sheet, and struggling with the last of the string that bound it, certain words caught my eye. Also the date at the top of the paper caught my eye, a date nearly a year old, or, to be quite accurate, a date fifty-one weeks old. It was an American paper and what it recorded was this:

"The body of Mr. Silas R. Hume, who committed suicide last week at the Hôtel Beau Site, Moulin sur Chalons, is to be buried at his house in Boston, Mass. The inquest held in Switzerland showed that he cut his throat with a razor, in an attack of delirium tremens induced by drink. In the cupboard of his room were found three dozen empty bottles of Scotch whisky . . ."

So far I had read when without warning the electric light went out, and I was left in, what seemed for the moment, absolute darkness. And again I knew I was not alone, and I knew now who it was who was with me in the room.

Then the absolute paralysis of fear seized me. As if a wind had blown over my head, I felt the hair of it stir and rise a little. My eyes also, I suppose, became accustomed to the sudden darkness, for they could now perceive the shape of the furniture in the room from the light of the starlit sky outside. They saw more too than the mere furniture. There was standing by the wash-stand between the two windows a figure, clothed only in night-garments, and its hands moved among the objects on the shelf above the basin. Then with two steps it made a sort of dive for the other bed, which was in shadow. And then the sweat poured on to my forehead.

Though the other bed stood in shadow I could still see dimly, but sufficiently, what was there. The shape of a head lay on the pillow, the shape of an arm lifted its hand to the electric bell that was close by on the wall, and I fancied I could hear it distantly ringing. Then a moment later came hurrying feet up the stairs and along the passage outside, and a quick rapping at my door.

"Monsieur's whisky, monsieur's whisky," said a voice just outside. "Pardon, monsieur, I brought it as quickly as I could."

The impotent paralysis of cold terror was still on me. Once I tried to speak and failed, and still the gentle tapping went on at the door, and the voice telling some one that his whisky was there. Then at a second attempt, I heard a voice which was mine saying hoarsely:

"For God's sake come in; I am alone with it."

There was the click of a turned door-handle, and as suddenly as it had gone out a few seconds before, the electric light came back again, and the room was in full illumination. I saw a face peer round the corner of the door, but it was at another face I looked, the face of a man sallow and shrunken, who lay in the other bed, staring at me with glazed eyes. He lay high in bed, and his throat was cut from ear to ear; and the lower part of the pillow was soaked in blood, and the sheet streamed with it.

Then suddenly that hideous vision vanished, and there was only a sleepy-eyed waiter looking into the room. But below the sleepiness terror was awake, and his voice shook when he spoke.

"Monsieur rang?" he asked.

No, monsieur had not rung. But monsieur made himself a couch in the billiard-room.

The Thing in the Hall

The following pages are the account given me by Dr. Assheton of the Thing in the Hall. I took notes, as copious as my quickness of hand allowed me, from his dictation, and subsequently read to him this narrative in its transcribed and connected form. This was on the day before his death, which indeed probably occurred within an hour after I had left him, and, as readers of inquests and such atrocious literature may remember, I had to give evidence before the coroner's jury. Only a week before Dr. Assheton had to give similar evidence, but as a medical expert, with regard to the death of his friend, Louis Fielder, which occurred in a manner identical with his own. As a specialist, he said he believed that his friend had committed suicide while of unsound mind, and the verdict was brought in accordingly. But in the inquest held over Dr. Assheton's body, though the verdict eventually returned was the same, there was more room for doubt.

For I was bound to state that only shortly before his death, I read what follows to him; that he corrected me with extreme precision on a few points of detail, that he seemed perfectly himself, and that at the end he used these words:

"I am quite certain as a brain specialist that I am completely sane, and that these things happened not merely in my imagination, but in the external world. If I had to give evidence again about poor Louis, I should be compelled to take a different line. Please put that down at the end of your account, or at the beginning, if it arranges itself better so."

There will be a few words I must add at the end of this story, and a few words of explanation must precede it. Briefly, they are these.

Francis Assheton and Louis Fielder were up at Cambridge together, and there formed the friendship that lasted nearly till their death. In general attributes no two men could have been less alike, for while Dr. Assheton had become at the age of thirty-five the first and final authority on his subject, which was the functions and diseases of the brain, Louis Fielder at the same age was still on the threshold of achievement. Assheton, apparently without any brilliance at all, had by careful and incessant work arrived at the top of his profession, while Fielder, brilliant at school, brilliant at college and brilliant ever afterwards, had never done anything. He was too eager, so it seemed to his friends, to set about the dreary work of patient investigation and logical deductions; he was for ever guessing and prying, and striking out luminous ideas, which he left burning, so to speak, to illumine the work of others. But at bottom, the two men had this compelling interest in common, namely, an insatiable curiosity after the unknown, perhaps the most potent bond yet devised between the solitary units that make up the race of man. Both – till the end – were absolutely fearless, and Dr. Assheton would sit by the bedside of the man stricken with bubonic plague to note the gradual surge of the tide of disease to the reasoning faculty with the same absorption as Fielder would study X-rays one week, flying machines the next, and spiritualism the third. The rest of the story, I think, explains itself – or does not quite do so. This, anyhow, is what I read to Dr. Assheton, being the connected narrative of what he had himself told me. It is he, of course, who speaks.

"After I returned from Paris, where I had studied under Charcot, I set up practice at home. The general doctrine of hypnotism, suggestion, and cure by such means had been accepted even in London by this time, and, owing to a few papers I had written on the subject, together with my foreign diplomas, I found that I was a busy man almost as soon as I had arrived in town. Louis Fielder had his ideas about how I should make my début (for he had ideas on every subject, and all of them original), and entreated me to come and live, not in the stronghold of doctors, 'Chloroform Square,' as he called it, but down in Chelsea, where there was a house vacant next his own.

"Who cares where a doctor lives," he said, "so long as he cures people? Besides you don't believe in old methods; why believe in old localities? Oh, there is an atmosphere of painless death in Chloroform Square! Come and make people live instead! And on most evenings I shall have so much to tell you; I can't 'drop in' across half London."

Now if you have been abroad for five years, it is a great deal to know that you have any intimate friend at all still left in the metropolis, and, as Louis said, to have that intimate friend next door is an excellent reason for going next door. Above all, I remembered from Cambridge days, what Louis' "dropping in" meant. Towards bed-time, when work was over, there would come a rapid step on the landing, and for an hour, or two hours, he would gush with ideas. He simply diffused life, which is ideas, wherever he went. He fed one's brain, which is the one thing which matters. Most people who are ill, are ill because their brain is starving, and the body rebels, and gets lumbago or cancer. That is the chief doctrine of my work such as it has been. All bodily disease springs from the brain. It is merely the brain that has to be fed and rested and exercised properly to make the body absolutely healthy, and immune from all disease. But when the brain is affected, it is as useful to pour medicines down the sink, as make your patient swallow them, unless – and this is a paramount limitation – unless he believes in them.

I said something of the kind to Louis one night, when, at the end of a busy day, I had dined with him. We were sitting over coffee in the hall, or so it is called, where he takes his meals. Outside, his house is just like mine, and ten thousand other small houses in London, but on entering, instead of finding a narrow passage with a door on one side, leading into the dining-room, which again communicates with a small back room called "the study," he has had the sense to eliminate all unnecessary walls, and consequently the whole ground floor of his house is one room, with stairs leading up to the first floor. Study, dining-room and passage have been knocked into one; you enter a big room from the front door. The only drawback is that the postman makes loud noises close to you, as you dine, and just as I made these commonplace observations to him about the effect of the brain on the body and the senses, there came a loud rap, somewhere close to me, that was startling.

"You ought to muffle your knocker," I said, "anyhow during the time of meals."

Louis leaned back and laughed.

"There isn't a knocker," he said. "You were startled a week ago, and said the same thing. So I took the knocker off. The letters slide in now. But you heard a knock, did you?"

"Didn't you?" said I.

"Why, certainly. But it wasn't the postman. It was the Thing. I don't know what it is. That makes it so interesting."

Now if there is one thing that the hypnotist, the believer in unexplained influences, detests and despises, it is the whole root-notion of spiritualism. Drugs are not more opposed to his belief than the exploded, discredited idea of the influence of spirits on our lives. And both are discredited for the same reason; it is easy to understand how brain can act on brain, just as it is easy to understand how body can act on body, so that there is no more difficulty in the reception of the idea that the strong mind can direct the weak one, than there is in the fact of a wrestler of greater strength overcoming one of less. But that spirits should rap at furniture and divert the course of events is as absurd as administering phosphorus to strengthen the brain. That was what I thought then.

However, I felt sure it was the postman, and instantly rose and went to the door. There were no letters in the box, and I opened the door. The postman was just ascending the steps. He gave the letters into my hand.

Louis was sipping his coffee when I came back to the table.

"Have you ever tried table-turning?" he asked. "It's rather odd."

"No, and I have not tried violet-leaves as a cure for cancer," I said.

"Oh, try everything," he said. "I know that that is your plan, just as it is mine. All these years that you have been away, you have tried all sorts of things, first with no faith, then with just a little faith, and finally with mountain-moving faith. Why, you didn't believe in hypnotism at all when you went to Paris."

He rang the bell as he spoke, and his servant came up and cleared the table. While this was being done we strolled about the room, looking at prints, with applause for a Bartolozzi that Louis had bought in the New Cut, and dead silence over a "Perdita" which he had acquired at considerable cost. Then he sat down again at the table on which we had dined. It was round, and mahogany-heavy, with a central foot divided into claws.

"Try its weight," he said; "see if you can push it about."

So I held the edge of it in my hands, and found that I could just move it. But that was all; it required the exercise of a good deal of strength to stir it.

"Now put your hands on the top of it," he said, "and see what you can do."

I could not do anything, my fingers merely slipped about on it. But I protested at the idea of spending the evening thus.

"I would much sooner play chess or noughts and crosses with you," I said, "or even talk about politics, than turn tables. You won't mean to push, nor shall I, but we shall push without meaning to."

Louis nodded.

"Just a minute," he said, "let us both put our fingers only on the top of the table and push for all we are worth, from right to left."

We pushed. At least I pushed, and I observed his finger-nails. From pink they grew to white, because of the pressure he exercised. So I must assume that he pushed too. Once, as we tried this, the table creaked. But it did not move.

Then there came a quick peremptory rap, not I thought on the front door, but somewhere in the room.

"It's the Thing," said he.

To-day, as I speak to you, I suppose it was. But on that evening it seemed only like a challenge. I wanted to demonstrate its absurdity.

"For five years, on and off, I've been studying rank spiritualism," he said. "I haven't told you before, because I wanted to lay before you certain phenomena, which I can't explain, but which now seem to me to be at my command. You shall see and hear, and then decide if you will help me."

"And in order to let me see better, you are proposing to put out the lights," I said.

"Yes; you will see why."

"I am here as a sceptic," said I.

"Scep away," said he.

Next moment the room was in darkness, except for a very faint glow of firelight. The window-curtains were thick, and no street-illumination penetrated them, and the familiar, cheerful sounds of pedestrians and wheeled traffic came in muffled. I was at the side of the table towards the door; Louis was opposite me, for I could see his figure dimly silhouetted against the glow from the smouldering fire.

"Put your hands on the table," he said, "quite lightly, and – how shall I say it – expect."

Still protesting in spirit, I expected. I could hear his breathing rather quickened, and it seemed to me odd that anybody could find excitement in standing in the dark over a large mahogany table, expecting. Then – through my finger-tips, laid lightly on the table, there began to come a faint vibration, like nothing so much as the vibration through the handle of a kettle when water is beginning to boil inside it. This got gradually more pronounced and violent till it was like the throbbing of a motor-car. It seemed to give off a low humming note. Then quite suddenly the table seemed to slip from under my fingers and began very slowly to revolve.

"Keep your hands on it and move with it," said Louis, and as he spoke I saw his silhouette pass away from in front of the fire, moving as the table moved.

For some moments there was silence, and we continued, rather absurdly, to circle round, keeping step, so to speak, with the table. Then Louis spoke again, and his voice was trembling with excitement.

"Are you there?" he said.

There was no reply, of course, and he asked it again. This time there came a rap like that which I had thought during dinner to be the postman. But whether it was that the room was dark, or that despite myself I felt rather excited too, it seemed to me now to be far louder than before. Also it appeared to come neither from here nor there, but to be diffused through the room.

Then the curious revolving of the table ceased, but the intense, violent throbbing continued. My eyes were fixed on it, though owing to the darkness I could see nothing, when quite suddenly a little speck of light moved across it, so that for an instant I saw my own hands. Then came another and another, like the spark of matches struck in the dark, or like fire-flies crossing the dusk in southern gardens. Then came another knock of shattering loudness, and the throbbing of the table ceased, and the lights vanished.

Such were the phenomena at the first séance at which I was present, but Fielder, it must be remembered, had been studying, "expecting," he called it, for some years. To adopt spiritualistic language (which at that time I was very far from doing), he was the medium, I merely the observer, and all the phenomena I had seen that night were habitually produced or witnessed by him. I make this limitation since he told me that certain of them now appeared to be outside his own control altogether. The knockings would come when his mind, as far as he knew, was entirely occupied in other matters, and sometimes he had even been awakened out of sleep by them. The lights were also independent of his volition.

Now my theory at the time was that all these things were purely subjective in him, and that what he expressed by saying that they were out of his control, meant that they had become fixed and rooted in the unconscious self, of which we know so little, but which, more and more, we see to play so enormous a part in the life of man. In fact, it is not too much to say that the vast majority of our deeds spring, apparently without volition, from this unconscious self. All hearing is the unconscious exercise of the aural nerve, all seeing of the optic, all walking, all ordinary movement seem to be done without the exercise of will on our part. Nay more, should we take to some new form of progression, skating, for instance, the beginner will learn with falls and difficulty the outside edge, but within a few hours of his having learned his balance on it, he will give no more thought to what he learned so short a time ago as an acrobatic feat, than he gives to the placing of one foot before the other.

But to the brain specialist all this was intensely interesting, and to the student of hypnotism, as I was, even more so, for (such was the conclusion I came to after this first séance), the fact that I saw and heard just what Louis saw and heard was an exhibition of thought-transference which in all my experience in the Charcot-schools I had never seen surpassed, if indeed rivalled. I knew that I was myself extremely sensitive to suggestion, and my part in it this evening I believed to be purely that of the receiver of suggestions so vivid that I visualised and heard these phenomena which existed only in the brain of my friend.

We talked over what had occurred upstairs. His view was that the Thing was trying to communicate with us. According to him it was the Thing that moved the table and tapped, and made us see streaks of light.

"Yes, but the Thing," I interrupted, "what do you mean? Is it a great-uncle – oh, I have seen so many relatives appear at séances, and heard so many of their dreadful platitudes – or what is it? A spirit? Whose spirit?"

Louis was sitting opposite to me, and on the little table before us there was an electric light. Looking at him I saw the pupil of his eye suddenly dilate. To the medical man – provided that some violent change in the light is not the cause of the dilation – that meant only one thing, terror. But it quickly resumed its normal proportion again.

Then he got up, and stood in front of the fire.

"No. I don't think it is great-uncle anybody," he said. "I don't know, as I told you, what the Thing is. But if you ask me what my conjecture is, it is that the Thing is an Elemental."

"And pray explain further. What is an Elemental?"

Once again his eye dilated.

"It will take two minutes," he said. "But, listen. There are good things in this world, are there not, and bad things? Cancer, I take it is bad, and – and fresh air is good; honesty is good, lying is bad. Impulses of some sort direct both sides, and some power suggests the impulses. Well, I went into this spiritualistic business impartially. I learned to 'expect,' to throw open the door into the soul, and I said, 'Anyone may come in.' And I think Something has applied for admission, the Thing that tapped and turned the table and struck matches, as you saw, across it. Now the control of the evil principle in the world is in the hands of a power which entrusts its errands to the things which I call Elementals. Oh, they have been seen; I doubt not that they will be seen again. I did not, and do not ask good spirits to come in. I don't want 'The Church's one foundation' played on a musical box. Nor do I *want* an Elemental. I only threw open the door. I believe the Thing has come into my house and is establishing communication with me. Oh, I want to go the whole hog. What is it? In the name of Satan, if necessary, what is it? I just want to know."

What followed I thought then might easily be an invention of the imagination, but what I believed to have happened was this. A piano with music on it was standing at the far end of the room by the door, and a sudden draught entered the room, so strong that the leaves turned. Next the draught troubled a vase of daffodils, and the yellow heads nodded. Then it reached the candles that stood close to us, and they fluttered burning blue and low. Then it reached me, and the draught was cold, and stirred my hair. Then it eddied, so to speak, and went across to Louis, and his hair also moved, as I could see. Then it went downwards towards the fire, and flames suddenly started up in its path, blown upwards. The rug by the fireplace flapped also.

"Funny, wasn't it?" he asked.

"And has the Elemental gone up the chimney?" said I.

"Oh, no," said he, "the Thing only passed us."

Then suddenly he pointed at the wall just behind my chair, and his voice cracked as he spoke.

"Look, what's that?" he said. "There on the wall."

Considerably startled I turned in the direction of his shaking finger. The wall was pale grey in tone, and sharp-cut against it was a shadow that, as I looked, moved. It was like the shadow of some enormous slug, legless and fat, some two feet high by about four feet long. Only at one end of it was a head shaped like the head of a seal, with open mouth and panting tongue.

Then even as I looked it faded, and from somewhere close at hand there sounded another of those shattering knocks.

For a moment after there was silence between us, and horror was thick as snow in the air. But, somehow, neither Louis nor I was frightened for more than one moment. The whole thing was so absorbingly interesting.

"That's what I mean by its being outside my control," he said. "I said I was ready for any – any visitor to come in, and by God, we've got a beauty."

Now I was still, even in spite of the appearance of this shadow, quite convinced that I was only taking observations of a most curious case of disordered brain accompanied by the most vivid and remarkable thought-transference. I believed that I had not seen a slug-like shadow at all, but that Louis had visualised this dreadful creature so intensely that I saw what he saw. I found also that his spiritualistic trash-books, which I thought a truer nomenclature than text-books, mentioned this as a common form for Elementals to take. He on the other hand was more firmly convinced than ever that we were dealing not with a subjective but an objective phenomenon.

For the next six months or so we sat constantly, but made no further progress, nor did the Thing or its shadow appear again, and I began to feel that we were really wasting time. Then it occurred to me, to get in a so-called medium, induce hypnotic sleep, and see if we could learn anything further. This we did, sitting as before round the dining-room table. The room was not quite dark, and I could see sufficiently clearly what happened.

The medium, a young man, sat between Louis and myself, and

without the slightest difficulty I put him into a light hypnotic sleep. Instantly there came a series of the most terrific raps, and across the table there slid something more palpable than a shadow, with a faint luminance about it, as if the surface of it was smouldering. At the moment the medium's face became contorted to a mask of hellish terror; mouth and eyes were both open, and the eyes were focussed on something close to him. The Thing, waving its head, came closer and closer to him, and reached out towards his throat. Then with a yell of panic, and warding off this horror with his hands, the medium sprang up, but It had already caught hold, and for the moment he could not get free. Then simultaneously Louis and I went to his aid, and my hands touched something cold and slimy. But pull as we could we could not get it away. There was no firm hand-hold to be taken; it was as if one tried to grasp slimy fur, and the touch of it was horrible, unclean, like a leper. Then, in a sort of despair, though I still could not believe that the horror was real, for it must be a vision of diseased imagination, I remembered that the switch of the four electric lights was close to my hand. I turned them all on. There on the floor lay the medium, Louis was kneeling by him with a face of wet paper, but there was nothing else there. Only the collar of the medium was crumpled and torn, and on his throat were two scratches that bled.

The medium was still in hypnotic sleep, and I woke him. He felt at his collar, put his hand to his throat and found it bleeding, but, as I expected, knew nothing whatever of what had passed. We told him that there had been an unusual manifestation, and he had, while in sleep, wrestled with something. We had got the result we wished for, and were much obliged to him.

I never saw him again. A week after that he died of blood-poisoning.

From that evening dates the second stage of this adventure. The Thing had materialised (I use again spiritualistic language which I still did not use at the time). The huge slug, the Elemental, manifested itself no longer by knocks and waltzing tables, nor yet by shadows. It was there in a form that could be seen and felt. But it still – this was my strong point – was only a thing of twilight; the sudden kindling of the electric light had shown us that there was nothing there. In this struggle perhaps the medium had clutched his own throat, perhaps I had grasped Louis' sleeve, he mine. But though I said these things to myself, I am not sure that I believed them in the same way that I believe the sun will rise to-morrow.

Now as a student of brain-functions and a student in hypnotic affairs, I ought perhaps to have steadily and unremittingly pursued this extraordinary series of phenomena. But I had my practice to attend to, and I found that with the best will in the world, I could think of nothing else except the occurrence in the hall next door. So I refused to take part in any further séance with Louis. I had another reason also. For the last four or five months he was becoming depraved. I have been no prude or Puritan in my own life, and I hope I have not turned a Pharisaical shoulder on sinners. But in all branches of life and morals, Louis had become infamous. He was turned out of a club for cheating at cards, and narrated the event to me with gusto. He had become cruel; he tortured his cat to death; he had become bestial. I used to shudder as I passed his house, expecting I knew not what fiendish thing to be looking at me from the window.

Then came a night only a week ago, when I was awakened by an awful cry, swelling and falling and rising again. It came from next door. I ran downstairs in my pyjamas, and out into the street. The policeman on the beat had heard it too, and it came from the hall of Louis' house, the window of which was open. Together we burst the door in. You know what we found. The screaming had ceased but a moment before, but he was dead already. Both jugulars were severed, torn open.

It was dawn, early and dusky when I got back to my house next door. Even as I went in something seemed to push by me, something soft and slimy. It could not be Louis' imagination this time. Since then I have seen glimpses of it every evening. I am awakened at night by tappings, and in the shadows in the corner of my room there sits something more substantial than a shadow."

Within an hour of my leaving Dr. Assheton, the quiet street was once more aroused by cries of terror and agony. He was already dead, and in no other manner than his friend, when they got into the house.

THE HOUSE WITH THE BRICK-KILN

The hamlet of Trevor Major lies very lonely and sequestered in a hollow below the north side of the south downs that stretch westward from Lewes, and run parallel with the coast. It is a hamlet of some three or four dozen inconsiderable houses and cottages much girt about with trees, but the big Norman church and the manor house which stands a little outside the village are evidence of a more conspicuous past. This latter, except for a tenancy of rather less than three weeks, now four years ago, has stood unoccupied since the summer of 1896, and though it could be taken at a rent almost comically small, it is highly improbable that either of its last tenants, even if times were very bad, would think of passing a night in it again. For myself – I was one of the tenants – I would far prefer living in a workhouse to inhabiting those low-pitched oak-panelled rooms, and I would sooner look from my garret windows on to the squalor and grime of Whitechapel than from the diamond-shaped and leaded panes of the Manor of Trevor Major on to the boskage of its cool thickets, and the glimmering of its clear chalk streams where the quick trout glance among the waving water-weeds and over the chalk and gravel of its sliding rapids.

It was the news of these trout that led Jack Singleton and myself to take the house for the month between mid-May and mid-June, but as I have already mentioned a short three weeks was all the time we passed there, and we had more than a week of our tenancy yet unexpired when we left the place, though on the very last afternoon we enjoyed the finest dry-fly fishing that has ever fallen to my lot. Singleton had originally seen the advertisement of the house in a Sussex paper, with the statement that there was good dry-fly fishing belonging to it, but it was with but faint hopes of the reality of the dry-fly fishing that we went down to look at the place, since we had before this so often inspected depopulated ditches which were offered to the unwary under high-sounding titles. Yet after a half-hour's stroll by the stream, we went straight back to the agent, and before nightfall had taken it for a month with option of renewal.

We arrived accordingly from town at about five o'clock on a cloudless afternoon in May, and through the mists of horror that now stand between me and the remembrance of what occurred later, I cannot forget the exquisite loveliness of the impression then conveyed. The garden, it is true, appeared to have been for years untended; weeds half-choked the gravel paths, and the flower-beds were a congestion of mingled wild and cultivated vegetations. It was set in a wall of mellowed brick, in which snap-dragon and stone-crop had found an anchorage to their liking, and beyond that there stood sentinel a ring of ancient pines in which the breeze made music as of a distant sea. Outside that the ground sloped slightly downwards in a bank covered with a jungle of wild-rose to the stream that ran round three sides of the garden, and then followed a meandering course through the two big fields which lay towards the village. Over all this we had fishing-rights; above, the same rights extended for another quarter of a mile to the arched bridge over which there crossed the road which led to the house. In this field above the house on the fourth side, where the ground had been embanked to carry the road, stood a brick-kiln in a ruinous state. A shallow pit, long overgrown with tall grasses and wild field-flowers, showed where the clay had been digged.

The house itself was long and narrow; entering, you passed direct into a square panelled hall, on the left of which was the dining-room which communicated with the passage leading to the kitchen and offices. On the right of the hall were two excellent sitting-rooms looking out, the one on to the gravel in front of the house, the other on to the garden. From the first of these you could see, through the gap in the pines by which the road approached the house, the brick-kiln of which I have already spoken. An oak staircase went up from the hall, and round it ran a gallery on to which the three principal bedrooms opened. These were commensurate with the dining-room and the two sitting-rooms below. From this gallery there led a long narrow passage shut off from the rest of the house by a red-baize door, which led to a couple more guest-rooms and the servants' quarters.

Jack Singleton and I share the same flat in town, and we had sent down in the morning Franklyn and his wife, two old and valued servants, to get things ready at Trevor Major, and procure help from the village to look after the house, and Mrs. Franklyn, with her stout comfortable face all wreathed in smiles, opened the door to us. She had had some previous experience of the "comfortable quarters" which go with fishing, and had come down prepared for the worst, but found it all of the best. The kitchen-boiler was not furred; hot and cold water was laid on in the most convenient fashion, and could be obtained from taps that neither stuck nor leaked. Her husband, it appeared, had gone into the village to buy a few necessaries, and she brought up tea for us, and then went upstairs to the two rooms over the dining-room and bigger sitting-room, which we had chosen for our bedrooms, to unpack. The doors of these were exactly opposite one another to right and left of the gallery, and Jack, who chose the bedroom above the sitting-room, had thus a smaller room, above the second sitting-room, unoccupied, next his and opening out from it.

We had a couple of hours' fishing before dinner, each of us catching three or four brace of trout, and came back in the dusk to the house. Franklyn had returned from the village from his errand, reported that he had got a woman to come in to do housework in the mornings, and mentioned that our arrival had seemed to arouse a good deal of interest. The reason for this was obscure; he could only tell us that he was questioned a dozen times as to whether we really intended to live in the house, and his assurance that we did produced silence and a shaking of heads. But the country-folk of Sussex are notable for their silence and chronic attitude of disapproval, and we put this down to local idiosyncrasy.

The evening was exquisitely warm, and after dinner we pulled out a couple of basket-chairs on to the gravel by the front door, and sat for an hour or so, while the night deepened in throbs of gathering darkness. The moon was not risen and the ring of pines cut off much of the pale starlight, so that when we went in, allured by the shining of the lamp in the sitting-room, it was curiously dark for a clear night in May. And at that moment of stepping from the darkness into the cheerfulness of the lighted house, I had a sudden sensation, to which, during the next fortnight, I became almost accustomed, of there being something unseen and unheard and dreadful near me. In spite of the warmth, I felt myself shiver, and concluded instantly that I had sat out-of-doors long enough, and without mentioning it to Jack, followed him into the smaller sitting-room in which we had scarcely yet set foot. It, like the hall, was oak-panelled, and in the panels hung some half-dozen of water-colour sketches, which we examined, idly at first, and then with growing interest, for they were executed with extraordinary finish and delicacy, and each represented some aspect of the house or garden. Here you looked up the gap in the fir-trees into a crimson sunset; here the garden, trim and carefully tended, dozed beneath some languid summer noon; here an angry wreath of storm-cloud brooded over the meadow where the trout-stream ran grey and leaden below a threatening sky, while another, the most careful and arresting of all, was a study of the brick-kiln. In this, alone of them all, was there a human figure; a man, dressed in grey, peered into the open door from which issued a fierce red glow. The figure was painted with miniature-like elaboration; the face was in profile, and represented a youngish man, clean-shaven, with a long aquiline nose and singularly square chin. The sketch was long and narrow in shape, and the chimney of the kiln appeared against a dark sky. From it there issued a thin stream of grey smoke.

Jack looked at this with attention.

"What a horrible picture!" he said, "and how beautifully painted! I feel as if it meant something, as if it was a representation of something that happened, not a mere sketch. By Jove!—"

He broke off suddenly and went in turn to each of the other pictures.

"That's a queer thing," he said. "See if you notice what I mean."

With the brick-kiln rather vividly impressed on my mind, it was not difficult to see what he had noticed. In each of the pictures appeared the brick-kiln, chimney and all, now seen faintly between trees, now in full view, and in each the chimney was smoking.

"And the odd part is that from the garden side, you can't really see the kiln at all," observed Jack, "it's hidden by the house, and yet the artist F. A., as I see by his signature, puts it in just the same."

"What do you make of that?" I asked.

"Nothing. I suppose he had a fancy for brick-kilns. Let's have a game of picquet."

A fortnight of our three weeks passed without incident, except that again and again the curious feeling of something dreadful being close at hand was present in my mind. In a way, as I said, I got used to it, but on the other hand the feeling itself seemed to gain in poignancy. Once just at the end of the fortnight I mentioned it to Jack.

"Odd you should speak of it," he said, "because I've felt the same. When do you feel it? Do you feel it now, for instance?"

We were again sitting out after dinner, and as he spoke I felt it with far greater intensity than ever before. And at the same moment the house-door which had been closed, though probably not latched, swung gently open, letting out a shaft of light from the hall, and as gently swung to again, as if something had stealthily entered.

"Yes," I said. "I felt it then. I only feel it in the evening. It was rather bad that time."

Jack was silent a moment.

"Funny thing the door opening and shutting like that," he said. "Let's go indoors."

We got up and I remember seeing at that moment that the windows of my bedroom were lit; Mrs. Franklyn probably was making things ready for the night. Simultaneously, as we crossed the gravel, there came from just inside the house the sound of a hurried footstep on the stairs, and entering we found Mrs. Franklyn in the hall, looking rather white and startled.

"Anything wrong?" I asked.

She took two or three quick breaths before she answered:

"No, sir," she said, "at least nothing that I can give an account of. I was tidying up in your room, and I thought you came in. But there was nobody, and it gave me a turn. I left my candle there; I must go up for it."

I waited in the hall a moment, while she again ascended the stairs, and passed along the gallery to my room. At the door, which I could see was open, she paused, not entering.

"What is the matter?" I asked from below.

"I left the candle alight," she said, "and it's gone out."

Jack laughed.

"And you left the door and window open," said he.

"Yes, sir, but not a breath of wind is stirring," said Mrs. Franklyn, rather faintly.

This was true, and yet a few moments ago the heavy hall-door had swung open and back again. Jack ran upstairs.

"We'll brave the dark together, Mrs. Franklyn," he said.

He went into my room, and I heard the sound of a match struck. Then through the open door came the light of the rekindled candle and simultaneously I heard a bell ring in the servants' quarters. In a moment came steps, and Franklyn appeared.

"What bell was that?" I asked.

"Mr. Jack's bedroom, sir," he said.

I felt there was a marked atmosphere of nerves about for which there was really no adequate cause. All that had happened of a disturbing nature was that Mrs. Franklyn had thought I had come into my bedroom, and had been startled by finding I had not. She had then left the candle in a draught, and it had been blown out. As for a bell ringing, that, even if it had happened, was a very innocuous proceeding.

"Mouse on a wire," I said. "Mr. Jack is in my room this moment lighting Mrs. Franklyn's candle for her."

Jack came down at this juncture, and we went into the sitting-room. But Franklyn apparently was not satisfied, for we heard him in the room above us, which was Jack's bedroom, moving about with his slow and rather ponderous tread. Then his steps seemed to pass into the bedroom adjoining and we heard no more.

I remember feeling hugely sleepy that night, and went to bed earlier than usual, to pass rather a broken night with stretches of dreamless sleep interspersed with startled awakenings, in which I passed very suddenly into complete consciousness. Sometimes the house was absolutely still, and the only sound to be heard was the sighing of the night breeze outside in the pines, but sometimes the place seemed full of muffled movements and once I could have sworn that the handle of my door turned. That required verification, and I lit my candle, but found that my ears must have played me false. Yet even as I stood there, I thought I heard steps just outside, and with a considerable qualm, I must confess, I opened the door and looked out. But the gallery was quite empty, and the house quite still. Then from Jack's room opposite I heard a sound that was somehow comforting, the snorts of the snorer, and I went back to bed and slept again, and when next I woke, morning was already breaking in red lines, on the horizon, and the sense of trouble that had been with me ever since last evening had gone.

Heavy rain set in after lunch next day, and as I had arrears of letter-writing to do, and the water was soon both muddy and rising, I came home alone about five, leaving Jack still sanguine by the stream, and worked for a couple of hours sitting at a writing-table in the room overlooking the gravel at the front of the house, where hung the water-colours. By seven I had finished, and just as I got up to light candles, since it was already dusk, I saw, as I thought, Jack's figure emerge from the bushes that bordered the path to the stream, on to the space in front of the house. Then instantaneously and with a sudden queer sinking of the heart quite unaccountable, I saw that it was not Jack at all, but a stranger. He was only some six yards from the window, and after pausing there a moment he came close up to the window, so that his face nearly touched the glass, looking intently at me. In the light from the freshly-kindled candles I could distinguish his features with great clearness, but though, as far as I knew, I had never seen him before, there was something familiar about both his face and figure. He appeared to smile at me, but the smile was one of inscrutable evil and malevolence, and immediately he walked on, straight towards the house door opposite him, and out of sight of the sitting-room window.

Now, little though I liked the look of the man, he was, as I have said, familiar to my eye, and I went out into the hall, since he was clearly coming to the front-door, to open it to him and learn his business. So without waiting for him to ring, I opened it, feeling sure I should find him on the step. Instead, I looked out into the empty gravel-sweep, the heavy-falling rain, the thick dusk. And even as I looked, I felt something that I could not see push by me through the half-opened door and pass into the house. Then the stairs creaked, and a moment after a bell rang.

Franklyn is the quickest man to answer a bell I have ever seen, and next instant he passed me going upstairs. He tapped at Jack's door, entered and then came down again.

"Mr. Jack still out, sir?" he asked.

"Yes. His bell ringing again?"

"Yes, sir," said Franklyn, quite imperturbably.

I went back into the sitting-room, and soon Franklyn brought a lamp. He put it on the table above which hung the careful and curious picture of the brick-kiln, and then with a sudden horror I saw why the stranger on the gravel outside had been so familiar to me. In all respects he resembled the figure that peered into the kiln; it was more than a resemblance, it was an identity. And what had happened to this man who had inscrutably and evilly smiled at me? And what had pushed in through the half-closed door?

At that moment I saw the face of Fear; my mouth went dry, and I heard my heart leaping and cracking in my throat. That face was only turned on me for a moment, and then away again, but I knew it to be the genuine thing; not apprehension, not foreboding, not a feeling of being startled, but Fear, cold Fear. And then though nothing had occurred to assuage the Fear, it passed, and a certain sort of reason usurped – for so I must say – its place. I had certainly seen somebody on the gravel outside the house; I had supposed he was going to the front-door. I had opened it, and found he had not come to the front-door. Or – and once again the terror resurged – had the invisible pushing thing been that which I had seen outside? And if so, what was it? And how came it that the face and figure of the man I had seen were the same as those which were so scrupulously painted in the picture of the brick-kiln?

I set myself to argue down the Fear for which there was no more foundation than this, this and the repetition of the ringing bell, and my belief is that I did so. I told myself, till I believed it, that a man – a human man – had been walking across the gravel outside, and that he had not come to the front-door but had gone, as he might easily have done, up the drive into the high-road. I told myself that it was mere fancy that was the cause of the belief that Something had pushed in by me, and as for the ringing of the bell, I said to myself, as was true, that this had happened before. And I must ask the reader to believe also that I argued these things away, and looked no longer on the face of Fear itself. I was not comfortable, but I fell short of being terrified.

I sat down again by the window looking on to the gravel in front of the house, and finding another letter that asked, though it did not demand, an answer, proceeded to occupy myself with it. Straight in front led the drive through the gap in the pines, and passed through the field where lay the brick-kiln. In a pause of page-turning I looked up and saw something unusual about it; at the same moment an unusual smell came to my nostril. What I saw was smoke coming out of the chimney of the kiln, what I smelt was the odour of roasting meat. The wind – such as there was – set from the kiln to the house. But as far as I knew the smell of roast meat probably came from the kitchen where dinner, so I supposed, was cooking. I had to tell myself this: I wanted reassurance, lest the face of Fear should look whitely on me again.

Then there came a crisp step on the gravel, a rattle at the front-door, and Jack came in.

"Good sport," he said, "you gave up too soon."

And he went straight to the table above which hung the picture of the man at the brick-kiln, and looked at it. Then there was silence; and eventually I spoke, for I wanted to know one thing.

"Seen anybody?" I asked.

"Yes. Why do you ask?"

"Because I have also; the man in that picture."

Jack came and sat down near me.

"It's a ghost, you know," he said. "He came down to the river about dusk and stood near me for an hour. At first I thought he was – was real, and I warned him that he had better stand further off if he didn't want to be hooked. And then it struck me he wasn't real, and I cast, well, right through him, and about seven he walked up towards the house."

"Were you frightened?"

"No. It was so tremendously interesting. So you saw him here too. Whereabouts?"

"Just outside. I think he is in the house now."

Jack looked round.

"Did you see him come in?" he asked.

"No, but I felt him. There's another queer thing too; the chimney of the brick-kiln is smoking."

Jack looked out of the window. It was nearly dark, but the wreathing smoke could just be seen.

"So it is," he said, "fat, greasy smoke. I think I'll go up and see what's on. Come too?"

"I think not," I said.

"Are you frightened? It isn't worth while. Besides, it is so tremendously interesting."

Jack came back from his little expedition still interested. He had found nothing stirring at the kiln, but though it was then nearly dark the interior was faintly luminous, and against the black of the sky he could see a wisp of thick white smoke floating northwards. But for the rest of the evening we neither heard nor saw anything of abnormal import, and the next day ran a course of undisturbed hours. Then suddenly a hellish activity was manifested.

That night, while I was undressing for bed, I heard a bell ring furiously, and I thought I heard a shout also. I guessed where the ring came from, since Franklyn and his wife had long ago gone to bed, and went straight to Jack's room. But as I tapped at the door I heard his voice from inside calling loud to me. "Take care," it said, "he's close to the door."

A sudden qualm of blank fear took hold of me, but mastering it as best I could, I opened the door to enter, and once again something pushed softly by me, though I saw nothing.

Jack was standing by his bed, half-undressed. I saw him wipe his forehead with the back of his hand.

"He's been here again," he said. "I was standing just here, a minute ago, when I found him close by me. He came out of the inner room, I think. Did you see what he had in his hand?"

"I saw nothing."

"It was a knife; a great long carving knife. Do you mind my sleeping on the sofa in your room to-night? I got an awful turn then. There was another thing too. All round the edge of his clothes, at his collar and at his wrists, there were little flames playing, little white licking flames."

But next day, again, we neither heard nor saw anything, nor that night did the sense of that dreadful presence in the house come to us. And then came the last day. We had been out till it was dark, and as I said, had a wonderful day among the fish. On reaching home we sat together in the sitting-room, when suddenly from overhead came a tread of feet, a violent pealing of the bell, and the moment after yell after yell as of someone in mortal agony. The thought occurred to both of us that this might be Mrs. Franklyn in terror of some fearful sight, and together we rushed up and sprang into Jack's bedroom.

The doorway into the room beyond was open, and just inside it we saw the man bending over some dark huddled object. Though the room was dark we could see him perfectly, for a light stale and impure seemed to come from him. He had again a long knife in his hand, and as we entered he was wiping it on the mass that lay at his feet. Then he took it up, and we saw what it was, a woman with head nearly severed. But it was not Mrs. Franklyn.

And then the whole thing vanished, and we were standing looking into a dark and empty room. We went downstairs without a word, and it was not till we were both in the sitting-room below that Jack spoke.

"And he takes her to the brick-kiln," he said rather unsteadily. "I say, have you had enough of this house? I have. There is hell in it."

About a week later Jack put into my hand a guide-book to Sussex open at the description of Trevor Major, and I read:

"Just outside the village stands the picturesque manor house, once the home of the artist and notorious murderer, Francis Adam. It was here he killed his wife, in a fit, it is believed, of groundless jealousy, cutting her throat and disposing of her remains by burning them in a brick-kiln. Certain charred fragments found six months afterwards led to his arrest and execution."

So I prefer to leave the house with the brick-kiln and the pictures signed F. A. to others.

"And the Dead Spake—"

There is not in all London a quieter spot, or one, apparently, more withdrawn from the heat and bustle of life than Newsome Terrace. It is a cul-de-sac, for at the upper end the roadway between its two lines of square, compact little residences is brought to an end by a high brick wall, while at the lower end, the only access to it is through Newsome Square, that small discreet oblong of Georgian houses, a relic of the time when Kensington was a suburban village sundered from the metropolis by a stretch of pastures stretching to the river. Both square and terrace are most inconveniently situated for those whose ideal environment includes a rank of taxicabs immediately opposite their door, a spate of 'buses roaring down the street, and a procession of underground trains, accessible by a station a few yards away, shaking and rattling the cutlery and silver on their dining tables. In consequence Newsome Terrace had come, two years ago, to be inhabited by leisurely and retired folk or by those who wished to pursue their work in quiet and tranquillity. Children with hoops and scooters are phenomena rarely encountered in the Terrace and dogs are equally uncommon.

In front of each of the couple of dozen houses of which the Terrace is composed lies a little square of railinged garden, in which you may often see the middle-aged or elderly mistress of the residence horticulturally employed. By five o'clock of a winter's evening the pavements will generally be empty of all passengers except the policeman, who with felted step, at intervals throughout the night, peers with his bull's-eye into these small front gardens, and never finds anything more suspicious there than an early crocus or an aconite. For by the time it is dark the inhabitants of the Terrace have got themselves home, where behind drawn curtains and bolted shutters they will pass a domestic and uninterrupted evening. No funeral (up to the time I speak of) had I ever seen leave the Terrace, no marriage party had strewed its pavements with confetti, and perambulators were unknown. It and its inhabitants seemed to be quietly mellowing like bottles of sound wine. No doubt there was stored within them the sunshine and summer of youth long past, and now, dozing in a cool place, they waited for the turn of the key in the cellar door, and the entry of one who would draw them forth and see what they were worth.

Yet, after the time of which I shall now speak, I have never passed down its pavement without wondering whether each house, so seemingly-tranquil, is not, like some dynamo, softly and smoothly bringing into being vast and terrible forces, such as those I once saw at work in the last house at the upper end of the Terrace, the quietest, you would have said, of all the row. Had you observed it with continuous scrutiny, for all the length of a summer day, it is quite possible that you might have only seen issue from it in the morning an elderly woman whom you would have rightly conjectured to be the housekeeper, with her basket for marketing on her arm, who returned an hour later. Except for her the entire day might often pass without there being either ingress or egress from the door. Occasionally a middle-aged man, lean and wiry, came swiftly down the pavement, but his exit was by no means a daily occurrence, and indeed when he did emerge, he broke the almost universal usage of the Terrace, for his appearances took place, when such there were, between nine and ten in the evening. At that hour sometimes he would come round to my house in Newsome Square to see if I was at home and inclined for a talk a little later on. For the sake of air and exercise he would then have an hour's tramp through the lit and noisy streets, and return about ten, still pale and unflushed, for one of those talks which grew to have an absorbing fascination for me. More rarely through the telephone I proposed that I should drop in on him: this I did not often do, since I found that if he did not come out himself, it implied that he was busy with some investigation, and though he made me welcome, I could easily see that he burned for my departure, so that he might get busy with his batteries and pieces of tissue, hot on the track of discoveries that never yet had presented themselves to the mind of man as coming within the horizon of possibility.

My last sentence may have led the reader to guess that I am indeed speaking of none other than that recluse and mysterious physicist Sir James Horton, with whose death a hundred half-hewn avenues into the dark forest from which life comes must wait completion till another pioneer as bold as he takes up the axe which hitherto none but himself has been able to wield.

Probably there was never a man to whom humanity owed more, and of whom humanity knew less. He seemed utterly independent of the race to whom (though indeed with no service of love) he devoted himself: for years he lived aloof and apart in his house at the end of the Terrace. Men and women were to him like fossils to the geologist, things to be tapped and hammered and dissected and studied with a view not only to the reconstruction of past ages, but to construction in the future. It is known, for instance, that he made an artificial being formed of the tissue, still living, of animals lately killed, with the brain of an ape and the heart of a bullock, and a sheep's thyroid, and so forth. Of that I can give no first-hand account; Horton, it is true, told me something about it, and in his will directed that certain memoranda on the subject should on his death be sent to me. But on the bulky envelope there is the direction, 'Not to be opened till January, 1925.' He spoke with some reserve and, so I think, with slight horror at the strange things which had happened on the completion of this creature. It evidently made him uncomfortable to talk about it, and for that reason I fancy he put what was then a rather remote date to the day when his record should reach my eye. Finally, in these preliminaries, for the last five years before the war, he had scarcely entered, for the sake of companionship, any house other than his own and mine. Ours was a friendship dating from school-days, which he had never suffered to drop entirely, but I doubt if in those years he spoke except on matters of business to half a dozen other people. He had already retired from surgical practice in which his skill was unapproached, and most completely now did he avoid the slightest intercourse with his colleagues, whom he regarded as ignorant pedants without courage or the rudiments of knowledge. Now and then he would write an epochmaking little monograph, which he flung to them like a bone to a starving dog, but for the most part, utterly absorbed in his own investigations, he left them to grope along unaided. He frankly told me that he enjoyed talking to me about such subjects, since I was utterly unacquainted with them. It clarified his mind to be obliged to put his theories and guesses and confirmations with such simplicity that anyone could understand them.

I well remember his coming in to see me on the evening of the 4th of August, 1914.

"So the war has broken out," he said, "and the streets are impassable with excited crowds. Odd, isn't it? Just as if each of us already was not a far more murderous battlefield than any which can be conceived between warring nations."

"How's that?" said I.

"Let me try to put it plainly, though it isn't that I want to talk about. Your blood is one eternal battlefield. It is full of armies eternally marching and counter-marching. As long as the armies friendly to you are in a superior position, you remain in good health; if a detachment of microbes that, if suffered to establish themselves, would give you a cold in the head, entrench themselves in your mucous membrane, the commander-in-chief sends a regiment down and drives them out. He doesn't give his orders from your brain, mind you – those aren't his headquarters, for your brain knows nothing about the landing of the enemy till they have made good their position and given you a cold."

He paused a moment.

"There isn't one headquarters inside you," he said, "there are many. For instance, I killed a frog this morning; at least most people would say I killed it. But had I killed it, though its head lay in one place and its severed body in another? Not a bit: I had only killed a piece of it. For I opened the body afterwards and took out the heart, which I put in a sterilised chamber of suitable temperature, so that it wouldn't get cold or be infected by any microbe. That was about twelve o'clock to-day. And when I came out just now, the heart was beating still. It was alive, in fact. That's full of suggestions, you know. Come and see it."

The Terrace had been stirred into volcanic activity by the news of war: the vendor of some late edition had penetrated into its quietude, and there were half a dozen parlour-maids fluttering about like black and white moths. But once inside Horton's door isolation as of an Arctic night seemed to close round me. He had forgotten his latch-key, but his housekeeper, then newly come to him, who became so regular and familiar a figure in the Terrace, must have heard his step, for before he rang the bell she had opened the door, and stood with his forgotten latch-key in her hand.

"Thanks, Mrs. Gabriel," said he, and without a sound the door shut behind us. Both her name and face, as reproduced in some illustrated daily paper, seemed familiar, rather terribly familiar, but before I had time to grope for the association, Horton supplied it.

"Tried for the murder of her husband six months ago," he said. "Odd case. The point is that she is the one and perfect housekeeper. I once had four servants, and everything was all mucky, as we used to say at school. Now I live in amazing comfort and propriety with one. She does everything. She is cook, valet, housemaid, butler, and won't have anyone to help her. No doubt she killed her husband, but she planned it so well that she could not be convicted. She told me quite frankly who she was when I engaged her."

Of course I remembered the whole trial vividly now. Her husband, a morose, quarrelsome fellow, tipsy as often as sober, had, according to the defence cut his own throat while shaving; according to the prosecution, she had done that for him. There was the usual discrepancy of evidence as to whether the wound could have been self-inflicted, and the prosecution tried to prove that the face had been lathered after his throat had been cut. So singular an exhibition of forethought and nerve had hurt rather than helped their case, and after prolonged deliberation on the part of the jury, she had been acquitted. Yet not less singular was Horton's selection of a probable murderess, however efficient, as housekeeper.

He anticipated this reflection.

"Apart from the wonderful comfort of having a perfectly appointed and absolutely silent house," he said, "I regard Mrs. Gabriel as a sort of insurance against my being murdered. If you had been tried for your life, you would take very especial care not to find yourself in suspicious proximity to a murdered body again: no more deaths in your house, if you could help it. Come through to my laboratory, and look at my little instance of life after death."

Certainly it was amazing to see that little piece of tissue still pulsating with what must be called life; it contracted and expanded faintly indeed but perceptibly, though for nine hours now it had been severed from the rest of the organisation. All by itself it went on living, and if the heart could go on living with nothing, you would say, to feed and stimulate its energy, there must also, so reasoned Horton, reside in all the other vital organs of the body other independent focuses of life.

"Of course a severed organ like that," he said, "will run down quicker than if it had the co-operation of the others, and presently I shall apply a gentle electric stimulus to it. If I can keep that glass bowl under which it beats at the temperature of a frog's body, in sterilised air, I don't see why it should not go on living. Food – of course there's the question of feeding it. Do you see what that opens up in the way of surgery? Imagine a shop with glass cases containing healthy organs taken from the dead. Say a man dies of pneumonia. He should, as soon as ever the breath is out of his body, be dissected, and though they would, of course, destroy his lungs, as they will be full of pneumococci, his liver and digestive organs are probably healthy. Take them out, keep them in a sterilised atmosphere with the temperature at 98.4, and sell the liver, let us say, to another poor devil who has cancer there. Fit him with a new healthy liver, eh?"

"And insert the brain of someone who has died of heart disease into the skull of a congenital idiot?" I asked.

"Yes, perhaps; but the brain's tiresomely complicated in its connections and the joining up of the nerves, you know. Surgery will have to learn a lot before it fits new brains in. And the brain has got such a lot of functions. All thinking, all inventing seem to belong to it, though, as you have seen, the heart can get on quite well without it. But there are other functions of the brain I want to study first. I've been trying some experiments already."

He made some little readjustment to the flame of the spirit lamp which kept at the right temperature the water that surrounded the sterilised receptacle in which the frog's heart was beating.

"Start with the more simple and mechanical uses of the brain," he said. "Primarily it is a sort of record office, a diary. Say that I rap your knuckles with that ruler. What happens? The nerves there send a message to the brain, of course, saying – how can I put it most simply – saying, 'Somebody is hurting me.' And the eye sends another, saying 'I perceive a ruler hitting my knuckles,' and the ear sends another, saying 'I hear the rap of it.' But leaving all that alone, what else happens? Why, the brain records it. It makes a note of your knuckles having been hit."

He had been moving about the room as he spoke, taking off his coat and waistcoat and putting on in their place a thin black dressing-gown, and by now he was seated in his favourite attitude cross-legged on the hearth-rug, looking like some magician or perhaps the afrit which a magician of black arts had caused to appear. He was thinking intently now, passing through his fingers his string of amber beads, and talking more to himself than to me.

"And how does it make that note?" he went on. "Why, in the manner in which phonograph records are made. There are millions of minute dots, depressions, pockmarks on your brain which certainly record what you remember, what you have enjoyed or disliked, or done or said. The surface of the brain anyhow is large enough to furnish writing-paper for the record of all these things, of all your memories. If the impression of an experience has not been acute, the dot is not sharply impressed, and the record fades: in other words, you come to forget it. But if it has been vividly impressed, the record is never obliterated. Mrs. Gabriel, for instance, won't lose the impression of how she lathered her husband's face after she had cut his throat. That's to say, if she did it.

"Now do you see what I'm driving at? Of course you do. There is stored within a man's head the complete record of all the memorable things he has done and said: there are all his thoughts there, and all his speeches, and, most well-marked of all, his habitual thoughts and the things he has often said; for habit, there is reason to believe, wears a sort of rut in the brain, so that the life principle, whatever it is, as it gropes and steals about the brain, is continually stumbling into it. There's your record, your gramophone plate all ready. What we want, and what I'm trying to arrive at, is a needle which, as it traces its minute way over these dots, will come across words or sentences which the dead have uttered, and will reproduce them. My word, what Judgment Books! What a resurrection!"

Here in this withdrawn situation no remotest echo of the excitement which was seething through the streets penetrated; through the open window there came in only the tide of the midnight silence. But from somewhere closer at hand, through the wall surely of the laboratory, there came a low, somewhat persistent murmur.

"Perhaps our needle – unhappily not yet invented – as it passed over the record of speech in the brain, might induce even facial expression," he said. "Enjoyment or horror might even pass over dead features. There might be gestures and movements even, as the words were reproduced in our gramophone of the dead. Some people when they want to think intensely walk about: some, there's an instance of it audible now, talk to themselves aloud."

He held up his finger for silence.

"Yes, that's Mrs. Gabriel," he said. "She talks to herself by the hour together. She's always done that, she tells me. I shouldn't wonder if she has plenty to talk about."

It was that night when, first of all, the notion of intense activity going on below the placid house-fronts of the Terrace occurred to me. None looked more quiet than this, and yet there was seething here a volcanic activity and intensity of living, both in the man who sat cross-legged on the floor and behind that voice just audible through the partition wall. But I thought of that no more, for Horton began speaking of the brain-gramophone again . . . Were it possible to trace those infinitesimal dots and pock-marks in the brain by some needle exquisitely fine, it might follow that by the aid of some such contrivance as translated the pock-marks on a gramophone record into sound, some audible rendering of speech might be recovered from the brain of a dead man. It was necessary, so he pointed out to me, that this strange gramophone record should be new; it must be that of one lately dead, for corruption and decay would soon obliterate these infinitesimal markings. He was not of opinion that unspoken thought could be thus recovered: the utmost he hoped for from his pioneering work was to be able to recapture actual speech, especially when such speech had habitually dwelt on one subject, and thus had worn a rut on that part of the brain known as the speech-centre.

"Let me get, for instance," he said, "the brain of a railway porter, newly dead, who has been accustomed for years to call out the name of a station, and I do not despair of hearing his voice through my gramophone trumpet. Or again, given that Mrs. Gabriel, in all her interminable conversations with herself, talks about one subject, I might, in similar circumstances, recapture what she had been constantly saying. Of course my instrument must be of a power and delicacy still unknown, one of which the needle can trace the minutest irregularities of surface, and of which the trumpet must be of immense magnifying power, able to translate the smallest whisper into a shout. But just as a microscope will show you the details of an object invisible to the eye, so there are instruments which act in the same way on sound. Here, for instance, is one of remarkable magnifying power. Try it if you like."

He took me over to a table on which was standing an electric battery connected with a round steel globe, out of the side of which sprang a gramophone trumpet of curious construction. He adjusted the battery, and directed me to click my fingers quite gently opposite an aperture in the globe, and the noise, ordinarily scarcely audible, resounded through the room like a thunderclap.

"Something of that sort might permit us to hear the record on a brain," he said.

After this night my visits to Horton became far more common than they had hitherto been. Having once admitted me into the region of his strange explorations, he seemed to welcome me there. Partly, as he had said, it clarified his own thought to put it into simple language, partly, as he subsequently admitted, he was beginning to penetrate into such lonely fields of knowledge by paths so utterly untrodden, that even he, the most aloof and independent of mankind, wanted some human presence near him. Despite his utter indifference to the issues of the war – for, in his regard, issues far more crucial demanded his energies – he offered himself as surgeon to a London hospital for operations on the brain, and his services, naturally, were welcomed, for none brought knowledge or skill like his to such work. Occupied all day, he performed miracles of healing, with bold and dexterous excisions which none but he would have dared to attempt. He would operate, often successfully, for lesions that seemed certainly fatal, and all the time he was learning. He refused to accept any salary; he only asked, in cases where he had removed pieces of brain matter, to take these away, in order by further examination and dissection, to add to the knowledge and manipulative skill which he devoted to the wounded. He wrapped these morsels in sterilised lint, and took them back to the Terrace in a box, electrically heated to maintain the normal temperature of a man's blood. His fragment might then, so he reasoned, keep some sort of independent life of its own, even as the severed heart of a frog had continued to beat for hours without connection with the rest of the body. Then for half the night he would continue to work on these sundered pieces of tissue scarcely dead, which his operations during the day had given him. Simultaneously, he was busy over the needle that must be of such infinite delicacy.

One evening, fatigued with a long day's work, I had just heard with a certain tremor of uneasy anticipation the whistles of warning which heralded an air-raid, when my telephone bell rang. My servants, according to custom, had already betaken themselves to the cellar, and I went to see what the summons was, determined in any case not to go out into the streets. I recognised Horton's voice. "I want you at once," he said.

"But the warning whistles have gone," said I. "And I don't like showers of shrapnel."

"Oh, never mind that," said he. "You must come. I'm so excited that I distrust the evidence of my own ears. I want a witness. Just come."

He did not pause for my reply, for I heard the click of his receiver going back into its place. Clearly he assumed that I was coming, and that I suppose had the effect of suggestion on my mind. I told myself that I would not go, but in a couple of minutes his certainty that I was coming, coupled with the prospect of being interested in something else than air-raids, made me fidget in my chair and eventually go to the street door and look out. The moon was brilliantly bright, the square quite empty, and far away the coughings of very distant guns. Next moment, almost against my will, I was running down the deserted pavements of Newsome Terrace. My ring at his bell was answered by Horton, before Mrs. Gabriel could come to the door, and he positively dragged me in.

"I shan't tell you a word of what I am doing," he said. "I want you to tell me what you hear. Come into the laboratory."

The remote guns were silent again as I sat myself, as directed, in a chair close to the gramophone trumpet, but suddenly through the wall I heard the familiar mutter of Mrs. Gabriel's voice. Horton, already busy with his battery, sprang to his feet.

"That won't do," he said. "I want absolute silence."

He went out of the room, and I heard him calling to her. While he was gone I observed more closely what was on the table. Battery, round steel globe, and gramophone trumpet were there, and some sort of a needle on a spiral steel spring linked up with the battery and the glass vessel, in which I had seen the frog's heart beat. In it now there lay a fragment of grey matter.

Horton came back in a minute or two, and stood in the middle of the room listening.

"That's better," he said. "Now I want you to listen at the mouth of the trumpet. I'll answer any questions afterwards."

With my ear turned to the trumpet, I could see nothing of what he was doing, and I listened till the silence became a rustling in my ears. Then suddenly that rustling ceased, for it was overscored by a whisper which undoubtedly came from the aperture on which my aural attention was fixed. It was no more than the faintest murmur, and though no words were audible, it had the timbre of a human voice.

"Well, do you hear anything?" asked Horton.

"Yes, something very faint, scarcely audible."

"Describe it," said he.

"Somebody whispering."

"I'll try a fresh place," said he.

The silence descended again; the mutter of the distant guns was still mute, and some slight creaking from my shirt front, as I breathed, alone broke it. And then the whispering from the gramophone trumpet began again, this time much louder than it had been before – it was as if the speaker (still whispering) had advanced a dozen yards – but still blurred and indistinct. More unmistakable, too, was it that the whisper was that of a human voice, and every now and then, whether fancifully or not, I thought I caught a word or two. For a moment it was silent altogether, and then with a sudden inkling of what I was listening to I heard something begin to sing. Though the words were still inaudible there was melody, and the tune was "Tipperary." From that convolvulus-shaped trumpet there came two bars of it.

"And what do you hear now?" cried Horton with a crack of exultation in his voice. "Singing, singing! That's the tune they all sang. Fine music that from a dead man. Encore! you say? Yes, wait a second, and he'll sing it again for you. Confound it, I can't get on to the place. Ah! I've got it: listen again."

Surely that was the strangest manner of song ever yet heard on the earth, this melody from the brain of the dead. Horror and fascination strove within me, and I suppose the first for the moment prevailed, for with a shudder I jumped up.

"Stop it!" I said. "It's terrible."

His face, thin and eager, gleamed in the strong ray of the lamp which he had placed close to him. His hand was on the metal rod from which depended the spiral spring and the needle, which just rested on that fragment of grey stuff which I had seen in the glass vessel.

"Yes, I'm going to stop it now," he said, "or the germs will be getting at my gramophone record, or the record will get cold. See, I spray it with carbolic vapour, I put it back into its nice warm bed. It will sing to us again. But terrible? What do you mean by terrible?"

Indeed, when he asked that I scarcely knew myself what I meant. I had been witness to a new marvel of science as wonderful perhaps as any that had ever astounded the beholder, and my nerves – these childish whimperers – had cried out at the darkness and the profundity. But the horror diminished, the fascination increased as he quite shortly told me the history of this phenomenon. He had attended that day and operated upon a young soldier in whose brain was embedded a piece of shrapnel. The boy was *in extremis*, but Horton had hoped for the possibility of saving him. To extract the shrapnel was the only chance, and this involved the cutting away of a piece of brain known as the speech-centre, and taking from it what was embedded there. But the hope was not realised, and two hours later the boy died. It was to this fragment of brain that, when Horton returned home, he had applied the needle of his gramophone, and had obtained the faint whisperings which had caused him to ring me up, so that he might have a witness of this wonder. Witness I had been, not to these whisperings alone, but to the fragment of singing.

"And this is but the first step on the new road," said he. "Who knows where it may lead, or to what new temple of knowledge it may not be the avenue? Well, it is late: I shall do no more to-night. What about the raid, by the way?"

To my amazement I saw that the time was verging on midnight. Two hours had elapsed since he let me in at his door; they had passed like a couple of minutes. Next morning some neighbours spoke of the prolonged firing that had gone on, of which I had been wholly unconscious.

Week after week Horton worked on this new road of research, perfecting the sensitiveness and subtlety of the needle, and, by vastly increasing the power of his batteries, enlarging the magnifying power of his trumpet. Many and many an evening during the next year did I listen to voices that were dumb in death, and the sounds which had been blurred and unintelligible mutterings in the earlier experiments, developed, as the delicacy of his mechanical devices increased, into coherence and clear articulation. It was no longer necessary to impose silence on Mrs. Gabriel when the gramophone was at work, for now the voice we listened to had risen to the pitch of ordinary human utterance, while as for the faithfulness and individuality of these records, striking testimony was given more than once by some living friend of the dead, who, without knowing what he was about to hear, recognised the tones of the speaker. More than once also, Mrs. Gabriel, bringing in syphons and whisky, provided us with three glasses, for she had heard, so she told us, three different voices in talk. But for the present no fresh phenomenon occurred; Horton was but perfecting the mechanism of his previous discovery and, rather grudging the time, was scribbling at a monograph, which presently he would toss to his colleagues, concerning the results he had already obtained. And then, even while Horton was on the threshold of new wonders, which he had already foreseen and spoken of as theoretically possible, there came an evening of marvel and of swift catastrophe.

I had dined with him that day, Mrs. Gabriel deftly serving the meal that she had so daintily prepared, and towards the end, as she was clearing the table for our dessert, she stumbled, I supposed, on a loose edge of carpet, quickly recovering herself. But instantly Horton checked some half-finished sentence, and turned to her.

"You're all right, Mrs. Gabriel?" he asked quickly.

"Yes, sir, thank you," said she, and went on with her serving.

"As I was saying," began Horton again, but his attention clearly wandered, and without concluding his narrative, he relapsed into silence, till Mrs. Gabriel had given us our coffee and left the room.

"I'm sadly afraid my domestic felicity may be disturbed," he said. "Mrs. Gabriel had an epileptic fit yesterday, and she confessed when she recovered that she had been subject to them when a child, and since then had occasionally experienced them."

"Dangerous, then?" I asked.

"In themselves not in the least," said he. "If she was sitting in her chair or lying in bed when one occurred, there would be nothing to trouble about. But if one occurred while she was cooking my dinner or beginning to come downstairs, she might fall into the fire or tumble down the whole flight. We'll hope no such deplorable calamity will happen. Now, if you've finished your coffee, let us go into the laboratory. Not that I've got anything very interesting in the way of new records. But I've introduced a second battery with a very strong induction coil into my apparatus. I find that if I link it up with my record, given that the record is a – a fresh one, it stimulates certain nerve centres. It's odd, isn't it, that the same forces which so encourage the dead to live would certainly encourage the living to die, if a man received the full current. One has to be careful in handling it. Yes, and what then? you ask."

The night was very hot, and he threw the windows wide before he settled himself cross-legged on the floor.

"I'll answer your question for you," he said, "though I believe we've talked of it before. Supposing I had not a fragment of brain-tissue only, but a whole head, let us say, or best of all, a complete corpse, I think I could expect to produce more than mere speech through the gramophone. The dead lips themselves perhaps might utter – God! what's that?"

From close outside, at the bottom of the stairs leading from the dining room which we had just quitted to the laboratory where we now sat, there came a crash of glass followed by the fall as of something heavy which bumped from step to step, and was finally flung on the threshold against the door with the sound as of knuckles rapping at it, and demanding admittance. Horton sprang up and threw the door open, and there lay, half inside the room and half on the landing outside, the body of Mrs. Gabriel. Round her were splinters of broken bottles and glasses, and from a cut in her forehead, as she lay ghastly with face upturned, the blood trickled into her thick grey hair.

Horton was on his knees beside her, dabbing his handkerchief on her forehead.

"Ah! that's not serious," he said; "there's neither vein nor artery cut. I'll just bind that up first."

He tore his handkerchief into strips which he tied together, and made a dexterous bandage covering the lower part of her forehead, but leaving her eyes unobscured. They stared with a fixed meaningless steadiness, and he scrutinised them closely.

"But there's worse yet," he said. "There's been some severe blow on the head. Help me to carry her into the laboratory. Get round to her feet and lift underneath the knees when I am ready. There! Now put your arm right under her and carry her."

Her head swung limply back as he lifted her shoulders, and he propped it up against his knee, where it mutely nodded and bowed, as his leg moved, as if in silent assent to what we were doing, and the mouth, at the extremity of which there had gathered a little lather, lolled open. He still supported her shoulders as I fetched a cushion on which to place her head, and presently she was lying close to the low table on which stood the gramophone of the dead. Then with light deft fingers he passed his hands over her skull, pausing as he came to the spot just above and behind her right ear. Twice and again his fingers groped and lightly pressed, while with shut eyes and concentrated attention he interpreted what his trained touch revealed.

"Her skull is broken to fragments just here," he said. "In the middle there is a piece completely severed from the rest, and the edges of the cracked pieces must be pressing on her brain."

Her right arm was lying palm upwards on the floor, and with one hand he felt her wrist with fingertips.

"Not a sign of pulse," he said. "She's dead in the ordinary sense of the word. But life persists in an extraordinary manner, you may remember. She can't be wholly dead: no one is wholly dead in a moment, unless every organ is blown to bits. But she soon will be dead, if we don't relieve the pressure on the brain. That's the first thing to be done. While I'm busy at that, shut the window, will you, and make up the fire. In this sort of case the vital heat, whatever that is, leaves the body very quickly. Make the room as hot as you can – fetch an oil-stove, and turn on the electric radiator, and stoke up a roaring fire. The hotter the room is the more slowly will the heat of life leave her."

Already he had opened his cabinet of surgical instruments, and taken out of it two drawers full of bright steel which he laid on the floor beside her. I heard the grating chink of scissors severing her long grey hair, and as I busied myself with laying and lighting the fire in the hearth, and kindling the oil-stove, which I found, by Horton's directions, in the pantry, I saw that his lancet was busy on the exposed skin. He had placed some vaporising spray, heated by a spirit lamp close to her head, and as he worked its fizzing nozzle filled the air with some clean and aromatic odour. Now and then he threw out an order.

"Bring me that electric lamp on the long cord," he said. "I haven't got enough light. Don't look at what I'm doing if you're squeamish, for if it makes you feel faint, I shan't be able to attend to you."

I suppose that violent interest in what he was doing overcame any qualm that I might have had, for I looked quite unflinching over his shoulder as I moved the lamp about till it was in such a place that it threw its beam directly into a dark hole at the edge of which depended a flap of skin. Into this he put his forceps, and as he withdrew them they grasped a piece of blood-stained bone.

"That's better," he said, "and the room's warming up well. But there's no sign of pulse yet. Go on stoking, will you, till the thermometer on the wall there registers a hundred degrees."

When next, on my journey from the coal-cellar, I looked, two more pieces of bone lay beside the one I had seen extracted, and presently referring to the thermometer, I saw, that between the oil-stove and the roaring fire and the electric radiator, I had raised the room to the temperature he wanted. Soon, peering fixedly at the seat of his operation, he felt for her pulse again.

"Not a sign of returning vitality," he said, "and I've done all I can. There's nothing more possible that can be devised to restore her."

As he spoke the zeal of the unrivalled surgeon relaxed, and with a sigh and a shrug he rose to his feet and mopped his face. Then suddenly the fire and eagerness blazed there again. "The gramophone!" he said. "The speech centre is close to where I've been working, and it is quite uninjured. Good heavens, what a wonderful opportunity. She served me well living, and she shall serve me dead. And I can stimulate the motor nerve-centre, too, with the second battery. We may see a new wonder to-night."

Some qualm of horror shook me.

"No, don't!" I said. "It's terrible: she's just dead. I shall go if you do."

"But I've got exactly all the conditions I have long been wanting," said he. "And I simply can't spare you. You must be witness: I must have a witness. Why, man, there's not a surgeon or a physiologist in the kingdom who would not give an eye or an ear to be in your place now. She's dead. I pledge you my honour on that, and it's grand to be dead if you can help the living."

Once again, in a far fiercer struggle, horror and the intensest curiosity strove together in me.

"Be quick, then," said I.

"Ha!. That's right," exclaimed Horton. "Help me to lift her on to the table by the gramophone. The cushion too; I can get at the place more easily with her head a little raised."

He turned on the battery and with the movable light close beside him, brilliantly illuminating what he sought, he inserted the needle of the gramophone into the jagged aperture in her skull. For a few minutes, as he groped and explored there, there was silence, and then quite suddenly Mrs. Gabriel's voice, clear and unmistakable and of the normal loudness of human speech, issued from the trumpet.

"Yes, I always said that I'd be even with him," came the articulated syllables. "He used to knock me about, he did, when he came home drunk, and often I was black and blue with bruises. But I'll give him a redness for the black and blue."

The record grew blurred; instead of articulate words there came from it a gobbling noise. By degrees that cleared, and we were listening to some dreadful suppressed sort of laughter, hideous to hear. On and on it went.

"I've got into some sort of rut," said Horton. "She must have laughed a lot to herself."

For a long time we got nothing more except the repetition of the words we had already heard and the sound of that suppressed laughter. Then Horton drew towards him the second battery.

"I'll try a stimulation of the motor nerve-centres," he said. "Watch her face."

He propped the gramophone needle in position, and inserted into the fractured skull the two poles of the second battery, moving them about there very carefully. And as I watched her face, I saw with a freezing horror that her lips were beginning to move.

"Her mouth's moving," I cried. "She can't be dead."

He peered into her face.

"Nonsense," he said. "That's only the stimulus from the current. She's been dead half an hour. Ah! what's coming now?"

The lips lengthened into a smile, the lower jaw dropped, and from her mouth came the laughter we had heard just now through the gramophone. And then the dead mouth spoke, with a mumble of unintelligible words, a bubbling torrent of incoherent syllables.

"I'll turn the full current on," he said.

The head jerked and raised itself, the lips struggled for utterance, and suddenly she spoke swiftly and distinctly.

"Just when he'd got his razor out," she said, "I came up behind him, and put my hand over his face, and bent his neck back over his chair with all my strength. And I picked up his razor and with one slit – ha, ha, that was the way to pay him out. And I didn't lose my head, but I lathered his chin well, and put the razor in his hand, and left him there, and went downstairs and cooked his dinner for him, and then an hour afterwards, as he didn't come down, up I went to see what kept him. It was a nasty cut in his neck that had kept him—"

Horton suddenly withdrew the two poles of the battery from her head, and even in the middle of her word the mouth ceased working, and lay rigid and open.

"By God!" he said. "There's a tale for dead lips to tell. But we'll get more yet."

Exactly what happened then I never knew. It appeared to me that as he still leaned over the table with the two poles of the battery in his hand, his foot slipped, and he fell forward across it. There came a sharp crack, and a flash of blue dazzling light, and there he lay face downwards, with arms that just stirred and quivered. With his fall the two poles that must momentarily have come into contact with his hand were jerked away again, and I lifted him and laid him on the floor. But his lips as well as those of the dead woman had spoken for the last time.

The Outcast

When Mrs. Acres bought the Gate-house at Tarleton, which had stood so long without a tenant, and appeared in that very agreeable and lively little town as a resident, sufficient was already known about her past history to entitle her to friendliness and sympathy. Hers had been a tragic story, and the account of the inquest held on her husband's body, when, within a month of their marriage, he had shot himself before her eyes, was recent enough, and of as full a report in the papers as to enable our little community of Tarleton to remember and run over the salient grimness of the case without the need of inventing any further details – which, otherwise, it would have been quite capable of doing.

Briefly, then, the facts had been as follows. Horace Acres appeared to have been a heartless fortune-hunter – a handsome, plausible wretch, ten years younger than his wife. He had made no secret to his friends of not being in love with her but of having a considerable regard for her more than considerable fortune. But hardly had he married her than his indifference developed into violent dislike, accompanied by some mysterious, inexplicable dread of her. He hated and feared her, and on the morning of the very day when he had put an end to himself he had begged her to divorce him; the case he promised would be undefended, and he would make it indefensible. She, poor soul, had refused to grant this; for, as corroborated by the evidence of friends and servants, she was utterly devoted to him, and stated with that quiet dignity which distinguished her throughout this ordeal, that she hoped that he was the victim of some miserable but temporary derangement, and would come to his right mind again. He had dined that night at his club, leaving his month-old bride to pass the evening alone, and had returned between eleven and twelve that night in a state of vile intoxication. He had gone up to her bedroom, pistol in hand, had locked the door, and his voice was heard screaming and yelling at her. Then followed the sound of one shot. On the table in his dressing-room was found a half-sheet of paper, dated that day, and this was read out in court. "The horror of my position," he had written, "is beyond description and endurance. I can bear it no longer: my soul sickens . . ." The jury, without leaving the court, returned the verdict that he had committed suicide while temporarily insane, and the coroner, at their request, expressed their sympathy and his own with the poor lady, who, as testified on all hands, had treated her husband with the utmost tenderness and affection.

For six months Bertha Acres had travelled abroad, and then in the autumn she had bought Gate-house at Tarleton, and settled down to the absorbing trifles which make life in a small country town so busy and strenuous.

Our modest little dwelling is within a stone's throw of the Gate-house; and when, on the return of my wife and myself from two months in Scotland, we found that Mrs. Acres was installed as a neighbour, Madge lost no time in going to call on her. She returned with a series of pleasant impressions. Mrs. Acres, still on the sunny slope that leads up to the tableland of life which begins at forty years, was extremely handsome, cordial, and charming in manner, witty and agreeable, and wonderfully well dressed. Before the conclusion of her call Madge, in country fashion, had begged her to dispose with formalities, and, instead of a frigid return of the call, to dine with us quietly next day. Did she play bridge? That being so, we would just be a party of four; for her brother, Charles Alington, had proposed himself for a visit . . .

I listened to this with sufficient attention to grasp what Madge was saying, but what I was really thinking about was a chess-problem which I was attempting to solve. But at this point I became acutely aware that her stream of pleasant impressions dried up suddenly, and she became stonily silent. She shut speech off as by the turn of a tap, and glowered at the fire, rubbing the back of one hand with the fingers of another, as is her habit in perplexity.

"Go on," I said.

She got up, suddenly restless.

"All I have been telling you is literally and soberly true," she said. "I thought Mrs. Acres charming and witty and good-looking and friendly. What more could you ask from a new acquaintance? And then, after I had asked her to dinner, I suddenly found for no earthly reason that I very much disliked her; I couldn't bear her."

"You said she was wonderfully well dressed," I permitted myself to remark . . . If the Queen took the Knight—

"Don't be silly!" said Madge. "I am wonderfully well dressed too. But behind all her agreeableness and charm and good looks I suddenly felt there was something else which I detested and dreaded. It's no use asking me what it was, because I haven't the slightest idea. If I knew what it was, the thing would explain itself. But I felt a horror – nothing vivid, nothing close, you understand, but somewhere in the background. Can the mind have a 'turn,' do you think, just as the body can, when for a second or two you suddenly feel giddy? I think it must have been that – oh! I'm sure it was that. But I'm glad I asked her to dine. I mean to like her. I shan't have a 'turn' again, shall I?"

"No, certainly not," I said . . . If the Queen refrained from taking the tempting Knight—

"Oh, do stop your silly chess-problem!" said Madge. "Bite him, Fungus!"

Fungus, so called because he is the son of Humour and Gustavus Adolphus, rose from his place on the hearthrug, and with a hoarse laugh nuzzled against my leg, which is his way of biting those he loves. Then the most amiable of bull-dogs, who has a passion for the human race, lay down on my foot and sighed heavily. But Madge evidently wanted to talk, and I pushed the chessboard away.

"Tell me more about the horror," I said.

"It was just horror," she said – "a sort of sickness of the soul." . . .

I found my brain puzzling over some vague reminiscence, surely connected with Mrs. Acres, which those words mistily evoked. But next moment that train of thought was cut short, for the old and sinister legend about the Gate-house came into my mind as accounting for the horror of which Madge spoke. In the days of Elizabethan religious persecutions it had, then newly built, been inhabited by two brothers, of whom the elder, to whom it belonged, had Mass said there every Sunday. Betrayed by the younger, he was arrested and racked to death. Subsequently the younger, in a fit of remorse, hanged himself in the panelled parlour. Certainly there was a story that the house was haunted by his strangled apparition dangling from the beams, and the late tenants of the house (which now had stood vacant for over three years) had quitted it after a month's occupation, in consequence, so it was commonly said, of unaccountable and horrible sights. What was more likely, then, than that Madge, who from childhood has been intensely sensitive to occult and psychic phenomena, should have caught, on that strange wireless receiver which is characteristic of "sensitives," some whispered message?

"But you know the story of the house," I said "Isn't it quite possible that something of that may have reached you? Where did you sit, for instance? In the panelled parlour?"

She brightened at that.

"Ah, you wise man!" she said. "I never thought of that. That may account for it all. I hope it does. You shall be left in peace with your chess for being so brilliant."

I had occasion half an hour later to go to the post-office, a hundred yards up High Street, on the matter of a registered letter which I wanted to despatch that evening. Dusk was gathering, but the red glow of sunset still smouldered in the west, sufficient to enable me to recognise familiar forms and features of passers-by. Just as I came opposite the post-office there approached from the other direction a tall, finely built woman, whom, I felt sure, I had never seen before. Her destination was the same as mine, and I hung on my step a moment to let her pass in first. Simultaneously I felt that I knew, in some vague, faint manner, what Madge had meant when she talked about a "sickness of the soul." It was no nearer realisation to me than is the running of a tune in the head to the audible external hearing of it, and I attributed my sudden recognition of her feeling to the fact that in all probability my mind had subconsciously been dwelling on what she had said, and not for a moment did I connect it with any external cause. And then it occurred to me who, possibly, this woman was . . .

She finished the transaction of her errand a few seconds before me, and when I got out into the street again she was a dozen yards down the pavement, walking in the direction of my house and of the Gate-house. Opposite my own door I deliberately lingered, and saw her pass down the steps that led from the road to the entrance of the Gate-house. Even as I turned into my own door the unbidden reminiscence which had eluded me before came out into the open, and I cast my net over it. It was her husband, who, in the inexplicable communication he had left on his dressing-room table, just before he shot himself, had written "my soul sickens." It was odd, though scarcely more than that for Madge to have used those identical words.

Charles Alington, my wife's brother, who arrived next afternoon, is quite the happiest man whom I have ever come across. The material world, that perennial spring of thwarted ambition, physical desire, and perpetual disappointment, is practically unknown to him. Envy, malice, and all uncharitableness are equally alien, because he does not want to obtain what anybody else has got, and has no sense of possession, which is queer, since he is enormously rich. He fears nothing, he hopes for nothing, he has no abhorrences or affections, for all physical and nervous functions are in him in the service of an intense inquisitiveness. He never passed a moral judgment in his life, he only wants to explore and to know. Knowledge, in fact, is his entire preoccupation, and since chemists and medical scientists probe and mine in the world of tinctures and microbes far more efficiently than he could do, as he has so little care for anything that can be weighed or propagated, he devotes himself, absorbedly and ecstatically, to that world that lies about the confines of conscious existence. Anything not yet certainly determined appeals to him with the call of a trumpet: he ceases to take an interest in a subject as soon as it shows signs of assuming a practical and definite status. He was intensely concerned, for instance, in wireless transmission, until Signor Marconi proved that it came within the scope of practical science, and then Charles abandoned it as dull. I had seen him last two months before, when he was in a great perturbation, since he was speaking at a meeting of Anglo-Israelites in the morning, to show that the Scone Stone, which is now in the Coronation Chair at Westminster, was for certain the pillow on which Jacob's head had rested when he saw the vision at Bethel; was addressing the Psychical Research Society in the afternoon on the subject of messages received from the dead through automatic script, and in the evening was, by way of a holiday, only listening to a lecture on reincarnation. None of these things could, as yet, be definitely proved, and that was why he loved them. During the intervals when the occult and the fantastic do not occupy him, he is, in spite of his fifty years and wizened mien, exactly like a schoolboy of eighteen back on his holidays and brimming with superfluous energy.

I found Charles already arrived when I got home next afternoon, after a round of golf. He was betwixt and between the serious and the holiday mood, for he had evidently been reading to Madge from a journal concerning reincarnation, and was rather severe to me . . .

"Golf!" he said, with insulting scorn. "What is there to know about golf? You hit a ball into the air—"

I was a little sore over the events of the afternoon.

"That's just what I don't do," I said. "I hit it along the ground!"

"Well, it doesn't matter where you hit it," said he. "It's all subject to known laws. But the guess, the conjecture: there's the thrill and the excitement of life. The charlatan with his new cure for cancer, the automatic writer with his messages from the dead, the reincarnationist with his positive assertions that he was Napoleon or a Christian slave – they are the people who advance knowledge. You have to guess before you know. Even Darwin saw that when he said you could not investigate without a hypothesis!"

"So what's your hypothesis this minute?" I asked.

"Why, that we've all lived before, and that we're going to live again here on this same old earth. Any other conception of a future life is impossible. Are all the people who have been born and have died since the world emerged from chaos going to become inhabitants of some future world? What a squash, you know, my dear Madge! Now, I know what you're going to ask me. If we've all lived before, why can't we remember it? But that's so simple! If you remembered being Cleopatra, you would go on behaving like Cleopatra; and what would Tarleton say? Judas Iscariot, too! Fancy knowing you had been Judas Iscariot! You couldn't get over it! you would commit suicide, or cause everybody who was connected with you to commit suicide from their horror of you. Or imagine being a grocer's boy who knew he had been Julius Cæsar . . . Of course, sex doesn't matter; souls, as far as I understand, are sexless – just sparks of life, which are put into physical envelopes, some male, some female. You might have been King David, Madge and poor Tony here one of his wives."

"That would be wonderfully neat," said I.

Charles broke out into a shout of laughter.

"It would indeed," he said. "But I won't talk sense any more to you scoffers. I'm absolutely tired out, I will confess, with thinking. I want to have a pretty lady to come to dinner, and talk to her as if she was just herself and I myself, and nobody else. I want to win two-and-sixpence at bridge with the expenditure of enormous thought. I want to have a large breakfast to-morrow and read *The Times* afterwards, and go to Tony's club and talk about crops and golf and Irish affairs and Peace Conferences, and all the things that don't matter one straw!"

"You're going to begin your programme to-night, dear," said Madge. "A very pretty lady is coming to dinner, and we're going to play bridge afterwards."

Madge and I were ready for Mrs. Acres when she arrived, but Charles was not yet down. Fungus, who has a wild adoration for Charles, quite unaccountable, since Charles has no feelings for dogs, was helping him to dress, and Madge, Mrs. Acres, and I waited for his appearance. It was certainly Mrs. Acres whom I had met last night at the door of the post-office, but the dim light of sunset had not enabled me to see how wonderfully handsome she was. There was something slightly Jewish about her profile: the high forehead, the very full-lipped mouth, the bridged nose, the prominent chin, all suggested rather than exemplified an Eastern origin. And when she spoke she had that rich softness of utterance, not quite hoarseness, but not quite of the clear-cut distinctness of tone which characterises northern nations. Something southern, something Eastern . . .

"I am bound to ask one thing," she said, when, after the usual greetings, we stood round the fireplace, waiting for Charles – "but have you got a dog?"

Madge moved towards the bell.

"Yes, but he shan't come down if you dislike dogs," she said. "He's wonderfully kind, but I know—"

"Ah, it's not that," said Mrs. Acres. "I adore dogs. But I only wished to spare your dog's feelings. Though I adore them, they hate me, and they're terribly frightened of me. There's something anti-canine about me."

It was too late to say more. Charles's steps clattered in the little hall outside, and Fungus was hoarse and amused. Next moment the door opened, and the two came in.

Fungus came in first. He lolloped in a festive manner into the middle of the room, sniffed and snored in greeting, and then turned tail. He slipped and skidded on the parquet outside, and we heard him bundling down the kitchen stairs.

"Rude dog," said Madge. "Charles, let me introduce you to Mrs. Acres. My brother, Mrs. Acres: Sir Charles Alington."

Our little dinner-table of four would not permit of separate conversations, and general topics, springing up like mushrooms, wilted and died at their very inception. What mood possessed the others I did not at that time know, but for myself I was only conscious of some fundamental distaste of the handsome, clever woman who sat on my right, and seemed quite unaffected by the withering atmosphere. She was charming to the eye, she was witty to the ear, she had grace and gracefulness, and all the time she was something terrible. But by degrees, as I found my own distaste increasing, I saw that my brother-in-law's interest was growing correspondingly keen. The "pretty lady" whose presence at dinner he had desired and obtained was enchaining him – not, so I began to guess, for her charm and her prettiness, but for some purpose of study, and I wondered whether it was her beautiful Jewish profile that was confirming to his mind some Anglo-Israelitish theory, whether he saw in her fine brown eyes the glance of the seer and the clairvoyante, or whether he divined in her some reincarnation of one of the famous or the infamous dead. Certainly she had for him some fascination beyond that of the legitimate charm of a very handsome woman; he was studying her with intense curiosity.

"And you are comfortable in the Gate-house?" he suddenly rapped out at her, as if asking some question of which the answer was crucial.

"Ah! but so comfortable," she said – "such a delightful atmosphere. I have never known a house that 'felt' so peaceful and home-like. Or is it merely fanciful to imagine that some houses have a sense of tranquillity about them and others are uneasy and even terrible?"

Charles stared at her a moment in silence before he recollected his manners.

"No, there may easily be something in it, I should say," he answered. "One can imagine long centuries of tranquillity actually investing a home with some sort of psychical aura perceptible to those who are sensitive."

She turned to Madge.

"And yet I have heard a ridiculous story that the house is supposed to be haunted," she said. "If it is, it is surely haunted by delightful, contented spirits."

Dinner was over. Madge rose.

"Come in very soon, Tony," she said to me, "and let's get to our bridge."

But her eyes said, "Don't leave me long alone with her."

Charles turned briskly round when the door had shut.

"An extremely interesting woman," he said.

"Very handsome," said I.

"Is she? I didn't notice. Her mind, her spirit – that's what intrigued me. What is she? What's behind? Why did Fungus turn tail like that? Queer, too, about her finding the atmosphere of the Gate-house so tranquil. The late tenants, I remember, didn't find that soothing touch about it!"

"How do you account for that?" I asked.

"There might be several explanations. You might say that the late tenants were fanciful, imaginative people, and that the present tenant is a sensible, matter-of-fact woman. Certainly she seemed to be."

"Or—" I suggested.

He laughed.

"Well, you might say – mind, I don't say so – but you might say that the – the spiritual tenants of the house find Mrs. Acres a congenial companion, and want to retain her. So they keep quiet, and don't upset the cook's nerves!"

Somehow this answer exasperated and jarred on me.

"What do you mean?" I said. "The spiritual tenant of the house, I suppose, is the man who betrayed his brother and hanged himself. Why should he find a charming woman like Mrs. Acres a congenial companion?"

Charles got up briskly. Usually he is more than ready to discuss such topics, but to-night it seemed that he had no such inclination.

"Didn't Madge tell us not to be long?" he asked. "You know how I run on if I once get on that subject, Tony, so don't give me the opportunity."

"But why did you say that?" I persisted.

"Because I was talking nonsense. You know me well enough to be aware that I am an habitual criminal in that respect."

It was indeed strange to find how completely both the first impression that Madge had formed of Mrs. Acres and the feeling that followed so quickly on its heels were endorsed by those who, during the next week or two, did a neighbour's duty to the newcomer. All were loud in praise of her charm, her pleasant, kindly wit, her good looks, her beautiful clothes, but even while this *Lobgesang* was in full chorus it would suddenly die away, and an uneasy silence descended, which somehow was more eloquent than all the appreciative speech. Odd, unaccountable little incidents had occurred, which were whispered from mouth to mouth till they became common property. The same fear that Fungus had shown of her was exhibited by another dog. A parallel case occurred when she returned the call of our parson's wife. Mrs. Dowlett had a cage of canaries in the window of her drawing-room. These birds had manifested symptoms of extreme terror when Mrs. Acres entered the room, beating themselves against the wires of their cage, and uttering the alarm-note . . . She inspired some sort of inexplicable fear, over which we, as trained and civilised human beings, had control, so that we behaved ourselves. But animals, without that check, gave way altogether to it, even as Fungus had done.

Mrs. Acres entertained; she gave charming little dinner-parties of eight, with a couple of tables at bridge to follow, but over these evenings there hung a blight and a blackness. No doubt the sinister story of the panelled parlour contributed to this.

This curious secret dread of her, of which as on that first evening at my house, she appeared to be completely unconscious differed very widely in degree. Most people, like myself, were conscious of it, but only very remotely so, and we found ourselves at the Gate-house behaving quite as usual, though with this unease in the background. But with a few, and most of all with Madge, it grew into a sort of obsession. She made every effort to combat it; her will was entirely set against it, but her struggle seemed only to establish its power over her. The pathetic and pitiful part was that Mrs. Acres from the first had taken a tremendous liking to her, and used to drop in continually, calling first to Madge at the window, in that pleasant, serene voice of hers, to tell Fungus that the hated one was imminent.

Then came a day when Madge and I were bidden to a party at the Gate-house on Christmas evening. This was to be the last of Mrs. Acres's hospitalities for the present, since she was leaving immediately afterwards for a couple of months in Egypt. So, with this remission ahead, Madge almost gleefully accepted the bidding. But when the evening came she was seized with so violent an attack of sickness and shivering that she was utterly unable to fulfil her engagement. Her doctor could find no physical trouble to account for this: it seemed that the anticipation of her evening alone caused it, and here was the culmination of her shrinking from our kindly and pleasant neighbour. She could only tell me that her sensations, as she began to dress for the party, were like those of that moment in sleep when somewhere in the drowsy brain nightmare is ripening. Something independent of her will revolted at what lay before her . . .

Spring had begun to stretch herself in the lap of winter when next the curtain rose on this veiled drama of forces but dimly comprehended and shudderingly conjectured; but then, indeed, nightmare ripened swiftly in broad noon. And this was the way of it.

Charles Alington had again come to stay with us five days before Easter, and expressed himself as humorously disappointed to find that the subject of his curiosity was still absent from the Gate-house. On the Saturday morning before Easter he appeared very late for breakfast, and Madge had already gone her ways. I rang for a fresh teapot, and while this was on its way he took up *The Times*.

"I only read the outside page of it," he said. "The rest is too full of mere materialistic dullnesses – politics, sports, money-market—"

He stopped, and passed the paper over to me.

"There, where I'm pointing," he said – "among the deaths. The first one."

What I read was this:

> ACRES, BERTHA. Died at sea, Thursday night, 30th March, and by her own request buried at sea. (Received by wireless from P. & O. steamer *Peshawar*.)

He held out his hand for the paper again, and turned over the leaves.

"Lloyd's," he said. "The *Peshawar* arrived at Tilbury yesterday afternoon. The burial must have taken place somewhere in the English Channel."

On the afternoon of Easter Sunday Madge and I motored out to the golf links three miles away. She proposed to walk along the beach just outside the dunes while I had my round, and return to the club-house for tea in two hours' time. The day was one of most lucid spring: a warm south-west wind bowled white clouds along the sky, and their shadows jovially scudded over the sandhills. We had told her of Mrs. Acres's death, and from that moment something dark and vague which had been lying over her mind since the autumn seemed to join this fleet of the shadows of clouds and leave her in sunlight. We parted at the door of the club-house, and she set out on her walk.

Half an hour later, as my opponent and I were waiting on the fifth tee, where the road crosses the links, for the couple in front of us to move on, a servant from the club-house, scudding along the road, caught sight of us, and, jumping from his bicycle, came to where we stood.

"You're wanted at the club-house, sir," he said to me. "Mrs. Carford was walking along the shore, and she found something left by the tide. A body, sir. 'Twas in a sack, but the sack was torn, and she saw – It's upset her very much, sir. We thought it best to come for you."

I took the boy's bicycle and went back to the club-house as fast as I could turn the wheel. I felt sure I knew what Madge had found, and, knowing that, realised the shock . . . Five minutes later she was telling me her story in gasps and whispers.

"The tide was going down," she said, "and I walked along the high-water mark . . . There were pretty shells; I was picking them up . . . And then I saw it in front of me – just shapeless, just a sack . . . and then, as I came nearer, it took shape; there were knees and elbows. It moved, it rolled over, and where the head was the sack was torn, and I saw her face. Her eyes were open, Tony, and I fled . . . All the time I felt it was rolling along after me. Oh, Tony! she's dead, isn't she? She won't come back to the Gate-house? Do you promise me? . . . There's something awful! I wonder if I guess. The sea gives her up. The sea won't suffer her to rest in it." . . .

The news of the finding had already been telephoned to Tarleton, and soon a party of four men with a stretcher arrived. There was no doubt as to the identity of the body, for though it had been in the water for three days no corruption had come to it. The weights with which at burial it had been laden must by some strange chance have been detached from it, and by a chance stranger yet it had drifted to the shore closest to her home. That night it lay in the mortuary, and the inquest was held on it next day, though that was a bank-holiday. From there it was taken to the Gate-house and coffined, and it lay in the panelled parlour for the funeral on the morrow.

Madge, after that one hysterical outburst, had completely recovered herself, and on the Monday evening she made a little wreath of the spring-flowers which the early warmth had called into blossom in the garden, and I went across with it to the Gate-house. Though the news of Mrs. Acres's death and the subsequent finding of the body had been widely advertised, there had been no response from relations or friends, and as I laid the solitary wreath on the coffin a sense of the utter loneliness of what lay within seized and encompassed me. And then a portent, no less, took place before my eyes. Hardly had the freshly gathered flowers been laid on the coffin than they drooped and wilted. The stalks of the daffodils bent, and their bright chalices closed; the odour of the wallflowers died, and they withered as I watched . . . What did it mean, that even the petals of spring shrank and were moribund?

I told Madge nothing of this; and she, as if through some pang of remorse, was determined to be present next day at the funeral. No arrival of friends or relations had taken place, and from the Gate-house there came none of the servants. They stood in the porch as the coffin was brought out of the house, and even before it was put into the hearse had gone back again and closed the door. So, at the cemetery on the hill above Tarleton, Madge and her brother and I were the only mourners.

The afternoon was densely overcast, though we got no rainfall, and it was with thick clouds above and a sea-mist drifting between the grave-stones that we came, after the service in the cemetery-chapel, to the place of interment. And then – I can hardly write of it now – when it came for the coffin to be lowered into the grave, it was found that by some faulty measurement it could not descend, for the excavation was not long enough to hold it.

Madge was standing close to us, and at this moment I heard her sob.

"And the kindly earth will not receive her," she whispered.

There was awful delay: the diggers must be sent for again, and meantime the rain had begun to fall thick and tepid. For some reason – perhaps some outlying feeler of Madge's obsession had wound a tentacle round me – I felt that I must know that earth had gone to earth, but I could not suffer Madge to wait. So, in this miserable pause, I got Charles to take her home, and then returned.

Pick and shovel were busy, and soon the resting-place was ready. The interrupted service continued, the handful of wet earth splashed on the coffin-lid, and when all was over I left the cemetery, still feeling, I knew not why, that all was *not* over. Some restlessness and want of certainty possessed me, and instead of going home I fared forth into the rolling wooded country inland, with the intention of walking off these bat-like terrors that flapped around me. The rain had ceased, and a blurred sunlight penetrated the sea-mist which still blanketed the fields and woods, and for half an hour, moving briskly, I endeavoured to fight down some fantastic conviction that had gripped my mind in its claws. I refused to look straight at that conviction, telling myself how fantastic, how unreasonable it was; but as often as I put out a hand to throttle it there came the echo of Madge's words: "The sea will not suffer her; the kindly earth will not receive her." And if I could shut my eyes to that there came some remembrance of the day she died, and of half-forgotten fragments of Charles's superstitious belief in reincarnation. The whole thing, incredible though its component parts were, hung together with a terrible tenacity.

Before long the rain began again, and I turned, meaning to go by the main-road into Tarleton, which passes in a wide-flung curve some half-mile outside the cemetery. But as I approached the path through the fields, which, leaving the less direct route, passes close to the cemetery and brings you by a steeper and shorter descent into the town, I felt myself irresistibly impelled to take it. I told myself, of course, that I wished to make my wet walk as short as possible; but at the back of my mind was the half-conscious, but none the less imperative need to know by ocular evidence that the grave by which I had stood that afternoon had been filled in, and that the body of Mrs. Acres now lay tranquil beneath the soil. My path would be even shorter if I passed through the graveyard, and so presently I was fumbling in the gloom for the latch of the gate, and closed it again behind me. Rain was falling now thick and sullenly, and in the bleared twilight I picked my way among the mounds and slipped on the dripping grass, and there in front of me was the newly turned earth. All was finished: the grave-diggers had done their work and departed, and earth had gone back again into the keeping of the earth.

It brought me some great lightening of the spirit to know that, and I was on the point of turning away when a sound of stir from the heaped soil caught my ear, and I saw a little stream of pebbles mixed with clay trickle down the side of the mound above the grave: the heavy rain, no doubt, had loosened the earth. And then came another and yet another, and with terror gripping at my heart I perceived that this was no loosening from without, but from within, for to right and left the piled soil was falling away with the press of something from below. Faster and faster it poured off the grave, and ever higher at the head of it rose a mound of earth pushed upwards from beneath. Somewhere out of sight there came the sound as of creaking and breaking wood, and then through that mound of earth there protruded the end of the coffin. The lid was shattered: loose pieces of the boards fell off it, and from within the cavity there faced me white features and wide eyes. All this I saw, while sheer terror held me motionless; then, I suppose, came the breaking-point, and with such panic as surely man never felt before I was stumbling away among the graves and racing towards the kindly human lights of the town below.

I went to the parson who had conducted the service that afternoon with my incredible tale, and an hour later he, Charles Alington, and two or three men from the undertaker's were on the spot. They found the coffin, completely disinterred, lying on the ground by the grave, which was now three-quarters full of the earth which had fallen back into it. After what had happened it was decided to make no further attempt to bury it; and next day the body was cremated.

Now, it is open to anyone who may read this tale to reject the incident of this emergence of the coffin altogether, and account for the other strange happenings by the comfortable theory of coincidence. He can certainly satisfy himself that one Bertha Acres did die at sea on this particular Thursday before Easter, and was buried at sea: there is nothing extraordinary about that. Nor is it the least impossible that the weights should have slipped from the canvas shroud, and that the body should have been washed ashore on the coast by Tarleton (why not Tarleton, as well as any other little town near the coast?); nor is there anything inherently significant in the fact that the grave, as originally dug, was not of sufficient dimensions to receive the coffin. That all these incidents should have happened to the body of a single individual is odd, but then the nature of coincidence is to be odd. They form a startling series, but unless coincidences are startling they escape observation altogether. So, if you reject the last incident here recorded, or account for it by some local disturbance, an earthquake, or the breaking of a spring just below the grave, you can comfortably recline on the cushion of coincidence . . .

For myself, I give no explanation of these events, though my brother-in-law brought forward one with which he himself is perfectly satisfied. Only the other day he sent me, with considerable jubilation, a copy of some extracts from a mediæval treatise on the subject of reincarnation which sufficiently indicates his theory. The original work was in Latin, which, mistrusting my scholarship, he kindly translated for me. I transcribe his quotations exactly as he sent them to me.

"We have these certain instances of his reincarnation. In one his spirit was incarnated in the body of a man; in the other, in that of a woman, fair of outward aspect, and of a pleasant conversation, but held in dread and in horror by those who came into more than casual intercourse with her . . . She, it is said, died on the anniversary of the day on which he hanged himself, after the betrayal, but of this I have no certain information. What is sure is that, when the time came for her burial, the kindly earth would receive her not, but though the grave was dug deep and well it spewed her forth again . . . Of the man in whom his cursed spirit was reincarnated it is said that, being on a voyage when he died, he was cast overboard with weights to sink him; but the sea would not suffer him to rest in her bosom, but slipped the weights from him, and cast him forth again on to the coast . . . Howbeit, when the full time of his expiation shall have come and his deadly sin forgiven, the corporal body which is the cursed receptacle of his spirit shall at length be purged with fire, and so he shall, in the infinite mercy of the Almighty, have rest, and shall wander no more."

The Horror-Horn

For the past ten days Alhubel had basked in the radiant midwinter weather proper to its eminence of over 6,000 feet. From rising to setting the sun (so surprising to those who have hitherto associated it with a pale, tepid plate indistinctly shining through the murky air of England) had blazed its way across the sparkling blue, and every night the serene and windless frost had made the stars sparkle like illuminated diamond dust. Sufficient snow had fallen before Christmas to content the skiers, and the big rink, sprinkled every evening, had given the skaters each morning a fresh surface on which to perform their slippery antics. Bridge and dancing served to while away the greater part of the night, and to me, now for the first time tasting the joys of a winter in the Engadine, it seemed that a new heaven and a new earth had been lighted, warmed, and refrigerated for the special benefit of those who like myself had been wise enough to save up their days of holiday for the winter.

But a break came in these ideal conditions: one afternoon the sun grew vapour-veiled and up the valley from the north-west a wind frozen with miles of travel over ice-bound hill-sides began scouting through the calm halls of the heavens. Soon it grew dusted with snow, first in small flakes driven almost horizontally before its congealing breath and then in larger tufts as of swansdown. And though all day for a fortnight before the fate of nations and life and death had seemed to me of far less importance than to get certain tracings of the skate-blades on the ice of proper shape and size, it now seemed that the one paramount consideration was to hurry back to the hotel for shelter: it was wiser to leave rocking-turns alone than to be frozen in their quest.

I had come out here with my cousin, Professor Ingram, the celebrated physiologist and Alpine climber. During the serenity of the last fortnight he had made a couple of notable winter ascents, but this morning his weather-wisdom had mistrusted the signs of the heavens, and instead of attempting the ascent of the Piz Passug he had waited to see whether his misgivings justified themselves. So there he sat now in the hall of the admirable hotel with his feet on the hot-water pipes and the latest delivery of the English post in his hands. This contained a pamphlet concerning the result of the Mount Everest expedition, of which he had just finished the perusal when I entered.

"A very interesting report," he said, passing it to me, "and they certainly deserve to succeed next year. But who can tell, what that final six thousand feet may entail? Six thousand feet more when you have already accomplished twenty-three thousand does not seem much, but at present no one knows whether the human frame can stand exertion at such a height. It may affect not the lungs and heart only, but possibly the brain. Delirious hallucinations may occur. In fact, if I did not know better, I should have said that one such hallucination had occurred to the climbers already."

"And what was that?" I asked.

"You will find that they thought they came across the tracks of some naked human foot at a great altitude. That looks at first sight like an hallucination. What more natural than that a brain excited and exhilarated by the extreme height should have interpreted certain marks in the snow as the footprints of a human being? Every bodily organ at these altitudes is exerting itself to the utmost to do its work, and the brain seizes on those marks in the snow and says 'Yes, I'm all right, I'm doing my job, and I perceive marks in the snow which I affirm are human footprints.' You know, even at this altitude, how restless and eager the brain is, how vividly, as you told me, you dream at night. Multiply that stimulus and that consequent eagerness and restlessness by three, and how natural that the brain should harbour illusions! What after all is the delirium which often accompanies high fever but the effort of the brain to do its work under the pressure of feverish conditions? It is so eager to continue perceiving that it perceives things which have no existence!"

"And yet you don't think that these naked human footprints were illusions," said I. "You told me you would have thought so, if you had not known better."

He shifted in his chair and looked out of the window a moment. The air was thick now with the density of the big snow-flakes that were driven along by the squealing north-west gale.

"Quite so," he said. "In all probability the human footprints were real human footprints. I expect that they were the footprints, anyhow, of a being more nearly a man than anything else. My reason for saying so is that I know such beings exist. I have even seen quite near at hand – and I assure you I did not wish to be nearer in spite of my intense curiosity – the creature, shall we say, which would make such footprints. And if the snow was not so dense, I could show you the place where I saw him."

He pointed straight out of the window, where across the valley lies the huge tower of the Ungeheuerhorn with the carved pinnacle of rock at the top like some gigantic rhinoceros-horn. On one side only, as I knew, was the mountain practicable, and that for none but the finest climbers; on the other three a succession of ledges and precipices rendered it unscalable. Two thousand feet of sheer rock form the tower; below are five hundred feet of fallen boulders, up to the edge of which grow dense woods of larch and pine.

"Upon the Ungeheuerhorn?" I asked.

"Yes. Up till twenty years ago it had never been ascended, and I, like several others, spent a lot of time in trying to find a route up it. My guide and I sometimes spent three nights together at the hut beside the Blumen glacier, prowling round it, and it was by luck really that we found the route, for the mountain looks even more impracticable from the far side than it does from this. But one day we found a long, transverse fissure in the side which led to a negotiable ledge; then there came a slanting ice couloir which you could not see till you got to the foot of it. However, I need not go into that."

The big room where we sat was filling up with cheerful groups driven indoors by this sudden gale and snowfall, and the cackle of merry tongues grew loud. The band, too, that invariable appanage of tea-time at Swiss resorts, had begun to tune up for the usual potpourri from the works of Puccini. Next moment the sugary, sentimental melodies began.

"Strange contrast!" said Ingram. "Here are we sitting warm and cosy, our ears pleasantly tickled with these little baby tunes and outside is the great storm growing more violent every moment, and swirling round the austere cliffs of the Ungeheuerhorn: the Horror-Horn, as indeed it was to me."

"I want to hear all about it," I said. "Every detail: make a short story long, if it's short. I want to know why it's *your* Horror-Horn?"

"Well, Chanton and I (he was my guide) used to spend days prowling about the cliffs, making a little progress on one side and then being stopped, and gaining perhaps five hundred feet on another side and then being confronted by some insuperable obstacle, till the day when by luck we found the route. Chanton never liked the job, for some reason that I could not fathom. It was not because of the difficulty or danger of the climbing, for he was the most fearless man I have ever met when dealing with rocks and ice, but he was always insistent that we should get off the mountain and back to the Blumen hut before sunset. He was scarcely easy even when we had got back to shelter and locked and barred the door, and I well remember one night when, as we ate our supper, we heard some animal, a wolf probably, howling somewhere out in the night. A positive panic seized him, and I don't think he closed his eyes till morning. It struck me then that there might be some grisly legend about the mountain, connected possibly with its name, and next day I asked him why the peak was called the Horror Horn. He put the question off at first, and said that, like the Schreckhorn, its name was due to its precipices and falling stones; but when I pressed him further he acknowledged that there was a legend about it, which his father had told him. There were creatures, so it was supposed, that lived in its caves, things human in shape, and covered, except for the face and hands, with long black hair. They were dwarfs in size, four feet high or thereabouts, but of prodigious strength and agility, remnants of some wild primeval race. It seemed that they were still in an upward stage of evolution, or so I guessed, for the story ran that sometimes girls had been carried off by them, not as prey, and not for any such fate as for those captured by cannibals, but to be bred from. Young men also had been raped by them, to be mated with the females of their tribe. All this looked as if the creatures, as I said, were tending towards humanity. But naturally I did not believe a word of it, as applied to the conditions of the present day. Centuries ago, conceivably, there may have been such beings, and, with the extraordinary tenacity of tradition, the news of this had been handed down and was still current round the hearths of the peasants. As for their numbers, Chanton told me that three had been once seen together by a man who owing to his swiftness on skis had escaped to tell the tale. This man, he averred, was no other than his grand-father, who had been benighted one winter evening as he passed through the dense woods below the Ungeheuerhorn, and Chanton supposed that they had been driven down to these lower altitudes in search of food during severe winter weather, for otherwise the recorded sights of them had always taken place among the rocks of the peak itself. They had pursued his grandfather, then a young man, at an extraordinarily swift canter, running sometimes upright as men run, sometimes on all-fours in the manner of beasts, and their howls were just such as that we had heard that night in the Blumen hut. Such at any rate was the story Chanton told me, and, like you, I regarded it as the very moonshine of superstition. But the very next day I had reason to reconsider my judgment about it.

"It was on that day that after a week of exploration we hit on the only route at present known to the top of our peak. We started as soon as there was light enough to climb by, for, as you may guess, on very difficult rocks it is impossible to climb by lantern or moonlight. We hit on the long fissure I have spoken of, we explored the ledge which from below seemed to end in nothingness, and with an hour's stepcutting ascended the couloir which led upwards from it. From there onwards it was a rock-climb, certainly of considerable difficulty, but with no heart-breaking discoveries ahead, and it was about nine in the morning that we stood on the top. We did not wait there long, for that side of the mountain is raked by falling stones loosened, when the sun grows hot, from the ice that holds them, and we made haste to pass the ledge where the falls are most frequent. After that there was the long fissure to descend, a matter of no great difficulty, and we were at the end of our work by midday, both of us, as you may imagine, in the state of the highest elation.

"A long and tiresome scramble among the huge boulders at the foot of the cliff then lay before us. Here the hill-side is very porous and great caves extend far into the mountain. We had unroped at the base of the fissure, and were picking our way as seemed good to either of us among these fallen rocks, many of them bigger than an ordinary house, when, on coming round the corner of one of these, I saw that which made it clear that the stories Chanton had told me were no figment of traditional superstition.

"Not twenty yards in front of me lay one of the beings of which he had spoken. There it sprawled naked and basking on its back with face turned up to the sun, which its narrow eyes regarded unwinking. In form it was completely human, but the growth of hair that covered limbs and trunk alike almost completely hid the sun-tanned skin beneath. But its face, save for the down on its cheeks and chin, was hairless, and I looked on a countenance the sensual and malevolent bestiality of which froze me with horror. Had the creature been an animal, one would have felt scarcely a shudder at the gross animalism of it; the horror lay in the fact that it was a man. There lay by it a couple of gnawed bones, and, its meal finished, it was lazily licking its protuberant lips, from which came a purring murmur of content. With one hand it scratched the thick hair on its belly, in the other it held one of these bones, which presently split in half beneath the pressure of its finger and thumb. But my horror was not based on the information of what happened to those men whom these creatures caught, it was due only to my proximity to a thing so human and so infernal. The peak, of which the ascent had a moment ago filled us with such elated satisfaction, became to me an Ungeheuerhorn indeed, for it was the home of beings more awful than the delirium of nightmare could ever have conceived.

"Chanton was a dozen paces behind me, and with a backward wave of my hand I caused him to halt. Then withdrawing myself with infinite precaution, so as not to attract the gaze of that basking creature, I slipped back round the rock, whispered to him what I had seen, and with blanched faces we made a long detour, peering round every corner, and crouching low, not knowing that at any step we might not come upon another of these beings, or that from the mouth of one of these caves in the mountain-side there might not appear another of those hairless and dreadful faces, with perhaps this time the breasts and insignia of womanhood. That would have been the worst of all.

"Luck favoured us, for we made our way among the boulders and shifting stones, the rattle of which might at any moment have betrayed us, without a repetition of my experience, and once among the trees we ran as if the Furies themselves were in pursuit. Well now did I understand, though I dare say I cannot convey, the qualms of Chanton's mind when he spoke to me of these creatures. Their very humanity was what made them so terrible, the fact that they were of the same race as ourselves, but of a type so abysmally degraded that the most brutal and inhuman of men would have seemed angelic in comparison."

The music of the small band was over before he had finished the narrative, and the chattering groups round the tea-table had dispersed. He paused a moment.

"There was a horror of the spirit," he said, "which I experienced then, from which, I verily believe, I have never entirely recovered. I saw then how terrible a living thing could be, and how terrible, in consequence, was life itself. In us all I suppose lurks some inherited germ of that ineffable bestiality, and who knows whether, sterile as it has apparently become in the course of centuries, it might not fructify again. When I saw that creature sun itself, I looked into the abyss out of which we have crawled. And these creatures are trying to crawl out of it now, if they exist any longer. Certainly for the last twenty years there has been no record of their being seen, until we come to this story of the footprint seen by the climbers on Everest. If that is authentic, if the party did not mistake the footprint of some bear, or what not, for a human tread, it seems as if still this bestranded remnant of mankind is in existence."

Now, Ingram, had told his story well; but sitting in this warm and civilised room, the horror which he had clearly felt had not communicated itself to me in any very vivid manner. Intellectually, I agreed, I could appreciate his horror, but certainly my spirit felt no shudder of interior comprehension.

"But it is odd," I said, "that your keen interest in physiology did not disperse your qualms. You were looking, so I take it, at some form of man more remote probably than the earliest human remains. Did not something inside you say 'This is of absorbing significance'?"

He shook his head.

"No: I only wanted to get away," said he. "It was not, as I have told you, the terror of what according to Chanton's story, might await us if we were captured; it was sheer horror at the creature itself. I quaked at it."

The snowstorm and the gale increased in violence that night, and I slept uneasily, plucked again and again from slumber by the fierce battling of the wind that shook my windows as if with an imperious demand for admittance. It came in billowy gusts, with strange noises intermingled with it as for a moment it abated, with flutings and moanings that rose to shrieks as the fury of it returned. These noises, no doubt, mingled themselves with my drowsed and sleepy consciousness, and once I tore myself out of nightmare, imagining that the creatures of the Horror-horn had gained footing on my balcony and were rattling at the window-bolts. But before morning the gale had died away, and I awoke to see the snow falling dense and fast in a windless air. For three days it continued, without intermission, and with its cessation there came a frost such as I have never felt before. Fifty degrees were registered one night, and more the next, and what the cold must have been on the cliffs of the Ungeheuerborn I cannot imagine. Sufficient, so I thought, to have made an end altogether of its secret inhabitants: my cousin, on that day twenty years ago, had missed an opportunity for study which would probably never fall again either to him or another.

I received one morning a letter from a friend saying that he had arrived at the neighbouring winter resort of St. Luigi, and proposing that I should come over for a morning's skating and lunch afterwards. The place was not more than a couple of miles off, if one took the path over the low, pine-clad foot-hills above which lay the steep woods below the first rocky slopes of the Ungeheuerhorn; and accordingly, with a knapsack containing skates on my back, I went on skis over the wooded slopes and down by an easy descent again on to St. Luigi. The day was overcast, clouds entirely obscured the higher peaks though the sun was visible, pale and unluminous, through the mists. But as the morning went on, it gained the upper hand, and I slid down into St. Luigi beneath a sparkling firmament. We skated and lunched, and then, since it looked as if thick weather was coming up again, I set out early about three o'clock for my return journey.

Hardly had I got into the woods when the clouds gathered thick above, and streamers and skeins of them began to descend among the pines through which my path threaded its way. In ten minutes more their opacity had so increased that I could hardly see a couple of yards in front of me. Very soon I became aware that I must have got off the path, for snow-cowled shrubs lay directly in my way, and, casting back to find it again, I got altogether confused as to direction. But, though progress was difficult, I knew I had only to keep on the ascent, and presently I should come to the brow of these low foot-hills, and descend into the open valley where Alhubel stood. So on I went, stumbling and sliding over obstacles, and unable, owing to the thickness of the snow, to take off my skis, for I should have sunk over the knees at each step. Still the ascent continued, and looking at my watch I saw that I had already been near an hour on my way from St. Luigi, a period more than sufficient to complete my whole journey. But still I stuck to my idea that though I had certainly strayed far from my proper route a few minutes more must surely see me over the top of the upward way, and I should find the ground declining into the next valley. About now, too, I noticed that the mists were growing suffused with rose-colour, and, though the inference was that it must be close on sunset, there was consolation in the fact that they were there and might lift at any moment and disclose to me my whereabouts. But the fact that night would soon be on me made it needful to bar my mind against that despair of loneliness which so eats out the heart of a man who is lost in woods or on mountain-side, that, though still there is plenty of vigour in his limbs, his nervous force is sapped, and he can do no more than lie down and abandon himself to whatever fate may await him . . . And then I heard that which made the thought of loneliness seem bliss indeed, for there was a worse fate than loneliness. What I heard resembled the howl of a wolf, and it came from not far in front of me where the ridge – was it a ridge? – still rose higher in vestment of pines.

From behind me came a sudden puff of wind, which shook the frozen snow from the drooping pine-branches, and swept away the mists as a broom sweeps the dust from the floor. Radiant above me were the unclouded skies, already charged with the red of the sunset, and in front I saw that I had come to the very edge of the wood through which I had wandered so long. But it was no valley into which I had penetrated, for there right ahead of me rose the steep slope of boulders and rocks soaring upwards to the foot of the Ungeheuerhorn. What, then, was that cry of a wolf which had made my heart stand still? I saw.

Not twenty yards from me was a fallen tree, and leaning against the trunk of it was one of the denizens of the Horror-Horn, and it was a woman. She was enveloped in a thick growth of hair grey and tufted, and from her head it streamed down over her shoulders and her bosom, from which hung withered and pendulous breasts.

And looking on her face I comprehended not with my mind alone, but with a shudder of my spirit, what Ingram had felt. Never had nightmare fashioned so terrible a countenance; the beauty of sun and stars and of the beasts of the field and the kindly race of men could not atone for so hellish an incarnation of the spirit of life. A fathomless bestiality modelled the slavering mouth and the narrow eyes; I looked into the abyss itself and knew that out of that abyss on the edge of which I leaned the generations of men had climbed. What if that ledge crumbled in front of me and pitched me headlong into its nethermost depths? . . .

In one hand she held by the horns a chamois that kicked and struggled. A blow from its hindleg caught her withered thigh, and with a grunt of anger she seized the leg in her other hand, and, as a man may pull from its sheath a stem of meadow-grass, she plucked it off the body, leaving the torn skin hanging round the gaping wound. Then putting the red, bleeding member to her mouth she sucked at it as a child sucks a stick of sweetmeat. Through flesh and gristle her short, brown teeth penetrated, and she licked her lips with a sound of purring. Then dropping the leg by her side, she looked again at the body of the prey now quivering in its death-convulsion, and with finger and thumb gouged out one of its eyes. She snapped her teeth on it, and it cracked like a soft-shelled nut.

It must have been but a few seconds that I stood watching her, in some indescribable catalepsy of terror, while through my brain there pealed the panic-command of my mind to my stricken limbs "Begone, begone, while there is time." Then, recovering the power of my joints and muscles, I tried to slip behind a tree and hide myself from this apparition. But the woman – shall I say? – must have caught my stir of movement, for she raised her eyes from her living feast and saw me. She craned forward her neck, she dropped her prey, and half rising began to move towards me. As she did this, she opened her mouth, and gave forth a howl such as I had heard a moment before. It was answered by another, but faintly and distantly.

Sliding and slipping, with the toes of my skis tripping in the obstacles below the snow, I plunged forward down the hill between the pine-trunks. The low sun already sinking behind some rampart of mountain in the west reddened the snow and the pines with its ultimate rays. My knapsack with the skates in it swung to and fro on my back, one ski-stick had already been twitched out of my hand by a fallen branch of pine, but not a second's pause could I allow myself to recover it. I gave no glance behind, and I knew not at what pace my pursuer was on my track, or indeed whether any pursued at all, for my whole mind and energy, now working at full power again under the stress of my panic, was devoted to getting away down the hill and out of the wood as swiftly as my limbs could bear me. For a little while I heard nothing but the hissing snow of my headlong passage, and the rustle of the covered undergrowth beneath my feet, and then, from close at hand behind me, once more the wolf-howl sounded and I heard the plunging of footsteps other than my own.

The strap of my knapsack had shifted, and as my skates swung to and fro on my back it chafed and pressed on my throat, hindering free passage of air, of which, God knew, my labouring lungs were in dire need, and without pausing I slipped it free from my neck, and held it in the hand from which my ski-stick had been jerked. I seemed to go a little more easily for this adjustment, and now, not so far distant, I could see below me the path from which I had strayed. If only I could reach that, the smoother going would surely enable me to outdistance my pursuer, who even on the rougher ground was but slowly overhauling me, and at the sight of that riband stretching unimpeded downhill, a ray of hope pierced the black panic of my soul. With that came the desire, keen and insistent, to see who or what it was that was on my tracks, and I spared a backward glance. It was she, the hag whom I had seen at her gruesome meal; her long grey hair flew out behind her, her mouth chattered and gibbered, her fingers made grabbing movements, as if already they closed on me.

But the path was now at hand, and the nearness of it I suppose made me incautious. A hump of snow-covered bush lay in my path, and, thinking I could jump over it, I tripped and fell, smothering myself in snow. I heard a maniac noise, half scream, half laugh, from close behind, and before I could recover myself the grabbing fingers were at my neck, as if a steel vice had closed there. But my right hand in which I held my knapsack of skates was free, and with a blind back-handed movement I whirled it behind me at the full length of its strap, and knew that my desperate blow had found its billet somewhere. Even before I could look round I felt the grip on my neck relax, and something subsided into the very bush which had entangled me. I recovered my feet and turned.

There she lay, twitching and quivering. The heel of one of my skates piercing the thin alpaca of the knapsack had hit her full on the temple, from which the blood was pouring, but a hundred yards away I could see another such figure coming downwards on my tracks, leaping and bounding. At that panic rose again within me, and I sped off down the white smooth path that led to the lights of the village already beckoning. Never once did I pause in my headlong going: there was no safety until I was back among the haunts of men. I flung myself against the door of the hotel, and screamed for admittance, though I had but to turn the handle and enter; and once more as when Ingram had told his tale, there was the sound of the band, and the chatter of voices, and there, too, was he himself, who looked up and then rose swiftly to his feet as I made my clattering entrance.

"I have seen them too," I cried. "Look at my knapsack. Is there not blood on it? It is the blood of one of them, a woman, a hag, who tore off the leg of a chamois as I looked, and pursued me through the accursed wood. I—"

Whether it was I who spun round, or the room which seemed to spin round me, I knew not, but I heard myself falling, collapsed on the floor, and the next time that I was conscious at all I was in bed. There was Ingram there, who told me that I was quite safe, and another man, a stranger, who pricked my arm with the nozzle of a syringe, and reassured me . . .

A day or two later I gave a coherent account of my adventure, and three or four men, armed with guns, went over my traces. They found the bush in which I had stumbled, with a pool of blood which had soaked into the snow, and, still following my ski-tracks, they came on the body of a chamois, from which had been torn one of its hindlegs and one eye-socket was empty. That is all the corroboration of my story that I can give the reader, and for myself I imagine that the creature which pursued me was either not killed by my blow or that her fellows removed her body . . . Anyhow, it is open to the incredulous to prowl about the caves of the Ungeheuerhorn, and see if anything occurs that may convince them.

Machaon

I was returning at the close of the short winter day from my visit to St. James's Hospital, where my old servant Parkes, who had been in my service for twenty years, was lying. I had sent him there three days before, not for treatment, but for observation, and this afternoon I had gone up to London, to hear the doctor's report on the case. He told me that Parkes was suffering from an internal tumour, the nature of which could not be diagnosed for certain, but all the symptoms pointed directly to its being cancerous. That, however, must not be regarded as proved; it could only be proved by an explanatory operation to reveal the nature and the extent of the growth, which must then, if possible, be excised. It might involve, so my old friend Godfrey Symes told me, certain tissues and would be found to be inoperable, but he hoped this would not be the case, and that it would be possible to remove it: removal gave the only chance of recovery. It was fortunate that the patient had been sent for examination in an early stage, for thus the chances of success were much greater than if the growth had been one of long standing. Parkes was not, however, in a fit state to stand the operation at once; a recuperative week or ten days in bed was advisable. In these circumstances Symes recommended that he should not be told at once what lay in front of him.

"I can see that he is a nervous fellow," he said, "and to lie in bed thinking of what he has got to face will probably undo all the good that lying in bed will bring to him. You don't get used to the idea of being cut open; the more you think about it, the more intolerable it becomes. If that sort of adventure faced me, I should infinitely prefer not to be told about it until they came to give me the anæsthetic. Naturally, he will have to consent to the operation, but I shouldn't tell him anything about it till the day before. He's not married, I think, is he?"

"No: he's alone in the world," said I. "He's been with me twenty years."

"Yes, I remember Parkes almost as long as I remember you. But that's all I can recommend. Of course, if the pain became severe, it might be better to operate sooner, but at present he suffers hardly at all, and he sleeps well, so the nurse tells me."

"And there's nothing else that you can try for it?" I asked.

"I'll try anything you like, but it will be perfectly useless. I'll let him have any quack nostrum you and he wish, as long as it doesn't injure his health, or make you put off the operation. There are X-rays and ultra-violet rays, and violet leaves and radium; there are fresh cures for cancer discovered every day, and what's the result? They only make people put off the operation till it's no longer possible to operate. Naturally, I will welcome any further opinion you want."

Now Godfrey Symes is easily the first authority on this subject, and has a far higher percentage of cures to his credit than any-one else.

"No, I don't want any fresh opinion," said I.

"Very well, I'll have him carefully watched. By the way, can't you stop in town and dine with me? There are one or two people coming, and among them a perfectly mad spiritualist who has more messages from the other world than I ever get on my telephone. Trunkcalls, eh? I wonder where the exchange is. Do come! You like cranks, I know!"

"I can't, I'm afraid," said I. "I've a couple of guests coming to stay with me to-day down in the country. They are both cranks: one's a medium."

He laughed.

"Well, I can only offer you one crank, and you've got two," he said. "I must get back to the wards. I'll write to you in about a week's time or so, unless there's any urgency which I don't foresee, and I should suggest your coming up to tell Parkes. Good-bye."

I caught my train at Charing Cross with about three seconds to spare, and we slid clanking out over the bridge through the cold, dense air. Snow had been falling intermittently since morning, and when we got out of the grime and fog of London, it was lying thickly on field and hedgerow, retarding by its reflection of such light as lingered the oncoming of darkness, and giving to the landscape an aloof and lonely austerity. All day I had felt that drowsiness which accompanies snowfall, and sometimes, half losing myself in a doze, my mind crept, like a thing crawling about in the dark, over what Godfrey Symes had told me. For all these years Parkes, as much friend as servant, had given me his faithfulness and devotion, and now, in return for that, all that apparently I could do was to tell him of his plight. It was clear, from what the surgeon had said, that he expected a serious disclosure, and I knew from the experience of two friends of mine who had been in his condition what might be expected of this "exploratory operation." Exactly similar had been these cases; there was clear evidence of an internal growth possibly not malignant, and in each case the same dismal sequence had followed. The growth had been removed, and within a couple of months there had been a recrudescence of it. Indeed, surgery had proved no more than a pruning-knife, which had stimulated that which the surgeon had hoped to extirpate into swifter activity. And that apparently was the best chance that Symes held out: the rest of the treatments were but rubbish or quackery . . .

My mind crawled away towards another subject: probably the two visitors whom I expected, Charles Hope and the medium whom he was bringing with him, were in the same train as I, and I ran over in my mind all that he had told me of Mrs. Forrest. It was certainly an odd story he had brought me two days before. Mrs. Forrest was a medium of considerable reputation in psychical circles, and had produced some very extraordinary book-tests which, by all accounts, seemed inexplicable, except on a spiritualistic hypothesis, and no imputation of trickery had, at any rate as yet, come near her. When in trance, she spoke and wrote, as is invariably the case with mediums, under the direction of a certain "control" – that is to say, a spiritual and discarnate intelligence which for the time was in possession of her. But lately there had been signs that a fresh control had inspired her, the nature of whom, his name, and his identity was at present unknown. And then came the following queer incident.

Last week only when in trance, and apparently under the direction of this new control, she began describing in considerable detail a certain house where the control said that he had work to do. At first the description aroused no association in Charles Hope's mind, but as it went on, it suddenly struck him that Mrs. Forrest was speaking of my house in Tilling. She gave its general features, its position in a small town on a hill, its walled-in garden, and then went on to speak with great minuteness of a rather peculiar feature in the house. She described a big room built out in the garden a few yards away from the house itself at right-angles to its front, and approached by half a dozen stone steps. There was a railing, so she said, on each side of them, and into the railing were twisted, like snake coils, the stems of a tree which bore pale mauve flowers. This was all a correct description of my garden room and the wistaria which writhes in and out of the railings which line the steps. She then went on to speak of the interior of the room. At one end was a fireplace, at the other a big bow-window looking out on to the street and the front of the house, and there were two other windows opposite each other, in one of which was a table, while the other, looking out on to the garden, was shadowed by the tree that twisted itself about the railings. Book-cases lined the walls, and there was a big sofa at right-angles to the fire . . .

Now all this, though it was a perfectly accurate description of a place that, as far as could be ascertained, Mrs. Forrest had never seen, might conceivably have been derived from Charles Hope's mind, since he knew the room well, having often stayed with me. But the medium added a detail which could not conceivably have been thus derived, for Charles believed it to be incorrect. She said that there was a big piano near the bow-window, while he was sure that there was not. But oddly enough I had hired a piano only a week or so ago, and it stood in the place that she mentioned. The "control" then repeated that there was work for him to do in that house. There was some situation or complication there in which he could help, and he could "get through" better (that is, make a clearer communication) if the medium could hold a séance there. Charles Hope then told the control that he believed he knew the house that he had been speaking of, and promised to do his best. Shortly afterwards Mrs. Forrest came out of trance, and, as usual, had no recollection of what had passed.

So Charles came to me with the story exactly as I have given it here, and though I could not think of any situation or complication in which an unknown control of a medium I had never seen could be of assistance, the whole thing (and in especial that detail about the piano) was so odd that I asked him to bring the medium down for a sitting or a series of sittings. The day of their arrival was arranged, but when three days ago Parkes had to go into hospital, I was inclined to put them off. But a neighbour away for a week obligingly lent me a parlour-maid, and I let the engagement stand. With regard to the situation in which the control would be of assistance, I can but assure the reader that as far as I thought about it at all, I only wondered whether it was concerned with a book on which I was engaged, which dealt (if I could ever succeed in writing it) with psychical affairs. But at present I could not get on with it at all. I had made half a dozen beginnings which had all gone into the waste-paper basket.

My guests proved not to have come by the same train as I, but arrived shortly before dinner-time, and after Mrs. Forrest had gone to her room, I had a few words with Charles, who told me exactly how the situation now stood.

"I know your caution and your captiousness in these affairs," he said, "so I have told Mrs. Forrest nothing about the description she gave of this house, or of the reason why I asked her to come here. I said only, as we settled, that you were a great friend of mine and immensely interested in psychical affairs, but a countrymouse whom it was difficult to get up to town. But you would be delighted if she would come down for a few days and give some sittings here."

"And does she recognise the house, do you think?" I asked.

"No sign of it. As I told you, when she comes out of trance she never seems to have the faintest recollection of what she has said or written. We shall have a séance, I hope, to-night after dinner."

"Certainly, if she will," said I. "I thought we had better hold it in the garden-room, for that was the place that was so minutely described. It's quite warm there, central-heating and a fire, and it's only half a dozen yards from the house. I've had the snow swept from the steps."

Mrs. Forrest turned out to be a very intelligent woman, well spiced with humour, gifted with a sane appreciation of the comforts of life, and most agreeably furnished with the small change of talk. She was inclined to be stout, but carried herself with briskness, and neither in body nor mind did she suggest that she was one who held communication with the unseen: there was nothing wan or occult about her. Her general outlook on life appeared to be rather materialistic than otherwise, and she was very interesting on the topic when, about half-way through dinner, the subject of her mediumship came on the conversational board.

"My gifts, such as they are," she said, "have nothing to do with this person who sits eating and drinking and talking to you. She, as Mr. Hope may have told you, is quite expunged before the subconscious part of me – that is the latest notion, is it not? – gets into touch with discarnate intelligences. Until that happens, the door is shut, and when it is over, the door is shut again, and I have no recollection of what I have said or written. The control uses my hand and my voice, but that is all. I know no more about it than a piano on which a tune has been played."

"And there is a new control who has lately been using you?" I asked.

She laughed.

"You must ask Mr. Hope about that," she said. "I know nothing whatever of it. He tells me it is so, and he tells me – don't you, Mr. Hope? – that he hasn't any idea who or what the new control is. I look forward to its development; my idea is that the control has to get used to me, as in learning a new instrument. I assure you I am as eager as anyone that he should gain facility in communication through me. I hope, indeed, that we are to have a séance to-night."

The talk veered again, and I learned that Mrs. Forrest had never been in Tilling before, and was enchanted with the snowy moonlit glance she had had of its narrow streets and ancient residences. She liked, too, the atmosphere of the house: it seemed tranquil and kindly; especially so was the little drawing-room where we had assembled before dinner.

I glanced at Charles.

"I had thought of proposing that we should sit in the garden-room," I said, "if you don't mind half a dozen steps in the open. It adjoins the house."

"Just as you wish," she said, "though I think we have excellent conditions in here without going there."

This confirmed her statement that she had no idea after she had come out of trance what she had said, for otherwise she must have recognised at the mention of the garden-room her own description of it, and when soon after dinner we adjourned there, it was clear that, unless she was acting an inexplicable part, the sight of it twanged no chord of memory. There we made the very simple arrangements to which she was accustomed.

As the procedure in such sittings is possibly unfamiliar to the reader, I will describe quite shortly what our arrangements were. We had no idea what form these manifestations – if there were any – might take, and therefore we, Charles and I, were prepared to record them on the spot. We three sat round a small table about a couple of yards from the fire, which was burning brightly; Mrs. Forrest seated herself in a big armchair. Exactly in front of her on the table were a pencil and a block of paper in case, as often happened, the manifestation took the form of automatic script – writing, that is, while in a state of trance. Charles and I sat on each side of her, also provided with pencil and paper in order to take down what she said if and when (as lawyers say) the control took possession of her. In case materialised spirits appeared, a phenomenon not as yet seen at her séances, our idea was to jot down as quickly as possible whatever we saw or thought we saw. Should there be rappings or movements of furniture, we were to make similar notes of our impressions. The lamp was then turned down, so that just a ring of flame encircled the wick, but the firelight was of sufficient brightness, as we tested before the séance began, to enable us to write and to see what we had written. The red glow of it illuminated the room, and it was settled that Charles should note by his watch the time at which anything occurred. Occasionally, throughout the séance a bubble of coal-gas caught fire, and then the whole room started into strong light. I had given orders that my servants should not interrupt the sitting at all, unless somebody rang the bell from the garden-room. In that case it was to be answered. Finally, before the séance began, we bolted all the windows on the inside and locked the door. We took no other precautions against trickery, though, as a matter of fact, Mrs. Forrest suggested that she should be tied into her chair. But in the firelight any movement of hers would be so visible that we did not adopt this precaution. Charles and I had settled to read to each other the notes we made during the sitting, and cut out anything that both of us had not recorded. The accounts, therefore, of this sitting and of that which followed next day are founded on our joint evidence. The sitting began.

Mrs. Forrest was leaning back at ease with her eyes open and her hands on the arms of her chair. Then her eyes closed and a violent trembling seized her. That passed, and shortly afterwards her head fell forward and her breathing became very rapid. Presently that quieted to normal pace again, and she began to speak at first in a scarcely audible whisper and then in a high shrill voice, quite unlike her usual tones.

I do not think that in all England there was a more disappointed man than I during the next half-hour. "Starlight," it appeared, was in control, and Starlight was a personage of platitudes. She had been a nun in the time of Henry VII, and her work was to help those who had lately passed over. She was very busy and very happy, and was in the third sphere where they had a great deal of beautiful music. We must all be good, said Starlight, and it didn't matter much whether we were clever or not. Love was the great thing; we had to love each other and help each other, and death was no more than the gate of life, and everything would be tremendously jolly . . . Starlight, in fact, might be better described as clap-trap, and I began thinking about Parkes . . .

And then I ceased to think about Parkes, for the shrill moralities of Starlight ceased, and Mrs. Forrest's voice changed again. The stale facility of her utterance stopped and she began to speak, quite unintelligibly, in a voice of low baritone range. Charles leaned across the table and whispered to me.

"That's the new control," he said.

The voice that was speaking stumbled and hesitated: it was like that of a man trying to express himself in some language which he knew very imperfectly. Sometimes it stopped altogether, and in one of these pauses I asked:

"Can you tell us your name?"

There was no reply, but presently I saw Mrs. Forrest's hand reach out for the pencil. Charles put it into her fingers and placed the writing-pad more handily for her. I watched the letters, in capitals, being traced. They were made hesitatingly, but were perfectly legible. "Swallow," she wrote, and again "Swallow," and stopped.

"The bird?" I asked.

The voice spoke in answer; now I could hear the words, uttered in that low baritone voice.

"No, not a bird," it said. "Not a bird, but it flies."

I was utterly at sea; my mind could form no conjecture whatever as to what was meant. And then the pencil began writing again. "Swallow, swallow," and then with a sudden briskness of movement, as if the guiding intelligence had got over some difficulty, it wrote "Swallow-tail."

This seemed more abstrusely senseless than ever. The only connection with swallow-tail in my mind was a swallow-tailed coat, but whoever heard of a swallow-tailed coat flying?

"I've got it," said Charles. "Swallow-tail butterfly. Is it that?"

There came three sudden raps on the table, loud and startling. These raps, I may explain, in the usual code mean "Yes." As if to confirm it the pencil began to write again, and spelled out "Swallow-tail butterfly."

"Is that your name?" I asked.

There was one rap, which signifies "No," followed by three, which means "Yes." I had not the slightest idea of what it all signified (indeed it seemed to signify nothing at all), but the sitting had become extraordinarily interesting if only for its very unexpectedness. The control was trying to establish himself by three methods simultaneously – by the voice, by the automatic writing, and by rapping. But how a swallow-tail butterfly could assist in some situation which was now existing in my house was utterly beyond me . . . Then an idea struck me: the swallow-tail butterfly no doubt had a scientific name, and that we could easily ascertain, for I knew that there was on my shelves a copy of Newman's *Butterflies and Moths of Great Britain*, a sumptuous volume bound in morocco, which I had won as an entomological prize at school. A moment's search gave me the book, and by the firelight I turned up the description of this butterfly in the index. Its scientific name was *Papilio Machaon*.

"Is Machaon your name?" I asked.

The voice came clear now.

"Yes, I am Machaon," it said.

With that came the end of the séance, which had lasted not more than an hour. Whatever the power was that had made Mrs. Forrest speak in that male voice and struggle, through that roundabout method of "swallow, swallow-tail, Machaon," to establish its identity, it now began to fail. Mrs. Forrest's pencil made a few illegible scribbles, she whispered a few inaudible words, and presently with a stretch and a sigh she came out of trance. We told her that the name of the control was established, but apparently Machaon meant nothing to her. She was much exhausted, and very soon I took her across to the house to go to bed, and presently rejoined Charles.

"Who was Machaon, anyhow?" he asked. "He sounds classical: more in your line than mine."

I remembered enough Greek mythology to supply elementary facts, while I hunted for a particular book about Athens.

"Machaon was the son of Asclepios," I said, "and Asclepios was the Greek god of healing. He had precincts, hydropathic establishments, where people went to be cured. The Romans called him Aesculapius."

"What can he do for you then?" asked Charles. "You're fairly fit, aren't you?"

Not till he spoke did a light dawn on me. Though I had been thinking so much of Parkes that day, I had not consciously made the connection.

"But Parkes isn't," said I. "Is that possible?"

"By Jove!" said he.

I found my book, and turned to the accounts of the precinct of Asclepios in Athens.

"Yes, Asclepios had two sons," I said – "Machaon and Podaleirios. In Homeric times he wasn't a god, but only a physician, and his sons were physicians too. The myth of his godhead is rather a late one—

I shut the book.

"Best not to read any more," I said. "If we know all about Asclepios, we shall possibly be suggesting things to the medium's mind. Let's see what Machaon can tell us about himself, and we can verify it afterwards."

It was therefore with no further knowledge than this on the subject of Machaon that we proposed to hold another séance the next day. All morning the bitter air had been laden with snow, and now the street in front of my house, a by-way at the best in the slender traffic of the town, lay white and untrodden, save on the pavement where a few passengers had gone by. Mrs. Forrest had not appeared at breakfast, and from then till lunch-time I sat in the bow-window of the garden-room, for the warmth of the central heating, of which a stack of pipes was there installed, and for securing the utmost benefit of light that penetrated this cowl of snow-laden sky, busy with belated letters. The drowsiness that accompanies snowfall weighed heavily on my faculties, but as far as I can assert anything, I can assert that I did not sleep. From one letter I went on to another, and then for the sixth or seventh time I tried to open my story. It promised better now than before, and searching for a word that would not come to my pen, I happened to look up along the street which lay in front of me. I expected nothing: I was thinking of nothing but my work; probably I had looked up like that a dozen times before, and had seen the empty street, with snow lying thickly on the roadway.

But now the roadway was not untenanted. Someone was walking

down the middle of it, and his aspect, incredible though it seemed, was not startling. Why I was not startled I have no idea: I can only say that the vision appeared perfectly natural. The figure was that of a young man, whose hair, black and curly, lay crisply over his forehead. A large white cloak reaching down to his knees enveloped him, and he had thrown the end of it over his shoulder. Below his knees his legs and feet were bare, so too was the arm up to the elbow, with which he pressed his cloak to him, and there he was walking briskly down the snowy street. As he came directly below the window where I sat, he raised his head and looked at me directly, and smiled. And now I saw his face: there was the low brow, the straight nose, the curved and sunny mouth, the short chin, and I thought to myself that this was none other than the Hermes of Praxiteles, he whose statue at Olympia makes all those who look on it grow young again. There, anyhow, was a boyish Greek god, stepping blithely and with gay, incomparable grace along the street, and raising his face to smile at this stolid, middle-aged man who blankly regarded him. Then with the certainty of one returning home, he mounted the steps outside the front door, and seemed to pass into and through it. Certainly he was no longer in the street, and, so real and solid-seeming had he been to my vision, that I jumped up, ran across the few steps of garden, and went into the house, and I should not have been amazed if I had found him standing in the hall. But there was no one there, and I opened the front door: the snow lay smooth and untrodden down the centre of the road where he had walked and on my doorstep. And at that moment the memory of the séance the evening before, about which up till now I had somehow felt distrustful and suspicious, passed into the realm of sober fact, for had not Machaon just now entered my house, with a smile as of recognition on some friendly mission?

We sat again that afternoon by daylight, and now, I must suppose, the control was more actively and powerfully present, for hardly had Mrs. Forrest passed into trance than the voice began, louder than it had been the night before, and far more distinct. He – Machaon I must call him – seemed to be anxious to establish his identity beyond all doubt, like some newcomer presenting his credentials, and he began to speak of the precinct of Asclepios in Athens. Often he hesitated for a word in English, often he put in a word in Greek, and as he spoke, fragments of things I had learned when an archæological student in Athens came back into my mind, and I knew that he was accurately describing the portico and the temple and the well. All this I toss to the sceptic to growl and worry over and tear to bits; for certainly it seems possible that my mind, holding these facts in its subconsciousness, was suggesting them to the medium's mind, who thereupon spoke of them and, conveying them back to me, made me aware that I had known them . . . My forgotten knowledge of these things and of the Greek language came flooding back on me, as he told us, now half in Greek, and half in English, of the patients who came to consult the god, how they washed in the sacred well for purification, and lay down to sleep in the portico. They often dreamed, and in the interpretation of their dreams, which they told to the priest next day, lay the indication of the cure. Or sometimes the god healed more directly, and accompanied by the sacred snake walked among the sleepers and by his touch made them whole. His temple was hung with *ex-votos*, the gifts of those whom he had cured. And at Epidaurus, where was another shrine of his, there were great mural tablets recording the same . . .

Then the voice stopped, and as if to prove identity by another means, the medium drew the pencil and paper to her, and in Greek characters, unknown apparently to her, she traced the words "Machaon, son of Asclepios . . ."

There was a pause, and I asked a direct question, which now had been long simmering in my mind.

"Have you come to help me about Parkes?" I asked. "Can you tell me what will cure him?"

The pencil began to move again, tracing out characters in Greek. It wrote *φέγγος ζ*, and repeated it. I did not at once guess what it meant, and asked for an explanation. There was no answer, and presently the medium stirred, stretched herself and sighed, and came out of trance. She took up the paper on which she had written.

"Did that come through?" she asked. "And what does it mean? I don't even know the characters . . ."

Then suddenly the possible significance of *φέγγος ζ* flashed on me, and I marvelled at my slowness. *φέγγος*, a beam of light, a ray, and the letter ζ, the equivalent of the English *x*. That had come in direct answer to my question as to what would cure Parkes, and it was without hesitation or delay that I wrote to Symes. I reminded him that he had said that he had no objection to any possible remedy, provided it was not harmful, being tried on his patient, and I asked him to treat him with X-rays. The whole sequence of events had been so frankly amazing, that I believe the veriest sceptic would not have done otherwise than I did.

Our sittings continued, but after this day we had no further evidence of this second control. It looked as if the intelligence (even the most incredulous will allow me, for the sake of convenience, to call that intelligence Machaon) that had described this room, and told Mrs. Forrest that he had work to do here, had finished his task. Machaon had said, or so my interpretation was, that X-rays would cure Parkes. In justification of this view it is proper to quote from a letter which I got from Symes a week later.

"There is no need for you to come up to break to Parkes that an operation lies in front of him. In answer to your request, and without a grain of faith in its success, I treated him with X-rays, which I assured you were useless. To-day, to speak quite frankly, I don't know what to think, for the growth has been steadily diminishing in size and hardness, and it is perfectly evident that it is being absorbed and is disappearing.

"The treatment through which I put Parkes is that of— Here in this hospital we have had patients to whom it brought no shadow of benefit. Often it had been continued on these deluded wretches till any operation which might possibly have been successful was out of the question owing to the encroachment of the growth. But from the first dose of the X-rays, Parkes began to get better, the growth was first arrested, and then diminished.

"I am trying to put the whole thing before you with as much impartiality as I can command. So, on the other side, you must remember that Parkes's was never a proved case of cancer. I told you that it could not be proved till the exploratory operation took place. All the symptoms pointed to cancer – you see, I am trying to save my own face – but my diagnosis, though confirmed by—, may have been wrong. If he only had what we call a benign tumour, the case is not so extraordinary; there have been plenty of cases when a benign tumour has disappeared by absorption or what not. It is unusual, but by no means unknown. For instance . . .

"But Parkes's case was quite different. I certainly believe he had a cancerous growth, and thought that an operation was inevitable if his life was to be saved. Even then, the most I hoped for was an alleviation of pain, as the disease progressed, and a year or two more, at the most, of life. Instead, I apply another remedy, at your suggestion, and if he goes on as he has been doing, the growth will be a nodule in another week or two, and I should expect it to disappear altogether. Taking everything into consideration, if you asked me the question whether this X-ray treatment was the cause of the cure, I should be obliged to say 'Yes.' I don't believe in such a treatment, but I believe it is curing him. I suppose that it was suggested to you by a fraudulent, spiritualistic medium in a feigned trance, who was inspired by Aesculapius or some exploded heathen deity, for I remember you said you were going down into the country for some spiritual business . . .

"Well, Parkes is getting better, and I am so old-fashioned a fellow that I would sooner a patient of mine got better by incredible methods, than died under my skilful knife . . . Of course, we trained people know nothing, but we have to act according to the best chances of our ignorance. I entirely believed that the knife was the only means of saving the man, and now, when I stand confuted, the only thing that I can save is my honesty, which I hereby have done. Let me know, at your leisure, whether you just thought you would, on your own idea, like me to try X-rays, or whether some faked voice from the grave suggested it.

"EVER YOURS,

"GODFREY SYMES.

"P.S. – If it was some beastly voice from the grave, you might tell me in confidence who the medium was. I want to be fair . . ."

That is the story; the reader will explain it according to his temperament. And as I have told Parkes, who is now back with me again, to look into the garden-room before post-time and take a registered packet to the office, it is time that I got it ready for him. So here is the completed packet in manuscript, to be sent to the printer's. From my window I shall see him go briskly along the street down which Machaon walked on a snowy morning.

Negotium Perambulans

The casual tourist in West Cornwall may just possibly have noticed, as he bowled along over the bare high plateau between Penzance and the Land's End, a dilapidated signpost pointing down a steep lane and bearing on its battered finger the faded inscription "Polearn 2 miles," but probably very few have had the curiosity to traverse those two miles in order to see a place to which their guide-books award so cursory a notice. It is described there, in a couple of unattractive lines, as a small fishing village with a church of no particular interest except for certain carved and painted wooden panels (originally belonging to an earlier edifice) which form an altar-rail. But the church at St. Creed (the tourist is reminded) has a similar decoration far superior in point of preservation and interest, and thus even the ecclesiastically disposed are not lured to Polearn. So meagre a bait is scarce worth swallowing, and a glance at the very steep lane which in dry weather presents a carpet of sharp-pointed stones, and after rain a muddy watercourse, will almost certainly decide him not to expose his motor or his bicycle to risks like these in so sparsely populated a district. Hardly a house has met his eye since he left Penzance, and the possible trundling of a punctured bicycle for half a dozen weary miles seems a high price to pay for the sight of a few painted panels.

Polearn, therefore, even in the high noon of the tourist season, is little liable to invasion, and for the rest of the year I do not suppose that a couple of folk a day traverse those two miles (long ones at that) of steep and stony gradient. I am not forgetting the postman in this exiguous estimate, for the days are few when, leaving his pony and cart at the top of the hill, he goes as far as the village, since but a few hundred yards down the lane there stands a large white box, like a sea-trunk, by the side of the road, with a slit for letters and a locked door. Should he have in his wallet a registered letter or be the bearer of a parcel too large for insertion in the square lips of the sea-trunk, he must needs trudge down the hill and deliver the troublesome missive, leaving it in person on the owner, and receiving some small reward of coin or refreshment for his kindness.

But such occasions are rare, and his general routine is to take out of the box such letters as may have been deposited there, and insert in their place such letters as he has brought. These will be called for, perhaps that day or perhaps the next, by an emissary from the Polearn post-office. As for the fishermen of the place, who, in their export trade, constitute the chief link of movement between Polearn and the outside world, they would not dream of taking their catch up the steep lane and so, with six miles farther of travel, to the market at Penzance. The sea route is shorter and easier, and they deliver their wares to the pier-head. Thus, though the sole industry of Polearn is sea-fishing, you will get no fish there unless you have bespoken your requirements to one of the fishermen. Back come the trawlers as empty as a haunted house, while their spoils are in the fish-train that is speeding to London.

Such isolation of a little community, continued, as it has been, for centuries, produces isolation in the individual as well, and nowhere will you find greater independence of character than among the people of Polearn. But they are linked together, so it has always seemed to me, by some mysterious comprehension: it is as if they had all been initiated into some ancient rite, inspired and framed by forces visible and invisible. The winter storms that batter the coast, the vernal spell of the spring, the hot, still summers, the season of rains and autumnal decay, have made a spell which, line by line, has been communicated to them, concerning the powers, evil and good, that rule the world, and manifest themselves in ways benignant or terrible . . .

I came to Polearn first at the age of ten, a small boy, weak and sickly, and threatened with pulmonary trouble. My father's business kept him in London, while for me abundance of fresh air and a mild climate were considered essential conditions if I was to grow to manhood. His sister had married the vicar of Polearn, Richard Bolitho, himself native to the place, and so it came about that I spent three years, as a paying guest, with my relations. Richard Bolitho owned a fine house in the place, which he inhabited in preference to the vicarage, which he let to a young artist, John Evans, on whom the spell of Polearn had fallen for from year's beginning to year's end he never let it. There was a solid roofed shelter, open on one side to the air, built for me in the garden, and here I lived and slept, passing scarcely one hour out of the twenty-four behind walls and windows. I was out on the bay with the fisher-folk, or wandering along the gorse-clad cliffs that climbed steeply to right and left of the deep combe where the village lay, or pottering about on the pier-head, or bird's-nesting in the bushes with the boys of the village. Except on Sunday and for the few daily hours of my lessons, I might do what I pleased so long as I remained in the open air. About the lessons there was nothing formidable; my uncle conducted me through flowering bypaths among the thickets of arithmetic, and made pleasant excursions into the elements of Latin grammar, and above all, he made me daily give him an account, in clear and grammatical sentences, of what had been occupying my mind or my movements. Should I select to tell him about a walk along the cliffs, my speech must be orderly, not vague, slip-shod notes of what I had observed. In this way, too, he trained my observation, for he would bid me tell him what flowers were in bloom, and what birds hovered fishing over the sea or were building in the bushes. For that I owe him a perennial gratitude, for to observe and to express my thoughts in the clear spoken word became my life's profession.

But far more formidable than my weekday tasks was the prescribed routine for Sunday. Some dark embers compounded of Calvinism and mysticism smouldered in my uncle's soul, and made it a day of terror. His sermon in the morning scorched us with a foretaste of the eternal fires reserved for unrepentant sinners, and he was hardly less terrifying at the children's service in the afternoon. Well do I remember his exposition of the doctrine of guardian angels. A child, he said, might think himself secure in such angelic care, but let him beware of committing any of those numerous offences which would cause his guardian to turn his face from him, for as sure as there were angels to protect us, there were also evil and awful presences which were ready to pounce; and on them he dwelt with peculiar gusto. Well, too, do I remember in the morning sermon his commentary on the carved panels of the altar-rails to which I have already alluded. There was the angel of the Annunciation there, and the angel of the Resurrection, but not less was there the witch of Endor, and, on the fourth panel, a scene that concerned me most of all. This fourth panel (he came down from his pulpit to trace its time-worn features) represented the lych-gate of the church-yard at Polearn itself, and indeed the resemblance when thus pointed out was remarkable. In the entry stood the figure of a robed priest holding up a Cross, with which he faced a terrible creature like a gigantic slug, that reared itself up in front of him. That, so ran my uncle's interpretation, was some evil agency, such as he had spoken about to us children, of almost infinite malignity and power, which could alone be combated by firm faith and a pure heart. Below ran the legend "Negotium perambulans in tenebris" from the ninety-first Psalm. We should find it translated there, "the pestilence that walketh in darkness," which but feebly rendered the Latin. It was more deadly to the soul than any pestilence that can only kill the body: it was the Thing, the Creature, the Business that trafficked in the outer Darkness, a minister of God's wrath on the unrighteous . . .

I could see, as he spoke, the looks which the congregation exchanged with each other, and knew that his words were evoking a surmise, a remembrance. Nods and whispers passed between them, they understood to what he alluded, and with the inquisitiveness of boyhood I could not rest till I had wormed the story out of my friends among the fisher-boys, as, next morning, we sat basking and naked in the sun after our bathe. One knew one bit of it, one another, but it pieced together into a truly alarming legend. In bald outline it was as follows:

A church far more ancient than that in which my uncle terrified us every Sunday had once stood not three hundred yards away, on the shelf of level ground below the quarry from which its stones were hewn. The owner of the land had pulled this down, and erected for himself a house on the same site out of these materials, keeping, in a very ecstasy of wickedness, the altar, and on this he dined and played dice afterwards. But as he grew old some black melancholy seized him, and he would have lights burning there all night, for he had deadly fear of the darkness. On one winter evening there sprang up such a gale as was never before known, which broke in the windows of the room where he had supped, and extinguished the lamps. Yells of terror brought in his servants, who found him lying on the floor with the blood streaming from his throat. As they entered some huge black shadow seemed to move away from him, crawled across the floor and up the wall and out of the broken window.

"There he lay a-dying," said the last of my informants, "and him that had been a great burly man was withered to a bag o' skin, for the critter had drained all the blood from him. His last breath was a scream, and he hollered out the same words as passon read off the screen."

"*Negotium perambulans in tenebris*," I suggested eagerly.

"Thereabouts. Latin anyhow."

"And after that?" I asked.

"Nobody would go near the place, and the old house rotted and fell in ruins till three years ago, when along comes Mr. Dooliss from Penzance, and built the half of it up again. But he don't care much about such critters, nor about Latin neither. He takes his bottle of whisky a day and gets drunk's a lord in the evening. Eh, I'm gwine home to my dinner."

Whatever the authenticity of the legend, I had certainly heard the truth about Mr. Dooliss from Penzance, who from that day became an object of keen curiosity on my part, the more so because the quarry-house adjoined my uncle's garden. The Thing that walked in the dark failed to stir my imagination, and already I was so used to sleeping alone in my shelter that the night had no terrors for me. But it would be intensely exciting to wake at some timeless hour and hear Mr. Dooliss yelling, and conjecture that the Thing had got him.

But by degrees the whole story faded from my mind, overscored by the more vivid interests of the day, and, for the last two years of my out-door life in the vicarage garden, I seldom thought about Mr. Dooliss and the possible fate that might await him for his temerity in living in the place where that Thing of darkness had done business. Occasionally I saw him over the garden fence, a great yellow lump of a man, with slow and staggering gait, but never did I set eyes on him outside his gate, either in the village street or down on the beach. He interfered with none, and no one interfered with him. If he wanted to run the risk of being the prey of the legendary nocturnal monster, or quietly drink himself to death, it was his affair. My uncle, so I gathered, had made several attempts to see him when first he came to live at Polearn, but Mr. Dooliss appeared to have no use for parsons, but said he was not at home and never returned the call.

After three years of sun, wind, and rain, I had completely outgrown my early symptoms and had become a tough, strapping youngster of thirteen. I was sent to Eton and Cambridge, and in due course ate my dinners and became a barrister. In twenty years from that time I was earning a yearly income of five figures, and had already laid by in sound securities a sum that brought me dividends which would, for one of my simple tastes and frugal habits, supply me with all the material comforts I needed on this side of the grave. The great prizes of my profession were already within my reach, but I had no ambition beckoning me on, nor did I want a wife and children, being, I must suppose, a natural celibate. In fact there was only one ambition which through these busy years had held the lure of blue and far-off hills to me, and that was to get back to Polearn, and live once more isolated from the world with the sea and the gorse-clad hills for play-fellows, and the secrets that lurked there for exploration. The spell of it had been woven about my heart, and I can truly say that there had hardly passed a day in all those years in which the thought of it and the desire for it had been wholly absent from my mind. Though I had been in frequent communication with my uncle there during his lifetime, and, after his death, with his widow who still lived there, I had never been back to it since I embarked on my profession, for I knew that if I went there, it would be a wrench beyond my power to tear myself away again. But I had made up my mind that when once I had provided for my own independence, I would go back there not to leave it again. And yet I did leave it again, and now nothing in the world would induce me to turn down the lane from the road that leads from Penzance to the Land's End, and see the sides of the combe rise steep above the roofs of the village and hear the gulls chiding as they fish in the bay. One of the things invisible, of the dark powers, leaped into light, and I saw it with my eyes.

The house where I had spent those three years of boyhood had been left for life to my aunt, and when I made known to her my intention of coming back to Polearn, she suggested that, till I found a suitable house or found her proposal unsuitable, I should come to live with her.

"The house is too big for a lone old woman," she wrote, "and I have often thought of quitting and taking a little cottage sufficient for me and my requirements. But come and share it, my dear, and if you find me troublesome, you or I can go. You may want solitude – most people in Polearn do – and will leave me. Or else I will leave you: one of the main reasons of my stopping here all these years was a feeling that I must not let the old house starve. Houses starve, you know, if they are not lived in. They die a lingering death; the spirit in them grows weaker and weaker, and at last fades out of them. Isn't this nonsense to your London notions? . . ."

Naturally I accepted with warmth this tentative arrangement, and on an evening in June found myself at the head of the lane leading down to Polearn, and once more I descended into the steep valley between the hills. Time had stood still apparently for the combe, the dilapidated signpost (or its successor) pointed a rickety finger down the lane, and a few hundred yards farther on was the white box for the exchange of letters. Point after remembered point met my eye, and what I saw was not shrunk, as is often the case with the revisited scenes of childhood, into a smaller scale. There stood the post-office, and there the church und close beside it the vicarage, and beyond, the tall shrubberies which separated the house for which I was bound from the road, and beyond that again the grey roofs of the quarry-house damp and shining with the moist evening wind from the sea. All was exactly as I remembered it, and, above all, that sense of seclusion and isolation. Somewhere above the tree-tops climbed the lane which joined the main road to Penzance, but all that had become immeasurably distant. The years that had passed since last I turned in at the well-known gate faded like a frosty breath, and vanished in this warm, soft air. There were law-courts somewhere in memory's dull book which, if I cared to turn the pages, would tell me that I had made a name and a great income there. But the dull book was closed now, for I was back in Polearn, and the spell was woven around me again.

And if Polearn was unchanged, so too was Aunt Hester, who met me at the door. Dainty and china-white she had always been, and the years had not aged but only refined her. As we sat and talked after dinner she spoke of all that had happened in Polearn in that score of years, and yet somehow the changes of which she spoke seemed but to confirm the immutability of it all. As the recollection of names came back to me, I asked her about the quarry-house and Mr. Dooliss, and her face gloomed a little as with the shadow of a cloud on a spring day.

"Yes, Mr. Dooliss," she said, "poor Mr. Dooliss, how well I remember him, though it must be ten years and more since he died. I never wrote to you about it, for it was all very dreadful, my dear, and I did not want to darken your memories of Polearn. Your uncle always thought that something of the sort might happen if he went on in his wicked, drunken ways, and worse than that, and though nobody knew exactly what took place, it was the sort of thing that might have been anticipated."

"But what more or less happened, Aunt Hester?" I asked.

"Well, of course I can't tell you everything, for no one knew it. But he was a very sinful man, and the scandal about him at Newlyn was shocking. And then he lived, too, in the quarry-house . . . I wonder if by any chance you remember a sermon of your uncle's when he got out of the pulpit and explained that panel in the altar-rails, the one, I mean, with the horrible creature rearing itself up outside the lych-gate?"

"Yes, I remember perfectly," said I.

"Ah. It made an impression on you, I suppose, and so it did on all who heard him, and that impression got stamped and branded on us all when the catastrophe occurred. Somehow Mr. Dooliss got to hear about your uncle's sermon, and in some drunken fit he broke into the church and smashed the panel to atoms. He seems to have thought that there was some magic in it, and that if he destroyed that he would get rid of the terrible fate that was threatening him. For I must tell you that before he committed that dreadful sacrilege he had been a haunted man: he hated and feared darkness, for he thought that the creature on the panel was on his track, but that as long as he kept lights burning it could not touch him. But the panel, to his disordered mind, was the root of his terror, and so, as I said, he broke into the church and attempted – you will see why I said 'attempted' – to destroy it. It certainly was found in splinters next morning, when your uncle went into church for matins, and knowing Mr. Dooliss's fear of the panel, he went across to the quarry-house afterwards and taxed him with its destruction. The man never denied it; he boasted of what he had done. There he sat, though it was early morning, drinking his whisky.

"'I've settled your Thing for you,' he said, 'and your sermon too. A fig for such superstitions.'

"Your uncle left him without answering his blasphemy, meaning to go straight into Penzance and give information to the police about this outrage to the church, but on his way back from the quarry-house he went into the church again, in order to be able to give details about the damage, and there in the screen was the panel, untouched and uninjured. And yet he had himself seen it smashed, and Mr. Dooliss had confessed that the destruction of it was his work. But there it was, and whether the power of God had mended it or some other power, who knows?"

This was Polearn indeed, and it was the spirit of Polearn that made me accept all Aunt Hester was telling me as attested fact. It had happened like that. She went on in her quiet voice.

"Your uncle recognised that some power beyond police was at work, and he did not go to Penzance or give informations about the outrage, for the evidence of it had vanished."

A sudden spate of scepticism swept over me.

"There must have been some mistake," I said. "It hadn't been broken . . ."

She smiled.

"Yes, my dear, but you have been in London so long," she said. "Let me, anyhow, tell you the rest of my story. That night, for some reason, I could not sleep. It was very hot and airless; I dare say you will think that the sultry conditions accounted for my wakefulness. Once and again, as I went to the window to see if I could not admit more air, I could see from it the quarry-house, and I noticed the first time that I left my bed that it was blazing with lights. But the second time I saw that it was all in darkness, and as I wondered at that, I heard a terrible scream, and the moment afterwards the steps of someone coming at full speed down the road outside the gate. He yelled as he ran; 'Light, light!' he called out. 'Give me light, or it will catch me!' It was very terrible to hear that, and I went to rouse my husband, who was sleeping in the dressing-room across the passage. He wasted no time, but by now the whole village was aroused by the screams, and when he got down to the pier he found that all was over. The tide was low, and on the rocks at its foot was lying the body of Mr. Dooliss. He must have cut some artery when he fell on those sharp edges of stone, for he had bled to death, they thought, and though he was a big burly man, his corpse was but skin and bones. Yet there was no pool of blood round him, such as you would have expected. Just skin and bones as if every drop of blood in his body had been sucked out of him!"

She leaned forward.

"You and I, my dear, know what happened," she said, "or at least can guess. God has His instruments of vengeance on those who bring wickedness into places that have been holy. Dark and mysterious are His ways."

Now what I should have thought of such a story if it had been told me in London I can easily imagine. There was such an obvious explanation: the man in question had been a drunkard, what wonder if the demons of delirium pursued him? But here in Polearn it was different.

"And who is in the quarry-house now?" I asked. "Years ago the fisher-boys told me the story of the man who first built it and of his horrible end. And now again it has happened. Surely no one has ventured to inhabit it once more?"

I saw in her face, even before I asked that question, that somebody had done so.

"Yes, it is lived in again," said she, "for there is no end to the blindness . . . I don't know if you remember him. He was tenant of the vicarage many years ago."

"John Evans," said I.

"Yes. Such a nice fellow he was too. Your uncle was pleased to get so good a tenant. And now—

She rose.

"Aunt Hester, you shouldn't leave your sentences unfinished," I said.

She shook her head.

"My dear, that sentence will finish itself," she said. "But what a time of night! I must go to bed, and you too, or they will think we have to keep lights burning here through the dark hours."

Before getting into bed I drew my curtains wide and opened all the windows to the warm tide of the sea air that flowed softly in. Looking out into the garden I could see in the moonlight the roof of the shelter, in which for three years I had lived, gleaming with dew. That, as much as anything, brought back the old days to which I had now returned, and they seemed of one piece with the present, as if no gap of more than twenty years sundered them. The two flowed into one like globules of mercury uniting into a softly shining globe, of mysterious lights and reflections. Then, raising my eyes a little, I saw against the black hill-side the windows of the quarry-house still alight.

Morning, as is so often the case, brought no shattering of my illusion. As I began to regain consciousness, I fancied that I was a boy again waking up in the shelter in the garden, and though, as I grew more widely awake, I smiled at the impression, that on which it was based I found to be indeed true. It was sufficient now as then to be here, to wander again on the cliffs, and hear the popping of the ripened seed-pods on the gorse-bushes; to stray along the shore to the bathing-cove, to float and drift and swim in the warm tide, and bask on the sand, and watch the gulls fishing, to lounge on the pier-head with the fisher-folk, to see in their eyes and hear in their quiet speech the evidence of secret things not so much known to them as part of their instincts and their very being. There were powers and presences about me; the white poplars that stood by the stream that babbled down the valley knew of them, and showed a glimpse of their knowledge sometimes, like the gleam of their white underleaves; the very cobbles that paved the street were soaked in it . . . All that I wanted was to lie there and grow soaked in it too; unconsciously, as a boy, I had done that, but now the process must be conscious. I must know what stir of forces, fruitful and mysterious, seethed along the hill-side at noon, and sparkled at night on the sea. They could be known, they could even be controlled by those who were masters of the spell, but never could they be spoken of, for they were dwellers in the innermost, grafted into the eternal life of the world. There were dark secrets as well as these clear, kindly powers, and to these no doubt belonged the *negotium perambulans in tenebris* which, though of deadly malignity, might be regarded not only as evil, but as the avenger of sacrilegious and impious deeds . . . All this was part of the spell of Polearn, of which the seeds had long lain dormant in me. But now they were sprouting, and who knew what strange flower would unfold on their stems?

It was not long before I came across John Evans. One morning, as I lay on the beach, there came shambling across the sand a man stout and middle-aged with the face of Silenus. He paused as he drew near and regarded me from narrow eyes.

"Why, you're the little chap that used to live in the parson's garden," he said. "Don't you recognise me?"

I saw who it was when he spoke: his voice, I think, instructed me, and recognising it, I could see the features of the strong, alert young man in this gross caricature.

"Yes, you're John Evans," I said. "You used to be very kind to me: you used to draw pictures for me."

"So I did, and I'll draw you some more. Been bathing? That's a risky performance. You never know what lives in the sea, nor what lives on the land for that matter. Not that I heed them. I stick to work and whisky. God! I've learned to paint since I saw you, and drink too for that matter. I live in the quarry-house, you know, and it's a powerful thirsty place. Come and have a look at my things if you're passing. Staying with your aunt, are you? I could do a wonderful portrait of her. Interesting face; she knows a lot. People who live at Polearn get to know a lot, though I don't take much stock in that sort of knowledge myself."

I do not know when I have been at once so repelled and interested. Behind the mere grossness of his face there lurked something which, while it appalled, yet fascinated me. His thick lisping speech had the same quality. And his paintings, what would they be like? . . .

"I was just going home," I said. "I'll gladly come in, if you'll allow me."

He took me through the untended and overgrown garden into the house which I had never yet entered. A great grey cat was sunning itself in the window, and an old woman was laying lunch in a corner of the cool hall into which the door opened. It was built of stone, and the carved mouldings let into the walls, the fragments of gargoyles and sculptured images, bore testimony to the truth of its having been built out of the demolished church. In one corner was an oblong and carved wooden table littered with a painter's apparatus and stacks of canvases leaned against the walls.

He jerked his thumb towards a head of an angel that was built into the mantelpiece and giggled.

"Quite a sanctified air," he said, "so we tone it down for the purposes of ordinary life by a different sort of art. Have a drink? No? Well, turn over some of my pictures while I put myself to rights."

He was justified in his own estimate of his skill: he could paint (and apparently he could paint anything), but never have I seen pictures so inexplicably hellish. There were exquisite studies of trees, and you knew that something lurked in the flickering shadows. There was a drawing of his cat sunning itself in the window, even as I had just now seen it, and yet it was no cat but some beast of awful malignity. There was a boy stretched naked on the sands, not human, but some evil thing which had come out of the sea. Above all there were pictures of his garden overgrown and jungle-like, and you knew that in the bushes were presences ready to spring out on you . . .

"Well, do you like my style?" he said as he came up, glass in hand. (The tumbler of spirits that he held had not been diluted.) "I try to paint the essence of what I see, not the mere husk and skin of it, but its nature, where it comes from and what gave it birth. There's much in common between a cat and a fuchsia-bush if you look at them closely enough. Everything came out of the slime of the pit, and it's all going back there. I should like to do a picture of you some day. I'd hold the mirror up to Nature, as that old lunatic said."

After this first meeting I saw him occasionally throughout the months of that wonderful summer. Often he kept to his house and to his painting for days together, and then perhaps some evening I would find him lounging on the pier, always alone, and every time we met thus the repulsion and interest grew, for every time he seemed to have gone farther along a path of secret knowledge towards some evil shrine where complete initiation awaited him . . . And then suddenly the end came.

I had met him thus one evening on the cliffs while the October sunset still burned in the sky, but over it with amazing rapidity there spread from the west a great blackness of cloud such as I have never seen for denseness. The light was sucked from the sky, the dusk fell in ever thicker layers. He suddenly became conscious of this.

"I must get back as quick as I can," he said. "It will be dark in a few minutes, and my servant is out. The lamps will not be lit."

He stepped out with extraordinary briskness for one who shambled and could scarcely lift his feet, and soon broke out into a stumbling run. In the gathering darkness I could see that his face was moist with the dew of some unspoken terror.

"You must come with me," he panted, "for so we shall get the lights burning the sooner. I cannot do without light."

I had to exert myself to the full to keep up with him, for terror winged him, and even so I fell behind, so that when I came to the garden gate, he was already half-way up the path to the house. I saw him enter, leaving the door wide, and found him fumbling with matches. But his hand so trembled that he could not transfer the light to the wick of the lamp.

"But what's the hurry about?" I asked.

Suddenly his eyes focused themselves on the open door behind me, and he jumped from his seat beside the table which had once been the altar of God, with a gasp and a scream.

"No, no!" he cried. "Keep it off! . . ."

I turned and saw what he had seen. The Thing had entered and now was swiftly sliding across the floor towards him, like some gigantic caterpillar. A stale phosphorescent light came from it, for though the dusk had grown to blackness outside, I could see it quite distinctly in the awful light of its own presence. From it too there came an odour of corruption and decay, as from slime that has long lain below water. It seemed to have no head, but on the front of it was an orifice of puckered skin which opened and shut and slavered at the edges. It was hairless, and slug-like in shape and in texture. As it advanced its fore-part reared itself from the ground, like a snake about to strike, and it fastened on him . . .

At that sight, and with the yells of his agony in my ears, the panic which had struck me relaxed into a hopeless courage, and with palsied, impotent hands I tried to lay hold of the Thing. But I could not: though something material was there, it was impossible to grasp it; my hands sunk in it as in thick mud. It was like wrestling with a nightmare.

I think that but a few seconds elapsed before all was over. The screams of the wretched man sank to moans and mutterings as the

Thing fell on him: he panted once or twice and was still. For a moment longer there came gurglings and sucking noises, and then it slid out even as it had entered. I lit the lamp which he had fumbled with, and there on the floor he lay, no more than a rind of skin in loose folds over projecting bones.

AT THE FARMHOUSE

The dusk of a November day was falling fast when John Aylsford came out of his lodging in the cobbled street and started to walk briskly along the road which led eastwards by the shore of the bay. He had been at work while the daylight served him, and now, when the gathering darkness weaned him from his easel, he was accustomed to go out for air and exercise and cover half a dozen miles before he returned to his solitary supper.

To-night there were but few folk abroad, and those scudded along before the strong south-westerly gale which had roared and raged all day, or, leaning forward, beat their way against it. No fishing-boats had put forth on that maddened sea, but had lain moored behind the quay-wall, tossing uneasily with the backwash of the great breakers that swept by the pier-head. The tide was low now, and they rested on the sandy beach, black blots against the smooth wet surface which sombrely reflected the last flames in the west. The sun had gone down in a wrack of broken and flying clouds, angry and menacing with promise of a wild night to come.

For many days past, at this hour John Aylsford had started eastwards for his tramp along the rough coast road by the bay. The last high tide had swept shingle and sand over sections of it, and fragments of seaweed, driven by the wind, bowled along the ruts. The heavy boom of the breakers sounded sullenly in the dusk, and white towers of foam appearing and disappearing showed how high they leaped over the reefs of rock beyond the headland. For half a mile or so, slanting himself against the gale he pursued this road, then turned up a narrow muddy lane sunk deep between the banks on either side of it. It ran steeply uphill, dipped down again, and joined the main road inland. Having arrived at the junction, John Aylsford went eastwards no more, but turned his steps to the west, arriving, half an hour after he had set out, on the top of the hill above the village he had quitted, though five minutes' ascent would have taken him from his lodgings to the spot where he now stood looking down on the scattered lights below him. The wind had blown all wayfarers indoors, and now in front of him the road that crossed this high and desolate table-land, sprinkled here and there with lonely cottages and solitary farms, lay empty and greyly glimmering in the wind-swept darkness, not more than faintly visible.

Many times during this past month had John Aylsford made this long detour, starting eastwards from the village and coming back by a wide circuit, and now, as on these other occasions, he paused in the black shelter of the hedge through which the wind hissed and whistled, crouching there in the shadow as if to make sure that none had followed him, and that the road in front lay void of passengers, for he had no mind to be observed by any on these journeyings. And as he paused he let his hate blaze up, warming him for the work the accomplishment of which alone could enable him to recapture any peace or profit from life. To-night he was determined to release himself from the millstone which for so many years had hung round his neck, drowning him in bitter waters. From long brooding over the idea of the deed, he had quite ceased to feel any horror of it. The death of that drunken slut was not a matter for qualms or uneasiness; the world would be well rid of her, and he more than well.

No spark of tenderness for the handsome fisher-girl who once had been his model and for twenty years had been his wife pierced the blackness of his purpose. Just here it was that he had seen her first when on a summer holiday he had lodged with a couple of friends in the farmhouse towards which his way now lay. She was coming up the hill with the late sunset gilding her face, and, breathing quickly from the ascent, had leaned on the wall close by with a smile and a glance for the young man. She had sat to him, and the autumn brought the sequel to the summer in his marriage. He had bought from her uncle the little farmhouse where he had lodged, adding to its modest accommodation a studio and a bedroom above it, and there he had seen the flicker of what had never been love, die out, and over the cold ashes of its embers the poisonous lichen of hatred spread fast. Early in their married life she had taken to drink, and had sunk into a degradation of soul and body that seemed bottomless, dragging him with her, down and down, in the grip of a force that was hardly human in its malignity.

Often during the wretched years that followed he had tried to leave her; he had offered to settle the farm on her and make adequate provision for her, but she had clung to the possession of him, not, it would seem, from any affection for him, but for a reason exactly opposite, namely, that her hatred of him fed and glutted itself on the sight of his ruin. It was as if, in obedience to some hellish power, she set herself to spoil his life, his powers, his possibilities, by tying him to herself. And by the aid of that power, so sometimes he had thought, she enforced her will on him, for, plan as he might to cut the whole dreadful business and leave the wreck behind him, he had never been able to consolidate his resolve into action. There, but a few miles away, was the station from which ran the train that would bear him out of this ancient western kingdom, where the beliefs in spells and superstitions grew rank as the herbage in that soft enervating air, and set him in the dry hard light of cities. The way lay open, but he could not take it; something unseen and potent, of grim inflexibility, held him back . . .

He had passed no one on his way here, and satisfied now that in the darkness he could proceed without fear of being recognised if a chance wayfarer came from the direction in which he was going, he left the shelter of the hedge, and struck out into the stormy sea of that stupendous gale. Even as a man in the grip of imminent death sees his past life spread itself out in front of him for his final survey before the book is closed, so now, on the brink of the new life from which the deed on which he was determined alone separated him, John Aylsford, as he battled his advance through this great tempest, turned over page after page of his own wretched chronicles, feeling already strangely detached from them; it was as if he read the sordid and enslaved annals of another, wondering at them, half-pitying, half-despising him who had allowed himself to be bound so long in this ruinous noose.

Yes; it had been just that, a noose drawn ever tighter round his neck, while he choked and struggled all unavailingly. But there was another noose which should very soon now be drawn rapidly and finally tight, and the drawing of that in his own strong hands would free him. As he dwelt on that for a moment, his fingers stroked and patted the hank of whipcord that lay white and tough in his pocket. A noose, a knot drawn quickly taut, and he would have paid her back with justice and swifter mercy for the long strangling which he had suffered.

Voluntarily and eagerly at the beginning had he allowed her to slip the noose about him, for Ellen Trenair's beauty in those days, so long past and so everlastingly regretted, had been enough to ensnare a man. He had been warned at the time, by hint and half-spoken suggestion, that it was ill for a man to mate with a girl of that dark and ill-famed family, or for a woman to wed a boy in whose veins ran the blood of Jonas Trenair, once Methodist preacher, who learned on one All-Hallows' Eve a darker gospel than he had ever preached before. What had happened to the girls who had married into that dwindling family, now all but extinct? One, before her marriage was a year old, had gone off her head, and now, a withered and ancient crone, mowed and gibbered about the streets of the village, picking garbage from the gutter and munching it in her toothless jaws. Another, Ellen's own mother, had been found hanging from the banister of her stairs, stark and grim. Then there was young Frank Pencarris, who had wed Ellen's sister. He had sunk into an awful melancholy, and sat tracing on sheets of paper the visions that beset his eyes, headless shapes, and foaming mouths, and the images of the spawn of hell . . . John Aylsford, in those early days, had laughed to scorn these old-wife tales of spells and sorceries: they belonged to ages long past, whereas fair Ellen Trenair was of the lovely present, and had lit desire in his heart which she alone could assuage. He had no use, in the brightness of her eye, for such shadows and superstitions; her beams dispelled them.

Bitter and black as midnight had his enlightenment been, darkening through dubious dusks till the mirk of the pit itself enveloped him. His laughter at the notion that in this twentieth century spells and sorceries could survive, grew silent on his lips. He had seen the cattle of a neighbour who had offended one whom it was wiser not to cross, dwindle and pine, though there were rich pastures for their grazing, till the rib-bones stuck out like the timbers of stranded wrecks. He had seen the spring on another farm run dry at lambing-time because the owner, sceptic like himself, had refused that bounty, which all prudent folk paid to the wizard of Mareuth, who, like Ellen, was of the blood of Jonas Trenair. From scorn and laughter he had wavered to an uneasy wonder, and from wonder his mind had passed to the conviction that there were powers occult and terrible which strove in darkness and prevailed, secrets and spells that could send disease on man and beast, dark incantations, known to few, which could maim and cripple, and of these few his wife was one. His reason revolted, but some conviction, deeper than reason, held its own. To such a view it seemed that the deed he contemplated was no crime, but rather an act of obedience to the ordinance "Thou shalt not suffer a witch to live." And the sense of detachment was over that, even as over the memories that oozed up in his mind. Somebody – not he – who had planned everything very carefully was in the next hour going to put an end to his bondage.

So the years had passed, he floundering ever deeper in the slough into which he was plunged, out of which while she lived he could never emerge. For the last year, she, wearying of his perpetual presence at the farm, had allowed him to take a lodging in the village. She did not loose her hold over him, for the days were few on which she did not come with demands for a handful of shillings to procure her the raw spirits which alone could slake her thirst. Sometimes as he sat at work there in the north room looking on to the small garden-yard, she would come lurching up the path, with her bloated crimson face set on the withered neck, and tap at his window with fingers shrivelled like bird's claws. Body and limbs were no more than bones over which the wrinkled skin was stretched, but her face bulged monstrously with layers of fat. He would give her whatever he had about him, and if it was not enough, she would plant herself there, grinning at him and wheedling him, or with screams and curses threatening him with such fate as he had known to overtake those who crossed her will. But usually he gave her enough to satisfy her for that day and perhaps the next, for thus she would the more quickly drink herself to death. Yet death seemed long in coming . . .

He remembered well how first the notion of killing her came into his head, just a little seed, small as that of mustard, which lay long in barrenness. Only the bare idea of it was there, like an abstract proposition. Then imperceptibly in the fruitful darkness of his mind, it must have begun to sprout, for presently a tendril, still soft and white, prodded out into the daylight. He almost pushed it back again, for fear that she, by some divining art, should probe his purpose. But when next she came for supplies, he saw no gleam of surmise in her red-rimmed eyes, and she took her money and went her way, and his purpose put forth another leaf, and the stem of it grew sappy. All autumn through it had flourished, and grown tree-like, and fresh ideas, fresh details, fresh precautions, flocked there like building birds and made it gay with singing. He sat under the shadow of it and listened with brightening hopes to their song; never had there been such peerless melody. They knew their tunes now, there was no need for any further rehearsal.

He began to wonder how soon he would be back on the road again, with face turned from this buffeting wind, and on his way home. His business would not take him long; the central deed of it would be over in a couple of minutes, and he did not anticipate delay about the setting to work on it, for by seven o'clock of the evening, as well he knew, she was usually snoring in the oblivion of complete drunkenness, and even if she was not as far gone as that, she would certainly be incapable of any serious resistance. After that, a quarter of an hour more would finish the job, and he would leave the house secure already from any chance of detection. Night after night during these last ten days he had been up here, peering from the darkness into the lighted room where she sat, then listening for her step on the stairs as she stumbled up to bed, or hearing her snorings as she slept in her chair below. The outhouse, he knew, was well stocked with paraffin; he needed no further apparatus than the whipcord and the matches he carried with him. Then back he would go along the exact route by which he had come, re-entering the village again from the eastwards, in which direction he had set out.

This walk of his was now a known and established habit; half the village during the last week or two had seen him every evening set forth along the coast road, for a tramp in the dusk when the light failed for his painting, and had seen him come back again as they hung about and smoked in the warm dusk, a couple of hours later. None knew of his detour to the main road which took him westwards again above the village and so to the stretch of bleak upland along which now he fought his way against the gale. Always round about the hour of eight he had entered the village again from the other side, and had stopped and chatted with the loiterers. To-night, no later than was usual, he would come up the cobbled road again, and give "good night" to any who lingered there outside the public-house. In this wild wind it was not likely that there would be such, and if so, no matter; he had been seen already setting forth on his usual walk by the coast of the bay, and if none outside saw him return, none could see the true chart of his walk. By eight he should be back to his supper, there would be a soused herring for him, and a cut of cheese, and the kettle would be singing on the hob for his hot whisky-toddy. He would have a keen edge for the enjoyment of them to-night; he would drink long healths to the damned and the dead. Not till to-morrow, probably, would the news of what had happened reach him, for the farmhouse lay lonely and sheltered by the wood of firs. However high might mount the beacon of its blazing, it would scarcely, screened by the tall trees, light up the western sky, and be seen from the village nestling below the steep hill-crest.

By now John Aylsford had come to the fir wood which bordered the road on the left, and, as he passed into its shelter, cut off from him the violence of the gale. All its branches were astir with the sound of some vexed, overhead sea, and the trunks that upheld them creaked and groaned in the fury of the tempest. Somewhere behind the thick scud of flying cloud the moon must have risen, for the road glimmered more visibly, and the tossing blackness of the branches was clear enough against the grey tumult overhead. Behind the tempest she rode in serene skies, and in the murderous clarity of his mind he likened himself to her. Just for half an hour more he would still grope and scheme and achieve in this hurly-burly, and then, like a balloon released, soar through the clouds and find serenity. A couple of hundred yards now would take him round the corner of the wood; from there the miry lane led from the high-road to the farm.

He hastened rather than retarded his going as he drew near, for the wood, though it roared with the gale, began to whisper to him of memories. Often in that summer before his marriage had he strayed out at dusk into it, certain that before he had gone many paces he would see a shadow flitting towards him through the firs, or hear the crack of dry twigs in the stillness. Here was their tryst; she would come up from the village with the excuse of bringing fish to the farmhouse, after the boats had come in, and deserting the high-road make a short cut through the wood. Like some distant blink of lightning the memory of those evenings quivered distantly on his mind, and he quickened his step. The years that followed had killed and buried those recollections, but who knew what stirring of corpses and dry bones might not yet come to them if he lingered there? He fingered the whipcord in his pocket, and launched out, beyond the trees, into the full fury of the gale.

The farmhouse was near now and in full view, a black blot against the clouds. A beam of light shone from an uncurtained window on the ground-floor, and the rest was dark. Even thus had he seen it for many nights past, and well knew what sight would greet him as he stole up nearer. And even so it was to-night, for there she sat in the studio he had built, betwixt table and fireplace with the bottle near her, and her withered hands stretched out to the blaze, and the huge bloated face swaying on her shoulders. Beside her to-night were the wrecked remains of a chair, and the first sight that he caught of her was to show her feeding the fire with the broken pieces of it. It had been too troublesome to bring fresh logs from the store of wood; to break up a chair was the easier task.

She stirred and sat more upright, then reached out for the bottle that stood beside her, and drank from the mouth of it. She drank and licked her lips and drank again, and staggered to her feet, tripping on the edge of the hearthrug. For the moment that seemed to anger her, and with clenched teeth and pointing finger she mumbled at it; then once more she drank, and lurching forward, took the lamp from the table. With it in her hand she shuffled to the door, and the room was left to the flickering firelight. A moment afterwards, the bedroom window above sprang into light, an oblong of bright illumination.

As soon as that appeared he crept round the house to the door. He gently turned the handle of it, and found it unlocked. Inside was a small passage entrance, on the left of which ascended the stairs to the bedroom above the studio. All was silent there, but from where he stood he could see that the door into the bedroom was open, for a shaft of light from the lamp she had carried up with her was shed on to the landing there . . . Everything was smoothing itself out to render his course most easy. Even the gale was his friend, for it would be bellows for the fire. He slipped off his shoes, leaving them on the mat, and drew the whipcord from his pocket. He made a noose in it, and began to ascend the stairs. They were well-built of seasoned oak, and no creak betrayed his advancing footfall.

At the top he paused, listening for any stir of movement within, but there was nothing to be heard but the sound of heavy breathing from the bed that lay to the left of the door and out of sight. She had thrown herself down there, he guessed, without undressing, leaving the lamp to burn itself out. He could see it through the open door already beginning to flicker; on the wall behind it were a couple of water-colours, pictures of his own, one of the little walled garden by the farm, the other of the pinewood of their tryst. Well he remembered painting them: she would sit by him as he worked with prattle and singing. He looked at them now quite detachedly; they seemed to him wonderfully good, and he envied the artist that fresh, clean skill. Perhaps he would take them down presently and carry them away with him.

Very softly now he advanced into the room, and looking round the corner of the door, he saw her, sprawling and fully dressed on the broad bed. She lay on her back, eyes closed and mouth open, her dull grey hair spread over the pillow. Evidently she had not made the bed that day, for she lay stretched on the crumpled back-turned blankets. A hair-brush was on the floor beside her; it seemed to have fallen from her hand. He moved quickly towards her.

He put on his shoes again when he came to the foot of the stairs, carrying the lamp with him and the two pictures which he had taken down from the wall, and went into the studio. He set the lamp on the table and drew down the blinds, and his eye fell on the half-empty whisky bottle from which he had seen her drinking. Though his hand was quite steady and his mind composed and tranquil, there was yet at the back of it some impression that was slowly developing, and a good dose of spirits would no doubt expunge that. He drank half a tumbler of it raw and undiluted, and though it seemed no more than water in his mouth, he soon felt that it was doing its work and sponging away from his mind the picture that had been outlining itself there. In a couple of minutes he was quite himself again, and could afford to wonder and laugh at the illusion, for it was no less than that, which had been gaining on him. For though he could distinctly remember drawing the noose tight, and seeing the face grow black, and struggling with the convulsive movements of those withered limbs that soon lay quiet again, there had sprung up in his mind some unaccountable impression that what he had left there huddled on the bed was not just the bundle of withered limbs and strangled neck, but the body of a young girl, smooth of skin and golden of hair, with mouth that smiled drowsily. She had been asleep when he came in, and now was half-awake, and was stirring and stretching herself. In what dim region of his mind that image had formed itself, he had no idea; all he cared about now was that his drink had shattered it again, and he could proceed with order and method to make all secure. Just one drop more first: how lucky it was that this morning he had been liberal with his money when she came to the village, for he would have been sorry to have gone without that fillip to his nerves.

He looked at his watch, and saw to his satisfaction that it was still only a little after seven o'clock. Half an hour's walking, with this gale to speed his steps, would easily carry him from door to door, round the detour which approached the village from the east, and a quarter of an hour, so he reckoned, would be sufficient to accomplish thoroughly what remained to be done here. He must not hurry and thus overlook some precaution needful for his safety, though, on the other hand, he would be glad to be gone from the house as soon as might be, and he proceeded to set about his work without delay. There was brushwood and fire-kindling to be brought in from the wood-shed in the yard, and he made three journeys, returning each time with his arms full, before he had brought in what he judged to be sufficient. Most of this he piled in a loose heap in the studio; with the rest he ascended once more to the bedroom above and made a heap of it there in the middle of the floor. He took the curtains down from the windows, for they would make a fine wick for the paraffin, and stuffed them into the pile. Before he left, he looked once more at what lay on the bed, and marvelled at the illusion which the whisky had dispelled, and as he looked, the sense that he was free mounted and bubbled in his head. The thing seemed scarcely human at all; it was a monster from which he had delivered himself, and now, with the thought of that to warm him, he was no longer eager to get through with his work and be gone, for it was all part of that act of riddance which he had accomplished, and he gloried in it. Soon, when all was ready, he would come back once more and soak the fuel and set light to it, and purge with fire the corruption that lay humped on the bed.

The fury of the gale had increased with nightfall, and as he went downstairs again he heard the rattle of loosened tiles on the roof, and the crash as they shattered themselves on the cobbles of the yard. At that a sudden misgiving made his breath to catch in his throat, as he pictured to himself some maniac blast falling on the house and crashing in the walls that now trembled and shuddered. Supposing the whole house fell, even if he escaped with his life from the toppling ruin, what would his life be worth? There would be search made in the fallen débris to find the body of her who lay strangled with the whipcord round her neck, and he pictured to himself the slow, relentless march of justice. He had bought whipcord only yesterday at a shop in the village, insisting on its strength and toughness . . . would it be wiser now, this moment, to untie the noose and take it back with him or add it to his brushwood? . . . He paused on the staircase, pondering that; but his flesh quaked at the thought, and master of himself though he had been during those few struggling minutes, he distrusted his power of making himself handle once more that which could struggle no longer. But even as he tried to screw his courage to the point, the violence of the squall passed, and the shuddering house braced itself again. He need not fear that; the gale was his friend that would blow on the flames, not his enemy. The blasts that trumpeted overhead were the voices of the allies who had come to aid him.

All was arranged then upstairs for the pouring of the paraffin and the lighting of the pyre; it remained but to make similar dispositions in the studio. He would stay to feed the flames till they raged beyond all power of extinction; and now he began to plan the line of his retreat. There were two doors in the studio: one by the fireplace which opened on to the little garden; the other gave into the passage entrance from which mounted the stairs and so to the door through which he had come into the house. He decided to use the garden-door for his exit; but when he came to open it, he found that the key was stiff in the rusty lock, and did not yield to his efforts. There was no use in wasting time over that; it made no difference through which door he finally emerged, and he began piling up his heap of wood at that end of the room. The lamp was burning low; but the fire, which only so few minutes ago she had fed with a broken chair, shone brightly, and a flaming ember from it would serve to set light to his conflagration. There was a straw mat in front of it, which would make fine kindling, and with these two fires, one in the bedroom upstairs and the other here, there would be no mistake about the incineration of the house and all that it contained. His own crime, if crime it was, would perish, too, and all evidence thereof, victim and whipcord, and the very walls of the house of sin and hate. It was a great deed and a fine adventure, and as the liquor he had drunk began to circulate more buoyantly through his veins, he gloried at the thought of the approaching consummation. He would slip out of the sordid tragedy of his past life, as from a discarded garment that he threw into the bonfire he would soon kindle.

All was ready now for the soaking of the fuel he had piled with the paraffin, and he went out to the shed in the yard where the barrel stood. A big tin ewer stood beside it, which he filled and carried indoors. That would be sufficient for the soaking of the pile upstairs, and fetching the smoky and flickering lamp from the studio, he went up again, and like a careful gardener watering some bed of choice blossoms, he sprinkled and poured till his ewer was empty. He gave but one glance to the bed behind him, where the huddled thing lay so quietly, and as he turned, lamp in hand, to go down again, the draught that came in through the window against which the gale blew, extinguished it. A little blue flame of burning vapour rose in the chimney and went out; so, having no further use for it, he pitched it on to the pile of soaked material. As he left the room he thought he heard some small stir of movement behind him, but he told himself that it was but something slipping in the heap he had built there.

Again he went out into the storm. The clouds that scudded overhead were thinner now, though the gale blew not less fiercely, and the blurred, watery moonlight was brighter. Once for a moment, as he approached the shed, he caught sight of the full orb plunging madly among the streaming vapours; then she was hidden again behind the wrack. Close in front of him were the fir trees of the wood where those sweet trysts had been held, and once again the vision of her as she had been broke into his mind and the queer conviction that it was no withered and bloated hag, who lay on the bed upstairs but the fair, comely limbs and the golden head. It was even more vivid now, and he made haste to get back to the studio, where he would find the trusty medicine that had dispelled that vision before. He would have to make two journeys at least with his tin ewer before he transported enough oil to feed the larger pyre below, and so, to save time, he took the barrel off its stand, and rolled it along the path and into the house. He paused at the foot of the stairs, listening to hear if anything stirred, but all was silent. Whatever had slipped up there was steady again; from outside only came the squeal and bellow of the wind.

The studio was brightly but fitfully lit by the flames on the hearth; at one moment a noonday blazed there, the next but the last smoulder of some red sunset. It was easier to decant from the barrel into his ewer than carry the heavy keg and sprinkle from it, and once and once again he filled and emptied it. One more application would be sufficient, and after that he could let what remained trickle out on to the floor. But by some awkward movement he managed to spill a splash of it down the front of his trousers: he must be sure, therefore (how quickly his brain responded with counsels of precautions), to have some accident with his lamp when he came in to his supper, which should account for this little misadventure. Or, probably, the wind through which he would presently be walking would dry it before he reached the village.

So, for the last time with matches ready in his hand, he mounted the stairs to set light to the fuel piled in the room above. His second dose of whisky sang in his head, and he said to himself, smiling at the humour of the notion, "She always liked a fire in her bedroom;

she shall have it now." That seemed a very comical idea, and it dwelt in his head as he struck the match which should light it for her. Then, still grinning, he gave one glance to the bed, and the smile died on his face, and the wild cymbals of panic crashed in his brain. The bed was empty; no huddled shape lay there.

Distraught with terror, he thrust the match into the soaked pile and the flame flared up. Perhaps the body had rolled off the bed. It must, in any case, be here somewhere, and when once the room was alight there would be nothing more to fear. High rose the smoky flame, and banging the door, he leaped down the stairs to set light to the pile below and be gone from the house. Yet, whatever monstrous miracle his eye had assured him of, it could not be that she still lived and had left the place where she lay, for she had ceased to breathe when the noose was tight round her neck, and her fight for life and air had long been stilled. But, if by some hideous witchcraft, she was not dead, it would soon be over now with her in the stupefaction of the smoke and the scorching flames. Let be; the door was shut and she within, for him it remained to be finished with the business, and flee from the house of terror, lest he leave the sanity of his soul behind him.

The red glare from the hearth in the studio lit his steps down the passage from the stairway, and already he could hear from above the dry crack and snap from the fire that prospered there. As he shuffled in, he held his hands to his head, as if pressing the brain back into its cool case, from which it seemed eager to fly out into the welter of storm and fire and hideous imagination. If he could only control himself for a few moments more, all would be done and he would escape from this disordered haunted place into the night and the gale, leaving behind him the blaze that would burn away all perilous stuff. Again the flames broke out in the embers on the hearth, bravely burning, and he took from the heart of the glare a fragment on which the fire was bursting into yellow flowers. He heeded not the scorching of his hand, for it was but for a moment that he held it, and then plunged it into the pile that dripped with the oil he had poured on it. A tower of flame mounted, licking the rafters of the low ceiling, then died away as if suffocated by its own smoke, but crept onwards, nosing its way along till it reached the straw mat, which blazed fiercely. That blaze kindled the courage in him; whatever trick his imagination had played on him just now, he had nothing to fear except his own terror, which now he mastered again, for nothing real could ever escape from the conflagration, and it was only the real that he feared. Spells and witchcrafts and superstitions, such as for the last twenty years had battened on him, were all enclosed in that tight-drawn noose.

It was time to be gone, for all was safe now, and the room was growing to oven-heat. But as he picked his way across the floor over which runnels of flames from the split barrel were beginning to spread this way and that, he heard from above the sound of a door unlatched, and footsteps light and firm tapped on the stairs. For one second the sheer catalepsy of panic seized him, but he recovered his control, and with hands that groped through the thick smoke he found the door. At that moment the fire shot up in a blaze of blinding flame, and there in the doorway stood Ellen. It was no withered body and bloated face that confronted him, but she with whom he had trysted in the wood, with the bloom of eternal youth upon her, and the smooth soft hand, on which was her wedding-ring, pointed at him.

It was in vain that he called on himself to rush forward out of that torrid and suffocating air. The front door was open, he had but to pass her and speed forth safe into the night. But no power from his will reached his limbs; his will screamed to him, "Go, go! Push by her: it is but a phantom which you fear!" but muscle and sinew were in mutiny, and step by step he retreated before that pointing finger and the radiant shape that advanced on him. The flames that flickered over the floor had discovered the paraffin he had spilt, and leaped up his leg.

Just one spot in his brain retained lucidity from the encompassing terror. Somewhere behind that barrier of fire there was the second door into the garden. He had but cursorily attempted to unlock its rusty wards; now, surely, the knowledge that there alone was escape would give strength to his hand. He leaped backwards through the flames, still with eyes fixed on her who ever advanced in time with his retreat, and turning, wrestled and strove with the key. Something snapped in his hand, and there still in the keyhole was the bare shaft.

Holding his breath, for the heat scorched his throat, he groped towards where he knew was the window through which he had first seen her that night. The flames licked fiercely round it, but there, beneath his hand, was the hasp, and he threw it open. At that the wind poured in as through the nozzle of a plied bellows, and Death rose high and bright around him. Through the flames, as he sank to the floor, a face radiant with revenge smiled on him.

INSCRUTABLE DECREES

I had found nothing momentous in the more august pages of *The Times* that morning, and so, just because I was lazy and unwilling to embark on a host of businesses that were waiting for me, I turned to the first page and, beginning with the seventh column, pondered profoundly over "Situations Vacant," and hoped that the "Gentlewoman fond of games," who desired the position of governess, would find the very thing to suit her. I glanced at the notices of lectures to be delivered under the auspices of various learned societies, and was thankful that I had not got to give or to listen to any of them. I debated over "Business Opportunities"; I vainly tried to conjecture clues to mysterious "Personal" paragraphs, and, still pursuing my sideways, crab-fashion course, came to "Deaths Continued."

There, with a shock of arrest, I saw that Sybil Rorke, widow of the late Sir Ernest Rorke, had died at Torquay, suddenly, at the age of thirty-two. It seemed strange that there should be only this bare announcement concerning a woman who at one time had been so well-known and dazzling a figure; and turning to the obituary notices, I found that my inattentive skimming had overlooked a paragraph there of appreciation and regret. She had died during her sleep, and it was announced that an inquest would be held. My laziness then had been of some use, for Archie Rorke, distant cousin but successor to Sir Ernest's estates and title, was arriving that evening to spend a few country days with me, and I was glad to have known this before he came. How it would affect him, or whether, indeed, it would affect him at all, I had no idea.

What a mysterious affair it had been! No one, I supposed, knew the history of it except he, now that Lady Rorke was dead. If anyone knew, it should have been myself, and yet Archie, my oldest friend, whose best man I was to have been, had never opened his lips to a syllable of explanation. I knew, in fact, no whit more than the whole world knew, namely, that a year after Sir Ernest Rorke's death the engagement of his widow to the new baronet, Sir Archibald Rorke, was made public, and that within a fortnight of the date fixed for the wedding it was laconically announced that the marriage would not take place. When, on seeing that, I rang Archie up on the telephone, I was told that he had already left London, and he wrote to me a few days later from Lincote – the place in Hampshire, which he had inherited from his cousin – saying that he had nothing to tell me about the breaking off of his engagement beyond the fact that it was true. The whole – he had written a word and carefully erased it – episode was now an excised leaf from his life. He was proposing to stay down at Lincote alone for a month or so, and would then turn on to the new page.

Lady Rorke, so I heard, had also left London immediately and passed the summer in Italy. Then she took a furnished house in Torquay, where she lived for the remainder of the year which intervened between the breaking off of her engagement and her death. She cut herself completely off from all her friends – and no woman, surely, ever commanded a larger host of them – saw nobody, seldom went outside her house and garden, and observed the same unbroken silence as did Archie about what had happened. And now, with all her youth and charm and beauty, she had gone down dumb into the Great Silence.

With the prospect of seeing Archie that evening it was no wonder that the thought of Lady Rorke ran all day in my head like a tune heard long ago which now recalled itself to my mind in scattered staves of melody. Meetings and talks with her, phrase by phrase, reconstructed themselves, and as these memories grew definite and complete I found that, even as before, when I was actually experiencing them, there lurked underneath the gay rhythms and joyousness something *macabre* and mysterious. To-day that was accentuated, whereas before when I listened for it, trying to isolate it from the rest and so perhaps dispel it, it was always overscored by some triumphant crescendo: her presence diverted eye and ear alike. Yet such a simile halts; perhaps, still in simile, I shall more accurately define this underlying "something" by saying that her presence was like some gorgeous rose-bush, full of flowers, and sun, and sweetness; then, even as one admired and applauded and inhaled, one saw that among its buds and blossoms there emerged the spikes of some other plant, bitter and poisonous, but growing from the same soil as the rose, and intertwined with it. But immediately a fresh glory met your eye, a fresh fragrance enchanted you.

As I rummaged among my memories of her, certain scenes which significantly illustrated this curiously vivid impression stirred and made themselves manifest to me, and now they were not broken in upon by her presence. One such occurred on the first evening that I ever met her, which was in the summer before the death of her husband. The moment that she entered the room where we were waiting before dinner for her arrival, the stale, sultry air of a June evening grew fresh and effervescent; never have I come across so radiant and infectious a vitality. She was tall and big, with the splendour of the Juno-type, and though she was then close on thirty, the iridescence of girlhood was still hers. Without effort she Pied-pipered a rather stodgy party to dance to her flutings, she caused everyone to become silly and pleased and full of laughter. At her bidding we indulged in ridiculous games, dumb-crambo, and what not, and after that the carpet was rolled up and we capered to the strains of a gramophone. And then the incident occurred.

I was standing with her, for a breath of air, on the balcony outside the drawing-room windows which faced the park. She had just made a great curtsey to a slip of the moon that rose above the trees and had borrowed a shilling of me in order to turn it.

"No, I can't swear that I believe in moon-luck," she said, "but after all it does no harm, and, in case it's true, you can't afford to make an enemy of her. Ah, what's that?"

A thrush, attracted by the lights inside, had flown between us, dashed itself against the window, and now lay fluttering on the ground at our feet. Instantly she was all pity and tenderness. She picked up the bird, examined it, and found that its wing was broken.

"Ah, poor thing!" she said. "Look, its wing-bone is snapped; the end protrudes. And how terrified it is! What are we to do?"

It was clear that the kindest thing to do would be to put the bird out of its pain, but when I suggested that, she took a step back from me, and covered it with her other hand. Her eyes gleamed, her mouth smiled, and I saw the tip of her tongue swiftly pass over her lips as if licking them.

"No, that would be a terrible thing to do," she said. "I shall take it home with me ever so carefully, and watch over it. I am afraid it is badly hurt. But it may live."

Suddenly – perhaps it was that swift licking of her lips that suggested the thought to me – I felt instinctively that she was not so much pitiful as pleased. She stood there with eyes fixed on it, as it feebly struggled in her hands.

And then her face clouded; over its brightness there came a look of displeasure, of annoyance.

"I'm afraid it is dying," she said. "Its poor frightened eyes are closing."

The bird fluttered once more, then its legs stretched themselves stiffly out, and it lay still. She tossed it out of her hands on to the paved balcony, with a little shrug of her shoulders.

"What a fuss over a bird," she said. "It was silly of it to fly against the glass. But I have too soft a heart; I cannot bear that the poor creatures should die. Let us go in and have one more romp. Oh, here is your shilling; I hope it will have brought me good luck. And then I must get home. My husband – do you know him? – always sits up till I get back, and he will scold me for being so late!"

There, then, was my first meeting with her, and there, too, were the spikes of the poisonous plant pushing up among the magnificence of her roses. And yet, so I thought to myself then, and so I think to myself now, I perhaps was utterly wrong about it all, in thus attributing to her a secret glee of which she was wholly incapable. So, with a certain effort I wiped the impression I had received off my mind, determining to consider myself quite mistaken. But, involuntarily, my mind as if to justify itself in having delineated such a picture, proceeded to delineate another.

Very shortly after that first meeting I received from her a charming note, asking me to dine with her on a date not far distant. I telephoned a delighted acceptance, for, indeed, I wanted then, even as I did this morning, to convince myself that I was wholly in error concerning my interpretation of that incident concerning the thrush. Though I hold that no man has the right to accept the hospitality offered by one he does not like, in all points except one I admired and liked Lady Rorke immensely and wished to get rid of that one. So I gratefully accepted, and then hurried out on a dismal and overdue visit to the dentist's. In the waiting-room was a girl of about twelve, with a hand nursing a rueful face, and from time to time she stifled a sob of pain or apprehension. I was just wondering whether it would be a breach of waiting-room etiquette to attempt to administer comfort or supply diversion, when the door opened and in came Lady Rorke. She laughed delightfully when she saw me.

"Hurrah! You're another occupant of the condemned cell," she said, "and very soon we shall both be sent for to the scaffold. I can't describe to you what a coward I am about it. Why haven't we got beaks like birds?—"

Her glance fell on the forlorn little figure by the window, with the rueful face and the wet eyes.

"Why, here's another of us," she said. "And have they sent you to the dentist's all alone, my dear?"

"Y – yes."

"How horrid of them!" said Lady Rorke. "They've sent me alone, too, and I think it's most unfeeling. But you shan't be alone, anyhow, I'll come in with you, and sit by you, if you like that, and box the man's ears for him if he hurts you. Or shall you and I set on him, as soon as we've got him by himself, and take out all his teeth one after the other? Just to teach him to be a dentist."

A faint smile began to break through the clouds.

"Oh, will you come in with me?" she asked. "I shan't mind nearly so much, then. It's – it's got to come out, you know, and I mayn't have gas."

Just the same gleam of a smile as I had seen on Lady Rorke's face once before quivered there now, a light not of pity, surely.

"Ah, but it won't ache any more after that," she said, "and after all, it is so soon over. You'll just open your mouth as if you were going to put the largest of all strawberries into it, and you'll hold tight on to my hand, and the dentist takes up something which you needn't look at—"

There was a want of tact in the vividness of this picture, and the child began to sob again.

"Oh, don't, don't!" she cried.

Again the door opened, and she clung to Lady Rorke.

"Oh, I know it's for me!" she wailed.

Lady Rorke bent over her, scanning her terrified face.

"Come along, my dear," she said, "and it will be over in no time. You'll be back here again before this gentleman can count a hundred, and he'll have all his troubles in front of him still."

Again this morning I tried to expunge from that picture, so trivial and yet so vivid to me, the sinister something which seemed to connect it with the incident about the thrush, and, leaving it, my mind strayed on over other reminiscences of Lady Rorke. Before the season was over I had got to know her well, and the better I knew her the more I marvelled at that many-petalled vitality, which never ceased unfolding itself. She entertained largely, and had that crowning gift of a good hostess, namely, that she enjoyed her own parties quite enormously. She was a very fine horse-woman, and after being up till dawn at some dance, she would be in the Row by half-past eight on a peculiarly vicious mare to whom she seemed to pay only the most cursory attention. She had a good knowledge of music, she dressed amazingly, she was charming to her meagre little husband, playing piquet with him by the hour (which was the only thing, apart from herself, that he cared about), and if in this modern democratic London there could be said to be a queen, there is no doubt who that season would have worn the crown. Less publicly, she was a great student of the psychical and occult, and I remembered hearing that she was herself possessed of very remarkable mediumistic gifts. But to me that was a matter of hearsay, for I never was present at any séance of hers.

Yet through the triumphant music of her pageant, there sounded, to my ears at least, fragments of a very ugly tune. It was not only in these two instances of its emergence that I heard it, it was chiefly and most persistently audible in her treatment of Archie Rorke, her husband's cousin. Everyone knew, for none could help knowing, that he was desperately in love with her, and it is impossible to imagine that she alone was ignorant of it. It is, no doubt, the instinct of many women to fan a passion which they do not share, and which they have no intention of indulging, just as the male instinct is to gratify a passion that he does not really feel, but there are limits to mercilessness. She was not "cruel to be kind"; she was kind to be demoniacally cruel. She had him always by her; she gave him those little touches and comrade-like licences which meant nothing to her, but crazed him with thirst; she held the glass close to his lips and then tilted it up and showed it him empty. The more charitable explanation was that she, perhaps, knew that her husband could not live long, and that she intended to marry Archie, and such, so it subsequently appeared, her intentions were. But when I saw her feeding him with husks and putting an empty glass to his lips, nothing, to my mind, could account for her treatment of him except a rapture of cruelty at the sight of his aching. And somehow, awfully and aptly, that seemed to fit in with the affair of the thrush, and the meeting with the forlorn child in the dentist's waiting-room. Yet ever, through that gruesome twilight, there blazed forth her charm and her beauty and the beam of her joyous vitality, and I would cudgel myself for my nasty interpretations.

It was early in the spring of next year that I was spending a week-end with her and her husband at Lincote. She had suggested my coming down on Saturday morning before the party assembled later in the day, and at lunch I was alone with her husband and her. Sir Ernest was very silent; he looked ill and haggard, and, in fact, hardly spoke a word except when suddenly he turned to the butler and said, "Has anything been heard of the child yet?" He was told that there was no news, and subsided into silence again. I thought that some queer shadow as of suspense or anxiety crossed Lady Rorke's face at the question; but on the answer, it cleared off again, and, as if to sweep the subject wholly away, she asked me if I could tolerate a saunter with her through the woods till her guests arrived.

Out she came like some splendid Diana of the Forests, and like the goddess's was the swift, swinging pace of her saunter. Spring all round was riotous in blossom and bird-song; it was just that ecstatic moment of the year when the hounds of spring have run winter to death, and as we gained the high ridge of down above the woods she stopped and threw her arms wide.

"Oh, the sense of spring!" she cried. "The daffodils, and the west wind, and the shadows of the clouds. How I wish I could take the whole lot into my arms and hug them. Miracles are flowering every moment now in the country, while the only miracle in London is the mud. What sunshine, what air! Drink them in, for they are the one divine medicine. One wants that medicine sometimes, for there are sad things and terrible things all round us, pain and anguish, and decay. Yet I suppose that even those call out the splendour of fortitude or endurance. Even when one looks on a struggle which one knows is hopeless, it warms the heart to see it."

The gleam that shone from her paled, her arms dropped, and she moved on. Then, soft of voice and soft of eye, she spoke again.

"Such a sad thing happened here two days ago," she said. "A small girl – now what was her name? Yes – Ellen Davenport – brought a note from the village up to the house. I was out, so she left it, and started, it is supposed, to go back home. She has not been seen since. Descriptions of her were circulated in all the villages for miles round; but, as you heard at lunch, there has been no news of her, and the copses and coverts in the park have been searched, but with no result. And yet out of that comes splendour. I went to see her mother yesterday, bowed down with grief, but she won't give up hope. 'If it is God's will,' she said to me, 'we shall find my Ellen alive; and if we find her dead, it will be God's will, too.'"

She paused.

"But I didn't ask you down here to moan over tragedies," she said. "I wanted you after all your weeks in town to come and have a spring-cleaning. Doesn't the wind take the dust out of you, like one of those sucking-machines which you put on to carpets? And the sun! Make a sponge of yourself and soak it up till you're dripping with it."

For a couple of miles, at the least, we kept along this high ridge of down, and the larks were springing from the grass, vocal with song uncongealed, as they aspired and sank again, dropping at last dumb and spent with rapture. Then we descended steeply, through the woods and glades of the park, past thickets of cat-kinned sallows, and of willows with soft moleskin buttons, and in the hollows the daffodils were dancing, and the herbs of the springtime were pushing up through the brittle withered stuff of the winter. Then, passing along the one street of the red-tiled village, in which my companion pointed me out the house where the poor vanished girl had lived, we turned homewards across the grass and joined the road again at the bottom of the great lake that lies below the terraced gardens of the house.

This lake was artificial, made a hundred years ago by the erection of a huge dam across the dip of the valley, so that the stream which flowed down it was thereby confined and must needs form this sheet of water before it found outlet again through the sluices. At the centre the dam is some twenty-five feet in height, and by the side of the road which crosses it clumps of rhododendrons lean out over the deep water. The margin on the side towards the lake is reinforced with concrete, now mossy and overgrown with herbage, and the face of it burrows down to the level of the bottom of the dam through four fathoms of dusky water. The lake was high and the overflow poured sonorously through the sluices, and the sun in the west made broken rainbows in the foam of its outpouring.

As we paused there a moment, my companion seemed the incarnation of the sights and sounds that went to the spell of the spring; singing larks and dancing daffodils, west wind and rain-bowed foam and, no less, the dark, deep water, were all distilled into her radiant vitality.

"And now for the house again," she said, going briskly up the steep slope. "Is it inhospitable of me to wish that no one was coming except, of course, our delightful Archie? A houseful brings London into the country, and we shall talk scandal and stir up mud instead of watching miracles."

Another faint memory of her lingered somewhere in the dusk, and I groped for it, as one gropes in slime for the roots of a water-plant, and pulled it out. A notorious murderer had been guillotined that morning in France, and in some Sunday paper next day there was a brutal, brilliant, inexcusable little sketch of his being led out between guards for the final scene at dawn outside the prison at Versailles. And, as I wrote my name in Lady Rorke's visitors' book on Monday morning, I spilt a blot of ink on the page and hastily had recourse to the blotting-pad on her writing-table in order to minimise the disfigurement. Inside it was this unpardonable picture, cut out and put away, and I thought of the thrush and the dentist's waiting-room—

A month afterwards her husband died, after three weeks of intolerable torment. The doctor insisted on his having two trained nurses, but Lady Rorke never left him. She was present at the painful dressings of the wound from the operation that only prolonged the misery of his existence, and even slept on the sofa of the room where he lay.

Archie Rorke arrived that evening. He let me know at once that he had seen the announcement of Lady Rorke's death, and said no more about it till later, when he and I were left alone over the fire in the smoking-room. He looked round to see that the door was shut behind the last bedgoer of my little party, and then turned to me.

"I've got to tell you something," he said. "It'll take half an hour, so to-morrow will do if you want to be off."

"But I don't," said I.

He pulled himself together from his sprawling sunkenness in his chair.

"Very well," he said. "What I want to tell you is the story of the breaking-off of my engagement with Sybil. I have often wanted to do so before, but while she was alive, as you will presently see, I could tell nobody. I shall ask you, when you know everything, whether you think I could have done otherwise. And please do not interrupt me till I have finished, unless there is something you don't understand, for it won't be very easy to get through with it. But I think I can make it intelligible."

He was silent a moment, and I saw his face working and twitching.

"I must tell somebody," he said, "and I choose you, unless you mind it awfully. But I simply can't bear it alone any more."

"Go on, then, old boy," I said. "I'm glad you chose me, do you know. And I won't interrupt."

Archie spoke.

"A week or two only before our marriage was to have taken place," he said, "I went down to Lincote for a couple of days. I had had the house done up and re-decorated, and now the work was finished and I wanted to see that all was in order. Nothing could be worthy of Sybil, but – well, you can guess, more or less, what my feelings were.

"For a week before there had been very heavy rains, and the lake – you know it – below the garden was very high, higher than I had ever seen it: the water poured over the road across the dam which leads to the village. Under the weight and press of it a great crack had appeared in the concrete with which it is faced, and there was danger of the dam being carried away. If that happened the whole lake would have been suddenly released and no end of damage might have been done. It was therefore necessary to draw off the water as fast as possible to relieve the pressure and repair the crack. This was done by means of big siphons. For two days we had them working, but the crack seemed to extend right to the foundations of the dam, and before it could be repaired all the water in the lake would have to be drawn off. I was just leaving for town, when the foreman came up to the house to tell me that they had found something there. In the ooze and mud at the base of the dam, twenty-five feet below water-level, they had come upon the body of a young girl."

He gripped the arms of his chair tight. Little did he know that I was horribly aware of what he was going to tell me next.

"About a month before my cousin Ernest's death," he said, "a mysterious affair happened in the village. A girl named Ellen Davenport had disappeared. She came up one afternoon to the house with a note, and was never seen again, dead or alive. Her disappearance was now explained. A chain of beads round the neck and various fragments of clothing established, beyond any doubt, the identity of what they had found at the bottom of the lake. I waited for the inquest, telegraphing to Sybil that business had detained me, and then returned to town, not intending to tell her what that business was, for our marriage was close at hand and it was not a topic one would choose. She was very superstitious, you know, and I thought that it would shock her. That she would feel it to be unlucky and ill-omened. So I said nothing to her.

"Sybil had extraordinary mediumistic powers. She did not often exercise them and she never would give a séance to any one she did not know extremely well, for she believed that people brought with them the spiritual influences with which they were surrounded, and that there was the possibility of very evil intelligences being set free. But she had sat several times with me, and I had witnessed some very remarkable manifestations. Her procedure was to put herself, by abstraction of her mind, into a state of trance, and spirits of the dead who were connected with the sitters could then communicate through her. On one occasion my mother, whom she had never seen, and who died many years ago, spoke through her and told me certain facts which Sybil could not have known, and which I did not know. But an old friend of my mother's, still alive, told me that they were correct. They were of an exceedingly private nature. Sybil also, so she told me, could produce materialisations, but up till now I had never seen any. A remarkable thing about her mediumship was that she would sometimes regain consciousness from her trance while still these communications were being made, and she knew what was going on. She could hear herself speak and be mentally aware of what she was saying. On the occasion, for instance, of which I have told you, when my mother spoke to me she was in this state. The same thing occurred at the sitting of which I shall now speak.

"That night, on my return to London, she and I dined alone. I felt a very strong desire, for which I could not account, that she should hold a sitting – just herself and me – and she consented. We sat in her room, with a shaded lamp, but there was sufficient illumination for me to see her quite distinctly, for her face was towards the light. There was a small table in front of us covered with a dark cloth. She sat close to it, in a high chair, composed herself, and almost immediately went into trance. Her head fell forward and by her slow breathing and her absolute immobility I knew she was unconscious. For a long time we sat there in silence, and I began to think that we should get no manifestations at all, and that the sitting, as sometimes was the case, would be a failure; but then I saw that something was happening."

His hands, with which he gripped the arms of his chair, were trembling. Twice he tried to speak, but it was not till the third attempt that he mastered himself.

"There was forming a mist above the table," he said. "It was slightly luminous and it spread upwards, pillar-shaped, in height between two and three feet. Then I saw that below the outlying skeins of it something was materialising. It moulded itself into human shape, rising waist-high from the table, and presently shoulders and arms and neck and head were visible, and features began to outline themselves. For some time it remained vague and fluid, swaying backwards and forwards a little; then very quickly it solidified, and there, close in front of me, was the half-figure of a young girl. The eyes were still closed, but now they opened. Round her neck was a chain of beads just such as I had seen laid by the body that had been found in the lake. And then I spoke to her, asking her who she was, though I already knew.

"Her answer was no more than a whisper, but quite distinct.

"'Ellen Davenport,' she said.

"A disordered terror seized me. Yet perhaps this little white figure, with its wide-gazing eyes, was some hallucination, something that had no objective existence at all. All day the thought of the poor kiddie whose remains I had seen taken out of the ooze at the bottom of the lake had been vivid in my mind, and I tried to think that what I saw was no more than some strange projection of my thought. And yet I felt it was not so; it was independent of myself. And why was it made manifest, and on what errand had it come? I had pressed Sybil to give me this séance, and God knows what I would have given not to have done so! For one thing I was thankful, namely, that she was in unconscious trance. Perhaps the phantom would fade again before she came out of it.

"And then I heard a stir of movement from the chair where she sat, and, turning, I saw that she had raised her head. Her eyes were open and on her face such a mask of terror as I have never known human being could wear. Recognition was there, too; I saw that Sybil knew who the phantom was.

"The figure that palely gleamed above the table turned its head towards her, and once more the white lips opened.

"'Yes, I am Ellen Davenport,' she said.

"The whisper grew louder.

"'You might have saved me,' she said, 'or you might have tried to save me; but you watched me struggling till I sank.'

"And then the apparition vanished. It did not die away; it was there clear and distinct one moment, at the next it was gone. Sybil and I were sitting alone in her room with the low-burning lamp, and the silence sang in my ears.

"I got up and turned on the switch that kindled the electric lights, and knew that something within me had grown cold and that something had snapped. She still sat where she was, not looking at me at all, but blankly in front of her. She said no word of denial in answer to the terrible accusation that had been uttered. And I think I was glad of that, for there are times when it is not only futility to deny, but blasphemy. For my part, I could neither look at her nor speak to her. I remember holding out my hands to the empty grate, as if there had been a fire burning there. And standing there I heard her rise, and drearily wondered what she would say and knew how useless it would be. And then I heard the whisper of her dress on the carpet and the noise of the door opening and shutting, and when I turned I found that I was alone in the room. Presently I let myself out of the house."

There was a long pause, but I did not break it, for I felt he had not quite finished.

"I had loved her with my whole heart," he said, "and she knew it. Perhaps that was why I never attempted to see her again and why she did not attempt to see me. That little white figure would always have been with us, for she could not deny the reality of it and the truth of that which it had spoken. That's my story, then. You needn't even tell me if you think I could have done differently, for I knew I couldn't. And she couldn't."

He rose.

"I see there is to be an inquest," he said. "I hope they will find that she killed herself. It will mean, won't it, that her remorse was unbearable. And that's atonement."

He moved towards the door.

"Inscrutable decrees," he said.

The Gardener

Two friends of mine, Hugh Grainger and his wife, had taken for a month of Christmas holiday the house in which we were to witness such strange manifestations, and when I received an invitation from them to spend a fortnight there I returned them an enthusiastic affirmative. Well already did I know that pleasant heathery country-side, and most intimate was my acquaintance with the subtle hazards of its most charming golf-links. Golf, I was given to understand, was to occupy the solid day for Hugh and me, so that Margaret should never be obliged to set her hand to the implements with which the game, so detestable to her, was conducted . . .

I arrived there while yet the daylight lingered, and as my hosts were out, I took a ramble round the place. The house and garden stood on a plateau facing south; below it were a couple of acres of pasture that sloped down to a vagrant stream crossed by a foot-bridge, by the side of which stood a thatched cottage with a vegetable patch surrounding it. A path ran close past this across the pasture from a wicket-gate in the garden, conducted you over the foot-bridge, and, so my remembered sense of geography told me, must constitute a short cut to the links that lay not half a mile beyond. The cottage itself was clearly on the land of the little estate, and I at once supposed it to be the gardener's house. What went against so obvious and simple a theory was that it appeared to be untenanted. No wreath of smoke, though the evening was chilly, curled from its chimneys, and, coming closer, I fancied it had that air of "waiting" about it which we so often conjure into unused habitations. There it stood, with no sign of life whatever about it, though ready, as its apparently perfect state of repair seemed to warrant, for fresh tenants to put the breath of life into it again. Its little garden, too, though the palings were neat and newly painted, told the same tale; the beds were untended and unweeded, and in the flower-border by the front door was a row of chrysanthemums, which had withered on their stems. But all this was but the impression of a moment, and I did not pause as I passed it, but crossed the foot-bridge and went on up the heathery slope that lay beyond. My geography was not at fault, for presently I saw the club-house just in front of me. Hugh no doubt would be just about coming in from his afternoon round, and so we would walk back together. On reaching the club-house, however, the steward told me that not five minutes before Mrs. Grainger had called in her car for her husband, and I therefore retraced my steps by the path along which I had already come. But I made a detour, as a golfer will, to walk up the fairway of the seventeenth and eighteenth holes just for the pleasure of recognition, and looked respectfully at the yawning sandpit which so inexorably guards the eighteenth green, wondering in what circumstances I should visit it next, whether with a step complacent and superior, knowing that my ball reposed safely on the green beyond, or with the heavy footfall of one who knows that laborious delving lies before him.

The light of the winter evening had faded fast, and when I crossed the foot-bridge on my return the dusk had gathered. To my right, just beside the path, lay the cottage, the whitewashed walls of which gleamed whitely in the gloaming; and as I turned my glance back from it to the rather narrow plank which bridged the stream I thought I caught out of the tail of my eye some light from one of its windows, which thus disproved my theory that it was untenanted. But when I looked directly at it again I saw that I was mistaken: some reflection in the glass of the red lines of sunset in the west must have deceived me, for in the inclement twilight it looked more desolate than ever. Yet I lingered by the wicket gate in its low palings, for though all exterior evidence bore witness to its emptiness, some inexplicable feeling assured me, quite irrationally, that this was not so, and that there was somebody there. Certainly there was nobody visible, but, so this absurd idea informed me, he might be at the back of the cottage concealed from me by the intervening structure, and, still oddly, still unreasonably, it became a matter of importance to my mind to ascertain whether this was so or not, so clearly had my perceptions told me that the place was empty, and so firmly had some conviction assured me that it was tenanted. To cover my inquisitiveness, in case there was someone there, I could inquire whether this path was a short cut to the house at which I was staying, and, rather rebelling at what I was doing, I went through the small garden, and rapped at the door. There was no answer, and, after waiting for a response to a second summons, and having tried the door and found it locked, I made the circuit of the house. Of course there was no one there, and I told myself that I was just like a man who looks under his bed for a burglar and would be beyond measure astonished if he found one.

My hosts were at the house when I arrived, and we spent a cheerful two hours before dinner in such desultory and eager conversation as is proper between friends who have not met for some time. Between

Hugh Grainger and his wife it is always impossible to light on a subject which does not vividly interest one or other of them, and golf, politics, the needs of Russia, cooking, ghosts, the possible victory over Mount Everest, and the income tax were among the topics which we passionately discussed. With all these plates spinning, it was easy to whip up any one of them, and the subject of spooks generally was lighted upon again and again.

"Margaret is on the high road to madness," remarked Hugh on one of these occasions, "for she has begun using planchette. If you use planchette for six months, I am told, most careful doctors will conscientiously certify you as insane. She's got five months more before she goes to Bedlam."

"Does it work?" I asked.

"Yes, it says most interesting things," said Margaret. "It says things that never entered my head. We'll try it to-night."

"Oh, not to-night," said Hugh. "Let's have an evening off."

Margaret disregarded this.

"It's no use asking planchette questions," she went on, "because there is in your mind some sort of answer to them. If I ask whether it will be fine to-morrow, for instance, it is probably I – though indeed I don't mean to push – who makes the pencil say 'yes.'"

"And then it usually rains," remarked Hugh.

"Not always: don't interrupt. The interesting thing is to let the pencil write what it chooses. Very often it only makes loops and curves – though they may mean something – and every now and then a word comes, of the significance of which I have no idea whatever, so I clearly couldn't have suggested it. Yesterday evening, for instance, it wrote 'gardener' over and over again. Now what did that mean? The gardener here is a Methodist with a chin-beard. Could it have meant him? Oh, it's time to dress. Please don't be late, my cook is so sensitive about soup."

We rose, and some connection of ideas about "gardener" linked itself up in my mind.

"By the way, what's that cottage in the field by the foot-bridge?" I asked. "Is that the gardener's cottage?"

"It used to be," said Hugh. "But the chin-beard doesn't live there: in fact nobody lives there. It's empty. If I was owner here, I should put the chin-beard into it, and take the rent off his wages. Some people have no idea of economy. Why did you ask?"

I saw Margaret was looking at me rather attentively.

"Curiosity," I said. "Idle curiosity."

"I don't believe it was," said she.

"But it was," I said. "It was idle curiosity to know whether the house was inhabited. As I passed it, going down to the club-house, I felt sure it was empty, but coming back I felt so sure that there was someone there that I rapped at the door, and indeed walked round it."

Hugh had preceded us upstairs, as she lingered a little.

"And there was no one there?" she asked. "It's odd: I had just the same feeling as you about it."

"That explains planchette writing 'gardener' over and over again," said I. "You had the gardener's cottage on your mind."

"How ingenious!" said Margaret. "Hurry up and dress."

A gleam of strong moonlight between my drawn curtains when I went up to bed that night led me to look out. My room faced the garden and the fields which I had traversed that afternoon, and all was vividly illuminated by the full moon. The thatched cottage with its white walls close by the stream was very distinct, and once more, I suppose, the reflection of the light on the glass of one of its windows made it appear that the room was lit within. It struck me as odd that twice that day this illusion should have been presented to me, but now a yet odder thing happened. Even as I looked the light was extinguished.

The morning did not at all bear out the fine promise of the clear night, for when I woke the wind was squealing, and sheets of rain from the south-west were dashed against my panes. Golf was wholly out of the question, and, though the violence of the storm abated a little in the afternoon, the rain dripped with a steady sullenness. But I wearied of indoors, and, since the two others entirely refused to set foot outside, I went forth mackintoshed to get a breath of air. By way of an object in my tramp, I took the road to the links in preference to the muddy short cut through the fields, with the intention of engaging a couple of caddies for Hugh and myself next morning, and lingered awhile over illustrated papers in the smoking-room. I must have read for longer than I knew, for a sudden beam of sunset light suddenly illuminated my page, and looking up, I saw that the rain had ceased, and that evening was fast coming on. So instead of taking the long detour by the road again, I set forth homewards by the path across the fields. That gleam of sunset was the last of the day, and once again, just as twenty-four hours ago, I crossed the foot-bridge in the gloaming. Till that moment, as far as I was aware, I had not thought at all about the cottage there, but now in a flash the light I had seen there last night, suddenly extinguished, recalled itself to my mind, and at the same moment I felt that invincible conviction that the cottage was tenanted. Simultaneously in these swift processes of thought I looked towards it, and saw standing by the door the figure of a man. In the dusk I could distinguish nothing of his face, if indeed it was turned to me, and only got the impression of a tallish fellow, thickly built. He opened the door, from which there came a dim light as of a lamp, entered, and shut it after him.

So then my conviction was right. Yet I had been distinctly told that the cottage was empty: who, then, was he that entered as if returning home? Once more, this time with a certain qualm of fear, I rapped on the door, intending to put some trivial question; and rapped again, this time more drastically, so that there could be no question that my summons was unheard. But still I got no reply, and finally I tried the handle of the door. It was locked. Then, with difficulty mastering an increasing terror, I made the circuit of the cottage, peering into each unshuttered window. All was dark within, though but two minutes ago I had seen the gleam of light escape from the opened door.

Just because some chain of conjecture was beginning to form itself in my mind, I made no allusion to this odd adventure, and after dinner Margaret, amid protests from Hugh, got out the planchette which had persisted in writing "gardener." My surmise was, of course, utterly fantastic, but I wanted to convey no suggestion of any sort to Margaret . . . For a long time the pencil skated over her paper making loops and curves and peaks like a temperature chart, and she had begun to yawn and weary over her experiment before any coherent word emerged. And then, in the oddest way, her head nodded forward and she seemed to have fallen asleep.

Hugh looked up from his book and spoke in a whisper to me.

"She fell asleep the other night over it," he said.

Margaret's eyes were closed, and she breathed the long, quiet breaths of slumber, and then her hand began to move with a curious firmness. Right across the big sheet of paper went a level line of writing, and at the end her hand stopped with a jerk, and she woke.

She looked at the paper.

"Hullo," she said. "Ah, one of you has been playing a trick on me!"

We assured her that this was not so, and she read what she had written.

"Gardener, gardener," it ran. "I am the gardener. I want to come in. I can't find her here."

"O Lord, that gardener again!" said Hugh.

Looking up from the paper, I saw Margaret's eyes fixed on mine, and even before she spoke I knew what her thought was.

"Did you come home by the empty cottage?" she asked.

"Yes: why?"

"Still empty?" she said in a low voice. "Or – or anything else?"

I did not want to tell her just what I had seen – or what, at any rate, I thought I had seen. If there was going to be anything odd, anything worth observation, it was far better that our respective impressions should not fortify each other.

"I tapped again, and there was no answer," I said.

Presently there was a move to bed: Margaret initiated it, and after she had gone upstairs Hugh and I went to the front door to interrogate the weather. Once more the moon shone in a clear sky, and we strolled out along the flagged path that fronted the house. Suddenly Hugh turned quickly and pointed to the angle of the house.

"Who on earth is that?" he said. "Look! There! He has gone round the corner."

I had but the glimpse of a tallish man of heavy build.

"Didn't you see him?" asked Hugh. "I'll just go round the house, and find him; I don't want anyone prowling round us at night. Wait here, will you, and if he comes round the other corner ask him what his business is."

Hugh had left me, in our stroll, close by the front door which was open, and there I waited until he should have made his circuit. He had hardly disappeared when I heard, quite distinctly, a rather quick but heavy footfall coming along the paved walk towards me from the opposite direction. But there was absolutely no one to be seen who made this sound of rapid walking. Closer and closer to me came the steps of the invisible one, and then with a shudder of horror I felt somebody unseen push by me as I stood on the threshold. That shudder was not merely of the spirit, for the touch of him was that of ice on my hand. I tried to seize this impalpable intruder, but he slipped from me, and next moment I heard his steps on the parquet of the floor inside. Some door within opened and shut, and I heard no more of him. Next moment Hugh came running round the corner of the house from which the sound of steps had approached.

"But where is he?" he asked. "He was not twenty yards in front of me – a big, tall fellow."

"I saw nobody," I said. "I heard his step along the walk, but there was nothing to be seen."

"And then?" asked Hugh.

"Whatever it was seemed to brush by me, and go into the house," said I.

There had certainly been no sound of steps on the bare oak stairs, and we searched room after room through the ground floor of the house. The dining-room door and that of the smoking-room were locked, that into the drawing-room was open, and the only other door which could have furnished the impression of an opening and a shutting was that into the kitchen and servants' quarters. Here again our quest was fruitless; through pantry and scullery and boot-room and servants' hall we searched, but all was empty and quiet. Finally we came to the kitchen, which too was empty. But by the fire there was set a rocking-chair, and this was oscillating to and fro as if someone, lately sitting there, had just quitted it. There it stood gently rocking, and this seemed to convey the sense of a presence, invisible now, more than even the sight of him who surely had been sitting there could have done. I remember wanting to steady it and stop it, and yet my hand refused to go forth to it.

What we had seen, and in especial what we had not seen, would have been sufficient to furnish most people with a broken night, and assuredly I was not among the strong-minded exceptions. Long I lay wide-eyed and open-eared, and when at last I dozed I was plucked from the border-land of sleep by the sound, muffled but unmistakable, of someone moving about the house. It occurred to me that the steps might be those of Hugh conducting a lonely exploration, but even while I wondered a tap came at the door of communication between our rooms, and, in answer to my response, it appeared that he had come to see whether it was I thus uneasily wandering. Even as we spoke the step passed my door, and the stairs leading to the floor above creaked to its ascent. Next moment it sounded directly above our heads in some attics in the roof.

"Those are not the servants' bedrooms," said Hugh. "No one sleeps there. Let us look once more: it must be somebody."

With lit candles we made our stealthy way upstairs, and just when we were at the top of the flight, Hugh, a step ahead of me, uttered a sharp exclamation.

"But something is passing by me!" he said, and he clutched at the empty air. Even as he spoke, I experienced the same sensation, and the moment afterwards the stairs below us creaked again, as the unseen passed down.

All night long that sound of steps moved about the passages, as if someone was searching the house, and as I lay and listened that message which had come through the pencil of the planchette to Margaret's fingers occurred to me. "I want to come in. I cannot find her here." . . . Indeed someone had come in, and was sedulous in his search. He was the gardener, it would seem. But what gardener was this invisible seeker, and for whom did he seek?

Even as when some bodily pain ceases it is difficult to recall with any vividness what the pain was like, so next morning, as I dressed, I found myself vainly trying to recapture the horror of the spirit which had accompanied these nocturnal adventures. I remembered that something within me had sickened as I watched the movements of the rocking-chair the night before and as I heard the steps along the paved way outside, and by that invisible pressure against me knew that someone had entered the house. But now in the sane and tranquil morning, and all day under the serene winter sun, I could not realise what it had been. The presence, like the bodily pain, had to be there for the realisation of it, and all day it was absent. Hugh felt the same; he was even disposed to be humorous on the subject.

"Well, he's had a good look," he said, "whoever he is, and whomever he was looking for. By the way, not a word to Margaret, please. She heard nothing of these perambulations, nor of the entry of – of whatever it was. Not gardener, anyhow: who ever heard of a gardener spending his time walking about the house? If there were steps all over the potato-patch, I might have been with you."

Margaret had arranged to drive over to have tea with some friends of hers that afternoon, and in consequence Hugh and I refreshed ourselves at the club-house after our game, and it was already dusk when for the third day in succession I passed homewards by the whitewashed cottage. But to-night I had no sense of it being subtly occupied; it stood mournfully desolate, as is the way of untenanted houses, and no light nor semblance of such gleamed from its windows. Hugh, to whom I had told the odd impressions I had received there, gave them a reception as flippant as that which he had accorded to the memories of the night, and he was still being humorous about them when we came to the door of the house.

"A psychic disturbance, old boy," he said. "Like a cold in the head. Hullo, the door's locked."

He rang and rapped, and from inside came the noise of a turned key and withdrawn bolts.

"What's the door locked for?" he asked his servant who opened it.

The man shifted from one foot to the other.

"The bell rang half an hour ago, sir," he said, "and when I came to answer it there was a man standing outside, and—"

"Well?" asked Hugh.

"I didn't like the looks of him, sir," he said, "and I asked him his business. He didn't say anything, and then he must have gone pretty smartly away, for I never saw him go."

"Where did he seem to go?" asked Hugh, glancing at me.

"I can't rightly say, sir. He didn't seem to go at all. Something seemed to brush by me."

"That'll do," said Hugh rather sharply.

Margaret had not come in from her visit, but when soon after the crunch of the motor wheels was heard Hugh reiterated his wish that nothing should be said to her about the impression which now, apparently, a third person shared with us. She came in with a flush of excitement on her face.

"Never laugh at my planchette again," she said. "I've heard the most extraordinary story from Maud Ashfield – horrible, but so frightfully interesting."

"Out with it," said Hugh.

"Well, there was a gardener here," she said. "He used to live at that little cottage by the foot-bridge, and when the family were up in London he and his wife used to be caretakers and live here."

Hugh's glance and mine met: then he turned away.

I knew, as certainly as if I was in his mind, that his thoughts were identical with my own.

"He married a wife much younger than himself," continued Margaret, "and gradually he became frightfully jealous of her. And one day in a fit of passion he strangled her with his own hands. A little while after someone came to the cottage, and found him sobbing over her, trying to restore her. They went for the police, but before they came he had cut his own throat. Isn't it all horrible? But surely it's rather curious that the planchette said 'Gardener. I am the gardener. I want to come in. I can't find her here.' You see I knew nothing about it. I shall do planchette again to-night. Oh dear me, the post goes in half an hour, and I have a whole budget to send. But respect my planchette for the future, Hughie."

We talked the situation out when she had gone, but Hugh, unwillingly convinced and yet unwilling to admit that something more than coincidence lay behind that "planchette nonsense," still insisted that Margaret should be told nothing of what we had heard and seen in the house last night, and of the strange visitor who again this evening, so we must conclude, had made his entry.

"She'll be frightened," he said, "and she'll begin imagining things. As for the planchette, as likely as not it will do nothing but scribble and make loops. What's that? Yes: come in!"

There had come from somewhere in the room one sharp, peremptory rap. I did not think it came from the door, but Hugh, when no response replied to his words of admittance, jumped up and opened it. He took a few steps into the hall outside, and returned.

"Didn't you hear it?" he asked.

"Certainly. No one there?"

"Not a soul."

Hugh came back to the fireplace and rather irritably threw a cigarette which he had just lit into the fender.

"That was rather a nasty jar," he observed; "and if you ask me whether I feel comfortable, I can tell you I never felt less comfortable in my life. I'm frightened, if you want to know, and I believe you are too."

I hadn't the smallest intention of denying this, and he went on.

"We've got to keep a hand on ourselves," he said. "There's nothing so infectious as fear, and Margaret mustn't catch it from us. But there's something more than our fear, you know. Something has got into the house and we're up against it. I never believed in such things before. Let's face it for a minute. *What* is it anyhow?"

"If you want to know what I think it is," said I, "I believe it to be the spirit of the man who strangled his wife and then cut his throat. But I don't see how it can hurt us. We're afraid of our own fear really."

"But we're up against it," said Hugh. "And what will it do? Good Lord, if I only knew what it would do I shouldn't mind. It's the not knowing . . . Well, it's time to dress."

Margaret was in her highest spirits at dinner. Knowing nothing of the manifestations of that presence which had taken place in the last twenty-four hours, she thought it absorbingly interesting that her planchette should have "guessed" (so ran her phrase) about the gardener, and from that topic she flitted to an equally interesting form of patience for three which her friend had showed her, promising to initiate us into it after dinner. This she did, and, not knowing that we both above all things wanted to keep planchette at a distance, she was delighted with the success of her game. But suddenly she observed that the evening was burning rapidly away, and swept the cards together at the conclusion of a hand.

"Now just half an hour of planchette," she said.

"Oh, mayn't we play one more hand?" asked Hugh.

"It's the best game I've seen for years. Planchette will be dismally slow after this."

"Darling, if the gardener will only communicate again, it won't be slow," said she.

"But it is such drivel," said Hugh.

"How rude you are! Read your book, then."

Margaret had already got out her machine and a sheet of paper, when Hugh rose.

"Please don't do it to-night, Margaret," he said.

"But why? You needn't attend."

"Well, I ask you not to, anyhow," said he.

Margaret looked at him closely.

"Hughie, you've got something on your mind," she said. "Out with it. I believe you're nervous. You think there is something queer about. What is it?"

I could see Hugh hesitating as to whether to tell her or not, and I gathered that he chose the chance of her planchette inanely scribbling.

"Go on, then," he said.

Margaret hesitated: she clearly did not want to vex Hugh, but his insistence must have seemed to her most unreasonable.

"Well, just ten minutes," she said, "and I promise not to think of gardeners."

She had hardly laid her hand on the board when her head fell forward, and the machine began moving. I was sitting close to her, and as it rolled steadily along the paper the writing became visible.

"I have come in," it ran, "but still I can't find her. Are you hiding her? I will search the room where you are."

What else was written but still concealed underneath the planchette I did not know, for at that moment a current of icy air swept round the room, and at the door, this time unmistakably, came a loud, peremptory knock. Hugh sprang to his feet.

"Margaret, wake up," he said, "something is coming!"

The door opened, and there moved in the figure of a man. He stood just within the door, his head bent forward, and he turned it from side to side, peering, it would seem, with eyes staring and infinitely sad, into every corner of the room.

"Margaret, Margaret," cried Hugh again.

But Margaret's eyes were open too; they were fixed on this dreadful visitor.

"Be quiet, Hughie," she said below her breath, rising as she spoke. The ghost was now looking directly at her. Once the lips above the thick, rust-coloured beard moved, but no sound came forth, the mouth only moved and slavered. He raised his head, and, horror upon horror, I saw that one side of his neck was laid open in a red, glistening gash . . .

For how long that pause continued, when we all three stood stiff and frozen in some deadly inhibition to move or speak, I have no idea: I suppose that at the utmost it was a dozen seconds. Then the spectre turned, and went out as it had come. We heard his steps pass along the parqueted floor; there was the sound of bolts withdrawn from the front door, and with a crash that shook the house it slammed to.

"It's all over," said Margaret. "God have mercy on him!"

Now the reader may put precisely what construction he pleases on this visitation from the dead. He need not, indeed, consider it to have been a visitation from the dead at all, but say that there had been impressed on the scene, where this murder and suicide happened, some sort of emotional record, which in certain circumstances could translate itself into images visible and invisible. Waves of ether, or what not, may conceivably retain the impress of such scenes; they may be held, so to speak, in solution, ready to be precipitated. Or he may hold that the spirit of the dead man indeed made itself manifest, revisiting in some sort of spiritual penance and remorse the place where his crime was committed. Naturally, no materialist will entertain such an explanation for an instant, but then there is no one so obstinately unreasonable as the materialist. Beyond doubt a dreadful deed was done there, and Margaret's last utterance is not inapplicable.

Mr. Tilly's Séance

Mr. Tilly had only the briefest moment for reflection, when, as he slipped and fell on the greasy wood pavement at Hyde Park Corner, which he was crossing at a smart trot, he saw the huge traction-engine with its grooved ponderous wheels towering high above him.

"Oh, dear! oh, dear!" he said petulantly, "it will certainly crush me quite flat, and I shan't be able to be at Mrs. Cumberbatch's séance! Most provoking! A-ow!"

The words were hardly out of his mouth, when the first half of his horrid anticipations was thoroughly fulfilled. The heavy wheels passed over him from head to foot and flattened him completely out. Then the driver (too late) reversed his engine and passed over him again, and finally lost his head, whistled loudly and stopped. The policeman on duty at the corner turned quite faint at the sight of the catastrophe, but presently recovered sufficiently to hold up the traffic, and ran to see what on earth could be done. It was all so much "up" with Mr. Tilly that the only thing possible was to get the hysterical engine-driver to move clear. Then the ambulance from the hospital was sent for, and Mr. Tilly's remains, detached with great difficulty from the road (so firmly had they been pressed into it), were reverently carried away into the mortuary . . .

Mr. Tilly during this had experienced one moment's excruciating pain, resembling the severest neuralgia as his head was ground beneath the wheel, but almost before he realised it, the pain was past, and he found himself, still rather dazed, floating or standing (he did no know which) in the middle of the road. There had been no break in his consciousness; he perfectly recollected slipping, and wondered how he had managed to save himself. He saw the arrested traffic, the policeman with white wan face making suggestions to the gibbering engine-driver, and he received the very puzzling impression that the traction engine was all mixed up with him. He had a sensation of red-hot coals and boiling water and rivets all around him, but yet no feeling of scalding or burning or confinement. He was, on the contrary, extremely comfortable, and had the most pleasant consciousness of buoyancy and freedom. Then the engine puffed and the wheels went round, and immediately, to his immense surprise, he perceived his own crushed remains, flat as a biscuit, lying on the roadway. He identified them for certain by his clothes, which he had put on for the first time that morning, and one patent leather boot which had escaped demolition.

"But what on earth has happened?" he said. "Here am I, and yet that poor pressed flower of arms and legs is me – or rather I – also. And how terribly upset the driver looks. Why, I do believe that I've been run over! It did hurt for a moment, now I come to think of it . . . My good man, where are you shoving to? Don't you see me?"

He addressed these two questions to the policeman, who appeared to walk right through him. But the man took no notice, and calmly came out on the other side: it was quite evident that he did not see him, or apprehend him in any way.

Mr. Tilly was still feeling rather at sea amid these unusual occurrences, and there began to steal into his mind a glimpse of the fact which was so obvious to the crowd which formed an interested but respectful ring round his body. Men stood with bared heads; women screamed and looked away and looked back again.

"I really believe I'm dead," said he. "That's the only hypothesis which will cover the facts. But I must feel more certain of it before I do anything. Ah! Here they come with the ambulance to look at me. I must be terribly hurt, and yet I don't feel hurt. I should feel hurt surely if I was hurt. I must be dead."

Certainly it seemed the only thing for him to be, but he was far from realising it yet. A lane had been made through the crowd for the stretcher-bearers, and he found himself wincing when they began to detach him from the road.

"Oh, do take care!" he said. "That's the sciatic nerve protruding there surely, isn't it? A-ow! No, it didn't hurt after all. My new clothes, too: I put them on to-day for the first time. What bad luck! Now you're holding my leg upside down. Of course all my money comes out of my trouser pocket. And there's my ticket for the séance; I must have that: I may use it after all."

He tweaked it out of the fingers of the man who had picked it up, and laughed to see the expression of amazement on his face as the card suddenly vanished. That gave him something fresh to think about, and he pondered for a moment over some touch of association set up by it.

"I have it," he thought. "It is clear that the moment I came into connection with that card, it became invisible. I'm invisible myself (of course to the grosser sense), and everything I hold becomes invisible. Most interesting! That accounts for the sudden appearances of small objects at a séance. The spirit has been holding them, and as long as he holds them they are invisible. Then he lets go, and there's the flower or the spirit-photograph on the table. It accounts, too, for the sudden disappearances of such objects. The spirit has taken them, though the scoffers say that the medium has secreted them about his person. It is true that when searched he sometimes appears to have done so; but, after all, that may be a joke on the part of the spirit. Now, what am I to do with myself . . . Let me see, there's the clock. It's just half-past ten. All this has happened in a few minutes, for it was a quarter past when I left my house. Half-past ten now: what does that mean exactly? I used to know what it meant, but now it seems nonsense. Ten what? Hours, is it? What's an hour?"

This was very puzzling. He felt that he used to know what an hour and a minute meant, but the perception of that, naturally enough, had ceased with his emergence from time and space into eternity. The conception of time was like some memory which, refusing to record itself on the consciousness, lies perdu in some dark corner of the brain, laughing at the efforts of the owner to ferret it out. While he still interrogated his mind over this lapsed perception, he found that space as well as time, had similarly grown obsolete for him, for he caught sight of his friend Miss Ida Soulsby, who he knew was to be present at the séance for which he was bound, hurrying with bird-like steps down the pavement opposite. Forgetting for the moment that he was a disembodied spirit, he made the effort of will which in his past human existence would have set his legs in pursuit of her, and found that the effort of will alone was enough to place him at her side.

"My dear Miss Soulsby," he said, "I was on my way to Mrs. Cumberbatch's house when I was knocked down and killed. It was far from unpleasant, a moment's headache—"

So far his natural volubility had carried him before he recollected that he was invisible and inaudible to those still closed in by the muddy vesture of decay, and stopped short. But though it was clear that what he said was inaudible to Miss Soulsby's rather large intelligent-looking ears, it seemed that some consciousness of his presence was conveyed to her finer sense, for she looked suddenly startled, a flush rose to her face, and he heard her murmur, "Very odd. I wonder why I received so vivid an impression of dear Teddy."

That gave Mr. Tilly a pleasant shock. He had long admired the lady, and here she was alluding to him in her supposed privacy as "dear Teddy." That was followed by a momentary regret that he had been killed: he would have liked to have been possessed of this information before, and have pursued the primrose path of dalliance down which it seemed to lead. (His intentions, of course, would, as always, have been strictly honourable: the path of dalliance would have conducted them both, if she consented, to the altar, where the primroses would have been exchanged for orange blossom.) But his regret was quite short-lived; though the altar seemed inaccessible, the primrose path might still be open, for many of the spiritualistic circle in which he lived were on most affectionate terms with their spiritual guides and friends who, like himself, had passed over. From a human point of view these innocent and even elevating flirtations had always seemed to him rather bloodless; but now, looking on them from the far side, he saw how charming they were, for they gave him the sense of still having a place and an identity in the world he had just quitted. He pressed Miss Ida's hand (or rather put himself into the spiritual condition of so doing), and could vaguely feel that it had some hint of warmth and solidity about it. This was gratifying, for it showed that though he had passed out of the material plane, he could still be in touch with it. Still more gratifying was it to observe that a pleased and secret smile overspread Miss Ida's fine features as he gave this token of his presence: perhaps she only smiled at her own thoughts, but in any case it was he who had inspired them. Encouraged by this, he indulged in a slightly more intimate token of affection, and permitted himself a respectful salute, and saw that he had gone too far, for she said to herself, "Hush, hush!" and quickened her pace, as if to leave these amorous thoughts behind.

He felt that he was beginning to adjust himself to the new conditions in which he would now live or, at any rate, was getting some sort of inkling as to what they were. Time existed no more for him, nor yet did space, since the wish to be at Miss Ida's side had instantly transported him there, and with a view to testing this further he wished himself back in his flat. As swiftly as the change of scene in a cinematograph show he found himself there, and perceived that the news of his death must have reached his servants, for his cook and parlour-maid with excited faces, were talking over the event.

"Poor little gentleman," said his cook. "It seems a shame it does. He never hurt a fly, and to think of one of those great engines laying him out flat. I hope they'll take him to the cemetery from the hospital: I never could bear a corpse in the house."

The great strapping parlour-maid tossed her head.

"Well, I'm not sure that it doesn't serve him right," she observed. "Always messing about with spirits he was, and the knockings and concertinas was awful sometimes when I've been laying out supper in the dining-room. Now perhaps he'll come himself and visit the rest of the loonies. But I'm sorry all the same. A less troublesome little gentleman never stepped. Always pleasant, too, and wages paid to the day."

These regretful comments and encomiums were something of a shock to Mr. Tilly. He had imagined that his excellent servants regarded him with a respectful affection, as befitted some sort of demigod, and the rôle of the poor little gentleman was not at all to his mind. This revelation of their true estimate of him, although what they thought of him could no longer have the smallest significance irritated him profoundly.

"I never heard such impertinence," he said (so he thought) quite out loud, and still intensely earth-bound, was astonished to see that they had no perception whatever of his presence. He raised his voice, replete with extreme irony, and addressed his cook.

"You may reserve your criticism on my character for your saucepans," he said. "They will no doubt appreciate them. As regards the arrangements for my funeral, I have already provided for them in my will, and do not propose to consult your convenience. At present—"

"Lor'!" said Mrs. Inglis, "I declare I can almost hear his voice, poor little fellow. Husky it was, as if he would do better by clearing his throat. I suppose I'd best be making a black bow to my cap. His lawyers and what not will be here presently."

Mr. Tilly had no sympathy with this suggestion. He was immensely conscious of being quite alive, and the idea of his servants behaving as if he were dead, especially after the way in which they had spoken about him, was very vexing. He wanted to give them some striking evidence of his presence and his activity, and he banged his hand angrily on the dining-room table, from which the breakfast equipage had not yet been cleared. Three tremendous blows he gave it, and was rejoiced to see that his parlour-maid looked startled. Mrs. Inglis's face remained perfectly placid.

"Why, if I didn't hear a sort of rapping sound," said Miss Talton. "Where did it come from?"

"Nonsense! You've the jumps, dear," said Mrs. Inglis, picking up a remaining rasher of bacon on a fork, and putting it into her capacious mouth.

Mr. Tilly was delighted at making any impression at all on either of these impercipient females.

"Talton!" he called at the top of his voice.

"Why, what's that?" said Talton. "Almost hear his voice, do you say, Mrs. Inglis? I declare I did hear his voice then."

"A pack o' nonsense, dear," said Mrs. Inglis placidly. "That's a prime bit of bacon, and there's a good cut of it left. Why, you're all of a tremble! It's your imagination."

Suddenly it struck Mr. Tilly that he might be employing himself much better than, with such extreme exertion, managing to convey so slight a hint of his presence to his parlour-maid, and that the séance at the house of the medium, Mrs. Cumberbatch, would afford him much easier opportunities of getting through to the earth-plane again. He gave a couple more thumps to the table and, wishing himself at Mrs. Cumberbatch's, nearly a mile away, scarcely heard the faint scream of Talton at the sound of his blows before he found himself in West Norfolk Street.

He knew the house well, and went straight to the drawing-room, which was the scene of the séances he had so often and so eagerly attended. Mrs. Cumberbatch, who had a long spoon-shaped face, had already pulled down the blinds, leaving the room in total darkness except for the glimmer of the night-light which, under a shade of ruby-glass, stood on the chimneypiece in front of the coloured photograph of Cardinal Newman. Round the table were seated Miss Ida Soulsby, Mr. and Mrs. Meriott (who paid their guineas at least twice a week in order to consult their spiritual guide Abibel and received mysterious advice about their indigestion and investments), and Sir John Plaice, who was much interested in learning the details of his previous incarnation as a Chaldean priest, completed the circle. His guide, who revealed to him his sacerdotal career, was playfully called Mespot. Naturally many other spirits visited them, for Miss Soulsby had no less than three guides in her spiritual household, Sapphire, Semiramis, and Sweet William, while Napoleon and Plato were not infrequent guests. Cardinal Newman, too, was a great favourite, and they encouraged his presence by the singing in unison of "Lead, kindly Light": he could hardly ever resist that . . .

Mr. Tilly observed with pleasure that there was a vacant seat by the table which no doubt had been placed there for him. As he entered, Mrs. Cumberbatch peered at her watch.

"Eleven o'clock already," she said, "and Mr. Tilly is not here yet. I wonder what can have kept him. What shall we do, dear friends? Abibel gets very impatient sometimes if we keep him waiting."

Mr. and Mrs. Meriott were getting impatient too, for he terribly wanted to ask about Mexican oils, and she had a very vexing heartburn.

"And Mespot doesn't like waiting either," said Sir John, jealous for the prestige of his protector, "not to mention Sweet William."

Miss Soulsby gave a little silvery laugh.

"Oh, but my Sweet William's so good and kind," she said; "besides, I have a feeling, quite a psychic feeling, Mrs. Cumberbatch, that Mr. Tilly is very close."

"So I am," said Mr. Tilly.

"Indeed, as I walked here," continued Miss Soulsby, "I felt that

Mr. Tilly was somewhere quite close to me. Dear me, what's that?"

Mr. Tilly was so delighted at being sensed, that he could not resist giving a tremendous rap on the table, in a sort of pleased applause. Mrs. Cumberbatch heard it too.

"I'm sure that's Abibel come to tell us that he is ready," she said. "I know Abibel's knock. A little patience, Abibel. Let's give Mr. Tilly three minutes more and then begin. Perhaps, if we put up the blinds, Abibel will understand we haven't begun."

This was done, and Miss Soulsby glided to the window, in order to make known Mr. Tilly's approach, for he always came along the opposite pavement and crossed over by the little island in the river of traffic. There was evidently some lately published news, for the readers of early editions were busy, and she caught sight of one of the advertisement boards bearing in large letters the announcement of a terrible accident at Hyde Park Corner. She drew in her breath with a hissing sound and turned away, unwilling to have her psychic tranquillity upset by the intrusion of painful incidents. But Mr. Tilly, who had followed her to the window and saw what she had seen, could hardly restrain a spiritual whoop of exultation.

"Why, it's all about me!" he said. "Such large letters, too. Very gratifying. Subsequent editions will no doubt contain my name."

He gave another loud rap to call attention to himself, and Mrs. Cumberbatch, sitting down in her antique chair which had once belonged to Madame Blavatsky, again heard.

"Well, if that isn't Abibel again," she said. "Be quiet, naughty. Perhaps we had better begin."

She recited the usual invocation to guides and angels, and leaned back in her chair. Presently she began to twitch and mutter, and shortly afterwards with several loud snorts, relapsed into cataleptic immobility. There she lay, stiff as a poker, a port of call, so to speak, for any voyaging intelligence. With pleased anticipation Mr. Tilly awaited their coming. How gratifying if Napoleon, with whom he had so often talked, recognised him and said, "Pleased to see you, Mr. Tilly. I perceive you have joined us . . ." The room was dark except for the ruby-shaded lamp in front of Cardinal Newman, but to Mr. Tilly's emancipated perceptions the withdrawal of mere material light made no difference, and he idly wondered why it was generally supposed that disembodied spirits like himself produced their most powerful effects in the dark. He could not imagine the reason for that, and, what puzzled him still more, there was not to his spiritual perception any sign of those colleagues of his (for so he might now call them) who usually attended Mrs. Cumberbatch's séances in such gratifying numbers. Though she had been moaning and muttering a long time now, Mr. Tilly was in no way conscious of the presence of Abibel and Sweet William and Sapphire and Napoleon: "They ought to be here by now," he said to himself.

But while he still wondered at their absence, he saw to his amazed disgust that the medium's hand, now covered with a black glove, and thus invisible to ordinary human vision in the darkness, was groping about the table and clearly searching for the megaphone-trumpet which lay there. He found that he could read her mind with the same ease, though far less satisfaction, as he had read Miss Ida's half an hour ago, and knew that she was intending to apply the trumpet to her own mouth and pretend to be Abibel or Semiramis or somebody, whereas she affirmed that she never touched the trumpet herself. Much shocked at this, he snatched up the trumpet himself, and observed that she was not in trance at all, for she opened her sharp black eyes, which always reminded him of buttons covered with American cloth, and gave a great gasp.

"Why, Mr. Tilly!" she said. "On the spiritual plane too!"

The rest of the circle was now singing "Lead, kindly Light" in order to encourage Cardinal Newman, and this conversation was conducted under cover of the hoarse crooning voices. But Mr. Tilly had the feeling that though Mrs. Cumberbatch saw and heard him as clearly as he saw her, he was quite imperceptible to the others.

"Yes, I've been killed," he said, "and I want to get into touch with the material world. That's why I came here. But I want to get into touch with other spirits too, and surely Abibel or Mespot ought to be here by this time."

He received no answer, and her eyes fell before his like those of a detected charlatan. A terrible suspicion invaded his mind.

"What? Are you a fraud, Mrs. Cumberbatch?" he asked. "Oh, for shame! Think of all the guineas I have paid you."

"You shall have them all back," said Mrs. Cumberbatch. "But don't tell of me."

She began to whimper, and he remembered that she often made that sort of sniffling noise when Abibel was taking possession of her.

"That usually means that Abibel is coming," he said, with withering sarcasm. "Come along, Abibel: we're waiting."

"Give me the trumpet," whispered the miserable medium. "Oh, please give me the trumpet!"

"I shall do nothing of the kind," said Mr. Tilly indignantly. "I would sooner use it myself."

She gave a sob of relief.

"Oh do, Mr. Tilly!" she said. "What a wonderful idea! It will be most interesting to everybody to hear you talk just after you've been killed and before they know. It would be the making of me! And I'm not a fraud, at least not altogether. I do have spiritual perceptions sometimes; spirits do communicate through me. And when they won't come through it's a dreadful temptation to a poor woman to – to supplement them by human agency. And how could I be seeing and hearing you now, and be able to talk to you – so pleasantly, I'm sure – if I hadn't super-normal powers? You've been killed, so you assure me, and yet I can see and hear you quite plainly. Where did it happen, may I ask, if it's not a painful subject?"

"Hyde Park Corner, half an hour ago," said Mr. Tilly. "No, it only hurt for a moment, thanks. But about your other suggestion—"

While the third verse of "Lead, kindly Light" was going on, Mr. Tilly applied his mind to this difficult situation. It was quite true that if Mrs. Cumberbatch had no power of communication with the unseen she could not possibly have seen him. But she evidently had, and had heard him too, for their conversation had certainly been conducted on the spirit-plane, with perfect lucidity. Naturally, now that he was a genuine spirit, he did not want to be mixed up in fraudulent mediumship, for he felt that such a thing would seriously compromise him on the other side, where, probably, it was widely known that Mrs. Cumberbatch was a person to be avoided. But, on the other hand, having so soon found a medium through whom he could communicate with his friends, it was hard to take a high moral view, and say that he would have nothing whatever to do with her.

"I don't know if I trust you," he said. "I shouldn't have a moment's peace if I thought that you would be sending all sorts of bogus messages from me to the circle, which I wasn't responsible for at all. You've done it with Abibel and Mespot. How can I know that when I don't choose to communicate through you, you won't make up all sorts of piffle on your own account?"

She positively squirmed in her chair.

"Oh, I'll turn over a new leaf," she said. "I will leave all that sort of thing behind me. And I am a medium. Look at me! Aren't I more real to you than any of the others? Don't I belong to your plane in a way that none of the others do? I may be occasionally fraudulent, and I can no more get Napoleon here than I can fly, but I'm genuine as well. Oh, Mr. Tilly, be indulgent to us poor human creatures! It isn't so long since you were one of us yourself."

The mention of Napoleon, with the information that Mrs. Cumberbatch had never been controlled by that great creature, wounded Mr. Tilly again. Often in this darkened room he had held long colloquies with him, and Napoleon had given him most interesting details of his life on St. Helena, which, so Mr. Tilly had found, were often borne out by Lord Rosebery's pleasant volume *The Last Phase*. But now the whole thing wore a more sinister aspect, and suspicion as solid as certainty bumped against his mind.

"Confess!" he said. "Where did you get all that Napoleon talk from? You told us you had never read Lord Rosebery's book, and allowed us to look through your library to see that it wasn't there. Be honest for once, Mrs. Cumberbatch."

She suppressed a sob.

"I will," she said. "The book was there all the time. I put it into an old cover called 'Elegant Extracts . . .' But I'm not wholly a fraud. We're talking together, you a spirit and I a mortal female. They can't hear us talk. But only look at me, and you'll see . . . You can talk to them through me, if you'll only be so kind. I don't often get in touch with a genuine spirit like yourself."

Mr. Tilly glanced at the other sitters and then back to the medium, who, to keep the others interested, was making weird gurgling noises like an undervitalised siphon. Certainly she was far clearer to him than were the others, and her argument that she was able to see and hear him had great weight. And then a new and curious perception came to him. Her mind seemed spread out before him like a pool of slightly muddy water, and he figured himself as standing on a header-board above it, perfectly able, if he chose, to immerse himself in it. The objection to so doing was its muddiness, its materiality; the reason for so doing was that he felt that then he would be able to be heard by the others, possibly to be seen by them, certainly to come into touch with them. As it was, the loudest bangs on the table were only faintly perceptible.

"I'm beginning to understand," he said.

"Oh, Mr. Tilly! Just jump in like a kind good spirit," she said. "Make your own test-conditions. Put your hand over my mouth to make sure that I'm not speaking, and keep hold of the trumpet."

"And you'll promise not to cheat any more?" he asked.

"Never!"

He made up his mind.

"All right then," he said, and, so to speak, dived into her mind.

He experienced the oddest sensation. It was like passing out of some fine, sunny air into the stuffiest of unventilated rooms. Space and time closed over him again: his head swam, his eyes were heavy. Then, with the trumpet in one hand, he laid the other firmly over her mouth. Looking round, he saw that the room seemed almost completely dark, but that the outline of the figures sitting round the table had vastly gained in solidity.

"Here I am!" he said briskly.

Miss Soulsby gave a startled exclamation.

"That's Mr. Tilly's voice!" she whispered.

"Why, of course it is," said Mr. Tilly. "I've just passed over at Hyde Park Corner under a traction engine . . ."

He felt the dead weight of the medium's mind, her conventional conceptions, her mild, unreal piety pressing in on him from all sides, stifling and confusing him. Whatever he said had to pass through muddy water . . .

"There's a wonderful feeling of joy and lightness," he said. "I can't tell you of the sunshine and happiness. We're all very busy and active, helping others. And it's such a pleasure, dear friends, to be able to get into touch with you all again. Death is not death: it is the gate of life . . ."

He broke off suddenly.

"Oh, I can't stand this," he said to the medium. "You make me talk such twaddle. Do get your stupid mind out of the way. Can't we do anything in which you won't interfere with me so much?"

"Can you give us some spirit lights round the room?" suggested Mrs. Cumberbatch in a sleepy voice. "You have come through beautifully, Mr. Tilly. It's too dear of you!"

"You're sure you haven't arranged some phosphorescent patches already?" asked Mr. Tilly suspiciously.

"Yes, there are one or two near the chimney-piece," said Mrs. Cumberbatch, "but none anywhere else. Dear Mr. Tilly, I swear there are not. Just give us a nice star with long rays on the ceiling!"

Mr. Tilly was the most good-natured of men, always willing to help an unattractive female in distress, and whispering to her, "I shall require the phosphorescent patches to be given into my hands after the séance," he proceeded, by the mere effort of his imagination, to light a beautiful big star with red and violet rays on the ceiling. Of course it was not nearly as brilliant as his own conception of it, for its light had to pass through the opacity of the medium's mind, but it was still a most striking object, and elicited gasps of applause from the company. To enhance the effect of it he intoned a few very pretty lines about a star by Adelaide Anne Procter, whose poems had always seemed to him to emanate from the topmost peak of Parnassus.

"Oh, thank you, Mr. Tilly!" whispered the medium. "It was lovely! Would a photograph of it be permitted on some future occasion, if you would be so kind as to reproduce it again?"

"Oh, I don't know," said Mr. Tilly irritably. "I want to get out. I'm very hot and uncomfortable. And it's all so cheap."

"Cheap?" ejaculated Mrs. Cumberbatch. "Why, there's not a medium in London whose future wouldn't be made by a real genuine star like that, say, twice a week."

"But I wasn't run over in order that I might make the fortune of mediums," said Mr. Tilly. "I want to go: it's all rather degrading. And I want to see something of my new world. I don't know what it's like yet."

"Oh, but, Mr. Tilly," said she. "You told us lovely things about it, how busy and happy you were."

"No, I didn't. It was you who said that, at least it was you who put it into my head."

Even as he wished, he found himself emerging from the dull waters of Mrs. Cumberbatch's mind.

"There's the whole new world waiting for me," he said. "I must go and see it. I'll come back and tell you, for it must be full of marvellous revelations . . ."

Suddenly he felt the hopelessness of it. There was that thick fluid of materiality to pierce, and, as it dripped off him again, he began to see that nothing of that fine rare quality of life which he had just begun to experience, could penetrate these opacities. That was why, perhaps, all that thus came across from the spirit-world, was so stupid, so banal. They, of whom he now was one, could tap on furniture, could light stars, could abound with commonplace, could read as in a book the mind of medium or sitters, but nothing more. They had to pass into the region of gross perceptions, in order to be seen of blind eyes and be heard of deaf ears.

Mrs. Cumberbatch stirred.

"The power is failing," she said, in a deep voice, which Mr. Tilly felt was meant to imitate his own. "I must leave you now, dear friends—"

He felt much exasperated.

"The power isn't failing," he shouted. "It wasn't I who said that."

But he had emerged too far, and perceived that nobody except the medium heard him.

"Oh, don't be vexed, Mr. Tilly," she said. "That's only a formula. But you're leaving us very soon. Not time for just one materialisation? They are more convincing than anything to most inquirers."

"Not one," said he. "You don't understand how stifling it is even to speak through you and make stars. But I'll come back as soon as I find there's anything new that I can get through to you. What's the use of my repeating all that stale stuff about being busy and happy? They've been told that often enough already.

Besides, I have got to see if it's true. Good-bye: don't cheat any more."

He dropped his card of admittance to the séance on the table and heard murmurs of excitement as he floated off.

The news of the wonderful star, and the presence of Mr. Tilly at the séance within half an hour of his death, which at the time was unknown to any of the sitters, spread swiftly through spiritualistic circles. The Psychical Research Society sent investigators to take independent evidence from all those present, but were inclined to attribute the occurrence to a subtle mixture of thought-transference and unconscious visual impression, when they heard that Miss Soulsby had, a few minutes previously, seen a news-board in the street outside recording the accident at Hyde Park Corner. This explanation was rather elaborate, for it postulated that Miss Soulsby, thinking of Mr. Tilly's non-arrival, had combined that with the accident at Hyde Park Corner, and had probably (though unconsciously) seen the name of the victim on another news-board and had transferred the whole by telepathy to the mind of the medium. As for the star on the ceiling, though they could not account for it, they certainly found remains of phosphorescent paint on the panels of the wall above the chimney-piece, and came to the conclusion that the star had been produced by some similar contrivance. So they rejected the whole thing, which was a pity, since, for once, the phenomena were absolutely genuine.

Miss Soulsby continued to be a constant attendant at Mrs. Cumberbatch's séance, but never experienced the presence of Mr. Tilly again. On that the reader may put any interpretation he pleases. It looks to me somewhat as if he had found something else to do.

Mrs. Amworth

The village of Maxley, where, last summer and autumn, these strange events took place, lies on a heathery and pine-clad upland of Sussex. In all England you could not find a sweeter and saner situation. Should the wind blow from the south, it comes laden with the spices of the sea; to the east high downs protect it from the inclemencies of March; and from the west and north the breezes which reach it travel over miles of aromatic forest and heather. The village itself is insignificant enough in point of population, but rich in amenities and beauty. Half-way down the single street, with its broad road and spacious areas of grass on each side, stands the little Norman Church and the antique graveyard long disused: for the rest there are a dozen small, sedate Georgian houses, red-bricked and long-windowed, each with a square of flower-garden in front, and an ampler strip behind; a score of shops, and a couple of score of thatched cottages belonging to labourers on neighbouring estates, complete the entire cluster of its peaceful habitations. The general peace, however, is sadly broken on Saturdays and Sundays, for we lie on one of the main roads between London and Brighton and our quiet street becomes a race-course for flying motor-cars and bicycles.

A notice just outside the village begging them to go slowly only seems to encourage them to accelerate their speed, for the road lies open and straight, and there is really no reason why they should do otherwise. By way of protest, therefore, the ladies of Maxley cover their noses and mouths with their handkerchiefs as they see a motor-car approaching, though, as the street is asphalted, they need not really take these precautions against dust. But late on Sunday night the horde of scorchers has passed, and we settle down again to five days of cheerful and leisurely seclusion. Railway strikes which agitate the country so much leave us undisturbed because most of the inhabitants of Maxley never leave it at all.

I am the fortunate possessor of one of these small Georgian houses, and consider myself no less fortunate in having so interesting and stimulating a neighbour as Francis Urcombe, who, the most confirmed of Maxleyites, has not slept away from his house, which stands just opposite to mine in the village street, for nearly two years, at which date, though still in middle life, he resigned his Physiological Professorship at Cambridge University and devoted himself to the study of those occult and curious phenomena which seem equally to concern the physical and the psychical sides of human nature. Indeed his retirement was not unconnected with his passion for the strange uncharted places that lie on the confines and borders of science, the existence of which is so stoutly denied by the more materialistic minds, for he advocated that all medical students should be obliged to pass some sort of examination in mesmerism, and that one of the tripos papers should be designed to test their knowledge in such subjects as appearances at time of death, haunted houses, vampirism, automatic writing, and possession.

"Of course they wouldn't listen to me," ran his account of the matter, "for there is nothing that these seats of learning are so frightened of as knowledge, and the road to knowledge lies in the study of things like these. The functions of the human frame are, broadly speaking, known. They are a country, anyhow, that has been charted and mapped out. But outside that lie huge tracts of undiscovered country, which certainly exist, and the real pioneers of knowledge are those who, at the cost of being derided as credulous and superstitious, want to push on into those misty and probably perilous places. I felt that I could be of more use by setting out without compass or knapsack into the mists than by sitting in a cage like a canary and chirping about what was known. Besides, teaching is very bad for a man who knows himself only to be a learner: you only need to be a self-conceited ass to teach."

Here, then, in Francis Urcombe, was a delightful neighbour to one who, like myself, has an uneasy and burning curiosity about what he called the "misty and perilous places"; and this last spring we had a further and most welcome addition to our pleasant little community, in the person of Mrs. Amworth, widow of an Indian civil servant. Her husband had been a judge in the North-West Provinces, and after his death at Peshawar she came back to England, and after a year in London found herself starving for the ampler air and sunshine of the country to take the place of the fogs and griminess of town. She had, too, a special reason for settling in Maxley, since her ancestors up till a hundred years ago had long been native to the place, and in the old churchyard, now disused, are many gravestones bearing her maiden name of Chaston. Big and energetic, her vigorous and genial personality speedily woke Maxley up to a higher degree of sociality than it had ever known. Most of us were bachelors or spinsters or elderly folk not much inclined to exert ourselves in the expense and effort of hospitality, and hitherto the gaiety of a small tea-party, with bridge afterwards and goloshes (when it was wet) to trip home in again for a solitary dinner, was about the climax of our festivities. But Mrs. Amworth showed us a more gregarious way, and set an example of luncheon-parties and little dinners, which we began to follow. On other nights when no such hospitality was on foot, a lone man like myself found it pleasant to know that a call on the telephone to Mrs. Amworth's house not a hundred yards off, and an inquiry as to whether I might come over after dinner for a game of piquet before bed-time, would probably evoke a response of welcome. There she would be, with a comrade-like eagerness for companionship, and there was a glass of port and a cup of coffee and a cigarette and a game of piquet. She played the piano, too, in a free and exuberant manner, and had a charming voice and sang to her own accompaniment; and as the days grew long and the light lingered late, we played our game in her garden, which in the course of a few months she had turned from being a nursery for slugs and snails into a glowing patch of luxuriant blossoming. She was always cheery and jolly; she was interested in everything, and in music, in gardening, in games of all sorts was a competent performer. Everybody (with one exception) liked her, everybody felt her to bring with her the tonic of a sunny day. That one exception was Francis Urcombe; he, though he confessed he did not like her, acknowledged that he was vastly interested in her. This always seemed strange to me, for pleasant and jovial as she was, I could see nothing in her that could call forth conjecture or intrigued surmise, so healthy and unmysterious a figure did she present. But of the genuineness of Urcombe's interest there could be no doubt; one could see him watching and scrutinising her. In matter of age, she frankly volunteered the information that she was forty-five; but her briskness, her activity, her unravaged skin, her coal-black hair, made it difficult to believe that she was not adopting an unusual device, and adding ten years on to her age instead of subtracting them.

Often, also, as our quite unsentimental friendship ripened, Mrs. Amworth would ring me up and propose her advent. If I was busy writing, I was to give her, so we definitely bargained, a frank negative, and in answer I could hear her jolly laugh and her wishes for a successful evening of work. Sometimes, before her proposal arrived, Urcombe would already have stepped across from his house opposite for a smoke and a chat, and he, hearing who my intending visitor was, always urged me to beg her to come. She and I should play our piquet, said he, and he would look on, if we did not object, and learn something of the game. But I doubt whether he paid much attention to it, for nothing could be clearer than that, under that penthouse of forehead and thick eyebrows, his attention was fixed not on the cards, but on one of the players. But he seemed to enjoy an hour spent thus, and often, until one particular evening in July, he would watch her with the air of a man who has some deep problem in front of him. She, enthusiastically keen about our game, seemed not to notice his scrutiny. Then came that evening, when, as I see in the light of subsequent events, began the first twitching of the veil that hid the secret horror from my eyes. I did not know it then, though I noticed that thereafter, if she rang up to propose coming round, she always asked not only if I was at leisure, but whether Mr. Urcombe was with me. If so, she said, she would not spoil the chat of two old bachelors, and laughingly wished me good night.

Urcombe, on this occasion, had been with me for some half-hour before Mrs. Amworth's appearance, and had been talking to me about the mediæval beliefs concerning vampirism, one of those borderland subjects which he declared had not been sufficiently studied before it had been consigned by the medical profession to the dust-heap of exploded superstitions. There he sat, grim and eager, tracing, with that pellucid clearness which had made him in his Cambridge days so admirable a lecturer, the history of those mysterious visitations. In them all there were the same general features: one of those ghoulish spirits took up its abode in a living man or woman, conferring supernatural powers of bat-like flight and glutting itself with nocturnal blood-feasts. When its host died it continued to dwell in the corpse, which remained undecayed. By day it rested, by night it left the grave and went on its awful errands. No European country in the Middle Ages seemed to have escaped them; earlier yet, parallels were to be found, in Roman and Greek and in Jewish history.

"It's a large order to set all that evidence aside as being moonshine," he said. "Hundreds of totally independent witnesses in many ages have testified to the occurrence of these phenomena, and there's no explanation known to me which covers all the facts. And if you feel inclined to say 'Why, then, if these are facts, do we not come across them now?' there are two answers I can make you. One is that there were diseases known in the Middle Ages, such as the black death, which were certainly existent then and which have become extinct since, but for that reason we do not assert that such diseases never existed. Just as the black death visited England and decimated the population of Norfolk, so here in this very district about three hundred years ago there was certainly an outbreak of vampirism, and Maxley was the centre of it. My second answer is even more convincing, for I tell you that vampirism is by no means extinct now. An outbreak of it certainly occurred in India a year or two ago."

At that moment I heard my knocker plied in the cheerful and peremptory manner in which Mrs. Amworth is accustomed to announce her arrival, and I went to the door to open it.

"Come in at once," I said, "and save me from having my blood curdled. Mr. Urcombe has been trying to alarm me."

Instantly her vital, voluminous presence seemed to fill the room.

"Ah, but how lovely!" she said. "I delight in having my blood curdled. Go on with your ghost-story, Mr. Urcombe. I adore ghost-stories."

I saw that, as his habit was, he was intently observing her.

"It wasn't a ghost-story exactly," said he. "I was only telling our host how vampirism was not extinct yet. I was saying that there was an outbreak of it in India only a few years ago."

There was a more than perceptible pause, and I saw that, if Urcombe was observing her, she on her side was observing him with fixed eye and parted mouth. Then her jolly laugh invaded that rather tense silence.

"Oh, what a shame!" she said. "You're not going to curdle my blood at all. Where did you pick up such a tale, Mr. Urcombe? I have lived for years in India and never heard a rumour of such a thing. Some story-teller in the bazaars must have invented it: they are famous at that."

I could see that Urcombe was on the point of saying something further, but checked himself.

"Ah! very likely that was it," he said.

But something had disturbed our usual peaceful sociability that night, and something had damped Mrs. Amworth's usual high spirits. She had no gusto for her piquet, and left after a couple of games. Urcombe had been silent too, indeed he hardly spoke again till she departed.

"That was unfortunate," he said, "for the outbreak of – of a very mysterious disease, let us call it, took place at Peshawar, where she and her husband were. And—"

"Well?" I asked.

"He was one of the victims of it," said he. "Naturally I had quite forgotten that when I spoke."

The summer was unreasonably hot and rainless, and Maxley suffered much from drought, and also from a plague of big black night-flying gnats, the bite of which was very irritating and virulent. They came sailing in of an evening, settling on one's skin so quietly that one perceived nothing till the sharp stab announced that one had been bitten. They did not bite the hands or face, but chose always the neck and throat for their feeding-ground, and most of us, as the poison spread, assumed a temporary goitre. Then about the middle of August appeared the first of those mysterious cases of illness which our local doctor attributed to the long-continued heat coupled with the bite of these venomous insects. The patient was a boy of sixteen or seventeen, the son of Mrs. Amworth's gardener, and the symptoms were an anæmic pallor and a languid prostration, accompanied by great drowsiness and an abnormal appetite. He had, too, on his throat two small punctures where, so Dr. Ross conjectured, one of these great gnats had bitten him. But the odd thing was that there was no swelling or inflammation round the place where he had been bitten. The heat at this time had begun to abate, but the cooler weather failed to restore him, and the boy, in spite of the quantity of good food which he so ravenously swallowed, wasted away to a skin-clad skeleton.

I met Dr. Ross in the street one afternoon about this time, and in answer to my inquiries about his patient he said that he was afraid the boy was dying. The case, he confessed, completely puzzled him: some obscure form of pernicious anæmia was all he could suggest. But he wondered whether Mr. Urcombe would consent to see the boy, on the chance of his being able to throw some new light on the case, and since Urcombe was dining with me that night, I proposed to Dr. Ross to join us. He could not do this, but said he would look in later. When he came, Urcombe at once consented to put his skill at the other's disposal, and together they went off at once. Being thus shorn of my sociable evening, I telephoned to Mrs. Amworth to know if I might inflict myself on her for an hour. Her answer was a welcoming affirmative, and between piquet and music the hour lengthened itself into two. She spoke of the boy who was lying so desperately and mysteriously ill, and told me that she had often been to see him, taking him nourishing and delicate food. But to-day – and her kind eyes moistened as she spoke – she was afraid she had paid her last visit. Knowing the antipathy between her and Urcombe, I did not tell her that he had been called into consultation; and when I returned home she accompanied me to my door, for the sake of a breath of night air, and in order to borrow a magazine which contained an article on gardening which she wished to read.

"Ah, this delicious night air," she said, luxuriously sniffing in the coolness. "Night air and gardening are the great tonics. There is nothing so stimulating as bare contact with rich mother earth. You are never so fresh as when you have been grubbing in the soil – black hands, black nails, and boots covered with mud." She gave her great jovial laugh.

"I'm a glutton for air and earth," she said. "Positively I look forward to death, for then I shall be buried and have the kind earth all round me. No leaden caskets for me – I have given explicit directions. But what shall I do about air? Well, I suppose one can't have everything. The magazine? A thousand thanks, I will faithfully return it. Good night: garden and keep your windows open, and you won't have anæmia."

"I always sleep with my windows open," said I.

I went straight up to my bedroom, of which one of the windows looks out over the street, and as I undressed I thought I heard voices talking outside not far away. But I paid no particular attention, put out my lights, and falling asleep plunged into the depths of a most horrible dream, distortedly suggested no doubt, by my last words with Mrs. Amworth. I dreamed that I woke, and found that both my bedroom windows were shut. Half-suffocating I dreamed that I sprang out of bed, and went across to open them. The blind over the first was drawn down, and pulling it up I saw, with the indescribable horror of incipient nightmare, Mrs. Amworth's face suspended close to the pane in the darkness outside, nodding and smiling at me. Pulling down the blind again to keep that terror out, I rushed to the second window on the other side of the room, and there again was Mrs. Amworth's face. Then the panic came upon me in full blast; here was I suffocating in the airless room, and whichever window I opened Mrs. Amworth's face would float in, like those noiseless black gnats that bit before one was aware. The nightmare rose to screaming point, and with strangled yells I awoke to find my room cool and quiet with both windows open and blinds up and a half-moon high in its course, casting an oblong of tranquil light on the floor. But even when I was awake the horror persisted, and I lay tossing and turning. I must have slept long before the nightmare seized me, for now it was nearly day, and soon in the east the drowsy eyelids of morning began to lift.

I was scarcely downstairs next morning – for after the dawn I slept late – when Urcombe rang up to know if he might see me immediately. He came in, grim and preoccupied, and I noticed that he was pulling on a pipe that was not even filled.

"I want your help," he said, "and so I must tell you first of all what happened last night. I went round with the little doctor to see his patient, and found him just alive, but scarcely more. I instantly diagnosed in my own mind what this anæmia, unaccountable by any other explanation, meant. The boy is the prey of a vampire."

He put his empty pipe on the breakfast-table, by which I had just sat down, and folded his arms, looking at me steadily from under his overhanging brows.

"Now about last night," he said. "I insisted that he should be moved from his father's cottage into my house. As we were carrying him on a stretcher, whom should we meet but Mrs. Amworth? She expressed shocked surprise that we were moving him. Now why do you think she did that?"

With a start of horror, as I remembered my dream that night before, I felt an idea come into my mind so preposterous and unthinkable that I instantly turned it out again.

"I haven't the smallest idea," I said.

"Then listen, while I tell you about what happened later. I put out all light in the room where the boy lay, and watched. One window was a little open, for I had forgotten to close it, and about midnight I heard something outside, trying apparently to push it farther open. I guessed who it was – yes, it was full twenty feet from the ground – and I peeped round the corner of the blind. Just outside was the face of Mrs. Amworth and her hand was on the frame of the window. Very softly I crept close, and then banged the window down, and I think I just caught the tip of one of her fingers."

"But it's impossible," I cried. "How could she be floating in the air like that? And what had she come for? Don't tell me such—"

Once more, with closer grip, the remembrance of my nightmare seized me.

"I am telling you what I saw," said he. "And all night long, until it was nearly day, she was fluttering outside, like some terrible bat, trying to gain admittance. Now put together various things I have told you."

He began checking them off on his fingers.

"Number one," he said: "there was an outbreak of disease similar to that which this boy is suffering from at Peshawar, and her husband died of it. Number two: Mrs. Amworth protested against my moving the boy to my house. Number three: she, or the demon that inhabits her body, a creature powerful and deadly, tries to gain admittance. And add this, too: in mediæval times there was an epidemic of vampirism here at Maxley. The vampire, so the accounts run, was found to be Elizabeth Chaston . . . I see you remember Mrs. Amworth's maiden name. Finally, the boy is stronger this morning. He would certainly not have been alive if he had been visited again. And what do you make of it?"

There was a long silence, during which I found this incredible horror assuming the hues of reality.

"I have something to add," I said, "which may or may not bear on it. You say that the – the spectre went away shortly before dawn."

"Yes."

I told him of my dream, and he smiled grimly.

"Yes, you did well to awake," he said. "That warning came from your subconscious self, which never wholly slumbers, and cried out to you of deadly danger. For two reasons, then, you must help me: one to save others, the second to save yourself."

"What do you want me to do?" I asked.

"I want you first of all to help me in watching this boy, and ensuring that she does not come near him. Eventually I want you to help me in tracking the thing down, in exposing and destroying it. It is not human: it is an incarnate fiend. What steps we shall have to take I don't yet know."

It was now eleven of the forenoon, and presently I went across to his house for a twelve-hour vigil while he slept, to come on duty again that night, so that for the next twenty-four hours either Urcombe or myself was always in the room where the boy, now getting stronger every hour, was lying. The day following was Saturday and a morning of brilliant, pellucid weather, and already when I went across to his house to resume my duty the stream of motors down to Brighton had begun. Simultaneously I saw Urcombe with a cheerful face, which boded good news of his patient, coming out of his house, and Mrs. Amworth, with a gesture of salutation to me and a basket in her hand, walking up the broad strip of grass which bordered the road. There we all three met. I noticed (and saw that Urcombe noticed it too) that one finger of her left hand was bandaged.

"Good morning to you both," said she. "And I hear your patient is doing well, Mr. Urcombe. I have come to bring him a bowl of jelly, and to sit with him for an hour. He and I are great friends. I am overjoyed at his recovery."

Urcombe paused a moment, as if making up his mind, and then shot out a pointing finger at her.

"I forbid that," he said. "You shall not sit with him or see him. And you know the reason as well as I do."

I have never seen so horrible a change pass over a human face as that which now blanched hers to the colour of a grey mist. She put up her hand as if to shield herself from that pointing finger, which drew the sign of the cross in the air, and shrank back cowering on to the road. There was a wild hoot from a horn, a grinding of brakes, a shout – too late – from a passing car, and one long scream suddenly cut short. Her body rebounded from the roadway after the first wheel had gone over it, and the second followed. It lay there, quivering and twitching, and was still.

She was buried three days afterwards in the cemetery outside Maxley, in accordance with the wishes she had told me that she had devised about her interment, and the shock which her sudden and awful death had caused to the little community began by degrees to pass off. To two people only, Urcombe and myself, the horror of it was mitigated from the first by the nature of the relief that her death brought; but, naturally enough, we kept our own counsel, and no hint of what greater horror had been thus averted was ever let slip. But, oddly enough, so it seemed to me, he was still not satisfied about something in connection with her, and would give no answer to my questions on the subject. Then as the days of a tranquil mellow September and the October that followed began to drop away like the leaves of the yellowing trees, his uneasiness relaxed. But before the entry of November the seeming tranquillity broke into hurricane.

I had been dining one night at the far end of the village, and about eleven o'clock was walking home again. The moon was of an unusual brilliance, rendering all that it shone on as distinct as in some etching. I had just come opposite the house which Mrs. Amworth had occupied, where there was a board up telling that it was to let, when I heard the click of her front gate, and next moment I saw, with a sudden chill and quaking of my very spirit, that she stood there. Her profile, vividly illuminated, was turned to me, and I could not be mistaken in my identification of her. She appeared not to see me (indeed the shadow of the yew hedge in front of her garden enveloped me in its blackness) and she went swiftly across the road, and entered the gate of the house directly opposite. There I lost sight of her completely.

My breath was coming in short pants as if I had been running – and now indeed I ran, with fearful backward glances, along the hundred yards that separated me from my house and Urcombe's. It was to his that my flying steps took me, and next minute I was within.

"What have you come to tell me?" he asked. "Or shall I guess?"

"You can't guess," said I.

"No; it's no guess. She has come back and you have seen her. Tell me about it."

I gave him my story.

"That's Major Pearsall's house," he said. "Come back with me there at once."

"But what can we do?" I asked.

"I've no idea. That's what we have got to find out."

A minute later, we were opposite the house. When I had passed it before, it was all dark; now lights gleamed from a couple of windows upstairs. Even as we faced it, the front door opened, and next moment Major Pearsall emerged from the gate. He saw us and stopped.

"I'm on my way to Dr. Ross," he said quickly, "My wife has been taken suddenly ill. She had been in bed an hour when I came upstairs, and I found her white as a ghost and utterly exhausted. She had been to sleep, it seemed – but you will excuse me."

"One moment, Major," said Urcombe. "Was there any mark on her throat?"

"How did you guess that?" said he. "There was: one of those beastly gnats must have bitten her twice there. She was streaming with blood."

"And there's someone with her?" asked Urcombe.

"Yes, I roused her maid."

He went off, and Urcombe turned to me. "I know now what we have to do," he said. "Change your clothes, and I'll join you at your house."

"What is it?" I asked.

"I'll tell you on our way. We're going to the cemetery."

He carried a pick, a shovel, and a screwdriver when he rejoined me, and wore round his shoulders a long coil of rope. As we walked, he gave me the outlines of the ghastly hour that lay before us.

"What I have to tell you," he said, "will seem to you now too fantastic for credence, but before dawn we shall see whether it outstrips reality. By a most fortunate happening, you saw the spectre, the astral body, whatever you choose to call it, of Mrs. Amworth, going on its grisly business, and therefore, beyond doubt, the vampire spirit which abode in her during life animates her again in death. That is not exceptional – indeed, all these weeks since her death I have been expecting it. If I am right, we shall find her body undecayed and untouched by corruption."

"But she has been dead nearly two months," said I.

"If she had been dead two years it would still be so, if the vampire has possession of her. So remember: whatever you see done, it will be done not to her, who in the natural course would now be feeding the grasses above her grave, but to a spirit of untold evil and malignancy, which gives a phantom life to her body."

"But what shall I see done?" said I.

"I will tell you. We know that now, at this moment, the vampire clad in her mortal semblance is out; dining out. But it must get back before dawn, and it will pass into the material form that lies in her grave. We must wait for that, and then with your help I shall dig up her body. If I am right, you will look on her as she was in life, with the full vigour of the dreadful nutriment she has received pulsing in her veins. And then, when dawn has come, and the vampire cannot leave the lair of her body, I shall strike her with this" – and he pointed to his pick – "through the heart, and she, who comes to life again only with the animation the fiend gives her, she and her hellish partner will be dead indeed. Then we must bury her again, delivered at last."

We had come to the cemetery, and in the brightness of the moonshine there was no difficulty in identifying her grave. It lay some twenty yards from the small chapel, in the porch of which, obscured by shadow, we concealed ourselves. From there we had a clear and open sight of the grave, and now we must wait till its infernal visitor returned home. The night was warm and windless, yet even if a freezing wind had been raging I think I should have felt nothing of it, so intense was my preoccupation as to what the night and dawn would bring. There was a bell in the turret of the chapel, that struck the quarters of the hour, and it amazed me to find how swiftly the chimes succeeded one another.

The moon had long set, but a twilight of stars shone in a clear sky, when five o'clock of the morning sounded from the turret. A few minutes more passed, and then I felt Urcombe's hand softly nudging me; and looking out in the direction of his pointing finger, I saw that the form of a woman, tall and large in build, was approaching from the right. Noiselessly, with a motion more of gliding and floating than walking, she moved across the cemetery to the grave which was the centre of our observation. She moved round it as if to be certain of its identity, and for a moment stood directly facing us. In the greyness to which now my eyes had grown accustomed, I could easily see her face, and recognise its features.

She drew her hand across her mouth as if wiping it, and broke into a chuckle of such laughter as made my hair stir on my head. Then she leaped on to the grave, holding her hands high above her head, and inch by inch disappeared into the earth. Urcombe's hand was laid on my arm, in an injunction to keep still, but now he removed it.

"Come," he said.

With pick and shovel and rope we went to the grave. The earth was light and sandy, and soon after six struck we had delved down to the coffin lid. With his pick he loosened the earth round it, and, adjusting the rope through the handles by which it had been lowered, we tried to raise it. This was a long and laborious business, and the light had begun to herald day in the east before we had it out, and lying by the side of the grave. With his screw-driver he loosed the fastenings of the lid, and slid it aside, and standing there we looked on the face of Mrs. Amworth. The eyes, once closed in death, were open, the cheeks were flushed with colour, the red, full-lipped mouth seemed to smile.

"One blow and it is all over," he said. "You need not look."

Even as he spoke he took up the pick again, and, laying the point of it on her left breast, measured his distance. And though I knew what was coming I could not look away . . .

He grasped the pick in both hands, raised it an inch or two for the taking of his aim, and then with full force brought it down on her breast. A fountain of blood, though she had been dead so long, spouted high in the air, falling with the thud of a heavy splash over the shroud, and simultaneously from those red lips came one long, appalling cry, swelling up like some hooting siren, and dying away again. With that, instantaneous as a lightning flash, came the touch of corruption on her face, the colour of it faded to ash, the plump cheeks fell in, the mouth dropped.

"Thank God, that's over," said he, and without pause slipped the coffin lid back into its place.

Day was coming fast now, and, working like men possessed, we lowered the coffin into its place again, and shovelled the earth over it . . . The birds were busy with their earliest pipings as we went back to Maxley.

In the Tube

"It's a convention," said Anthony Carling cheerfully, "and not a very convincing one. Time, indeed! There's no such thing as Time really; it has no actual existence. Time is nothing more than an infinitesimal point in eternity, just as space is an infinitesimal point in infinity. At the most, Time is a sort of tunnel through which we are accustomed to believe that we are travelling. There's a roar in our ears and a darkness in our eyes which makes it seem real to us. But before we came into the tunnel we existed for ever in an infinite sunlight, and after we have got through it we shall exist in an infinite sunlight again. So why should we bother ourselves about the confusion and noise and darkness which only encompass us for a moment?"

For a firm-rooted believer in such immeasurable ideas as these, which he punctuated with brisk application of the poker to the brave sparkle and glow of the fire, Anthony has a very pleasant appreciation of the measurable and the finite, and nobody with whom I have acquaintance has so keen a zest for life and its enjoyments as he. He had given us this evening an admirable dinner, had passed round a port beyond praise, and had illuminated the jolly hours with the light of his infectious optimism. Now the small company had melted away, and I was left with him over the fire in his study. Outside the tattoo of wind-driven sleet was audible on the window-panes, over-scoring now and again the flap of the flames on the open hearth, and the thought of the chilly blasts and the snow-covered pavement in Brompton Square, across which, to skidding taxicabs, the last of his other guests had scurried, made my position, resident here till to-morrow morning, the more delicately delightful. Above all there was this stimulating and suggestive companion, who, whether he talked of the great abstractions which were so intensely real and practical to him, or of the very remarkable experiences which he had encountered among these conventions of time and space, was equally fascinating to the listener.

"I adore life," he said. "I find it the most entrancing plaything. It's a delightful game, and, as you know very well, the only conceivable way to play a game is to treat it extremely seriously. If you say to yourself, 'It's only a game,' you cease to take the slightest interest in it. You have to know that it's only a game, and behave as if it was the one object of existence. I should like it to go on for many years yet. But all the time one has to be living on the true plane as well, which is eternity and infinity. If you come to think of it, the one thing which the human mind cannot grasp is the finite, not the infinite, the temporary, not the eternal."

"That sounds rather paradoxical," said I.

"Only because you've made a habit of thinking about things that seem bounded and limited. Look it in the face for a minute. Try to imagine finite Time and Space, and you find you can't. Go back a million years, and multiply that million of years by another million, and you find that you can't conceive of a beginning. What happened before that beginning? Another beginning and another beginning? And before that? Look at it like that, and you find that the only solution comprehensible to you is the existence of an eternity, something that never began and will never end. It's the same about space. Project yourself to the farthest star, and what comes beyond that? Emptiness? Go on through the emptiness, and you can't imagine it being finite and having an end. It must needs go on for ever: that's the only thing you can understand. There's no such thing as before or after, or beginning or end, and what a comfort that is! I should fidget myself to death if there wasn't the huge soft cushion of eternity to lean one's head against. Some people say – I believe I've heard you say it yourself – that the idea of eternity is so tiring; you feel that you want to stop. But that's because you are thinking of eternity in terms of Time, and mumbling in your brain, 'And after that, and after that?' Don't you grasp the idea that in eternity there isn't any 'after,' any more than there is any 'before'? It's all one. Eternity isn't a quantity: it's a quality."

Sometimes, when Anthony talks in this manner, I seem to get a glimpse of that which to his mind is so transparently clear and solidly real, at other times (not having a brain that readily envisages abstractions) I feel as though he was pushing me over a precipice, and my intellectual faculties grasp wildly at anything tangible or comprehensible. This was the case now, and I hastily interrupted.

"But there is a 'before' and 'after,'" I said. "A few hours ago you gave us an admirable dinner, and after that – yes, after – we played bridge. And now you are going to explain things a little more clearly to me, and after that I shall go to bed—"

He laughed.

"You shall do exactly as you like," he said, "and you shan't be a slave to Time either to-night or to-morrow morning. We won't even mention an hour for breakfast, but you shall have it in eternity whenever you awake. And as I see it is not midnight yet, we'll slip the bonds of Time, and talk quite infinitely. I will stop the clock, if that will assist you in getting rid of your illusion, and then I'll tell you a story, which to my mind, shows how unreal so-called realities are; or, at any rate, how fallacious are our senses as judges of what is real and what is not."

"Something occult, something spookish?" I asked, pricking up my ears, for Anthony has the strangest clairvoyances and visions of things unseen by the normal eye.

"I suppose you might call some of it occult," he said, "though there's a certain amount of rather grim reality mixed up in it."

"Go on; excellent mixture," said I.

He threw a fresh log on the fire.

"It's a longish story," he said. "You may stop me as soon as you've had enough. But there will come a point for which I claim your consideration. You, who cling to your 'before' and 'after,' has it ever occurred to you how difficult it is to say *when* an incident takes place? Say that a man commits some crime of violence, can we not, with a good deal of truth, say that he really commits that crime when he definitely plans and determines upon it, dwelling on it with gusto? The actual commission of it, I think we can reasonably argue, is the mere material sequel of his resolve: he is guilty of it when he makes that determination. When, therefore, in the term of 'before' and 'after,' does the crime truly take place? There is also in my story a further point for your consideration. For it seems certain that the spirit of a man, after the death of his body, is obliged to re-enact such a crime, with a view, I suppose we may guess, to his remorse and his eventual redemption. Those who have second sight have seen such re-enactments. Perhaps he may have done his deed blindly in this life; but then his spirit re-commits it with its spiritual eyes open, and able to comprehend its enormity. So, shall we view the man's original determination and the material commission of his crime only as preludes to the real commission of it, when with eyes unsealed he does it and repents of it? . . . That all sounds very obscure when I speak in the abstract, but I think you will see what I mean, if you follow my tale. Comfortable? Got everything you want? Here goes, then."

He leaned back in his chair, concentrating his mind, and then spoke:

"The story that I am about to tell you," he said, "had its beginning a month ago, when you were away in Switzerland. It reached its conclusion, so I imagine, last night. I do not, at any rate, expect to experience any more of it. Well, a month ago I was returning late on a very wet night from dining out. There was not a taxi to be had, and I hurried through the pouring rain to the tube-station at Piccadilly Circus, and thought myself very lucky to catch the last train in this direction. The carriage into which I stepped was quite empty except for one other passenger, who sat next the door immediately opposite to me. I had never, to my knowledge, seen him before, but I found my attention vividly fixed on him, as if he somehow concerned me. He was a man of middle age, in dress-clothes, and his face wore an expression of intense thought, as if in his mind he was pondering some very significant matter, and his hand which was resting on his knee clenched and unclenched itself. Suddenly he looked up and stared me in the face, and I saw there suspicion and fear, as if I had surprised him in some secret deed.

"At that moment we stopped at Dover Street, and the conductor threw open the doors, announced the station and added, 'Change here for Hyde Park Corner and Gloucester Road.' That was all right for me since it meant that the train would stop at Brompton Road, which was my destination. It was all right apparently, too, for my companion, for he certainly did not get out, and after a moment's stop, during which no one else got in, we went on. I saw him, I must insist, after the doors were closed and the train had started. But when I looked again, as we rattled on, I saw that there was no one there. I was quite alone in the carriage.

"Now you may think that I had had one of those swift momentary dreams which flash in and out of the mind in the space of a second, but I did not believe it was so myself, for I felt that I had experienced some sort of premonition or clairvoyant vision. A man, the semblance of whom, astral body or whatever you may choose to call it, I had just seen, would sometime sit in that seat opposite to me, pondering and planning."

"But why?" I asked. "Why should it have been the astral body of a living man which you thought you had seen? Why not the ghost of a dead one?"

"Because of my own sensations. The sight of the spirit of someone dead, which has occurred to me two or three times in my life, has always been accompanied by a physical shrinking and fear, and by the sensation of cold and of loneliness. I believed, at any rate, that I had seen a phantom of the living, and that impression was confirmed, I might say proved, the next day. For I met the man himself. And the next night, as you shall hear, I met the phantom again. We will take them in order.

"I was lunching, then, the next day with my neighbour Mrs. Stanley: there was a small party, and when I arrived we waited but for the final guest. He entered while I was talking to some friend, and presently at my elbow I heard Mrs. Stanley's voice—

"'Let me introduce you to Sir Henry Payle,' she said.

"I turned and saw my *vis-à-vis* of the night before. It was quite unmistakably he, and as we shook hands he looked at me I thought with vague and puzzled recognition.

"'Haven't we met before, Mr. Carling?' he said. 'I seem to recollect—'

"For the moment I forgot the strange manner of his disappearance from the carriage, and thought that it had been the man himself whom I had seen last night.

"Surely, and not so long ago,' I said. 'For we sat opposite each other in the last tube-train from Piccadilly Circus yesterday night.'

"He still looked at me, frowning, puzzled, and shook his head.

"'That can hardly be,' he said. 'I only came up from the country this morning.'

"Now this interested me profoundly, for the astral body, we are told, abides in some half-conscious region of the mind or spirit, and has recollections of what has happened to it, which it can convey only very vaguely and dimly to the conscious mind. All lunch-time I could see his eyes again and again directed to me with the same puzzled and perplexed air, and as I was taking my departure he came up to me.

"'I shall recollect some day,' he said, 'where we met before, and I hope we may meet again. Was it not—?' – and he stopped. 'No: it has gone from me,' he added."

The log that Anthony had thrown on the fire was burning bravely now, and its high-flickering flame lit up his face.

"Now, I don't know whether you believe in coincidences as chance things," he said, "but if you do, get rid of the notion. Or if you can't at once, call it a coincidence that that very night I again caught the last train on the tube going westwards. This time, so far from my being a solitary passenger, there was a considerable crowd waiting at Dover Street, where I entered, and just as the noise of the approaching train began to reverberate in the tunnel I caught sight of Sir Henry Payle standing near the opening from which the train would presently emerge, apart from the rest of the crowd. And I thought to myself how odd it was that I should have seen the phantom of him at this very hour last night and the man himself now, and I began walking towards him with the idea of saying, 'Anyhow, it is in the tube that we meet to-night.' . . . And then a terrible and awful thing happened. Just as the train emerged from the tunnel he jumped down on to the line in front of it, and the train swept along over him up the platform.

"For a moment I was stricken with horror at the sight, and I remember covering my eyes against the dreadful tragedy. But then I perceived that, though it had taken place in full sight of those who were waiting, no one seemed to have seen it except myself. The driver, looking out from his window, had not applied his brakes, there was no jolt from the advancing train, no scream, no cry, and the rest of the passengers began boarding the train with perfect nonchalance. I must have staggered, for I felt sick and faint with what I had seen, and some kindly soul put his arm round me and supported me into the train. He was a doctor, he told me, and asked if I was in pain, or what ailed me. I told him what I thought I had seen, and he assured me that no such accident had taken place.

"It was clear then to my own mind that I had seen the second act, so to speak, in this psychical drama, and I pondered next morning over the problem as to what I should do. Already I had glanced at the morning paper, which, as I knew would be the case, contained no mention whatever of what I had seen. The thing had certainly not happened, but I knew in myself that it would happen. The flimsy veil of Time had been withdrawn from my eyes, and I had seen into what you would call the future. In terms of Time of course it was the future, but from my point of view the thing was just as much in the past as it was in the future. It existed, and waited only for its material fulfilment. The more I thought about it, the more I saw that I could do nothing."

I interrupted his narrative.

"You did nothing?" I exclaimed. "Surely you might have taken some step in order to try to avert the tragedy."

He shook his head.

"What step precisely?" he said. "Was I to go to Sir Henry and tell him that once more I had seen him in the tube in the act of committing suicide? Look at it like this. Either what I had seen was pure illusion, pure imagination, in which case it had no existence or significance at all, or it was actual and real, and essentially it had happened. Or take it, though not very logically, somewhere between the two. Say that the idea of suicide, for some cause of which I knew nothing, had occurred to him or would occur. Should I not, if that was the case, be doing a very dangerous thing, by making such a suggestion to him? Might not the fact of my telling him what I had seen put the idea into his mind, or, if it was already there, confirm it and strengthen it? 'It's a ticklish matter to play with souls,' as Browning says."

"But it seems so inhuman not to interfere in any way," said I, "not to make any attempt."

"What interference?" asked he. "What attempt?"

The human instinct in me still seemed to cry aloud at the thought of doing nothing to avert such a tragedy, but it seemed to be beating itself against something austere and inexorable. And cudgel my brain as I would, I could not combat the sense of what he had said. I had no answer for him, and he went on.

"You must recollect, too," he said, "that I believed then and believe now that the thing had happened. The cause of it, whatever that was, had begun to work, and the effect, in this material sphere, was inevitable. That is what I alluded to when, at the beginning of my story, I asked you to consider how difficult it was to say when an action took place. You still hold that this particular action, this suicide of Sir Henry, had not yet taken place, because he had not yet thrown himself under the advancing train. To me that seems a materialistic view. I hold that in all but the endorsement of it, so to speak, it had taken place. I fancy that Sir Henry, for instance, now free from the material dusks, knows that himself."

Exactly as he spoke there swept through the warm lit room a current of ice-cold air, ruffling my hair as it passed me, and making the wood flames on the hearth to dwindle and flare. I looked round to see if the door at my back had opened, but nothing stirred there, and over the closed window the curtains were fully drawn. As it reached Anthony, he sat up quickly in his chair and directed his glance this way and that about the room.

"Did you feel that?" he asked.

"Yes: a sudden draught," I said. "Ice-cold."

"Anything else?" he asked. "Any other sensation?"

I paused before I answered, for at the moment there occurred to me Anthony's differentiation of the effects produced on the beholder by a phantasm of the living and the apparition of the dead. It was the latter which accurately described my sensations now, a certain physical shrinking, a fear, a feeling of desolation. But yet I had seen nothing. "I felt rather creepy," I said.

As I spoke I drew my chair rather closer to the fire, and sent a swift and, I confess, a somewhat apprehensive scrutiny round the walls of the brightly lit room. I noticed at the same time that Anthony was peering across to the chimney-piece, on which, just below a sconce holding two electric lights, stood the clock which at the beginning of our talk he had offered to stop. The hands I noticed pointed to twenty-five minutes to one.

"But you saw nothing?" he asked.

"Nothing whatever," I said. "Why should I? What was there to see? Or did you—"

"I don't think so," he said.

Somehow this answer got on my nerves, for the queer feeling

which had accompanied that cold current of air had not left me. If anything it had become more acute.

"But surely you know whether you saw anything or not?" I said.

"One can't always be certain," said he. "I say that I don't think I saw anything. But I'm not sure, either, whether the story I am telling you was quite concluded last night. I think there may be a further incident. If you prefer it, I will leave the rest of it, as far as I know it, unfinished till to-morrow morning, and you can go off to bed now."

His complete calmness and tranquillity reassured me.

"But why should I do that?" I asked.

Again he looked round on the bright walls.

"Well, I think something entered the room just now," he said, "and it may develop. If you don't like the notion, you had better go. Of course there's nothing to be alarmed at; whatever it is, it can't hurt us. But it is close on the hour when on two successive nights I saw what I have already told you, and an apparition usually occurs at the same time. Why that is so, I cannot say, but certainly it looks as if a spirit that is earth-bound is still subject to certain conventions, the conventions of time for instance. I think that personally I shall see something before long, but most likely you won't. You're not such a sufferer as I from these – these delusions—"

I was frightened and knew it, but I was also intensely interested, and some perverse pride wriggled within me at his last words. Why, so I asked myself, shouldn't I see whatever was to be seen? . . .

"I don't want to go in the least," I said. "I want to hear the rest of your story."

"Where was I, then? Ah, yes: you were wondering why I didn't do something after I saw the train move up to the platform, and I said that there was nothing to be done. If you think it over, I fancy you will agree with me . . . A couple of days passed, and on the third morning I saw in the paper that there had come fulfilment to my vision. Sir Henry Payle, who had been waiting on the platform of Dover Street Station for the last train to South Kensington, had thrown himself in front of it as it came into the station. The train had been pulled up in a couple of yards, but a wheel had passed over his chest, crushing it in and instantly killing him.

"An inquest was held, and there emerged at it one of those dark stories which, on occasions like these, sometimes fall like a midnight shadow across a life that the world perhaps had thought prosperous. He had long been on bad terms with his wife, from whom he had lived apart, and it appeared that not long before this he had fallen desperately in love with another woman. The night before his suicide he had appeared very late at his wife's house, and had a long and angry scene with her in which he entreated her to divorce him, threatening otherwise to make her life a hell to her. She refused, and in an ungovernable fit of passion he attempted to strangle her. There was a struggle and the noise of it caused her manservant to come up, who succeeded in overmastering him. Lady Payle threatened to proceed against him for assault with the intention to murder her. With this hanging over his head, the next night, as I have already told you, he committed suicide."

He glanced at the clock again, and I saw that the hands now pointed to ten minutes to one. The fire was beginning to burn low and the room surely was growing strangely cold.

"That's not quite all," said Anthony, again looking round. "Are you sure you wouldn't prefer to hear it to-morrow?"

The mixture of shame and pride and curiosity again prevailed.

"No: tell me the rest of it at once," I said.

Before speaking, he peered suddenly at some point behind my chair, shading his eyes. I followed his glance, and knew what he meant by saying that sometimes one could not be sure whether one saw something or not. But was that an outlined shadow that intervened between me and the wall? It was difficult to focus; I did not know whether it was near the wall or near my chair. It seemed to clear away, anyhow, as I looked more closely at it.

"You see nothing?" asked Anthony.

"No: I don't think so," said I. "And you?"

"I think I do," he said, and his eyes followed something which was invisible to mine. They came to rest between him and the chimney-piece. Looking steadily there, he spoke again.

"All this happened some weeks ago," he said, "when you were out in Switzerland, and since then, up till last night, I saw nothing further. But all the time I was expecting something further. I felt that, as far as I was concerned, it was not all over yet, and last night, with the intention of assisting any communication to come through to me from – from beyond, I went into the Dover Street tube-station at a few minutes before one o'clock, the hour at which both the assault and the suicide had taken place. The platform when I arrived on it was absolutely empty, or appeared to be so, but presently, just as I began to hear the roar of the approaching train, I saw there was the figure of a man standing some twenty yards from me, looking into the tunnel. He had not come down with me in the lift, and the moment before he had not been there. He began moving towards me, and then I saw who it was, and I felt a stir of wind icy-cold coming towards me as he approached. It was not the draught that heralds the approach of a train, for it came from the opposite direction. He came close up to me, and I saw there was recognition in his eyes. He raised his face towards me and I saw his lips move, but, perhaps in the increasing noise from the tunnel, I heard nothing come from them. He put out his hand, as if entreating me to do something, and with a cowardice for which I cannot forgive myself, I shrank from him, for I knew, by the sign that I have told you, that this was one from the dead, and my flesh quaked before him, drowning for the moment all pity and all desire to help him, if that was possible. Certainly he had something which he wanted of me, but I recoiled from him. And by now the train was emerging from the tunnel, and next moment, with a dreadful gesture of despair, he threw himself in front of it."

As he finished speaking he got up quickly from his chair, still looking fixedly in front of him. I saw his pupils dilate, and his mouth worked.

"It is coming," he said. "I am to be given a chance of atoning for my cowardice. There is nothing to be afraid of: I must remember that myself . . ."

As he spoke there came from the panelling above the chimney-piece one loud shattering crack, and the cold wind again circled about my head. I found myself shrinking back in my chair with my hands held in front of me as instinctively I screened myself against something which I knew was there but which I could not see. Every sense told me that there was a presence in the room other than mine and Anthony's, and the horror of it was that I could not see it. Any vision, however terrible, would, I felt, be more tolerable than this clear certain knowledge that close to me was this invisible thing. And yet what horror might not be disclosed of the face of the dead and the crushed chest . . . But all I could see, as I shuddered in this cold wind, was the familiar walls of the room, and Anthony standing in front of me stiff and firm, making, as I knew, a call on his courage. His eyes were focused on something quite close to him, and some semblance of a smile quivered on his mouth. And then he spoke again.

"Yes, I know you," he said. "And you want something of me. Tell me, then, what it is."

There was absolute silence, but what was silence to my ears could not have been so to his, for once or twice he nodded, and once he said, "Yes: I see. I will do it." And with the knowledge that, even as there was someone here whom I could not see, so there was speech going on which I could not hear, this terror of the dead and of the unknown rose in me with the sense of powerlessness to move that accompanies nightmare. I could not stir, I could not speak. I could only strain my ears for the inaudible and my eyes for the unseen, while the cold wind from the very valley of the shadow of death streamed over me. It was not that the presence of death itself was terrible; it was that from its tranquillity and serene keeping there had been driven some unquiet soul unable to rest in peace for whatever ultimate awakening rouses the countless generations of those who have passed away, driven, no less, from whatever activities are theirs, back into the material world from which it should have been delivered. Never, until the gulf between the living and the dead was thus bridged, had it seemed so immense and so unnatural. It is possible that the dead may have communication with the living, and it was not that exactly that so terrified me, for such communication, as we know it, comes voluntarily from them. But here was something icy-cold and crime-laden, that was chased back from the peace that would not pacify it.

And then, most horrible of all, there came a change in these unseen conditions. Anthony was silent now, and from looking straight and fixedly in front of him, he began to glance sideways to where I sat and back again, and with that I felt that the unseen presence had turned its attention from him to me. And now, too, gradually and by awful degrees I began to see . . .

There came an outline of shadow across the chimney-piece and the panels above it. It took shape: it fashioned itself into the outline of a man. Within the shape of the shadow details began to form themselves, and I saw wavering in the air, like something concealed by haze, the semblance of a face, stricken and tragic, and burdened with such a weight of woe as no human face had ever worn. Next, the shoulders outlined themselves, and a stain livid and red spread out below them, and suddenly the vision leaped into clearness. There he stood, the chest crushed in and drowned in the red stain, from which broken ribs, like the bones of a wrecked ship, protruded. The mournful, terrible eyes were fixed on me, and it was from them, so I knew, that the bitter wind proceeded . . .

Then, quick as the switching off of a lamp, the spectre vanished, and the bitter wind was still, and opposite to me stood Anthony, in a quiet, bright-lit room. There was no sense of an unseen presence any more; he and I were then alone, with an interrupted conversation still dangling between us in the warm air. I came round to that, as one comes round after an anæsthetic. It all swam into sight again, unreal at first, and gradually assuming the texture of actuality.

"You were talking to somebody, not to me," I said. "Who was it? What was it?"

He passed the back of his hand over his forehead, which glistened in the light.

"A soul in hell," he said.

Now it is hard ever to recall mere physical sensations, when they have passed. If you have been cold and are warmed, it is difficult to remember what cold was like: if you have been hot and have got cool, it is difficult to realise what the oppression of heat really meant. Just so, with the passing of that presence, I found myself unable to recapture the sense of the terror with which, a few moments ago only, it had invaded and inspired me.

"A soul in hell?" I said. "What are you talking about?"

He moved about the room for a minute or so, and then came and sat on the arm of my chair.

"I don't know what you saw," he said, "or what you felt, but there has never in all my life happened to me anything more real than what these last few minutes have brought. I have talked to a soul in the hell of remorse, which is the only possible hell. He knew, from what happened last night, that he could perhaps establish communication through me with the world he had quitted, and he sought me and found me. I am charged with a mission to a woman I have never seen, a message from the contrite . . . You can guess who it is . . ."

He got up with a sudden briskness.

"Let's verify it anyhow," he said. "He gave me the street and the number. Ah, there's the telephone book! Would it be a coincidence merely if I found that at No. 20 in Chasemore Street, South Kensington, there lived a Lady Payle?"

He turned over the leaves of the bulky volume.

"Yes, that's right," he said.

Roderick's Story

My powers of persuasion at first seemed quite ineffectual; I could not induce my friend Roderick Cardew to strike his melancholy tent in Chelsea, and (leaving it struck) steal away like the Arabs and spend this month of spring with me at my newly acquired house at Tilling to observe the spell of April's wand making magic in the country. I seemed to have brought out all the arguments of which I was master; he had been very ill, and his doctor recommended a clearer air with as mild a climate as he could conveniently attain; he loved the great stretches of drained marsh-land which lay spread like a pool of verdure round the little town; he had not seen my new home which made a breach in the functions of hospitality, and he really could not be expected to object to his host, who, after all, was one of his oldest friends. Besides (to leave no stone unturned) as he regained his strength he could begin to play golf again, and it entailed, as he well remembered, a very mild exertion for him to keep me in my proper position in such a pursuit.

At last there was some sign of yielding.

"Yes. I should like to see the marsh and the big sky once more," he said.

A rather sinister interpretation of his words "once more," made a sudden flashed signal of alarm in my mind. It was utterly fanciful, no doubt, but that had better be extinguished first.

"Once more?" I asked. "What does that mean?"

"I always say 'once more,'" he said. "It's greedy to ask for too much."

The very fact that he fenced so ingeniously deepened my suspicion.

"That won't do," I said. "Tell me, Roddie."

He was silent a moment.

"I didn't intend to," he said, "for there can be no use in it. But if you insist, as apparently you mean to do, I may as well give in. It's what you think; 'once more' will very likely be the most. But you mustn't fuss about it; I'm not going to. No proper person fusses about death; that's a train which we are all sure to catch. It always waits for you."

I have noticed that when one learns tidings of that sort, one feels, almost immediately, that one has known them a long time. I felt so now.

"Go on," I said.

"Well, that's about all there is. I've had sentence of death passed upon me, and it will probably be carried out, I'm delighted to say, in the French fashion. In France, you know, they don't tell you when you are to be executed till a few minutes before. It is likely that I shall have even less than that, so my doctor informs me. A second or two will be all I shall get. Congratulate me, please."

I thought it over for a moment.

"Yes, heartily," I said. "I want to know a little more though."

"Well, my heart's all wrong, quite unmendably so. Heart-disease! Doesn't it sound romantic? In mid-Victorian romance, heroes and heroines alone die of heart-disease. But that's by the way. The fact is that I may die at any time without a moment's warning. I shall give a couple of gasps, so he told me when I insisted on knowing details, and that'll be all. Now, perhaps, you understand why I was unwilling to come and stay with you. I don't want to die in your house; I think it's dreadfully bad manners to die in other people's houses. I long to see Tilling again, but I think I shall go to an hotel. Hotels are fair game, for the management overcharges those who live there to compensate themselves for those who die there. But it would be rude of me to die in your house; it might entail a lot of bother for you, and I couldn't apologize—"

"But I don't mind your dying in my house," I said. "At least you see what I mean—"

He laughed.

"I do, indeed," he said. "And you couldn't give a warmer assurance of friendship. But I couldn't come and stay with you in my present plight without telling you what it was, and yet I didn't mean to tell you. But there we are now. Think again; reconsider your decision."

"I don't," I said. "Come and die in my house by all means, if you've got to. I would much sooner you lived there: your dying will, in any case, annoy me immensely. But it would annoy me even more to know that you had done it in some beastly hotel among plush and looking glasses. You shall have any bedroom you like. And I want you dreadfully to see my house, which is adorable . . . O Roddie, what a bore it all is!"

It was impossible to speak or to think differently. I knew well how trivial a matter death was to my friend, and I was not sure that at heart I did not agree with him. We were quite at one, too, in that we had so often gossiped about death with cheerful conjecture and interested surmise based on the steady assurance that something of new and delightful import was to follow, since neither of us happened to be of that melancholy cast of mind that can envisage annihilation. I had promised, in case I was the first to embark on the great adventure, to do my best to "get through," and give him some irrefutable proof of the continuance of my existence, just by way of endorsement of our belief, and he had given a similar pledge, for it appeared to us both, that, whatever the conditions of the future might turn out to be, it would be impossible when lately translated there, not to be still greatly concerned with what the present world still held for us in ties of love and affection. I laughed now to remember how he had once imagined himself begging to be excused for a few minutes, directly after death, and saying to St. Peter: "May I keep your Holiness waiting for a minute before you finally lock me into Heaven or Hell with those beautiful keys? I won't be a minute, but I do want so much to be a ghost, and appear to a friend of mine who is on the look-out for such a visit. If I find I can't make myself visible I will come back at once . . . Oh, *thank* you, your Holiness."

So we agreed that I should run the risk of his dying in my house, and promised not to make any reproaches posthumously (as far as he was concerned) in case he did so. He on his side promised not to die if he could possibly help it, and next week or so he would come down to me in the heart of the country that he loved, and see April at work.

"And I haven't told you anything about my house yet," I said. "It's right at the top of the hill, square and Georgian and red-bricked. A panelled hall, dining-room and panelled sitting-room downstairs, and more panelled rooms upstairs. And there's a garden with a lawn, and a high brick wall round it, and there is a big garden-room, full of books, with a bow-window looking down the cobbled street. Which bedroom will you have? Do you like looking on to the garden or on to the street? You may even have my room if you like."

"He looked at me a moment with eager attention. "I'll have the square panelled bedroom that looks out on to the garden, please," he said. "It's the second door on the right when you stand at the top of the stairs."

"But how do you know?" I asked.

"Because I've been in the house before, once only, three years ago," he said. "Margaret Alton took it furnished and lived there for a year or so. She died there, and I was with her. And if I had known that this was your house, I should never have dreamed of hesitating whether I should accept your invitation. I should have thrown my good manners about not dying in other people's houses to the winds. But the moment you began to describe the garden and garden-room I knew what house it was. I have always longed to go there again. When may I come, please? Next week is too far ahead. You're off there this afternoon, aren't you?"

I rose: the clock warned me that it was time for me to go to the station.

"Yes. Come this afternoon," I suggested. "Come with me."

"I wish I could, but I take that to mean that it will suit you if I come to-morrow. For I certainly will. Good Lord! To think of your having got just that house! It ought to be a wonderfully happy one, for I saw— But I'll tell you about that perhaps when I'm there. But don't ask me to: I'll tell you if and when I can, as the lawyers say. Are you really off?"

I was really off, for I had no time to spare, but before I got to the door he spoke again.

"Of course, the room I have chosen was *the* room," he said, and there was no need for me to ask what he meant by *the* room.

I knew no more than the barest and most public outline of that affair, distant now by the space of many years, but, so I conceived, ever green in Roderick's heart, and, as my train threaded its way through the gleams of this translucent spring evening, I retraced this outline as far as I knew it. It was the one thing of which Roderick never spoke (even now he was not sure that he could manage to tell me the end of it), and I had to rummage in my memory for the reconstruction of the half-obliterated lines.

Margaret – her maiden-name would not be conjured back into memory – had been an extremely beautiful girl when Roderick first met her, and, not without encouragement, he had fallen head over ears in love with her. All seemed to be going well with his wooing, he had the air of a happy lover, when there appeared on the scene that handsome and outrageous fellow, Richard Alton. He was the heir to his uncle's barony and his really vast estates, and the girl, when he proceeded to lay siege, very soon capitulated. She may have fallen in love with him, for he was an attractive scamp, but the verdict at the time was that it was her ambition, not her heart, that she indulged. In any case, there was the end of Roderick's wooing, and before the year was out she had married the other.

I remembered seeing her once or twice in London about this time, splendid and brilliant, of a beauty that dazzled, with the world very much at her feet. She bore him two sons; she succeeded to a great position; and then with the granting of her heart's desire, the leanness withal followed. Her husband's infidelities were numerous and notorious; he treated her with a subtle cruelty that just kept on the right side of the law, and, finally, seeking his freedom, he deserted her, and openly lived with another woman. Whether it was pride that kept her from divorcing him, or whether she still loved him (if she had ever done so) and was ready to take him back, or whether it was out of revenge that she refused to have done with him legally, was an affair of which I knew nothing. Calamity followed on calamity; first one and then the other of her sons was killed in the European War, and I remembered having heard that she was the victim of some malignant and disfiguring disease, which caused her to lead a hermit life, seeing nobody. It was now three years or so since she had died.

Such, with the addition that she had died in my house, and that Roderick had been with her, was the sum of my meagre knowledge, which might or might not, so he had intimated, be supplemented by him. He arrived next day, having motored down from London for the avoidance of fatigue, and certainly as we sat after dinner that night in the garden-room, he had avoided it very successfully, for never had I seen him more animated.

"Oh, I have been so right to come here," he said, "for I feel steeped in tranquillity and content. There's such a tremendous sense of Margaret's presence here, and I never knew how much I wanted it. Perhaps that is purely subjective, but what does that matter so long as I feel it? How a scene soaks into the place where it has been enacted; my room, which you know was her room, is alive with her. I want nothing better than to be here, prowling and purring over the memory of the last time, which was the only one, that I was here. Yes, just that; and I know how odd you must think it. But it's true, it was here that I saw her die, and instead of shunning the place, I bathe myself in it. For it was one of the happiest hours of my life."

"Because—" I began.

"No; not because it gave her release, if that's in your mind," he said. "It's because I saw—"

He broke off, and remembering his stipulation that I should ask him nothing, but that he would tell me "if and when" he could, I put no question to him. His eyes were dancing with the sparkle of fire that burned on the hearth, for though April was here, the evenings were still chilly, and it was not the fire that gave them their light, but a joyousness that was as bright as glee, and as deep as happiness.

"No, I'm not going on with that now," he said, "though I expect I shall before my days are out. At present I shall leave you wondering why a place that should hold such mournful memories for me, is such a well-spring. And as I am not for telling you about me, let me inquire about you. Bring yourself up to date; what have you been doing, and much more important, what have you been thinking about?"

"My doings have chiefly been confined to settling into this house," I said. "I've been pulling and pushing furniture into places where it wouldn't go, and cursing it."

He looked round the room.

"It doesn't seem to bear you any grudge," he said. "It looks contented. And what else?"

"In the intervals, when I couldn't push and curse any more," I said, "I've been writing a few spook stories. All about the borderland, which I love as much as you do."

He laughed outright.

"Do you, indeed?" he said. "Then it's no use my saying that it is quite impossible. But I should like to know your views on the borderland."

I pointed to a sheaf of typewritten stuff that littered my table.

"Them's my sentiments," I said, "and quite at your service."

"Good; then I'll take them to bed with me when I go, if you'll allow me. I've always thought that you had a pretty notion of the creepy, but the mistake that you make is to imagine that creepiness is characteristic of the borderland. No doubt there are creepy things there, but so there are everywhere, and a thunder-storm is far more terrifying than an apparition. And when you get really close to the borderland, you see how enchanting it is, and how vastly more enchanting the other side must be. I got right on to the borderland once, here in this house, as I shall probably tell you, and I never saw so happy and kindly a place. And without doubt I shall soon be careering across it in my own person. That'll be, as we've often determined, wildly interesting, and it will have the solemnity of a first night at a new play about it. There'll be the curtain close in front of you, and presently it will be raised, and you will see something you never saw before. How well, on the whole, the secret has been kept, though from time to time little bits of information, little scraps of dialogue, little descriptions of scenery have leaked out. Enthrallingly interesting; one wonders how they will come into the great new drama."

"You don't mean the sort of thing that mediums tell us?" I asked.

"Of course I don't. I hate the sloshy – really there's no other word for it, and why should there be, since that word fits so admirably – the sloshy utterances of the ordinary high-class, beyond-suspicion medium at half a guinea a sitting, who asks if there's anybody present who once knew a Charles, or if not Charles, Thomas or William. Naturally somebody has known a Charles, Thomas or William who has passed over, and is the son, brother, father or cousin of a lady in black. So when she claims Thomas, he tells her that he is very busy and happy, helping people . . . O Lord, what rot! I went to one such séance a month ago, just before I was taken ill, and the medium said that Margaret wanted to get into touch with somebody. Two of us claimed Margaret, but Margaret chose me and said she was the spirit of my wife. Wife, you know! You must allow that this was a very unfortunate shot. When I said that I was unmarried, Margaret said that she was my mother, whose name was Charlotte. Oh dear, oh dear! Well, I shall go to bed with joy, bringing your spooks with me . . ."

"Sheaves," said I.

"Yes, but aren't they the sheaves? Isn't one's gleaning of sheaves in this world what they call spooks? That is, the knowledge of what one takes across?"

"I don't understand one word," said I.

"But you must understand. All the knowledge – worth anything – which you or I have collected here, is the beginning of the other life. We toil and moil, and make our gleanings and our harvestings, and all our decent efforts help us to realise what the real harvest is. Surely we shall take with us exactly that which we have reaped . . ."

After he had gone up to bed I sat trying to correct the errors of a typist, but still between me and the pages there dwelt that haunting sense of all that we did here being only the grist for what was to come. Our achievements were rewarded, so he seemed to say, by a glimpse. And those glimpses – so I tried to follow him – were the hints that had leaked out of the drama for which the curtain was twitching. Was that it?

Roderick came down to breakfast next morning, superlatively frank and happy.

"I didn't read a single line of your stories," he said. "When I got into my bedroom I was so immeasurably content that I couldn't risk getting interested in anything else. I lay awake a long time, pinching myself in order to prolong my sheer happiness, but the flesh was weak, and at last, from sheer happiness, I slept and probably snored. Did you hear me? I hope not. And then sheer happiness dictated my dreams, though I don't know what they were, and the moment I was called I got up, because . . . because I didn't want to miss anything. Now, to be practical again, what are you doing this morning?"

"I was intending to play golf," I said, "unless—"

"There isn't an 'unless,' if you mean Me. My plan made itself for me, and I intend – this is my plan – to drive out with you, and sit in the hollow by the fourth tee, and read your stories there. There's a great southwesterly wind, like a celestial housemaid, scouring the skies, and I shall be completely sheltered there, and in the intervals of my reading, I shall pleasantly observe the unsuccessful efforts of the golfers to carry the big bunker. I can't personally play golf any more, but I shall enjoy seeing other people attempting to do it."

"And no prowling or purring?" I asked.

"Not this morning. That's all right: it's there. It's so much all right that I want to be active in other directions. Sitting in a windless hollow is about the range of my activities. I say that for fear that you should."

I found a match when we arrived at the club-house, and Roderick strolled away to the goal of his observations. Half an hour afterwards I found him watching with criminally ecstatic joy the soaring drives that, in the teeth of the great wind, were arrested and blown back into the unholiest bunker in all the world or the low clever balls that never rose to the height of the shored-up cliff of sand. The couple in front of my partner and me were sarcastic dogs, and bade us wait only till they had delved themselves over the ridge, and then we might follow as soon as we chose. After violent deeds in the bunker they climbed over the big dune, thirty yards beyond which lay the green on which they would now be putting.

As soon as they had disappeared, Roderick snatched my driver from my hand.

"I can't bear it," he said. "I must hit a ball again. Tee it low, caddie . . . No, no tee at all."

He hit a superb shot, just high enough to carry the ridge, and not so high that it caught the opposing wind and was stopped towards the end of its flight. He gave a loud croak of laughter.

"That'll teach them not to insult my friend," he said. "It must have been pitched right among their careful puttings. And now I shall read his ghost-stories."

I have recorded this athletic incident because better than any analysis of his attitude towards life and death it conveys just what that attitude was. He knew perfectly well that any swift exertion might be fatal to him, but he wanted to hit a golf ball again as sweetly and as hard as it could be hit. He had done it: he had scored off death. And as I went on my way I felt perfectly confident that if, with that brisk free effort, he had fallen dead on the tee, he would have thought it well worth while, provided only that he had made that irreproachable shot. While alive, he proposed to partake in the pleasures of life, amongst which he had always reckoned that of hitting golf balls, not caring, though he liked to be alive, whether the immediate consequence was death, just because he did not in the least object to being dead. The choice was of such little consequence . . . The history of that I was to know that evening.

The stories which Roderick had taken to read were designed to be of an uncomfortable type: one concerned a vampire, one an elemental, the third the reincarnation of a certain execrable personage, and as we sat in the garden-room after tea, he with these pages on his knees, I had the pleasure of seeing him give hasty glances round, as he read, as if to assure himself that there was nothing unusual in the dimmer corners of the room . . . I liked that; he was doing as I intended that a reader should.

Before long he came to the last page.

"And are you intending to make a book of them?" he asked. "What are the other stories like?"

"Worse," said I, with the complacency of the horror-monger.

"Then – did you ask for criticism? I shall give it in any case – you will make a book that not only is inartistic, all shadows and no light, but a false book. Fiction can be false, you know, inherently false. You play godfather to your stories, you see: you tell them in the first person, those at least that I have read, and that, though it need not be supposed that those experiences were actually yours, yet gives a sort of guarantee that you believe the borderland of which you write to be entirely terrible. But it isn't: there are probably terrors there – I think for instance that I believe in elemental spirits, of some ghastly kind – but I am sure that I believe that the borderland, for the most part, is almost inconceivably delightful. I've got the best of reasons for believing that."

"I'm willing to be convinced," said I.

Again, as he looked at the fire, his eye sparkled, not with the reflected flame, but with the brightness of some interior vision.

"Well, there's an hour yet before dinner," he said, "and my story won't take half of that. It's about my previous experience of this house; what I saw, in fact, in the room which I now occupy. It was because of that, naturally, that I wanted the same room again. Here goes, then.

"For the twenty years of Margaret's married life," he said, "I never saw her except quite accidentally and casually. Casually, like that, I had seen her at theatres and what not with her two boys whom thus I knew by sight. But I had never spoken to either of them, nor, after her marriage, to their mother. I knew, as all the world knew, that she had a terrible life, but circumstances being what they were, I could not bring myself to her notice, the more so because she made no sign or gesture of wanting me. But I am sure that no day passed on which I did not long to be able to show her that my love and sympathy were hers. Only, so I thought, I had to know that she wanted them.

"I heard, of course, of the death of her sons. They were both killed in France within a few days of each other; one was eighteen, the other nineteen. I wrote to her then formally, so long had we been strangers, and she answered formally. After that, she took this house, where she lived alone. A year later, I was told that she had now for some months been suffering from a malignant and disfiguring disease.

"I was in London, strolling down Piccadilly when my companion mentioned it, and I at once became aware that I must go to see her, not to-morrow or soon, but now. It is difficult to describe the quality of that conviction, or tell you how instinctive and over-mastering it was. There are some things which you can't help doing, not exactly because you desire to do them, but because they must be done. If, for instance, you are in the middle of the road, and see a motor coming towards you at top-speed, you have to step to the side of the road, unless you deliberately choose to commit suicide. It was just like that; unless I intended to commit a sort of spiritual suicide there was no choice.

"A few hours later I was at your door here, asked to see her, and was told that she was desperately ill and could see nobody. But I got her maid to take the message that I was here, and presently her nurse came down to tell me that she would see me. I should find Margaret, she said, wearing a veil so as to conceal from me the dreadful ravages which the disease had inflicted on her face, and the scars of the two operations which she had undergone. Very likely she would not speak to me, for she had great difficulty in speaking at all, and in any case I was not to stay for more than a few minutes. Probably she could not live many hours: I had only just come in time. And at that moment I wished I had done anything rather than come here, for though instinct had driven me here, yet instinct now recoiled with unspeakable horror. The flesh wars against the spirit, you know, and under its stress I now suggested that it was better perhaps that I should not see her . . . But the nurse merely said again that Margaret wished to see me, and guessing perhaps the cause of my unwillingness, 'Her face will be quite invisible,' she added. 'There will be nothing to shock you.'

"I went in alone: Margaret was propped up in bed with pillows, so that she sat nearly upright, and over her head was a dark veil through which I could see nothing whatever. Her right hand lay on the coverlet, and as I seated myself by her bedside, where the nurse had put a chair for me, Margaret advanced her hand towards me, shyly, hesitatingly, as if not sure that I would take it. But it was a sign, a gesture."

He paused, his face beaming and radiant with the light of that memory.

"I am speaking of things unspeakable," he said. "I can no more convey to you all that meant than by a mere enumeration of colours can I steep your soul in the feeling of a sunset . . . So there I sat, with her hand covered and clasped in mine. I had been told that very likely she would not speak, and for myself there was no word in the world which would not be dross in the gold of that silence.

"And then from behind her veil there came a whisper.

"'I couldn't die without seeing you,' she said. 'I was sure you would come. I've one thing to say to you. I loved you, and I tried to choke my love. And for years, my dear, I have been reaping the harvest of what I did. I tried to kill love, but it was so much stronger than I. And now the harvest is gathered. I have suffered cruelly, you know, but I bless every pang of it. I needed it all . . .'

"Only a few minutes before, I had quaked at the thought of seeing her. But now I could not suffer that the veil should cover her face.

"'Put up your veil, darling,' I said. 'I must see you.'

"'No, no,' she whispered. 'I should horrify you. I am terrible.'

"'You can't be terrible to me,' I said. 'I am going to lift it.'

"I raised her veil. And what did I see? I might have known, I think: I might have guessed that at this moment, supreme and perfect, I should see with vision.

"There was no scar or ravage of disease or disfigurement there. She was far lovelier than she had ever been, and on her face there shone the dawn of the everlasting day. She had shed all that was perishable and subject to decay, and her immortal spirit was manifested to me, purged and punished if you will, but humble and holy. There was granted to my frail mortal sight the power of seeing truly; it was permitted to me to be with her beyond the bounds of mortality . . .

"And then, even as I was lost in an amazement of love and wonder, I saw we were not alone in the room. Two boys, whom I recognised, were standing at the other side of the bed, looking at her. It seemed utterly natural that they should be there.

"'We've been allowed to come for you, mother darling,' said one. 'Get up.'

"She turned her face to them.

"'Ah, my dears,' she said. 'How lovely of you. But just one moment.'

"She bent over towards me and kissed me.

"'Thank you for coming, Roderick,' she said. 'Good-bye, just for a little while.'

"At that my power of sight – my power of true sight – failed. Her head fell back on the pillows and turned over on one side. For one second, before I let the veil drop over it again, I had a glimpse of her face, marred and cruelly mutilated. I saw that, I say, but never then nor afterwards could I remember it. It was like a terrible dream, which utterly fades on the awaking. Then her hand, which had been clasping mine, in that moment of her farewell slackened its hold, and dropped on to the bed. She had just moved away, somewhere out of sight, with her two boys to look after her."

He paused.

"That's all," he said. "And do you wonder that I chose that room? How I hope that she will come for me."

My room was next to Roderick's, the head of his bed being just opposite the head of mine on the other side of the wall. That night I had undressed, lain down, and had just put out my light, when I heard a sharp tap just above me. I thought it was some fortuitous noise, as of a picture swinging in a draught, but the moment after it was repeated, and it struck me that it was perhaps a summons from Roderick who wanted something. Still quite unalarmed, I got out of bed, and, candle in hand, went to his door. I knocked, but receiving no answer, opened it an inch or two.

"Did you want anything?" I asked, and, again receiving no answer, I went in.

His lights were burning, and he was sitting up in bed. He did not appear to see me or be conscious of my presence, and his eyes were fixed on some point a few feet away in front of him. His mouth smiled, and in his eyes was just such a joy as I had seen there when he told me his story. Then, leaning on his arm, he moved as if to rise.

"Oh, Margaret, my dear . . .,' he cried.

He drew a couple of short breaths, and fell back.

RECONCILIATION

Garth Place lies low in a dip of the hills which, north, east and west, enclose its sequestered valley as in the palm of a hollowed hand. To the south the valley broadens out and the encompassing hills merge themselves into the wide strip of flat country once reclaimed from the sea, and now, with intersections of drainage dykes, forming the fat pasture of the scattered farms. Thick woods of beech and oak, which climb the hillsides above the house up to the top of the ridge, give it further shelter, and it dozes in a soft and sundered climate of its own when the bleak uplands above it are swept by the east winds of spring or the northerly blasts of winter; and, sitting in its terraced garden in the mild sunshine of a clear December day you may hear the gale roaring through the tree-tops on the upper slopes, and see the clouds scudding high above you, yet never feel a breath of the wind that shreds them seawards. The clearings in these woods are thick with anemones and fullblown clumps of primroses a month before the tiniest bud has appeared in the copses of the upland, and its gardens are still bright with the red blossoms of the autumn long after the flower-borders in the village that huddles on the hilltop to the west have been blackened by the frosts. Only when the south wind blows is its tranquillity disturbed, and then the sound of the waves is heard, and the wind is salt with the sea.

The house itself dates from the beginning of the seventeenth century, and has miraculously escaped the destructive hand of the restorer. Its three low storeys are built of the grey stone of the district, the roof is made of thin slabs of the same, between which the blown seeds have found anchorage, and the broad mullioned windows are many-paned. Never a creak comes from its oaken floors, solid and broad are its staircases, its panelling is as firm as the walls in which it is laid.

A faint odour of wood smoke from the centuries of fires that have burned on its open hearths pervades it, that and an extraordinary silence. A man who lay awake all night in one of its chambers would hear no whisper of cracking woodwork, or rattling pane, and all night long there would come to his listening ears no sound from outside but the hoot of the tawny owl, or in June the music of the nightingale. At the back a strip of garden has been anciently levelled out of the hillside, in front the slope has been built up to form a couple of terraces. Below, a spring feeds a small sheet of water, bordered by marshy ground set with tufts of rushes, and out of it a stream much stifled in herbage wanders exiguously past the kitchen garden, and joins the slow-flowing little river which, after a couple of miles of lazy travel, debouches through broadening mud-flats into the English Channel. Along the further margin of the stream a footpath with right-of-way leads from the village of Garth on the hill above to the main road across the plain. Just below the house a small stone bridge with a gate crosses the stream and gives access to this footpath.

I first saw the house to which now for so many years I have been a constant visitor when I was an undergraduate at Cambridge. Hugh Verrall, the only son of its widowed owner, was a friend of mine, and he proposed to me one August that we should have a month there together. His father, he explained, was spending the next six weeks at a foreign health resort. Mine, so he understood, was tied in London, and this really seemed a more agreeable way of getting through August than that he should inhabit his house in melancholy solitude, and that I should stew in town. So if the notion at all appealed to me, I had but to get the parental permission; it had already received his father's sanction. Hugh, in fact, produced Mr. Verrall's letter, in which he stated his views as to his son's disposal of his time with great lucidity.

> I won't have you hanging about at Marienbad all August, (*he said,*) for you'll only get into mischief, and spend the rest of your allowance for the year. Besides, there's your work to

> think of; you didn't do a stroke, so your tutor informed me, all last term, so you'd better make up for it now. Go down to Garth, and get some pleasant, idle scamp like yourself to stay with you, and then you'll have to work, for you won't find anything else to do! Besides, nobody wants to do anything at Garth.

"All right, the idle scamp will come," said I. I knew my father didn't want me to be in London, either.

"Mark you, the idle scamp has to be pleasant," said Hugh. "Well, you'll come, anyhow; that's ripping. You'll see what my father means by not wanting to do anything. That's Garth."

The end of the next week saw us installed there, and never in all the first sights of the various splendours of the world that have since then been accorded to me have I felt so magical and potent a spell as that which caught the breath in my throat when on the evening of that hot August day I first saw Garth. For a mile before the road had lain through the woods that clothe the slope above it; from there my cab emerged as from a tunnel, and there in the clear twilight, with sunset flaming overhead, was the long grey facade, with the green lawns about it, and its air of antique and native tranquillity. It seemed an incarnation of the very soul and spirit of England: there on the south was the line of sea, and all round it the immemorial woods. Like its oaks, like the velvet of its lawns, the house had grown from the very soil, and the life of the soil still richly nurtured it. Venice was not more authentically born from the sea, nor Egypt from the mystery of the Nile, than Garth was born from the woods of England.

There was time for a stroll round before dinner, and Hugh casually recounted the history of it. His forebears had owned it since the time of Queen Anne.

"But we're interlopers," he said, "and not very creditable ones. Before that, my people had been tenants of the farm you passed at the top of the hill, and the Garths were in possession. It was a Garth who built the house in the reign of Elizabeth."

"Ah, then you've got a ghost," I said. "That makes it quite complete. Don't tell me that there isn't a Garth who haunts the house?"

"Anything to oblige," said he, "but that I am afraid I can't manage for you. You're too late: a hundred years ago it certainly was supposed to be haunted by a Garth."

"And then?" I asked.

"Well, I know nothing about spooks, but it looks as if the haunt wore itself out. It must be tiresome, you know, for a spirit to be chained to a place, and have to walk about the garden in the evening, and patrol the passages and bedrooms at night, if nobody pays any attention to it. My forebears didn't care the least, it appears, whether the ghost haunted the place or not. In consequence, it evaporated."

"And whose ghost was it supposed to be?" I asked.

"The ghost of the last Garth, who lived here in the time of Queen Anne. What happened was this. A younger son of my family, Hugh Verrall – same name as me – went up to London to seek his fortune. He made a lot of money in a very short time, and when he was a middle-aged man he retired, and took it into his head that he would like to be a country gentleman with an estate of his own. He was always fond of this country, and came to live at a house in the village up there, while he looked about, and no doubt he had ulterior purposes. For Garth Place was at that time in the hands of a wild fellow called Francis Garth, a drunkard and a great gambler, and Hugh Verrall used to come down here night after night and thoroughly fleece him. Francis had one daughter, who of course was heiress to the place; and at first Hugh made up to her with the idea of marrying her, but when that was no use, he took to the other way of getting hold of it. Eventually, in the fine traditional manner, Francis Garth, who by that time owed my ancestor something like thirty thousand pounds, staked the Garth property against his debt and lost. There was a tremendous excitement over it, with stories of loaded dice and marked cards, but nothing could be proved, and Hugh evicted Francis and took possession. Francis lived for some years yet, in a labourer's cottage in the village, and every evening he used to walk down the path there, and, standing opposite the house, curse the inhabitants. At his death the haunt began and then, simply, it died out."

"Perhaps it's storing force," I suggested. "Perhaps it's intending to come out strong again. You ought to have a ghost here, you know."

"Not a trace of one, I'm afraid," said Hugh; "or I wonder if you'll think there is still a trace of it. But it's such a silly trace that I'm almost ashamed to tell you about it."

"Go on quickly," said I.

He pointed up to the gable above the front door. Underneath it, in an angle formed by the roof, there was a big square stone, evidently of later date than the wall. The surface of it was in contrast to the rest of the wall, much crumbled, but it had evidently been carved, and the shape of a heraldic shield could be seen on it, though of the arms it carried there was nothing left.

"It's too silly," said Hugh, "but it is a fact that my father remembers that stone being placed there. His father put it up, and it bore our coat of arms: you can just see the shape of the shield.

But though it was of the stone of the district, exactly like the rest of the house, it had hardly been put up when the surface began to decay, and in ten years our arms were absolutely obliterated. Odd, that just that one stone should have perished so quickly, when all the rest really seems to have defied time."

I laughed.

"That's Francis Garth's work beyond a doubt," I said. "There's life in the old dog yet."

"Sometimes I think there is," he said. "Mind you, I've never seen or heard anything here which is in the smallest way suggestive of spooks, but constantly I feel that there is something here that waits and watches. It never manifests itself, but it's there."

As he spoke, I caught some faint psychical glimpse of what he meant. There was something there, something sinister and malevolent. But the impression was of the most momentary sort; hardly had it conveyed itself to me when it vanished again, and the amazing beauty and friendliness of the house overwhelmingly reasserted itself. If ever there was an abode of ancient peace, it was here.

We settled down at once into a delightful existence. Being very great friends, we were completely at ease with each other; we talked as we felt disposed, but if a silence fell there was no constraint about it, and it would continue, perfectly happily, till one of us was moved to speak again. In the morning for three hours or so we applied ourselves very studiously to our books, but by lunchtime they were closed for the day, and we would walk across the marsh for a swim in the sea, or stray through the woods, or play bowls on the lawn behind the house. The weather, blazing hot, predisposed to laziness, and in that cupped hollow of the hills, where the house stood, it was almost impossible to remember what it felt like to be energetic. But, as Hugh's father had indicated, that was the proper state of body and mind to be in when you resided at Garth. You must be sleepy and hungry and well, but without desires or energies; life moved along there as on some lotus-eater's shore, very softly and quietly without disturbance. To be lazy without scruple or compunction but with a purring content was to act in accordance with the spirit of Garth. But as the days went on I knew that below this content there was something in us both that grew ever more alert and watchful for that which was watching us.

We had been there about a week when on an afternoon of still and sultry heat we went down to the sea for a dip before dinner. There was clearly a storm coming up, but it seemed possible to get a bathe and return before it broke. It came up, however, more quickly than we had thought, and we were still a mile from home when the rain began, heavy and windless. The clouds, which had spread right across the sky, made a darkness as of late twilight, and when we struck the little public footpath on the far side of the stream in front of the house, we were both drenched to the skin. Just as we got to the bridge I saw the figure of a man standing there, and it struck me at once as odd that he should wait out in this deluge and not seek shelter. He stood quite still, looking towards the house, and as I passed him I had one good stare at his face and instantly knew that I had seen a face very like it before, though I could not localize my memory. He was of middle-age, clean-shaven, and there was something curiously sinister about that lean, dark-skinned profile.

However, it was no business of mine if a stranger chose to stand out in the rain and look at Garth Place, and I went on a dozen steps, and then spoke to Hugh in a low voice.

"I wonder what that man's doing there," I said.

"Man? What man?" said Hugh.

"The man by the bridge whom we passed just now," I said.

He turned round to look.

"There's no one there," he said.

Now it seemed quite impossible that this stranger who had certainly been there so few seconds ago could have vanished into the darkness, thick as it was, and at that moment for the first time it occurred to me that this was no creature of flesh and blood into whose face I had looked. But Hugh had hardly spoken when he pointed to the path up which we had come.

"Yes, there is someone there," he said. "Odd that I didn't see him as we passed. But if he likes to stand about in the rain, I suppose he can."

We went on quickly up to the house, and as I changed I cudgelled my brain to think when and where I had seen that face before. I knew it was quite lately, and I knew I had looked with interest at it. And then suddenly the solution came to me. I had never seen the man before, but only a picture of him, and that picture hung in the long gallery at the front of the house, into which Hugh had taken me the first day that I was here, but I had not been there since. Portraits of Verralls and Garths hung on the walls, and the portrait in question was that of Francis Garth. Before going downstairs I verified this, and there was no doubt whatever about it. The man whom I had passed on the bridge was the living image of him who, in the time of Anne, had forfeited the house to Hugh's ancestral namesake.

I said nothing about this identification to Hugh, for I did not want to put any suggestion into his mind. For his part, he made no further allusion to our encounter; it had evidently made no particular impression on him and we spent the evening as usual. Next morning we sat at our books in the parlour overlooking the bowling-green. After an hour's work, Hugh got up for a few minutes' relaxation, and strolled, whistling, to the window. I was not following his movements with any attention, but I noticed that his whistling stopped in the middle of a phrase. Presently he spoke in rather a queer voice.

"Come here a minute," he said.

I joined him, and he pointed out of the window.

"Is that the man you saw yesterday by the bridge?" he said. There he was at the far end of the bowling-green, looking straight at us.

"Yes, that's he," I said.

"I shall go and ask him what he's doing here," said Hugh. "Come with me!"

We went together out of the room and down the short passage to the garden door. The quiet sunlight slept on the grass, but there was no one there.

"That's queer," said Hugh. "That's very queer. Come up to the picture gallery a minute."

"There's no need," said I.

"So you've seen the likeness too," he said. "I say – it is a likeness only, or is it Francis Garth? Whatever it is, it's that which is watching us."

The apparition which, from that time, we both thought and spoke of as Francis Garth, had now been seen twice. During the next week it seemed to be drawing nearer to the house that had once been its haunt, for Hugh saw it just outside the porch by the front door, and a day or two afterwards, as I sat at twilight in the room overlooking the bowling-alley waiting for him to come down to dinner, I saw it close outside the window looking narrowly into the room with malevolent scrutiny. Finally, a few days only before my visit here came to an end, as we returned one evening from a ramble in the woods, we saw it together, standing by the big open fireplace in the hall. This time its appearance was not momentary, for on our entry it remained where it was, taking no notice of us for perhaps ten seconds, and then moved away towards the far doorway. There it stopped and turned, looking directly at Hugh. At that he spoke to it, and without answer it passed out through the door. It had now definitely come inside; and from that time onwards was seen only within the house. Francis Garth had taken possession again.

Now I do not pretend that the sight of this apparition did not affect my nerves. It affected them very unpleasantly; fright, perhaps, is too superficial a word with which to describe the effect it had on me. It was rather some still, dark horror of the spirit that closed over me, not (to be precise) at the moment when I actually saw it, but some few seconds before, so that I knew by this dire terror that invaded me that the apparition was about to manifest itself. But mingled with that was an intense interest and curiosity as to the nature of this strange visitant, who, though long dead, still wore the semblance of the living, and clothed itself in the body which had long crumbled to dust. Hugh, however, felt nothing of this; the spectre alarmed him as little now on its second inhabiting of the house as it had alarmed those who lived here when first it appeared.

"And it's so interesting," he said, as he saw me off on the conclusion of my visit. "It's got some business here, but what can that business be? I'll let you know if there's any further development."

From that time onwards the ghost was constantly seen. It alarmed some people, it interested others, but it harmed none. Often during the next five years or so I stayed there, and I do not think that any visit passed without my seeing it once or twice. But always to me its appearance was heralded by that terror of which I have spoken, in which neither Hugh nor his father shared. And then quite suddenly Hugh's father died. After the funeral Hugh came up to London for interviews with lawyers and for the settlement of affairs connected with the will, and told me that his father was not nearly so well-off as had been supposed, and that he hardly knew if he could afford to live at Garth Place at all. He intended, however, to shut up part of the house, and with a greatly reduced household to attempt to continue there.

"I don't want to let it," he said; "in fact, I should hate to let it. And I don't really believe that there's much chance of my being able to do so. The story of its being haunted is widely known now, and I don't fancy it would be very easy to get a tenant for it. However, I hope it won't be necessary."

But six months later he found that in spite of all economies it was no longer possible to live there, and one June I went down for a final visit, after which, unless he succeeded in getting a tenant, the house would be shut up.

"I can't tell you how I dislike having to go," he said, "but there's no help for it. And what are the ethics of letting a haunted house, do you think? Ought one to tell an intending tenant? I advertised the house last week in *Country Life*, and there's been an inquirer already. In fact, he's coming down with his daughter to see the house to-morrow morning. Name of Francis Jameson."

"I hope he'll hit it off with the other Francis," I said. "Have you seen him much lately?"

Hugh jumped up.

"Yes, fairly often," he said. "But there's an odd thing I want to show you. Come out of doors a minute."

He took me out to the front of the house, and pointed to the gable below which was the shield containing his obliterated arms.

"I'll give you no hint," he said. "But look at it and make any comment."

"There's something appearing there," said I. "I can see two bends crossing the shield, and some device between them."

"And you're sure you didn't see them there before?" he asked.

"I certainly thought the surface had quite perished," I said. "Of course, it can't have. Or have you had it restored?"

He laughed.

"I certainly haven't," he said. "In fact, what you see there isn't part of my arms at all, but the Garth arms."

"Nonsense. It's some chance cracks and weatherings that have come on the stone, rather regular, certainly, but accidental."

He laughed again.

"You don't really believe that," he said. "Nor do I, for that matter. It's Francis: Francis is busy."

I had gone up to the village next morning, over some small business, and as I came back down the footpath opposite the house saw a motor drive up to the door, and concluded that this was Mr. Jameson who had just arrived. I went indoors, and into the hall, and next moment was standing there with staring eyes and open mouth. For just inside were three people talking together: there was Hugh, there was a very charming-looking girl, obviously Miss Jameson, and the third, so my eyes told me, was Francis Garth. As surely as I had recognized the spectre as him whose portrait hung in the gallery, so surely was this man the living and human incarnation of the spectre itself. You could not say it was a likeness: it was an identity.

Hugh introduced me to his two visitors, and I saw in his glance that he had been through much the same experience as I. The interview and the inquiries had evidently only just begun, for after this little ceremony Mr. Jameson turned to Hugh again.

"But before we see the house or garden," he said, "there is one most important question I have to ask, and if your answer to that is unsatisfactory I shall but waste your time in asking you to show me over."

I thought that some inquiry about the ghost was sure to follow, but was quite wrong. This paramount consideration was climate, and Mr. Jameson began explaining to Hugh, with all the ardour of the invalid, his requirements. A warm, soft air, with an absence of easterly and northerly winds in winter, was what he was seeking for – a sheltered and sunny situation.

The replies to these questions were sufficiently satisfactory to warrant an inspection of the house, and presently all four of us were starting on our tour.

"Go on first, my dear Peggy, with Mr. Verrall," said Mr. Jameson to his daughter, "and leave me to follow a little more leisurely with this gentleman, if he will kindly give me his escort. We will receive our impressions independently, too, in that way."

It occurred to me once again that he wanted to make some inquiry about the house, and preferred to get his information not from the owner, but from someone who knew the place, but was in no way connected with the business of letting it. And again I waited to hear some questions about the ghost. But what came surprised me much more.

He waited, evidently with purpose, till the other two had passed some distance on, and then turned to me.

"Now a most extraordinary thing has happened," he said. "I have never set eyes on this house before, and yet I know it intimately. As soon as we came to the front door I knew what this room would be like, and I can tell you what we shall see when we follow the others. At the end of the passage up which they have gone there are two rooms of which the one looks out on to a bowling-green behind the house, the other on to a path close below the windows from which you can look into the room. A broad staircase ascends from there in two short flights to the first floor, there are bedrooms at the back, along the front runs a long, panelled room with pictures. Beyond that again are two bedrooms with a bathroom in between. A smaller staircase, rather dark, ascends from there to the second floor. Is that correct?"

"Absolutely," said I.

"Now you mustn't think I've dreamed these things," he said. "They are in my consciousness, not as a dream at all, but as actual things I knew in my own life. And they are accompanied by a feeling of hostility in my mind. I can tell you this also, that about two hundred years ago my ancestor in the direct line married a daughter of Francis Garth and assumed her arms. This is Garth Place. Was a family of Garth ever here, or is the house simply named after the village?"

"Francis Garth was the last of the Garths who lived here," said I. "He gambled the place away, losing it to the direct ancestor of the present owner; his name also was Hugh Verrall."

He looked at me a moment with a puzzled air, that gave his face a curiously sharp and malevolent expression.

"What does it all mean?" he said. "Are we dreaming, or awake? And there's another thing I wanted to ask you. I have heard – it may be mere gossip – that the house is haunted. Can you tell me anything about that? Have you ever seen anything of the sort here? Let us call it a ghost, though I don't believe in the existence of such a thing. But have you ever seen any inexplicable appearance?"

"Yes, frequently," I said.

"And may I ask what it was?"

"Certainly. It was the apparition of the man of whom we have been speaking. At least, the first time I saw it I at once recognized it as the ghost – if I may use the word – of Francis Garth, whose portrait hangs in the gallery you have correctly described."

I hesitated a moment, wondering if I had better tell him that not only had I recognized the apparition from the portrait, but that I had recognized him from the apparition. He saw my hesitation.

"There is something more," he said.

I made up my mind.

"There is something more," I said, "but I think it would be better if you saw the portrait for yourself. Possibly it will tell you more directly and convincingly what that is."

We went up the stairs, which he had described without first visiting the other rooms on the ground floor, from which I heard the voice of Hugh and his companion. There was no need for me to point out to Mr. Jameson the portrait of Francis Garth, for he went straight to it, and looked at it for a long while in silence. Then he turned to me.

"So it's I who ought to be able to tell you about the ghost," he said, "instead of your telling me."

The others joined us at this moment, and Miss Jameson came up to her father.

"Oh, Daddy, it's the most delicious home-like house," she said. "If you won't take it, I shall."

"Have a look at my portrait, Peggy," said he.

We changed partners after that, and presently Miss Peggy and I were strolling round the outside of the house while the others lingered within. Opposite the front door she stopped and looked up at the gable.

"Those arms," she said. "It's hard to make them out, and I suppose they're Mr. Verrall's? But they're wonderfully like my father's."

After we had lunched, Hugh and his proposed tenant had a private talk together, and soon after his visitors left.

"It's practically settled," he said as we turned back into the hall again after seeing them off. "Mr. Jameson wants a year's lease with option to renew. And now what do you make of it all?"

We talked it out lengthways and sideways and right way up and upside down, and theory after theory was tried and found wanting, for some pieces seemed to fit together, but we could not dovetail them in with others. Eventually, after hours of talk, we reasoned it out, granting that it was all inexplicable, in a manner that may or may not commend itself to the reader, but seems to cover the facts and to present what I may perhaps call a uniform surface of inexplicability.

To start, then, at the beginning, shortly summing up the facts, Francis Garth, dispossessed, possibly with fraud, of his estate, had cursed the incomers and apparently haunted it after his death. Then came a long intermission from any ghostly visitant, and once more the haunt began again at the time when I first stayed here with Hugh. Then to-day there had come to the house a direct descendant of Francis Garth, who was the living image of the apparition we had both so constantly seen, which, by the portrait, was also identified with Francis Garth himself. And already, before Mr. Jameson had entered the house, he was familiar with it and knew what was within, its staircases and rooms and corridors, and remembered that he had often been here with hostility in his soul, even as we had seen hostility on the face of the apparition. What, then (here is the theory that slowly emerged), if we see in Francis Jameson some reincarnation of Francis Garth, purged, so to speak, of his ancient hostility, and coming back to the house which two hundred years ago was his home, and finding a home there once more? Certainly from that day no apparition, hostile and malevolent, has looked in through its windows, or walked in its bowling-alley.

In the sequel, too, I cannot help seeing some correspondence between what happened now and what happened when, in the time of Anne, Hugh Verrall took possession; here was what we may think of as the reverse of the coin that was hot-minted then. For now another Hugh Verrall, unwilling, for reasons that soon became very manifest, to leave the place altogether, established himself in a house in the village, even as his ancestor had done, and amazingly frequent were his visits to the home of his fathers, which was for the present the house of those whose family had owned it before the first of his forefathers came there. I see, too, a correspondence, which Hugh certainly would be the last to pass lightly over, in the fact that Francis Jameson, like Francis Garth, had a daughter. At that point, however I am bound to say that strict correspondence is rudely broken, for whereas Hugh Verrall the first had no luck when he went a-wooing the daughter of Francis Garth, a much better fortune attended the venture of Hugh Verrall the second. In fact, I have just returned from their marriage.

The Face

Hester Ward, sitting by the open window on this hot afternoon in June, began seriously to argue with herself about the cloud of foreboding and depression which had encompassed her all day, and, very sensibly, she enumerated to herself the manifold causes for happiness in the fortunate circumstances of her life. She was young, she was extremely good-looking, she was well-off, she enjoyed excellent health, and above all, she had an adorable husband and two small, adorable children. There was no break, indeed, anywhere in the circle of prosperity which surrounded her, and had the wishing-cap been handed to her that moment by some beneficent fairy, she would have hesitated to put it on her head, for there was positively nothing that she could think of which would have been worthy of such solemnity. Moreover, she could not accuse herself of a want of appreciation of her blessings; she appreciated enormously, she enjoyed enormously, and she thoroughly wanted all those who so munificently contributed to her happiness to share in it.

She made a very deliberate review of these things, for she was really anxious, more anxious, indeed, than she admitted to herself, to find anything tangible which could possibly warrant this ominous feeling of approaching disaster. Then there was the weather to consider; for the last week London had been stiflingly hot, but, if that was the cause, why had she not felt it before? Perhaps the effect of these broiling, airless days had been cumulative. That was an idea, but, frankly, it did not seem a very good one, for, as a matter of fact, she loved the heat; Dick, who hated it, said that it was odd he should have fallen in love with a salamander.

She shifted her position, sitting up straight in this low window-seat, for she was intending to make a call on her courage. She had known from the moment she awoke this morning what it was that lay so heavy on her, and now, having done her best to shift the reason of her depression on to anything else, and having completely failed, she meant to look the thing in the face. She was ashamed of doing so, for the cause of this leaden mood of fear which held her in its grip was so trivial, so fantastic, so excessively silly.

"Yes, there never was anything so silly," she said to herself. "I must look at it straight, and convince myself how silly it is." She paused a moment, clenching her hands.

"Now for it," she said.

She had had a dream the previous night, which, years ago, used to be familiar to her, for again and again when she was a child she had dreamed it. In itself the dream was nothing, but in those childish days whenever she had this dream which had visited her last night, it was followed on the next night by another, which contained the source and the core of the horror, and she would awake screaming and struggling in the grip of overwhelming nightmare. For some ten years now she had not experienced it, and would have said that, though she remembered it, it had become dim and distant to her. But last night she had had that warning dream, which used to herald the visitation of the nightmare, and now that whole store-house of memory, crammed as it was with bright things and beautiful, contained nothing so vivid.

The warning dream, the curtain that was drawn up on the succeeding night, and disclosed the vision she dreaded, was simple and harmless enough in itself. She seemed to be walking on a high sandy cliff covered with short down-grass; twenty yards to the left came the edge of this cliff, which sloped steeply down to the sea that lay at its foot. The path she followed led through fields bounded by low hedges, and mounted gradually upwards. She went through some half-dozen of these, climbing over the wooden stiles that gave communication; sheep grazed there, but she never saw another human being, and always it was dusk, as if evening was falling, and she had to hurry on, because someone (she knew not whom) was waiting for her, and had been waiting not a few minutes only, but for many years. Presently, as she mounted this slope, she saw in front of her a copse of stunted trees, growing crookedly under the continual pressure of the wind that blew from the sea, and when she saw those she knew her journey was nearly done, and that the nameless one, who had been waiting for her so long, was somewhere close at hand. The path she followed was cut through this wood, and the slanting boughs of the trees on the sea-ward side almost roofed it in; it was like walking through a tunnel. Soon the trees in front began to grow thin, and she saw through them the grey tower of a lonely church. It stood in a graveyard, apparently long disused, and the body of the church, which lay between the tower and the edge of the cliff, was in ruins, roofless, and with gaping windows round which ivy grew thickly.

At that point this prefatory dream always stopped. It was a

troubled, uneasy dream, for there was over it the sense of dusk and of the man who had been waiting for her so long, but it was not of the order of nightmare. Many times in childhood had she experienced it, and perhaps it was the subconscious knowledge of the night that so surely followed it which gave it its disquiet. And now last night it had come again, identical in every particular but one. For last night it seemed to her that in the course of these ten years which had intervened since last it had visited her the glimpse of the church and churchyard was changed. The edge of the cliff had come nearer to the tower, so that it now was within a yard or two of it, and the ruined body of the church, but for one broken arch that remained, had vanished. The sea had encroached, and for ten years had been busily eating at the cliff.

Hester knew well that it was this dream and this alone which had darkened the day for her, by reason of the nightmares that used to follow it, and, like a sensible woman, having looked it once in the face, she refused to admit into her mind any conscious calling-up of the sequel. If she let herself contemplate that, as likely or not the very thinking about it would be sufficient to ensure its return, and of one thing she was very certain, namely, that she didn't at all want it to do so. It was not like the confused jumble and jangle of ordinary nightmare, it was very simple, and she felt it concerned the nameless one who waited for her. . . . But she must not think of it; her whole will and intention was set on not thinking of it, and to aid her resolution there was the rattle of Dick's latchkey in the front door, and his voice calling her

She went out into the little square front hall; there he was, strong and large, and wonderfully undream-like.

"This heat's a scandal, it's an outrage, it is an abomination of desolation," he cried, vigorously mopping. "What have we done that Providence should place us in this frying-pan? Let us thwart him, Hester! Let us drive out of this inferno and have our dinner at – I'll whisper it so that he shan't overhear – at Hampton Court!"

She laughed: this plan suited her excellently. They would return late, after the distraction of a fresh scene; and dining out at night was both delicious and stupefying.

"The very thing," she said, "and I'm sure Providence didn't hear. Let's start now!"

"Rather. Any letters for me?"

He walked to the table where there were a few rather uninteresting-looking envelopes with half-penny stamps.

"Ah, receipted bill," he said. "Just a reminder of one's folly in paying it. Circular . . . unasked advice to invest in German marks . . . Circular begging letter, beginning, 'Dear Sir or Madam'. Such impertinence to ask one to subscribe to something without ascertaining one's sex . . . Private view, portraits at the Walton Gallery . . . Can't go; business meetings all day. You might like to have a look in, Hester. Someone told me there were some fine Vandycks. That's all: let's be off."

Hester spent a thoroughly reassuring evening, and though she thought of telling Dick about the dream that had so deeply imprinted itself on her consciousness all day, in order to hear the great laugh he would have given her for being such a goose, she refrained from doing so, since nothing that he could say would be so tonic to these fantastic fears as his general robustness. Besides, she would have to account for its disturbing effect, tell him that it was once familiar to her, and recount the sequel of the nightmares that followed. She would neither think of them nor mention them: it was wiser by far just to soak herself in his extraordinary sanity, and wrap herself in his affection . . . They dined out-of-doors at a riverside restaurant and strolled about afterwards, and it was very nearly midnight when, soothed with coolness and fresh air, and the vigour of his strong companionship, she let herself into the house, while he took the car back to the garage. And now she marvelled at the mood which had beset her all day, so distant and unreal had it become. She felt as if she had dreamed of shipwreck, and had awoke to find herself in some secure and sheltered garden where no tempest raged nor waves beat. But was there, ever so remotely, ever so dimly, the noise of far-offbreakers somewhere?

He slept in the dressing-room which communicated with her bedroom, the door of which was left open for the sake of air and coolness, and she fell asleep almost as soon as her light was out, and while his was still burning. And immediately she began to dream.

She was standing on the seashore; the tide was out, for level sands strewn with stranded jetsam glimmered in a dusk that was deepening into night. Though she had never seen the place it was awfully familiar to her. At the head of the beach there was a steep cliff of sand, and perched on the edge of it was a grey church tower. The sea must have encroached and undermined the body of the church, for tumbled blocks of masonry lay close to her at the bottom of the cliff, and there were gravestones there, while others still in place were silhouetted whitely against the sky. To the right of the church tower there was a wood of stunted trees, combed sideways by the prevalent sea wind, and she knew that along the top of the cliff a few yards inland there lay a path through fields, with wooden stiles to climb, which led through a tunnel of trees and so out into the churchyard. All this she saw in a glance, and waited, looking at the sand-cliff crowned by the church tower, for the terror that was going to reveal itself. Already she knew what it was, and as so many times before, she tried to run away. But the catalepsy of nightmare was already on her; frantically she strove to move, but her utmost endeavour could not raise a foot from the sand. Frantically she tried to look away from the sand-cliffs close in front of her, where in a moment now the horror would be manifested . . .

It came. There formed a pale oval light, the size of a man's face, dimly luminous in front of her and a few inches above the level of her eyes. It outlined itself: short reddish hair grew low on the forehead; below were two grey eyes, set very close together, which steadily and fixedly regarded her. On each side the ears stood noticeably away from the head, and the lines of the jaw met in a short, pointed chin. The nose was straight and rather long, below it came a hairless lip, and last of all the mouth took shape and colour, and there lay the crowning terror. One side of it, soft-curved and beautiful, trembled into a smile, the other side, thick and gathered together as by some physical deformity, sneered and lusted.

The whole face, dim at first, gradually focused itself into clear outline: it was pale and rather lean, the face of a young man. And then the lower lip dropped a little, showing the glint of teeth, and there was the sound of speech. "I shall soon come for you now," it said, and on the words it drew a little nearer to her, and the smile broadened. At that the full, hot blast of nightmare poured in upon her. Again she tried to run, again she tried to scream, and now she could feel the breath of that terrible mouth upon her. Then with a crash and a rending like the tearing asunder of soul and body she broke the spell, and heard her own voice yelling and felt with her fingers for the switch of her light. And then she saw that the room was not dark, for Dick's door was open, and the next moment, not yet undressed, he was with her.

"My darling, what is it?" he said. "What's the matter?"

She clung desperately to him, still distraught with terror.

"Ah, he has been here again," she cried. "He says he will soon come to me. Keep him away, Dick."

For one moment her fear infected him, and he found himself glancing round the room.

"But what do you mean?" he said. "No one has been here."

She raised her head from his shoulder.

"No, it was just a dream," she said. "But it was the old dream, and I was terrified. Why, you've not undressed yet. What time is it?"

"You haven't been in bed ten minutes, dear," he said. "You had hardly put out your light when I heard you screaming."

She shuddered.

"Ah, it's awful," she said. "And he will come again . . ."

He sat down by her.

"Now tell me all about it," he said.

She shook her head.

"No, it will never do to talk about it," she said, "it will only make it more real. I suppose the children are all right, are they?"

"Of course they are. I looked in on my way upstairs."

"That's good. But I'm better now, Dick. A dream hasn't anything real about it, has it? It doesn't mean anything?"

He was quite reassuring on this point, and soon she quieted down. Before he went to bed he looked in again on her, and she was asleep.

Hester had a stern interview with herself when Dick had gone down to his office next morning. She told herself that what she was afraid of was nothing more than her own fear. How many times had that ill-omened face come to her in dreams, and what significance had it ever proved to possess? Absolutely none at all, except to make her afraid. She was afraid where no fear was: she was guarded, sheltered, prosperous, and what if a nightmare of childhood returned? It had no more meaning now than it had then, and all those visitations of her childhood had passed away without trace ... And then, despite herself, she began thinking over that vision again. It was grimly identical with all its previous occurrences, except ... And then, with a sudden shrinking of the heart, she remembered that in earlier years those terrible lips had said: "I shall come for you when you are older," and last night they had said: "I shall soon come for you now." She remembered, too, that in the warning dream the sea had encroached, and it had now demolished the body of the church. There was an awful consistency about these two changes in the otherwise identical visions. The years had brought their change to them, for in the one the encroaching sea had brought down the body of the church, in the other the time was now near ...

It was no use to scold or reprimand herself, for to bring her mind to the contemplation of the vision meant merely that the grip of terror closed on her again; it was far wiser to occupy herself, and starve her fear out by refusing to bring it the sustenance of thought. So she went about her household duties, she took the children out for their airing in the park, and then, determined to leave no moment unoccupied, set off with the card of invitation to see the pictures in the private view at the Walton Gallery. After that her day was full enough; she was lunching out, and going on to a matinée, and by the time she got home Dick would have returned, and they would drive down to his little house at Rye for the week-end. All Saturday and Sunday she would be playing golf, and she felt that fresh air and physical fatigue would exorcise the dread of these dreaming fantasies.

The gallery was crowded when she got there; there were friends among the sightseers, and the inspection of the pictures was diversified by cheerful conversation. There were two or three fine

Raeburns, a couple of Sir Joshuas, but the gems, so she gathered, were three Vandycks that hung in a small room by themselves. Presently she strolled in there, looking at her catalogue. The first of them, she saw, was a portrait of Sir Roger Wyburn. Still chatting to her friend she raised her eye and saw it . . .

Her heart hammered in her throat, and then seemed to stand still altogether. A qualm as of some mental sickness of the soul overcame her, for there in front of her was he who would soon come for her. There was the reddish hair, the projecting ears, the greedy eyes set close together, and the mouth smiling on one side, and on the other gathered up into the sneering menace that she knew so well. It might have been her own nightmare rather than a living model which had sat to the painter for that face.

"Ah, what a portrait, and what a brute!" said her companion. "Look, Hester, isn't that marvellous?"

She recovered herself with an effort. To give way to this ever-mastering dread would have been to allow nightmare to invade her waking life, and there, for sure, madness lay. She forced herself to look at it again, but there were the steady and eager eyes regarding her; she could almost fancy the mouth began to move. All round her the crowd bustled and chattered, but to her own sense she was alone there with Roger Wyburn.

And yet, so she reasoned with herself, this picture of him – for it was he and no other – should have reassured her. Roger Wyburn, to have been painted by Vandyck, must have been dead near on two hundred years; how could he be a menace to her? Had she seen that portrait by some chance as a child; had it made some dreadful impression on her, since overscored by other memories, but still alive in the mysterious subconsciousness, which flows eternally, like some dark underground river, beneath the surface of human life? Psychologists taught that these early impressions fester or poison the mind like some hidden abscess. That might account for this dread of one, nameless no longer, who waited for her.

That night down at Rye there came again to her the prefatory dream, followed by the nightmare, and clinging to her husband as the terror began to subside, she told him what she had resolved to keep to herself. Just to tell it brought a measure of comfort, for it was so outrageously fantastic, and his robust common sense upheld her. But when on their return to London there was a recurrence of these visions, he made short work of her demur and took her straight to her doctor.

"Tell him all, darling," he said. "Unless you promise to do that, I will. I can't have you worried like this. It's all nonsense, you know, and doctors are wonderful people for curing nonsense."

She turned to him.

"Dick, you're frightened," she said quietly.

He laughed.

"I'm nothing of the kind," he said, "but I don't like being awakened by your screaming. Not my idea of a peaceful night. Here we are."

The medical report was decisive and peremptory. There was nothing whatever to be alarmed about; in brain and body she was perfectly healthy, but she was run down. These disturbing dreams were, as likely as not, an effect, a symptom of her condition, rather than the cause of it, and Dr. Baring unhesitatingly recommended a complete change to some bracing place. The wise thing would be to send her out of this stuffy furnace to some quiet place to where she had never been. Complete change; quite so. For the same reason her husband had better not go with her; he must pack her off to, let us say, the East coast. Sea-air and coolness and complete idleness. No long walks; no long bathings; a dip, and a deck-chair on the sands. A lazy, soporific life. How about Rushton? He had no doubt that Rushton would set her up again. After a week or so, perhaps, her husband might go down and see her. Plenty of sleep – never mind the nightmares – plenty of fresh air.

Hester, rather to her husband's surprise, fell in with this suggestion at once, and the following evening saw her installed in solitude and tranquillity. The little hotel was still almost empty, for the rush of summer tourists had not yet begun, and all day she sat out on the beach with the sense of a struggle over. She need not fight the terror any more; dimly it seemed to her that its malignancy had been relaxed. Had she in some way yielded to it and done its secret bidding? At any rate no return of its nightly visitations had occurred, and she slept long and dreamlessly, and woke to another day of quiet. Every morning there was a line for her from Dick, with good news of himself and the children, but he and they alike seemed somehow remote, like memories of a very distant time. Something had driven in between her and them, and she saw them as if through glass. But equally did the memory of the face of Roger Wyburn, as seen on the master's canvas or hanging close in front of her against the crumbling sand-cliff, become blurred and indistinct, and no return of her nightly terrors visited her. This truce from all emotion reacted not on her mind alone, lulling her with a sense of soothed security, but on her body also, and she began to weary of this day-long inactivity.

The village lay on the lip of a stretch of land reclaimed from the sea. To the north the level marsh, now beginning to glow with the pale bloom of the sea-lavender, stretched away featureless till it lost itself in distance, but to the south a spur of hill came down to the shore ending in a wooded promontory. Gradually, as her physical health increased, she began to wonder what lay beyond this ridge which cut short the view, and one afternoon she walked across the intervening level and strolled up its wooded slopes. The day was close and windless, the invigorating sea breeze which till now had spiced the heat with freshness had died, and she looked forward to finding a current of air stirring when she had topped the hill. To the south a mass of dark cloud lay along the horizon, but there was no imminent threat of storm. The slope was easily surmounted, and presently she stood at the top and found herself on the edge of a tableland of wooded pasture, and following the path, which ran not far from the edge of the cliff, she came out into more open country. Empty fields, where a few sheep were grazing, mounted gradually upwards. Wooden stiles made a communication in the hedges that bounded them. And there, not a mile in front of her, she saw a wood, with trees growing slantingly away from the push of the prevalent sea winds, crowning the upward slope, and over the top of it peered a grey church tower.

For the moment, as the awful and familiar scene identified itself, Hester's heart stood still: the next a wave of courage and resolution poured in upon her. Here, at last, was the scene of that prefatory dream, and here was she presented with the opportunity of fathoming and dispelling it. Instantly her mind was made up, and under the strange twilight of the shrouded sky she walked swiftly on through the fields she had so often traversed in sleep, and up to the wood, beyond which he was waiting for her. She closed her ears against the clanging bell of terror, which now she could silence for ever, and unfalteringly entered that dark tunnel of wood. Soon in front of her the trees began to thin, and through them, now close at hand, she saw the church tower. In a few yards farther she came out of the belt of trees, and round her were the monuments of a graveyard long disused. The cliff was broken off close to the church tower: between it and the edge there was no more of the body of the church than a broken arch, thick-hung with ivy. Round this she passed and saw below the ruin of fallen masonry, and the level sands strewn with headstones and disjected rubble, and at the edge of the cliff were graves already cracked and toppling. But there was no one here, none waited for her, and the churchyard where she had so often pictured him was as empty as the fields she had just traversed.

A huge elation filled her; her courage had been rewarded, and all the terrors of the past became to her meaningless phantoms. But there was no time to linger, for now the storm threatened, and on the horizon a blink of lightning was followed by a crackling peal. Just as she turned to go her eye fell on a tombstone that was balanced on the very edge of the cliff, and she read on it that here lay the body of Roger Wyburn.

Fear, the catalepsy of nightmare, rooted her for the moment to the spot; she stared in stricken amazement at the moss-grown letters; almost she expected to see that fell terror of a face rise and hover over his resting-place. Then the fear which had frozen her lent her wings, and with hurrying feet she sped through the arched pathway in the wood and out into the fields. Not one backward glance did she give till she had come to the edge of the ridge above the village, and, turning, saw the pastures she had traversed empty of any living presence. None had followed; but the sheep apprehensive of the coming storm, had ceased to feed, and were huddling under shelter of the stunted hedges.

Her first idea, in the panic of her mind, was to leave the place at once, but the last train for London had left an hour before, and besides, where was the use of flight if it was the spirit of a man long dead from which she fled? The distance from the place where his bones lay did not afford her safety; that must be sought for within. But she longed for Dick's sheltering and confident presence; he was arriving in any case to-morrow, but there were long dark hours before to-morrow, and who could say what the perils and dangers of the coming night might be? If he started this evening instead of to-morrow morning, he could motor down here in four hours, and would be with her by ten o'clock or eleven. She wrote an urgent telegram:

Come at once, (*she said*). Don't delay.

The storm which had flickered in the south now came quickly up, and soon after it burst in appalling violence. For preface there were but a few large drops that splashed and dried on the roadway as she came back from the post-office, and just as she reached the hotel again the roar of the approaching rain sounded, and the sluices of heaven were opened.

Through the deluge flared the fire of the lightning, the thunder crashed and echoed overhead, and presently the street of the village was a torrent of sandy, turbulent water, and sitting there in the dark, one picture leapt floating before her eyes – that of the tombstone of Roger Wyburn, already tottering to its fall at the edge of the cliff of the church tower. In such rains as these, acres of the cliffs were loosened; she seemed to hear the whisper of the sliding sand that would precipitate those perished sepulchres and what lay within to the beach below.

By eight o'clock the storm was subsiding, and as she dined she was handed a telegram from Dick, saying that he had already started and sent this off *en route*. By half past ten, therefore, if all was well, he would be here, and somehow he would stand between her and her fear. Strange how a few days ago both it and the thought of him had become distant and dim to her; now the one was as vivid as the other, and she counted the minutes to his arrival. Soon the rain ceased altogether, and looking out of the curtained window of her sitting-room where she sat watching the slow circle of the hands of the clock, she saw a tawny moon rising over the sea. Before it had climbed to the zenith, before her clock had twice told the hour again, Dick would be with her.

It had just struck ten when there came a knock at her door, and the pageboy entered with the message that a gentleman had come for her. Her heart leaped at the news; she had not expected Dick for half an hour yet, and now the lonely vigil was over. She ran downstairs, and there was the figure standing on the step outside. His face was turned away from her; no doubt he was giving some order to his chauffeur. He was outlined against the white moonlight, and in contrast with that, the gas-jet in the entrance just above his head gave his hair a warm, reddish tinge.

She ran across the hall to him.

"Ah, my darling, you've come," she said. "It was good of you. How quick you've been!" Just as she laid her hand on his shoulder he turned. His arm was thrown out round her, and she looked into a face with eyes close-set, and a mouth smiling on one side, the other, thick and gathered together as by some physical deformity, sneered and lusted.

The nightmare was on her; she could neither run nor scream, and supporting her dragging steps, he went forth with her into the night.

Half an hour later Dick arrived. To his amazement he heard that a man had called for his wife not long before, and that she had gone out with him. He seemed to be a stranger here, for the boy who had taken his message to her had never seen him before, and presently surprise began to deepen into alarm; inquiries were made outside the hotel, and it appeared that a witness or two had seen the lady whom they knew to be staying there walking, hatless, along the top of the beach with a man whose arm was linked in hers. Neither of them knew him, but one had seen his face and could describe it.

The direction of the search thus became narrowed down, and though with a lantern to supplement the moonlight they came upon footprints which might have been hers, there were no marks of any who walked beside her. But they followed these until they came to an end, a mile away, in a great landslide of sand, which had fallen from the old churchyard on the cliff, and had brought down with it half the tower and a gravestone, with the body that had lain below.

The gravestone was that of Roger Wyburn, and his body lay by it, untouched by corruption or decay, though two hundred years had elapsed since it was interred there. For a week afterwards the work of searching the landslide went on, assisted by the high tides that gradually washed it away. But no further discovery was made.

Spinach

Ludovic Byron and his sister Sylvia had adopted these pretty, though quite incredible, names because those for which their injudicious parents and godparents were responsible were not so suitable, though quite as incredible. They rightly felt that there was a lack of spiritual suggestiveness in Thomas and Caroline Carrot which would be a decided handicap in their psychical careers, and would cool rather than kindle the faith of those inquirers who were so eager to have séances with the Byrons.

The change, however, had not been made without earnest thought on their parts, for they were two very scrupulous young people, and wondered whether it would be "acting a lie" thus to profess to be what they were not, and whether, in consequence, the clearness of their psychical sight would be dimmed. But they found to their great joy that their spiritual guides or controls, Asteria and Violetta, communicated quite as freely with the Byrons as with the Carrots, and by now they called each other by their assumed names quite naturally, and had almost themselves forgotten that they had ever been other than what they were styled on their neat professional engagement-cards.

While it would be tedious to trace Ludovic's progress from the time when it was first revealed to him that he had rare mediumistic gifts down to the present day, when he was quite at the head of his interesting profession, it is necessary to explain the manner in which his powers were manifested. When the circle was assembled (fees payable in advance), he composed himself in his chair, and seemed to sink into a sort of trance, in which Asteria took possession of him and communicated through his mouth with the devotees. Asteria, when living on the material plane had been a Greek maiden of ancient Athens, who had become a Christian and suffered martyrdom in Rome about the same time as St. Peter. She had wonderful things to tell them all about her experiences on this earth, a little vague, perhaps, as was only natural after so long a lapse of time, but she spoke dreamily yet convincingly about the Parthenon and the Forum and the Ægean sea (so blue), and the catacombs (so black), and the beautiful Italian and Greek sunsets, and this was all the more remarkable because Ludovic had never been outside the country of his birth.

But far more interesting to the circle, any of whom could take a ticket for Rome or Athens and see the sunsets and the catacombs for themselves, were the encouraging things she said about her present existence. Everyone was wonderfully happy and busy helping those who had lately passed over to the other side, and they all lived in an industrious ecstasy of spiritual progress. There were refreshments and relaxations as well, quantities of the most beautiful flowers and exquisite fruits and crystal rivers and azure mountains, and flowing robes and delightful habitations. None of these things was precisely material; you "thought" a flower or a robe, and there it was!

Asteria knew many of the friends and relatives, who had passed over, of Ludovic's circle, and they sent through her loving messages and sweet thoughts. There was George, for instance – did any of the sitters know George? Very often somebody did know George. George was the late husband of one of the sitters, or the father of another, or the little son, who had passed over, of a third, and so George would say how happy he was, and how much love he sent. Then Asteria would tell them that Jane wanted to talk to her dear one, and if nobody knew Jane, it was Mary. And Asteria explained quite satisfactorily how it was that, among all the thousands who were continually passing over, just those who had friends and relations among the ladies and gentlemen who sat with Ludovic Byron were clever enough to "spot" Asteria as being his spiritual guide, who would put them into communication with their loved ones. This was due to currents of sympathy which immediately drew them to her.

Then, when the séance had gone on for some time, Asteria would say that the power was getting weak, and she would bid them good-bye and fade into silence. Presently Ludovic came out of his trance, and they would all tell him how wonderful it had been. At other séances he would not go into trance at all, but Asteria used his hand and his pencil, and wrote pages of automatic script in quaint, slightly foreign English, with here and there a word in strange and undecipherable characters, which was probably Greek. George and Jane and Mary were then dictating to Asteria, who caused Ludovic to write down what she said, and sometimes they were very playful, and did not like their wife's hat or their husband's tie, just by way of showing that they were really there. And then any member of the circle could ask Asteria questions, and she gave them beautiful answers.

Sylvia and her guide, Violetta, were not in so advanced a stage of development as Ludovic and Asteria; indeed, it was only lately that Sylvia had discovered that she had psychical gifts and had got into touch with her guide. Violetta had been a Florentine lady of noble birth, and was born (on the material plane) in the year 1492, which was a very interesting date, as it made her an exact contemporary of Savonarola and Leonardo da Vinci. She had often heard Savonarola preach, and had seen Leonardo at his easel, and it was splendid to know that Savonarola often preached now to enraptured audiences, and that Leonardo was producing pictures vastly superior to anything he had done on earth. They were not material pictures exactly, but thought-pictures. He thought them, and there the pictures were. This corresponded precisely with what Asteria had said about the flowers, and was therefore corroborative evidence.

This winter and spring had been a very busy time for Ludovic, and Mrs. Sapson, one of the most regular attendants at his séances, had been trying to persuade him to go for a short holiday. He was very unwilling to do so, for he was giving five full séances every day (which naturally "mounted up"), and he was loth to abandon, even for a short time, the work that so many people found so enlightening. But then Mrs. Sapson had been very clever, and had asked Asteria at one of the séances whether he ought not to take a rest, and Asteria distinctly said: "Wisdom counsels prudence; be it so." After the séance was over, therefore, Mrs. Sapson, strong in spiritual support, renewed her arguments with redoubled force. She was a large, emphatic widow, who received no end of messages from her husband William. He had been a choleric stockbroker on this plane, but his character had marvellously mellowed and improved, and now he knew what a waste of time it had been to make so much money and lose so much temper.

"Dear Mr. Ludovic," she said, "you must have a rest. You can't fly in the face of sweet Asteria. Besides, I have just got a lovely plan for you. I own a charming little cottage near Rye, which is vacant. My tenant has – has suddenly quitted it. It is a dear little place, everything quite ready for you. No expense at all, except what you eat and drink, and seabathing and golf at your door. Such a place for quiet and meditation, and – who knows – some wonderful visitor (not earthly, of course, for there are no bothering neighbours) might come to you there."

Of course, this charming offer made a great difference. Ludovic felt that he could give up his spiritual work for a fortnight with less of a wrench than was possible when he thought that he would have to pay for lodgings. He expressed his gratitude in suitable terms, and promised to consult Sylvia, who at the moment was engaged with Violetta. She leaped at the idea when it was referred to her, and the matter was instantly settled.

The two were chatting together on the eve of their departure.

"Wonderfully kind of Mrs. Sapson," said Ludovic. "But it's odd that she didn't offer us the cottage before. She was wanting me to take a holiday a month ago."

"Perhaps the tenant has only just left," said Sylvia. "That may be so. Dear me, the country and seabreezes! How nice. But I don't mean to be idle."

"Golf?" suggested Sylvia. "Isn't it very difficult?" He walked across to the table and took up a square parcel, which had just been delivered.

"No, not golf," he said. "But I am going to take up spirit photography. It pays very – I mean it's very helpful. So I've bought a camera and some rolls of films, and the developing and fixing solutions. I shall do it all myself. I used to photograph when I was a boy."

"That must have cost a good deal of money," said Sylvia, who had a great gift for economy.

"Ten pounds, but don't look pained; I think it's worth it. Besides, we get our lodging free. And if I have the power of spirit-photography, it will repay us over and over again."

"Explain the process to me," said Sylvia.

"Well, it's very mysterious, but there's no doubt that if a medium who has got the gift takes a photograph, there sometimes appears on the negative what is called an 'extra'. In other words, if I took a photograph of you there might appear on the film not only your photograph, but that of some spirit, connected with you or the place, standing by you, or perhaps its face floating in the air near you. It would make another branch of our work, it would bring in fresh clients. The old ones too; I think they want something new. Mrs. Sapson would love a photograph of herself with her William leaning over her shoulder. Anyhow, it's worth trying. I shall practise down at the cottage."

He put the parcel containing the photographic apparatus with other property for packing, and made himself comfortable in his chair.

"I want you to work too," he said. "I want you to develop your *rapport* with Violetta. There's nothing like practice. Mediumistic power is just as much a gift as music. But you must practise on the piano to be able to play."

The two were alone, and the utmost confidence existed between them. They talked to each other with a frankness which would have appalled their sitters.

"Sometimes I wonder whether I have any mediumistic power at all," she said. "I get in a dreamy sort of state when I am writing automatic script; but is Violetta really communicating, or am I only putting down the thoughts of my subconscious self? Or when Asteria speaks through you is she really an independent intelligence, or is she part of your own?"

Ludovic was in a very candid mood.

"I don't know, and I don't care," he said. "But my conscious self certainly can't invent all the things Asteria says, so they come from outside my normal perceptions. And then, after all, Asteria tells things about George and Jane, and so on, concerning their life on earth, which I never knew at all."

"But their relations who are sitting with you know them," said Sylvia. "Isn't it possible that you may get at those facts through telepathy?"

"Yes, but then that's extremely clever of me if I do," said Ludovic. "And it's just as reasonable to say that it's Asteria. Besides, if it's all me, how do you account for it that Asteria sometimes says something which goes against all my intentions and inclinations? For instance, when she said, 'Wisdom counsels prudence: be it so,' in answer to Mrs. Sapson's asking if I was not overworked and wanted a holiday, that quite contradicted my own wishes. I didn't want to go for a holiday at all. Therefore it looks as if Asteria was an external intelligence controlling me."

"Subconsciously you might have known you wanted a holiday," said the ingenious Sylvia.

"That's far-fetched. Better stick to Asteria. Besides, I sincerely believe that sometimes things come to me from outside my consciousness. And I don't know – not always, that's to say – what Asteria has been telling them while I'm in trance. Sometimes it really astonishes me."

He poured out a moderate whisky-and-soda.

"I'm looking forward to a holiday from séances," he said, "now that it's settled, for, frankly, Asteria has been a little thin and feeble lately. And I'm not sure that Mrs. Sapson doesn't think so too. I think she feels that she's heard about all that Asteria has got to say, and it would never do to lose her as a sitter. That's why I should very much like to find that I can produce spirit photographs. It – it would vary the menu."

They took with them a grim and capable general servant called

Gramsby, and arrived next afternoon at Mrs. Sapson's cottage. It was romantically situated near a range of great sand-dunes which ran along the coast, and was only a few minutes' walk from the sea. The place was very remote; a minute village with a shop or two and a cluster of fishermen's huts stood half a mile away, and inland there stretched the empty levels of the Romney marsh away to Rye, which smouldered distantly in the afternoon sunlight. The cottage itself was an enchanting abode, built of timber and rough-cast, with a broad verandah facing south, and a gay little garden in front. Inside, on the ground floor, there were kitchen and dining-room, and a large living-room with access to the verandah. This was well and plainly furnished and had an open fireplace with a wide hearth for a wood fire and an immense chimney. Logs were ready laid there and, indeed, the whole house had the aspect of having been lately tenanted. Upstairs there were sunny bedrooms facing south, which, overlooking the sand-dunes, gave a restful view of the sea beyond; it was impossible to conceive a more tranquil haven for an overworked medium.

They had a hasty cup of tea, and hurried out to enjoy the last hours of daylight in exploration among the sand-dunes and along the beach, and came back soon after sunset. Though the day had been warm, the evening air had a nip in it, and Sylvia gave a little shiver as they stepped in from the verandah to the sitting-room.

"It's rather cold," she said. "I think I'll light the fire."

Ludovic shared her sensations.

"An excellent idea," he said. "And we'll draw the curtains and be cosy. What a charming room! I shall take some interiors to-morrow – time exposure, I think they told me, for an interior."

Their supper was soon ready, and presently they came back to the sitting-room and laid out a hectic Patience. But they were both strangely absent-minded, neglecting the most glaring opportunities for getting spaces and putting up kings.

"I can't concentrate on it to-night," said Ludovic. "I feel as if someone was trying to attract my attention . . . I wonder if Asteria wants to communicate."

Sylvia looked up at him.

"Now it's very odd that you should say that," she observed. "I feel exactly as if Violetta was wanting to come through, and yet it doesn't seem quite like Violetta."

He gave an uneasy glance round the room.

"A curious sensation," he said. "I have the consciousness of some presence here which isn't quite Asteria. But it may be she. Tiresome of her, if it is, for she ought to know I came down here for a holiday, considering that she recommended it herself. I think I'll get a pencil and paper, and see if she wants to say anything."

He composed himself in a chair, with the stationery for Asteria on his knee.

"Ask her a question or two, Sylvia," he said, "when I go off."

Sylvia waited till her brother's eyelids fluttered and fell.

"Is that you, Asteria?" she asked.

His hand twitched and quivered. Then the pencil scribbled "Certainly not" in large, firm letters, quite unlike Asteria's pretty writing.

Sylvia asked if it was Violetta, but got an emphatic denial.

"Who is it, then?" she said.

And then a very absurd thing happened. The pencil spelt out "Thomas Spinach".

Sylvia was puzzled for a moment. Then the explanation occured to her, and she laughed.

"Wake up, dear," she said to Ludovic. "It says it is Thomas Spinach. Of course, that's your sub-conscious self trying to remember Carrot."

But Ludovic did not stir, and to her surprise the pencil began writing again.

"I don't know who you are," wrote the unknown control. "But I'm Spinach, young Spinach. And" – there was a long pause – "I want you to help me. I can't remember . . . I'm very unhappy."

As she followed the words, there suddenly came a very loud rap on the wall just above her, which considerably startled her, for why, if "Spinach" was an attempt on the part of Ludovic's subconsciousness to write "Carrot", should he announce his presence? She sprang up, and shook Ludovic by the shoulder.

"Wake up," she said. "There's a strange spirit here, and I don't like it. Wake up, Ludovic."

He came drowsily to himself.

"Hullo!" he said. "Anything been happening? Was it Asteria?"

His eye fell on the paper.

"What's all this?" he said. "Thomas Spinach? That's only me. My subconsciousness said it was Asparagus once."

"But look what it has been writing," said Sylvia.

He read it.

"That's queer," he said. "That can't be me. I'm not very unhappy. I don't want my own help. I know who I am."

He jumped up.

"Most interesting," he said. "It looks like a new control. Young Spinach must be powerful, too; he came through the first time he tried. We'll investigate this, Sylvia. It would be fine to get a new control for our séances."

"But not to-night, Ludovic," said she. "I really shouldn't sleep if you went on now. And he's violent. He made the loudest rap I ever heard."

"Did he, indeed?" said Ludovic. "I must have been in deep trance then, for I never heard it. We'll certainly try to snap him with the camera to-morrow."

The morning was bright and sunny, and directly after breakfast Ludovic set to work with his photography. The first three or four films showed nothing but impenetrable blackness, and a consultation of his handbook convinced him that they must have been over-exposed. He corrected this, and after a few errors on the other side, produced a negative which quite clearly showed Sylvia sitting by the long window into the verandah. This, though it revealed no "extra", was an encouraging achievement, and he took half a dozen more exposures, with which he hurried away into the small dark cupboard under the stairs, where he had installed his developing and fixing baths. Shortly afterwards Sylvia heard her name called in crowing, exultant tones, and ran to see what had happened.

"Don't open the door," he called, "or you'll spoil it. But I've got a picture of you with a magnificent extra – a face hanging in the air by your shoulder."

"How lovely!" shouted Sylvia. "Do be quick and fix it."

There was no sort of doubt about it. There she sat by the window, and close by her was a strange, inexplicable face. So much could be seen from the negative, and when a print was taken of it the details were wonderfully clear. It was the face of a young man; his handsome features wore an expression of agonized entreaty.

"Poor boy!" said Sylvia sympathetically. "So good-looking too; but somehow I don't like him."

Then a brilliant idea struck her.

"Oh, Ludovic," she said, "is it young Spinach?"

He snatched the print from her.

"I must fix it," he said, "or it will be ruined. Of course it's young Spinach. Who else could it be, I should like to know? We'll find out more about him this evening. Fancy obtaining that the very first morning!"

They spent the afternoon on the beach, in order to get in an elevated frame of mind by contemplating the beauties of nature, and after a light supper, prepared for a double séance. Two hooks, so to speak, were baited for Spinach, for in one chair sat Sylvia, with pencil and paper, ready to take down his slightest word, and in another Ludovic, similarly equipped. They both let themselves sink into that drowsy and vacant condition which they knew to be favourable to communications from the unseen, but for a long time they neither of them got a bite. Then Ludovic heard the dash and clatter of his sister's pencil, suddenly beginning to write very rapidly, and this aroused in him disturbing feelings of envy and jealousy, for something was coming through to Sylvia and not to him.

This inharmonious emotion quite dissipated the tranquillity which was a *sine qua non* of the receptive state, and he got up to see what was coming through to her. Probably some mawkish rubbish from Violetta about Savonarola's sermons. But the moment he saw her paper he was thrilled to the marrow.

"Yes, I'm Thomas Spinach," he read, "and I'm very unhappy. I came and stood by you this morning when the man was photographing. I want you to help me. Oh, do help me! It's something I've forgotten, though it is so important. I want you to look everywhere and see if you can't find something very unusual, and tell them. It is somewhere here. It must be, because I put it there, and I hardly like to tell you what it is, because it's terrible . . ."

The pencil stopped. Ludovic was wildly excited, and his jealousy of Sylvia was almost forgotten. After all, it was he who had taken Spinach's photograph . . .

Sylvia's hand continued idle so long that Ludovic, in order to stir it into activity again, began to ask questions.

"Have you passed over, Spinach?" he said.

Her hand began to write in a swift and irritated manner. "Of course I have," it scribbled. "Otherwise I should know where it was."

"Used you to live here?" asked Ludovic. "And when did you pass over?"

"Yes, I lived here," came the answer. "I passed over a week ago. Very suddenly. There was a thunderstorm that night, and I had just finished it all, and was in the garden cooling down, when lightning struck me, and when I came to – on this side, you understand – I couldn't remember where it was."

"Where what was?" asked Ludovic. "Do you mean the thing you had finished? What was it you had finished?"

The pencil seemed to give a loud squeak, as if it was a slate pencil.

"Oh, here it is again," it wrote in trembling characters. "I can't go on now. It's terrible. I'm so frightened. Please, please find it."

Just as on the previous evening, there came an appalling rap somewhere on the wall close to him, and, seriously startled, Ludovic sprang up, and shook Sylvia into consciousness. Whoever this spirit was, it was not a good, kind, mild one like Asteria, who, whenever she rapped, did so very softly and pleasantly.

Sylvia yawned and stretched herself.

"Spinach?" she said, drowsily. "Any Spinach?"

"Yes, dear, quantities," said Ludovic.

"And what did he say? Oh, I went off deep then, Ludovic. I don't know what's been happening. Violetta isn't nearly so powerful. Such an odd feeling! Did I write all that?"

"Yes, in answer to some pretty good questions of mine," he said. "It's really wonderful. We're on the track of young Spinach, or, rather, he's on ours."

Sylvia was reading her manuscript.

"'I passed over a week ago,'" she said. "'Very suddenly – there was a thunderstorm that night—' Why, Ludovic, there was! That's quite true. You slept through it, but I didn't, and I remember reading in the paper that it had been very violent in the Rye district. How strange!"

Ludovic clicked his fingers.

"I know what I'll do," he said. "I shall send a telegram to Mrs. Sapson. Give me a piece of paper. She said that wonderful visitors might perhaps come to me here."

Sylvia grasped his thoughts.

"I see!" she cried. "You mean to tell her that her late tenant, young Thomas Spinach, who was killed by lightning last week, has communicated with us. That will impress her tremendously, if you think she's had enough of Asteria. Indeed, I shouldn't wonder if she lent us this cottage just in order to test us, and see if we really received messages from the other side. What a score!"

She hastily scribbled on a leaf of her writing-block, counting up the words on her fingers. Her economical mind exerted itself to contrive the message in exactly twelve words.

"There!" she read out triumphantly. "Listen! 'Sapson, 29 Brompton Avenue, London. Tenant Spinach killed last week, thunderstorm, communicated.' Just twelve. You needn't sign it, as it will have the Rye postmark."

"My dear," said he, "it's no time for such petty economies. Better spend a few pence more and make it impressive and rather more intelligible. Give me some paper; I asked you before. And we must make it clear that it's not a chance word of local gossip that has inspired it. I shall tell her about the photograph too."

Before they went to bed, Ludovic composed a more explicit telegram, and in the course of the next morning he received an enthusiastic reply from Mrs. Sapson.

> All quite correct and most wonderful (*she wrote*). Delighted you have got into communication. Find out more, and ask him about his uncle. Wire again if fresh revelations occur.

In order to secure themselves from the possibility of interruption, Sylvia gave Gramsby an afternoon out, which she proposed to spend in the excitements of Rye, and as soon as she was gone the mediums prepared for a séance. As Spinach seemed to fancy Sylvia, she composed herself for the trance-condition, with pencil and paper handy, and Ludovic sat by to ask questions. Very soon Sylvia's eyes closed, her head fell forward, and the pencil she held began to tremble violently, like a motor-car ready to start.

"Are you Spinach?" asked Ludovic, observing these signs of possession. Instantly the pencil began to write.

"Yes. Have you found it?"

"We don't know what it is," said Ludovic. Then he remembered Mrs. Sapson's telegram. "Has it anything to do with your uncle?" he asked.

There was a long pause. Then the pencil began to move again.

"Please find him," it wrote.

"But how are we to find your uncle?" asked Ludovic. "We don't know where to look or what he's like. Tell us where to look."

The pencil moved in a most agitated fashion.

"I don't know," it wrote. "If I knew I would tell you. But it's somewhere about. I had just put it somewhere, when the lightning came and killed me, and I can't remember. My memory's gone like – like after concussion of the brain."

An uneasy thought struck Ludovic. Why did young Spinach allude to his uncle as "it"?

"Is your uncle dead?" he asked. "Is it his body that you mean by 'it'?"

Sylvia's fingers writhed as if in mortal agony. Then the pencil jerked out, "Yes."

Ludovic, accustomed as he was to spirits, felt an icy shudder run through him. But he waited in silence, for the pencil looked as if it had something more to write. Then – great heavens – it came.

"I will tell you all," it wrote. "I killed him, and I can't remember where I put him."

A spasm of moral indignation seized Ludovic.

"That was very wrong of you," he justly observed. "But we'll try to help you if you will tell us all about it. Come; you're dead. Nobody can hang you."

Shocked as Ludovic was, and extremely uneasy also at the thought of the proximity not only of the spirit of a murderer, but the corpse of young Spinach's uncle, it was only natural that he should feel an overwhelming professional interest in the revelations that appeared to be imminent. It would be a glorious thing for his career to receive from a departed spirit the first-hand account of this undetected crime, and to be able to corroborate it by the discovery of the corpse. Though he had come down here for a holiday, the chance of such a unique piece of work made him feel quite rested already, for it was impossible to conceive a more magnificent advertisement. What a wonderful confirmation it would be also to Mrs. Sapson's wavering faith in his psychical powers. She would publish the news of it far and wide, and the séances would be more popular than ever. Moreover, there was the chance of learning all sorts of fresh information about the conditions that prevailed on the other side, of a far more sensational and exciting quality than the method of the production of thought-flowers and flowing robes and general love and helpfulness . . . He waited with the intensest expectation for anything that Spinach might vouchsafe.

At last it began, and now there was no need for further questions, for the pencil streamed across the page. Sheet after sheet of the writing-block was filled, and twice Ludovic had to sharpen Sylvia's pencil, for the point was quite worn down with these remarkable disclosures, and only made illegible scratches on the paper. For half an hour it careered over the sheets; then finally it made a great scrawl, and Sylvia's hand dropped inert. She stretched and yawned, and came to herself.

The next hour was the most absorbing that Ludovic had ever spent in his professional work. Together they read the account of the crime. Alexander Spinach, the uncle, was the most wicked of elderly gentlemen, who made his nephew's life an intolerable burden to him. He had found out that the orphan boy had committed a petty forgery with regard to a cheque which he had signed with his uncle's name, and, holding exposure and arrest over his head, had made him work for him day and night, fishing and farming and doing the work of the house without a penny-piece of wages, while he himself boozed his days away in the chimney-corner.

Long brooding over his wrongs and the misery of his life made young Spinach (very properly, as he still thought) determine to kill the odious old wretch, and he adroitly poisoned his whisky with weed-killer. He went out to his work next morning as usual, leaving the corpse in the locked-up house, and casually mentioned to the folk he came across that his uncle had gone up to London and would probably not be back for some time. When he returned in the evening he hid the body somewhere, meaning to dig a handsome excavation in the garden, and having buried it, plant some useful vegetables above it. But hardly had he made this temporary disposition of the corpse, than he was struck by lightning in the terrific storm that visited the district a week ago, and killed. When he came to himself on the spiritual plane he could not remember what he had done with the body.

So far the story was ordinary enough, apart from the interest in the manner of its communication, but now came that part of the confession which these ardent young psychicists saw would be a veritable gold-mine to them. For on emerging on the other side young Spinach found himself terrifyingly haunted not by the spirit, but by the body of his uncle. Just as on the material plane, so he explained, murderers are sometimes haunted by the spirit of their victim, so on the spiritual plane, quite logically, they may be haunted by the body of their victim. His uncle's bodily and palpable presence grimly pursued him wherever he went; even as he gathered sweet thought-flowers or thought-fruits, the terrible body appeared. If he woke at night he found it watching by his bed, if he bathed in the crystal rivers it swam beside him, and he had learned that he could never find peace till it was given proper burial. No doubt, he said, Ludovic had heard of the skeletons of murdered folk being walled up in secret chambers, and how their spirits haunted the place till their bones were discovered and interred. The converse was true on the other side, and while murdered corpses lay about unburied in the material world, their bodies haunted the perpetrator of the crime.

It was here that poor young Spinach's difficulty came in. The sudden lightning-stroke had bereft him of all memory of what he was doing just before, and, puzzle as he might, he could not recollect where he had put the corpse . . . Then he broke out into passionate entreaties: "Help me, help me, kind mediums," he wrote. "I know it is somewhere about, so search for it and get it buried. He was an awful old man and I can't describe the agony of being haunted by his beastly body. Find it and have it buried, and then I shall be free from its dreadful presence."

They read this unique document together by the fading light, strung up to the highest pitch of professional interest, and yet peering awfully round from time to time in vague apprehension of what might happen next. During the séance the wind had got up, and now it was moaning round the corners of the house, and dusk was falling rapidly, with prospects of a wild night to follow. The curtains bulged and bellied in the draught, hollow voices sounded in the chimney, and Sylvia clung to her brother.

"I don't like it," she wailed. "I don't like this spirit of Spinach; Violetta and Asteria are far preferable. And then there's 'It'. It is somewhere about, and it may be anywhere."

Ludovic made an attempt at gaiety.

"It may be anywhere, as you say," he remarked, "but it actually is somewhere. And we've got to find it, dear. Better find it before it gets dark. And think of the sensation there will be when we publish the account of how, in answer to the entreaty of a remorseful spirit—"

"But he isn't remorseful," said Sylvia. "There's not a word of remorse, but only terror at being haunted. There's not only a corpse about, but the spirit of an unrepentant murderer. It isn't pleasant. I would sooner be in expensive lodgings than here."

"Oh, nonsense," said Ludovic. "Besides, young Spinach is friendly enough to us. We're his one hope. And if we find it he will certainly be very grateful. I shouldn't wonder if he sent us many more revelations. Even as it is, how deeply interesting! Nobody ever guessed that there were material ghosts in the spiritual world. But now we must get busy and search for Alexander. Fix your mind on what a tremendously paying experience this will be. Now, where shall we begin? There's the house and the garden—"

"Oh, I hope it will be in the garden," said Sylvia. "But there's no chance of that, for he meant to bury it in the garden afterwards."

"True. We'll begin with the house, then. Now most murderers bury the body under the floor of the kitchen, cover it with quicklime, and fill in with cement."

"But he wouldn't have had time for that," said Sylvia. "Besides, this was to be only a temporary resting-place."

"Perhaps he cut it up," said Ludovic, "and we shall find a piece here and a piece there."

The search began. In the growing dusk, with the wild wind increasing to a gale, they annealed themselves for the gruesome business. They investigated the coal-cellar, they peered into housemaids' cupboards, and with quaking hearts examined the woodshed. Here there were signs that its contents had been disturbed, and the sight of an old boot peeping out from behind some logs nearly caused Sylvia to collapse. Then Ludovic got a ladder, and, climbing up to the roof, interrogated the water-tank, from the contents of which they had already drunk. But all their explorations were in vain; there was no sign of the corpse. For a nerve-racking hour they persevered, and a dismal idea occurred to Ludovic.

"It can't be a practical joke on the part of Spinach, can it?" he said. "That would be in the worst possible taste. Good gracious, what's that?"

There came a loud tapping at the front door, and Sylvia hid her face on his shoulder.

"That's Spinach," she whispered. "That terrible Spinach!"

They tottered to the door and opened it. On the threshold was a man, who told them he was the carrier from Rye, and brought a note for Miss Byron.

"I'm going back in half an hour, miss," he said, "if there's any answer. A box, I understood."

The note was from Gramsby, who, though unwilling to "upset" them, declined to come back to the cottage. She had heard things, and she didn't like it, and she would be obliged if they would pack her box and send it in.

"The coward!" said Sylvia, trembling violently. "She shan't have her box unless she comes to fetch it."

They went back into the sitting-room, lit the fire, and made it as cheerful as they could with many candles. Their flames wagged ominously in the eddying draughts, and the two drew their chairs close to the hearth. By now the full fury of the gale was unloosed, the whole house shuddered at the blasts, doors creaked, curtains whispered, flurries of rain were flung against the windows, and strange noises and stirrings muttered in the chimney.

"I shall just get warm," said Ludovic, "and then go on with the search. I shan't know a moment's peace till I find it."

"I shan't know a moment's peace when you do!" wailed Sylvia.

They were sitting in the fire almost, and suddenly something up the chimney caught Ludovic's eye.

"What's that?" he said.

He got a candle and held it up the chimney.

"It's a rope," he said, "tied round a staple in the wall."

His look met hers, and read the answering horror there.

"I'm going to undo it," he said. "Step back, Sylvia."

There was no need to say that, for she had already retreated to the farthest corner of the room. He pulled the rope off the staple and let it go.

There was a scrambling, shuffling noise from high up in the chimney, and in a cloud of soot "It" fell, with a heavy thud, sprawling across the hearth.

They fled into the night; the carrier had only just got to the garden gate.

"Take us into Rye," cried Ludovic. "Take us to the police-station. Murder has been done!"

The account of these amazing events duly appeared in all the psychical papers and many others. Long queues of would-be sitters formed up for the Byron séances, in the hopes of getting fresh revelations from young Spinach. But from association with Asteria and Violetta he gradually became quite common-place, and only told them about thought-flowers and white robes.

Bagnell Terrace

I had been for ten years an inhabitant of Bagnell Terrace, and, like all those who have been so fortunate as to secure a footing there, was convinced that for amenity, convenience, and tranquillity it is unrivalled in the length and breadth of London. The houses are small; we could, none of us, give an evening party or a dance, but we who live in Bagnell Terrace do not desire to do anything of the kind. We do not go in for sounds of revelry at night, nor, indeed, is there much revelry during the day, for we have gone to Bagnell Terrace in order to be anchored in a quiet little backwater. There is no traffic through it, for the terrace is a cul-de-sac, closed at the far end by a high brick wall, along which, on summer nights, cats trip lightly on visits to their friends. Even the cats of Bagnell Terrace have caught something of its discretion and tranquillity, for they do not hail each other with long-drawn yells of mortal agony like their cousins in less well-conducted places, but sit and have quiet little parties like the owners of the houses in which they condescend to be lodged and boarded.

But, though I was more content to be in Bagnell Terrace than anywhere else, I had not got, and was beginning to be afraid I never should get the particular house which I coveted above all others. This was at the top end of the terrace adjoining the wall that closed it, and in one respect it was unlike the other houses, which so much resemble each other. The others have little square gardens in front of them, where we have our bulbs abloom in the spring, when they present a very gay appearance, but the gardens are too small, and London too sunless to allow of any very effective horticulture. The house, however, to which I had so long turned envious eyes, had no garden in front of it; instead, the space had been used for the erection of a big, square room (for a small garden will make a very well-sized room) connected with the house by a covered passage. Rooms in Bagnell Terrace, though sunny and cheerful, are not large, and just one big room, so it occurred to me, would give the final touch of perfection to those delightful little residences.

Now, the inhabitants of this desirable abode were something of a mystery to our neighbourly little circle; though we knew that a man lived there (for he was occasionally seen leaving or entering his house), he was personally unknown to us. A curious point was that, though we had all (though rarely) encountered him on the pavements, there was a considerable discrepancy in the impression he had made on us. He certainly walked briskly, as if the vigour of life was still his, but while I believed that he was a young man, Hugh Abbot, who lived in the house next his, was convinced that, in spite of his briskness, he was not only old, but very old. Hugh and I, lifelong bachelor friends, often discussed him in the ramble of conversation when he had dropped in for an after-dinner pipe, or I had gone across for a game of chess. His name was not known to us, so, by reason of my desire for his house, we called him Naboth. We both agreed that there was something odd about him, something baffling and elusive.

I had been away for a couple of months one winter in Egypt; the night after my return Hugh dined with me, and after dinner I produced those trophies which the strongest-minded are unable to refrain from purchasing, when they are offered by an engaging burnoused ruffian in the Valley of the Tombs of the Kings. There were some beads (not quite so blue as they had appeared there), a scarab or two, and for the last I kept the piece of which I was really proud, namely, a small lapis-lazuli statuette, a few inches high, of a cat. It sat square and stiff on its haunches, with upright forelegs, and, in spite of the small scale, so good were the proportions and so accurate the observation of the artist, that it gave the impression of being much bigger. As it stood on Hugh's palm it was certainly small, but if, without the sight of it, I pictured it to myself, it represented itself as far larger than it really was.

"And the old thing is," I said, "that though it is far and away the best thing I picked up, I cannot for the life of me remember where I bought it. Somehow I feel that I've always had it."

He had been looking very intently at it. Then he jumped up from his chair and put it down on the chimney-piece.

"I don't think I quite like it," he said, "and I can't tell you why. Oh, a jolly bit of workmanship; I don't mean that. And you can't remember where you got it, did you say? That's odd . . . Well, what about a game of chess?"

We played a couple of games, without much concentration or fervour, and more than once I saw him glance with a puzzled look at my little image on the chimney-piece. But he said nothing more about it, and when our games were over he gave me the discursive news of the Terrace. A house had fallen vacant and been instantly snapped up.

"Not Naboth's?" I asked.

"No, not Naboth's. Naboth is in possession still. Very much in possession; going strong."

"Anything new?" I asked.

"Oh, just bits of things. I've seen him a good many times lately, and yet I can't get any clear idea of him. I met him three days ago, as I was coming out of my gate, and had a good look at him, and for a moment I agreed with you and thought he was a young man. Then he turned and stared me in the face for a second, and I thought I had never seen anyone so old. Frightfully alive, but more than old – antique, primeval."

"And then?" I asked.

"He passed on, and I found myself, as has so often happened before, quite unable to remember what his face was like. Was he old or young? I didn't know. What was his mouth like, or his nose? But it was the question of his age which was the most baffling."

Hugh stretched his feet out towards the blaze, and sank back in his chair, with one more frowning look at my lapis lazuli cat.

"Though after all, what is age?" he said. "We measure age by time, we say 'so many years', and forget that we're in eternity here and now, just as we say we're in a room or in Bagnell Terrace, though we're much more truly in infinity."

"What has that got to do with Naboth?" I asked.

Hugh beat his pipe out against the bars of the grate before he answered.

"Well, it will probably sound quite cracked to you," he said, "unless Egypt, the land of ancient mystery, has softened your rind of materialism, but it struck me then that Naboth belonged to eternity much more obviously than we do. We belong to it, of course; we can't help that; but he's less involved in this error or illusion of time than we are. Dear me, it sounds amazing nonsense when I put it into words."

I laughed.

"I'm afraid my rind of materialism isn't soft enough yet," I said. "What you say implies that you think Naboth is a sort of apparition, a ghost, a spirit of the dead that manifests itself as a human being, though it isn't one!"

He drew his legs up to him again.

"Yes; it must be nonsense," he said. "Besides, he has been so much in evidence lately, and we can't all be seeing a ghost. It doesn't happen. And there have been noises coming from his house, loud and cheerful noises, which I've never heard before. Somebody plays an instrument like a flute in that big, square room you envy so much, and somebody beats an accompaniment as if with drums. Odd sort of music; it goes on often now at night . . . Well, it's time to go to bed."

Again he glanced up at the chimney-piece.

"Why, it's quite a little cat," he said.

This rather interested me, for I had said nothing to him about the impression left on my mind that it was bigger than its actual dimensions.

"Just the same size as ever," I said.

"Naturally. But I had been thinking of it as lifesize for some reason," said he.

I went with him to the door, and strolled out with him into the darkness of an overcast night. As we neared his house I saw that big patches of light shone into the road from the windows of the square room next door. Suddenly Hugh laid his hand on my arm.

"There!" he said. "The flutes and drums are at it to-night."

The night was very still, but, listen as I would, I could hear nothing but the rumble of traffic in the street beyond the terrace.

"I can't hear it," I said.

Even as I spoke, I heard it, and the wailing noise whisked me back to Egypt again. The boom of the traffic became for me the beat of the drum, and upon it floated just that squeal and wail of the little reed-pipes which accompany the Arab dances, tuneless and rhythmless, and as old as the temples of the Nile.

"It's like the Arab music that you hear in Egypt," I said.

As we stood listening it ceased to his ears as well as mine, as suddenly as it had begun, and simultaneously the lights in the windows of the square room were extinguished.

We waited a moment in the roadway opposite Hugh's house, but from next door came no sound at all, nor glimmer of illumination from any of its windows . . .

I turned; it was rather chilly to one lately arrived from the south.

"Good night," I said; "we'll meet to-morrow sometime."

I went straight to bed, slept at once, and woke with the impress of a very vivid dream on my mind. There was music in it, familiar Arab music, and there was an immense cat somewhere. Even as I tried to recall it, it faded, and I had but time to recognize it as a hash-up of the happenings of the evening before I went to sleep again.

The normal habits of life quickly reasserted themselves. I had work to do, and there were friends to see; all the minute events of each day stitched themselves into the tapestry of life. But somehow a new thread began to be woven into it, though at the time I did not recognize it as such. It seemed trivial and extraneous that I should so often hear a few staves of that odd music from Naboth's house, or that as often as it fixed my attention it was silent again, as if I had imagined, rather than actually heard it. It was trivial, too, that I should so often see Naboth entering or leaving his house. And then one day I had a sight of him which was unlike any previous experience of mine.

I was standing one morning in the window of my front room. I had idly picked up my lapis lazuli cat, and was holding it in the splash of sunlight that poured in, admiring the texture of its surface which, though it was of hard stone, somehow suggested fur. Then, quite casually, I looked up, and there, a few yards in front of me, leaning on the railings of my garden, and intently observing not me, but what I held, was Naboth. His eyes, fixed on it, blinked in the April sunshine with some purring sensuous content, and Hugh was right on the question of his age; he was neither old nor young, but timeless.

The moment of perception passed; it flashed on and off my mind like the revolving beam of some distant lighthouse. It was just a ray of illumination, and was instantly shut off again, so that it appeared to my conscious mind like some hallucination. He suddenly seemed aware of me, and, turning, walked briskly off down the pavement.

I remember being rather startled, but the effect soon faded, and the incident became to me one of those trivial little things that make a momentary impression and vanish. It was odd, too, but in no way remarkable, that more than once I saw one of those discreet cats of which I have spoken sitting on the little balcony outside my front room, and gravely regarding the interior. I am devoted to cats, and several times I got up in order to open the window and invite it to enter; but each time on my movement it jumped down and slunk away. And April passed into May.

I came back after dining out one night in this month, and found a telephone message from Hugh that I should ring him up on my return. A rather excited voice answered me.

"I thought you would like to know at once," he said. "An hour ago a board was put up on Naboth's house to say that the freehold was for sale. Martin and Smith are the agents. Good night; I'm in bed already."

"You're a true friend," I said.

Early next morning, of course, I presented myself at the house-agent's. The price asked was very moderate, the title perfectly satisfactory. He could give me the keys at once, for the house was empty, and he promised that I could have a couple of days to make up my mind, during which time I was to have the prior right of purchase if I was disposed to pay the full price asked. If, however, I only made an offer, he could not guarantee that the trustees would accept it . . . Hot-foot, with the keys in my pocket, I sped back up the Terrace again.

I found the house completely empty, not of inhabitants only, but of all else. There was not a blind, not a strip of drugget, not a curtain-rod in it from garret to cellar. So much the better, thought I, for there would be no tenants' fixtures to take on. Nor was there any debris of removal, of straw and waste-paper; the house looked as if it was prepared for an occupant instead of just rid of one. All was in apple-pie order, the windows clean, the floors swept, the paint and woodwork bright; it was a clean and polished shell ready for its occupier. My first inspection, of course, was of the big built-out room, which was its chief attraction, and my heart leaped at the sight of its plain spaciousness. On one side was an open fireplace, on the other a coil of pipes for central heating, and at the end, between the windows, a niche let into the wall, as if a statue had once stood there; it might have been designed expressly for my bronze Perseus. The rest of the house presented no particular features; it was on the same plan as my own, and my builder, who inspected it that afternoon, pronounced it to be in excellent condition.

"It looks as if it had been newly done up, and never lived in," he said, "and at the price you mention is a decided bargain."

The same thing struck Hugh when, on his return from his office, I dragged him over to see it.

"Why, it all looks new," he said, "and yet we know that Naboth has been here for years, and was certainly here a week ago. And then there's another thing. When did he remove his furniture? There have been no vans at the house that I have seen."

I was much too pleased at getting my heart's desire to consider anything except that I had got it.

"Oh, I can't bother about little things like that," I said. "Look at my beautiful big room. Piano there, bookcases all along the wall, sofa in front of the fire, Perseus in the niche. Why, it was made for me."

Within the specified two days the house was mine, and within a month papering and distempering, electric fittings, and blinds and curtain-rods were finished, and my move began. Two days were sufficient for the transport of my goods, and at the close of the second my old house was dismantled, except for my bedroom, the contents of which would be moved next day. My servants were installed in the new abode, and that night, after a hurried dinner with Hugh, I went back for a couple more hours' work of hauling and tugging and arranging books in the large room, which it was my purpose to finish first. It was a chilly night for May, and I had had a log-fire lit on the hearth, which from time to time I replenished, in intervals of dusting and arranging. Eventually, when the two hours had lengthened themselves into three, I determined to give over for the present, and, much tired, sat down for a recuperative pause on the edge of my sofa and contemplated with satisfaction the result of my labours. At that moment I was conscious that there was a stale, but aromatic, smell in the room that reminded me of the curious odour that hangs about an Egyptian temple. But I put it down to the dust from my books and the smouldering logs.

The move was completed next day, and after another week I was installed as firmly as if I had been there for years. May slipped by, and June, and my new house never ceased to give me a vivid pleasure; it was always a treat to return to it. Then came a certain afternoon when a strange thing happened.

The day had been wet, but towards evening it cleared up; the pavements soon dried, but the road remained moist and miry. I was close to my house on my way home when I saw form itself on the paving-stones a few yards in front of me the mark of a wet shoe, as if someone invisible to the eye had just stepped off the road. Another and yet another briskly imprinted themselves, going up towards my house. For the moment I stood stock-still, and then, with a thumping heart I followed. The marks of these strange footsteps preceded me right up to my door; there was one on the very threshold faintly visible.

I let myself in, closing the door, I confess, very quickly behind me. As I stood there I heard a resounding crash from my room, which, so to speak, startled my fright from me, and I ran down the little passage and burst in. There, at the far end of the room was my bronze Perseus fallen from its niche and lying on the floor. And I knew, by what sixth sense I cannot tell, that I was not alone in the room and that the presence there was no human presence.

Now fear is a very odd thing; unless it is overmastering and overwhelming it always produces its own reaction. Whatever courage we have rises to meet it, and with courage comes anger that we have given entrance to this unnerving intruder. That, at any rate, was my case now, and I made an effective emotional resistance. My servant came running in to see what the noise was, and we set Perseus on his feet again and examined into the cause of his fall. It was clear enough; a big piece of plaster had broken away from the niche, and that must be repaired and strengthened before we reinstated him. Simultaneously my fear and the sense of an unaccountable presence in the room slipped from me. The footsteps outside were still unexplained and I told myself that if I was to shudder at everything I did not understand there would be an end to tranquil existence for ever.

I was dining with Hugh that night; he had been away for the last week, only returning to-day, and he had come in before these slightly agitating events happened to announce his arrival and suggest dinner. I noticed that as he stood chatting for a few minutes, he had once or twice sniffed the air, but he had made no comment, nor had I asked him if he perceived the strange faint odour that every now and then manifested itself to me. I knew it was a great relief to some secretly quaking piece of my mind that he was back, for I was convinced that there was some psychic disturbance going on, either subjectively in my mind, or a real invasion from without. In either case his presence was comforting, not because he is of that stalward breed which believes in nothing beyond the material facts of life, and pooh-poohs these mysterious forces which surround and so strangely interpenetrate existence, but because, while thoroughly believing in them, he has the firm confidence that the deadly and evil powers which occasionally break through into the seeming security of existence are not really to be feared, since they are held in check by forces stronger yet, ready to assist all who realize their protective care. Whether I meant to tell him what had occurred to-day I had not fully determined.

It was not till after dinner that such subjects came up at all, but I had seen there was something on his mind of which he had not spoken yet.

"And your new house," he said at length, "does it still remain as all your fancy painted?"

"I wonder why you ask that," I said.

He gave me a quick glance.

"Mayn't I take any interest in your well-being?" he said.

I knew that something was coming, if I chose to let it.

"I don't think you've ever liked my house from the first," I said. "I believe you think there's something queer about it. I allow that the manner in which I found it empty was odd."

"It was rather," he said. "But so long as it remains empty, except for what you've put in it, it is all right."

I wanted now to press him further.

"What was it you smelt this afternoon in the big room?" I said. "I saw you nosing and sniffing. I have smelt something too. Let's see if we smelt the same thing."

"An odd smell," he said. "Something dusty and stale, but aromatic."

"And what else have you noticed?" I asked.

He paused a moment.

"I think I'll tell you," he said. "This evening from my window I saw you coming up the pavement, and simultaneously I saw, or thought I saw, Naboth cross the road and walk on in front of you. I wondered if you saw him too, for you paused as he stepped on to the pavement in front of you, and then you followed him."

I felt my hands grow suddenly cold, as if the warm current of my blood had been chilled.

"No, I didn't see him," I said, "but I saw his step."

"What do you mean?"

"Just what I say. I saw footprints in front of me which continued on to my threshold."

"And then?"

"I went in, and a terrific crash startled me. My bronze Perseus had fallen from his niche. And there was something in the room."

There was a scratching noise at the window. Without answering, Hugh jumped up and drew aside the curtain. On the sill was seated a large grey cat, blinking in the light. He advanced to the window, and on his approach the cat jumped down into the garden. The light shone out into the road, and we both saw, standing on the pavement just outside, the figure of a man. He turned and looked at me, and then moved away towards my house next door.

"It's he," said Hugh.

He opened the window and leaned out to see what had become of him. There was no sign of him anywhere, but I saw that light shone from behind the blinds of my room.

"Come on," I said. "Let's see what is happening. Why is my room lit?"

I opened the door of my house with my latchkey, and followed by Hugh went down the short passage to the room. It was perfectly dark, and when I turned the switch, we saw that it was empty. I rang the bell, but no answer came, for it was already late, and doubtless my servants had gone to bed.

"But I saw a strong light from the windows two minutes ago," I said, "and there has been no one here since."

Hugh was standing by me in the middle of the room. Suddenly he threw out his arm as if striking at something. That thoroughly alarmed me.

"What's the matter?" I asked. "What are you hitting at?"

He shook his head.

"I don't know," he said. "I thought I saw . . . But I'm not sure. But we're in for something if we stop here. Something is coming, though I don't know what."

The light seemed to me to be burning dim; shadows began to collect in the corner of the room, and though outside the night had been clear, the air here was growing thick with a foggy vapour, which smelt dusty and stale and aromatic. Faintly, but getting louder as we waited there in silence, I heard the throb of drums and the wail of flutes. As yet I had no feeling that there were other presences in the place beyond ours, but in the growing dimness I knew that something was coming nearer. Just in front of me was the empty niche from which my bronze had fallen, and looking at it, I saw that something was astir. The shadow within it began to shape itself into a form, and out of it there gleamed two points of greenish light. A moment more and I saw that they were eyes of antique and infinite malignity.

I heard Hugh's voice in a sort of hoarse whisper.

"Look there!" he said. "It's coming! Oh, my God, it's coming!"

Sudden as the lightning that leaps from the heart of the night it came. But it came not with blaze and flash of light, but, as it were, with a stroke of blinding darkness, that fell not on the eye, or on any material sense, but on the spirit, so that I cowered under it in some abandonment of terror. It came from those eyes which gleamed in the niche, and which now I saw to be set in the face of the figure that stood there. The form of it, naked but for a loin-cloth, was that of a man, the head seemed now human, now to be that of some monstrous cat. And as I looked I knew that if I continued looking there I should be submerged and drowned in that flood of evil that poured from it. As in some catalepsy of nightmare I struggled to tear my eyes from it, but still they were riveted there, gazing on incarnate hate.

Again I heard Hugh's whisper.

"Defy it," he said. "Don't yield an inch."

A swarm of disordered and hellish images were buzzing in my brain, and now I knew as surely as if actual words had been spoken to us that the presence there told me to come to it.

"I've got to go to it," I said. "It's making me go."

I felt his hand tighten on my arm.

"Not a step," he said. "I'm stronger than it is. It will know that soon. Just pray – pray."

Suddenly his arm shot out in front of me, pointing at the presence.

"By the power of God!" he shouted. "By the power of God!"

There was dead silence. The light of those eyes faded, and then came dawn on the darkness of the room. It was quiet and orderly, the niche was empty, and there on the sofa by me was Hugh, his face white and streaming with sweat.

"It's over," he said, and without pause fell fast asleep.

Now we have often talked over together what happened that evening. Of what seemed to happen I have already given the account, which anyone may believe or not, precisely as they please. He, as I, was conscious of a presence wholly evil, and he tells me that all the time that those eyes gleamed from the niche, he was trying to realize what he believed, namely, that only one power in the world is Omnipotent, and that the moment he gained that realization the presence collapsed. What exactly that presence was it is impossible to say. It looks as if it was the essence or spirit of one of those mysterious Egyptian cults, of which the force survived, and was seen and felt in this quiet Terrace. That it was embodied in Naboth seems (among all these incredibilities) possible, and Naboth certainly has never been seen again. Whether or not it was connected with the worship and cult of cats might occur to the mythological mind, and it is perhaps worthy of record that I found next morning my little lapis lazuli image, which stood on the chimney-piece, broken into fragments. It was too badly damaged to mend, and I am not sure that, in any case, I should have attempted to have it restored.

Finally, there is no more tranquil and pleasant room in London than the one built out in front of my house in Bagnell Terrace.

A Tale of an Empty House

It had been a disastrous afternoon: rain had streamed incessantly from a low grey sky, and the road was of the vilest description. There were sections consisting of sharp flints, newly laid down and not yet rolled into amenity, and the stretches in between were worn into deep ruts and bouncing holes, so that it was impossible anywhere to travel at even a moderate speed. Twice we had punctured, and now, as the stormy dusk began to fall, something went wrong with the engine, and after crawling on for a hundred yards or so we stopped. My driver, after a short investigation, told me that there was a half-hour's tinkering to be done, and after that we might, with luck, trundle along in a leisurely manner, and hope eventually to arrive at Crowthorpe, which was the proposed destination.

We had come, when this stoppage occurred, to a crossroad. Through the driving rain I could see on the right a great church, and in front a huddle of houses. A consultation of the map seemed to indicate that this was the village of Riddington, The guide-book added the information that Riddington possessed an hotel, and the signpost at the corner endorsed them both. To the right along the main road, into which we had just struck, was Crowthorpe, fifteen miles away and straight in front of us, half a mile distant, was the hotel.

The decision was not difficult. There was no reason why I should get to Crowthorpe to-night instead of to-morrow, for the friend whom I was to meet there would not arrive until next afternoon and it was surely better to limp half a mile with a spasmodic engine than to attempt fifteen on this inclement evening.

"We'll spend the night here," I said to my chauffeur. "The road dips downhill, and it's only half a mile to the hotel. I dare say we shall get there without using the engine at all. Let's try, anyhow."

We hooted and crossed the main road, and began to slide very slowly down a narrow street. It was impossible to see much, but on either side there were little houses with lights gleaming through blinds, or with blinds still undrawn, revealing cosy interiors. Then the incline grew steeper, and close in front of us I saw masts against a sheet of water that appeared to stretch unbroken into the rain-shrouded gloom of the gathering night.

Riddington, then, must be on the open sea, though how it came about that boats should be tied up to an open quay-wall was a puzzle, but perhaps there was some jetty, invisible in the darkness, which protected them. I heard the chauffeur switch on his engine as we made a sharp turn to the left, and we passed below a long row of lighted windows, shining out on to a rather narrow road, on the right edge of which the water lapped. Again he turned sharply to the left, described a half-circle on crunching gravel, and drew up at the door of the hotel. There was a room for me, there was a garage, there was a room for him, and dinner had not long begun.

Among the little excitements and surprises of travel there is none more delightful than that of waking in a new place at which one has arrived after nightfall on the previous evening. The mind has received a few hints and dusky impressions, and probably during sleep it has juggled with these, constructing them into some sort of coherent whole, and next morning its anticipations are put to the proof. Usually the eye has seen more than it has consciously registered, and the brain has fitted together as in the manner of a jigsaw puzzle a very fair presentment of its immediate surroundings. When I woke next morning a brilliantly sunny sky looked in at my windows; there was no sound of wind or of breaking waves, and before getting up and verifying my impressions of the night before I lay and washed in my imagined picture. In front of my windows there would be a narrow roadway bordered by a quay-wall: there would be a breakwater, forming a harbour for the boats that lay at anchor there, and away, away to the horizon would stretch an expanse of still and glittering sea. I ran over these points in my mind; they seemed an inevitable inference from the glimpses of the night before and then, assured of my correctness, I got out of bed and went to the window.

I have never experienced so complete a surprise. There was no harbour, there was no breakwater, and there was no sea. A very narrow channel, three-quarters choked with sand-banks on which now rested the boats whose masts I had seen the previous evening, ran parallel to the road, and then turned at right-angles and went off into the distance. Otherwise no water of any sort was visible; right and left and in front stretched a limitless expanse of shining grasses with tufts of shrubby growth, and great patches of purple sea-lavender. Beyond were tawny sand-banks, and further yet a line of shingle and scrub and sand-dunes. But the sea which I had expected to fill the whole circle of the visible world till it met the sky on the horizon had totally disappeared.

After the first surprise at this colossal conjuring trick was over, I dressed quickly, in order to ascertain from local authorities how it was done. Unless some hallucination had poisoned my perceptive faculties, there must be an explanation of this total disappearance, alternately, of sea and land, and the key, when supplied, was simple enough. That line of shingle and scrub and sand-dunes on the horizon was a peninsula running for four or five miles parallel with the land, forming the true beach, and it enclosed this vast basin of sand-banks and mud-banks and level lavender-covered marsh, which was submerged at high tide, and made an estuary. At low tide it was altogether empty but for the stream that struggled out through various channels to the mouth of it two miles away to the left, and there was easy passage across it for a man who carried his shoes and stockings, to the far sand-dunes and beaches which terminated at Riddington Point, while at high tide you could sail out from the quay just in front of the hotel and be landed there.

The tide would be out of the estuary for five or six hours yet; I could spend the morning on the beach, or, taking my lunch, walk out to the Point, and be back before the returning waters rendered the channel impassable. There was good bathing on the beach, and there was a colony of terns who nested there.

Already, as I ate my breakfast at a table in the window overlooking the marsh, the spell and attraction of it had begun to work. It was so immense and so empty; it had the allure of the desert about it, with none of the desert's intolerable monotony, for companies of chiding gulls hovered over it, and I could hear the pipe of redshank and the babble of curlews. I was due to meet Jack Granger in Crowthorpe that evening, but if I went I knew that I should persuade him to come back to Riddington, and from my knowledge of him I was aware that he would feel the spell of the place not less potent than I. So, having ascertained that there was a room for him here, I wrote him a note saying that I had found the most amazing place in the world, and told my chauffeur to take the car into Crowthorpe to meet the train that afternoon and bring him here. And with a perfectly clear conscience I set off with a towel and a packet of lunch in my pocket to explore vaguely and goallessly that beckoning immensity of lavender-covered, bird-haunted expanse.

My way, as pointed out to me, led first along a sea-bank which defended the drained pastureland on the right of it from the high tides, and at the corner of that I struck into the basin of the estuary. A contour-line of jetsam, withered grass, strands of seaweed, and the bleached shells of little crabs showed where the last tide had reached its height, and inside it the marsh-growth was still wet. Then came a stretch of mud and pebbles, and presently I was wading through the stream that flowed down to the sea. Beyond that were banks of ribbed sand swept by the incoming tides, and soon I regained the wide green marshes on the further side, beyond which was the bar of shingle that fringed the sea.

I paused as I reshod myself. There was not a sign of any living human being within sight, but never have I found myself in so exhilarating a solitude. Right and left were spread the lawns of sea-lavender, starred with pink tufts of thrift and thickets of suæda bushes. Here and there were pools left in depressions of the ground by the retreated tide, and here were patches of smooth black mud, out of which grew, like little spikes of milky-green asparagus, a crop of glasswort, and all these happy vegetables flourished in sunshine, or rain, or the salt of the flooding tides with impartial amphibiousness. Overhead was the immense arc of the sky, across which flew now a flight of duck, hurrying with necks outstretched, and now a lonely black-backed gull, flapping his ponderous way seawards. Curlews were bubbling, and redshank and ringed plover fluting, and now as I trudged up the shingle-bank, at the bottom of which the marsh came to an end, the sea, blue and waveless, lay stretched and sleeping, bordered by a strip of sand, on which far off a mirage hovered. But from end to end of it, as far as eye could see, there was no sign of human presence.

I bathed and basked on the hot beach, walked along for half a mile, and then struck back across the shingle into the marsh. And then with a pang of disappointment I saw the first evidence of the intrusion of man into this paradise of solitude, for on a stony spit of ground that ran like some great rib into the amphibious meadows, there stood a small square house built of brick, with a tall flagstaff set up in front of it. It had not caught my eye before, and it seemed an unwarrantable invasion of the emptiness. But perhaps it was not so gross an infringement of it as it appeared, for it wore an indefinable look of desertion, as if man had attempted to domesticate himself here and had failed. As I approached it this impression increased, for the chimney was smokeless, and the closed windows were dim with the film of salt air and the threshold of the closed door was patched with lichen and strewn with debris of withered grasses. I walked twice round it, decided that it was certainly uninhabited, and finally, leaning against the sunbaked wall, ate my lunch.

The glitter and heat of the day were at their height. Warmed and exercised, and invigorated by my bathe, I felt strung to the supreme pitch of physical well-being, and my mind, quite vacant except for these felicitous impressions, followed the example of my body, and basked in an unclouded content. And, I suppose by a sense of the Lucretian luxury of contrast, it began to picture to itself, in order to accentuate these blissful conditions, what this sunlit solitude would be like when some November night began to close in underneath a low, grey sky and a driving storm of sleet. Its solitariness would be turned into an abominable desolation: if from some unconjecturable cause one was forced to spend the night here, how the mind would long for any companionship, how sinister would become the calling of the birds, how weird the whistle of the wind round the cavern of this abandoned habitation. Or would it be just the other way about, and would one only be longing to be assured that the seeming solitude was real, and that no invisible but encroaching presence, soon to be made manifest, was creeping nearer under cover of the dusk, and be shuddering to think that the wail of the wind was not only the wind, but the cry of some discarnate being, and that it was not the curlews who made that melancholy piping? By degrees the edge of thought grew blunt, and melted into inconsequent imaginings, and I fell asleep.

I woke with a start from the trouble of a dream that faded with waking, but felt sure that some noise close at hand had aroused me. And then it came again: it was the footfall of someone moving about inside the deserted house, against the wall of which my back was propped. Up and down it went, then paused and began again; it was like that of a man who waited with impatience for some expected arrival. I noticed also that the footfall had an irregular beat, as if the walker went with a limp. Then in a minute or two the sound ceased altogether.

An odd uneasiness came over me, for I had been so certain that the house was uninhabited. Then turning my head I noticed that in the wall just above me was a window, and the notion, wholly irrational and unfounded, entered my mind that the man inside who tramped was watching me from it. When once that idea got hold of me, it became impossible to sit there in peace any more, and I got up and shovelled into my knapsack my towel and the remains of my meal. I walked a little further down the spit of land which ran out into the marsh, and turning looked at the house again, and again to my eyes it seemed absolutely deserted. But, after all, it was no concern of mine and I proceeded on my walk, determining to inquire casually on my return to the hotel who it was that lived in so hermetical a place, and for the present dismissed the matter from my mind.

It was some three hours later that I found myself opposite the house again, after a long, wandering walk. I saw that, by making an only slightly longer detour, I could pass close to the house again, and I knew that the sound of those footsteps within it had raised in me a curiosity that I wanted to satisfy. And then, even as I paused, I saw that a man was standing by the door: how he came there I had no idea, for the moment before he had not been there, and he must have come out of the house. He was looking down the path that led through the marsh, shielding his eyes against the sun, and presently he took a step or two forward, and he dragged his left leg as he walked, limping heavily. It was his step, then, which I had heard within, and any mystery about the matter was of my own making. I therefore took the shorter path, and got back to the hotel to find that Jack Granger had just arrived.

We went out again in the gleam of the sunset, and watched the tide sweeping in and pouring up the dykes, until again the great conjuring trick was accomplished, and the stretch of marsh with its fields of sea-lavender was a sheet of shining water. Far away across it stood the house by which I had lunched, and just as we turned Jack pointed to it.

"That's a queer place for a house," he said. "I suppose no one lives there."

"Yes, a lame man," said I; "I saw him to-day. I'm going to ask the hotel porter who he is."

The result of this inquiry was unexpected.

"No; the house has been uninhabited several years," he said. "It used to be a watch-house from which the coastguards signalled if there was a ship in distress, and the lifeboat went out from here. But now the lifeboat and the coastguards are at the end of the Point."

"Then who is the lame man I saw walking about there, and heard inside the house?" I asked.

He looked at me, I thought, queerly.

"I don't know who that could be," he said. "There's no lame man about here to my knowledge."

The effect on Jack of the marshes and their gorgeous emptiness, of the sun and the sea, was precisely what I had anticipated. He vowed that any day spent anywhere than on these beaches and fields of sea-lavender was a day wasted, and proposed that the tour, of which the main object had originally been the golf links of Norfolk, should for the present be cancelled. In particular, it was the birds of this long solitary headland that enchanted him.

"After all, we can play golf anywhere," he said.

"There's an oyster-catcher scolding, do you hear? – and how silly to whack a little white ball – ringed plover, but what's that calling as well? – when you can spend the day like this! Oh, don't let us go and bathe yet: I want to wander along that edge of the marsh – ha, there's a company of turnstones; they make a noise like the drawing of a cork – there they are, those little chaps with chestnut-coloured patches! Let's go along the near edge of the marsh, and come out by the house where your lame man lives."

We took, therefore, the path with the longer detour, which I had abandoned last night. I had said nothing to him of what the hotel porter had told me that the house was unlived in, and all he knew was that I had seen a lame man, apparently in occupation there. My reason for not doing so (to make the confession at once) was that I already half believed that the steps I had heard inside, and the lame man I had seen watching outside, did not imply in the porter's sense of the word that the house was occupied, and I wanted to see whether Jack as well as myself would be conscious of any such tokens of a presence there. And then the oddest thing happened.

All the way up to the house his attention was alert on the birds, and in especial on a piping note which was unfamiliar to him. In vain he tried to catch sight of the bird that uttered it, and in vain I tried to hear it. "It doesn't sound like any bird I know," he said; "in fact, it doesn't sound like a bird at all, but like some human being whistling. There it is again! Is it possible you don't hear it?"

We were now quite close to the house.

"There must be someone there who is whistling," he said; "it must be your lame man . . . Lord, yes, it comes from inside the house. So that's explained, and I hoped it was some new bird. But why can't you hear it?"

"Some people can't hear a bat's squeak," said I.

Jack, satisfied with the explanation, took no more interest in the matter, and we struck across the shingle, bathed and lunched, and tramped on to the tumble of sand-dunes in which the Point ended. For a couple of hours we strolled and lazed there in the liquid and sunny air, and reluctantly returned in order to cross the ford before the tide came in. As we retraced our way, I saw coming up from the west a huge continent of cloud; and just as we reached the spit of land on which the house stood, a jagged sword of lightning flickered down to the low-lying hills across the estuary, and a few big raindrops plopped on the shingle.

"We're in for a drenching," he said. "Ha! Let's ask for shelter at your lame man's house. Better run for it!" Already the big drops were falling thickly, and we scuttled across the hundred yards that lay between us and the house, and came to the door just as the sluices of heaven were pulled wide. He rapped on it, but there came no answer; he tried the handle of it, but the door did not yield, and then, by a sudden inspiration, he felt along the top of the lintel and found a key. It fitted into the wards and next moment we stood within.

We found ourselves in a slip of a passage, at the end of which went up the staircase to the floor above. On each side of it was a room, one a kitchen, the other a living-room, but in neither was there any stick of furniture. Discoloured paper was peeling off the walls, the windows were thick with spidery weavings, the air heavy with unventilated damp.

"Your lame man dispenses with the necessities as well as the luxuries of life," said Jack. "A spartan fellow."

We were standing in the kitchen: outside the hiss of the rain had grown to a roar, and the bleared window was suddenly lit up with a flare of lightning. A crack of thunder answered it, and in the silence that followed there came from just outside, audible now to me, the sound of a piping whistle. Immediately afterwards I heard the door by which we had just entered violently banged, and I remembered that I had left it open.

His eyes met mine.

"But there's no breath of wind," I said. "What made it bang like that?"

"And that was no bird that whistled," said he.

There was the shuffle in the passage outside of a limping step: I could hear the drag of a man's lame foot along the boards.

"He has come in," said Jack.

Yes, he had come in, and who had come in? At that moment not fright, but fear, which is a very different matter, closed in on me. Fright, as I understand it, is an emotion, startling, but not unnerving; you may under the finger of fright spring aside, you may scream, you may shout, you have the command of your muscles. But as that limping step moved down the passage I felt fear, the hand of the nightmare that, as it clutches, paralyses and inhibits not action only, but thought. I waited frozen and speechless for what should happen next.

Exactly opposite the open door of the kitchen in which we stood the step stopped. And then, soundlessly and invisibly, the presence that had made itself manifest to the outward ear entered. Suddenly I heard Jack's breath rattle in his throat.

"Oh, my God!" he cried in a voice hoarse and strangled, and he threw his left arm across his face as if defending himself, and his right arm, shooting out seemed to hit at something which I could not see, and his fingers crooked themselves as if clutching at that which had evaded his blow. His body was bent back as if resisting some invisible pressure, then lunged forward again, and I heard the noise of a resisting joint, and saw on his throat the shadow (or so it seemed) of a clutching hand. At that some power of movement came back to me, and I remember hurling myself at the empty space between him and me, and felt under my grip the shape of a shoulder and heard on the boards of the floor the slip and scoop of a foot. Something invisible, now a shoulder, now an arm, struggled in my grasp, and I heard a panting respiration that was not Jack's, nor mine, and now and then in my face I felt a hot breath that stank of corruption and decay. And all the time this physical contention was symbolical only: what he and I wrestled with was not a thing of flesh and blood, but some awful spiritual presence. And then . . .

There was nothing. The ghostly invasion ceased as suddenly as it had begun, and there was Jack's face gleaming with sweat close to mine, as we stood with dropped arms opposite each other in an empty room, with the rain beating on the roof and the gutters chuckling. No word passed between us, but next moment we were out in the pelting rain, running for the ford. The deluge was sweet to my soul, it seemed to wash away that horror of great darkness and that odour of corruption in which we had been plunged.

Now, I have no certain explanation to give of the experience which has here been shortly recounted, and the reader may or may not connect with it a story that I heard a week or two later on my return to London.

A friend of mine and I had been dining at my house one evening, and we had discussed a murder trial then going on of which the papers were full.

"It isn't only the atrocity that attracts," he said, "I think it is the place where the murder occurs that is the cause of the interest in it. A murder at Brighton, or Margate, or Ramsgate, any place which the public associates with pleasure trips, attracts them because they know the place and can visualize the scene. But when there is a murder at some small, unknown spot, which they have never heard of, there is no appeal to their imagination. Last spring, for instance, there was the murder at that small village on the coast of Norfolk. I've forgotten the name of the place, though I was in Norwich at the time of the trial and was present in court. It was one of the most awful stories I ever heard, as ghastly and sensational as this last affair, but it didn't attract the smallest attention. Odd that I can't remember the name of the place when all the rest is so vivid to me!"

"Tell me about it," I said; "I never heard of it."

"Well, there was this little village, and just outside it was a farm, owned by a man called John Beardsley. He lived there with his only daughter, an unmarried woman of about thirty, a good-looking, sensible creature apparently, the last in the world you would have thought to do anything unexpected. There worked at the farm as a day-labourer a young fellow called Alfred Maldon, who in the trial of which I am speaking was the prisoner. He had one of the most dreadful faces I ever saw, a catlike receding forehead, a broad, short nose, and a great red sensual mouth, always on the grin. He seemed positively to enjoy being the central figure around whom all the interest of those ghoulish women who thronged the court was concentrated, and when he shambled into the witness-box—"

"Shambled?" I asked.

"Yes; he was lame; his left foot dragged along the floor as he walked. As he shambled into the witness-box he nodded and smiled to the judge, and clapped his counsel on the shoulder, and leered at the gallery . . . He worked on the farm, as I was saying, doing jobs that were within his capacity, among which was certain house-work, carrying coals and what-not, for John Beardsley, though very well-off, kept no servant, and this daughter Alice – that was her name – ran the house. And what must she do but fall in love, it was no less than that, with this monstrous and misshapen fellow. One afternoon her father came home unexpectedly and caught them together in the parlour, kissing and cuddling. He turned the man out of the house, neck and crop, gave him his week's wages, and dismissed him, threatening him with a fine thrashing if he ever caught him hanging about the place. He forbade his daughter ever to speak to him again, and in order to keep watch over her, got in a woman from the village who would be there all day while he was out on the farm.

"Young Maldon, deprived of his job, tried to get work in the village, but none would employ him, for he was a black-tempered fellow ready to pick a quarrel with anyone, and an unpleasant opponent, for, with all his lameness, he was of immense muscular strength. For some weeks he idled about in the village, getting a chance job occasionally, and no doubt, as you will see, Alice Beardsley managed to meet him. The village – its name still escapes me – lay on the edge of a big tidal estuary, full at high water, but on the ebb of a broad stretch of marsh and sand and mud-banks, beyond which ran a long belt of shingle that formed the seaward side of the estuary. On it stood a disused coastguard house, a couple of miles away from the village, and in as lonely a place as you would find anywhere in England. At low tide there was a shallow ford across to it, and in the sand-banks round about it some beds of cockle. Maldon, unable to get regular work, took to cockle-digging, and during the summer, when the tide was low, Alice (it was no new thing with her) used to go over the ford to the beach beyond and bathe. She would go across the sandbanks where the cockle-diggers, Maldon among them, were at work, and if he whistled as she passed that was the signal between them that he would slip away presently and join her at the disused coastguard house, and there throughout the summer they used to meet.

"As the weeks went on her father saw the change that was coming in her, and suspecting the cause, often left his work and, hidden behind some sea-bank, used to watch her. One day he saw her cross the ford, and soon after she had passed he saw Maldon, recognizable from a long way off by his dragging leg, follow her. He went up the path to the coastguard house, and entered. At that John Beardsley crossed the ford, and hiding in the bushes near the house, saw Alice coming back from her bathe. The house was off the direct path to the ford, but she went round that way, and the door was opened to her, and closed behind her. He found them together, and mad with rage attacked the man. They fought and Maldon got him down and then and there in front of his daughter strangled him.

"The girl went off her head, and is in the asylum at Norwich now. She sits all day by the window whistling. The man was hanged."

"Was Riddington the name of the village?" I asked.

"Yes. Riddington, of course," he said. "I can't think how I forgot it."

NABOTH'S VINEYARD

Ralph Hatchard had for the last twenty years been making a very good income at the Bar; no one could marshal facts so tellingly as he, no one could present a case to a jury in so persuasive and convincing a way, nor make them see the situation he pictured to them with so sympathetic an eye. He disdained to awaken sentiment by moving appeals to humanity, for he had not, either in his private or his public life, any use for mercy, but demanded mere justice for his client. Many were the cases in which, not by distorting facts, but merely by focusing them for the twelve intelligent men whom he addressed, had he succeeded in making them look through the telescope of his mind, and see at the end of it precisely what he wished them to see. But if he had been asked of which out of all his advocacies he was most intellectually proud, he would probably have mentioned one in which that advocacy had not been successful. This was in the famous Wraxton case of seven years ago, in which he had defended a certain solicitor, Thomas Wraxton, on a charge of embezzlement and conversion to his own use of the money of a client.

As the case was presented by the prosecution, it seemed as if any defence would merely waste the time of the Court, but when the speech for the defence was concluded, most of them who heard it, not the public alone, but the audience of trained legal minds, would probably have betted (had betting been permitted in a court of justice) that Thomas Wraxton would be acquitted. But the twelve intelligent men were among the minority, and after being absent from Court for three hours had brought in a verdict of guilty. A sentence of seven years was passed on Thomas Wraxton, and his counsel, thoroughly disgusted that so much ingenuity should have been thrown away, felt, ever afterward, a sort of contemptuous irritation with him. The irritation was rendered more acute by an interview he had with Wraxton after sentence had been passed. His client raged and stormed at him for the stupidity and lack of skill he had shown in his defence.

Hatchard was a bachelor; he had little opinion of women as

companions, and it was enough for him in town when his day's work was over to take his dinner at the club, and after a stern rubber or two at bridge, to retire to his flat, and more often than not work at some case in which he was engaged till the small hours. Apart from the dinner-table and the card-table, the only companion he wanted was an opponent at golf for Saturday and Sunday, when he went down for his week-end to the seaside links at Scarling. There was a pleasant dormy-house in the town, at which he put up, and in the summer he was accustomed to spend the greater part of the long vacation here, renting a house in the neighbourhood. His only near relation was a brother who had a Civil Service appointment at Bareilly, in the North-West province of India, whom he had not seen for some years, for he spent the hot season in the hills and but seldom came to England.

Hatchard got from acquaintances all the friendship that he needed, and though he was a solitary man, he was by no means to be described as a lonely one. For loneliness implies the knowledge that a man is alone, and his wish that it were otherwise. Hatchard knew he was alone, but preferred it. His golf and his bridge of an evening gave him all the companionship he needed; a further recreation of his was botany. "Plants are good to look at; they're interesting to study, and they don't bore you by unwished-for conversation," would have been his manner of accounting for so unexpected a hobby. He intended, when he retired from practice, to buy a house with a good garden in some country town, where he could enjoy at leisure this trinity of innocuous amusements. Till then, there was no use in having a garden from which his work would sever him for the greater part of the year.

He always took the same house at Scarling when he came to spend his long vacation there. It suited him admirably, for it was within a few doors of the local club, where he could get a rubber in the evening, and find a match at golf for next day, and the motor omnibuses that plied along the seaside-road to the links passed his door. He had long ago settled in his mind that Scarling was to be the home of his late and leisured years, and of all the houses in that compact mediæval little town the one which he most coveted lay close to that which he was now accustomed to take for the summer months. Opposite his windows ran the long, red-brick wall of its garden, and from his bedroom above he could look over this and see the amenities which in its present proprietorship seemed so sadly undervalued.

An acre of lawn with a gnarled and sprawling mulberry tree lay there, a pergola of rambler-roses separated this from the kitchen garden, and all round in the shelter of the walls which defended them from the chill northerly and easterly blasts lay deep flower beds. A paved terrace faced the garden side of Telford House, but weeds were sprouting there, the grass of the lawn had been suffered to grow long and rank, and the flower beds were an untended jungle. The house, too, seemed exactly what would suit him; it was of Queen Anne date, and he could conjecture the square, panelled rooms within. He had been to the house-agent's in Scarling to ask if there was any chance of obtaining it, and had directed him to make inquiries of the occupying tenant or proprietor as to whether he had any thoughts of getting rid of it to a purchaser who was prepared to negotiate at once for it. But it appeared that it had only been bought some six years ago by the present owner, Mrs. Pringle, when she came to live at Scarling, and she had no idea of parting with it.

Ralph Hatchard, when he was at Scarling, took no part whatever in the local life and society of the place except in so far as he encountered it among the men whom he met in the card-room of the club and out at the links, and it appeared that Mrs. Pringle was as recluse as he. Once or twice in casual conversation mention had been made by one or another of her house or its owner, but nothing was forthcoming about her. He learned that when she had come there first, the usual country-town civilities had been paid her, but she either did not return the call or soon suffered the acquaintanceship to drop, and at the present time she appeared to see nobody except occasionally the vicar of the church or his wife. Hatchard made no particular note of all this, and did not construct any such hypothesis as might be supposed to divert the vagrant thoughts of a legal mind by picturing her as a woman hiding from justice or from the exposure that justice had already subjected her to. As far as he was aware he had never set eyes on her, nor had he any object in wishing to do so, as long as she was not willing to part with her house; it was sufficient for a man who was not in the least inquisitive (except when conducting a cross-examination) to suppose that she liked her own company well enough to dispense with that of others. Plenty of sensible folk did that, and he thought no worse of them for it.

More than six years had now elapsed since the Wraxton trial, and Hatchard was spending the last days of the long vacation at the house that overlooked that Naboth's vineyard of a garden. The day was one of squealing wind and driving rain, and even he, who usually defied the elements to stop his couple of rounds of golf, had not gone out to the links today. Towards evening, however, it cleared, and he set out to get a mouthful of fresh air and a little exercise, and returned just about sunset past the house he coveted. There were two women standing on the threshold as he approached, one of them hatless, and it came into his mind that here, no doubt, was the retiring Mrs. Pringle. She stood sideface to him for that moment, and at once he knew that he had seen her before; her face and her carriage were perfectly but remotely familiar to him. Then she turned and saw him; she gave him but one glance, and without pause went back into the house and shut the door. The sight he had of her was but instantaneous, but sufficient to convince him not only that he had seen her before, but that she was in no way desirous of seeing him again.

Mrs. Grampound, the vicar's wife, had been talking to her, and Hatchard raised his hat, for he had been introduced to her one day when he had been playing golf with her husband. He alluded to the malignity of the weather, which, after being wet all day, was clearly going to be uselessly fine all night.

"And that lady, I suppose," he said, "with whom you were speaking, was Mrs. Pringle? A widow, perhaps? One does not meet her husband at the club."

"No; she is not a widow," said Mrs. Grampound. "Indeed, she told me just now that she expected her husband home before long. He has been out in India for some years."

"Indeed! I heard only to-day from my brother, who is also in India. I expect him home in the spring for six months' leave. Perhaps I shall find that he knows Mr. Pringle."

They had come to his house, and he turned in. Somehow Mrs. Pringle had ceased to be merely the owner of the house he so much desired. She was somebody else, and good though his memory was, he could not recall where he had met her before. He could not in the least remember the sound of her voice, perhaps he had never heard it. But he knew her face.

During the winter he was often down at Scarling again for his week-ends, and now he was definitely intending to retire from practice before the summer. He had made sufficient money to live with all possible comfort, and he was certainly beginning to feel the strain of his work. His memory was not quite what it had been, and he who had been robust as a piece of ironwork all his life had several times been in the doctor's hands. It was clearly time, if he was going to enjoy the long evening of life, to begin doing so while the capacity for enjoyment was still unimpaired and not linger on at work till his health suffered. He could not concentrate as he had been used; even when he was most occupied in his own argument the train of his thought would grow dim, and through it, as if through a mist, vague images of thought would fleetingly appear, images not fully tangible to his mind, and evade him before he could grasp them.

That logical constructive brain of his was certainly getting tired with its years of incessant work, and knowing that, he longed more than ever to have done with business, and more vividly than ever he saw himself established in that particular house and garden at Scarling. The thought of it bid fair to become an obsession with him; he began to look upon Mrs. Pringle as an enemy standing in the way of the fulfilment of his dream, and still he cudgelled his brain to think when and where and how he had seen her before. Sometimes he seemed close to the solution of that conundrum, but just as he pounced on it, it slipped away again, like some object in the dusk.

He was down here one week-end in March, and instead of playing golf, spent his Saturday morning in looking over a couple of houses which were for sale. His brother, whom he now expected back in a week or two, and who, like himself, was a bachelor, would be living with him all the summer, and now, at last despairing of getting the house he wanted, he must resign himself to the inevitable and get some other permanent home. One of these two houses, he thought, would do for him fairly well, and after viewing it he went to the house agent's and secured the first refusal of it, with a week in which to make up his mind.

"I shall almost certainly purchase it," he said, "for I suppose there is still no chance of my getting Telford House."

The agent shook his head.

"I'm afraid not, sir," he said. "Mr. Pringle, you may have heard, has come home and lives there now."

As he left the office an idea occurred to him. Though Mrs. Pringle might not, when living there alone, have felt disposed to face the inconvenience of moving, it was possible that a firm and adequate offer made to her husband might effect something. He had only just come there; it was not to be supposed that he had any very strong attachment to the house, and a definite offer of so many thousand pounds down might perhaps induce him to give it up. Hatchard determined, before definitely purchasing another house, to make a final effort to get that on which his heart was set.

He went straight to Telford House and rang. He gave the maid his card, asking if he could see Mr. Pringle, and at that moment a man came into the little hall from the door into the garden, and seeing someone there paused as he entered. He was a tall fellow, but bent; and walked limpingly with the aid of a stick. He wore a short, grey beard and moustache, his eyes were sunk deep below the overhanging brows.

Hatchard gave one glance at him, and a curious thing happened. Instantly there sprang into his mind not, first of all, the knowledge of who this man was, but the knowledge which had so long evaded him. He remembered everything: Mrs. Pringle's white, drawn face as she looked at the jury filing into the box again at the end of their consultation, in which they had decided the guilt or the innocence of Thomas Wraxton. No wonder she was all suspense and anxiety, for it was her husband's fate that was being decided. And then, a moment afterwards, he could trace in the face of the man who stood at the garden door the shattered identity of him who had stood in the dock. But had it not been for his wife, he thought he would not have recognized him, so terribly had suffering changed him. He looked very ill, and the high colour in his face clearly pointed to a weakness of the heart rather than a vigorous circulation.

Hatchard turned to him. He did not intend to use his deadliest weapon unless it was necessary. But at that moment he told himself that Telford House would be his.

"You will excuse me, Mr. Pringle," he said, "for calling on you so unceremoniously. My name is Hatchard, Ralph Hatchard, and I should be most grateful if you would let me have a few minutes' conversation with you."

Pringle took a step forward. He told himself that he had not been recognized; that was no wonder. But the shock of the encounter had left him trembling.

"Certainly," he said; "shall we go into my room here?"

The two went into a little sitting-room close by the front door.

"My business is quite short," said Hatchard. "I am on the look-out for a house here, and of all the houses in Scarling yours is the one which I have long wanted. I am willing to pay you six thousand pounds for it. I may add that there is an extremely pleasant house, which I have the option to purchase, which you can obtain for half that sum."

Pringle shook his head.

"I am not thinking of parting with my house," he said.

"If it is a matter of price," said Hatchard, "I am willing to make it six thousand five hundred pounds."

"It is not a matter of price," said Pringle. "The house suits my wife and me, and it is not for sale."

Hatchard paused a moment. The man had been his client, but a guilty and a very ungrateful one.

"I am quite determined to get this house, Mr. Pringle," he said. "You will make, I feel sure, a very handsome profit by accepting the price I offer, and if you are attached to Scarling you will be able to purchase a very convenient residence."

"The house is not for sale," said Pringle.

Hatchard looked at him closely.

"You will be more comfortable in the other house," he said. "You will live there, I assure you, in peace and security, and I hope you will spend many pleasant years there as Mr. Pringle from India. That will be better than being known as Mr. Thomas Wraxton, of His Majesty's prison."

The wretched man shrunk into a mere nerveless heap in his chair, and wiped his forehead.

"You know me, then?" he said.

"Intimately, I may say," retorted Hatchard.

Five minutes later Hatchard left the house. He had in his pocket Mr. Pringle's acceptance of his offer of £6,500 for Telford House with possession in a month's time. That night the doctor was hurriedly sent for to Telford House, but his skill was of no avail against the heart-attack which proved fatal to his patient.

Ralph Hatchard was sitting on the flagged terrace on the garden side of his newly acquired house one warm evening in May. He had spent his morning on the links with his brother Francis, his afternoon in the garden, weeding and planting, and now he was glad enough to sprawl in his low easy basket-chair and glance at the paper which he had not yet read. He had been a month here, and looking back through his happy and busy life he could not recollect having ever been busier and happier. It was said, how falsely he now knew, that if a man gave up his work he often went downhill both in mind and body, growing stout and lazy and losing that interest in life which keeps old age in the background, but the very opposite had been his own experience. He played his golf and his bridge with just as much zest as when they had been the recreation from his work, and he found time now for serious reading. He gardened, too, you might say with gluttony; awaking in the morning found him refreshed and eager for the pleasurable toil and exercise of the day, and every evening found him ready for bed and long, dreamless sleep.

He sat, alone for the time being, content to take his ease and glance at the news. Even now he gave but a cursory attention to it and his eye wandered over the lawn, and the long-neglected flower-beds, which the joint labours of the gardener and himself were quickly bringing back into orderly cultivation. The lawn must be cut to-morrow, and there were some late-flowering roses to be planted . . . Then perhaps he dozed a little, for though he had heard no one approach there was the sound of steps somewhere at his back quite close to him, and the tapping of a stick on the paving-stones of the terrace. He did not look round, for of course it must be Francis returned from his shopping; he had occasional twinges of rheumatism which made him a little lame, but Ralph had not noticed till to-day that he limped like that.

"Is your rheumatism bothering you, Francis?" he said, still not looking round. There was no answer, and he turned his head. The terrace was quite empty: neither his brother nor anyone else was there.

For the moment he was startled: then he was aware that he certainly had been dozing, for his paper had slipped off his knee without his noticing it. No doubt this impression was the fag-end of some dream. Confirmation of that immediately came, for there in the street outside was the noise of a tapping footfall; it was that no doubt that had mingled itself with some only half-waking impression. He had dreamed, too, now that he came to think about it; he had dreamed something about poor Wraxton. What it was he could not recollect, beyond that Wraxton was angry with him and railed at him just as he had done after that long sentence had been passed on him.

The sun had set, and there was a slight chill in the air which caused him a moment's goose-flesh. So getting out of his basket-chair he took a turn along the gravel path which bordered the lawn, his eye dwelling with satisfaction on the labours of the day. The bed had been smothered in weeds a week ago; now there was not a weed to be seen on it . . . Ah, just one; that small piece of chickweed had evaded notice, and he bent down to root it up. At that moment he heard the limping step again, not in the street at all, but close to him on the terrace, and the basket-chair creaked, as if someone had sat down in it. But again the terrace was void of occupants, and his chair empty.

It would have been strange indeed if a man so hard-headed and practical as Hatchard had allowed himself to be disturbed by an echoing stone and a creaking chair, and it was with no effort that he dismissed them. He had plenty to occupy him without that, but once or twice in the next week he received impressions which he definitely chucked into the lumber-room of his mind as among the things for which he had no use. One morning, for instance, after the gardener had gone to his dinner, he thought he saw him standing on the far side of the mulberry tree, half screened by the foliage. He took the trouble to walk round the tree on this occasion, but found no one there, neither his gardener nor any other, and coming back to the place where he had received this impression, he saw (and was secretly relieved to see) that a splash of light on the wall beyond might have tricked him into constructing a human figure there. But though his waking moments were still untroubled he began to sleep badly, and when he slept to be the prey of vivid and terrible dreams, from which he would awake in disordered panic.

The recollection of these was vague, but always he had been pursued by something invisible and angry that had come in from the garden, and was limping swiftly after him upstairs and along the passage at the end of which his room lay. Invariably, too, he just escaped into his room before the pursuer clutched him, and banged his door, the crash of which (in his dream) awoke him. Then he would turn on the light, and, despite himself, cast a glance at the door, and the oblong of glass above it which gave light to this dark end of the passage, as if to be sure that nothing was looking through it; and once, upbraiding himself for his cowardice, he had gone to the door and opened it, and turned on the light in the passage outside. But it was empty.

By day he was master of himself, though he knew that his self-control was becoming a matter that demanded effort. Often and often, though still nothing was visible, he heard the limping steps on the terrace and along the weeded gravel path; but instead of becoming used to so harmless an hallucination, which seemed to usher in nothing further, he grew to fear it. But until a certain day it was only in the garden that he heard that step . . .

July was now half way through, when a broiling morning was succeeded by a storm that raced up from the south. Thunder had been remotely muttering for an hour or two, and now, as he worked on the garden beds, the first large tepid drops of rain warned him that the downpour was imminent, and he had scarcely reached the door into the hall when it descended. The sluices of heaven were opened, and thick as a tropical tempest the rain splashed and steamed on the terrace. As he stood in the doorway he heard the limping step come slowly and unhurried through the deluge and up to the door where he stood. But it did not pause there; he felt something invisible push by him, he heard the steps limp across the hall within, and the door of the sitting-room, where he had sat one morning in March and watched Wraxton's tremulous signature traced on the paper, swing open and close again.

Ralph Hatchard stood steady as a rock, holding himself firmly in hand. "So it's come into the house," he said to himself. "So it's come in – ha! – out of the rain," he added. But he knew, when that unseen presence had pushed by him to the door, that at that moment terror real and authentic had touched some inmost fibre of him. That touch had quitted him now; he could reassert his dominion over himself, and be steady, but as surely as that unseen presence had entered the house, so surely had fear found entry into his soul.

All the afternoon the rain continued; golf and gardening were alike out of the question, and presently he went round to the club to find a rubber of bridge. He was wise to be occupied; occupation was always good, especially for one who now had in his mind a prohibited area where it was better not to graze. For something invisible and angry had come into the house, and he must starve it into quitting it again, not by facing it and defying it, but by the subtler and the safe process of denying and disregarding it. A man's soul was his own enclosed garden, nothing could obtain admittance there without his invitation and permission. He must forget it till he could afford to laugh at the fantastic motive of its existence . . . Besides, the perception of it was purely subjective, so he argued to himself: it had no real existence outside himself; his brother, for instance, and the servants were quite unaware of the limping steps that so constantly were heard by him. The invisible phantom was the product of some derangement of his own senses, some misfunction of the nerves. To convince himself of that, as he passed through the hall on his way to the club, he went into the room into which the limping steps had passed. Of course there was nothing there, it was just the small, quiet, unoccupied sitting-room that he knew.

There was some brisk bridge, which he enjoyed in his usual grim and magisterial manner, and dusk, hastened on by the thick pall of cloud which still overset the sky, was falling when he got back home again. He went into the panelled sitting-room looking out on the garden, and found Francis there, cheery and robust. The lamps were lit, but the blinds and curtains not yet drawn, and outside an illuminated oblong of light lay across the terrace.

"Well, pleasant rubbers?" asked Francis.

"Very decent," said Ralph. "You've not been out?"

"No; why go out in the rain, when there's a house to keep you dry? By the way, have you seen your visitor?"

Ralph knew that his heart checked and missed a beat. Had that which was invisible to him become visible to another? . . . Then he pulled himself together; why shouldn't there have been a visitor to see him?"

"No," he said. "Who was it?"

Francis beat out his pipe against the bars of the grate.

"I'm sure I don't know," he said. "But ten minutes ago I passed through the hall, and there was a man sitting on a chair there. I asked him what he wanted, and he said he was waiting to see you. I supposed it was somebody who had called by appointment, and I said you would no doubt be in presently, and suggested that he would be more comfortable in that little sitting-room than waiting in the hall. So I showed him in there, and shut the door on him."

Ralph rang the bell.

"Who is it who has called to see me?" he asked the parlourmaid.

"Nobody, sir, that I know of," she said; "I haven't let anyone in!"

"Well, somebody has called," he said, "and he's in the little sitting-room near the front door. Just see who it is; and ask him his name and his business."

He paused a moment, making a call on his courage.

"No; I'll go myself," he said.

He came back in a few seconds.

"Whoever it was, he has gone," he said. "I suppose he got tired of waiting. What was he like, Francis?"

"I couldn't see him very distinctly, for it was pretty dark in the hall. He had a grey beard, I saw that, and he walked with a limp."

Ralph turned to the window to pull down the blind. At that moment he heard a step on the terrace outside, and there stepped into the illuminated oblong the figure of a man. He leaned heavily on a stick as he walked, and came close up to the window, his eyes blazing with some devilish fury, his mouth mumbling and working in his beard . . . Then down came the blind, and the rattle of the curtain-rings along the pole followed.

The evening passed quietly enough: the two brothers dined together, and played a few hands at piquet afterwards, and before going up to bed looked out into the garden to see what promise the weather gave. But the rain still dripped, and the air was sultry with storm. Lightning quivered now and again in the west, and in one of these blinks Francis suddenly pointed towards the mulberry tree.

"Who is that?" he said.

"I saw no one," said Ralph.

Once more the lightning made things visible, and Francis laughed.

"Ah, I see," he said. "It's only the trunk of the tree and that grey patch of sky through the leaves. I could have sworn there was somebody there. That's a good example of how ghost stories arise. If it had not been for that second flash we should have searched the garden, and, finding nobody, I should have been convinced I had seen a ghost!"

"Very sound," said Ralph.

He lay long awake that night, listening to the hiss of the rain on the shrubs outside his window, and to a footfall that moved about the house . . .

The next few days passed without the renewal of any direct manifestations of the presence that had entered the house. But the cessation of it brought no relief to the pressure of some force that seemed combing in over Ralph Hatchard's mind. When he was out on the links or at the club it relaxed its hold on him, but the moment he entered his door it gripped him again. It mattered not that he neither saw nor heard anything for which there was no normal and material explanation; the power, whatever it was, was about his path and about his bed, driving terror into him. He confessed to strange lassitude and depression, and eventually yielded to his brother's advice, and made an appointment with his doctor in town for next day.

"Much the wisest course," said Francis. "Doctors are a splendid institution. Whenever I feel down I go and see one, and he always tells me there's nothing the matter. In consequence I feel better at once. Going up to bed? I shall follow in half an hour. There's an amusing tale I'm in the middle of."

"Put out the light, then," said Ralph, "and I'll tell the servants they can go to bed."

The half-hour lengthened into an hour, and it was not much before midnight that Francis finished his tale. There was a switch in the hall to be turned off, and another half-way up the stairs. As his finger was on this, he looked up to see that the passage above was still lit, and saw, leaning on the banister at the top of the stairs, the figure of a man. He had already put out the light on the stairs, and this figure was silhouetted in black against the bright background of the lit passage. For a moment he supposed that it must be his brother, and then the man turned, and he saw that he was grey-bearded, and limped as he walked.

"Who the devil are you?" cried Francis.

He got no reply, but the figure moved away up the passage, at the end of which was Ralph's room. He was now in full pursuit after it, but before he had traversed one half of the passage it was already at the end of it, and had gone into his brother's room. Strangely bewildered and alarmed, he followed, knocked on Ralph's door, calling him loudly by name, and turned the handle to enter. But the door did not yield for all his pushing, and again, "Ralph! Ralph!" he called aloud, but there was no answer.

Above the door was a glass pane that gave light to the passage and looking up he saw that this was black, showing that the room was in darkness within. But even as he looked it started into light, and simultaneously from inside there rose a cry of mortal agony.

"Oh, my God, my God!" rang out his brother's voice, and again that cry of agony resounded.

Then there was another voice, speaking low and angry . . .

"No, no!" yelled Ralph again, and again in a panic of fear. Francis put his shoulder to the door and strove quite in vain to open it, for it seemed as if the door had become a part of the solid wall.

Once more that cry of terror burst out, and then whatever was taking place within was all over, for there was dead silence. The door which had resisted his most frenzied efforts now yielded to him, and he entered.

His brother was in bed, his legs drawn up close under him, and his hands, resting on his knees, seemed to be attempting to beat off some terrible intruder. His body was pressed against the wall at the head of the bed, and the face was a mask of agonized horror and fruitless entreaty. But the eyes were already glazed in death, and before Francis could reach the bed the body had toppled over and lay inert and lifeless. Even as he looked, he heard a limping step go down the passage outside.

Expiation

Philip Stuart and I, unattached and middle-aged persons, had for the last four or five years been accustomed to spend a month or six weeks together in the summer, taking a furnished house in some part of the country, which, by an absence of attractive pursuits, was not likely to be overrun by gregarious holiday-makers. When, as the season for getting out of London draws near, and we scan the advertisement columns which set forth the charms and the cheapness of residences to be let for August, and see the mention of tennis-clubs and esplanades and admirable golf-links within a stone's throw of the proposed front door, our offended and disgusted eyes instantly wander to the next item.

For the point of a holiday, according to our private heresy, is not to be entertained and occupied and jostled by glad crowds, but to have nothing to do, and no temptation which might lead to any unseasonable activity. London has held employments and diversion enough; we want to be without both. But vicinity to the sea is desirable, because it is easier to do nothing by the sea than anywhere else, and because bathing and basking on the shore cannot be considered an employment, but only an apotheosis of loafing. A garden also is a requisite, for that tranquillizes any fidgety notion of going for a walk.

In pursuance of this sensible policy we had this year taken a house on the south coast of Cornwall, for a relaxing climate conduces to laziness. It was too far off for us to make any personal inspection of it, but a perusal of the modestly worded advertisement carried conviction. It was close to the sea; the village Polwithy, outside which it was situated, was remote, and, as far as we knew, unknown; it had a garden, and there was attached to it a cook-housekeeper who made for simplification. No mention of golf-links or attractive resorts in the neighbourhood defiled the bald and terse specification, and though there was a tennis-court in the garden, there was no clause that bound the tenants to use it. The owner was a Mrs. Hearne, who had been living abroad, and our business was transacted with a house-agent in Falmouth.

To make our household complete, Philip sent down a parlourmaid, and I a housemaid, and after leaving them a day in which to settle in, we followed. There was a six-mile drive from the station across high uplands, and at the end a long, steady descent into a narrow valley, cloven between the hills, that grew ever more luxuriant in verdure as we descended. Great trees of fuchsia spread up to the eaves of the thatched cottages which stood by the wayside, and a stream, embowered in green thickets, ran babbling along. Presently we came to the village, no more than a dozen houses, built of the grey stone of the district, and on a shelf just above it a tiny church with parsonage adjoining. High above us now flamed the gorse-clad slopes of the hills on each side, and now the valley opened out at its lower end, and the still, warm air was spiced and renovated by the breeze that drew up it from the sea. Then round a sharp angle of the road we came alongside a stretch of brick wall, and stopped at an iron gate above which flowed a riot of rambler rose.

It seemed hardly credible that it was this of which that terse and laconic advertisement had spoken; I had pictured something of villa-ish kind – yellow-bricked perhaps, with a roof of purplish slate, a sitting-room one side of the entrance, a dining-room the other; with a tiled hall and a pitch-pine staircase – and instead, here was this little gem of an early Georgian manor house, mellow and gracious, with mullioned windows and a roof of stone slabs. In front of it was a paved terrace, below which blossomed a herbaceous border, tangled and tropical, with no inch of earth visible through its luxuriance. Inside, too, was fulfilment of this fair exterior: a broad-balustered staircase led up from the odiously entitled "lounge hall", which I had pictured as a medley of Benares ware and saddle-bagged sofas, but which proved to be cool, broad and panelled with a door opposite that through which we entered, leading on to the further area of garden at the back. There was the advertised but innocuous tennis-court, bordered on the length of its far side by a steep grass bank, along which was planted a row of limes, once pollarded, but now allowed to develop at will. Thick boughs, some fourteen or fifteen feet from the ground, interlaced with each other, forming an arcaded row; above them, where Nature had been permitted to go her own way, the trees broke into feathered and honey-scented branches. Beyond lay a small orchard climbing upwards; above that the hillside rose more steeply, in broad spaces of short-cropped turf and ablaze with gorse, the Cornish gorse that flowers all the year round, and spreads its sunshine from January to December.

There was time for a stroll through this perfect little domain before dinner, and for a short interview with the housekeeper, a quiet, capable-looking woman, slightly aloof, as is the habit of her race, from strangers and foreigners, for so the Cornish account the English, but who proved herself at the repast that followed to be as capable as she appeared. The evening closed in hot and still, and after dinner we took chairs out on to the terrace in front of the house.

"Far the best place we've struck yet," observed Philip. "Why did no one say Polwithy before?"

"Because nobody had ever heard of it, luckily," said I.

"Well, I'm a Polwithian. At least, I am in spirit. But how aware Mrs. – Mrs. Criddle made me feel that I wasn't really."

Philip's profession, a doctor of obscure nervous diseases, has made him preternaturally acute in the diagnosis of what other people feel, and for some reason quite undefined I wanted to know what exactly he meant by this. I was in sympathy with his feeling, but I could not analyse it.

"Describe your symptoms," I said.

"I have. When she came up and talked to us, and hoped we should be comfortable, and told us that she would do her best, she was just gossiping. Probably it was perfectly true gossip. But it wasn't she. However, as that's all that matters, there's no reason why we should probe further."

"Which means that you have," I said.

"No; it means that I tried to and couldn't. She gave me an extraordinary sense of her being aware of something which we knew nothing of; of being on a plane which we couldn't imagine. I constantly meet such people; they aren't very rare. I don't mean that there's anything the least uncanny about them, or that they know things that are uncanny. They are simply aloof, as hard to understand as your dog or your cat. She would find us equally aloof if she succeeded in analysing her sensations about us, but like a sensible woman she probably feels not the smallest interest in us. She is there to bake and to boil, and we are there to eat her bakings and appreciate her boilings."

The subject dropped, and we sat on in the dusk that was rapidly deepening into night. The door into the hall was open at our backs, and a panel of light from the lamps within was cast out on to the terrace. Wandering moths, invisible in the darkness, suddenly became manifest as they fluttered into this illumination, and vanished again as they passed out of it. One moment they were there, living things with life and motion of their own, the next they had quite disappeared. How inexplicable that would be, I thought, if one did not know from long familiarity that light of the appropriate sort and strength is needed to make material objects visible.

Philip must have been following precisely the same train of thought, for his voice broke in, carrying it a little further.

"Look at that moth," he said, "and even while you look it has gone like a ghost, even as like a ghost it appeared. Light made it visible. And there are other sorts of light, interior psychical light which similarly makes visible the beings which people the darkness of our blindness."

Just as he spoke I thought for the moment that I heard the tingle of a telephone bell. It sounded very faintly, and I could not have sworn that I had actually heard it. At the most it gave one staccato little summons and was silent again.

"Is there a telephone in the house?" I asked. "I haven't noticed one."

"Yes, by the door into the back garden," said he. "Do you want to telephone?"

"No, but I thought I heard it ring. Didn't you?"

He shook his head, then smiled.

"Ah, that was it," he said.

Certainly now there was the clink of glass, rather bell-like, as the parlourmaid came out of the dining-room with a tray of syphon and decanter, and my reasonable mind was quite content to accept this very probable explanation. But behind that, quite unreasonably, some little obstinate denizen of my consciousness rejected it. It told me that what I had heard was like the moth that came out of darkness and went on into darkness again . . .

My room was at the back of the house, overlooking the lawn-tennis-court, and presently I went up to bed. The moon had risen, and the lawn lay in bright illumination bordered by a strip of dark shadow below the pollarded limes. Somewhere along the hillside an owl was foraging, softly hooting, and presently it swept whitely across the lawn. No sound is so intensely rural, yet none, to my mind, so suggests a signal. But it seemed to signal nothing, and, tired with the long, hot journey, and soothed by the deep tranquillity of the place, I was soon asleep. But often during the night I woke, though never to more than a dozing, dreamy consciousness of where I was, and each time I had the notion that some slight noise had roused me, and each time I found myself listening to hear whether the tingle of a telephone bell was the cause of my disturbance. There came no repetition of it, and again I slept, and again I woke with drowsy attention for the sound which I felt I expected, but never heard.

Daylight banished these imaginations, but though I must have slept many hours all told, for these wakings had been only brief and partial, I was aware of a certain weariness, as if though my bodily senses had been rested, some part of me had been wakeful and watching all night. This was fanciful enough to disregard, and certainly during the day I forgot it altogether. Soon after breakfast we went down to the sea, and a short ramble along a shingly shore brought us to a sandy cove framed in promontories of rock that went down into deep water. The most fastidious connoisseur in bathing could have pictured no more ideal scene for his operations, for with hot sand to bask on and rocks to plunge from, and a limpid ocean and a cloudless sky, there was indeed no lacuna in perfection. All morning we loafed here, swimming and sunning ourselves, and for the afternoon there was the shade of the garden, and a stroll later on up through the orchard and to the gorse-clad hillside. We came back through the churchyard, looked into the church, and coming out, Philip pointed to a tombstone which from its newness among its dusky and moss-grown companions easily struck the eye. It recorded without pious or scriptural reflection the date of the birth and death of George Hearne; the latter event had taken place close on two years ago, and we were within a week of the exact anniversary. Other tombstones near were monuments to those of the same name, and dated back for a couple of centuries and more.

"Local family," said I, and strolling on we came to our own gate in the long brick wall. It was opened from inside just as we arrived at it, and there came out a brisk, middle-aged man in clergyman's dress, obviously our vicar.

He very civilly introduced himself.

"I heard that Mrs. Hearne's house had been taken, and that the tenants had come," he said, "and I ventured to leave my card."

We performed our part of the ceremony, and in answer to his inquiry professed our satisfaction with our quarters and our neighbourhood.

"That is good news," said Mr. Stephens; "I hope you will continue to enjoy your holiday. I am Cornish myself, and like all natives think there is no place like Cornwall!"

Philip pointed with his stick towards the churchyard. "We noticed that the Hearnes are people of the place," he said. Quite suddenly I found myself understanding what he had meant by the aloofness of the race. Something between reserve and suspicion came into Mr. Stephens' face.

"Yes, yes, an old family here," he said, "and large landowners. But now some remote cousin . . . The house, however, belongs to Mrs. Hearne for life."

He stopped, and by that reticence confirmed the impression he had made. In consequence, for there is something in the breast of the most incurious which, when treated with reserve becomes inquisitive, Philip proceeded to ask a direct question.

"Then I take it that the George Hearne who, as I have just seen, died two years ago, was the husband of Mrs. Hearne, from whom we took the house?"

"Yes; he was buried in the churchyard," said Mr. Stephens quickly. Then, for no reason at all, he added:

"Naturally he was buried in the churchyard here."

Now my impression at that moment was that Mr. Stephens had said something he did not mean to say, and had corrected it by saying the same thing again.

He went on his way, back to the vicarage, with an amiably expressed desire to do anything that was in his power for us, in the way of local information, and we went in through the gate. The post had just arrived; there was the London morning paper and a letter for Philip which cost him two perusals before he folded it up and put it into his pocket. But he made no comment, and presently, as dinner-time was near, I went up to my room. Here in this deep valley with the great westerly hill towering above us, it was already dark, and the lawn lay beneath a twilight as of deep, clear water. Quite idly as I brushed my hair in front of the glass on the table in the window, of which the blinds were not yet drawn, I looked out and saw that on the bank along which grew the pollarded limes there was lying a ladder. It was just a shade odd that it should be there, but the oddity of it was quite accounted for by the supposition that the gardener had had business among the trees in the orchard, and had left it there, for the completion of his labours to-morrow. It was just as odd as that, and no odder, just worth a twitch of the imagination to account for it, but now completely accounted for.

I went downstairs, and passing Philip's door heard the swish of ablutions which implied he was not quite ready, and in the most loaferlike manner I strolled round the corner of the house. The kitchen window which looked on to the tennis-court was open, and there was a good smell, I remember, coming from it. And still without thought of the ladder I had just seen, I mounted the slope of grass on to the tenniscourt. Just across it was the bank where the pollarded limes grew; but there was no ladder lying there. Of course the gardener must have remembered he had left it, and had returned to remove it exactly as I came downstairs. There was nothing singular about that, and I could not imagine why the thing interested me at all. But for some inexplicable reason I found myself saying: "But I did see the ladder just now."

A bell – no telephone bell, but a welcome harbinger to a hungry man – sounded from inside the house, and I went back on to the terrace, just as Philip got downstairs. At dinner our speech rambled pleasantly over the accomplishments of to-day, and the prospects of to-morrow, and in due course we came to the consideration of Mr. Stephens. We settled that he was an aloof fellow, and then Philip said:

"I wonder why he hastened to tell us that George Hearne

was buried in the churchyard, and then added that naturally he was!"

"It's the natural place to be buried in," said I.

"Quite. That's just why it was hardly worth mentioning."

I felt then, just momentarily, just vaguely, as if my mind was regarding stray pieces of a jigsaw puzzle. The fancied ringing of the telephone bell last night was one of them, this burial of George Hearne in the churchyard was another, and, even more inexplicably, the ladder I had seen under the trees was a third. Consciously I made nothing whatever out of them, and did not feel the least inclination to devote any ingenuity to so fortuitous a collection of pieces. Why shouldn't I add, for that matter, our morning's bathe, or the gorse on the hillside? But I had the sensation that, though my conscious brain was presently occupied with piquet, and was rapidly growing sleepy with the day of sun and sea, some sort of mole inside it was digging passages and connecting-corridors below the soil.

Five eventless days succeeded; there were no more ladders, no more phantom telephone bells, and emphatically no more Mr. Stephens. Once or twice we met him in the village street and got from him the curtest salutation possible short of a direct cut. And yet somehow he seemed charged with information, so we lazily concluded, and he made for us a field of imaginative speculation. I remember that I constructed a highly fanciful romance, which postulated that George Hearne was not dead at all, but that Mr. Stephens had murdered some inconvenient blackmailer, whom he had buried with the rites of the Church. Or – these romances always broke down under cross-examination from Philip – Mr. Stephens himself was George Hearne, who had fled from justice, and was supposed to have died. Or Mrs. Hearne was really George Hearne, and our admirable housekeeper was the real Mrs. Hearne. From such indications you may judge how the intoxication of the sun and the sea had overpowered us.

But there was one explanation of why Mr. Stephens had so hastily assured us that George Hearne was buried in the churchyard which never passed our lips. It was just because both Philip and I really believed it to be the true one that we did not mention it. But just as if it was some fever or plague, we both knew that we were sickening with it. And then these fanciful romances stopped because we knew that the Real Thing was approaching. There had been faint glimpses of it before, like distant sheet-lightning; now the noise of it, authentic and audible, began to rumble.

There came a day of hot, overclouded weather. We had bathed in the morning, and loafed in the afternoon, but Philip, after tea, had refused to come for our usual ramble, and I set out alone. That morning Mrs. Criddle had rather peremptorily told me that a room in the front of the house would prove much cooler for me, for it caught the sea breeze, and though I objected that it would also catch the southerly sun, she had clearly made up her mind that I was to move from the bedroom overlooking the tennis-court and the pollarded limes, and there was no resisting so polite and yet determined a woman.

When I set out for my ramble after tea, the change had already been effected, and my brain nosed slowly about as I strolled, sniffing for her reason, for no self-respecting brain could accept the one she gave. But in this hot, drowsy air, I entirely lacked nimbleness, and when I came back the question had become a mere silly, unanswerable riddle. I returned through the churchyard, and saw that in a couple of days we should arrive at the anniversary of George Hearne's death.

Philip was not on the terrace in front of the house, and I went in at the door of the hall, expecting to find him there or in the back garden. Exactly as I entered my eye told me that there he was, a black silhouette against the glass door, at the end of the hall, which was open, and led through into the back garden. He did not turn round at the sound of my entry, but took a step or two in the direction of the far door, still framed in the oblong of it. I glanced at the table, where the post lay, found letters both for me and him, and looked up again. There was no one there.

He had hastened his steps, I supposed, but simultaneously I thought how odd it was that he had not taken his letters, if he was in the hall, and that he had not turned when I entered. However, I should find him just round the corner, and with his post and mine in my hand I went towards the far door. As I approached it I felt a sudden cold stir of air, rather unaccountable, for the day was notably sultry, and went out. He was sitting at the far end of the tennis-court.

I went up to him with his letters.

"I thought I saw you just now in the hall," I said. But I knew already that I had not seen him in the hall.

He looked up quickly.

"And have you only just come in?" he said.

"Yes; this moment. Why?"

"Because half an hour ago I went in to see if the post had come, and thought I saw you in the hall."

"And what did I do?" I asked.

"You went out on to the terrace. But I didn't find you there."

There was a short pause as he opened his letters.

"Damned interesting," he observed. "Because there's someone here who isn't you or me."

"Anything else?" I asked.

He laughed, pointing at the row of trees.

"Yes, something too silly for words," he said. "Just now I saw a piece of rope dangling from the big branch of that pollarded lime. I saw it quite distinctly. And then there wasn't any rope there at all, any more than there is now."

Philosophers have argued about the strongest emotion known to man. Some say "love", others "hate", others "fear". I am disposed to put "curiosity" on a level, at least, with these august sensations, just mere simple inquisitiveness. Certainly at the moment it rivalled fear in my mind, and there was a hint of that.

As he spoke the parlourmaid came out into the garden with a telegram in her hand. She gave it to Philip, who without a word scribbled a line on the reply-paid form inside it, and handed it back to her.

"Dreadful nuisance," he said, "but there's no help for it. A few days ago I got a letter which made me think I might have to go up to town, and this telegram makes it certain. There's an operation possible on a patient of mine, which I hoped might have been avoided, but my locum tenens won't take the responsibility of deciding whether it is necessary or not."

He looked at his watch.

"I can catch the night train," he said, "and I ought to be able to catch the night train back from town to-morrow. I shall be back, that is to say, the day after to-morrow in the morning. There's no help for it. Ha, that telephone of yours will come in useful. I can get a taxi from Falmouth, and needn't start till after dinner."

He went into the house, and I heard him rattling and tapping at the telephone. Soon he called for Mrs. Criddle, and presently came out again.

"We're not on the telephone service," he said. "It was cut off a year ago, only they haven't removed the apparatus. But I can get a trap in the village, Mrs. Criddle says, and she's sent for it. If I start at once I shall easily be in time. Spicer's packing a bag for me, and I'll take a sandwich."

He looked sharply towards the pollarded trees.

"Yes, just there," he said. "I saw it plainly, and equally plainly I saw it not. And then there's that telephone of yours."

I told him now about the ladder I had seen below the tree where he saw the dangling rope.

"Interesting," he said, "because it's so silly and unexpected. It is really tragic that I should be called away just now, for it looks as if the – well, the matter were coming out of the darkness into a shaft of light. But I'll be back, I hope, in thirty-six hours. Meantime do observe very carefully, and whatever you do, don't make a theory. Darwin says somewhere that you can't observe without a theory, but to make a theory is a great danger to an observer. It can't help influencing your imagination; you tend to see or hear what falls in with your hypothesis. So just observe; be as mechanical as a phonograph and a photographic lens."

Presently the dog-cart arrived, and I went down to the gate with him. "Whatever it is that is coming through, is coming through in bits," he said. "You heard a telephone; I saw a rope. We both saw a figure, but not simultaneously nor in the same place. I wish I didn't have to go."

I found myself sympathizing strongly with this wish, when after dinner I found myself with a solitary evening in front of me, and the pledge to "observe" binding me. It was not mainly a scientific ardour that prompted this sympathy, and the desire for independent combination, but, quite emphatically, fear of what might be coming out of the huge darkness which lies on all sides of human experience. I could no longer fail to connect together the fancied telephone bell, the rope, and the ladder, for what made the chain between them was the figure that both Philip and I had seen. Already my mind was seething with conjectural theory, but I would not let the ferment of it ascend to my surface consciousness; my business was not to aid, but rather stifle, my imagination.

I occupied myself, therefore, with the ordinary devices of a solitary man, sitting on the terrace, and subsequently coming into the house, for a few spots of rain began to fall. But though nothing disturbed the outward tranquillity of the evening, the quietness administered no opiate to that seething mixture of fear and curiosity that obsessed me. I heard the servants creep bedwards up the back stairs and presently I followed them. Then, forgetting for the moment that my room had been changed, I tried the handle of the door of that which I had previously occupied. It was locked.

Now here, beyond doubt, was the sign of a human agency, and at once I was determined to get into the room. The key, I could see, was not in the door, which must therefore have been locked from outside. I therefore searched the usual cache for keys along the top of the door-frame, found it, and entered.

The room was quite empty, the blinds not drawn, and after looking round it I walked across to the window. The moon was up, and though obscured behind clouds, gave sufficient light to enable me to see objects outside with tolerable distinctness. There was the row of pollarded limes, and then with a sudden intake of my breath I saw that a foot or two below one of the boughs there was suspended something whitish and oval which oscillated as it hung there. In the dimness I could see nothing more than that, but now conjecture crashed into my conscious brain. But even as I looked it was gone again; there was nothing there but deep shadow, the trees steadfast in the windless air. Simultaneously I knew that I was not alone in the room.

I turned swiftly about, but my eyes gave no endorsement of that conviction, and yet their evidence that there was no one here except myself failed to shake it. The presence, somewhere close to me, needed no such evidence; it was self-evident though invisible, and I knew that my forehead was streaming with the abject sweat of terror. Somehow I knew that the presence was that of the figure both Philip and I had seen that evening in the hall, and, credit it or not as you will, the fact that it was invisible made it infinitely the more terrible. I knew, too, that though my eyes were blind to it, it had got into closer touch with me; I knew more of its nature now: it had had tragic and awful commerce with evil and despair. Some sort of catalepsy was on me, while it thus obsessed me; presently, minutes afterwards, or perhaps mere seconds, the grip and clutch of its power was relaxed, and with shaking knees I crossed the room and went out, and again locked the door. Even as I turned the key I smiled at the futility of that. With my emergence the terror completely passed; I went across the passage leading to my room, got into bed, and was soon asleep. But I had no more need to question myself as to why Mrs. Criddle made the change. Another guest, she knew, would come to occupy it as the season arrived when George Hearne died and was buried in the churchyard.

The night passed quietly and then succeeded a day hot and still and sultry beyond belief. The very sea had lost its coolness and vitality, and I came in from my swim tired and enervated instead of refreshed. No breeze stirred; the trees stood motionless as if cast in iron, and from horizon to horizon the sky was overlaid by an ever-thickening pall of cloud. The cohorts of storm and thunder were gathering in the stillness, and all day I felt that power, other than that of these natural forces, was being stored for some imminent manifestation.

As I came near to the house the horror deepened, and after dinner I had a mind to drop into the viçarage, according to Mr. Stephens' general invitation, and get through an hour or two with other company than my own. But I delayed till it was past any reasonable time for such an informal visit, and ten o'clock still saw me on the terrace in front of the house. My nerves were all on edge, a stir or step in the house was sufficient to make me turn round in apprehension of seeing I knew not what, but presently it grew still. One lamp burned in the hall behind me; by it stood the candle which would light me to bed.

I went indoors soon after, meaning to go up to bed, then suddenly, ashamed of this craven imbecility of mind, took the fancy to walk round the house for the purpose of convincing myself that all was tranquil and normal, and that my fear, that nameless indefinable load on my spirit, was but a product of this close and thundery night. The tension of the weather could not last much longer; soon the storm must break and the relief come, but it would be something to know that there was nothing more than that. Accordingly I went out again on to the terrace, traversed it and turned the corner of the house where lay the tennis-lawn.

To-night the moon had not yet risen, and the darkness was such that I could barely distinguish the outline of the house, and that of the pollarded limes, but through the glass door that led from this side of the house into the hall there shone the light of the lamp that stood there. All was absolutely quiet, and half reassured I traversed the lawn, and turned to go back. Just as I came opposite the lit door, I heard a sound very close at hand from under the deep shadow of the pollarded limes. It was as if some heavy object had fallen with a thump and rebound on the grass, and with it there came the noise of a creaking bough suddenly strained by some weight. Then interpretation came upon me with the unreasoning force of conviction, though in the blackness I could see nothing. But at the sound a horror such as I have never felt laid hold on me. It was scarcely physical at all: it came from some deep-seated region of the soul.

The heavens were rent, a stream of blinding light shot forth, and straight in front of my eyes, a few yards from where I stood, I saw. The noise had been of a ladder thrown down on the grass, and from the bough of the pollarded lime there was the figure of a man, white-faced against the blackness, oscillating and twisting on the rope that strangled him. Just that I saw before the stillness was torn to atoms by the roar of thunder, and as from a hose the rain descended. Once again, even before that first appalling riot had died, the clouds were shredded again by the lightning, and my eyes which had not moved from the place, saw only the framed shadows of the trees, and their upper branches bowed by the pelting rain. All night the storm raged and bellowed, making sleep impossible, and for an hour at least, between the peals of thunder, I heard the ringing of the telephone bell.

Next morning Philip returned, to whom I told exactly what is written here, but watch and observe as we might, neither of us, in the three further weeks which we spent at Polwithy, heard or saw anything that could interest the student of the occult. Pleasant lazy days succeeded each other; we bathed and rambled and played piquet of an evening, and incidentally we made friends with the vicar. He was an interesting man, full of curious lore concerning local legends and superstitions, and one night, when in our ripened acquaintanceship he had dined with us, he asked Philip directly whether either of us had experienced anything unusual during our tenancy.

Philip nodded towards me.

"My friend saw most," he said.

"May I hear it?" asked the vicar.

When I had finished, he was silent awhile.

"I think the – shall we call it explanation? – is yours by right," he said. "I will give it you if you care to hear it."

Our silence, I supposed, answered him.

"I remember meeting you two on the day after your arrival here," he said, "and you inquired about the tombstone in the churchyard erected to the memory of George Hearne. I did not want to say more of him then, for a reason that you will presently know. I told you, I recollect, perhaps rather hurriedly, that it was Mrs. Hearne's husband who was buried there. Already, I imagine, you guess that I concealed something. You may even have guessed it at the time."

He did not wait for any confirmation or repudiation of this. Sitting out on the terrace in the deep dusk, his communication was very impersonal. It was just a narrating voice, without identity, an anonymous chronicle.

"George Hearne succeeded to the property here, which is considerable, only two years before his death. He was married shortly after he succeeded. According to any decent standard, his life both before and after his marriage was vile. I think – God forgive me if I wrong him – he made evil his good; he liked evil for its own sake. But out of the middle of the mire of his own soul there sprang a flower: he was devoted to his wife. And he was capable of shame.

"A fortnight before his – his death, she got to know what his life was like, and what he was in himself. I need not tell you what was the particular disclosure that came to her knowledge; it is sufficient to say that it was revolting. She was here at the time; he was coming down from London that night. When he arrived he found a note from her saying that she had left him and could never come back. She told him that he must give her opportunity for her to divorce him, and threatened him with exposure if he did not.

"He and I had been friends, and that night he came to me with her letter, acknowledged the justice of it, but asked me to intervene. He said that the only thing that could save him from utter damnation was she, and I believe that there he spoke sincerely. But, speaking as a clergyman, I should not have called him penitent. He did not hate his sin, but only the consequences of it. But it seemed to me that if she came back to him he might have a chance, and next day

I went to her. Nothing that I could say moved her one atom, and after a fruitless day I came back, and told him of the uselessness of my mission.

"Now, according to my view, no man who deliberately prefers evil to good, just for the sake of wickedness, is sane, and this refusal of hers to have anything more to do with him I fully believe upset the unstable balance of his soul altogether. There was just his devotion to her which might conceivably have restored it, but she refused – and I can quite understand her refusal – to come near him. If you knew what I know you could not blame her. But the effect of it on him was portentous and disastrous, and three days afterwards I wrote to her again, saying quite simply that the damnation of his soul would be on her head unless, leaving her personal feelings altogether out of the question, she came back. She got that letter the next evening, and already it was too late.

"That afternoon, two years ago, on the fifteenth of August, there was washed up in the harbour here a dead body, and that night George Hearne took a ladder from the fruit-wall in the kitchen garden and hanged himself. He climbed into one of the pollarded limes, tied the rope to a bough, and made a slip-knot at the other end of it. Then he kicked the ladder away.

"Mrs. Hearne meantime had received my letter. For a couple of hours she wrestled with her own repugnance and then decided to come to him. She rang him up on the telephone, but the housekeeper here, Mrs. Criddle, could only tell her that he had gone out after dinner. She continued ringing him up for a couple of hours, but there was always the same reply.

"Eventually she decided to waste no more time, and motored over from her mother's house where she was staying at the north end of the county. By then the moon had risen, and looking out from his bedroom window she saw him."

He paused.

"There was an inquest," he said, "and I could truthfully testify that I believed him to be insane. The verdict of suicide during temporary insanity was brought in, and he was buried in the churchyard. The rope was burned, and the ladder was burned."

The parlourmaid brought out drinks, and we sat in silence till she had gone again.

"And what about the telephone my friend heard?" asked Philip.

He thought a moment.

"Don't you think that great emotion like that of Mrs. Hearne's may make some sort of record," he asked, "so that if the needle of a sensitive temperament comes in contact with it a reproduction takes place? And it is the same perhaps about that poor fellow who hanged himself. One can hardly believe that his spirit is bound to visit and revisit the scene of his follies and his crimes year by year."

"Year by year?" I asked.

"Apparently. I saw him myself last year; Mrs. Criddle did also."

He got up.

"How can one tell?" he said. "Expiation, perhaps. Who knows?"

Home, Sweet Home

It was pleasant to get out of the baked train into an atmosphere that tingled with the subtle vitality of the sea, and though nothing could be duller than the general prospect of flat fields and dusty hedgerows, and the long white road that lay straight as a ruled line between them, I surmised that when it had climbed that long upward slope there would be a new horizon altogether, grey and liquid. Eyethorpe Junction was the name of the station, and though that appeared a strange misnomer, for nothing seemed to join anything, I presently perceived a weedy, derelict branchline, and a loquacious porter explained that the line to Eyethorpe had long been untraversed by railway traffic. There had once been high hopes that it would develop into a popular watering-place. But the public had preferred its established favourites.

The affairs that led to my disembarkation on this broiling August day at a jointless junction had been conducted in my sister Margery's most characteristic style. Her husband, Walter Mostyn, the eminent nerve specialist, had been threatened during July with a breakdown owing to overstrain in his work, and, in obedience to the ironical ordinance of, "Physician, heal thyself", had prescribed for himself a complete rest. His idea of resting his mind was not, as is the usual practice of those on holiday, to overtire his body, but to get away to some place where there was no temptation to do anything of the kind. There must be no golf-links, or he would want to play golf, and he would prefer his retreat to be by the sea, because the very fact of being in a boat at all made him feel seasick, and he hated bathing. A rest-cure in a nursing-home would be horrible to him, and he thought that if Margery could find some deadly seaside resort, where there was nothing that could tempt him into activity of mind or body, that would do just as well. He wanted to be a beast of the field, and recover his nervous force by sheer vegetation.

Margery, with these instructions to guide her, had thereupon set off, and scoured the coasts of Kent and Sussex, discovering on the second day of her wild career this amazing and unique Eyethorpe. There was a house there to let, which she at once saw was just what she was looking for, and with that most unfeminine instinct of hers of knowing that she had got what she wanted, and not making any further search, she went straight to the house-agent at Hastings and took "The Firs" for a month as from to-morrow. She drove back to London that evening, informed Walter what she had done, sent down her servants next morning, and took down her husband the same evening. A fortnight later she wrote to me that the cure was progressing splendidly, and that he, emerging from his languor, was getting rather cross and argumentative, which she took to be the sign of returning vitality. He was excessively bored with her, and wanted some man in the house, and had grudgingly said that I would "do". So would I come soon for a couple of weeks? In fact, I must, and she would expect me on Thursday. It was Thursday now, and, in consequence, I was driving up the straight, white road from Eyethorpe Junction.

We topped the rise, and there, as I had expected, was a new horizon. The sea sprang up to eye-level, the ground declined steeply over a stretch of open downland dotted with furze bushes to a line of low cliffs that fringed the shore. Along the edge of these was a huddle of red-roofed cottages, among which rose a conspicuous church-tower, and presently we jolted over the level-crossing of the line from Eyethorpe Junction, which the public had scorned. On the left was a small abandoned station with weed-grown platform, and a board, much defaced by the weather, bearing the inscription, "Eyethorpe and Coltham." The name Coltham stirred some remote vibration in my mind; I felt that I had heard the name before, but could not recall the reason for its faint familiarity. The road forked, the left-hand branch of it leading up the village street; the other, which we took, had a signpost with the information that Coltham was one mile distant. We traversed, I should have guessed, two or three furlongs, and there, close at hand, separated from the highway by a field, through which led a grass-grown drive, stood a big mellow-walled farmhouse. A clump of rather fine Scotch firs at one end of it was sufficient indication of its identity.

I was taken into and through a broad passage (you might call it a hall) which intersected the house, and from which a dignified staircase led to the upper storey. At its further end a glass-paned door opened into the garden. But there was no one here, and the servant supposed that they had gone strolling, perhaps down to the beach. The afternoon was still very hot, and, deciding to wait for them rather than vaguely pursue, I admired the luck that had attended Margery's search for a tranquil sanatorium. Not a house was visible; the clean emptiness of the downland was laid like a broad green riband east and west, and in front, through a V-shaped gap, gleamed the sea. A one-storied wing, evidently a later addition, sprouted from the west end of the house; this cast just now a very welcome shade over the square space, laid with old paving-stones, where long, low chairs and the tea-table stood. The added wing, it is scarcely necessary to mention, was of far more antique design than the house, and, looking in through its open door which gave on to this flagged space, I found a very big, pleasant room, with rafters in the ceiling, and small diamond-shaped panes in the mullioned windows. The oak floor was bare but for a few rugs, and at the far end, near an open fireplace, stood a grand piano. The lid was open, and I read there, to my great surprise, the world-famous name of Barenstein. That, too, was just like Margery, to take a remote farmhouse and find a Barenstein grand waiting for her very gifted fingers, and this fine spacious room. How cool it was in here, too – more than cool, it was positively cold; and at that moment, hearing familiar voices outside, I stepped out again on to the paved space from which I had entered.

Certainly Walter did not look as if a fortnight ago he had been on the edge of nervous breakdown. His face was bronzed and ruddy, he strode along with a firm step, and was talking in that loud, confident voice that had so often brought comfort to sufferers.

"But I tell you, darling," he was saying, "that it isn't that our senses occasionally deceive us, they habitually deceive us. Ah, there he is. Welcome, my dear Ted. You have come to a place beyond the limits of the civilized world, and it has done me a world of good already. Distractions, things that interest us are what starves the nerves. Boredom, there's the panacea for nerves. I've never been so bored in my life, and I'm a new man."

Margery laughed.

"I wonder how often you've told your patients exactly the opposite," she said. (Ted, there's a magnificent Barenstein here; did you ever know such luck?) But isn't it so, Walter? You always say that there's hope even for people who take an interest in postage-stamps. Never mind. You hate being consistent, and I won't press it. What about the senses habitually deceiving us?"

"Obvious. Your eyes, for instance. If you see a house half a mile off your eyes tell you it is about a quarter of an inch in height. If another train passes you as yours is standing in a station, they will tell you that you are moving in the opposite direction. Smell and taste are the same; if you shut your eyes you have no idea whether your cigarette is alight. Your sense of warmth and cold too; if you put your hand on a piece of very cold metal, it gives you the sensation of burning. I'm just as bad as you, perhaps worse, for my senses tell me that that room in there is bitterly cold to-day, but the thermometer says it is sixty-five degrees. I was suffering from some subjective disturbance, that was all, and my imbecile senses told me it was cold. There was the thermometer saying it was warm. The senses, as I tell you, are habitually deceptive. Liars!"

There was all his usual vehemence in this, and, so I thought, a little more. He was clearly upset at this divergence of view between his senses and the thermometer.

"But I'm on the side of your senses," I said. "I went in there just now, and I swear it was more than chilly."

He threw a quick glance over to Margery before he answered.

"More liars, then!" he said. "Another instance of the deceptiveness of the senses."

He said this with the air of bringing the discussion to an end; our talk became desultory and trivial, and before long Margery closed it by saying that, whatever anybody else did, she intended to have a dip in the sea before dinner. Presently she appeared again, with sandals and a dressing-gown over her bathing-suit, for there was but this strip of empty downland between the garden and the steep short descent on the beach. She insisted on my accompanying her as far as that V-shaped gap, and her very casual manner made me sure that she had some communication to make. It came as soon as we were out of earshot.

"Walter's ever so much better, as you can see for yourself," she said, "and till to-day he has been lying fallow with the most excellent results. But now that awful activity of his mind has begun to work again, and twenty times since lunch he has alluded to that strange feeling of chill in the big room in the wing. He keeps on saying that it's subjective, but you and I know him, and that means he thinks there's something queer about it. And you felt it too, apparently."

"I thought I did, but then I had just come into it from the broiling air outside. But hadn't he felt it before?"

"No, for the simple reason that he hadn't been into the room before," said she. "When we came here, and, indeed, till this morning, it was locked and shuttered. The gardener, who has been caretaker here, told me that the owner had stored things in it, and that it was to be left closed. Till this morning Walter did not seem to mind whether it was shut or open, but to-day he told the gardener that it was all nonsense to keep the biggest room in the house shut up, and demanded the key. Denton, that's his name, talked about disobeying his owner, but Walter insisted, and he produced the key. There was nothing stored there, and I drove over to the house-agent's at Hastings that morning to ask if there was any such order. None at all. What does it mean?"

"Nothing," said I, "except that Denton was a lazy brute, and didn't want the bother of airing and dusting the room before you came, and of putting it to rights again after you'd gone. Perhaps also the owner didn't want to prohibit your playing the great Barenstein, but hoped you wouldn't. Also this accounts for the fact that Walter and I found the room very chilly after it had been shut up for so long. When was the house last occupied, by the way?"

"I don't know. It had been unlet for some time, so the agent told me, and I didn't care in the least about its history provided I got it for Walter now."

Her jolly brown eyes made a complete circuit round my head, instead of looking at me straight when she answered.

"Don't be so foolish, Margery," I said, "but look straight at me. You told me just now that Walter thought there was something queer about the room. What do you think?"

Her eyes rested on mine.

"I think there's something queer about the house," she said. "I find myself looking up suddenly from a book or a paper to see who is in the room. And I think Walter does the same. But he – he thinks he hears something, and then finds he hasn't, just as I think I see something, and find I haven't. I cock an eye, he cocks an ear. But don't say a word to him. He hates the idea of anything you can't account for by the ordinary functions of the senses, which, he says, habitually deceive you. But since that room was opened he's been arguing with himself."

"Oh, put the stopper in," said I. "Do you remember the gurgle of the hot-water pipes in the nursery thirty years ago, and how you knew it was the groan of a murdered woman? You frightened me out of my wits then, but I'm too old to be frightened now. You haven't seen anything, and he hasn't heard anything; eye hath not seen nor ear heard. Don't imagine things; half the trouble in the world comes from imagining. Have a nice bathe, and wash it all off."

For a moment, as she looked at me, I saw somewhere behind her eyes a sense of uneasiness, but it vanished.

"I shan't wash off my gladness that you've joined us," she said, and ran off down the steep little path to the beach.

I strolled back through the garden thinking how unlike Margery it was to be within the grip of vague apprehension like this, or to imagine that there was anything "queer" about the house, for, in spite of the famous episode of the gurgling pipes, she was singularly free from imagined alarms. Even more unusual, if she was right about him, was it that Walter should be affected in the same sort of way. Margery certainly showed her good sense in demanding that her odd apprehensions should be kept apart from his, and not be given the meeting-ground of discussion. But she had noticed, or imagined, his, and I was soon to learn that he was not blind to hers.

Walter had gone up to his room when I got back, and I went into the lately opened sitting-room, where I found that my books and papers had been disposed on a big table, which was thus clearly consecrated to my use. I was engaged on a memoir which it interested me to write, though I had grave doubts about its interesting anybody else to read. The piano stood a little beyond my table, with the keyboard towards me; between it and me, on my left, was the open window looking on to the garden. The room still seemed chilly, but I speedily forgot that and, indeed, everything else but my delightful task.

How long I had been at work I had no idea, when suddenly – even as I turned a page to carry on the note I had begun – I became vividly aware of my surroundings again and knew with absolute conviction that I was not alone. I glanced up and saw that there was a man outside the window looking at the piano. For a second or two he gazed fixedly at it, and then, turning his head, perceived me at my table. He had not, I imagined, observed that there was anyone here, for he touched his hat, and would have gone away, but I called to him.

"Do you want anything?" I asked. "Denton, is it?"

"Yes, sir. I – I was only just looking to see if the room was all right," and immediately he withdrew. But, oddly enough, I felt that it was not Denton's presence at the window that gave me the sense that there was someone here; it had nothing to do with Denton. And why, I asked myself, as the man walked briskly off, why on earth should Denton look in to see if the room was all right? It was the piano that riveted him; did he want to be sure that all was well with the piano?

I tried to attach myself to my work again, but the connection would no longer hold. There was still that sense of some presence in the room, which came between me and my page. Time and again I held my mind down to its task, but it slipped away, and presently at its bidding my eyes left the paper and scrutinized the room. Certainly there was nothing behind me, nor at my side, but I found myself – was it Denton's example which had infected me? – looking at the piano as if what I sought was invisibly there. Its japanned case, darkly, like black glass, reflected my table, the white keys gleamed in their ebony setting. And then I saw that some of them were moving – a group, three of four at a time, and now a succession of single notes sank and recovered as if under the pressure of fingers.

I cannot hope to describe the curiosity and the dismay with which this filled my mind. I gazed fascinated at this inexplicable movement, but at the same time my mind cried out in horror at the invisible cause of it. Then, as suddenly as it had begun, this fantastic spectacle ceased, but the presence was still there. Then from outside there came the sound of steps. Walter entered.

"Margery here?" he asked. "No? Was it you playing, then?"

"Deceptive senses," I said. "I haven't touched the piano."

He looked at me a moment, puzzled.

"But I would swear I heard the piano," he said.

Instantly I made up my mind not to tell Walter what I had seen, and already, so fantastic was it, I was beginning to doubt if I had seen anything. Yet deep in my mind remained that intense curiosity, and deeper yet some unreasoning terror.

The evening passed quite normally; Walter bewailed the hideous necessity of going in to Hastings next day to have his hair cut, and even the darker fate of having the vicar of Eyethorpe to dinner.

It was still early when we went up to bed and, conscious of an overwhelming somnolence, I instantly fell asleep. I woke, staring wide awake, with the answer to the question which had slightly worried me yesterday, as to why the name of the neighbouring Coltham was remotely familiar to me, clear in my mind. There had occurred there, about a year before, a very brutal murder, which still remained among the unsolved mysteries of criminal history. An elderly spinster lady, living with her spinster sister at some house there, had been found strangled on the floor of her sitting-room. It was supposed that robbery was the motive for the crime, but the murderer seemed to have heard some stir in the house, and left a cashbox containing thirty or forty pounds in the drawer he had just opened. I could remember no further details, but I thought I would stroll over to Coltham next morning and, with that appetite for the horrible which lurks in us all, find out which the house was.

The two went off to Hastings next morning and, in pursuance of my plan, I strolled up the road to Coltham. It was a melancholy little bunch of cottages perched on the edge of the downs, and I had just decided that a rather stricken-looking house, with a board up to say it was to let, was a suitable site for the murder, when I saw Denton coming down the little street.

"Which was the house where that murder took place last year, Denton?" I asked him.

He stared at me a moment, and I saw his throat-apple jerk up and down. Then he pointed to the house I had picked out.

"That was the one, sir," he said.

"And what was the name of the old lady?" I asked.

"Miss Ellershaw," said he, and rather abruptly, much in the manner in which he had retreated from the window last night, he turned and left me. Rather pleased with myself for my perspicacity I strolled homewards again.

Margery and Walter, he shorn and self-respecting again, came back about one o'clock, and Margery announced her determination of writing overdue letters till the really intolerable heat of the day had declined.

"Hopeless arrears," she said, "bills and bills, and the rent of the house for the next fortnight, which ought to have been paid two days ago. But I'll send it straight to our landlord – or is it landlady? – instead of the agent; that will save a day."

The clear burning of the sun had given place to an extreme sultriness; the sky was overcast with clouds which all afternoon thickened to a still density portending thunder. Margery retired to the piano-room to perform her overdues, Walter fell asleep, and, leaving him on the paved space, I joined Margery for coolness. She jumped up as I entered.

"I was dying to be interrupted," she said, "because I long to see what's in that cupboard by the piano. I've muddled up your papers, Ted, I'm afraid. Unmuddle them again while I have an interval."

She had, indeed, muddled my papers up. Half-finished letters, and addressed envelopes, and bills were mixed up with my notes. As I disentangled them, I came across a cheque she had drawn. It was made out to Miss Ellershaw. There was also a half-sheet on which Mrs. Mostyn "much regretted not having sent cheque for a fortnight's rent sooner" . . . So Miss Ellershaw was owner of "The Firs", and two Miss Ellershaws, one of whom had been murdered, lived together. Had they lived in that house at Coltham, where Denton had told me the murder was committed, or had they—

Margery interrupted these rather disquieting thoughts.

"What a disappointment!" she said. "Empty cupboard, all but one leaf of a book of English songs, and that's 'Home, Sweet Home'! You may laugh at it, but it's a wonderful melody. I must just play it, and then I shall get on with my jobs."

The window close to which I sat commanded a view of the garden. Out of it, I could see Denton plucking sweet-peas. As the notes of the old-fashioned tune streamed out through the open window, I saw him drop his basket and stop his ears. Simultaneously I knew that there was some presence here in the room not Margery's nor mine.

She played two lines and stopped. She turned round and faced me.

"What is there here?" she said. "And what—"

Walter, whom I had left asleep, looked in at the door.

"Ah, it's you playing," he said. "That's all right."

By strange interweavings of emotion, that common consciousness between us all of the presence of something that came not from among the humming wheels of life but from the grey mists that encompassed it, grew thicker in texture. There was some presence in the room – not mine, nor Margery's, nor Walter's – here now, though invisible, and somehow gathering strength from our recognition of its existence. In our different ways we all contributed to it in that moment of absolute and appalling silence.

Some sort of babble broke it. I babbled of the disorder of my papers, Margery babbled apology and promised to put them straight, if she might be allowed to deal with them. Some sort of crisis passed. I can explain it no better than that.

As evening drew on the clouds gathered even more thickly. The sea was leaden, the air dead, and when, about half past ten that night, Mr. Bird, who had proved himself a charming guest, said good night, and I went with him to the door, we looked out on to a pit of impenetrable darkness. I saw the opportunity I wanted, and assuring him that I should really like a stroll to get such air as there was, insisted on fetching a lantern and lighting him back as far as the village. I then went straight to the point.

"There was a fearful tragedy in Coltham last year," I said. "Denton pointed me out the house where the murder was committed."

Mr. Bird stopped dead.

"Denton pointed you out the house?" he asked.

"Yes, but perhaps he was wrong," said I. "In fact, Mr. Bird, I should be very much obliged to you if you would tell me whether I am not right in thinking that the scene of the tragedy was 'The Firs'. My sister and brother-in-law know nothing about it, and I hope they won't. But I learned accidentally to-day that she pays the rent to Miss Ellershaw, which I think is the name. And I hazard the guess that the precise scene was the room outside which we sat to-night."

He did not reply for a moment.

"I can't deny what you suggest," he said, "and my mere refusal to reply would do no good. You are quite right. Denton's telling you, by the way, that the scene was in the village, itself, is quite intelligible, for Miss Ellershaw, who does not intend to live in the house again, wants to let it, and if it was known that the murder took place there it would be prejudicial; Denton knows that. And in turn I want to ask you something. Why do you guess that particular room?"

I hesitated as to whether I should tell him about the crop of strange impressions which were growing up round it, but decided not to.

"There are queer things," I said. "My sister was told, for instance, that there were orders that the room should not be used. Denton told her that."

"I can understand that too," he said. "The room has terrible memories for those who were in the house at the time. Any more queer things?"

"None that I can think of at present," I said. "But I will wish you good night here, as the rest of your way is clear."

I retraced my steps, and found that Walter and Margery had both gone upstairs. There was a lamp still burning on the paved space where we had sat after dinner, and I went out there, disinclined to go to bed, with my nerves all strung up by the stimulus of the approaching storm. All feeling of fear about what was creeping out into the light concerning this room, and what might, I felt, suddenly burst forth with some blaze of revelation, was gone, and I was conscious only of intense curiosity, as I summed up in my mind what I believed, owing to these strange hints and signals out of the mists, had actually taken place. I figured Miss Ellershaw as having been sitting at the piano when the strangling cord was slipped round her neck; I figured her as having been playing "Home, Sweet Home"; I figured Denton as having heard her. Then there would have been silence, but for some few gasps, some quivering convulsions, like the shaking of leaves in a tree, and then the discovery, perhaps by Denton, of the crime which was still unexplained. Certainly that afternoon the fragment of the tune which Margery had played gave him a sudden shock of horror . . .

The night was absolutely still; neither from inside the house nor from outside came the slightest stir of life, and the silence rang in my ears. And then from the room close at hand I heard, faint but distinct, the tinkle of the piano. A couple of bars of the familiar tune were played, and some voice, thin and quavering, began to sing the air. Curiosity, violent and irresistible, drowned all other feeling in my mind, and taking up the lamp, I opened the door of the room and entered. It burned brightly, and by its light, which gleamed on the keys of the piano, I could see that the room was empty. But the tune went on, softly played and faintly sung, and looking more closely at the piano I saw that once more the keys were moving. At that the sense of fear which till then had lain coiled and quiet in my mind began to stir. But I felt absolutely powerless to go; fear, now in swift invasion of my mind, held me where I was.

Something began to form in the air by the piano, a mist, a greyness. Then in a second it solidified, and there sat with her back to me the figure of a little whitehaired woman. Then the singing stopped, her arms shot up with quivering, clutching fingers; she struggled, she turned, and I saw her face, swollen and purple, with gasping mouth and protruding eyes. Her head lolled and nodded; her body swayed backwards and forwards, and she slid off the music-stool to the ground. At that moment a blaze of light poured through the unsheltered windows, and I saw pressed against the pane, and seemingly quite unaware of my presence, Denton's white and staring countenance. His eyes were fixed on the piano. Simultaneously with the light came an appalling crack of thunder. The storm had burst.

For that moment Denton and I faced each other; the next he had gone, and I heard his feet running down the garden path. I had seen enough too, and with my mind submerged in terror I stumbled from the room. As I paused for a moment outside, another flash flooded the gross darkness, and I saw him scudding across the down to the white edge of the cliffs. Then down came the rain, solid and hissing; my lamp was extinguished, and by the flare of the lightning, standing still between the flashes, I groped my way up to bed.

All night the prodigious storm streamed and rattled, but about dawn, as I lay still sleepless, and quaking with the prodigy of horror I had looked upon, it passed away, and I dozed and then slept deeply, and woke to find the morning tranquil and fresh and sunny. All the intolerable depression of the day before, not physical alone, seemed to me to have vanished, the house was wholesome as the breeze from the sea, and so, too, when, not without making a strong call on my courage, I entered it, I found the room where last night I had witnessed that ghastly pageantry. In no way could I account for that inward conviction, even less could I question it; all I knew was that some tragic stain had passed from it.

I was down before either of the others, and strolling through the garden as I waited for them, I saw advancing along the paved walk the figure of the vicar.

"A very dreadful thing has happened," he said. "Denton's body was found half an hour ago by some fishermen at the foot of the cliff down there. His head was smashed in; he must have fallen sheer on to the rocks."

Now the reader may put any interpretation he pleases on the events which I have here briefly recorded and on certain facts which may or may not seem to him to be connected with them, namely, that Miss Ellershaw, the elder of the two sisters who lived together at "The Firs", was found strangled on the floor by the piano in the room which juts out into the garden; that her sister not many minutes before her body was found had heard her singing "Home, Sweet Home" to her own accompaniment, and that the author of the murder had never been found. It is a fact also that late on the night of which I have been speaking I saw Denton looking in through the window of that room, and shortly afterwards running across the strip of downland towards the cliff, at the bottom of which next morning his body was found.

But beyond that point we deal not with material facts, but with impressions. Three separate people fancied that there was something strange about the room; one of them found herself expecting to see some unaccountable appearance; one of them thought there was a peculiar chill in the room, and also that he heard the piano being played when nobody had touched it; the third, as I have related, believed that he both saw and heard things in that room which he cannot explain. Whether Denton shared that experience we cannot tell, nor can we tell for certain whether it was a pure accident that he fell over the cliff, or whether he had seen and heard something which drove him to make an end of himself.

It remains only to add that Walter and Margery agreed that some strange sense, which they had both felt as of an unexplained presence in that room, had passed away from it during the night on which Denton met his death. Walter was inclined to attribute our original impressions to some purely subjective disturbance of the nerves caused by the approach of that great storm. Not then, but later, when, thoroughly restored, he had gone back to his work, I told him and Margery what I had seen that night and what, perhaps, Denton had seen.

"And No Bird Sings"

The red chimneys of the house for which I was bound were visible from just outside the station at which I had alighted, and, so the chauffeur told me, the distance was not more than a mile's walk if I took the path across the fields. It ran straight till it came to the edge of that wood yonder, which belonged to my host, and above which his chimneys were visible. I should find a gate in the paling of this wood, and a track traversing it, which debouched close to his garden. So, on this adorable afternoon of early May, it seemed a waste of time to do other than walk through meadows and woods, and I set off on foot, while the motor carried my traps.

It was one of those golden days which every now and again leak out of paradise and drip to earth. Spring had been late in coming, but now it was here with a burst, and the whole world was boiling with the sap of life. Never have I seen such a wealth of spring flowers, or such vividness of green, or heard such melodious business among the birds in the hedgerows; this walk through the meadows was a jubilee of festal ecstasy. And best of all, so I promised myself, would be the passage through the wood newly fledged with milky green that lay just ahead. There was the gate, just facing me, and I passed through it into the dappled lights and shadows of the grass-grown track.

Coming out of the brilliant sunshine was like entering a dim tunnel; one had the sense of being suddenly withdrawn from the brightness of the spring into some subaqueous cavern. The tree-tops formed a green roof overhead, excluding the light to a remarkable degree. I moved in a world of shifting obscurity. Presently, as the trees grew more scattered, their place was taken by a thick growth of hazels, which met over the path, and then, the ground sloping downwards, I came upon an open clearing, covered with bracken and heather, and studded with birches. But though now I walked once more beneath the luminous sky, with the sunlight pouring down, it seemed to have lost its effulgence. The brightness – was it some odd optical illusion? – was veiled as if it came from crape. Yet there was the sun still well above the tree-tops in an unclouded heaven, but for all that the light was that of a stormy winter's day, without warmth or brilliance. It was oddly silent too; I had thought that the bushes and trees would be ringing with the song of mating-birds, but listening, I could hear no note of any sort, neither the fluting of thrush or blackbird, nor the cheerful whirr of the chaffinch, nor the cooing wood-pigeon, nor the strident clamour of the jay. I paused to verify this odd silence; there was no doubt about it. It was rather eerie, rather uncanny, but I supposed the birds knew their own business best, and if they were too busy to sing it was their affair.

As I went on it struck me also that since entering the wood I had not seen a bird of any kind; and now, as I crossed the clearing, I kept my eyes alert for them, but fruitlessly, and soon I entered the further belt of thick trees which surrounded it. Most of them I noticed were beeches, growing very close to each other, and the ground beneath them was bare but for the carpet of fallen leaves, and a few thin bramble-bushes. In this curious dimness and thickness of the trees, it was impossible to see far to right or left of the path, and now, for the first time since I had left the open, I heard some sound of life. There came the rustle of leaves from not far away, and I thought to myself that a rabbit, anyhow, was moving. But somehow it lacked the staccato patter of a small animal; there was a certain stealthy heaviness about it, as if something much larger were stealing along and desirous of not being heard. I paused again to see what might emerge, but instantly the sound ceased. Simultaneously I was conscious of some faint but very foul odour reaching me, a smell choking and corrupt, yet somehow pungent, more like the odour of something alive rather than rotting. It was peculiarly sickening, and not wanting to get any closer to its source, I went on my way.

Before long I came to the edge of the wood; straight in front of me was a strip of meadow-land, and beyond an iron gate between two brick walls, through which I had a glimpse of lawn and flower-beds. To the left stood the house, and over house and garden there poured the amazing brightness of the declining afternoon.

Hugh Granger and his wife were sitting out on the lawn, with the usual pack of assorted dogs: a Welsh collie, a yellow retriever, a fox-terrier, and a Pekinese. Their protest at my intrusion gave way to the welcome of recognition, and I was admitted into the circle. There was much to say, for I had been out of England for the last three months, during which time Hugh had settled into this little estate left him by a recluse uncle, and he and Daisy had been busy during the Easter vacation with getting into the house. Certainly it was a most attractive legacy; the house, through which I was presently taken, was a delightful little Queen Anne manor, and its situation on the edge of this heather-clad Surrey ridge quite superb. We had tea in a small panelled parlour overlooking the garden, and soon the wider topics narrowed down to those of the day and the hour. I had walked, had I, asked Daisy, from the station: did I go through the wood, or follow the path outside it?

The question she thus put to me was given trivially enough; there was no hint in her voice that it mattered a straw to her which way I had come. But it was quite clearly borne in upon me that not only she but Hugh also listened intently for my reply. He had just lit a match for his cigarette, but held it unapplied till he heard my answer. Yes, I had gone through the wood; but now, though I had received some odd impressions in the wood, it seemed quite ridiculous to mention what they were. I could not soberly say that the sunshine there was of very poor quality, and that at one point in my traverse I had smelt a most iniquitous odour. I had walked through the wood; that was all I had to tell them.

I had known both my host and hostess for a tale of many years, and now, when I felt that there was nothing except purely fanciful stuff that I could volunteer about my experiences there, I noticed that they exchanged a swift glance, and could easily interpret it. Each of them signalled to the other an expression of relief; they told each other (so I construed their glance) that I, at any rate, had found nothing unusual in the wood, and they were pleased at that. But then, before any real pause had succeeded to my answer that I had gone through the wood, I remembered that strange absence of bird-song and bird, and as that seemed an innocuous observation in natural history, I thought I might as well mention it.

"One odd thing struck me," I began (and instantly I saw the attention of both riveted again), "I didn't see a single bird or hear one from the time I entered the wood to when I left it."

Hugh lit his cigarette.

"I've noticed that too," he said, "and it's rather puzzling. The wood is certainly a bit of primeval forest, and one would have thought that hosts of birds would have nested in it from time immemorial. But, like you, I've never heard or seen one in it. And I've never seen a rabbit there either."

"I thought I heard one this afternoon," said I. "Something was moving in the fallen beech leaves."

"Did you see it?" he asked.

I recollected that I had decided that the noise was not quite the patter of a rabbit.

"No, I didn't see it," I said, "and perhaps it wasn't one. It sounded, I remember, more like something larger."

Once again and unmistakably a glance passed between Hugh and his wife, and she rose.

"I must be off," she said. "Post goes out at seven, and I lazed all morning. What are you two going to do?"

"Something out of doors, please," said I. "I want to see the domain."

Hugh and I accordingly strolled out again with the cohort of dogs. The domain was certainly very charming; a small lake lay beyond the garden, with a reed bed vocal with warblers, and a tufted margin into which coots and moorhens scudded at our approach. Rising from the end of that was a high heathery knoll full of rabbit holes, which the dogs nosed at with joyful expectations, and there we sat for a while overlooking the wood which covered the rest of the estate. Even now, in the blaze of the sun near to its setting, it seemed to be in shadow, though like the rest of the view it should have basked in brilliance, for not a cloud flecked the sky and the level rays enveloped the world in a crimson splendour. But the wood was grey and darkling. Hugh, also, I was aware, had been looking at it, and now, with an air of breaking into a disagreeable topic, he turned to me.

"Tell me," he said, "does anything strike you about that wood?"

"Yes: it seems to lie in shadow."

He frowned.

"But it can't, you know," he said. "Where does the shadow come from? Not from outside, for sky and land are on fire."

"From inside, then?" I asked.

He was silent a moment.

"There's something queer about it," he said at length. "There's something there, and I don't know what it is. Daisy feels it too; she won't ever go into the wood, and it appears that birds won't either. Is it just the fact that, for some unexplained reason, there are no birds in it that has set all our imaginations at work?"

I jumped up.

"Oh, it's all rubbish," I said. "Let's go through it now and find a bird. I bet you I find a bird."

"Sixpence for every bird you see," said Hugh.

We went down the hillside and walked round the wood till we came to the gate where I had entered that afternoon. I held it open after I had gone in for the dogs to follow. But there they stood, a yard or so away, and none of them moved.

"Come on, dogs," I said, and Fifi, the fox-terrier, came a step nearer and then, with a little whine, retreated again.

"They always do that," said Hugh; "not one of them will set foot inside the wood. Look!"

He whistled and called, he cajoled and scolded, but it was no use. There the dogs remained, with little apologetic grins and signallings of tails, but quite determined not to come.

"But why?" I asked.

"Same reason as the birds, I suppose, whatever that happens to be. There's Fifi, for instance, the sweetest-tempered little lady; once I tried to pick her up and carry her in, and she snapped at me. They'll have nothing to do with the wood; they'll trot round outside it and go home."

We left them there and, in the sunset light which was now beginning to fade, began the passage. Usually the sense of eeriness disappears if one has a companion, but now to me, even with Hugh walking by my side, the place seemed even more uncanny than it had done that afternoon, and a sense of intolerable uneasiness, that grew into a sort of waking nightmare, obsessed me. I had thought before that the silence and loneliness of it had played tricks with my nerves; but with Hugh here it could not be that, and indeed I felt that it was not any such notion that lay at the root of this fear, but rather the conviction that there was some presence lurking there, invisible as yet, but permeating the gathered gloom. I could not form the slightest idea of what it might be, or whether it was material or ghostly; all I could diagnose of it from my own sensations was that it was evil and antique.

As we came to the open ground in the middle of the wood, Hugh stopped, and though the evening was cool I noticed that he mopped his forehead.

"Pretty nasty," he said. "No wonder the dogs don't like it. How do you feel about it?"

Before I could answer he shot out his hand, pointing to the belt of trees that lay beyond.

"What's that?" he said in whisper.

I followed his finger, and for one half-second thought I saw against the black of the wood some vague flicker, grey or faintly luminous. It waved as if it had been the head and forepart of some huge snake rearing itself, but it instantly disappeared, and my glimpse had been so momentary that I could not trust my impression.

"It's gone," said Hugh, still looking in the direction he had pointed; and as we stood there I heard again what I had heard that afternoon, a rustle among the fallen beech-leaves. But there was no wind nor breath of breeze astir.

He turned to me.

"What on earth was it?" he said. "It looked like some enormous slug standing up. Did you see it?"

"I'm not sure whether I did or not," I said. "I think I just caught sight of what you saw."

"But what was it?" he said again. "Was it a real material creature, or was it—"

"Something ghostly, do you mean?" I asked.

"Something half-way between the two," he said. "I'll tell you what I mean afterwards, when we've got out of this place."

The thing, whatever it was, had vanished among the trees to the left of where our path lay, and in silence we walked across the open till we came to where it entered tunnel-like among the trees. Frankly I hated and feared the thought of plunging into that darkness with the knowledge that not so far off there was something the nature of which I could not ever so faintly conjecture, but which, I now made no doubt, was that which filled the wood with some nameless terror. Was it material, was it ghostly, or was it (and now some inkling of what Hugh meant began to form itself into my mind) some being that lay on the borderland between the two? Of all the sinister possibilities that appeared the most terrifying.

As we entered the trees again I perceived that reek, alive and yet corrupt, which I had smelt before, but now it was far more potent, and we hurried on, choking with the odour that I now guessed to be not the putrescence of decay, but the living substance of that which crawled and reared itself in the darkness of the wood where no bird would shelter. Somewhere among those trees lurked the reptilian thing that defied and yet compelled credence.

It was a blessed relief to get out of that dim tunnel into the wholesome air of the open and the clear light of evening. Within doors, when we returned, windows were curtained and lamps lit. There was a hint of frost, and Hugh put a match to the fire in his room, where the dogs, still a little apologetic, hailed us with thumpings of drowsy tails.

"And now we've got to talk," said he, "and lay our plans, for whatever it is that is in the wood we've got to make an end of it. And, if you want to know what I think it is, I'll tell you."

"Go ahead," said I.

"You may laugh at me, if you like," he said, "but I believe it's an elemental. That's what I meant when I said it was a being half-way between the material and the ghostly. I never caught a glimpse of it till this afternoon; I only felt there was something horrible there. But now I've seen it, and it's like what spiritualists and that sort of folk describe as an elemental. A huge phosphorescent slug is what they tell us of it, which at will can surround itself with darkness."

Somehow, now safe within doors, in the cheerful light and warmth of the room, the suggestion appeared merely grotesque. Out there in the darkness of that uncomfortable wood something within me had quaked, and I was prepared to believe any horror, but now common sense revolted.

"But you don't mean to tell me you believe in such rubbish?" I said. "You might as well say it was a unicorn. What *is* an elemental, anyway? Who has ever seen one except the people who listen to raps in the darkness and say they are made by their aunts?"

"What is it, then?" he asked.

"I should think it is chiefly our own nerves," I said. "I frankly acknowledge I got the creeps when I went through the wood first, and I got them much worse when I went through it with you. But it was just nerves; we are frightening ourselves and each other."

"And are the dogs frightening themselves and each other?" he asked. "And the birds?"

That was rather harder to answer; in fact, I gave it up.

Hugh continued.

"Well, just for the moment we'll suppose that something else, not ourselves, frightened us and the dogs and the birds," he said, "and that we did see something like a huge phosphorescent slug. I won't call it an elemental, if you object to that; I'll call it It. There's another thing, too, which the existence of It would explain."

"What's that?" I asked.

"Well, It is supposed to be some incarnation of evil; it is a corporeal form of the devil. It is not only spiritual, it is material to this extent – that it can be seen, bodily in form, and heard, and, as you noticed, smelt, and, God forbid, handled. It has to be kept alive by nourishment. And that explains perhaps why, every day since I have been here, I've found on that knoll we went up some half-dozen dead rabbits."

"Stoats and weasels," said I.

"No, not stoats and weasels. Stoats kill their prey and eat it. These rabbits have not been eaten; they've been drunk."

"What on earth do you mean?" I asked.

"I examined several of them. There was just a small hole in their throats, and they were drained of blood. Just skin and bones, and a sort of grey mash of fibre, like – like the fibre of an orange which has been sucked. Also there was a horrible smell lingering on them. And was the thing you had a glimpse of like a stoat or a weasel?"

There came a rattle at the handle of the door.

"Not a word to Daisy," said Hugh as she entered.

"I heard you come in," she said. "Where did you go?"

"All round the place," said I, "and came back through the wood. It is odd; not a bird did we see; but that is partly accounted for because it was dark."

I saw her eyes search Hugh's, but she found no communication there. I guessed that he was planning some attack on It next day, and he did not wish her to know that anything was afoot.

"The wood's unpopular," he said. "Birds won't go there, dogs won't go there, and Daisy won't go there. I'm bound to say I share the feeling too, but having braved its terrors in the dark I've broken the spell."

"All quiet, was it?" asked she.

"Quiet wasn't the word for it. The smallest pin could have been heard dropping half a mile off."

We talked over our plans that night after she had gone up to bed. Hugh's story about the sucked rabbits was rather horrible, and though there was no certain connection between those empty rinds of animals and what we had seen, there seemed a certain reasonableness about it. But anything, as he pointed out, which could feed like that was clearly not without its material side – ghosts did not have dinner, and if it was material it was vulnerable.

Our plans, therefore, were very simple; we were going to tramp through the wood, as one walks up partridges in a field of turnips, each with a shotgun and a supply of cartridges. I cannot say that I looked forward to the expedition, for I hated the thought of getting into closer quarters with that mysterious denizen of the woods; but there was a certain excitement about it, sufficient to keep me awake a long time, and when I got to sleep to cause very vivid and awful dreams.

The morning failed to fulfil the promise of the clear sunset; the sky was lowering and cloudy and a fine rain was falling. Daisy had shopping errands which took her into the little town, and as soon as she had set off we started on our business. The yellow retriever, mad with joy at the sight of guns, came bounding with us across the garden, but on our entering the wood he slunk back home again.

The wood was roughly circular in shape, with a diameter perhaps of half a mile. In the centre, as I have said, there was an open clearing about a quarter of a mile across, which was thus surrounded by a belt of thick trees and copse a couple of hundred yards in breadth. Our plan was first to walk together up the path which led through the wood, with all possible stealth, hoping to hear some movement on the part of what we had come to seek. Failing that, we had settled to tramp through the wood at the distance of some fifty yards from each other in a circular track; two or three of these circuits would cover the whole ground pretty thoroughly. Of the nature of our quarry, whether it would try to steal away from us, or possibly attack, we had no idea; it seemed, however, yesterday to have avoided us.

Rain had been falling steadily for an hour when we entered the wood; it hissed a little in the tree-tops overhead; but so thick was the cover that the ground below was still not more than damp. It was a dark morning outside; here you would say that the sun had already set and that night was falling. Very quietly we moved up the grassy path, where our footfalls were noiseless, and once we caught a whiff of that odour of live corruption; but though we stayed and listened not a sound of anything stirred except the sibilant rain over our heads. We went across the clearing and through to the far gate, and still there was no sign.

"We'll be getting into the trees, then," said Hugh. "We had better start where we got that whiff of it."

We went back to the place, which was towards the middle of the encompassing trees. The odour still lingered on the windless air.

"Go on about fifty yards," he said, "and then we'll go in. If either of us comes on the track of it we'll shout to each other."

I walked on down the path till I had gone the right distance, signalled to him, and we stepped in among the trees.

I have never known the sensation of such utter lonelinesss. I knew that Hugh was walking parallel with me, only fifty yards away, and if I hung on my step I could faintly hear his tread among the beechleaves. But I felt as if I was quite sundered in this dim place from all companionship of man; the only live thing that lurked here was that monstrous mysterious creature of evil. So thick were the trees that I could not see more than a dozen yards in any direction; all places outside the wood seemed infinitely remote, and infinitely remote also everything that had occurred to me in normal human life. I had been whisked out of all wholesome experiences into this antique and evil place. The rain had ceased, it whispered no longer in the tree-tops, testifying that there did exist a world and a sky outside, and only a few drops from above pattered on the beech-leaves.

Suddenly I heard the report of Hugh's gun, followed by his shouting voice.

"I've missed it," he shouted; "it's coming in your direction."

I heard him running towards me, the beech-leaves rustling, and no doubt his footsteps drowned a stealthier noise that was close to me. All that happened now, until once more I heard the report of Hugh's gun, happened, I suppose, in less than a minute. If it had taken much longer I do not imagine I should be telling it to-day.

I stood there then, having heard Hugh's shout, with my gun cocked, and ready to put to my shoulder, and I listened to his running footsteps. But still I saw nothing to shoot at and heard nothing. Then between two beech trees, quite close to me, I saw what I can only describe as a ball of darkness. It rolled very swiftly towards me over the few yards that separated me from it, and then, too late, I heard the dead beech-leaves rustling below it. Just before it reached me, my brain realized what it was, or what it might be, but before I could raise my gun to shoot at that nothingness it was upon me. My gun was twitched out of my hand, and I was enveloped in this blackness, which was the very essence of corruption. It knocked me off my feet, and I sprawled flat on my back, and upon me, as I lay there, I felt the weight of this invisible assailant.

I groped wildly with my hands and they clutched something cold and slimy and hairy. They slipped off it, and next moment there was laid across my shoulder and neck something which felt like an india-rubber tube. The end of it fastened on to my neck like a snake, and I felt the skin rise beneath it. Again, with clutching hands, I tried to tear that obscene strength away from me, and as I struggled with it I heard Hugh's footsteps close to me through this layer of darkness that hid everything.

My mouth was free, and I shouted at him.

"Here, here!" I yelled. "Close to you, where it is darkest."

I felt his hands on mine, and that added strength detached from my neck that sucker that pulled at it. The coil that lay heavy on my legs and chest writhed and struggled and relaxed. Whatever it was that our four hands held, slipped out of them, and I saw Hugh standing close to me. A yard or two off, vanishing among the beech trunks, was that blackness which had poured over me. Hugh put up his gun, and with his second barrel fired at it.

The blackness dispersed, and there, wriggling and twisting like a huge worm lay what we had come to find. It was alive still, and I picked up my gun which lay by my side and fired two more barrels into it. The writhings dwindled into mere shudderings and shakings, and then it lay still.

With Hugh's help I got to my feet, and we both reloaded before going nearer. On the ground there lay a monstrous thing, half slug, half worm. There was no head to it; it ended in a blunt point with an orifice. In colour it was grey, covered with sparse black hairs; its length, I suppose, was some four feet, its thickness at the broadest part was that of a man's thigh, tapering towards each end. It was shattered by shot at its middle. There were stray pellets which had hit it elsewhere, and from the holes they had made there oozed not blood, but some grey viscous matter.

As we stood there some swift process of disintegration and decay began. It lost outline, it melted, it liquefied, and in a minute more we were looking at a mass of stained and coagulated beech leaves. Again and quickly that liquor of corruption faded, and there lay at our feet no trace of what had been there. The overpowering odour passed away, and there came from the ground just the sweet savour of wet earth in springtime, and from above the glint of a sunbeam piercing the clouds. Then a sudden pattering among the dead leaves sent my heart into my mouth again, and I cocked my gun. But it was only Hugh's yellow retriever who had joined us.

We looked at each other.

"You're not hurt?" he said.

I held my chin up.

"Not a bit," I said. "The skin's not broken, is it?"

"No; only a round red mark. My God, what was it? What happened?"

"Your turn first," said I. "Begin at the beginning."

"I came upon it quite suddenly," he said. "It was lying coiled like a sleeping dog behind a big beech. Before I could fire, it slithered off in the direction where I knew you were. I got a snapshot at it among the trees, but I must have missed, for I heard it rustling away. I shouted to you and ran after it. There was a circle of absolute darkness on the ground, and your voice came from the middle of it. I couldn't see you at all, but I clutched at the blackness and my hands met yours. They met something else too."

We got back to the house and had put the guns away before Daisy came home from her shopping. We had also scrubbed and brushed and washed. She came into the smoking-room.

"You lazy folk," she said. "It has cleared up, and why are you still indoors? Let's go out at once."

I got up.

"Hugh has told me you've got a dislike of the wood," I said, "and it's a lovely wood. Come and see; he and I will walk on each side of you and hold your hands. The dogs shall protect you as well."

"But not one of them will go a yard into the wood," said she.

"Oh yes, they will. At least, we'll try them. You must promise to come if they do."

Hugh whistled them up, and down we went to the gate. They sat panting for it to be opened, and scuttled into the thickets in pursuit of interesting smells.

"And who says there are no birds in it?" said Daisy. "Look at that robin! Why, there are two of them. Evidently house-hunting."

THE CORNER HOUSE

Firham-by-Sea had long been known to Jim Purley and myself, though we had been careful not to talk about it, and for years we had been accustomed to skulk quietly away from London, either alone or together, for a day or two of holiday at that delightful and unheard-of little village. It was not, I may safely say, any secretive or dog-in-the-manger instinct of keeping a good thing to ourselves that was the cause of this reticence, but it was because if Firham had become known at all the whole charm of it would have vanished. A popular Firham, in fact, would cease to be Firham, and while we should lose it nobody else would gain it. Its remoteness, its isolation, its emptiness were its most essential qualities; it would have been impossible, so we both of us felt, to have gone to Firham with a party of friends, and the idea of its little inn being peopled with strangers, or its odd little nine-hole golf-course with the small corrugated-iron shed for its club-house becoming full of serious golfers would certainly have been sufficient to make us desire never to play there again. Nor, indeed, were we guilty of any selfishness in keeping the knowledge of that golf-course to ourselves, for the holes were short and dull and the fairway badly kept. It was only because we were at Firham that we so often strolled round it, losing balls in furze bushes and marshy ground, and considering it quite decent putting if we took no more than three putts on a green. It was bad golf, in fact, and no one in his senses would think of going to Firham to play bad golf, when good golf was so vastly more accessible. Indeed, the only reason why I have spoken of the golf-links is because in an indirect and distant manner they were connected with the early incidents of the story which strung itself together there, and which, to me at any rate, has destroyed the secure tranquillity of our remote little hermitage.

To get to Firham at all from London, except by a motor drive of some hundred and twenty miles, is a slow progress, and after two changes the leisurely railway eventually lands you no nearer than five miles from your destination. After that a switchback road terminating in a long decline brings you off the inland Norfolk hills, and into the broad expanse of lowland, once reclaimed from the sea, and now protected from marine invasion by big banks and dykes. From the top of the last hill you get your first sight of the village, its brick-built houses with their tiled roofs smouldering redly in the sunset, like some small, glowing island anchored in that huge expanse of green, and, a mile beyond it the dim blue of the sea. There are but few trees to be seen on that wide landscape, and those stunted and slanted in their growth by the prevailing wind off the coast, and the great sweep of the country is composed of featureless fields intersected with drainage dykes, and dotted with sparse cattle. A sluggish stream, fringed with reed-beds and loose-strife, where moorhens chuckle, passes just outside the village, and a few hundred yards below it is spanned by a bridge and a sluice-gate. From there it broadens out into an estuary, full of shining water at high tide, and of grey mud banks at the ebb, and passes between rows of tussocked sand-dunes out to sea.

The road, descending from the higher inlands, strikes across these reclaimed marshes, and after a mile of solitary travel enters the village of Firham. To right and left stand a few outlying cottages, white-washed and thatched, each with a strip of gay garden in front and perhaps a fisherman's net spread out to dry on the wall, but before they form anything that could be called a street the road takes a sudden sharp-angled turn, and at once you are in the square which, indeed, forms the entire village. On each side of the broad cobbled space is a line of houses, on one side a post-office and police-station with a dozen small shops where may be bought the more rudimentary needs of existence: a baker's, a butcher's, a tobacconist's. Opposite is a row of little residences midway between villa and cottage, while at the far end stands the dumpy grey church with the vicarage, behind green and rather dilapidated palings, beside it. At the near end is the "Fisherman's Arms", the modest hostelry at which we always put up, flanked by two or three more small red-brick houses, of which the farthest, where the road leaves the square again, is the Corner House of which this story treats.

The Corner House was an object of mild curiosity to Jim and me, for while the rest of the houses in the square, shops and residences alike, had a tidy and well-cared-for appearance, with an air of prosperity on a small, contented scale, the Corner House presented a marked and curious contrast. The faded paint on the door was blistered and patchy, the step of the threshold always unwhitened and partly overgrown with an encroachment of moss, as if there was little traffic across it. Over the windows inside were stretched dingy casement curtains, and the Virginia creeper which straggled untended up the discoloured front of the house drooped over the dull panes like the hair over a terrier's eyes. Sometimes in one or other of these windows, between the curtains and the glass, there sat a mournful grey cat; but all day long no further sign of life within gave evidence of occupation. Behind the house was a spacious square of garden enclosed by a low brick wall, and from the upper windows of "The Fisherman's Arms" it was possible to look into it. There was a gravel path running round it, entirely overgrown, and a flower-bed underneath the wall was a jungle of rank weeds among which, in summer, two or three neglected rose trees put out a few meagre flowers. A broken water-butt stood at the end of it, and in the middle a rusty iron seat, but never at morning or at noon or at evening did I see any human figure in it; it seemed entirely derelict and unvisited.

At dusk shabby curtains were drawn across the windows that looked into the square, and then between chinks you could see that one room was lit within. The house, it was evident, had once been a very dignified little residence; it was built of red-brick and was early Georgian in date, square and comfortable with its enclosed plot behind; one wondered, as I have said, with mild curiosity what blight had fallen on it, what manner of folk moved silent and unseen behind the dingy casement curtains all day and sat in that front room when night had fallen.

It was not only to us but also to the Firhamites generally that the inhabitants of the Corner House were veiled in some sort of mystery. The landlord of our inn, for instance, in answer to casual questions, could tell us very little of their life nowadays, but what he knew of them indicated that something rather grim lurked behind the drawn curtains. It was a married couple who lived there, and he could remember the arrival of Mr. and Mrs. Labson some ten years before.

"She was a big, handsome woman," he said, "and her age might have been thirty. He was a good deal younger; at that time he looked hardly out of his teens, a slim little slip of a fellow, half a head shorter than his wife. I dare say you've seen him on the golf-links, knocking a ball about by himself, for he goes out there every afternoon."

I had more than once noticed a man playing alone, and carrying a couple of clubs. If he was on a green, and saw us coming up, he always went hurriedly on or stood aside at a little distance, with back turned, and waited for us to pass. But neither of us had paid any particular attention to him.

"She doesn't go out with him?" I asked.

"She never leaves the house at all to my knowledge," said the landlord, "though to be sure it wasn't always like that. When first they came here they were always out together, playing golf, or boating, or fishing, and in the evening there would be the sound of singing or piano-playing from that front room of theirs. They didn't live here entirely, but came down from London, where they had a house, for two or three months in the summer and perhaps a month at Christmas and another month at Easter. There would be friends staying with them much of the time, and merriment and games always going on, and dancing, too, with a gramophone to play their tunes for them till midnight and later. And then, all of a sudden, five years ago now or perhaps a little more, something happened and everything was changed. Yes, that was a queer thing, and sudden, as I say, like a clap of thunder."

"Interesting," said Jim. "What was it that happened?"

"Well, as we saw it, it was like this," said he. "Mr. and Mrs. Labson were down here together in the summer, and one morning as I passed their door I heard her voice inside scolding and swearing at him or at someone. Him it must have been, as we knew later. All that day she went on at him; it was a wonder to think that a woman had so much breath in her body or so much rage in her mind. Next day all their servants, five or six they kept then, butler and lady's maid and valet and housemaid and cook, were all dismissed, and off they went. The gardener got his month's wages too, and was told he'd be wanted no more, and so there were Mr. and Mrs. Labson alone in the house. But half that day, too, she went on shouting and yelling, so it must have been him she was scolding and swearing at. Like a mad woman she was, and never a word from him. Then there would be silence a bit and she'd break out again, and day after day it was like that, silence and then that screaming voice of hers. As the weeks went on, silence shut down on them; now and then she'd break out again, even as she does to this day, but a month and more will pass now, and you'll never hear a sound from within the house."

"And what had been the cause of it all?" I asked.

"That came out in the papers," said he, "when Mr. Labson was made a bankrupt. He had been speculating on the Stock Exchange, not with his own money alone, but with hers, and had lost nigh every penny. His house in London was sold, and all they had left was this house which belonged to her, and a bit of money he hadn't got at, which brings them in a pound or two a week. They keep no servants, and every morning Mr. Labson goes out early with his basket on his arm and brings provisions for their dinner with the shilling or two she gives him. They say he does the cooking as well, and the housework too, though there's not too much of that, if you can judge from what you see from outside, while she sits with her hands in her lap doing nothing from morning till night. Sitting there and hating him, you may say."

It was a weird, grim sort of story, and from that moment the house, to my mind, took on, as with a deeper dye of forbiddingness, something of its quality.

Its desolate and untended aspect was fully earned; the uncleaned windows and discoloured door seemed a fit expression of the spirit that dwelt there; the house was the faithful expression of those who lived in it, of the man whose folly or knavery had brought them to a penury that was near ruin, and of the woman who was never seen, but sat behind the dirty curtained windows hating him, and making him her drudge. He was her slave; those hours when she screamed and raved at him must surely have broken his spirit utterly, or, whatever his fault had been, he must have rebelled against so servile and dismal an existence. Just that hour or two of remission she gave him in the afternoon that he might get air and exercise to keep his health, and continue his life of bondage, and then back again he went to the seclusion and the simmering hostility.

As sometimes happens when a subject has got started, the round of trivial, everyday experiences begins to bristle with allusions and hints that bear on it, so now when this matter of the Corner House had been set going, Jim and I began to be constantly aware of its ticking. It was just that: it was as if a clock had been wound up and started off, and now we were aware in a way we had not been before that it was steadily ticking on, and the hands silently moving towards some unconjecturable hour. Fancifully and fantastically enough I wondered what the hour would be towards which the silent pointers were creeping. Would there be some sort of jarring whirr that gave warning that the hour was imminent, or should we miss that, and be suddenly startled by some reverberating shock? Such an idea was, of course purely an invention of the imagination; but somehow it had got hold of me, and I used to pass the Corner House with an uneasy glance at its dingy windows, as if they were the dial that interpreted the progress of the sombre mechanism within.

The reader must understand that all this formed no continuous series of impressions. Jim and I were at Firham only on short visits, with intervals of weeks or even of months in between. But certainly after the subject had been started we had more frequent glimpses of Mr. Labson. Day after day we saw his flitting figure on the links, keeping its distance, and retreating before us; but once we approached close up to him before he was aware of our presence. It was an afternoon that threatened rain, and in order to be nearer shelter if the storm burst suddenly we had cut two holes and walked across an intervening tract of rough ground to a hole which took us in a homeward direction. He was just addressing his ball on this teeing-ground when, looking up, he saw that we were beside him; he gave a little squeal as of terror, picked up his ball, and scuttled away, at a shuffling run, with abject terror written on his lean white face. Not a word did he give us in answer to Jim's begging him to precede us, not once did he look round.

"But the man's quaking with fear," said I, as he disappeared. "He could hardly pick up his ball."

"Poor devil!" said Jim. "There's something formidable at the Corner House."

He had hardly spoken when the rain began in torrents, and we trotted with the best speed of middle-aged gentlemen towards the corrugated-iron shed of the club-house. But Mr. Labson did not join us there for shelter; for we saw him plodding homewards through the downpour rather than face his fellow-creatures.

That close glimpse of Mr. Labson had made the affair of the Corner House much more real. Behind the curtains where the light was lit in the evening there sat a man in whose soul terror was enthroned. Was it terror of his companion who sat there with him that reigned so supreme that even when he was away out on the links it still was master of him? Had it also so drained from him all dregs of manhood and of courage that he could not even run away, but must return to the grim house for fear of his fear, as a rabbit on whose track is a weasel has not the courage to gallop off and easily save itself from the sharp white teeth? Or were there ties of affection between him and the woman whom his folly had brought to penury, so that as a willing penance he cooked and drudged for her? And then I thought of the voice that had yelled at him all day; it was more likely that, as Jim had said, there was something formidable at the Corner House, before which he cowered and from which he had not the strength to fly.

There were other glimpses of him as, with his basket on his arm in the early morning, he brought home bread and milk and some cheap cut from the butcher's. Once I saw him enter his house on his return from his marketing. He must have locked the door before going out, for now he unlocked it again, slipped in, and I heard the key click in the wards again. Once, too, though only in featureless outline, I saw her who shared his solitude, for passing by the Corner House in the dusk, the lamp had been lit within, and I had a glimpse through the thin casement blinds of a carpetless room, a blackened ceiling and one big armchair drawn up to the fire. And at that moment the form of a woman silhouetted itself between me and the light. She was very tall, and immensely broad and stout, and her hands, large as a man's, grasped the curtain. Next moment, with a jingle of running rings, she had drawn it, and shut up herself and the man for the long winter evening and the night that followed.

The same evening, I remember, Jim had occasion to go to the post-office, and came back to our snug little sitting-room with something of horror in his eyes.

"You've seen her to-day," he said, "and I've heard her."

"Who? Oh, at the Corner House?" I asked.

"Yes. I was just passing it when she began. I tell you it scared me. It was scarcely like a human voice at all, or at any rate not like a sane voice. A shrill, swearing gabble all on one note, and going on without a pause. Maniac."

The conjectured picture of the two grew more grim. It was an awful thought that behind those dingy curtains in the bare room there were the pair of them, the little terrified man, and that greater monster of a woman, yelling and bawling at him. Yet what could we do? It seemed impossible to interfere in any way. It was not the business of a couple of visitors from London to intrude on the domestic differences of total strangers. And yet the sequel showed that any interference would have been justified.

The day following was wet from morning till night. A gale of rain mingled with sleet roared in from the north-east, and neither of us stirred abroad, but kept close by the fire, listening to the wind bugling in the chimney, and the gale flinging the sheets of water solidly against the window-pane. But after nightfall the wind abated and the sky cleared, and when I went up to bed, sleepy with the day indoors, I saw the shadows of the window-bars black against a brightness outside, and pulling up the blind looked on to a blaze of moonlight. Below, a little to the left, was the neglected garden of the Corner House, and there, standing on the grass-grown path, was the figure of the woman I had seen in black silhouette against the lamplight in her room. Now the moonlight shone full on her face and my breath caught in my throat as I looked on that appalling countenance. It was fat and bloated beyond belief, the eyes were but slits above her cheeks, and the lines of her mouth were invisible in their shadows. But even the whiteness of the moonlight gave no pallor to her face, for it was flushed with some purplish hue that seemed nearly black. One glimpse only I had, for perhaps she had heard the rattle of my blind, and she looked up and next minute had stepped back into the house again. But that moment was enough; I felt that I had looked on something hellish, something almost outside the wide range of humanity. It was not only the appalling physical ugliness of that monstrous face that was so shocking; it was the expression in the eyes and mouth, visible in that second when she raised her face to look upwards to my window. An inhuman hatred and cruelty were there that made the heart quake; the featureless outline was filled in with details more awful than I had ever conjectured.

We were out on the links again next afternoon on a day of liquid sunshine and brisk air, but some nameless oppression of the spirits held me sundered from the genial and bracing warmth. The idea of that frightened little man being imprisoned all day and night, but for his brief outing, with her who at any moment might break into that screaming torrent of speech, was like a nightmare that came between me and the sun. It would have been something to have seen him out to-day, and know that he was having a respite from that terrible presence; but we caught no sight of him, and when we returned and passed the Corner House the curtains were already drawn, and, as usual, there was silence within.

Jim touched me on the arm as we walked by the windows.

"But there's no light inside this evening," he said.

This was quite true; the curtains were torn, as I knew, in half a dozen places, but neither through these holes nor from the chinks at their edges was there any light showing. Somehow this gave an added horror which set my nerves jangling.

"Well, we can't knock and tell them they've forgotten to light the lamp," I said.

We had halted for a moment, and even as I spoke I saw coming across the square towards us in the gathering dusk the figure of the man whom we had missed on the links that afternoon. Though I had not seen him approach, nor heard the noise of his footfall on the cobbles, he was now within a few yards of us.

"Here *he* is, anyhow," I said.

Jim turned.

"Where?" he asked.

We were standing perhaps two yards apart, and as he asked that the man stepped between us and advanced to the door of the Corner House. And then, instantaneously, I saw that Jim and I were alone. The door of the Corner House had not opened, but there was no one there.

Jim gave a startled exclamation.

"What was that?" he said. "Something brushed by me."

"Didn't you see anything?" I asked.

"No, but I felt something. I don't know what it was."

"I saw him," said I.

My jangled nerves seemed to have infected Jim.

"Nonsense!" he said. "How could you have seen him? Where has he gone if you saw him? And I don't know what we're standing here for."

Before I could answer I heard from within the Corner House the sound of heavy and shuffling steps; a key grated in the lock, and the door was flung open. Out of it, panting and heaving with some strange agitation, came the woman I had seen last night in her garden.

She had shut the door and locked it before she saw us. She was hatless and shod in great carpet-slippers the heels of which tapped on the pavement as she moved, and on her face was the vacancy of some nameless terror. Her mouth, a cavern in that mountain of flesh, was wide, and now there came from it something between a gasp and a rattle. Then, seeing us, quick as a lizard, she whisked round again, fumbled for a moment with the key which she still held in her hand, and there once more was the shut door and the empty pavement. The whole scene passed like a blink of strong light seen in the dusk and vanishing again. She had come out, driven by some terror of her own; she had gone back in terror, it would seem, of us.

It was without a word passing between us that we went back to the inn. Just then there was nothing to be said; for myself, at least. I knew that there was, covering my brain, so to speak, some frozen surface of abject fear which must be thawed. I knew that I had seen, I knew that Jim had felt, something which had no tangible existence in the material world. He had felt what I had seen, and I had seen the form and bodily semblance of the man who lived at the Corner House. But what his wife had seen that drove her from the house, and why, seeing us, she had whisked back into it again I had no notion. Perhaps when a certain physical horror in my brain was uncongealed I should know.

Presently we were sitting in the small, cosy room, with our tea ready for us, and the fire burning bright on the hearth. We talked, odd as it may appear, of anything else but *that*. But the silences between the abandonment of our topic and the introduction of another grew longer, and at last Jim spoke.

"Something has happened," he said. "You saw what wasn't there and I felt what wasn't there. What did we see or feel? And what did *she* see or feel?"

He had hardly spoken when there came a rap at the door, and our landlord entered. For the moment during which the door was open I heard from the bar of the inn a shrill, gabbling voice, which I had never heard before, but which I knew Jim had heard.

"There's Mrs. Labson come into the bar, gentlemen," he said, "and she wants to know if it was you who were standing outside her house ten minutes ago. She's got a notion . . ."

He paused.

"It's hard to make out what she's after," he said. "Her husband has not been at home all day, and he's not home yet, and she thinks you may have seen him on the golf-links. And then she says she's thinking of letting her house for a month, and wonders if you would care to take it, but she runs on so—"

The door opened again, and there she stood, filling the doorway. She had on her head a great feathered hat, and over her shoulders a red satin evening cloak now moth-eaten and ragged, while on her feet were still those carpet-slippers.

"So odd it must seem to you for a lady to intrude like this," she said, "but you are the gentlemen, are you not, whom I saw admiring my house just now?"

Her eyes, now utterly vacant, now suddenly keen and searching, fell on the window. The curtains were not drawn and outside the last of the daylight was fading. She shuffled quickly across the floor and rattled the blind down, first peering out into the dusk.

"I'm sure I don't wonder at that," she gabbled on, "for my house is much admired by visitors here. I was thinking of letting it for a few weeks, though I am not sure that it would be convenient to do so just yet, and even if I did, I should have to put some of my treasures away in a little attic at the top of the house and lock that up. Some heirlooms, you understand. But that's all by the way. I came in, a very odd intrusion, I know, to ask if either of you had seen my husband, Mr. Labson – I am Mrs. Labson, as I should have told you – if you'd seen him on the golf-links this afternoon. He went out about two o'clock, and he's not been back. Most unusual, for there's his tea ready for him always at half past four."

She paused and seemed to listen intently, then went across to the window again and drew the blind aside.

"I thought I heard a step in my garden just out there," she said, "and I wondered if it was Mr. Labson. Such a pleasant little garden, a bit over-grown maybe; I think I saw one of you gentlemen looking down into it last night, when I was taking a breath of air. Or even if you didn't care to take the whole of my house, perhaps you would like a couple of rooms there. I could make everything most comfortable for you, for Mr. Labson always said I was a wonderful cook and manager, and not a word of complaint have I ever had from him all these years. Still, if he's taken it into his head to go off suddenly like this, I should be pleased to have a lodger in the house, for I'm not accustomed to be alone. Being alone in a house was a thing I never could bear."

She turned to our landlord:

"I'll take a room here for to-night," she said, "if Mr. Labson doesn't come back. Perhaps you would send across for a bag into which I have put what I shall want. No; that would never do; I'll go and get it myself, if you would be so good as to come with me as far as the door. One never knows who is about at this time of night. And if Mr. Labson should come here to look for me, don't let him in whatever you do. Say I'm not here; say I've left home for a day or two and have given no address. You don't want Mr. Labson here, for he's not got a penny of his own, and couldn't pay for his board and lodging, and I won't support him in idleness any longer. He ruined me and I'll be even with him yet. I told him—"

The stream of insane babble suddenly ceased; her eyes, fixing themselves on a dusky corner of the room behind where I stood, grew wide with terror, and her mouth gaped. Simultaneously I heard a gasp of startled amazement from Jim, and turned quickly to see what he and Mrs. Labson were looking at.

There he stood, he whom I had seen half an hour ago appearing suddenly in the square, and as suddenly disappearing as he came to the Corner House. Next minute she had flung the door wide and bolted out. Jim and I followed and saw her rush down the passage outside, and through the open door of the bar into the square. Terror winged her feet, and that great misshapen bulk sped away and was lost in the darkness of the fallen night.

We went straight to the police-station, and the country was scoured for the mad woman who, I felt sure, was also a murderess. The river was dragged, and about midnight two fishermen found the body below the sluice-gate at the head of the estuary. Search meantime had been made in the Corner House, and her husband's corpse was discovered, strangled with a silk handkerchief, behind the water-butt in the corner of the garden. Close by was a half-dug excavation, where no doubt she had intended to bury him.

Corstophine

Fred Bennet had proposed himself for a visit of a couple of nights, and had said in his letter that he had a curious story to tell me. The date he suggested was perfectly convenient, and he arrived just before dinner. We were alone, but when I hinted that I was more than ready to hear his curious story he said that would come later.

"I want to clear the ground first," he said, "for it is always better to agree or disagree on a principle before you advance your illustration."

"Spook?" I asked, knowing that the occult side of life is far more real to him than the happenings of normal existence.

"I really don't know whether you'll think it is spooky or not," he said. "You may think it is only a coincidence. But, you see, I don't believe in coincidences. There isn't such a thing as blind chance, to my mind: what we call chance is only the working out of a law which we are ignorant of."

"Explain," said I.

"Well, take the rising of the sun. If we were ignorant of the movement of the earth we should think it a coincidence that the sun will rise to-morrow very nearly at the same time as it rose to-day. But we don't call it a coincidence because we know, more or less, the law that makes it do so. That's clear, isn't it?"

"That will do for the present," I said. "I won't argue yet."

"Right. Now since we know about the movement of the earth, we can safely prophesy that the sun will rise to-morrow. Our knowledge of what is past makes us able to see into the future, and, in fact, we shouldn't call it prophecy at all if we were told the sun would rise to-morrow. In just the same way, if a man had known the exact movement of a certain iceberg, and the exact course of the *Titanic*, he would have been able to prophesy that the *Titanic* would founder on that iceberg at a certain moment. Our knowledge of the future, in a word, depends entirely on our knowledge of the past, and if we knew absolutely all about the past, we should know absolutely all about the future."

"Not quite," said I. "A fresh factor might come."

"But that factor would be dependent on the past too," he said.

"Is the story going to be as difficult as the preliminaries?" I asked.

He laughed.

"Much more difficult," he said. "At least, the explanation is much more difficult, if you don't accept these very simple facts. To my mind the idea that the past and present and future are all really one is the only possible way of accounting for it."

He pushed back his plate and leaned his elbows on the table, looking fixedly at me. He has the most extraordinary eyes I have ever seen; they seem sometimes to look quite through what they are regarding, and then to come back as from some remote focus to your face again.

"Of course, time, the whole sum of time, cannot be more than an infinitesimal point in eternity," he said, "even if it is as much as that. When we get out of time, when we die, in fact, we shall regard time as just a point, visible all round, so to speak. Some people, even now, get glimpses of it in its entirety. We call them clairvoyants: they have visions of the future which are actually and literally fulfilled. Or, perhaps, they have, when they see such things, some revelation of the past which enables them, like the man prophesying about the sinking of the *Titanic*, to foretell the future. If he had found people to believe him a disaster like that might have been averted. Take it which way you like."

Now Fred, as I already knew, had more than once in his life

experienced this mysterious enlightenment, and I guessed now the nature of the curious story of which he had spoken.

"You've seen something," I said, rising. "I long to hear all about it."

The night was very hot, and instead of adjourning to another room, we went out into the garden, where there was some coolness of breeze and dew. The sun was set, but light still lingered in the sky; screeching companies of swifts wheeled overhead, and the warmth drew out in subtle distillation the fragrance from the rose-beds. My servant had already put out a little encampment of basket-chairs, and a table with cards, if we felt so disposed, on the lawn, and here we settled ourselves.

"And above all things," I said, "tell me your story fully and at length. Otherwise I shall only be asking questions as to details, and that will interrupt you."

With his permission I give the story very much as he told it me. As he spoke the night darkened round us, the swifts ceased their shrill foraging, and bats took their place with shriller and barely audible squeakings. Occasionally there was the flare of a lit match, and the creak of a basket-chair, but there was no other interruption.

"One evening, about three weeks ago," he said, "I was dining with Arthur Temple. His wife and his sister-in-law were there, but about half past ten they went out to a ball. He hates dancing as much as I do, and proposed that we should have a game of chess. I adore chess, and play it quite atrociously, but when I am playing chess I can think of nothing whatever else. That night, however, things went strangely well, and with trembling excitement I saw that after some twenty moves the unwonted prospect of winning my game was opening out in front of me. I mention this to show that I was very wide-awake and concentrated on what I was doing.

"As I meditated the move which was soon to prove fatal to my adversary, a vision such as I have had once or twice before leaped into being before my eyes. My hand was raised to take hold of my queen, when the chess-board at which I was looking and my actual surroundings entirely vanished, and I was standing on the platform of a railway station. There was a train drawn up by it, out of which I was aware I had just stepped, and I knew I had an hour to wait for the one that was to take me on to my unknown destination. Just opposite me was the board on which was painted the name of the station; this I shall not tell you at present, because you might guess what my story is going to be. But though it seemed perfectly natural that I should be there, I had never at that time, to the best of my knowledge, heard of the name of the station before. There was my luggage on the platform, and I gave it in charge of a porter who was exactly like Arthur Temple, told him that I was going for a walk, and would be back before my train was due.

"It was a very dark afternoon – somehow I knew it was afternoon – and the air oppressively close and sultry, as if a storm was coming up. I walked through the booking-office of the station and out into a big yard. To the right were some allotment gardens, beyond which the ground rose rapidly up to a distant line of moors; to the left were rows upon rows of sheds, with tall chimneys vomiting smoke, and in front a long street with huddled houses stretching right and left. They were built of grey, discoloured stone, with slate roofs, mean and dismal dwellings, and neither in the station yard nor in the long perspective of the street in front of me was there a sign of any human being. Probably, I thought, the men and women of the place were engaged in those manufacturing buildings; but there were no children playing on the pavements. The place seemed absolutely deserted, and somehow disquieting and appalling.

"I stood there a moment, hesitating as to whether I should start on a walk among such charmless surroundings or stop in the station and while away the hour with my book. Then I became aware that there was waiting for me something which very closely concerned me, and that, whatever it was, it lay beyond that long untenanted street. I had to go, though I had no idea where I was going or what I should find. I crossed the yard and started to walk up the street.

"As soon as I got on the move that sense of being obliged to go completely vanished; it had given me the required push, I suppose, and I realized that I was just waiting for my train and filling in the time. The street stretched endlessly in front of me, up a steepish hill, and on each side were these low two-storey houses. Their doors and windows, in spite of the stifling heat, were all shut, and never a face showed from within, nor was there a single footstep but my own to break the silence. No sparrow fluttered in the eaves or foraged in the gutters; no cat slunk along the house-walls or blinked on the doorsteps; there was nothing visible nor audible of the evidence of life.

"On and on I walked, and presently the street began to show signs of coming to an end. The houses on one side ceased, and I looked over long stretches of grimy fields, tenantless of any grazing beasts. At that, like a blink of distant lightning, there flashed on my mind the notion that I did not see any living things because I no longer had anything to do with the living. All about me probably were children and men and women, and cats and sparrows, but I did not belong to them. I was there in some other capacity, and whatever it was that was of significance for me in this desolate place it was not concerned with life. I can't express it more definitely than that, because the notion itself was indefinite, and it flashed upon me but for a moment and was gone again. Then the houses on the other side of the street came to an end also, and I was walking along a black country road, with stunted hedges on each side. Meantime the dusk was coming rapidly on, a thick and murky dusk, hot and windless. The road made a sharp right-angled turn, and while it was open to the fields on one side the other was bounded by a high stone wall that rose above my head. I was beginning to wonder what this enclosure was when I came to a big iron gate in it, and I saw through the bars that it was a graveyard. Row upon row the tombstones glimmered faintly in the dusk, and at the far end of it, only just visible in the gathering darkness, were the roofs and small spire of a cemetery chapel. The gate was open, and feeling that there was something here which concerned me, I entered and began walking up an unweeded gravel path in the direction of the chapel. As I did this, I looked at my watch and saw that half of my hour of waiting was nearly spent, and that I must soon be retracing my steps. But I knew I had business here which must be performed.

"The tombstones came to an end, and there was a broad space of open grass between me and the chapel. Then I saw that there was one grave standing alone there, and with that odd curiosity that prompts us to read the names on tombstones I left the path and went to it.

"Though it appeared rather new, glimmering whitely in the dusk, I saw that already moss and lichen had covered the face of it, and I wondered whether it was the grave of some stranger who had died a lonely death here, and had no one, friend or relation, who looked after it. The name, whatever it was, was quite overgrown, and with some impulse of pity for him who lay below, and had so soon been forgotten, I began scraping it with the ferrule of my stick. The moss peeled off quite easily, coming away in long shreds and fibres, and presently I saw that the name was visible. But as I worked the darkness had so gathered that I could not read it, and I lit a match and held it to the surface of the stone. And the name I read there was my own.

"I heard myself give some exclamation of surprise and horror, and immediately afterwards I heard Arthur Temple's laugh, and then again I was in his room, staring at the chess-board, and looking with dismay at the move he had made. I had not anticipated that, and my wonderful plan was ruined.

"'For half a minute,' he said, 'I thought you had got me.' A few moves were sufficient to bring the game to a most undesired conclusion, and after a short chat I went home. The vision apparently had lasted just the space of his own move, for mine was already being made when it began."

He paused, and I supposed the story was over.

"What an odd affair!" I said. "It's just one of those meaningless but interesting intrusions into everyday life, coming from God knows where, which doesn't lead to anything. What was the name of the station, by the way? Did you take the trouble to find out whether your vision resembled the actual place? Was that the coincidence?"

I was, I confess, rather disappointed, though, indeed, he had been telling his story very well. But like so many of these strange glimpses which clair voyantes and mediums seem genuinely to get into the world of powers and unseen agencies, which we know lies so closely round us and sometimes manifests itself to the senses of those who are still on the material plane, it seemed so pointless. Even if it turned out that eventually he was buried in the cemetery of this twilit, untenanted town, what good would it have done him to have known of that before it happened? What is the use of communications between this world and some other world inaccessible to the ordinary perceptions of mankind if these communications contain nothing that is of value or interest?

He looked at me with that distant penetrating glance which seemed to be focused on some inconceivable remoteness, and laughed.

"No, that wasn't the coincidence," he said, "at least, that coincidence, if you call it so, is not the point of the story. As for the name of the station, that will come very soon now."

"Oh, there is more, then, is there?" I asked.

"Certainly; you told me to tell it you at length. That's only the prologue, or the first act. Shall I go on?"

"Yes, of course. Sorry."

"Well, there I was again in Arthur's room; the whole vision had lasted perhaps a minute, and he was quite unaware that I had done anything but stare at the chess-board, and when he made that move which upset my plans, give a cry of surprise and dismay . . . And then as I told you, we talked for a little, and he mentioned that he and his wife were possibly going up to Yorkshire for Whitsuntide, to a place called Helyat, which she had lately inherited on the death of an uncle. It was up on the moors, he said, with a little shooting in the autumn, and just now some rather good trout-fishing. If they went, they would be there for a fortnight or so; perhaps I would come up for a week, if I was doing nothing particular. I said I should be delighted to, but this was contingent, of course, on their going, and the matter was left vague. I saw neither of them again, nor did I hear any more till, ten days afterwards, I got a telegram from him – he always sends a telegram in preference to a letter, because he says it receives more attention – asking me to come up as soon as ever I liked. If I would let him know the day and the time of my train, they would meet me: their station was Helyat. Helyat, I may say, was not the name of the station in the vision I have told you.

"There was an ABC time-table in the house. I looked out Helyat, found a train that started and arrived at convenient hours, and I telegraphed to Arthur that I would travel by it next day. So that was settled.

"The weather in London that week had been extremely oppressive, and I welcomed the idea of getting up on to the Yorkshire moors. Moreover, since the day when I had experienced that odd vision I had gone about with a strong sense of some impending disaster. I told myself, in the way one does, that the heat and sultriness of town were responsible for my depressed spirits, but I knew very well that it was the vision that lay at the root of them. I never shook off the consciousness of it; it lay like some leaden weight upon me, it got between the normal sunlight of life and myself like some menacing thunder-cloud. And now, the moment that I had sent off that telegram, the exhilaration at the thought of getting into a high and bracing air completely passed, and the dread of some imminent peril took such possession of me that I nearly sent a second telegram on the heels of the first to say that I could not manage to come after all. But why I connected these forebodings with my journey or my stay at Helyat I had no idea, and search my mind as I might there was no conceivable reason for doing so. I told myself that this was one of those causeless fears which sometimes obsess people of the steadiest nerves, and that to yield to it was to take a definite step in the direction of mental unbalance. It would never do to let oneself become the prey of such unreasonable terrors.

"I made up my mind therefore to go through with it, not only for the sake of not losing a pleasant week in the country, but even more for the sake of proving to myself the unreasonableness of my fears. I arrived accordingly at the terminus next morning, with a quarter of an hour to spare, found a corner seat, engaged a place in the restaurant-car for lunch, and settled down. Just before the train started the ticket-inspector came round, and as he clipped my ticket, looked at the name of my destination.

"'Change at Corstophine, sir,' he said, and now you know the name of the station at which I alighted in that vision.

"I felt panic invading my very bones, but I asked one question.

"'Do I wait there long?' I said.

"He consulted a time-table which he pulled out of his pocket.

"'Just an hour, sir,' he said. 'A branch line takes you on to Helyat.'"

I broke my determination not to interrupt him.

"Corstophine?" I said. "I've seen that name lately in the paper."

"So have I. We're just coming to that," said he. "And then the panic grew beyond my control. I could not resist it any longer, and I got out of the train. With some difficulty I managed to obtain my luggage from the van, and I sent a telegram to Arthur Temple saying I was detained. A minute later the train started, and there I was on the platform, already terribly ashamed of myself, but knowing in some interior cell of my brain that I was right in doing what I had done. In some manner, as yet inscrutable to me, I had obeyed the warning which I had received ten days ago.

"I dined that evening at my club, and after dinner read in an evening paper about a terrible railway accident that had occurred during the afternoon at Corstophine. The fast train from London, by which I should have travelled, stopped there at two-fifty-three p.m.; the train taking the branch line which goes up into the moors and stops at Helyat was due to start at three-fifty-four. It starts, so said the account, from the down platform, crosses on to the up line, along which it runs for some hundred yards, and then branches off to the right. About the same time an up-express is due to pass through Corstophine without stopping. Usually the local train to Helyat waits on the down line for it to pass; this afternoon, however, the express was late, and the Helyat train was signalled to start. Whether owing to a mistake of the signalman, who had not put up the signal against the express, or whether the driver of the express had not seen it, was not yet clear, but what had happened was that while the Helyat train was on the section of the up line, the express, running at full speed to make up time, dashed into it. The engine and front carriage of the express was wrecked, and the other train reduced simply to matchwood: the express had gone through it like a bullet."

Again he paused; this time I did not interrupt.

"So, there was my vision," he said, "and there was the interpretation of the warning it sent me. But there remains a little more to tell you, which, to my mind, is as curious from the point of view of the scientific investigator of such phenomena as anything yet. It is this:

"I instantly made up my mind to start for Helyat next day. Vision and fulfilment alike, as far as I was concerned, had done their work, and I had an immense curiosity to ascertain whether all the imagery and scenery of the vision had an actual existence here on earth, or whether it was an impulse, so to speak, from the immaterial world, clothing itself in forms of time and space. I must confess that I hoped it was the former, that I should find at Corstophine what I imagined I had seen there, for that would show me how closely the two worlds are interlinked or dovetailed together, so that the one can use for our mortal sense the scenery of the other . . . So I telegraphed again to Arthur Temple, saying that I should arrive at the same hour next day.

"Again, therefore, I went to the London terminus, and again the ticket inspector told me I must change at Corstophine. The papers that morning were full of this terrible accident, but he assured me that the line was already clear, and that I should get through. An hour before we were due there we passed into the black country of collieries and manufacture; the sun was hidden in the murk of the smoke-belching chimneys, and when we stopped at the station where I was to change the earth was shrouded under that gross and unnatural twilight in which I had seen it before. And, exactly as before, I gave my luggage in charge of the porter, and set out to explore a place I had never seen, but knew with a vividness which no normal exercise of memory can give. There on the right of the station yard were the allotment gardens, behind which rose the line of moors, among which, no doubt, Helyat lay, and there, to the left, were the roofs of sheds, with tall chimneys vomiting smoke, and there in front of me was the mean, steep street stretching into an endless perspective. But to-day, instead of finding a dead and uninhabited town, it was full of busy crowds hurrying about. Children were playing in the gutters, cats sat and made their toilets on doorsteps; the sparrows pecked at the refuse heaps that strewed the road. That seemed natural; when my spirit, or my astral body or whatever you care to call it, visited Corstophine before I belonged, potentially, to the dead, and the living were outside my ken. Now, potentially, I belonged to the living, and they swarmed about me.

"I went quickly up the street, for from my previous experience I knew that there was not more than time to go to the place which I must visit, and return to catch my train. It was swelteringly hot, and curiously dark; the darkness increased every moment as I hurried along. Then the houses on the left came to an end, and I looked over grimy fields, and then the houses on the right ceased also, and the road made a sharp turn. Presently I was walking below the stone wall, too high to look over, and there was the iron gate ajar, and the rows of tombstones within, and against the blackened sky the roofs and spire of the cemetery chapel. Once more I passed up the grass-grown gravel, and there was an empty space in front of the chapel, with just one gravestone standing apart from the rest.

"I crossed the grass to it and saw that it was overgrown with moss and lichen. I scraped with my stick the surface of the stone on which was cut the name of the man who lay below it – or woman, maybe – and then, lighting a match, for it was impossible to read the letters in the darkness, I saw that it was my own name and none other that was chiselled there. There was no date, there was no text; there was just my name and nothing else."

He paused again. Some time during the course of his story my servant must have brought out a tray of syphons and whisky, and put on the table a lamp that now burned there unwaveringly in the still air. But I had not been aware of his coming or going; I had known no more of it than Fred had known of his opponent's move at chess while the vision filled the field of his conscious perceptions. He helped himself to something; I did the same, and he spoke again.

"It is arguable," he said, "that at some time in my life I had been to Corstophine, and had done exactly what I did in my vision. I can't prove that I haven't, because I can't account for every day that I have spent since I was born. I can only say that I have absolutely no recollection of having done so, or of ever having heard of such a place as Corstophine. But if I had, it is on the cards that my vision was only a recollection, and that its preventing my going to Corstophine on a particular day when, if I had gone there, I should certainly have been killed in a railway accident was only a coincidence. If that had happened, and if my body had been identified, my remains would certainly have been buried in that cemetery, because my executor would have found in my will the wish that, unless there were strong reasons for the contrary, I should be buried in the graveyard nearest to the place in which I had died. Naturally I don't care what happens to my body when I have done with it, and I don't want it be to a sentimental nuisance to other people."

He sat up, stretched himself, and laughed.

"That would have been a very elaborate coincidence," he said, "and the coincidence would have had a longer arm than ever if they had observed that close to my grave there was buried another Fred Bennett. I must say that the simpler explanation appeals to me more."

"And what is the simpler explanation?" I asked.

"The one that you really believe in, though your reason revolts against it because it has not the faintest idea of the law that lies behind it. It's a law all the same, though it doesn't manifest itself so often as that which governs the rising of the sun. Let's say, then, that it's a law loosely analogous to that which regulates the appearance of comets, though of course it is far more frequent in its manifestations. Perhaps it requires for its manifestation a certain psychical perception given to some people and not to others, just in the same way as it requires a certain physical perception to hear the squeal of those bats which are flitting overhead. I can't hear them personally, but I think you told me before that you can. I perfectly accept your word for it, though the noise doesn't reach my senses."

"And the law?" I asked.

"The law is that in the real world, in the true existence beyond the 'muddy vesture of decay', the past and the present and the future are one. They are a point in eternity which can be perceived, and handled all round. Difficult to express, but that's the kind of thing. Occasionally, and in the case of some people, the muddy vesture can be stripped off, though only intermittently and for a moment, and then they perceive and know. It's very simple really, and, as a matter of fact, you believe it all the time."

"I know I do," said I, "but just because it is so rare, and because it is so abnormal, I want to try to account for everything of the sort which I hear by an extension of the physical senses. Thought-reading, telepathy, suggestion; all these are natural phenomena. We know a little about them, and we've got to exclude them first before we accept anything so strange as a vision of the future."

"Exclude them, then," he said. "I'm quite with you. But you mustn't think that I put clairvoyance or knowledge of the future on a different plane to any of those. It's only an extension of a natural law, a branch line, so to speak, that led to Helyat, off the main line. It's part of the system."

There was something to think about there, and we were both silent. I could hear the squeak of the bats, and Fred couldn't, but I should have thought it very materialistic of him to deny that I heard them just because his ears were deaf to them. I thought over the story, point by point; and, as he had said, I knew I really agreed with him on the principle that from somewhere out of what we think of as the great void, merely because we do not rightly know what is there, there did come, and had come, and would come, these wireless messages to the receivers that were in tune with them. There was the dead town of his vision, uninhabited, because potentially he was of the dead, and then it became a live town, because, having taken the warning, he was of the living. And then a bright and brilliant and go-to-bed notion struck me.

"Ha! I've picked a hole," I said. "When you saw the vision, Corstophine was without inhabitants, because you were dead. Wasn't it so?"

He laughed again.

"I know exactly what you are going to ask," he said. "You're going to ask about the porter at the station, to whom I gave my luggage. I can't explain that. Perhaps his appearance was like the last conscious view of the anæsthetist, who stands by you when you are having gas, and is the final link with the material world. He was like Arthur Temple, you will remember."

The Temple

Frank Ingleton and I had left London early in July with the intention of spending a couple of months at least in Cornwall. This sojourn was not by any means to be a complete holiday, for he was a student of those remains of prehistoric civilization which are found in such mysterious abundance in the ancient county, and I was employed on a book which should have already been approaching completion, but which was still lamentably far from its consummation. Naturally there was to be a little golf and a little sea-bathing for relaxation, but we were both keen on our work and meant to have gathered in a respectable harvest of industry before we returned.

The village of St. Caradoc's, from all accounts, seemed likely to be favourable to our projects, for there were remains in the neighbourhood which had never been thoroughly investigated by any archæologist, and its position on the map, remote from any of the more celebrated holiday centres, promised a reasonable tranquillity. It supplied, also, the desirable relaxations; the club-house of a pleasantly hazardous golf-course stood at the bottom of the hotel garden, and five minutes' walk across the sand-dunes among which the holes were placed led to the beach. The hotel was comfortable, and at present half empty, and Fortune seemed to smile on our undertakings. We settled down, therefore, without further plans. Frank meant, before he left, to visit other parts of the county, but here, within a mile of the hotel, was that curious circle of monoliths, like some Stonehenge in miniature, known as the "Council of Penruth". It had always been supposed, so Frank told me, that it was some place of Druidical worship, but he distrusted the conclusion and wanted to study it minutely on the spot.

I went there with him by way of an evening saunter on the second day after our arrival. The shortest way was along the sand-dunes, and thence up a steep, grassy slope on to the ploughed stretches of the uplands. In that warm, soft climate the wheat was in full ear, and beginning already to turn ripe and tawny. A very narrow path led across these cornfields to our destination, and from far off one could see the circle of stones, four to five feet high, standing there, black and austere, against the yellowing grain. Though all the country round was in cultivation no plough had furrowed the interior of the circle, and inside was the ancient turf of the downs, short and velvety, with patches of thyme and harebells. It seemed odd; a plough could have passed backwards and forwards between the monoliths and a half-acre of land have been made fruitful.

"But why isn't it ploughed?" I asked.

"Oh, you're in the land of superstitions and ancient sorceries," he said. "These circles are never touched or made use of. And do you see, the path across the fields by which we have come passes round it; it doesn't run across it. There it goes again on the far side, pursuing the same line after making the detour."

He laughed.

"The farmer of the land was up here this morning when I was making some measurements," he said. "He went round it, I noticed, and when his dog came inside after some interesting smell, he called it back, and cuffed it, and rapped out: 'Come out of that there; and never do you go within again.'"

"But what's the idea?" I asked.

"Something clings to it, some curse, some abomination. They think, no doubt, just as the archæologists do, that the place has been a Druidical temple, where dreadful rites were performed and human sacrifices made. But they are all wrong; this was never a temple at all, it was a Council Chamber, and the very name of it, the 'Council of Penruth', confirms that. No doubt there was a temple somewhere about; dearly should I like to find it."

It had been hot work climbing up that steep slippery hillside from the village, and we sat down within the circle, leaning our backs against two adjacent stones, and as we sat and rested Frank explained to me the grounds of his belief.

"If you care to count them," he said, "you'll find there are twenty-one of these monoliths, against two of which you and I are leaning, and if you care to measure the distances between them you will find that they are all equal. Each stone, in fact, represents the seat of a member of the council of twenty-one. But if the place had been a temple there would have been a larger gap between two of the stones towards the east, where the gate of the temple was, facing the rising sun, and somewhere within the circle, probably exactly in the middle, there would have been a large, flat stone, which was the stone of sacrifice, where no doubt human victims were offered. Or, if the stone had disappeared, there would have been a depression where it once was. Those are the distinguishing marks of a temple, and this place lacks them. It has always been assumed that it was a temple, and it has been described as such. But I am sure I am right about it."

"But there is a temple somewhere about?" I asked.

"Certain to be. If any of these prehistoric settlements was large enough to have a council hall, it would certainly have had a temple, though the remains of it have very likely disappeared. When the country was Christianized, the old religion – if you can call it a religion – was reckoned an abomination, and the places of worship were destroyed, just as the Israelites destroyed the groves of Baal. But I mean to explore very thoroughly here: there may be remains in some of those woods down there. This is just the sort of remote place where the temple might have escaped destruction."

"And what was the ancient religion?" I asked.

"Very little is known about it. It certainly was a religion not of love, but fear. The gods were the blind powers of nature, manifesting themselves in storms and destruction and plague, and had to be propitiated with human sacrifices. And the priests, of course, dealt in magic and sorcery. They were the governing class, and kept their power alive by terror. If you offended them, as likely as not you would be sent for and told that the gods required your eldest son as a blood-offering next midsummer day at sunrise, when the first beams of morning shone through the eastern gate of the temple. It was wise to be a good churchman in those days."

"It looks a kindly country nowadays," I said. "The temples of the old gods are empty."

"Yes, but it's extraordinary how old superstitions linger. It isn't a year ago that there was a witchcraft trial in Penzance. The cattle belonging to some farmer near here began to pine and die, and he went to an old woman, who said that a spell had been cast on them, and that if he paid her she could remove it. He went on paying and paying, and at last got tired of that and prosecuted her instead."

He looked at his watch.

"Let's take a stroll before dinner," he said. "Instead of going back the way we came, we might make a ramble down the hillside in front and through the woods. They look rather attractive."

"And may conceal a pagan temple," said I, getting up.

We skirted the harvest fields, and found a path leading through a big fir-wood that climbed up the hillside. The trees were of no great growth as regards height, and the prevalent wind from the south-west, to which they stood exposed, had combed and pressed their branches landwards. But the foliage of the tree-tops was very dense, making a curious sombre twilight as we penetrated deeper into the wood. There was no undergrowth whatever below them, the ground was spread thick and smooth with fallen pine-needles, and with the tree trunks rising straight and column-like and that thick roof of branches above, the place looked like some great hall of Nature's building. No whisper of wind moved overhead, and so dark and still was it that you might easily have conceived yourself to be walking up the aisle of some walled-in place. The smell of the firs was thick in the air like incense, and the foot went noiselessly as over spread carpets. No birds flitted between the tree trunks or called to each other; the only noise was the murmurous buzz of flies, which sounded like some long-held organ note.

It had been hot enough outside in the fresh draught off the sea, but here, where no breeze winnowed the air, it was stiflingly close, and as we plunged deeper into the dimness I was conscious of some gathering oppression of the spirit. It was an uncomfortable place, it seemed thick with unseen presences. And the same notion must have struck Frank as well.

"I feel as if we were being watched," he said. "There are eyes peeping at us from behind the trunks, and they don't like us. Now what makes so silly an idea enter my head?"

"A grove of Baal, is it?" I suggested. "One that has escaped destruction and is full of the spirits of murderous priests."

"I wish it was," he said. "Then we could inquire the way to the temple."

Suddenly he pointed ahead.

"Hullo, what's that?" he said.

I followed the direction of his finger, and for one half-second thought I saw the glimmer of something white moving among the trees. But before I could focus it, it was gone. Somehow, the heat and the oppression had got on my nerves.

"Well, it's not our wood," I said. "I suppose other people have just as much right to walk here. But I've had enough of tree trunks; I should like to have done with the wood."

Even as I spoke I saw it was getting lighter in front of us; glimmers of day began to show between the thick-set trunks, and presently we found ourselves threading the last row of the trees. The light of day poured in again and the stir of the sea breeze; it was like coming out of some crowded and airless building into the open air.

We emerged into a delectable place; a broad stretch of downland turf was spread in front of us, smooth and ancient turf like that in the circle, jewelled with thyme and centaury and bugloss. The path we had been following lay straight across this, and dipping down over the edge of it we came suddenly on the most enchanting little house, low and two-storied, standing in a small enclosure of lawn and garden-beds. The hill behind it had evidently once been quarried, but long ago, for now the sheer sides of it were overgrown with a tangle of ivy and bryony, and at their base lay a pool of water. Beyond and bordering the lawn was a copse of birches and hornbeams, which half encircled the clearing in which stood house and garden. The house itself, smothered in honeysuckle and climbing fuchsia, seemed unoccupied, for the chimneys were smokeless and the blinds drawn down over the windows. As we turned the corner of its low fence and came on to the front of it, the impression was verified, for there by the gate was a notice proclaiming that it was to be let furnished, and directing that application should be made to a house-agent in St. Caradoc's.

"But it's a pocket Paradise," said I. "Why shouldn't we—"

Frank interrupted me.

"Of course there's no reason why we shouldn't," he said. "In fact, there's every reason why we should. The manager at the hotel told me they were filling up next week and wanted to know for how long we should stop. We'll make inquiries to-morrow morning, and find the agent and the keys."

The keys next morning revealed a charm within that came up to the promise of what we had seen without, and, what was as wonderful, the agent could provide our staff as well. This consisted of a rotund and capable Cornishwoman who, with her daughter to help her, would arrive early every morning, and remain till she had served our dinner, and then go back to her cottage in St. Caradoc's. If that would suffice us, she was ready to be in charge as soon as we settled to take the little house; it must be understood, however, that she would not sleep there. Without making any further inquiries, the assurance that she was a clean and capable cook and competent in every way was enough, and two days afterwards we entered into possession. The rent asked was extraordinarily low, and my suspicious mind, as we went through the house, visualized an absence of water-supply, or a kitchen range that, while getting red hot, left its ovens as in the chill of an Arctic night. But no such dispiriting discoveries awaited us; Mrs. Fennell turned taps and manipulated dampers, and, scouring capably through the house, pronounced on her solemn guarantee that we should be very comfortable. "But I go back to my own house at night, gentlemen," she said, "and I promise you the water will be hot and your breakfast ready for you by eight in the morning."

We entered that afternoon; our luggage had been sent up an hour before, and when we arrived the portmanteaux were already unpacked and clothes bestowed in their drawers, and tea ready in the sitting-room. It and its adjoining dining-room, with a small parqueted hall, formed the ground floor accommodation. Beyond the dining-room was the kitchen, the convenience of which had already satisfied Mrs. Fennell. Upstairs there were two good bedrooms, and above the kitchen two smaller servants' rooms, which, by our arrangement, would be unoccupied. There was a bathroom between the two bedrooms with a door into it from each; for two friends occupying the house nothing could have been more exactly what was wanted with nothing to spare. Mrs. Fennell gave us an admirable plain dinner, and by nine o'clock she had locked the outer kitchen door and left us.

Before going to bed we wandered out into the garden, marvelling at our luck. The hotel, as the manager had told us, was already beginning to fill up, the dining-room to-night would have been a cackle of voices, the sitting-room crowded, and surely it was a wonderfully good exchange to be housed in this commodious little tranquillity of a place, with our own unobtrusive establishment that came at dawn and left at night. It remained only to see if this paragon who was so proficient in her kitchen would be as punctual in the morning.

"But I wonder why she and her daughter would not establish themselves here," said Frank. "They live alone down in the village. You'd have thought that they would have shut their cottage up, and saved themselves a morning and evening tramp."

"Gregariousness," said I. "They like to know that there are people, just people, close at hand and to right and left. I like to know that there are not. I like—"

As I spoke we turned at the garden gate, where the notice that the house was to let had been, and my eyes, quite idly, travelled across the space of open down-land to the black fringe of the wood that stood above it, and for a moment, bright, and then quenched again like the line of fire made by a match that has been struck and has not flared, I saw a light there. It was only for a second that it was visible, but it must have been somewhere inside the wood, for against that luminous streak I saw the shape of the fir trunks.

"Did you see that?" I said to Frank.

"A light in the wood?" he asked. "Yes, it has appeared there several times. Just for a moment and then disappearing again. Some farmer, perhaps, finding his way home."

That was a very sensible conclusion, and, for some reason that I did not trouble to probe, my mind hastened to adopt it. After all, who was more likely to be passing through the wood than men from the upland farms going home at closing time from the Red Lion at St. Caradoc's?

I was roused next morning out of very deep sleep by the entry of Mrs. Fennell with hot water; it was a struggle to join myself up with the waking world again. I had the impression of having dreamed very vividly of things dark and dim, and of perilous places, and though I had certainly slept for something like eight hours at a stretch I felt curiously unrefreshed. At breakfast Frank was more silent than his wont, but presently we were making plans for the day. He proposed to explore the wood again, while I was busy with my work; in the afternoon a round of golf would bring us to tea-time. Before he started and I settled down, we strolled about the garden that dozed tranquilly in the hot morning sun, and again congratulated ourselves on our exchange from the hotel. We went down to the pool below the quarried cliff, and there I left him to return to the house, while he, in order to start exploring at once, followed an overgrown path that led into the copse of birch and hornbeam of which I have spoken. But I had not crossed the lawn before I heard myself called.

"Come here a minute," he shouted; "I've found something interesting." I retraced my steps, and pushing through the trees found him standing by a tall, black granite stone that pushed its moss-green head above the undergrowth.

"It's a monolith," he said excitedly. "It's like one of those stones in the circle. Perhaps there has been another circle here, or perhaps it's a stone of the temple. It's deep in the earth; it looks as if it was in place. Let's see if we can find another in this copse."

He pushed on into the thick-growing trees to the right of the path, and I, infected with his enthusiasm, made an exploration to the left. Before long I came upon another stone of the same character as the first, and my shout of discovery was echoed by his. Yet another rewarded his hunting, and as I emerged from the copse on the edge of the quarry pool I found a fifth, standing but fallen forward in a bed of rushes that fringed the water.

In the excitement of this find, my planned studiousness was, of course, abandoned; so, too, when we had eaten a hearty lunch, was the projected game of golf, and before evening we had arrived at a rough scheme of the entire place. Most of the stones were in the belt of copse that half encircled the house, and with a tape-measure we found that these were set at uniform intervals from each other except that exactly twice that interval separated the two stones that lay due east of the circle. In the bank that lay to the south of the house several were missing, but in each case, by digging at the proper intervals, we found fragments of granite grassed over in the soil, which indicated that these stones had been broken up and used, probably, for building materials, and this conjecture of Frank's was confirmed by the discovery of pieces of granite built into the walls of the house we occupied.

He had jotted down the approximate position of the stones, and passed over to me the paper on which he had drawn his plan.

"Without doubt it's a temple," he said; "there's the double interval at the east, which I told you about, and which was the gate into it."

I looked at what he had drawn.

"Then our house stands just in the centre of it," I said.

"Yes. What vandals they were to build it just there!" said he. "Probably the stone of sacrifice lies somewhere below it.

Good Lord, dinner ready, Mrs. Fennell? I had no idea it was so late."

The sky had clouded over during the afternoon, and while we sat at dinner, a windless and heavy rain began to fall and thunder to mutter over the sea. Mrs. Fennell came in to inquire into our tastes for to-morrow, and as there was every appearance of a violent storm approaching, I asked her whether she and her girl would not stop here for the night and save themselves a wetting.

"No, I'll be off now, sir, thank you," she said. "We don't mind a wetting in Cornwall."

"But not very good for your rheumatism," I said. She had mentioned that she was a sufferer in this respect.

A blink of lightning flashed rather vividly across the uncurtained windows, and the rain hissed more heavily.

"No, I'll be off now," she said, "for it's late already. Good night, gentlemen."

We heard her turn the key in the kitchen door, and presently the figures of herself and her girl passed the window.

"Not even umbrellas," said Frank. "They'll be drenched before they get down."

"I wonder why they wouldn't stop," said I.

Frank was soon employed on preparations for a plan to scale that he was meaning to make to-morrow, and he began putting in the house, which he had ascertained stood just in the centre of the temple. The size of the ground plan of it was all he required on the scale he intended for the complete plan, and after measuring the sitting-room, passage, and dining-room, he went through into the kitchen. Meanwhile, I had settled down to the work I had intended to do this morning, and proposed to get a couple of solid hours at it before I went to bed. It was rather hard to get the thread of it again, and for some time I floundered with false starts and erased sentences, but before long I got into better form, and was already happily absorbed in it when he called me from the kitchen.

"Oh, I can't come," I said; "I'm busy."

"Just a moment, please," he shouted.

I laid down my pen and went to him. He had moved the kitchen table aside and turned up the drugget that covered the floor.

"Look there!" he said.

The floor was paved with stone of the district, very likely from the quarry just outside. But in the centre was an oblong slab of granite, some six feet by four in dimensions.

"That's a whacking big stone," I said. "Odd of them to have been at the trouble of putting that there."

"They didn't," said he. "I'll bet it was there when they laid the floor!"

Then I understood.

"The stone of sacrifice?" I asked.

"Rather. Granite, and just in the centre of the temple. It can't be anything else."

Some sudden thrill of horror seized me. It was on that stone that young boys and maidens, torn from their mother's arms and bound hand and foot, were laid, while the priest, with one hand over the victim's eyes, plunged the flint knife into the smooth, white throat, sawing through the tissue till the blood spurted from the severed artery . . . In the flickering light of the candle Frank carried the stone seemed wet and darkly glistening, and was that noise only the rain volleying on the roof, or the beating of drums to drown the cries of the victim? . . .

"It's terrible," I said. "I wish you hadn't found it."

Frank was on his knees by it, examining the surface of it. "I can't say I agree with you," he said. "It just puts the final touch of certainty on my discovery. Besides, whether I had found it or not, it would have been there just the same."

"Well, I'm going on with my work," I said. "It's more cheerful than stones of sacrifice."

He laughed.

"I hope it's as interesting," he said.

It appeared, when I went back to it, that it was not, and try as I would I could not recapture the interest which is necessary to production of any kind. Even my eye wandered from the words I wrote; as for my mind, it would give only the most cursory glance at that for which I demanded its fixed attention. It was busy elsewhere. I found myself, at its bidding, scrutinizing the shadowy corners of the room; but there was nothing there, and all the time some strange darkness, blacker than that which pressed in upon the house, began to grow upon my spirit. There was fear mingled with it, though I did not know what I was afraid of; but chiefly it was some sort of despair and depression, distant as yet and undefined, but quietly closing in upon me . . . As I sat with my pen still in my hand, trying to analyse these perturbed and troubled sensations, I heard Frank call out sharply from the kitchen, the door of which, on my return, I had left open.

"Hullo!" he cried. "What's that? Is anyone there?"

I jumped from my seat and went to join him. He was standing close to the stove, holding his candle above his head, and looking at the door into the garden, which Mrs. Fennell had locked on her departure.

"What's the matter?" I asked.

He looked round at me, startled by the sound of my voice.

"Curious," he said; "I was just measuring the stone, when out of the corner of my eye I thought I saw that door open. But it's locked, isn't it?"

He tried the handle, but sure enough it was locked.

"Optical illusion," he said. "Well, I've finished here for the present. But what a night! Frightfully oppressive, isn't it? And not a breath of air stirring."

We went back to the sitting-room. I put away my laboured manuscript and we got out the cards for a game of piquet. But after one *partie*, he rose with a yawn.

"I really don't think I could keep awake for another," he said; "I'm heavy with sleep. Let's have a breath of air, the rain seems to have stopped, and go to bed. Or are you going to sit up and work?"

I had not meant to do so, but his suggestion made me determine to have another try. There was certainly some mysterious pall of depression on me, and the wisest thing to do was to fight it.

"I shall try for half an hour," I said, "and see how it goes," and I followed him to the front door of the house. The rain, as he said, had ceased, but the darkness was impenetrable, and shuffling with our feet we took a few steps along the gravel path to the corner of the house. There the light from the sitting-room windows cast a circle of illumination, and one could see the flower-beds glistening with the wet. Though it was night, the air was still so hot that the gravel path was steaming. Beyond that nothing was visible of the lawn or the hill that sloped up to the firwood. But, as we stood there, I saw, as last night, a light moving up there. Now, however, it seemed to be outside the wood, for its progress was not interrupted by the tree trunks.

Frank saw it too, and pointed at it.

"It's too wet to-night," he said, "but to-morrow evening I vote we go up there, and see who these nightly wanderers are. It's coming closer, and there's another of them."

Even as we looked a third light sprang up, and in another moment all had vanished again.

I carried out my intention of trying to work, but I could make nothing of it, and presently I found myself nodding over a page that contained nothing but erasures. With head bent forward, I drifted into a doze and from dozing into sleep, and when I woke I found the lamp burning low and the wick smouldering. I seemed to have come back from some very distant place, and, only half awake, I lit a candle and quenched the lamp and went to the windows to bolt them. And then my heart stood still, for I thought I saw someone standing outside and looking in through the intervening glass. But it must have been a sleepy fancy, for now, broad awake again, I was staring at my own reflection cast by the candle on the window. I told myself that what I had seen was no more than that, but as I creaked my way upstairs I found myself asking if I really believed that . . .

As I dressed next morning, after another long but unrefreshing night, I began puzzling over a lost memory to which I had tried to find the clue yesterday. There was a bookcase in the sitting-room with some two or three dozen volumes in it, and opening one or two of these I had found the name Samuel Townwick inscribed in them. I knew I had seen that name not so many months ago in the daily Press, but I could not recapture the connection in which I had read it; but from the recurrence of it in these books it was reasonable to conjecture that he was the owner of the house we occupied. In taking it, his name had not come up; the house-agent had plenary powers, and our deposit of a fortnight's rent clinched the contract. But this morning the name still haunted me. And since I had other small businesses in St. Caradoc's, I settled to walk down there and make some definite inquiry at the agent's. Frank was too busy with his plan to accompany me, and I set out alone.

The feeling of depression and vague foreboding was more leaden than ever this morning, and I was aware, by that sixth sense which needs no speech or language, that he was a prey to the same causeless weight. But I had not gone fifty yards from the house when the burden of it was lifted from me, and I knew again the exhilaration proper to such a morning. The rain of last evening had cleared the air, the sea breeze drew lightly landwards, and, as if I had come out of some tunnel, I rejoiced in the morning splendour. The village hummed with holiday: Mr. Cranston received me with polite enquiries as to our comfort and Mrs. Fennell's capability, and having assured him on that score, I approached my point.

"Mr. Samuel Townwick is the owner, is he not?" I asked.

The agent's smile faded a little.

"He was, sir," he said. "I act for the executors."

Suddenly, in a flash, some of what I had been groping for came back to me. "I begin to remember," I said. "He died suddenly; there was an inquest. I want to know the rest. Hadn't you better tell me?"

He shifted his glance and came back to me again.

"It was a painful affair," he said. "The executors naturally do not want it talked about."

Another glimpse of what I had forgotten blinked on my memory.

"Suicide," I said. "The usual verdict of unsound mind was brought in. And – and is that why Mrs. Fennell won't sleep in the house? She left last night in a deluge of rain."

I readily gave him my promise of secrecy, for I had not the slightest desire to tell Frank, and he told me the rest. Mr. Townwick had been for some days in a very depressed state of mind, and one morning the servants coming down had found him lying underneath the kitchen table with his throat cut. Beside him was a sharp, curiously shaped fragment of flint covered with blood. The jagged nature of the wound had confirmed the idea that he had sawn at his throat till he had severed the jugular vein. Murder was ruled out, for he was a strong man, and there were no marks on his body or about the room of there having been any struggle, nor any sign of an assailant having entered. Both kitchen doors were locked on the inside, his valuables were untouched, and from the position of the body the only reasonable inference was that he had laid down under the table, and there deliberately done himself to death . . . I repeated my assurance of silence and went out.

I knew now what the source of my nameless horror and depression had been. It was no haunting spectre of Townwick that I feared; it was the power, whatever that was, which had driven him to kill himself on the stone of sacrifice.

I went back up the hill: there was the garden blazing in the July noon, and the sweet tranquillity of the place was spread abroad in the air. But I had no sooner passed the copse and come within the circle than the dead weight of something unseen began to lay its burden on me again. There *was* something here, horrible and menacing and potent.

I found Frank in the sitting-room. His head was bent over his plan, and he started as I entered.

"Hullo!" he said. "I've made all my measurements and I want to sit tight and finish my plan today. I don't know why, but I feel I must hurry about it and get it done. And I've got the most awful fit of the blues. I can't account for it, but, anyhow, occupation is the best thing. Go into lunch, will you; I don't want any."

I looked at him and saw some indefinable change had come over his face. There was terror in his eyes that came from within; I can express it in no other way than that.

"Anything wrong?" I asked.

"No; just blues. I want to go on working. This evening, you know, we have to see where those lights come from."

All afternoon he sat close over his work, and it was not till the day was fading that he got up.

"That's done," he said. "Good Lord, we have found a temple and a half! And I'm horribly tired. I shall have a snooze till dinner."

The invasion of fear beleaguered me, it seemed to pour in through the open windows in the gathering dusk; it gathered its reinforcements outside, ready to support the onrush of it. And yet how childish it was to yield to it. By now we were alone in the house, for we had told Mrs. Fennell that a cold meal would serve us in this heat, and while Frank slept I had heard the lock of the outside kitchen door turn and she and the girl went by the window.

Presently he stirred and awoke. I had lit the lamp, and I saw his hand feel in his waistcoat pocket, and he drew out a small object which he held out to me.

"A flint knife," he said. "I picked it up in the garden this morning. It's got a fine edge to it."

At that I felt a prickle of terror run through the hair of my head, and I jumped up.

"Look here," I said, "you've had no walk to-day, and that always gives you the blues. Let's go down and dine at the hotel."

His head was outside the illumination of the lamp, and from the dimness there came a curious cackle of laughter.

"But I can't," he said. "How strange that you don't know that I can't! They've surrounded the place, and there's no way out. Listen! Can't you hear the drums and the squeal of their pipes? And their hands are about me. Christ! It's terrible to die."

He got up and began to move with curious little shuffling steps towards the kitchen. I had laid the flint knife down on the table and he snatched it up. The horror of presences unseen and multitudinous closed in round me, but I knew they were concentrated not on me, but on him. They poured in, not through the window alone, but through the solid walls of the house; outside on the lawn there were lights moving, slow and orderly.

I had still control of my mind; the awfulness and the imminence of what so closely beset us gave me the courage and clearness of despair. I darted from my chair and stood with my back to the kitchen door.

"You're not to go in there," I said. "You must come away with me out of this. Pull yourself together, Frank. We'll get through yet; once outside the garden we're safe."

He paid no attention to what I said; it was as if he did not hear me. He laid his hand on my shoulder, and I felt his fingers press through the muscles and grind like points of steel on the underlying bone. Some maniac force possessed them, and he pulled me aside as if I had been a feather.

There was one thing only to be done. With my disengaged arm I hit him full on the chin, and he fell like a log across the floor. Without pausing for a second I gripped him round the knees and began dragging him, senseless and inert, towards the door.

It is difficult to state in words what those next few minutes held. I saw nothing. I heard nothing. I felt no touch of invisible hands upon me, but I can imagine no grinding agony of pain that wrenches body and soul asunder to equal that war of the evil and the unseen that raged about me. I struggled against no visible adversary, and there was the horror of it, for I am sure that no phantom of the dead that die not could have evoked so unnerving a terror.

Before those intangible hosts had fully closed in round me and my unconscious burden I had got him on to the lawn, and it was then that the full stress of their beleaguering might poured in upon me. Strange fugitive lights wavered round me and muttered voices filled the air, and as I dragged Frank over the grass his weight seemed to grow till it was not a man's body that I was pulling along, but something well-nigh immovable, so that I had to tug and pant for breath and tug again.

"God help us both," I heard myself muttering. "Deliver us from our ghostly enemies . . ." And again I tugged and panted for breath. Close at hand now was the ring of enclosing copse, where the stones of the circle stood, and I made one final effort of concentration, for I knew that my spirit was spent, and soon there would be no power of fight left in me at all.

"In the name of the Holiest, and by the power of the Highest!" I cried aloud, and waited for a moment, gathering what dregs of strength were still left in me. And then I leaned forward, and the strained sinews of my legs were slackened as the weight of Frank's body moved after me, and I made another step, and yet another, and we had passed beyond the copse, and out of the accursed precinct.

I knew no more after that. I had fallen forwards half across him, and when I regained my senses he was stirring, and the dew of the grass was on my face. There stood the house, with the lamp still burning in the window of the sitting-room, and the quiet night was around us, with a clear and starry heaven.

The Step

John Cresswell was returning home one night from the Britannia Club at Alexandria, where, as was his custom three or four times in the week, he had dined very solidly and fluidly, and played bridge afterwards as long as a table could be formed. It had been rather an expensive evening, for all his skill at cards had been unable to cope with such a continuous series of ill-favoured hands as had been his. But he had consoled himself with reasonable doses of whisky, and now he stepped homewards in very cheerful spirits, for his business affairs were going most prosperously and a loss of twenty-five or thirty pounds to-night would be amply compensated for in the morning. Besides, his bridge-account for the year showed a credit which proved that cards were a very profitable pleasure.

It was a hot night of October, and, being a big plethoric man, he strolled at a very leisurely pace across the square and up the long street at the far end of which was his house. There were no taxis on the rank, or he would have taken one and saved himself this walk of nearly a mile; but he had no quarrel with that, for the night air with a breeze from the sea was refreshing after so long a session in a smoke-laden atmosphere. Above, a moon near to its full cast a very clear white light on his road. There was a narrow strip of sharp-cut shadow beneath the houses on his right, but the rest of the street and the pavement on the left of it, where he walked, were in bright illumination.

At first his way lay between rows of shops, European for the most part, with here and there a café where a few customers still lingered. Pleasant thoughts beguiled his progress; the Egyptian sugar-crop, in which he was much interested, had turned out very well and he saw a big profit on his options. Not less satisfactory were other businesses in which he did not figure so openly. He lent money, for instance, on a large scale, to the native population, and these operations extended far up the Nile. Only last week he had been at Luxor, where he had concluded a transaction of a very remunerative sort. He had made a loan some months ago to a small merchant there and now the appropriate interest on this was in default: in consequence the harvest of a very fruitful acreage of sugar-cane was his. A similar and even richer windfall had just come his way in Alexandria, for he had advanced money a year ago to a Levantine tobacco merchant on the security of his freehold store. This had brought him in very handsome interest, but a day or two ago the unfortunate fellow had failed, and Cresswell owned a most desirable freehold. The whole affair had been very creditable to his enterprise and sagacity, for he had privately heard that the municipality was intending to lay out the neighbourhood, a slum at present, where this store was situated, in houses of flats, and make it a residential quarter, and his newly acquired freehold would thus become a valuable property.

At present the tobacco merchant lived with his family in holes and corners of the store, and they must be evicted to-morrow morning. John Cresswell had already arranged for this, and had told the man that he would have to quit: he would go round there in the forenoon and see that they and their sticks of furniture were duly bundled out into the street. He would see personally that this was done, and looked forward to doing so. The old couple were beastly creatures, the woman a perfect witch who eyed him and muttered, but there was a daughter who was not ill-looking, and someone of the beggared family would be obliged to earn bread. He did not dwell on this, but the thought just flitted through his brain . . . Then doors would be locked and windows barred in the store that was now his, and he would lunch at the club afterwards. He was popular there; he had a jovial geniality about him, and a habit of offering drinks before they could be offered to him. That, too, was good for business.

Ten minutes' strolling brought him to the end of the shops and cafés that formed the street, and now the road ran between residential houses, each detached and with a space of garden surrounding it, where dry-leaved palms rattled in this wind from the sea. He was approaching the flamboyant Roman Catholic church, to which was attached a monastic establishment, a big white barrack-looking house where the Brothers of Poverty or some such order lived. Something to do with St. Mark, he vaguely remembered, who by tradition had brought Christianity to Egypt nearly nineteen hundred years ago. Often he met one of these odd sandal-footed creatures with his brown habit, his rosary and his cowled head going in or out of their gate, or toiling in their garden. He did not like them: lousy fellows he would have called them. Sometimes in their mendicant errands they came to his door asking alms for the indigent Copts. Not long ago he had found one actually ringing the bell of his front door, instead of going humbly round to the back, as befitted his quality, and Cresswell told him that he would loose his bulldog on the next of their breed who ventured within his garden gate. How the fellow had skipped off when he heard talk of the dog! He dropped one of his sandals in his haste to be gone, and not sparing the time to adjust it again, had hopped and hobbled over the sharp gravel to gain the street. Cresswell had laughed aloud to see his precipitancy, and the best of the joke was that he had not got any sort of dog on his premises at all. At the remembrance of that humorous incident he grinned to himself as he passed the porch of the church.

He paused a moment to mop his forehead and to light a cigarette, looking about him in great good humour. Before him and behind the road was quite empty: lights gleamed behind venetian shutters from a few upper windows of the houses, but all the world was in bed or on its way there. There were still three or four hundred yards to go before he came to his house, and as he turned his face homewards again and walked a little more briskly, he heard a step behind him, sharp and distinct, not far in his rear. He paid no heed: someone, late like himself, was going home, walking in the same direction, for the step followed him.

His cigarette was ill-lit; a little core of burning stuff fell from it on to the pavement and he stopped to rekindle it. Possibly some subconscious region of his mind was occupied with the step which had sprung up so oddly behind him in the empty street, for while he was getting his cigarette to burn again he noticed that the step had ceased. It was hardly worth while to turn round (so little the matter interested him), but a casual glance showed him that the wayfarer must have turned into one of the houses he had just passed, for the whole street, brightly moonlit, was as empty as when he surveyed it a few minutes before. Soon he came to his own gate and clanged it behind him.

The eviction of the Levantine merchant took place in the morning, and Cresswell watched his porters carrying out the tawdry furniture – a few tables, a few chairs, a sofa covered in tattered crimson plush, a couple of iron bedsteads, a bundle of dirty sheets and blankets. He was not certain in his own mind whether these paltry articles did not by rights belong to him, but they were fit for nothing except the dust-heap, and he had no use for them. There they stood in the clean bright sunshine, rubbish and no more, blocking the pavement, and a policeman told their owner that he had best clear them away at once unless he wanted trouble. There was the usual scene to which he was quite accustomed: the man's wife snivelling and slovenly, witch-like and early old, knelt and kissed his hand, and wheezingly besought his compassion. She called him "Excellency," she promised him her prayers, which he desired as little as her pots and pans. She invoked blessings on his head, for she knew that out of his pity he would give them a little more time. They had nowhere to go nor any roof to shelter them: her husband had money owing to him, and he would collect these debts and pay his default as sure as there was a God in heaven. This was a changed note from her mutterings of yesterday, but of course Cresswell had a deaf ear for this oily rigmarole, and presently he went into the store to see that everything had been removed.

It was in a filthy, dirty state; floors were rotten and the paint peeling, but the whole place would soon be broken up and he was not going to spend a piastre on it, so long as the ground on which it stood was his. Then he saw to the barring of the windows and the doors, and he gave the policeman quite a handsome tip to keep an eye on the place and take care that these folk did not get ingress again. When he came out, he found that the old man had procured a hand-cart, and he and his son were loading it up, so of course they had somewhere to go: it was all a pack of lies about their being homeless. The old hag was squatting against the house wall, but now there were no more prayers and blessings for him, and she had taken to her mutterings again. As for the daughter, seen in the broad daylight, she had a handsome face, but she was sullen and dirty and forbidding, and he gave no further thought to her. He hailed a taxi and went off to the club for lunch.

Though Cresswell, in common parlance, "did himself well," taking his fill of food and drink and tobacco, he was also careful of that great strong body of his, and the occasions were few when he omitted, at the end of the day's work, to walk out in the direction of Ramleh for a brisk hour or two, or, during the hotter months, to have a good swim in the sea and a bask in the sun. On the day following this eviction he took a tramp along the firm sands of the coast, and then, turning inland, struck the road that would bring him back to his own house. This stood quite at the end of the rows of detached houses past which he had walked two evenings before: beyond, the road ran between tumbled sand-dunes and scrub-covered flats. Here and there in sheltered hollows a few Arab goat-herds and such had made themselves nomadic tent-like habitations of a primitive sort: half a dozen posts set in the sand supported a roof of rugs and blankets stitched together. If they encroached too near the outskirts of the town the authorities periodically made a clearance of them, for they were apt to be light-fingered, pilfering folk, whose close vicinity was not desirable.

To-day as he returned from his walk, Cresswell saw that a tent of this kind had newly been set up within twenty yards of his own garden wall. That would not do at all, that must be seen to, and he determined as soon as he had had his bath and his change of clothes to ring up his very good friend the chief inspector of police and request its removal. As he got nearer to it he saw that it was not quite of the usual type. The roof was clearly an outworn European carpet, and standing outside it on the sand were chairs and a sofa. Somehow these seemed familiar to him, though he could not localize the association. Then out of the tent came that old Levantine hag who had kissed his hand and knelt to him yesterday, invoking on him all sorts of blessings and prosperities, if only he would have compassion. She saw him, for now not more than a few dozen yards separated them, and then, suddenly pointing at him, she broke out into a gabble and yell of curses. That made him smile.

"So you've changed your tune again, have you?" he thought, "for that doesn't sound much like good wishes. Curse away, old woman, if it relieves your mind, for it doesn't hurt me. But you'll have to be shifting once more, for I'm not going to have you and your like squatting there."

Cresswell rang up his friend the chief inspector of police, and was most politely told that matter should be seen to in the morning. Sure enough when he set out to go to his office next day, he saw that it was being attended to, for the European carpet which had served for a roof was already down, and the handcart was being laden with the stuff. He noticed, quite casually, that the two women and the boy were employed in lading it; the Levantine was lying on the sand and taking no part in the work. Two days later he had occasion to pass the pauper cemetery of Alexandria, where the poorest kind of funeral was going on. The coffin was being pushed to the side of the shallow grave on a handcart: a boy and two women followed it. He could see who they were.

He dined that night at the club in rare good-humour with the affairs of life. Already the municipality had offered him for his newly acquired freehold a sum that was double the debt for which it had been security, and though possibly he might get more if he stuck out for a higher price he had accepted it, and the money had been paid into his bank that day. To get a hundred per cent in a week was very satisfactory business, and who knew but that some new scheme of improvement might cause them to change their plans, leaving him with a ramshackle building on his hands for which he had no manner of use? He enjoyed his dinner and his wine, and particularly did he enjoy the rubber of bridge that followed. All went well with his finesses; he doubled his adversaries two or three times with the happiest results, they doubled him and were sorry for having spoken, and there would be a very pleasant item to enter in his card-account that evening.

It was later than usual when he quitted the club. Just outside there was a beggar-woman squatting at the edge of the pavement, who held her palm towards him and whined out blessings. Good-naturedly he fumbled in his pocket for a couple of piastres, and the blessings poured out in greater shrillness and copiousness as she pushed back the black veil that half shrouded her face to thank him for his beneficence to the needy widow. Next moment she threw his alms on the pavement, she spat at him, and like a moth she flitted away into the shadows.

Cresswell recognized her even as she had recognized him and picked up his piastres. It was amusing to think that the old hag so hated him that even his alms were abhorrent to her. "I'll drop them into that collecting-box outside the church," he thought to himself.

To-night, late though it was, there were many folk about in the square, natives for the most part, padding softly along, and there were still a few taxis on the rank. But he preferred to walk home, for he had been so busy all day that he had given his firm fat body no sort of exercise. So crossing the square he went up the street which led to his house. Here the cafés were already closed, and soon the pavements grew empty. The waning moon had risen, and though the lights of the street grew more sparse as he emerged into the residential quarter, his way lay bright before him. In his hand he still held the two piastres which had been flung back at him ready for the collection-box. He walked briskly, for the night was cool, and it was no exercise to saunter. Not a breath of wind stirred the air, and the clatter of the dry palm-leaves was dumb.

He was now approaching the Roman Catholic church, when a step suddenly sounded out crisp and distinct behind him. He remembered then for the first time what had happened some nights ago and halted and listened: not a sound broke the stillness. He whisked round, but the street seemed empty. On he went again, now and more slowly, and there was the following step again, neither gaining on him nor falling behind; to judge by the loudness of it, it could not be more than a dozen paces in his rear. Then a very obvious explanation occurred to him: no doubt this was some echo of his own footsteps. He went more quickly, and the steps behind him quickened; he stopped and they stopped. The whole thing was clear enough, and not a shadow of uneasiness, or anything approaching it, was in his mind. He slipped his ironical alms into the collecting-box outside the church, and was amused to hear that they evoked no tinkle from within. "Quite a little windfall for those brown-gowned fellows; they'll buy another rosary," he said to himself, and soon, with the echo of his own steps following, he turned in at his gate. Once inside, he slipped behind a myrtle bush that stood at the edge of the gravel walk, to see if by chance anyone passed on the road outside. But nothing happened, and his theory of the echo, though it was odd that he should never have noticed it till so lately, seemed quite confirmed.

From that night onwards he made it a practice, if he dined at the club, to walk home. Sometimes the step followed him, but not always, and this was an objection to that sensible echo theory. But the matter was no sort of worry to him except sometimes when he woke in the night, and found that his brain, still drowsy and not in complete control, was brooding over it with an ever-increasing preoccupation. Often that misgiving faded away and he dropped off to dreamless sleep again; sometimes it was sufficiently disquieting to bring him broad awake, and then with all his senses about him, it vanished. But there was this condition, half-way between waking and sleeping, when in the twilight chamber of his brain something listened, something feared. When fully awake he no more thought of it than he thought of that frowsy Levantine tobacco merchant whom he had evicted and whose funeral he chanced to have seen.

Early in December his cousin and partner in the sugar-business came down from Cairo to spend a week with him. Bill Cresswell may be succinctly described as "a hot lot," and often after dinner at the club he left his cousin to his cronies and the sedater pleasures of bridge, and went out with a duplicate latchkey in his pocket on livelier private affairs. One night, the last of Bill's sojourn here, there was "nothing doing" and the two set forth together homewards from the club.

"Nice night, let's walk," said John. "Nothing like a walk when there's liquid on board. Clears the brain for you and I must have a final powwow tonight, if you're off to-morrow. There are some bits of things still to go through."

Bill acquiesced. The cafés were all closed, there was nothing very promising.

"Night life here ain't a patch on Cairo," he observed. "Everyone seems to go to bed here just about when we begin to get going. Not but what I haven't enjoyed my stay with you. Capital good fellows at your club and brandy to match."

He stopped and ruefully scanned the quiet and emptiness of the street.

"Not a soul anywhere," he said. "Shutters up, all gone to bed. Nothing for it but a powwow, I guess."

They walked on in silence for a while. Then behind them, firm and distinct to John's ears, there sprang up the sound of the footsteps, for which now he knew that he waited and listened. He wheeled round.

"What's up?" asked Bill.

"Curious thing," said John. "Night after night now, though not every night, when I walk home, I hear a step following me. I heard it then."

Bill gave a vinous giggle.

"No such luck for me," he said. "I like to hear a step following me about one of a morning. Something agreeable may come of it. Wish I could hear it."

They walked on, and again, clearer than before, John heard what was inaudible to the other. He told himself, as he often did now, that it was an echo. But it was odd that the echo only repeated the footfalls of one of them. As he recognized this, he felt for the first time, when he was fully awake, some sudden chill of fear. It was as if a cold hand closed for a moment on his heart, just pressing it softly, almost tenderly. But they were now close to his own gate, and presently it clanged behind them.

Bill returned next day to the gladder life of Cairo. John Cresswell saw him off at the station and was passing out into the street again through the crowd of loungers and porters and passengers when there defined itself to his ear the sound of that footstep which he now knew so well. How he recognized it and isolated it from the tread of so many other feet he had no idea: simply his brain told him that it was following him again. He took a taxi to his office, and as he mounted the white stone stairs once more it was on his track. Once more the gentle pressure of cold fingers seemed to assure him of the presence that, though invisible, was very close to him, and now it was as if those fingers were pressed on some bell-push in his brain, and there sounded out a shrill tingle of fear. So hard-headed and sensible a man, of course, had nothing but scorn for all the clap-trap bogy tales of spirits and ghosts and hauntings, and he would have welcomed any sort of apparition in which the step manifested itself, in order to have the pleasure of laughing in its face. He would have liked to see a skeleton or some shrouded figure stand close to him; he would have slashed at it with his stick and convinced himself that there was nothing there. Whatever his own eyes appeared to see could not be so unnerving as these tokens of the invisible.

A stiff drink pulled him together again, and for the rest of the day there occurred no repetition of that tapping step which had begun to sprout with terror for him. In any case he was determined to fight it, for he realized that it was chiefly his own fear that troubled him. No doubt he was suffering from some small nervous derangement; he had been working very hard, and after Christmas, if the thing continued to worry him, probably he would see a doctor, who would prescribe him some tonic or some sedative which would send the step into the limbo from which it had come. But it was more probable that his cure was in his own hands: his own resistance was all the medicine he needed.

It was in pursuance of this very sane policy that he set out that night after an evening at the club to walk home: he faced it just because he knew that some black well was digging itself into his soul. To yield, to take a taxi, was to retreat, and if he did that, if he gave way an inch, he guessed that he might be soon flying in panic before an invading and imaginary host of phantoms. He had no use for phantoms; the solid satisfactions of life were enough occupation. Once more, as he drew near the church, the step sprang up, and now he sought no longer to tell himself it was an echo. Instead he fixed his mind on it, saying to himself, "There it is and it can't hurt me. Let it walk all day and night behind me if it chooses. It's got a fancy for me." Then his garden gate shut behind him, and with a sigh of relief he knew that he had passed out of its beat, for when once he was within, it never came farther.

He stood for a moment on his threshold, after he had opened his door, pleased with himself for having faced it. The bright light shone full on to the straight gravel walk he had just traversed. It was quite empty, and nothing was looking in through his gate. Then he heard from close at hand the crunch of the gravel underneath the heel of some invisible wayfarer. Now was the time to assert himself again, to look his fear in the eyes and mock at it.

"Come along, whoever you are," he called, "and have a drink before you get back to hell. Something cooling. Drop of cold water, isn't it?"

Thick sweat had broken out on his forehead, and his hand on the door-knob shook as with ague as he stood there looking out on to the bright empty path. But he did not flinch from the lesson he was teaching himself. The seconds ticked away: he could count them from the pulse that hammered in his throat. "I'll give it a hundred beats," he said to himself, "and then I'll say good night to Mr. Nothing-at-all."

He counted his hundred, he gave ten beats more for good luck. "Good night, you old fraud," he said, and went in and secured the door.

It seemed indeed for the week that followed that he had rightly gauged the nature of the hallucination which had threatened to establish its awful dominion over him. Never once, whether by day or night, did there come to his ears that footfall which he feared and listened for, nor, if in the dead hours of the darkness he lay for a while between sleep and waking, did he quake with a sense that something unseen and aware was watching him. A little courage, a flat denial of his fears had been sufficient not only to scotch them, but to snuff out the manifestation which had caused them. He kept his thoughts well in hand, he would not even conjecture what had been the cause of that visitation. Occasionally, while it still vexed him, he had cast about for the origin of it, he had wondered whether that shrill Levantine hag calling curses on him could somehow have found root in his mind. But now it was past and done with: he would have a few days' remission from work, if it was overwork that had been at the bottom of it, at Christmas, and perhaps it would be prudent not to be quite so free with the club brandy.

On Christmas Eve he and his friends sat at their bridge till close on midnight, then lingered over a drink, wished each other seasonable greetings and dispersed. Cresswell hesitated as to whether he should not take a taxi home, for the object with which he had trudged back there so often seemed to be gained, and he no longer feared the recurrence of the step. But he thought he would just set the seal on his victory and went on foot.

He had come to the point in his walk where he had first heard the step. To-night, as usual, there was none, and he stopped a moment looking round him securely and serenely. It was a bright night, luminous with a moon a little after the full, and it amazed him to think that he had ever fashioned a terror to himself in this quiet, orderly street. From not far ahead there came the sound of the bells of the church saluting Christmas morning. They would have been holding their midnight Mass there. He breathed the night air with content, and throwing the butt of his spent cigar into the roadway, he walked on again.

With a sudden sinking of his heart, he heard behind him the step which he thought he had silenced for ever. It was faint at first, but to-night, instead of keeping at a uniform distance behind him, it was approaching. Louder and more crisp it sounded, until it was close to him. On and on it came, still gaining on him, and now there brushed by him, though not quite touching him, the figure of a man in European dress, with his head wrapped in a shawl.

"Hullo, you there," called Cresswell. "You're the skunk who's been following me, are you, and slipping out of sight again? No more of your damned conjuring tricks. Let's have a look at you."

The figure, now some two or three yards ahead of him, stopped at the sound of his voice and turned round. The shawl covered its face, but for a narrow chink between the edges.

"So you understand English," said Cresswell. "Now I'll thank you to take that shawl off your face, and let me see who it is that's been dogging me."

The man raised his hands and threw back the shawl. The moonlight shone on his face, and that face was just a slab of smooth yellowish flesh extending from ear to ear, empty as the oval of an egg without eyes or nose or mouth. From the upper edge of the shawl where it crossed the forehead there depended a few wisps of grey hair.

Cresswell looked, and a wave of panic fear submerged his very soul. He gave a little thin squeal and started to run, listening the while in an agony of terror to hear if the steps of that nameless, faceless, creature were following. He must run, he must run, to get away from that thing out of hell which had manifested itself.

Then close at hand he saw the lights of the church, and there perhaps he could find sanctuary from it. The door was open, and he sprang up the steps. Close by there were lights burning on the altar of a side chapel, and he flung himself on his knees. Not for years had he attempted to pray, and now in the agony of his soul he could but say in a gabbling whisper, "O my God: O my God." Over and over he said it.

By degrees some sort of self-control came back to him. There were holy images, there was a sacred picture above the altar, a smell of hallowing incense was in the air. Surely there was protection here, a power that would intervene between him and the terror of that face. A sort of tranquillity overscored his panic, and he began to look round.

The church was darker than it had been when he entered, and he saw that some of those cowled brown-habited men of the order were moving quietly about, quenching the lights. Those at the altar in front of which he knelt were still bright, and now he saw one of these cowled figures move up close to him, as if waiting for him to finish his devotions. He was calm now, his panic had quite passed, and he rose from his knees.

"I've had a terrible fright, Father," he said to the monk. "I saw something just now out in the street which must have come out of hell."

The figure turned a little towards him: the cowl concealed its face altogether, and the voice came muffled.

"Indeed, my son," he said. "Tell me what it is that frightened you."

Cresswell felt some backwash of his panic returning

"A man passed me as I was going back to my house," he said, "and I told him to stop and let me have a look at him. He wore a shawl over his head and he threw it back. Oh, my God, that face!"

The monk quietly raised his hands and grasped the edges of his cowl. Then with a quick movement he threw it back.

"That sort of face?" he said.

THE BED BY THE WINDOW

My friend Lionel Bailey understands the works of Mr. Einstein, and he reads them with the rapt, thrilled attention that more ordinary people give to detective stories. He says they are so exciting that he cannot put them down: they make him late for dinner. It may be owing to this unusual mental conformation of his that he talks about time and space in a manner that is occasionally puzzling, for he thinks of them as something quite different from our accepted notions of them, and tonight, as we sat over my fire hearing a spring-gale of March bugling outside, and dashing solid sheets of rain against my window, I had found him very difficult to follow. But though he thinks in terms which the average man finds unintelligible, he is always ready (though with an effort) to quit the austere heights on which he naturally roams, and explain. And his explanations are often so lucid that the average man (I allude to myself) can generally get some idea of what he means. Just now he had made some extremely cryptic remark about the real dimensions of time, and of the palpable incorrectness of our conception of it; but rightly interpreting the moaning sound with which I received this, he very kindly came to my aid.

"You see, time, as we think of it," he said, "is a most meaningless convention. We talk of the future and the past as if they were opposite poles, whereas they are really the same. What we thought of as the future a minute ago or a century ago, we now see to be the past; the future is always in process of becoming the past. The two are the same, as I said just now, looked at from different points."

"But they aren't the same," said I, rather inincautiously. "The future may become the past, but the past never becomes the future."

Lionel sighed.

"A most unfortunate remark," he said. "Why, the whole of the future is made up of the past; it entirely depends on it; the future consists of nothing else but the past."

I did see what he meant. There was no denying it, so I tried something else.

"A slippery slidey affair altogether," I said. "The future becomes the past, and the past the future. But luckily there's one firm spot in this welter, and that's the present. That's solid; there's nothing wrong with the present, is there?"

Lionel moved slightly in his chair – an indulgent, patient movement.

"Oh dear, oh dear," he said. "You've chosen as your firm, solid point the most shifting and unstable of all. What is the present? By the time you've said 'This is the present,' it has slid away into the past. The past has got some sort of real existence and we know that the future will blossom out of it. But the present hardly can be said to exist at all, for the moment you say that it is here, it has changed. It is far the most elusive part of the phantom which we call Time. It is the door, that is the most that can be said for it, through which the future passes into the past. And somehow, though it scarcely exists, we can see from it into the past and into the future."

I felt I could venture to contradict that.

"Thank heaven we can't," I said. "It would be the ultimate terror to be able to see into the future. It's bad enough sometimes to be able to remember the past."

He shook his head.

"But we can see into the future," he said. "The future is entirely evolved out of the past, and if we knew everything about the past, we should equally know everything about the future. Everything that happens is merely a fresh link in the chain of unalterable consequences. The little we know about the solar system, for instance, makes it a certainty that the sun will rise to-morrow."

"Oh, that kind of thing," said I. "Just material, mathematical deductions."

"No, all kinds of things. For instance, I'm sure you know the certainty that we all have now and then that somebody present is about to say some particular definite sentence. A few seconds pass, and then out it comes precisely as we had known it would. That's not so material and mathematical. It's a little instance of a very big thing called clairvoyance."

"I know what you mean," I said. "But it may be some trick of the brain. It isn't a normal experience."

"Everything is normal," said Lionel. "Everything depends on some rule. We only call things abnormal when we don't know what the rule is. Then there are mediums: mediums constantly see into the future, and to some extent everyone is a medium: we've all had glimpses."

He paused a moment.

"And there is such a simple explanation," he said. "You see, we're all existing in eternity, though just for the span of our lifetime we're also existing in Time. But there's eternity outside Time: Time is a sort of mist lying round us. Now and then the mist clears, and then – how shall I express anything so simple? – then we look down on Time, like a little speck of an island below us, quite clear, future and past and present, and awfully small. We get just a glimpse, no more, and then the mist closes round us again. But on these occasions we can see into the future just as clearly as we can look into the past, and we can see not only those who have passed outside the mist of material phenomena, whom we call ghosts, but the future or the past of those who are still inside it. They all appear to us then as they are in eternity, where there is neither past nor future."

I suddenly found that my grip on what he was saying was beginning to give way.

"That's enough for one night," said I flippantly. "The future is the past, and the past is the future, and there isn't any present, and ghosts may come from what has happened or what will happen. I should like to see a ghost out of the future . . . And as you've had a whisky and soda in the immediate past, I feel sure you will have one in the immediate future, as it's the same thing. Say when."

I was off into the country next day in order to make amends for a couple of months of wilful idleness in London by hermitizing myself in a small village on the coast of Norfolk, where I knew nobody, and where, I was credibly informed, there was nothing to do; I should thus have to work in order to get through the hours of the day. There was a house there, kept by a man and his wife who took in lodgers, and there I proposed to plant myself till I had got through these criminal arrears. Mr. Hopkins had been a butler, and his wife a cook, and – so I was told by a friend who had made trial of their ministrations – they made their inmates extremely comfortable. There were a couple of other folk, Mr. Hopkins had written to me, now staying in the house, and he regretted he could not give me a sitting-room to myself. But he could provide me with a big double bedroom, where there was ample room for a writing-table and my books. That was good enough.

Hopkins had ordered a car to convey me from the nearest railway-station, six miles distant, to Faringham, and a little before sunset, on a bright windy day of March, I came to the village. Though I had certainly never been here before, I had some odd sense of remote familiarity with it, and I supposed I must have seen and forgotten some hamlet which was like it. There was just one street lined with fishermen's houses, built of rounded flints, with nets hung up to dry on the walls of small plots in front, and a few miscellaneous shops. We passed through the length of this, and came at the end to a much bigger, three-storied house, at the gate of which we stopped. A spacious square of garden separated it from the road, with espaliered pear-trees bordering the path that led to the front door; beyond flat open country stretched away to the horizon, intersected with big dykes and ditches, across which I could see, a mile distant, a line of white shingle where lay the sea. My arrival was hooted on the motor-horn, and Hopkins, a prim dark spare man, came out to see to my luggage. His wife was waiting inside, and she took me up to my room. Certainly it would do very well: there were two windows commanding a view of the marsh eastwards, in one of which was set a big writing-table. A fire sparkled on the hearth, two beds stood in opposite angles of the room, one near the second window, the other by the fireplace, in front of which was a large arm-chair. This arm-chair had a footstool, under the table was a waste-paper basket, and on it one of those old-fashioned but convenient contrivances which show the day of the month and the day of the week, with pegs to adjust them. Everything had been thought out for comfort, everything looked spotlessly clean and cared-for, and at once I felt myself at home here.

"But what a charming room, Mrs. Hopkins," I said. "It's just what I want."

She moved away from the door as I spoke, to let her husband enter with my bags. She gave him one swift ugly look, and I found myself thinking, "How she dislikes him!" But the impression was momentary, and having elected to sleep in the bed by the fireplace, I went downstairs with her for a cup of tea, while her husband unpacked for me.

When I came up again the unpacking was over, and all my effects disposed, clothes laid in drawers and cupboards, and my books and papers neatly stacked on the table. There was no settling down to be done; I had stepped into possession of this pleasant room as if I had long lived and worked in it. Then my eye fell on the little adjustable contrivance on the table for displaying the current date, and I saw that this one detail had escaped the vigilance of my hosts, for it marked Tuesday, May 8th, instead of the true date, Thursday, March 22nd. I was rather pleased to observe that the Hopkinses were not too perfect, and after twisting the record back to the correct date I instantly settled down to work, for there was nothing to get used to before I felt at home.

A plain and excellent dinner was served some three hours later, and I found that one of my fellow-guests was an elderly sepulchral lady with a genteel voice who spoke but rarely and then about the weather. She had by her on the table a case of Patience cards and a bottle of medicine. She took a dose of the latter before and after her meal, and at once retired to the common sitting-room, where that night and every night she played long sad games of

Patience. The other was a ruddy young man who confided to me that he was making a study of the minute fresh-water fleas that infest fresh-water snails, for which daily he dragged the dykes. He had been so fortunate as to find a new species which would undoubtedly be called Pulex Dodsoniana in his honour. Hopkins waited on us with soft velvet-footed attention, and his wife brought in the admirable fruits of her kitchen. Once there was some slight collision of crockery in her tray, and happening to look up I saw the glance he gave her. It was not mere dislike that inspired it, but some quiet, deadly hatred. Dinner over, I went in for a few minutes to the sitting-room, where the sepulchral lady was sitting down to her Patience and Mr. Dodson to his microscope, and very soon betook myself upstairs to resume my work.

The room was pleasantly warm, my things laid out for the night, and for a couple of hours I busied and buried myself. Then the door of the room, without any enquiry of knocking, silently opened, and Mrs. Hopkins stood there. She gave a little gasp of dismay as she saw me.

"I'm sure I beg your pardon, sir," she said. "I quite forgot; so stupid of me. But this is the room my husband and I usually occupy, if it is not being used. So forgetful of me."

I awoke next morning after long traffic with troubled, nonsensical dreams to find the sun pouring in at the windows as Hopkins drew up the blinds. I thought that Mr. Dodson had come in to show me a collection of the diamond-shaped fleas that battened on Patience cards, or, rather, that would be hatched on Tuesday, May 8th, for, as he pointed out, there were none there now since the present had no existence. And then Hopkins, who had been bending over the bed by the window, apologized for being in my room, and explained that he could hate his wife more intensely here: he hoped that I had not been disturbed by him. Then there was the crack of some explosion, which resolved itself into the rattle of the up-going blind, and there indeed he was . . . I was soon out of bed and dressing, but somehow that farrago of dream-stuff concocted out of actual experience, hung about me. I could not help feeling that there was significance in it, if I could only find the clue. It did not, as is usual with dreams, fade and evaporate with my waking; it seemed to retreat into hidden caves and recesses of my brain and wait in ambush there till it was called out.

Then my eye fell on the date-recorder on my table, and I saw with surprise that it still registered Tuesday, May 8th, though I would have been willing to swear that last night I had adjusted it to the correct date. And with that surprise was mingled a faint and rather uncomfortable misgiving, and involuntarily I asked myself *what* Tuesday, *what* May 8th was indicated there. Was it some day in past years, or in years yet to come? I knew that such a question was an outrage on common sense; probably I imagined that I had screwed the cylinders back to the present, but had not actually done so. But now I felt that this date referred to some event that had happened or was to happen. It recorded the past, or . . . was it like a railway-signal suddenly hoisted at night at some wayside station? The line lay empty, but presently out of the darkness would come a yell and a roar from the approaching train . . . This time, anyhow, there should be no mistake, and I knew that I moved the date back again.

The days passed slowly at first, as is their wont in new surroundings, and then began to move with ever-accelerating speed as I settled into an industrious routine. I worked all morning, turned myself unwillingly out of doors for a couple of hours in the afternoon, and worked again after tea and once more till round about midnight. My task prospered, I was well, and the house most comfortable, but all the time there was some instinct bidding me leave the place, or, since I successfully resisted that, to get through with my work as soon as might be and be gone. That strong tonic air of the coast often made me drowsy when I came in, and I would slip from my desk into the big arm-chair and sleep for a while. But always after these short recuperative naps, I would wake with a start, feeling that Hopkins had come silently into the room as I slept, and in some inexplicable panic of mind I would wheel round, dreading to see him. Yet it was not, if I may so express it, his bodily presence which I feared, but some psychical phantom of him, which had sinister business on hand in this room. His thoughts were here – was that it? – something in him that hated and schemed. That business was not concerned with me; I seemed to be but a spectator waiting for the curtain to rise on some grim drama. Then, as this confused and fearful moment of waking passed, the horror slipped away, not dispersing exactly, but concealing itself and ready to emerge again.

Yet all the time the routine of the well-ordered house went smoothly on. Hopkins was busy with his jobs, doing much of the housework, and valeting and waiting at table; his wife continued to ply her admirable skill in the kitchen. Sometimes its door would be open, as I went upstairs after dinner, and I had a glimpse of them as I passed, sitting friendly at their supper. Indeed, I began to wonder whether that gleam of dislike on the one side and of sheer hate on the other which I fancied I had seen was not a fiction of my own mind, for if it was real there would surely be some betrayal of the truth, a voice raised in anger, and a sudden shrill answer. But there was none; quietly and efficiently the two went about their work, and sometimes late at night I could hear them pass to the attic-floor above, where they slept. A few footsteps would sound muffled overhead, and then there was silence, till, early in the morning, I, half-awake, heard the discreet movements begin again, and soft footfalls pass my door on their way downstairs.

This room of mine, where for three weeks now I had been so prosperously at work, was growing a haunted and a terrible place to me. Never once had I seen in it anything outside the ordinary, nor heard any sound that betokened another presence except my own and that of the flapping flames on the hearth, and I told myself that it was I, or, more exactly, my fanciful sense of the unseen and the unheard that was troubling me and causing this ghostly invasion. Yet the room itself had a share in it too, for downstairs, or out in the windy April day, or even just outside the door of the room, I was wholly free of this increasing obsession. Something had happened here which had left its mark not on material things, and which was imperceptible to the organs of sight and hearing, the effect of which was trickling not merely into my brain but filtering through it into the very source of life. Yet the explanation that a phantom was arising out of the past would not wholly fit, for whatever this haunting was, it was getting nearer, and though its lineaments were not yet visible, they were forming with greater distinctness below the veil that hid them. It was establishing touch with me, as if it was some denizen of a remote world that reached across time and space, and was already laying its fingers on me, and it took advantage of small physical happenings in that room to encompass me with its influence. For instance, when one evening I was brushing my hair before dinner, a white featureless face peered over my shoulder, and then, with an arrested shudder, I saw that this was only the reflection of the oval looking-glass on the ceiling. Or, as I lay in bed, before putting out my light, a puff of wind came in through the open sash, making the striped curtain to belly, and before I could realize the physical cause of it, there was a man in striped pyjamas bending over the bed by the window. Or a wheeze of escaping gas came from the coals on the hearth, and to my ears it sounded like a strangled gasp of someone in the room. Something was at work, using the trivial sounds and sights for its own ends, kneading away in my brain to make it ready and receptive for the revelation it was preparing for it. It worked very cleverly, for the morning after the curtain had shaped itself into the pyjamaed figure bending over the other bed, Hopkins, when he called me, apologized for his attire. He had overslept himself, and in order not to delay further, had come down in a coat over his striped pyjamas. Another night the breeze lifted the cretonne covering that lay over the bed by the window, inflating it into the shape of a body there. It stirred and turned before it was deflated again, and it was just then that the coal on the hearth gasped and choked.

But by now my work was completed; I had determined not to yield to the fear of any strange and troubling fancies until that was done, and to-night, very late, I scrawled a dash across the page below the final words, and added the date. I sat back in my chair, yawning and tired and pleased that I was now free to go back to London next day. For nearly a week now I had been the only lodger in the house, and I reflected how natural it was that, diving into myself all day over my work, and seeing nobody, I had been creating phantoms, to keep me company. Idly enough, my glance lighted on the record of the day of the week and the month, and I saw that once more it showed Tuesday, May 8th . . . Next moment I perceived that my eyes had played me false; they had visualized something that was inside my brain, for a second glance told me that the day indicated there was indeed Tuesday, but April 24th.

"Certainly it's time I went away," I said to myself.

The fire was out, and the room rather cold. Feeling very sleepy, and also very content that I had finished my task, I undressed quickly, not troubling to open the window by the other bed. But the curtains were undrawn and the blind was up, and the last thing I saw before I went to sleep was a narrow slip of moonlight on the floor.

I awoke, at any rate I thought I awoke. The moonlight had broadened to a thick oblong patch, very bright. The bed beyond it was in shadow, but clearly visible, and I saw that there was someone sleeping there. And there was someone standing at the foot of the bed, a man in striped pyjamas. He took a couple of steps across the patch of moonlight, and then swiftly thrusting his arms forward, he bent over the bed. The figure that lay there moved: the knees shot up, and an arm came out from beneath the coverlet. The bed creaked and shuddered with the struggle that was going on, but the man held tight to what he was grasping. He jumped on to the bed, crushing the knees flat again, and over his shoulder I saw and recognized the face of the woman who lay there. Once she got her neck free from the strangle-hold and I heard a long straining gasp for breath. Then the man's fingers found their place again: once more the bed shook as with the quivering of leaves in a wind, and after that all was still.

The man got up; he stood for a moment in the patch of moonlight, wiping the sweat from his face, and I could see him clearly. And then I knew that I was sitting up in bed, looking out into the familiar room. It was bright with the big patch of moonlight that lay on the floor, and empty and quiet. There was the other bed with its cretonne covering, flat and tidy.

The sequel is probably familiar to most people as the Faringham murder. On the morning of May 8 according to the account given by Hopkins to the police, he came downstairs as usual from the attic where he had slept about half-past seven, and found that the lock of the front door of his house had been forced, and the door was open. His wife was not yet down, and he went upstairs to the room on the first floor where they often slept together, when it was not being used by their guests, and found her lying strangled in her bed. He instantly rang up the police and also the doctor, though he felt sure she was dead, and while waiting for them observed that a drawer of the table, in which she was accustomed to keep the money she had in the house, had been broken open. She had been to the bank the day before and cashed a cheque for fifty pounds, in order to pay the bills of last month, and the notes were missing. He had seen her place them in the drawer when she brought them back. Questioned as to his having slept in the attic, while his wife had slept alone below, he said that this room had been lately occupied, and would be occupied again in a few days; he had not therefore thought it worth while to move down, though his wife had done so.

But there were two weak points in this story. The first was that the woman had been strangled as she lay in bed, full length, with the blankets and sheet over her. But if the supposed burglar had throttled her, because she had been awakened by his entrance, and threatened to raise the alarm, it seemed incredible that she should have remained lying there with the bedclothes up to her chin. Again, though the drawer into which she had put her money had been forced, it had not been locked. The burglar had only got to pull the handle of it, and it would have opened. Hopkins was detained, and the house searched, and the missing roll of notes was found in the lining of an old great-coat of his in the attic. Before he suffered the extreme penalty, he confessed his crime and told the manner of its execution. He had come down from his bedroom, entered his wife's room and strangled her. He had then forced the front door from outside, and, unnecessarily, the drawer where she had put her money . . . Reading it, I thought of Lionel Bailey's theory, and my own experience in the room where the murder was committed.

JAMES LAMP

Mr. John Storely, bachelor, of middle-age, and very comfortable circumstances, had lately retired from his extensive practice in London, while still in sound health and activity, for, as he justly remarked, what was the good of keeping in harness till you were too old and infirm to enjoy a well-earned leisure. He still spent most of the year in town, for he was of sociable habits, and the country, so he thought, was a very dreary place for a single man, who neither hunted nor shot, from the time when the autumn leaves began to fall until spring had definitely established itself again. There were fogs and darkness, it was true, in London, but there were also gas-lamps and pavements, and a walk along lighted streets to his club, where he would find a rubber of bridge before dinner was infinitely preferable to a tramp in dim and dripping country lanes, and the return again to his house at Trench, a small country-town at the edge of the Romney Marsh, where he would spend a solitary evening. Winter days in the country closed in early, a servant came round and drew the curtain, and then you were shut up in your box till morning, whereas in London there were many friends about, and pleasant dinners at home or abroad, amusements of all sorts ready to hand. As for going to some winter resort like the Riviera, the thought was anathema to him. People went to the Riviera to get sunshine and all they got was blizzards and possibly pneumonia. London, to his mind, was the ideal place in which to spend the winter.

He had therefore arranged his life on these lines. His delightful little house down at Trench was in the hands of a caretaker and his wife from November till April; during the late spring and earlier autumn Storely was often down there for a week or a week-end, and then Mr. and Mrs. Lamp looked after him, she as cook with housemaid's help got in from the town, and her husband as general manservant. When summer arrived he moved his London household down there for four or five solid months, while the caretakers took charge of his house in London. Like a sensible man, he knew that a motor, now that he had no rounds of professional visits to pay, was a mere encumbrance in town, and accordingly he left his car at Trench throughout the winter.

He had bought this house some three years ago, just before he retired, and I had often been down to stay with him for these week-ends of spring and autumn, and for longer periods during the summer. It stood half-way down one of those steep, cobbled streets for which Trench is famous, and was the most adorable establishment. Three small gables of timber and rough-cast faced the road, and from the front it seemed rather shut in, but once inside, it opened out into a dignified and spacious privacy. There was a little panelled hall with an oak staircase leading up to the first floor, and on each side of it a big ceiling-beamed room with wide open fireplace, and all looked out at the back on to a full acre of unexpected lawn and garden, screened by high red brick walls from the intrusion of neighbouring eyes. He had done the house up with due regard for its picturesque antiquity but with an equal regard for all possible demands of modern comfort: electric light was most conveniently installed, central heating supplemented the log-burning, open hearths, and the three big bedrooms on the first floor had each its own bathroom. Just as perfect were the ministrations of the caretaking couple when Storely went down for the shorter periods of his sojourn, Lamp, deft and silent-footed, and his wife, mostly invisible in her kitchen, manifesting her presence there by the most admirable meals. One saw her occasionally when she came up after breakfast to submit to Storely her proposed caterings for the day, a handsome, high-coloured woman, with a hard smart air about her, and considerably younger than her husband; sometimes one met her in the town with her marketing-basket, and many smiles and ribands.

I was engaged in the spring of this year to spend a week at Easter with my friend. A few days before I met him in the card-room at the club, and we cut into a table of bridge together. After a couple of rubbers we cut out again, and he beckoned me aside to a remote corner, where we could talk privately.

"Upsetting news from Trench yesterday morning," he said. "A couple of days ago Mrs. Lamp, my caretaker's wife; do you remember her?"

"Indeed, I do," said I.

"Well, she disappeared, and has not been seen since. She used often to take long walks in the country by herself when the two were alone there in the winter, and a couple of days ago she appears to have started for one, as was quite usual with her, but when the evening closed in and it had got dark she had not returned. Lamp behaved very sensibly and properly: he went to a house or two in the town where his wife sometimes visited, but no one had seen her, and about eleven o'clock that night, now feeling very uneasy, he went to the police-station, and told the inspector that she was still missing. They telephoned to various villages in the neighbourhood, and to wayside stations on the line, but got no news of her; beyond that there was nothing more that could be done that night. Morning came, but there was still no sign of her, and Lamp telephoned to me to say what had happened. I went down there after breakfast this morning, and he disclosed to me a state of things of which I had no suspicion at all."

"A man?" I asked.

"Yes; the foreman in some builder's establishment in Hastings. Lamp and his wife had had words about him before, and a fortnight ago, in consequence of what he had seen, he had told the man he mustn't set foot in the house again, but he had been seen in Trench on the day that his wife disappeared. All this Lamp told me, but he had not mentioned it to the police, since naturally he did not want scandal to get about. But now, when his wife disappeared, it seemed to us that it was necessary to let the police know, in case she had gone to him, and I sent for the inspector and told him about it. He made enquiries in Hastings, but nothing could be heard about her. The foreman admitted that he had been in Trench that day, but said he had not seen her. He admitted also, when he was closely questioned, that he and Mrs. Lamp had agreed that she should leave her husband and come to live with him. They intended to marry if Lamp would divorce her."

"And how is Lamp taking it?" I asked.

"My own opinion is that he will be much happier without her. He believes that she has gone to this foreman, though why, if she has, they should try to make a secret about it, it is impossible to say. But that is his firm conviction. The two, so Lamp told me, have had a horrible time of it this winter, and if she was never heard of again I don't think he would be sorry. She certainly has made their life together a wretched business."

"But at present there's no clue as to what has happened to her?" I asked.

"Absolutely none. The police expect loss of memory and sense of identity, as they always do when anyone disappears, and they're keeping an eye on this man in Hastings. It was painful to hear Lamp tell the story of all this, but he did it very frankly, and they're convinced that he has told all he knows. Apparently there is quite sufficient evidence for him to get his divorce, and if she tries to come back to him again, he means to do it.

Storely got up.

"I thought I would just tell you," he said, "for we'll go down there as arranged the day after tomorrow. Lamp says he can get a woman from Trench to come in and cook, and like a sensible fellow he wants to get back to work again. Far the best thing for him to do."

So we went down together as had been settled: Trench looked more attractive and idyllic than ever in this sudden burst of spring and warm April weather. Its red-brick houses climbing up the hill glowed in the mellow sunshine, its gardens were gay with fresh leaf and blossom. In the reclaimed marshland outside, the hawthorn hedges were in bud, innumerable lambs bleated and gambolled over the meadows, and the woods in the country round about were tapestried with primroses and anemone and curled bracken-shoots. It is a land of greenness and streams and slow rivers wending over the levels to the sea: on the east side of the small town the Roop wanders along under the steep hills, on the west side the bigger Inglis sweeps widely past the south of the town and joins the other. Half-way down this western slope of the hill was Storely's house, looking out on to the narrow cobbled street lined with gabled cottages. At the bottom of it, not fifty yards from his door stand granaries and warehouses on the banks of the River Inglis, up which, at high tide, vessels of considerable tonnage can come to anchor and discharge their freights. The road to Hastings passes along this bank, then crosses the river by a bridge, at the side of which are sluice-gates to be opened or shut to let through or limit the tide.

We strolled out after tea on the day of our arrival, Storely and I, across this bridge. The tide was low, and one could see how deeply the flows and ebbs of the water had scooped out, below the sluice, great holes lined with soft shining mud, while others deeper yet were still undiscovered. From there we strolled into a path leading across the daisied meadows of the marsh and bordered by dykes still brimming with the winter rains and fringed with the new growth of the reeds that pricked up through the dead raffle of last year. The sun was low to its setting, and now after this hot day skeins of mist were beginning to form over the level in the chill of the evening, shallow at present but so opaque that at a little distance they appeared like sheets of grey flood-water through which stood up the trunks of the scattered thorn-trees. Then turning we set our faces towards Trench, the topmost houses of which, set on the hill, still glowed in the sunlight though now on this lower land we walked in the shadow. As we crossed the bridge over the Inglis the mist had formed very thick upon the river, and like a tide had crept across the quayside, and out in the Channel fog-horns were mooing. We stepped briskly across the vaporous lake to the foot of the steep cobbled street, half-way up which stood Storely's house. The pavement was narrow, not giving room for two to walk abreast, and I fell behind him. Just here there joined this street on our right a narrow footway faced with houses leading round to the south face of the hill, and as we passed this, I saw there was a woman standing there. Her back was towards me, and she was looking up the street in the direction of Storely's house. He was a few paces ahead of me, and as I came directly opposite her she turned, and I felt sure that her face was familiar to me though for the moment I could not recollect who she was. Then close on the heels of that came recognition, and I knew that she was Mrs. Lamp. It was dusk, it was misty and I could not see her face very precisely, but I had no doubt of her identity.

I took a few quick steps forward, and touched Storely on the shoulder.

"Turn round," I said quietly, "and have a look at that woman standing at the corner just below. See if you recognize her!"

He turned, peering into the dusk.

"But I don't see any woman at all," he said. "There's no one there."

I turned also, and even as Storely had said, she was no longer there. I ran back to the corner where the footpath joined the street, and there she was moving up it away from us. I beckoned to him, pointing up this footway.

"But what's all this about?" he asked.

"I want you to see her," said I. "She's walking up that path. Be quick, or she'll have gone."

He laughed.

"But I really can't go in pursuit of women in the dusk about the streets of Trench," he said. "Who is it that you want me to identify?"

"I feel sure it's Mrs. Lamp," I answered.

Instantly he joined me.

"What? Mrs. Lamp?" he said in a changed voice. "Where? That woman ahead there? I'll soon see."

I waited at the corner while he went quickly after her. They both passed out of sight round a bend in the footpath. In a couple of minutes he returned.

"I lost sight of her somehow," he said. "She must have turned into one of those houses there, though I didn't see her do so. Are you sure it was she?"

"No: that's why I wanted you to see her. But if it wasn't she, it was somebody most extraordinarily like her."

He thought a moment.

"I think we had better not say anything either to Lamp or the police at present," he said. "We're not certain enough, for it's dusk, and after all you've only seen her a few times before. But if it is she, you may depend upon it that someone else will see her. We shall soon know."

Lamp was in the sitting-room when we got to the house. It was already chilly, and he had just put a match to the fire of logs and brushwood on the hearth, had turned the lights on, and was now drawing the curtains; I thought he peered oddly and intently up and down the street before he pulled the heavy folds across the windows. Somehow the sight (or so I believed) of the missing woman, had roused an uneasy feeling in my mind, but how utterly illogical and senseless that was. For if it was she, all fear of her having come to some ill end was over, while if it was not she, there could be nothing unsettling in having seen some other woman who strangely reminded me of her. But it was odd, it was also regrettable that Storely had lost sight of her like that. If he had only had one decent look at her, the question would have been settled.

We spent a quiet evening, playing a rather serious game of chess after dinner. About ten o'clock, while the game was still in progress, Lamp brought in a tray of water and spirits, and while he was in the room their came a soft tapping, very light, against the low diamond-paned window behind the curtain, looking out onto the street. At the moment he was pouring some whisky into a glass, and looking up, I saw he had paused as if listening.

"What was that tapping?" asked Storely absently, as he considered his move.

"A butterfly, sir," said Lamp. "I saw one fluttering about the window when I drew the curtains this evening."

"Must have been encouraged to come out after the winter by this hot sun," said Storely. "That's all we shall want, Lamp. You can go to bed: I'll put out the lights.

Lamp left us, Storely made his move, and as I was considering mine the soft tapping came again. He rose and went to the window.

"It sounded just as if someone was tapping at the pane from outside," he said.

He parted the curtain and looked out. There was silence for a moment.

"Just come here," he said to me.

The light from inside the room as he drew the curtain back cast a field of illumination into the street, and outside looking into the window was the figure of a woman. I could see her face clearly, and it was certainly that of her whom I had seen that evening in the flesh as we returned from our walk. She looked at Storely, then at me, and then between us into the room behind as if she was wanting somebody but not one of us.

"Stop there and watch her," said Storely to me, and he went out into the hall, and I heard him unlock the front door. The woman turned at the sound, and moved away from the window into the darkness. I heard Storely's step on the pavement outside, and he beckoned and called to me through the window.

"She's gone," he said. "Did you see which way she went?"

"I think down the hill," I said, and I heard his steps following her. I went out after him into the street. It was an exceedingly dark night and misty: I could not see more than a few yards in any direction. The light in the hall shone out of the open door, and I saw also that at the top of the house was a lit window against which was framed a man's head. Lamp had evidently gone up to bed, and, hearing the sound of Storely's voice in the street, was looking out. In a few minutes I heard Storely's returning steps.

"Come in," he said, "I lost her at once, for the fog is fearfully thick at the bottom of the hill."

He closed the door, and we sat down again on either side of our chess-board. Though the game was only half over he began putting the pieces back in the box.

"What am I to do?" he said. "There's no doubt who it was. But why is she here, and why does she come at night and tap at the window and then make off again? Did you see her looking between us as if she wanted somebody else? And if it's Lamp she wants, why doesn't she come and ask for him? Anyhow I must go round to the police station in the morning to tell them they needn't make any further enquiries about her, as she has certainly been seen. They aren't concerned about her connubial affairs, but only about her disappearance, and now that we're sure she's alive there's nothing more for them to investigate. Hullo, I've scrapped our game." He stared into the smouldering embers of the fire for a moment in silence, then wheeled round to me.

"It's all rather odd," he said. "I've no doubt it is she; absolutely none. But why did she come here at all, if it was only to sheer off again in that mysterious way? I wonder if by any chance Lamp has seen her? Surely he would have told me if he had."

Even as he spoke the door opened and Lamp came in.

"I beg your pardon, sir," he said, "but I had just gone up to bed when I heard you go out and call from the street. I came down to see if you were wanting anything."

Storely pointed to the window.

"Your wife was standing outside there a few minutes ago," he said. "I went out to see what she was doing here."

I was watching Lamp closely now, for an idea, wild and fantastic no doubt, had entered my head. He was standing by the electric light, and I saw sudden beads of perspiration break out on his forehead, and his lips moved as if for speech, but no words came. But he quickly recovered himself.

"Indeed, sir?" he said. "And may I ask if you got speech with her?"

"No, she disappeared in the fog before I could come up with her. But you can dismiss from your mind now any fear that some accident has happened to her. I shall go round to the police-station in the morning, and tell them they need not continue their search for her."

"Thank you very much, sir," said Lamp. "But I was never really afraid of that. I always thought that she had gone off with that man of hers . . . And there's another thing, sir, if you wouldn't mind my mentioning it. I'll get all her clothes and bits of things ready packed for her, if it's that she's hanging about for, but I hope you won't allow her into the house again after what she's done."

"No, that's reasonable," said Storely, "I won't let her bother you if I can help it. You haven't seen her I suppose?"

Again I watched Lamp. I saw him gulp in his throat before he spoke, and moisten his lips.

"No, sir, and I don't want to," he said.

Storely nodded.

"That's all then, Lamp," he said. "I'll go to the police to-morrow."

"Thank you, sir," said Lamp again. "Of course it's a great relief to me to learn that she's come to no bodily harm."

"But you said you weren't afraid of that," said Storely.

"I wasn't, sir," he said. "But it's another thing to be certain of it."

Now Storely, like most people accounted sensible, both distrusts and despises all theories that admit the existence of occult and unexplained phenomena. So I did not say anything to him about the notion which had entered my head, and which proved, when I had got to bed, to be very uncomfortably established there. In a word, I did not believe that the woman we had both seen was the living and material presentment of Lamp's wife. I believed that it was some bodiless phantom of her, and that Lamp also had seen her, and that he knew it was not her actual bodily presence we had all beheld. He had seen, I felt sure, what we had seen, and was terrified of it. His explanation and suggestion were certainly plausible enough; he would pack up her clothes and have them ready, and it was natural that he did not want her to come inside the house at all. But it was not the thought of that which made the sweat to stand on his forehead, and his throat to gulp, but something very different. The thought haunted me: often I half dropped off to sleep, but as many times I woke again with the sense that there was something creeping up to the house, like the fog that was now thick outside my window, and seeking admittance. And often in these wakenings, I heard from the room above, which was Lamp's, a soft footfall going backwards and forwards. It went to the window, and then I heard the creak of the opening sash: then the window was closed again, and the blind drawn down over it. But towards morning I slept more soundly, and woke to find him already in my room, deftly putting out my clothes.

Storely went off to the police-station directly after breakfast. He had told Lamp to bring the car round from the garage which adjoined the house, for we were to spend the day on the links. The fog had quite cleared under a breath of north wind, the morning was of a crystalline brightness, and while waiting for Storely I strolled down the street and out on to the river-side. In this radiant day of spring I almost thought that my uneasy imaginings were but nightmare notions, and unreal as dreams. Certainly they had left the surface of my conscious mind, and I cared little whether they had dispersed altogether or were lurking in the shadows within, so long as they did not trouble me . . . When I got back to the house the car was standing at the door, and casually glancing into it, as I passed, I thought I saw that huddled up on the back seat was sprawling the figure of a woman. The impression was absolutely momentary for at once it restored itself into a medley of coat and rug with a patch of oval sunlight for a face. A good lesson, thought I, of the tricks the imagination can play, for clearly this was a piece of that nightmare stuff which had been troubling me, and which had no existence in fact.

It was dusk when we drew up at the door again that evening after a salubrious day in the open. A tranquil, pleasant fatigue possessed me: I looked forward to my bath and my dinner, and cosy fireside hours before bedtime. Storely had passed into the house, leaving the front door open, and I lingered at the threshold a minute, watching Lamp back the car into the garage. As I stood there, I felt something brush by me, and pass invisibly into the house. Simultaneously I heard Storely's voice from the hall inside call out, "Hullo, what's that?" I came in, shutting the door.

"What was it?" I asked.

"I don't know. I was reading my letters at the table, when something brushed by me, and I thought it was you. But there was nothing to be seen. The door into the sitting-room swung open and closed again. Where's Lamp?"

"He's putting the car into the garage," I said.

"But something did go in there," he said. "Turn on the light."

I found the switch and turned it, and the dark room leaped into brightness. But it was quite empty.

"Odd," he said. "It must have been a draught. But it felt more solid than that."

"It brushed by me, too, as I stood in the doorway," I said.

"Of course it was a draught then," he said. "Strong eddies of air often come up this narrow street. I will shut them all out."

We drew our chairs up near the fire, for the evening had turned chilly again. I had looked forward to this drowsy hour, with the evening paper to glance at, and a book to doze over, but instead I found myself eagerly alert. But I could not give my attention to my book because something was going on far more arresting than anything which the world of books could contain. It was no subjective unrest that kept me thus on wires; it was that the whole of my mind was waiting for something quite outside myself to develop, and it, whatever it was, was in the room. It watched, it moved about, it waited, and now the air was growing misty, and I supposed that the fog had formed again outside, and was leaking in. But when I went up to dress I looked out from my bedroom window, and saw that the sky overhead was full of bright-burning stars, and that the street below, though dark, was so clear that I could see the dew which had fallen and lay on the cobbles shimmering in the starlight.

During dinner I noticed that Storely as well as I was observing Lamp. The man was evidently not himself, ordinarily deft-handed and silent-footed, he clattered with his dishes, and when he stood waiting for us to eat our course he kept glancing uneasily round. At the end of the dinner, as he poured out a glass of port for his master, he made some awkward jerk with his hand, and upset it. An impatient exclamation was on the tip of Storely's tongue, but he checked it.

"Anything the matter, Lamp?" he asked, as he mopped up the spilt wine. "Aren't you well?"

"No, sir, I'm right enough," he said. "But it's queer how the house is full of fog. The kitchen: why you can hardly see across it."

Presently we were back in the sitting-room where the chess-board was already set. The woman who came in to cook did not sleep in the house, and soon I heard the tapping of her steps down the flagged kitchen passage, and the opening and shutting of the back door: then came the sound of Lamp locking and bolting it. During the next hour, while our game was in progress, he must have come into the room half a dozen times: his hands trembled as he swept up the hearth, his face was ashen, and it was evident that he was in a state of acute nervous tension, and made any excuse to himself for coming into the room instead of biding alone in the kitchen. Finally, Storely told him that we wanted nothing more that night, and that he could get to bed. But we heard him moving about the house overhead, and when an hour later we finished our game, and went upstairs, he was still astir in the room above me.

I got to bed and instantly fell asleep, and woke again with the faint light of early dawn shining in through the window, knowing that some noise had aroused me. There was the sound of steps coming from the floor above, and they passed my door, and went on downstairs into the hall. I got out of bed, turned on my light and went to the door and opened it. But not a yard could I see in front of me, so dense was the fog that filled the passage. Yet somebody – were there not the steps of two people? – had just passed quickly by as if it was full daylight. Then suddenly from below came the sound of voices and with a thrill of nameless horror I heard that one of them was the voice of a woman.

"So now you've got to come with me, James Lamp," it said, "and take me where you took me before. You'll drive me down in the car, as you drove me before, and you'll come down into the water where you threw me, and I'll be waiting for you there, so close and loving."

Then came the other voice. It was Lamp's voice, and it rose to a scream as it spoke.

"No, no," he cried. "No, not that. I won't come. I tell you. Ah, take your hand off me: it's hot as fire, and I can't bear it."

"Come on then obediently," said the other. "It's cool in the water."

The door of Storely's room, just opposite mine, opened. I heard him click on the switch in the passage, and very faintly above our heads, in the dense air, there shone out white but hardly luminous the electric light from the ceiling.

"Ah, you've heard it, too," he said, seeing me. "What is it? What's happening? There were voices, and a yell . . . And then the front door opened and shut again. Come down!"

We groped our way along the passage, but on the stairs it was absolutely pitch dark. There was a switch somewhere there, but he could not find it, and he went back to his room to get a box of matches. With the help of that light he got hold of the switch, but even so we had to proceed with shuffling steps, so dense was the fog. We crossed the hall, and after fumbling at the front door, he threw it open, and there came in the faint clear light of the dawn. Even as we stood on the threshold the motor emerged from the garage close by, and I saw that by the side of Lamp, who drove it, there sat a woman. It turned and went swiftly down the street towards the river.

"But, good God, what's happening?" cried Storely. "That's Lamp. But where is he going? And who was that woman with him. Couldn't you see?"

And in the grey light of morning we read the answering horror in each other's faces.

The rest of the story, as it came out at the inquest held next day at Trench, is probably known to my readers. Storely's empty car was found by a labourer going out to his work drawn up on the bridge across the river Inglis, and the deep pool below the sluice was dragged. Two bodies were found there, one of a woman, the other of James Lamp. The woman's body had evidently been in the water for several days, his only for a few hours. But her hands were so tightly locked round the throat of the man that it was with difficulty that the two could be separated. In the woman's head was a wound caused by a revolver bullet: it had entered the back of her skull and was embedded in her brain. Medical evidence showed that she was certainly dead before she had been thrown into the water, and round her neck was a heavy iron weight. The body was quite recognizable as being that of Lamp's wife.

The Dance

Philip Hope had been watching with little neighing giggles of laughter the battle between a spider and a wasp that had been caught in its web. Once or twice the wasp nearly broke free, it hung with one wing only entangled in the tough light threads and he feared it would escape. But its adversary was always too quick and too clever; it swarmed about on its silken ladders, lean and nimble, and, by some process too rapid for Philip to follow, wound a new coil round head or struggling leg.

"Why, it's noosing its neck I believe," chuckled Philip, putting on his glasses, "like a hangman at work at eight o'clock in the morning. And it's got grey tips to its paws, like a hangman's gloves. Adorable!"

Clever spider! Philip's sympathy was entirely with it: he backed brains and agility against the buzzing, clumsy creature which had that curved sting, one stroke of which, if it could find its due target in the fat, round, mottled body of the other, would put an end to the combat. And the spider seemed to know that there was death in that horny scimitar so furiously stabbing, and skirted round it, keeping out of striking distance, while it spun its gossamers round the less dangerous members of its prey. The other wing was neatly tied up now, and then suddenly the spider pounced on the thread-like waist that joined the striped body to the thorax, and appeared to tear or to bite it in half.

The body dropped from the web, and the spider made a parcel of the rest, and took it into the woven tunnel at the centre of its home. Never was anything more neat and cruel; and neatness and cruelty were admirable qualities. Philip left the bed of dahlias, where he had watched this enthralling little spectacle, and stood still a moment thinking of some fresh entertainment. In person he was notably small and slight, narrow-chested, with spindle arms and legs. He leaned on a stick as he walked, for one of his knees was permanently stiff, but he was quick and nimble in spite of his limping gait. His clothes were fantastic; he wore a bright mustard-coloured suit, a green silk tie, a pink, silk shirt, with a low collar, above which rose a rather long neck supporting his very small sharp-chinned face, quite hairless and looking as if no razor had ever plied across it. His eyes were steel grey, and had no lashes on either lid: whether they looked up or down, they gave the impression of a mocking and amused vigilance. They saw much and derived much entertainment. He was hatless, and the thick crop of auburn hair that covered his head could deceive nobody, nor indeed did he intend that it should.

Beyond the lawn where he stood, half-screened by a row of shrubs, was the *en tout cas* court where, half an hour ago, he had left his wife and his secretary, Julian Weston, playing tennis. In point of age he might have been the father of either of them, and their combined years, twenty-two and twenty-three, just equalled his own forty-five. He could not catch any glimpse of their darting white-clad figures through the interstices of the hedge, and he supposed they had finished their game. He had told them that he intended to go for a motor drive, and no doubt they thought that he had gone, but there was no reason why he should not have a peep at them, to see what they were doing; and he walked quietly up to the screening shrubs. There they were, silly fools, only a few yards from him, sitting one on each side of the summer house. Sybil bounced a tennis ball on the tiled floor in the open space between them; Julian caught it and bounced it back. It was worth while to watch them for a little, and see what they would do when they tired of that. Five or six times the ball passed between them and then Julian missed it, and it rolled away, disregarded, under the table in the corner. They sat there, looking at each other. Philip, crouching down, moved a little nearer still invisible to them. He wanted to hear as well as to see. His face, satyr-like with its sharp chin and prominent ears, was alight with some secret merriment, and his small white teeth closed on his lower lip to prevent his laughing outright.

For the last week he had watched those two young creatures falling in love with each other. They had made friends at once when Julian came here a month ago, with the frank attraction of the young for each other: they rode, they played games, they bathed together in light-hearted enjoyment. But very soon Philip had seen that behind this natural comradeship there was stirring something that both troubled and kindled them. Their eyes were alight in each other's presence, their ears listened for each other. Sometimes each feigned an unconsciousness of the other till some swift glance betrayed the silly pretence. They would soon be as helpless in the silken web that enwrapped them as the wasp he had been watching, and indeed he himself was like the clever spider; for he had certainly helped to spread the net for them, encouraging their comradeship for the very purpose that they should get entangled. All this amused Philip, and it would be amusing to begin petting and making love to his wife again; that would touch both of them up. He would be very neat and dainty in device.

Suddenly these agreeable plans faded from his mind, and he became intensely alert. Julian got up, and Sybil also, and they stood facing each other.

"Does he know? Does he guess, do you think?" he asked.

She gave no audible answer. Then, which of them moved first it was difficult to say, but next moment they were clasped to each other, and then as suddenly stood apart again.

Philip, shaking with laughter, stole quietly away, for he had no notion of disclosing himself; that would spoil it all. Something in the abruptness of what he had seen made him feel certain that they had never passionately kissed like that before; for, if so, they would not have leaped to it thus and then instantly have recoiled from what they had done. But the time was ripe for him to intervene, and he promised himself an amusing week or two. Intensely amusing, too, was Julian's question as to whether Sybil thought that he knew. Did the boy take him for an idiot?

"I'll answer that question in my own way," thought Philip. "It will be great sport."

It was too late to go for his motor drive now, and, passing through the house, he went for a short stroll along the edge of the sand-cliffs that rose a hundred sheer feet above the sea. He had been married now for three years, having been over forty when first he met Sybil Mannering. At once he had determined that he must possess this golden girl of nineteen. He was not in the least in love with her, but her beauty and her child-like vitality nourished him: it would be delicious to have the right to pet and caress her. She was poor, but he was rich, which was all to the good, for that made an ally of her mother. He made the appeal of the weak to the strong, of the pitiful little loving *crétin* (so he called himself) to the young Juno, and her compassion had aided his suit. Then, as she got to know him, there grew in her a horror of him, and that was pleasant; her fright and her horror were grand nourishment, for they fed his dainty sadism. He loaded her with jewels, he designed her dresses. He took her about everywhere, boring himself with parties and balls for the sake of seeing the admiration she excited. But when he had had enough he would go to his hostess and say, "Such a charming evening, but Sybil will scold me if we stop any longer."

Then as they drove home he would say to her, "Loving little wifie, aren't I good to you, taking you out of the gutter and covering you with pearls? You must be good to me. Give me a kiss," and he would burst out into his little goat-like laugh at the touch of her cold lips. Then he had tired of that sport, but to-day, as he limped perkily along the cliff-edge, he thought he would renew his caresses. She shuddered at them before, she would shudder now with a far more acute loathing, and Julian would be there to see. Then he must make some needful alterations in his will. The chances were a hundred to one that she would survive him, and though nothing could prevent her from marrying Julian, he must make it as disagreeable as he could; make her feel that he wasn't quite done with yet. "I wonder if the dead can return," he thought. "What fun they might have!" He did not in the least contemplate dying for a long while yet, but in case anything happened to him he would get his lawyer to frame a codicil. That, however, was not so important as the neat little comedy that he was planning.

It was growing dark; the revolving beams from the Cromer lighthouse swept across the golf-links like the spokes of a luminous wheel, and shone where he walked and then passed on and scoured the sea. The house he had built here stood within a hundred yards of the cliff-edge, queer and rococo, with two sharp turrets like the pricked ears of some wary animal. A big hall-like sitting room with a gallery above running along the length of it, and communicating with the bedrooms, occupied the most of the ground floor. Out of it opened a small dining room hatched to the kitchen, and close to the front door was Philip's sitting-room where a tape-machine ticked out Stock Exchange prices and the news of the day. You could scarcely call him a gambler, so acute and so well-reasoned were his conclusions as to the effect of the news of the day on markets, and often he spent the entire evening here, making out what would be the effect of the latest news on the market next day, and selling or buying first thing in the morning.

But to-night he had a more amusing diversion; there was to be dancing. He had the furniture in the hall moved away to the sides of the room and the rugs rolled up, and the polished boards made a very decent floor for one couple. He sat himself by the gramophone with jazz records handy, and watched the two with little squeals of pleasure.

"You beautiful creatures," he cried. "Why, you're positively made for each other! Dance again! I'll find a more exciting tune. Hold her close, Julian. Bend your head down to her a little as if you wanted to kiss her. Forget that there's old hubby watching you. Look into his eyes, Sybil. Try to think that you're in love with him."

He gave his little goat-like laugh.

"Now we'll have a contrast," he cried. "You shall dance with me, darling. I can hop round in spite of my poor stiff leg."

He hugged her close to him, he skipped and capered round her, dragging her after him.

"Faster, more fire!" he cried. "Aren't I grotesque, and isn't it fun? I'm sure you never guessed I could be so nimble. Good Lord, how hot it makes one! Wait a second, while I take off my wig."

He threw it into a chair: his head was as hairless as an egg, and gleamed with sweat.

"Now come along again," he said. "You are kind to your poor little cripple! . . . Now have another turn with Julian, while I cool down. But give me a kiss first."

He gave her half a dozen little butterfly kisses, then kissed her on the mouth, cackling with laughter to see her eyes grow stale.

Every day he made traps and tortures for them. One night he went to bed early, passing with his limping tread along the gallery above the hall that led to the bedrooms beyond, knowing that, in spite of his injunction that they should sit up and amuse themselves together, he had poisoned the hour for them. He was right, and it was but a few minutes later that he heard them come upstairs, and Sybil went into her room next door, and Julian's step passed on.

He went in to see her before long in his yellow silk dressing-gown, and sent her maid away, saying that he would brush her hair for her. He kissed the nape of her neck, he talked to her about Julian, the handsomest boy he had ever seen: did not she think so? But did she think he was well? Sometimes he seemed to have something on his mind . . .

The next morning it would be Julian's turn. Philip told him he must be getting married soon. Wasn't there some nice girl he was fond of? Then he consulted him about Sybil. He thought she had something on her mind. Julian must find out – they were such friends – what was it, and tell him, and whatever it was, it must be put right. Sybil mustn't worry over any secret disquietude. They would dance again to-night, and dress up for it. What should Julian wear? Could he not make a costume – Sybil and he would help – out of a couple of leopard skins? Julian should be a young Dionysus, and Sybil a Maenad, wearing that Grecian frock that he had designed for her. They would have dinner in the loggia in the walled garden, and dance on the grass, and Julian should chase his Maenad over the lawn through moonlight and shadow. He laughed to see the boy's eyes gleam and then grown cold with hate. He was on the rack and no wonder, and the levers could be pulled over a little farther yet.

Then he had other devices for a day or two; he never let them be alone together for a moment, to see if that suited them better. He kept Julian at work all morning, he took Sybil out with him all afternoon, and there were prospectuses for his secretary to read and report on when dinner was over. He nagged at Sybil; he made mock of her before the servants, and it was amusing to see the angry blood leap to Julian's face, and the whiteness come to hers. Rare sport: they would have killed him, he thought, if they had the spirit of a louse between them.

"What happy times we're having," he said one day. "We'll stop on here into October, for we're such a loving harmonious little party. Do put your mother off, Sybil; she will spoil our lovely little triangle. Yet we've both got reason to be grateful to her for bringing us together. What about your marrying Mother Mannering, Julian? It would be nice to have you in the family. She can't be more than sixty, and as tough as a guinea-fowl without the guineas."

There they were then: they were bound on wheels for his breaking. He could wrench this one or that as he pleased, and the other could do nothing but look on impotently. For a day or two yet it was pleasant to make sport with them, but the edge was wearing off his enjoyment and it was time to make an end.

He took Julian for a stroll along the cliff one afternoon.

"I've got something to say to you, dear fellow," he said. "I hope it will meet with your approval, not that it matters very much. Now cudgel your clever brains, and see if you can guess what it is."

"I've no idea, sir," said Julian.

"Dull of you, sir. Not even if I give you three guesses? . . . Well, it's just this. I've had enough of you, and you can take yourself off to-morrow. A week's wages or a month's wages of course, which is right. My reason? Just that Sybil and I will be so very happy alone. That's all. What damned idiots you and she have been making of yourselves. So off you go, and there will be a little discipline for her. You must think of us dancing in the evening. So that's all pleasantly settled."

He was walking on the very edge of the cliff, and, as he finished speaking, he turned and looked out seawards. A yard behind him there was an irregular zigzag crack in the turf, and now it ran this way and that, spreading and widening. Next moment the riband of earth on which he stood suddenly slipped down a foot or two, and with a shrill cry of fright he jumped for the solid. But the poised lump slid away altogether from him, and all he could do was to clutch with his fingers at the broken edge.

"Quick, get hold of my hands, you senseless ape," he squealed.

Julian did not move. If he had thrown himself on the ground and grasped at the fingers which clutched the crumbling earth he might perhaps have saved him. But for that crucial second of time his body made no response: if it could have moved at all, it must have leaped and danced at the thought of what would presently befall, and he looked smiling and unwavering into those lashless, panic-stricken eyes. Next moment he was alone on the empty down. He felt no smallest pang of remorse; he told himself that by no possibility could he have saved him. But, soft as the fall of a single snow-flake, fear settled on his heart and then melted.

A flock of sheep were feeding not far away, and they scattered before him as he ran back to the house to get the help which his heart rejoiced to know must be unavailing.

The house remained shut up for a year and the turrets pricked their ears in vain to hear the sounds of life returning to it. Philip, by the codicil he had executed the day before his death, had revoked his previous will, and had left to Sybil only certain marriage settlements which he had no power to touch and this house "where" (so ran his phrase) "we are now passing such loving and harmonious days." During this year Julian's father had died, and their marriage took place in the autumn.

To-day they came to spend here their month of honeymoon. Fenton Philip's butler, and his wife had been living here as caretakers, the garden had been well looked after, and all was exactly as it had been a year ago. But the shadow of the mocking malevolence had passed for ever from it, and the spring sunshine in their hearts was as tranquil as the autumn radiance that lay on the lawns. Everything, flower-beds and winding path and sun-steeped wall, was full of memories from which all bitterness was purged; it was sweet to remember what had been, in a babble of talk.

"And there's the tennis court," said he, "with the summer house where we sat—".

"Yes, and bounced a ball to and fro between us—" she interrupted.

"And then I missed it and it rolled away, and we thought no more about it. Then I asked you if you thought he had guessed, and we kissed."

"Just here we stood," she said.

"And it was on that day that he began to mock us," he said. "How he enjoyed it! It made sport for him."

"I think he must have seen us," she said. "You could never tell what Philip saw. And he wove webs for us. Look, there's a wasp caught in a spider's web. I must let it free. I hate spiders. If ever I have a nightmare it's always about a spider. Oh, what a pity! The sunlight is fading. There's a sea fog coming up. How chilly it gets at once! Let's go indoors. And we won't talk about those things any more."

The mist formed rapidly, and before they got in it had spread white and low-lying over the lawn. A fire of logs burned in the hall, and as they sat over them in the fading light, a hundred memories which now they left unspoken, began to move about in their minds, like sparks crawling about the ashes of burnt paper that has flared and seems consumed. There was the cabinet gramophone to which they had danced . . . there was the chair on to which Philip had thrown his wig; above, running the length of the hall, was the gallery along which his limping footstep had passed when he left them to go early to bed, bidding them stay up and divert themselves. How the sparks crawled about the thin crinkling ash! Presently it would all be consumed, and the past collapse into the grey nothingness of forgotten things.

Outside the mist had grown vastly denser, it beleaguered the house, and nothing was to be seen from the windows except a woolly whiteness. From the sea there came the mournful hooting of fog-horns.

"I like that," said Sybil. "It makes me feel comfortable. We're safe, we're at home, and we don't want anyone to know where we are, like those lost ships. But pull the curtains, it shuts us in more."

As Julian rattled the rings across the rod he paused, listening.

"Telephone wasn't it?" he said.

"It can't have been," said she. "Why, it's standing close by my chair, and I heard nothing. It was the curtain-rings."

"But there it is again," said he. "It isn't from this instrument, it sounds as if it came from the study. I think I'll go and see. The servants won't have heard it there."

"If it's for me, say I'm in my bath," said Sybil.

Julian went along the passage to the room that had been Philip's workroom close to the front door. It was dark now, and, as he fumbled for the switch by the door, the bell sounded again, rather faint, rather thin, as if the fog outside muffled it.

He took off the receiver.

"Hullo!" he said.

There came a little goat-like laugh, just audible, and then a voice.

"Settled in comfortably, dear boy?" it asked. "I'll look in on you before long."

"Who's speaking?" said Julian. He heard his voice crack as he asked.

Silence. Once more he asked and there came no reply.

Julian felt the snowflakes of fear settle on him again. But the notion that had flashed out of the darkness into his mind was surely the wildest nonsense. The laugh, the voice, had for that moment sounded unmistakable, but his sane self knew the absurdity of such an idea. He turned out the light and went back to Sybil.

"The telephone did ring, dear," he said, "but I couldn't make out who it was. Somebody is going to look before long. Not at home, I think."

The fog cleared during the night before a light wind from the sea, and a crystalline October morning awaited them. Sybil had some household businesses that claimed her attention, and Julian walked along the shore until she was ready to come out. Not half a mile away was the precise spot he wished to visit, namely, that belt of shingle at the base of the cliff where, a little more than a year ago, they had found the shattered body on its back with wide-open eyes. He had dreamed of the place last night; he thought that he came here, and that, as he looked, the shingle began to stir and formed itself into the figure of a man lying there, and the dreamer had watched this odd process with interest, wondering what would come next. Then skin began to grow like swiftly spreading grey lichen over the head, and eyes and mouth moulded themselves on a face that was coming to life again; the eyes turned and looked into his, the mouth moved, and Julian awoke in the grip of nightmare. Even when the night was over and the morning luminous the taste of that terror still lingered, and he had to come to the place and convince himself of the emptiness of his dream. There lay the shingle shining and wet from the recession of the tide, and the wholesome sunlight dwelt on it.

Dusk had already fallen when they got home from a motor-drive that afternoon. As she got out Sybil stepped on the side of her foot and gave a little cry of pain. But it was nothing, she said, just a bit of a wrench, and she hobbled into the house.

As Julian returned from taking the car to the garage he noticed that there was a light in Philip's room by the front door. Sybil perhaps had gone in there, but, when he entered, he found the room was empty. The fire had been lit, and was beginning to burn up. No doubt the housemaid had thought he meant to use the room, and after lighting the fire had forgotten to turn off the switch.

He went on into the hall. Sybil was not there and she must have gone upstairs to take off her cloak and fur tippet and veil. He sat down to look at the evening paper, got interested in a political article, and heard with only half an ear the opening of the door to the bedroom passage at the end of the gallery that crossed the hall. The floor of it was of polished oak boards, uncarpeted, and he heard her step coming along it, and she limped as she walked. Her ankle still hurts her, he thought, and went on with his reading. He wondered then what had happened to her, for she had crossed the gallery several minutes ago, and she had not yet appeared. He had made no doubt that that limping step was hers.

The door at the end of the hall into the kitchen-quarters opened and she came in. She was still in her cloak and furs.

"So sorry, dear," she said, "but there was a bit of a domestic upset. Fenton told the housemaid to light the fire in the study, and she came running back, rather hysterical, saying that as she was lighting it she saw a man outside in the dusk looking in at the window, and she was frightened."

"Perhaps she saw me looking in," said Julian, "When I came back from the garage I saw there was a light in the room."

"No doubt that was it. But Fenton and the gardener have gone to have a look round."

"And the foot?" he asked.

She stripped herself of her wrappings and threw them into a chair.

"Perfectly all right," she said. "It only lasted a minute."

Motoring had made Julian sleepy, and when, after tea, Sybil gathered up her things and went upstairs he must have fallen into a doze. He did not appear to himself to have gone to sleep, for there was no change of consciousness or of scene, and he thought he was still looking into the fire, and wondering to himself, with an uneasiness that he would not admit, what that limping footstep had been. He had felt no doubt at the time that it was Sybil's, but she had not been upstairs, nor did she halt in her walk. And he thought of that nightmare of his about the shingle on which Philip had fallen, and of the voice that he had heard on the telephone, and the familiar laugh, and the promise that the speaker would soon be here. Was he here in some bodiless form? Was he giving token of his unseen presence? Then (in his dream) he reached out for the paper he had been reading to divert his thoughts. As he did so his eye fell on the chair from which Sybil had picked up the cloak and veil and fur tippet she had thrown there, but apparently she had forgotten to take the tippet. Then he looked more closely at it and saw it was a wig.

He woke: there was Fenton standing by him.

"The dressing-bell has gone a quarter of an hour ago, sir," he said.

Julian looked at the chair beside him. There was nothing there: it was all a dream, but the dream had brought the sweat to his forehead.

"Has it really?" he said. "I must have fallen asleep. "Oh, by the way, you went to see if there was anyone hanging about in the garden. Did you find anything?"

"No, sir. All quite quiet," said Fenton.

Sybil lingered behind in the dining-room after dinner to pour fresh water into the bowl of touzle-headed chrysanthemums that stood on the table, and Julian strolled on into the hall. The furniture was pushed aside from the centre of the room and the rugs rolled up, leaving the floor clear. Sybil had said nothing about that to him, but it would be fun to dance. Presently she followed him.

"Oh, Julian, what a good idea," she said. "How quick you've been. Turn on the gramophone. Why, it's a year since I have danced. Do you remember? . . . No, don't remember: forget it . . ."

Julian, standing with his back to her, picked out a record. Just as the first gay bars of the tune blared out, Sybil shrieked and shrieked again.

"Something's holding me," she cried. "Something's pressing against me. Something's laughing. Julian, come to me! Oh, my God, it's he!"

She was struggling in the grip of some invisible force. With her head craned back away from it, her hands wrestled furiously with the empty air, and, still violently resisting, her feet began to make steps on the floor, now tip-toeing in a straight line, now circling. Julian rushed to her, he felt the shape of the unseen horror, he tore at the head and the shoulders of it, but his hands slipped away as if on slime, and fear sucked his strength from him. Then, as if suddenly released, Sybil dropped to the ground, and he knew that all the hellish forces of the unseen were turned on him.

It played on him like a blast of fire or freezing, and he fled from the room, for that was its will. Down the passage he ran with it on his heels, and out into the moonlit night. He dodged this way and that, he tried to bolt back into the house again but it drove him where it would, past the tennis-court and the bed of dahlias, and out of the garden gate and on to the cliff, where the beams of the lighthouse swept across the downs. There was a flock of sheep which scattered as he rushed in among them. There were a boy and a girl, who, as he fled by them, called to him to beware of the cliff-edge that lay directly in front of him. The pencil of light swept across it now, and as he plunged over the edge he saw the line of ripple breaking on to the shingle a hundred feet below, where, one evening, he and the fisherfolk found the shattered body of Philip staring with lashless eyes into the sky.

THE HANGING OF ALFRED WADHAM

I had been telling Father Denys Hanbury about a very extraordinary séance which I had attended a few days before. The medium in trance had said a whole series of things which were unknown to anybody but myself and a friend of mine who had lately died, and who, so she said, was present and was speaking to me through her. Naturally, from the strictly scientific point of view in which alone we ought to approach such phenomena, such information was not really evidence that the spirit of my friend was in touch with her, for it was already known to me, and might by some process of telepathy have been communicated to the medium from my brain and not through the agency of the dead. She spoke, too, not in her own ordinary voice, but in a voice which certainly was very like his. But his voice was also known to me; it was in my memory even as were the things she had been saying. All this, therefore, as I was remarking to Father Denys, must be ruled out as positive evidence that communications had been coming from the other side of death.

"A telepathic explanation was possible," I said, "and we have to accept any known explanation which covers the facts before we conclude that the dead have come back into touch with the material world."

The room was quite warm, but I saw that he shivered slightly and, hitching his chair a little nearer the fire, he spread out his hands to the blaze. Such hands they were: beautiful and expressive of him, and so like the praying hands of Albert Dürer: the blaze shone through them as through rose-red alabaster. He shook his head.

"It's a terribly dangerous thing to attempt to get into communication with the dead," he said. "If you seem to get into touch with them you run the risk of establishing connection not with them but with awful and perilous intelligences. Study telepathy by all means, for that is one of the marvels of the mind which we are meant to investigate like any other of the wonderful secrets of Nature. But I interrupt you: you said something else occurred. Tell me about it."

Now I knew Father Denys's creed about such things and deplored it. He holds, as his church commands him, that intercourse with the spirits of the dead is impossible, and that when it appears to occur, as it undoubtedly does, the enquirer is really in touch with some species of dramatic demon, who is impersonating the spirit of the dead. Such a thing has always seemed to me as monstrous as it is without foundation, and there is nothing I can discover in the recognized sources of Christian doctrine which justifies such a view.

"Yes: now comes the queer part," I said. "For, still speaking in the voice of my friend the medium told me something which instantly I believed to be untrue. It could not therefore have been drawn telepathically from me. After that the séance came to an end, and in order to convince myself that this could not have come from him, I looked up the diary of my friend which had been left me at his death, and which had just been sent me by his executors, and was still unpacked. There I found an entry which proved that what the medium had said was absolutely correct. A certain thing – I needn't go into it – had occurred precisely as she had stated, though I should have been willing to swear to the contrary. That cannot have come into her mind from mine, and there is no source that I can see from which she could have obtained it except from my friend. What do you say to that?"

He shook his head.

"I don't alter my position at all," he said. "That information, given it did not come from your mind, which certainly seems to be impossible, came from some discarnate agency. But it didn't come from the spirit of your friend: it came from some evil and awful intelligence."

"But isn't that pure assumption?" I asked. "It is surely much simpler to say that the dead can, under certain conditions, communicate with us. Why drag in the devil?"

He glanced at the clock.

"It's not very late," he said. "Unless you want to go to bed, give me your attention for half-an-hour, and I will try to show you."

The rest of my story is what Father Denys told me, and what happened immediately afterwards.

"Though you are not a Catholic," he said, "I think you would agree with me about an institution which plays a very large part in our ministry, namely Confession, as regards the sacredness and the inviolability of it. A soul laden with sin comes to his Confessor knowing that he is speaking to one who has the power to pronounce or withhold forgiveness, but who will never, for any conceivable reason, repeat or hint at what has been told him. If there was the slightest chance of the penitent's confession being made known to anyone, unless he himself, for purposes of expiation or of righting some wrong, chooses to repeat it, no one would ever come to Confession at all. The Church would lose the greatest hold it possesses over the souls of men, and the souls of men would lose that inestimable comfort of knowing (not hoping merely, but knowing) that their sins are forgiven them. Of course the priest may withhold absolution, if he is not convinced that he is dealing with a true penitent, and before he gives it, he will insist that the penitent makes such reparation as is in his power for the wrong he has done. If he has profited by his dishonesty he must make good: whatever crime he has committed he must give warrant that his penitence is sincere. But I think you would agree that in any case the priest cannot, whatever the result of his silence may be, repeat what has been told him. By doing so he might right or avert some hideous wrong, but it is impossible for him to do so. What he has heard, he has heard under the seal of confession, concerning the sacredness of which no argument is conceivable."

"It is possible to imagine awful consequences resulting from it," I said. "But I agree."

"Before now awful consequences have come of it," he said, "but they don't touch the principle. And now I am going to tell you of a certain confession that was once made to me."

"But how can you?" I said. "That's impossible, surely."

"For a certain reason, which we shall come to later," he said, "you will see that secrecy is no longer incumbent on me. But the point of my story is not that: it is to warn you about attempting to establish communication with the dead. Signs and tokens, voices and apparitions appear to come through to us from them, but who sends them? You will see what I mean."

I settled myself down to listen.

"You will probably not remember with any distinctness, if at all, a murder committed a year ago, when a man called Gerald Selfe met his death. There was no enticing mystery about it, no romantic accessories, and it aroused no public interest. Selfe was a man of loose life, but he held a respectable position, and it would have been disastrous for him if his private irregularities had come to light. For some time before his death he had been receiving blackmailing letters regarding his relations with a certain married woman, and, very properly, he had put the matter into the hands of the police. They had been pursuing certain clues, and on the afternoon before Selfe's death one of the officers of the Criminal Investigation Department had written to him that everything pointed to his man servant, who certainly knew of his intrigue, being the culprit. This was a young man named Alfred Wadham: he had only lately entered Selfe's service, and his past history was of the most unsavoury sort. They had baited a trap for him, of which details were given, and suggested that Selfe should display it, which, within an hour or two, he successfully did. This information and these instructions were conveyed in a letter which after Selfe's death was found in a drawer of his writing-table, of which the lock had been tampered with. Only Wadham and his master slept in his flat; a woman came in every morning to cook breakfast and do the housework, and Selfe lunched and dined at his club, or in the restaurant on the ground floor of this house of flats, and here he dined that night. When the woman came in next morning she found the outer door of the flat open, and Selfe lying dead on the floor of his sitting-room with his throat cut. Wadham had disappeared, but in the slop-pail of his bedroom was water which was stained with human blood. He was caught two days afterwards and at his trial elected to give evidence. His story was that he suspected he had fallen into a trap, and that while Mr. Selfe was at dinner he searched his drawers and found the letter sent by the police, which proved that this was the case. He therefore decided to bolt, and he left the flat that evening before his master came back to it after dinner. Being in the witness-box, he was of course subjected to a searching cross-examination, and contradicted himself in several particulars. Then there was that incriminating evidence in his room, and the motive for the crime was clear enough. After a very long deliberation the jury found him guilty, and he was sentenced to death. His appeal which followed was dismissed.

"Wadham was a Catholic, and since it is my office to minister to Catholic prisoners at the gaol where he was lying under sentence of death, I had many talks with him, and entreated him for the sake of his immortal soul to confess his guilt. But though he was even eager to confess other misdeeds of his, some of which it was ugly to speak of, he maintained his innocence on this charge of murder. Nothing shook him, and though as far as I could judge he was sincerely penitent for other misdeeds, he swore to me that the story he told in court was, in spite of the contradictions in which he had involved himself, essentially true, and that if he was hanged he died unjustly. Up till the last afternoon of his life, when I sat with him for two hours, praying and pleading with him, he stuck to that. Why he should do that, unless indeed he was innocent, when he was eager to search his heart for the confession of other gross wickednesses, was curious; the more I pondered it, the more inexplicable I found it, and during that afternoon doubt as to his guilt began to grow in me. A terrible thought it was, for he had lived in sin and error, and to-morrow his life was to be broken like a snapped stick. I was to be at the prison again before six in the morning, and I still had to determine whether I should give him the Sacrament. If he went to his death guilty of murder, but refusing to confess, I had no right to give it him, but if he was innocent, my withholding of it was as terrible as any miscarriage of justice. Then on my way out I had a word with one of the warders, which brought my doubt closer to me.

"'What do you make of Wadham?' I asked.

"He drew aside to let a man pass, who nodded to him: somehow I knew that he was the hangman.

"'I don't like to think of it, sir,' he said. 'I know he was found guilty, and that his appeal failed. But if you ask me whether I believe him to be a murderer, why no, I don't.'

"I spent the evening alone: about ten o'clock as I was on the point of going to bed, I was told that a man called Horace Kennion was below, and wanted to see me. He was a Catholic, and though I had been friends with him at one time, certain things had come to my knowledge which made it impossible for me to have anything more to do with him, and I had told him so. He was wicked – oh, don't misunderstand me; we all do wicked things constantly; the life of us all is a tissue of misdeeds, but he alone of all men I had ever met seemed to me to love wickedness for its own sake. I said I could not see him, but the message came back that his need was urgent, and up he came. He wanted, he told me, to make his confession, not to-morrow, but now, and his Confessor was away. I could not, as a priest, resist that appeal. And his confession was that he had killed Gerald Selfe.

"For a moment I thought this was some impious joke, but he swore he was speaking the truth, and still under the seal of confession gave me a detailed account. He had dined with Selfe that night, and had gone up afterwards to his flat for a game of piquet. Selfe told him with a grin that he was going to lay his servant by the heels to-morrow for blackmail. 'A smart spry young man to-day,' he said. 'Perhaps a bit off colour to-morrow at this time.' He rang the bell for him to put out the card-table: then saw it was ready, and he forgot that his summons remained unanswered. They played high points and both had drunk a good deal. Selfe lost partie after partie and eventually accused Kennion of cheating. Words ran high and boiled over into blows, and Kennion, in some rough and tumble of wrestling and hitting, picked up a knife from the table and stabbed Selfe in the throat, through jugular vein and carotid artery. In a few minutes he had bled to death. . . . Then Kennion remembered that unanswered bell, and went tiptoe to Wadham's room. He found it empty; empty, too, were the other rooms in the flat. Had there been anyone there, his idea was to say he had come up at Selfe's invitation, and found him dead. But this was better yet: there was no more than a few spots of blood on him, and he washed them in Wadham's room, emptying the water into his slop-pail. Then leaving the door of the flat open he went downstairs and out.

"He told me this in quite a few sentences, even as I have told it you, and looked up at me with a smiling face.

"'So what's to be done next, Venerable Father?' he said gaily.

"'Ah, thank God you've confessed!' I said. 'We're in time yet to save an innocent man. You must give yourself up to the police at once.' But even as I spoke my heart misgave me.

"He rose, dusting the knees of his trousers.

"'What a quaint notion,' he said. 'There's nothing further from my thoughts.'

"I jumped up.

"'I shall go myself then,' I said.

"He laughed outright at that.

"'Oh, no, indeed you won't,' he said. 'What about the seal of confession? Indeed, I rather fancy it's a deadly sin for a priest ever to think of violating it. Really I'm ashamed of you, my dear Denys. Naughty fellow! But perhaps it was only a joke; you didn't mean it.'

"'I do mean it,' I said. 'You shall see if I mean it.' But even as I spoke, I knew I did not. 'Anything is allowable to save an innocent man from death.'

"He laughed again.

"'Pardon me: you know perfectly well, that it isn't,' he said. 'There's one thing in our creed far worse than death, and that is the damnation of the soul. You've got no intention of damning yours. I took no risk at all when I confessed to you.'

"'But it will be murder if you don't save this man,' I said.

"'Oh, certainly, but I've got murder on my conscience already,' he said. 'one gets used to it very quickly. And having got used to it, another murder doesn't seem to matter an atom. Poor young Wadham: to-morrow isn't it? I'm not sure it won't be a sort of rough justice. Blackmail is a disgusting offence.'

"I went to the telephone, and took off the receiver.

"'Really this is most interesting' he said. 'Walton Street is the nearest police-station. You don't need the number: just say Walton Street Police. But you can't. You can't say "I have a man with me now, Horace Kennion, who has confessed to me that he murdered Selfe." So why bluff? Besides, if you could do any such thing, I should merely say that I had done nothing of the kind. Your word, the word of a priest who has broken the most sacred vow, against mine. Childish!'

"'Kennion,' I said, 'for the love of God, and for the fear of hell, give yourself up! What does it matter whether you or I live a few years less, if at the end we pass into the vast infinite with our sins confessed and forgiven. Day and night I will pray for you.'

"'Charming of you,' said he. 'But I've no doubt that now you will give Wadham full absolution. So what does it matter if he goes into – into the vast infinite at eight o'clock to-morrow morning?'

"'Why did you confess to me then,' I asked, 'if you had no intention of saving him, and making atonement?'

"'Well, not long ago you were very nasty to me,' he said. 'You told me no decent man would consort with me. So it struck me, quite suddenly, only to-day, that it would be pleasant to see you in the most awful hole. I daresay I've got Sadic tastes, too, and they are being wonderfully indulged. You're in torment, you know: you would choose any physical agony rather than to be in such a torture-chamber of the soul. It's entrancing: I adore it. Thank you very much, Denys.'

"He got up.

"'I kept my taxi waiting,' he said. 'No doubt you'll be busy to-night. Can I give you a lift anywhere? Pentonville?'

"There are no words to describe certain darknesses and ecstasies that come to the soul, and I can only tell you that I can imagine no hell of remorse that could equal the hell that I was in. For in the bitterness of remorse we can see that our suffering is a needful and salutary experience: only through it can our sin be burned away. But here was a torture blank and meaningless . . . And then my brain stirred a little, and I began to wonder whether, without breaking the seal of confession, I might not be able to effect something. I saw from my window that the light was burning in the clock-tower at Westminster: the House therefore was sitting, and it seemed possible that without violation I might tell the Home Secretary that a confession had been made me, whereby I knew that Wadham was innocent. He would ask me for any details I could give him, and I could tell him – And then I saw that I could tell him nothing: I could not say that the murderer had gone up with Selfe to his room, for through that information it might be found that Kennion had dined with him. But before I did anything, I must have guidance, and I went to the Cardinal's house by our Cathedral. He had gone to bed, for it was now after midnight, but in answer to the urgency of my request he came down to see me. I told him without giving any clue, what had happened, and his verdict was what in my heart I knew it would be. Certainly I might see the Home Secretary and tell him that such a confession had been made me, but no word or hint must escape me which could lead to identification. Personally, he did not see how the execution could be postponed on such information as I could give.

"'And whatever you suffer, my son,' he said, 'be sure that you are suffering not from having done wrong, but from having done right. Placed as you are, your temptation to save an innocent man comes from the devil, and whatever you may be called upon to endure for not yielding to it, is of that origin also.'

"I saw the Home Secretary in his room at the House within the hour. But unless I told him more, and he realized that I could not, he was powerless to move.

"'He was found guilty at his trial,' he said,' and his appeal was dismissed. Without further evidence I can do nothing.'

"He sat thinking a moment: then jumped up.

"'Good God, it's ghastly,' he said. 'I entirely believe, I needn't tell you, that you've heard this confession, but that doesn't prove it's true. Can't you see the man again? Can't you put the fear of God into him? If you can do anything at all, which gives me any justification for acting, up till the moment the drop falls, I will give a reprieve at once. There's my telephone number: ring me up here or at my house at any hour.'

"I was back at the prison before six in the morning. I told Wadham that I believed in his innocence, and I gave him absolution for all else. He received the Holy and Blessed Sacrament with me, and went without flinching to his death."

Father Denys paused.

"I have been a long time coming to that point in my story," he said, "which concerns that séance you spoke of, but it was necessary for your understanding of what I am going to tell you now, that you should know all this. I said that these messages and communications from the dead come not from them but from some evil and awful power impersonating them. You answered, I remember, "Why drag in the Devil?" I will tell you.

"When it was over, when the drop on which he stood yawned open, and the rope creaked and jumped, I went home. It was a dark winter's morning, still barely light, and in spite of the tragic scene I had just witnessed I felt serene and peaceful. I did not think of Kennion at all, only of the boy – he was little more – who had suffered unjustly, and that seemed a pitiful mistake, but no more. It did not touch him, his essential living soul, it was as if he had suffered the sacred expiation of martyrdom. And I was humbly thankful that I had been enabled to act rightly, and had Kennion now, through my agency, been in the hands of the police and Wadham alive, I should have been branded with the most terrible crime a priest can commit.

"I had been up all night, and after I had said my office I lay down on my sofa to get a little sleep. And I dreamed that I was in the cell with Wadham and that he knew I had proof of his innocence. It was within a few minutes of the hour of his death, and I heard along the stone-flagged corridor outside the steps of those who were coming for him. He heard them too, and stood up, pointing at me.

"'You're letting an innocent man die, when you could save him,' he said. 'You can't do it, Father Denys. Father Denys!' he shrieked, and the shriek broke off in a gulp and a gasp as the door opened.

"I woke, knowing that what had roused me was my own name, screamed out from somewhere close at hand, and I knew whose voice it was. But there I was alone in my quiet, empty room, with the dim day peering in. I had been asleep, I saw, for only a few minutes, but now all thought or power of sleep had fled, for somewhere by me, invisible but awfully present, was the spirit of the man whom I had allowed to perish. And he called me.

"But presently I convinced myself that this voice coming to me in sleep was no more than a dream, natural enough in the circumstances, and some days passed tranquilly enough. And then one day when I was walking down a sunny crowded street, I felt some definite and dreadful change in what I may call the psychic atmosphere which surrounds us all, and my soul grew black with fear and with evil imaginings. And there was Wadham coming towards me along the pavement gay and debonair. He looked at me, and his face became a mask of hate. 'We shall meet often I hope, Father Denys,' he said, as he passed. Another day I returned home in the twilight, and suddenly, as I entered my room, I heard the creak and strain of a rope, and his body, with head covered by the deathcap, swung in the window against the sunset. And sometimes when I was at my books the door opened quietly and closed again, and I knew he was there. The apparition or the token of it did not come often or perhaps my resistance would have been quickened, for I knew it was devilish in origin. But it came when I was off my guard at long intervals, so that I thought I had vanquished it, and then sometimes I felt my faith to reel. But always it was preceded by this sense of evil power bearing down on me, and I made haste to seek the shelter of the House of Defence which is set very high. And this last Sunday only—"

He broke off, covering his eyes with his hand, as if shutting out some appalling spectacle.

"I had been preaching," he resumed, "for one of our missions. The church was full, and I do not think there were another thought or desire in my soul but to further the holy cause for which I was speaking. It was a morning service, and the sun poured in through the stained-glass windows in a glow of coloured light. But in the middle of my sermon some bank of cloud drove up, and with it this horrible forewarning of the approach of a tempest of evil. So dark it got that, as I was drawing near the end of my sermon, the lights in the church were switched on, and it leaped into brightness. There was a lamp on the desk in the pulpit, where I had placed my notes, and now when it was kindled it shone full on the pew just below. And there with his head turned upwards towards me, with his face purple and eyes protruding and with the strangling noose round his neck, sat Wadham.

"My voice faltered a second, and I clutched at the pulpit-rail as he stared at me and I at him. A horror of the spirit, black as the eternal night of the lost closed round me, for I had let him go innocent to his death, and my punishment was just . . . And then like a star shining out through some merciful rent in this soul-storm came again that ray of conviction that as a priest I could not have done otherwise, and with it the sure knowledge that this apparition could not be of God, but of the devil, to be resisted and defied even as we defy with contempt some sweet and insidious temptation. It could not therefore be the spirit of the man at which I gazed, but some diabolical counterfeit.

"And I looked back from him to my notes, and went on with my sermon, for that alone was my business. That pause had seemed to me eternal: it had the quality of timelessness, but I learned afterwards that it had been barely perceptible. And from my own heart I learned that it was no punishment that I was undergoing, but the strengthening of a faith that had faltered."

Suddenly he broke off. There came into his eyes as he fixed them on the door a look not of fear at all but of savage relentless antagonism.

"It's coming," he said to me, "and now if you hear or see anything, despise it, for it is evil."

The door swung open and closed again, and though nothing visible entered, I knew that there was now in the room a living intelligence other than Father Denys's and mine, and it affected my being, my self, just as some horrible odour of putrefaction affects one physically: my soul sickened in it. Then, still seeing nothing, I perceived that the room, warm and comfortable just now, with a fire of coal prospering in the grate, was growing cold, and that some strange eclipse was veiling the light. Close to me on the table stood an electric lamp: the shade of it fluttered in the icy draught that stirred in the air, and the illuminant wire was no longer incandescent, but red and dull like the embers in the grate. I scrutinized the dimness, but as yet no material form manifested itself.

Father Denys was sitting very upright in his chair, his eyes fixed and focused on something invisible to me. His lips were moving and muttering, his hands grasped the crucifix he was wearing. And then I saw what I knew he was seeing, too: a face was outlining itself on the air in front of him, a face swollen and purple, with tongue lolling from the mouth, and as it hung there it oscillated to and fro. Clearer and clearer it grew, suspended there by the rope that now became visible to me, and though the apparition was of a man hanged by the neck, it was not dead but active and alive, and the spirit that awfully animated it was no human one, but something diabolical.

Suddenly Father Denys rose to his feet, and his face was within an inch or two of that suspended horror. He raised his hands which held the sacred emblem.

"Begone to your torment," he cried, "until the days of it are over, and the mercy of God grants you eternal death."

There rose a wailing in the air: some blast shook the room so that the corners of it quaked, and then the light and the warmth were restored to it, and there was no one there but our two selves. Father Denys's face was haggard and dripping with the struggle he had been through, but there shone on it such radiance as I have never seen on human countenance.

"It's over," he said. "I saw it shrivel and wither before the power of His presence . . . And your eyes tell me you saw it too and you know now that what wore the semblance of humanity was pure evil."

We talked a little longer, and he rose to go.

"Ah, I forgot," he said. "You wanted to know how I could reveal to you what was told me in confession. Horace Kennion died this morning by his own hand. He left with his lawyer a packet to be opened on his death, with instructions that it should be published in the daily Press. I saw it in an evening paper, and it was a detailed account of how he killed Gerald Selfe. He wished it to have all possible publicity."

"But why?" I asked.

Father Denys paused.

"He gloried in his wickedness, I think," he said. "He loved it, as I told you, for its own sake, and he wanted everyone to know of it, as soon as he was safely away."

PIRATES

For many years this project of sometime buying back the house had simmered in Peter Graham's mind, but whenever he actually went into the idea with practical intention, stubborn reasons had presented themselves to deter him. In the first place it was very far off from his work, down in the heart of Cornwall, and it would be impossible to think of going there just for week-ends, and if he established himself there for longer periods what on earth would he do with himself in that soft remote Lotus-land? He was a busy man who, when at work, liked the diversion of his club and of the theatres in the evening, but he allowed himself few holidays away from the City, and those were spent on salmon river or golf links with some small party of solid and likeminded friends. Looked at in these lights, the project bristled with objections.

Yet through all these years, forty of them now, which had ticked away so imperceptibly, the desire to be at home again at Lescop had always persisted, and from time to time it gave him shrewd little unexpected tugs, when his conscious mind was in no way concerned with it. This desire, he was well aware, was of a sentimental quality, and often he wondered at himself that he, who was so well-armoured in the general jostle of the world against that type of emotion, should have just this one joint in his harness. Not since he was sixteen had he set eyes on the place, but the memory of it was more vivid than that of any other scene of subsequent experience. He had married since then, he had lost his wife, and though for many months after that he had felt horribly lonely, the ache of that loneliness had ceased, and now, if he had ever asked himself the direct question, he would have confessed that bachelor existence was more suited to him than married life had ever been. It had not been a conspicuous success, and he never felt the least temptation to repeat the experiment.

But there was another loneliness which neither married life nor his keen interest in his business had ever extinguished, and this was directly connected with his desire for that house on the green slope of the hills above Truro. For only seven years had he lived there, the youngest but one of a family of five children, and now out of all that gay company he alone was left. One by one they had dropped off the stem of life, but as each in turn went into this silence, Peter had not missed them very much: his own life was too occupied to give him time really to miss anybody, and he was too vitally constituted to do otherwise than look forwards.

None of that brood of children except himself, and he childless, had married, and now when he was left without intimate tie of blood to any living being, a loneliness had gathered thickly round him. It was not in any sense a tragic or desperate loneliness: he had no wish to follow them on the unverified and unlikely chance of finding them all again. Also, he had no use for any disembodied existence: life meant to him flesh and blood and material interests and activities, and he could form no conception of life apart from such. But sometimes he ached with this dull gnawing ache of loneliness, which is worse than all others, when he thought of the stillness that lay congealed like clear ice over these young and joyful years when Lescop had been so noisy and alert and full of laughter, with its garden resounding with games, and the house with charades and hide-and-seek and multitudinous plans. Of course there had been rows and quarrels and disgraces, hot enough at the time, but now there was no one to quarrel with. "You can't really quarrel with people whom you don't love," thought Peter, "because they don't matter." . . . Yet it was ridiculous to feel lonely; it was even more than ridiculous, it was weak, and Peter had the kindly contempt of a successful and healthy and unemotional man for weaknesses of that kind. There were so many amusing and interesting things in the world, he had so many irons in the fire to be beaten, so to speak, into gold when he was working, and so many palatable diversions when he was not (for he still brought a boyish enthusiasm to work and play alike), that there was no excuse for indulging in sentimental sterilities. So, for months together, hardly a stray thought would drift towards the remote years lived in the house on the hill-side above Truro.

He had lately become chairman of the board of that new and highly promising company, the British Tin Syndicate. Their property included certain Cornish mines which had been previously abandoned as nonpaying propositions, but a clever mineralogical chemist had recently invented a process by which the metal could be extracted far more cheaply than had hitherto been possible. The British Tin Syndicate had bought the patent, and having acquired these derelict Cornish mines was getting very good results from ore that had not been worth treating. Peter had very strong opinions as to the duty of a chairman to make himself familiar with the practical side of his concerns, and was now travelling down to Cornwall to make a personal inspection of the mines where this process was at work. He had with him certain technical reports which he had received to read during the uninterrupted hours of his journey, and it was not till his train had left Exeter behind that he finished his perusal of them, and, putting them back in his despatch-case, turned his eye at the swiftly passing panorama of travel. It was many years since he had been to the West Country, and now with the thrill of vivid recognition he found the red cliffs round Dawlish, interspersed between stretches of sunny sea-beach, startlingly familiar. Surely he must have seen them quite lately, he thought to himself, and then, ransacking his memory, he found it was forty years since he had looked at them, travelling back to Eton from his last holidays at Lescop. The intense sharp-cut impressions of youth!

His destination to-night was Penzance, and now, with a strangely keen sense of expectation, he remembered that just before reaching Truro station the house on the hill was visible from the train, for often on these journeys to and from school he had been all eyes to catch the first sight of it and the last. Trees perhaps would have grown up and intervened, but as they ran past the station before Truro he shifted across to the other side of the carriage, and once more looked out for that glimpse . . . There it was, a mile away across the valley, with its grey stone front and the big beech-tree screening one end of it, and his heart leaped as he saw it. Yet what use was the house to him now? It was not the stones and the bricks of it, nor the tall hay-fields below it, nor the tangled garden behind that he wanted, but the days when he had lived in it. Yet he leaned from the window till a cutting extinguished the view of it, feeling that he was looking at a photograph that recalled some living presence. All those who had made Lescop dear and still vivid had gone, but this record remained, like the image on the plate . . . And then he smiled at himself with a touch of contempt for his sentimentality.

The next three days were a whirl of enjoyable occupation: tin-mines in the concrete were new to Peter, and he absorbed himself in these, as in some new game or ingenious puzzle. He went down the shafts of mines which had been opened again, he inspected the new chemical process, seeing it at work and checking the results, he looked into running expenses, comparing them with the value of the metal recovered. Then, too, there were substantial traces of silver in some of these ores, and he went eagerly into the question as to whether it would pay to extract it. Certainly even the mines which had previously been closed down ought to yield a decent dividend with this process, while those where the lode was richer would vastly increase their profits. But economy, economy . . . Surely it would save in the end, though at a considerable capital expenditure now, to lay a light railway from the works to the rail-head instead of employing these motor-lorries. There was a piece of steep gradient, it was true, but a small detour, with a trestle-bridge over the stream, would avoid that.

He walked over the proposed route with the engineer and scrambled about the stream-bank to find a good take-off for his trestle-bridge. And all the time at the back of his head, in some almost subconscious region of thought, were passing endless pictures of the house and the hill, its rooms and passages, its fields and garden, and with them, like some accompanying tune, ran that ache of loneliness. He felt that he must prowl again about the place: the owner, no doubt, if he presented himself, would let him just stroll about alone for half an hour. Thus he would see it all altered and overscored by the life of strangers living there, and the photograph would fade into a mere blur and then blankness. Much better that it should.

It was in this intention that, having explored every avenue for dividends on behalf of his company, he left Penzance by an early morning train in order to spend a few hours in Truro and go up to London later in the day. Hardly had he emerged from the station when a crowd of memories, forty years old, but more vivid than any of those of the last day or two, flocked round him with welcome for his return. There was the level-crossing and the road leading down to the stream where his sister Sybil and he had caught a stickleback for their aquarium, and across the bridge over it was the lane sunk deep between high crumbling banks that led to a footpath across the fields to Lescop. He knew exactly where was that pool with long ribands of water-weed trailing and waving in it, which had yielded them that remarkable fish: he knew how campions red and white would be in flower on the lane-side, and in the fields the meadow-orchis. But it was more convenient to go first into the town, get his lunch at the hotel, and to make enquiries from a house-agent as to the present owner of Lescop; perhaps he would walk back to the station for his afternoon train by that short cut.

Thick now as flowers on the steppe when spring comes, memories bright and fragrant shot up round him. There was the shop where he had taken his canary to be stuffed (beautiful it looked!): and there was the shop of the "undertaker and cabinet-maker," still with the same name over the door, where on a memorable birthday, on which his amiable family had given him, by request, the tokens of their good-will in cash, he had ordered a cabinet with five drawers and two trays, varnished and smelling of newly cut wood, for his collection of shells . . . There was a small boy in jersey and flannel trousers looking in at the window now, and Peter suddenly said to himself, "Good Lord, how like I used to be to that boy: same kit, too." Strikingly like indeed he was, and Peter, curiously interested, started to cross the street to get a nearer look at him. But it was market-day, a drove of sheep delayed him, and when he got across the small boy had vanished among the passengers. Farther along was a dignified house-front with a flight of broad steps leading up to it, once the dreaded abode of Mr. Tuck, dentist. There was a tall girl standing outside it now, and again Peter involuntarily said to himself, "Why, that girl's wonderfully like Sybil!" But before he could get more than a glimpse of her, the door was opened and she passed in, and Peter was rather vexed to find that there was no longer a plate on the door indicating that Mr. Tuck was still at his wheel . . . At the end of the street was the bridge over the Fal just below which they used so often to take a boat for a picnic on the river. There was a jolly family party setting off just now from the quay, three boys, he noticed, and a couple of girls, and a woman of young middle-age. Quickly they dropped downstream and went forth, and with half a sigh he said to himself, "Just our number with Mamma."

He went to the Red Lion for his lunch: that was new ground and uninteresting, for he could not recall having set foot in that hostelry before. But as he munched his cold beef there was some great fantastic business going on deep down in his brain: it was trying to join up (and it believed it could) that boy outside the cabinet-maker's, that girl on the threshold of the house once Mr. Tuck's, and that family party starting for their picnic on the river. It was in vain that he told himself that neither the boy nor the girl nor the picnic-party could possibly have anything to do with him: as soon as his attention relaxed that burrowing underground chase, as of a ferret in a rabbit-hole, began again . . . And then Peter gave a gasp of sheer amazement, for he remembered with clear-cut distinctness how on the morning of that memorable birthday, he and Sybil started earlier than the rest from Lescop, he on the adorable errand of ordering his cabinet, she for a dolorous visit to Mr. Tuck. The others followed half an hour later for a picnic on the Fal to celebrate the great fact that his age now required two figures (though one was a nought) for expression. "It'll be ninety years, darling," his mother had said, "before you want a third one, so be careful of yourself."

Peter was almost as excited when this momentous memory burst on him as he had been on the day itself. Not that it meant anything, he said to himself, as there's nothing for it to mean. But I call it odd. It's as if something from those days hung about here still . . .

He finished his lunch quickly after that, and went to the house agent's to make his enquiries. Nothing could be easier than that he should prowl about Lescop, for the house had been untenanted for the last two years. No card "to view" was necessary, but here were the keys: there was no caretaker there.

"But the house will be going to rack and ruins," said Peter

indignantly. "Such a jolly house, too. False economy not to put a caretaker in. But of course it's no business of mine. You shall have the keys back during the afternoon: I'll walk up there now."

"Better take a taxi, sir," said the man. "A hot day, and a mile and a half up a steep hill."

"Oh, nonsense," said Peter. "Barely a mile. Why, my brother and I used often to do it in ten minutes."

It occurred to him that these athletic feats of forty years ago would probably not interest the modern world . . .

Pyder Street was as populous with small children as ever, and perhaps a little longer and steeper than it used to be. Then turning off to the right among strange new-built suburban villas he passed into the well-known lane, and in five minutes more had come to the gate leading into the short drive up to the house. It drooped on its hinges, he must lift it off the latch, sidle through and prop it in place again. Overgrown with grass and weeds was the drive, and with another spurt of indignation he saw that the stile to the pathway across the field was broken down and had dragged the wires of the fence with it. And then he came to the house itself, and the creepers trailed over the windows, and, unlocking the door, he stood in the hall with its discoloured ceiling and patches of mildew growing on the damp walls. Shabby and ashamed it looked, the paint perished from the window-sashes, the panes dirty, and in the air the sour smell of chambers long unventilated. And yet the spirit of the house was there still, though melancholy and reproachful, and it followed him wearily from room to room – "You are Peter, aren't you?" it seemed to say. "You've just come to look at me, I see and not to stop. But I remember the jolly days just as well as you." . . . From room to room he went, dining-room, drawing-room, his mother's sitting-room, his father's study: then upstairs to what had been the school-room in the days of governesses, and had then been turned over to the children for a play-room. Along the passage was the old nursery and the night-nursery, and above that attic-rooms, to one of which, as his own exclusive bedroom, he had been promoted when he went to school. The roof of it had leaked, there was a brown-edged stain on the sagging ceiling just above where his bed had been. "A nice state to let my room get into," muttered Peter. "How am I to sleep underneath that drip from the roof? Too bad!"

The vividness of his own indignation rather startled him. He had really felt himself to be not a dual personality, but the same Peter Graham at different periods of his existence. One of them, the chairman of the British Tin Syndicate, had protested against young Peter Graham being put to sleep in so damp and dripping a room, and the other (oh, the ecstatic momentary glimpse of him!) was indeed young Peter back in his lovely attic again, just home from school and now looking round with eager eyes to convince himself of that blissful reality, before bouncing downstairs again to have tea in the children's room. What a lot of things to ask about! How were his rabbits, and how were Sybil's guinea-pigs, and had Violet learned that song "Oh 'tis nothing but a shower," and were the wood-pigeons building again in the lime-tree? All these topics were of the first importance . . .

Peter Graham the elder sat down on the window-seat. It overlooked the lawn, and just opposite was the lime-tree, a drooping lime making a green cave inside the skirt of its lower branches, but with those above growing straight, and he heard the chuckling coo of the wood-pigeons coming from it. They were building there again then: that question of young Peter's was answered.

"Very odd that I should just be thinking of that," he said to himself: somehow there was no gap of years between him and young Peter, for his attic bridged over the decades which in the clumsy material reckoning of time intervened between them. Then Peter the elder seemed to take charge again.

The house was a sad affair, he thought: it gave him a stab of loneliness to see how decayed was the theatre of their joyful years, and no evidence of newer life, of the children of strangers and even of their children's children growing up here could have overscored the old sense of it so effectually. He went out of young Peter's room and paused on the landing: the stairs led down in two short flights to the story below, and now for the moment he was young Peter again, reaching down with his hand along the banisters, and preparing to take the first flight in one leap. But then old Peter saw it was an impossible feat for his less supple joints.

Well, there was the garden to explore, and then he would go back to the agent's and return the keys. He no longer wanted to take that short cut down the steep hill to the station, passing the pool where Sybil and he had caught the stickleback, for his whole notion, sometimes so urgent, of coming back here, had wilted and withered. But he would just walk about the garden for ten minutes, and as he went with sedate step downstairs, memories of the garden, and of what they all did there began to invade him. There were trees to be climbed, and shrubberies – one thicket of syringa particularly where goldfinches built – to be searched for nests and moths, but above all there was that game they played there, far more exciting than lawn-tennis or cricket in the bumpy field (though that was exciting enough) called Pirates . . . There was a summer-house, tiled and roofed and of solid walls at the top of the garden, and that was "home" or "Plymouth Sound," and from there ships (children that is) set forth at the order of the Admiral to pick a trophy without being caught by the Pirates. There were two Pirates who hid anywhere in the garden and jumped out, and (counting the Admiral who, after giving his orders, became the flagship) three ships, which had to cruise to orchard or flower-bed or field and bring safely home a trophy culled from the ordained spot. Once, Peter remembered, he was flying up the winding path to the summer-house with a pirate close on his heels, when he fell flat down, and the humane pirate leaped over him for fear of treading on him, and fell down too. So Peter got home, because Dick had fallen on his face and his nose was bleeding . . .

"Good Lord, it might have happened yesterday," thought Peter. "And Harry called him a bloody pirate, and Papa heard and thought he was using shocking language till it was explained to him."

The garden was even worse than the house, neglected utterly and rankly overgrown, and to find the winding path at all, Peter had to push through briar and thicket. But he persevered and came out into the rose-garden at the top, and there was Plymouth Sound with roof collapsed and walls bulging, and moss growing thick between the tiles of the floor.

"But it must be repaired at once," said Peter aloud . . . "What's that?" He whisked round towards the bushes through which he had pushed his way, for he had heard a voice, faint and far off coming from there, and the voice was familiar to him, though for thirty years it had been dumb. For it was Violet's voice which had spoken and she had said, "Oh, Peter: *here* you are!"

He knew it was her voice, and he knew the utter impossibility of it. But it frightened him, and yet how absurd it was to be frightened, for it was only his imagination, kindled by old sights and memories, that had played him a trick. Indeed, how jolly even to have imagined that he had heard Violet's voice again.

"Vi!" he called aloud, but of course no one answered. The wood-pigeons were cooing in the lime, there was a hum of bees and a whisper of wind in the trees and all round the soft enchanted Cornish air, laden with dream-stuff.

He sat down on the step of the summer-house, and demanded the presence of his own common sense. It had been an uncomfortable afternoon, he was vexed at this ruin of neglect into which the place had fallen, and he did not want to imagine these voices calling to him out of the past, or to see these odd glimpses which belonged to his boyhood. He did not belong any more to that epoch over which grasses waved and headstones presided, and he must be quit of all that evoked it, for, more than anything else, he was director of prosperous companies with big interests dependent on him. So he sat there for a calming five minutes, defying Violet, so to speak, to call to him again. And then, so unstable was his mood to-day, that presently he was listening for her. But Violet was always quick to see when she was not wanted, and she must have gone, to join the others . . ..

He retraced his way, fixing his mind on material environments. The golden maple at the head of the walk, a sapling like himself when last he saw it, had become a stout-trunked tree, the shrub of bay a tall column of fragrant leaf, and just as he passed the syringa, a goldfinch dropped out of it with dipping flight. Then he was back at the house again where the climbing fuchsia trailed its sprays across the window of his mother's room and hot thick scent (how well-remembered!) spilled from the chalices of the great magnolia.

"A mad notion of mine to come and see the house again," he said to himself. "I won't think about it any more: it's finished. But it was wicked not to look after it."

He went back into the town to return the keys to the house-agent.

"Much obliged to you," he said. "A pleasant house, when I knew it years ago. Why was it allowed to go to ruin like that?"

"Can't say, sir," said the man. "It has been let once or twice in the last ten years, but the tenants have never stopped long. The owner would be very pleased to sell it."

An idea, fanciful, absurd, suddenly struck Peter.

"But why doesn't he live there?" he asked. "Or why don't the tenants stop long? Was there something they didn't like about it? Haunted: anything of that sort? I'm not going to take it or purchase it: so that won't put me off."

The man hesitated a moment.

"Well, there were stories," he said, "if I may speak confidentially. But all nonsense, of course."

"Quite so," said Peter. "You and I don't believe in such rubbish. I wonder now: was it said that children's voices were heard calling in the garden?"

The discretion of a house-agent reasserted itself.

"I can't say, sir, I'm sure," he said. "All I know is that the house is to be had very cheap. Perhaps you would take our card."

Peter arrived back in London late that night. There was a tray of sandwiches and drinks waiting for him, and having refreshed himself, he sat smoking awhile thinking of his three days' work in Cornwall at the mines: there must be a directors' meeting as soon as possible to consider his suggestions . . . Then he found himself staring at the round rosewood table where his tray stood. It had been in his mother's sitting-room at Lescop, and the chair in which he sat, a fine Stuart piece, had been his father's chair at the dinner-table, and that book-case had stood in the hall, and his Chippendale card-table . . . he could not remember exactly where that had been. That set of Browning's poems had been Sybil's: it was from the shelves in the children's room. But it was time to go to bed, and he was glad he was not to sleep in young Peter's attic.

It is doubtful whether, if once an idea has really thrown out roots in a man's mind, he can ever extirpate it. He can cut off its sprouting suckers, he can nip off the buds it bears, or, if they come to maturity, destroy the seed, but the roots defy him. If he tugs at them something breaks, leaving a vital part still embedded, and it is not long before some fresh evidence of its vitality pushes up above the ground where he least expected it. It was so with Peter now: in the middle of some business-meeting, the face of one of his co-directors reminded him of that of the coachman at Lescop; if he went for a week-end of golf to the Dormy House at Rye, the bow-window of the billiard-room was in shape and size that of the drawing-room there, and the bank of gorse by the tenth green was no other than the clump below the tennis-court: almost he expected to find a tennis ball there when he had need to search it. Whatever he did, wherever he went, something called him from Lescop, and in the evening when he returned home, there was the furniture, more of it than he had realized, asking to be restored there: rugs and pictures and books, the silver on his table all joined in the mute appeal. But Peter stopped his ears to it: it was a senseless sentimentality, and a purely materialistic one to imagine that he could recapture the life over which so many years had flowed, and in which none of the actors but himself remained, by restoring to the house its old amenities and living there again. He would only emphasize his own loneliness by the visible contrast of the scene, once so alert and populous, with its present emptiness. And this "butting-in" (so he expressed it) of materialistic sentimentality only confirmed his resolve to have done with Lescop. It had been a bitter sight but tonic, and now he would forget it.

Yet even as he sealed his resolution, there would come to him, blown as a careless breeze from the west, the memory of that boy and girl he had seen in the town, of the gay family starting for their river-picnic, of the faint welcoming call to him from the bushes in the garden, and, most of all, of the suspicion that the place was supposed to be haunted. It was just because it was haunted that he longed for it, and the more savagely and sensibly he assured himself of the folly of possessing it, the more he yearned after it, and constantly now it coloured his dreams. They were happy dreams; he was back there with the others, as in old days, children again in holiday time, and like himself they loved being at home there again, and they made much of Peter because it was he who had arranged it all. Often in these dreams he said to himself 'I have dreamed this before, and then I woke and found myself elderly and lonely again, but this time it is real!'

The weeks passed on, busy and prosperous, growing into months, and one day in the autumn, on coming home from a day's golf, Peter fainted. He had not felt very well for some time, he had been languid and easily fatigued, but with his robust habit of mind he had labelled such symptoms as mere laziness, and had driven himself with the whip. But now it might be as well to get a medical overhauling just for the satisfaction of being told there was nothing the matter with him. The pronouncement was not quite that . . .

"But I simply can't," he said. "Bed for a month and a winter of loafing on the Riviera! Why, I've got my time filled up till close on Christmas, and then I've arranged to go with some friends for a short holiday. Besides, the Riviera's a pestilent hole. It can't be done. Supposing I go on just as usual: what will happen?"

Dr. Dufflin made a mental summary of his wilful patient.

"You'll die, Mr. Graham," he said cheerfully. "Your heart is not what it should be, and if you want it to do its work, which it will for many years yet, if you're sensible, you must give it rest. Of course, I don't insist on the Riviera: that was only a suggestion for I thought you would probably have friends there, who would help to pass the time for you. But I do insist on some mild climate, where you can loaf out of doors. London with its frosts and fogs would never do."

Peter was silent for a moment.

"How about Cornwall?" he asked.

"Yes, if you like. Not the north coast of course."

"I'll think it over," said Peter. "There's a month yet."

Peter knew that there was no need for thinking it over. Events were conspiring irresistibly to drive him to that which he longed to do, but against which he had been struggling, so fantastic was it, so irrational. But now it was made easy for him to yield and his obstinate colours came down with a run. A few telegraphic exchanges with the house-agent made Lescop his, another gave him the address of a reliable builder and decorator, and with the plans of the house, though indeed there was little need of them, spread out on his counterpane, Peter issued urgent orders. All structural repairs, leaking roofs and dripping ceilings, rotted woodwork and crumbling plaster must be tackled at once, and when that was done, painting and papering followed. The drawing-room used to have a Morris-paper; there were spring flowers on it, blackthorn, violets, and fritillaries, a hateful wriggling paper, so he thought it, but none other would serve. The hall was painted duck-egg green, and his mother's room was pink, "a beastly pink, tell them," said Peter to his secretary, "with a bit of blue in it: they must send me sample by return of post, big pieces, not snippets." . . . Then there was furniture: all the furniture in the house here which had once been at Lescop must go back there. For the rest, he would send down some stuff from London, bedroom appurtenances, and linen and kitchen utensils: he would see to carpets when he got there. Spare bedrooms could wait; just four servants' rooms must be furnished, and also the attic which he had marked on the plan, and which he intended to occupy himself. But no one must touch the garden till he came: he would superintend that himself, but by the middle of next month there must be a couple of gardeners ready for him.

"And that's all," said Peter, "just for the present." "All?" he thought, as, rather bored with the direction of matters that usually ran themselves, he folded up his plans. "Why, it's just the beginning: just underwriting."

The month's rest-cure was pronounced a success, and with strict orders not to exert mind or body, but to lie fallow, out of doors whenever possible, with quiet strolls and copious restings, Peter was allowed to go to Lescop, and on a December evening he saw the door opened to him and the light of welcome stream out on to his entry. The moment he set foot inside he knew, as by some interior sense, that he had done right, for it was not only the warmth and the ordered comfort restored to the deserted house that greeted him, but the firm knowledge that they whose loss made his loneliness were greeting him . . . That came in a flash, fantastic and yet soberly convincing; it was fundamental, everything was based on it. The house had been restored to its old aspect, and though he had ventured to turn the small attic next door to young Peter's bedroom into a bathroom, "after all," he thought, "it's my house, and I must make myself comfortable. They don't want bathrooms, but I do, and there it is." There indeed it was, and there was electric light installed, and he dined, sitting in his father's chair, and then pottered from room to room, drinking in the old friendly atmosphere, which was round him wherever he went, for They were pleased. But neither voice nor vision manifested that, and perhaps it was only his own pleasure at being back that he attributed to them. But he would have loved a glimpse or a whisper, and from time to time, as he sat looking over some memoranda about the British Tin Syndicate, he peered into corners of the room, thinking that something moved there, and when a trail of creeper tapped against the window he got up and looked out. But nothing met his scrutiny but the dim starlight falling like dew on the neglected lawn. "They're here, though," he said to himself, as he let the curtain fall back.

The gardeners were ready for him next morning, and under his directions began the taming of the jungly wildness. And here was a pleasant thing, for one of them was the son of the cowman, Calloway, who had been here forty years ago, and he had childish memories still of the garden where with his father he used to come from the milking-shed to the house with the full pails. And he remembered that Sybil used to keep her guinea-pigs on the drying-ground at the back of the house. Now that he said that Peter remembered it too, and so the drying-ground all overgrown with brambles and rank herbage must be cleared.

"Iss, sure, nasty little vermin I thought them," said Calloway the younger, "but 'twas here Miss Sybil had their hutches and a wired run for 'em. And a rare fuss there was when my father's terrier got in and killed half of 'em, and the young lady crying over the corpses."

That massacre of the innocents was dim to Peter; it must have happened in term-time when he was at school, and by the next holidays, to be sure, the prolific habits of her pets had gladdened Sybil's mourning.

So the drying-ground was cleared and the winding path up the shrubbery to the summer-house which had been home to the distressed vessels pursued by pirates. This was being rebuilt now, the roof timbered up, the walls rectified and whitewashed, and the steps leading to it and its tiled floor cleaned of the encroaching moss. It was soon finished, and Peter often sat there to rest and read the papers after a morning of prowling and supervising in the garden, for an hour or two on his feet oddly tired him, and he would doze in the sunny shelter. But now he never dreamed about coming back to Lescop or of the welcoming presences. "Perhaps that's because I've come," he thought, "and those dreams were only meant to drive me. But I think they might show that they're pleased: I'm doing all I can."

Yet he knew they were pleased, for as the work in the garden progressed, the sense of them and their delight hung about the cleared paths as surely as the smell of the damp earth and the uprooted bracken which had made such trespass. Every evening Calloway collected the gleanings of the day, piling it on the bonfire in the orchard. The bracken flared, and the damp hazel stems fizzed and broke into flame, and the scent of the wood smoke drifted across to the house. And after some three weeks' work all was done, and that afternoon Peter took no siesta in the summer-house, for he could not cease from walking through flower-garden and kitchen-garden and orchard now perfectly restored to their old order. A shower fell, and he sheltered under the lime where the pigeons built, and then the sun came out again, and in that gleam at the close of the winter day he took a final stroll to the bottom of the drive, where the gate now hung firm on even hinges. It used to take a long time in closing, if, as a boy, you let it swing, penduluming backwards and forwards with the latch of it clicking as it passed the hasp: and now he pulled it wide, and let go of it, and to and fro it went in lessening movement till at last it clicked and stayed. Somehow that pleased him immensely: he liked accuracy in details.

But there was no doubt he was very tired: he had an unpleasant sensation, too, as of a wire stretched tight across his heart, and of some thrumming going on against it. The wire dully ached, and this thrumming produced little stabs of sharp pain. All day he had been conscious of something of the sort, but he was too much taken up with the joy of the finished garden to heed little physical beckonings. A good long night would make him fit again, or, if not, he could stop in bed to-morrow. He went upstairs early, not the least anxious about himself, and instantly went to sleep. The soft night air pushed in at his open window, and the last sound that he heard was the tapping of the blind-tassel against the sash.

He woke very suddenly and completely, knowing that somebody had called him. The room was curiously bright, but not with the quality of moonlight; it was like a valley lying in shadow, while somewhere, a little way above it, shone some strong splendour of noon. And then he heard again his name called, and knew that the sound of the voice came in through the window. There was no doubt that Violet was calling him: she and the others were out in the garden.

"Yes, I'm coming," he cried, and he jumped out of bed. He seemed – it was not odd – to be already dressed: he had on a jersey and flannel trousers, but his feet were bare and he slipped on a pair of shoes, and ran downstairs, taking the first short flight in one leap, like young Peter. The door of his mother's room was open, and he looked in, and there she was, of course, sitting at the table and writing letters.

"Oh, Peter, how lovely to have you home again," she said. "They're all out in the garden, and they've been calling you, darling. But come and see me soon, and have a talk."

Out he ran along the walk below the windows, and up the winding path through the shrubbery to the summer-house, for he knew they were going to play Pirates. He must hurry, or the pirates would be abroad before he got there, and as he ran, he called out:

"Oh, do wait a second: I'm coming."

He scudded past the golden maple and the bay tree, and there they all were in the summer-house which was home. And he took a flying leap up the steps and was among them.

It was there that Calloway found him next morning. He must indeed have run up the winding path like a boy, for the new-laid gravel was spurned at long intervals by the toe-prints of his shoes.

The Wishing-Well

The village of St. Gervase lies at the seaward base of that broad triangular valley which lies scooped-out among the uplands of the north Cornish moors, and not even among the fells of Cumberland could you find so remote a cluster of human habitations. Four miles of by-road, steep and stony, lies between it and the highway along which in tourist-time the motor-buses pound dustily to Bude and Newquay, and eight more separate it from railhead. Scarcely once in the summer does an inquisitive traveller think it worth while to visit a village which his guide-book dismisses with the very briefest reference to the ancient wishing-well that lies near the lych-gate of the churchyard there. The world, in fact, takes very little heed of St. Gervase, and St. Gervase hardly more of the outer world. Seldom do you see man or woman waiting at the corner, where the road from the village joins the highway, for the advent of the motor-bus, and seldom does it pause there to set down one of its passengers. An occasional trolley laden with sacks of coal and cargo of beer-barrels jolts heavily down the lane; for the rest the farms of the valley and the kitchen-gardens of the cottagers supply it with the needs of life and its few fishingboats bring in their harvest from the sea. Nor does St. Gervase seek after any fruits of science or culture or religion save such as spring from its soil, which furnishes its wise women with herbs of healing for ailing bodies, and from its tradition of spells and superstition of a darker sort to be used in the service of love or of vengeance. These latter are not publicity spoken of save in one house at St. Gervase, but are muttered and whispered in quiet consultations, and thus the knowledge has been handed down from mother to daughter since the days when, three centuries ago, a screeching handcuffed band of women were driven from here to Bodmin, and, after a parody of a trial, burned at the stake.

It was strange that the Vicarage which might have been expected to be unblackened by the smoke of legendary learning was the one house where magic and witchcraft were openly and sedulously studied, but such study was purely academical, the Reverend Lionel Eusters being the foremost authority in England as a writer on folk-lore. His parochial duties were light and his leisure plentiful, for a couple of services on Sunday were, to judge by the congregation, sufficient for the spiritual needs of his parish, and for the rest of the week he was busy in the library of the creeper-covered vicarage that stood hard by the lych-gate that led to the churchyard. Here, patient but unremitting, he worked at his great book on witchcraft which had engaged him so many years, occasionally printing some sub-section of it as a pamphlet: the origin of the witch's broomstick, for instance, had furnished curious reading. He was a wealthy man with no expensive tastes save that for books on his subject and the big library he had built on to the Vicarage had now few empty shelves. Twenty years ago, when ill-health had driven him from the chill clays of Cambridge, he had been appointed to this remote college living, and the warm soft climate and the strange primitive traditions that hung about the place suited both his health and his hobby.

Mr. Eusters had long been a widower, and his daughter Judith, now a woman of forty years old, kept house for him. The time of her more marriageable maidenhood had been spent here in complete isolation from her own class, and though sometimes when she saw the courtships and childbirths of the village the sense of what she had missed made a bitter brew for her, she had long known that St. Gervase had cast some spell upon her, and that had a wooer from without sought her he must indeed be a magnet to her heart if he could draw her from this secluded valley into the world that lay beyond the moors. In the few visits she had paid to relations of her father and mother, she had always pined to be home again, and to wake to the glinting of the sun on the gorse-clad hills, or to the bellowing roar of some westerly gale that threw the sheets of rain against the window: a stormy day at home was worth all the alien sunshine, and the sandy beach of the bay with the waves asleep or toppling in, foam-laced and thunderous, was better than the brilliance of southern seas. Here alone her mind knew that background of content which is brighter than all the pleasures the world offers: here every day the spell of St. Gervase was like some magic shuttle weaving its threads through her.

Since her mother's death Judith's days had been of a uniform monotony. Household cares claimed a short hour of the morning, and then she went to the library where her father worked to transcribe his words if he had a section of his work ready for dictation, or to look up endless references in the volumes that lined the room, if he was preparing the notes which formed the material of his dictation. Some branch of witchcraft was always the subject of it, some magical rite for the fertility of the cattle, some charm for child-bearing, some philtre for love, or (what had by degrees got to interest her most), one that caused the man on whom a girl's heart was set, but who had nought for her, to wither in the grip of some nameless sickness and miserably to perish. Month by month as her father pushed his patient way forward through the ancient mists, these Satanic spells that blighted grew to be a fascination with Judith.

Just now he was deep in an exploration into wishing-wells, and there she sat this morning, pencil in hand for his dictation, as he walked up and down the library, glancing now and then at his memoranda spread out on the table.

"These wishing-wells," he said, "are common to the whole of early European beliefs, but nowhere do we find that the power which supposedly presided over them was at the beck and call of any chance persons who invoked their efficacy. Only witches and those who had occult powers could set the spell working, and the origin of that spell was undoubtedly Satanic, and not till Christian times were these wells used for any purpose but that of invoking evil. The form of these wells is curiously similar; an arch or shelter of stonework is invariably built over them, and in the sides are cut small niches where, in Christian days, candles were placed or thank-offerings deposited. What they were previously used for is uncertain, but they were beyond doubt connected with the evil spells, and I conjecture that the name of the person devoted to destruction was scratched on a coin, or written on a slip of linen or paper, to await the action of the diabolical power. The most perfectly preserved of these wishing-wells known to me, is that of St. Gervase in Cornwall; its arched shelter is in excellent condition, and the well, as is usual, very deep. The local belief in its efficacy has survived to this day, though its power is never invoked, as far as I can ascertain, for evil purposes. A woman in pregnancy, for instance, will drink of the well and pray beside it, a girl whose lover has gone to sea will scratch her name on a silver coin and drop it into the water, thus insuring his safe return. The village folk are curiously reticent about such practices, but I can personally vouch for cases of this kind . . .

He paused, fingering the short Vandyck beard that grew greyly from his chin.

"My dear, I wonder if that is quite discreet," he said to Judith. "But after all it is highly improbable that any copy of my work published by the University at a guinea, will find its way here. I think I will chance it . . . Dear me, the bell for luncheon already! We will resume our work this evening, if you are at leisure, as I have much ready for dictation."

Judith smiled to herself as she paged the sheets . . . She knew very much more about her father's parishioners than he, for he, scholar, recluse, and parson only lived on the fringe of their lives, whereas she, in chatty visits to the women who sat and knitted at their cottage-doors, had got into real touch with an inner life to which he was a stranger. She knew, for instance, that old Sally Trenair, whose death less than a week ago had been a source of such relief to her neighbours, was universally held to be a witch, and Sally was always muttering and mumbling round the wishing-well. None who crossed her will prospered, their cows went dry or threw stillborn calves, their sheep wilted, the atrocious henbane, fatal to cattle, appeared in their fields: so the prudent wished Sally a polite good day, and sent her honey from their hives and a cut of prime bacon when the pig was killed. But from some vein of secretiveness, Judith did not tell her father of such talk, whispered to her over the knitting-needles, which would have inclined him to modify his view about the surviving association of the wishing-well with evil invocations. It was idle gossip, perhaps, for if you had challenged her to say whether she believed such tales of old Sally, she would have certainly denied it . . . And yet something deep down in her would have whispered "I don't only believe: I *know*."

To-day, when luncheon was finished, her father returned to his desk and Judith started to walk a couple of miles up the valley to the farm of John Penarth, whose family from time immemorial had owned those rich acres. For the last eight years he and his wife had lived there alone, for their only son Steven had gone out to America at the age of sixteen to seek his fortune. But fortune had not sought him, and now, when his father was growing old and his health declining, Steven was coming home with the intention of settling down here. Judith remembered him well, a big handsome boy with the blue of the sea in his eyes and the sunshine in his hair, and she wondered into what sort of man he would have grown. She had heard that he was already come, but though she was curious to see him, the motive for her visit was really the same as that which so often drew her to the Penarth farm, namely, to have a talk with Steven's mother. There was no one, thought Judith, who was so learned in what was truly worth knowing as Mrs. Penarth. She could not have pointed you India on the big globe that stood in her parlour, or have answered the simplest board-school question about Queen Elizabeth, or have added five to four without counting on her fingers, but she had rarer knowledge in the stead of such trivialities. She had the healing touch for man and beast: she stroked an ailing cow and next day it would be at pasture again, she whispered in the ear of a feverish child, plucking gently at its forehead and pulled the headache out so that the child slept. And she, alone of all the village, paid no court to Sally Trenair nor sought to propitiate her. One day, as she passed Sally's cottage, Sally had screamed curses on her, and followed her, yelling, half-way to the farm. Then suddenly Mrs. Penarth had turned and shot out her finger at her. " You silly tipsy old crone," she had cried. "Down on your knees and crave my pardon, and then get home and don't cross my way again."

Sure enough Sally knelt on the stones, and slunk off home, and thereafter, if Mrs. Penarth was down in the village, she would make haste to get into her cottage, and shut the door. Mrs. Penarth, it seemed, knew more than Sally.

Judith swung her easy way up the steep hill, hatless in spite of the hot sun, and unbreathed by the ascent. She was a tall woman, black-haired and comely, her skin clear and healthy with the bloom on it that only sun and air can give. Her full-lipped mouth hinted that passion smouldered there, her eyebrows, fine and level nearly met across the base of her forehead, her eyes big and black looked ever so slightly inwards. So small was the convergence that it was no disfigurement: when she looked directly at you it was not perceptible, but if she was immersed in her own thoughts, then it was there. Most noticeable was it when her father was dictating to her some grim story of malign magic or witchcraft . . . But now she had come to the paved path through the garden of the farm-house set with flowers and herbs in front of the espaliered apple-trees, and there was Mrs. Penarth, knitting in the shade of the house during these hot hours before she went out again to chicken-run and milkingshed.

"Eh, but you're a welcome sight, Miss Judith," she said in the soft Cornish speech. "And you hatless in the sun, as ever, but indeed you're one of the wise who have made sun and rain their friends, and 'tis far you'd have to search ere you found better. Come in, dear soul, and have a glass of currant-water after your walk, and tell me the doings down to St. Gervase."

Judith always fell into their mode of speech when she was with the native folk!

"Sure, there's little to tell," she said. "There was a grand catch two days agone, and yesterday was the burying of old Sally Trenair."

Mrs. Penarth poured out for her a glass of the clear ruby liquor for which she was famous.

"Strange how the folk were scared of that tipsy old poppet," she said. "She had nobbut a few rhymes to gabble and a foul tongue to flap at them. A tale of curses she blew off at me one day, and I doubt not she hid my name in the wishing-well, though I never troubled to look."

"Hid your name in the wishing-well?" asked Judith, thinking of the morning's dictation.

Mrs. Penarth shot a swift oblique glance at her. There were certain things she had noticed about Judith, and they interested her.

"Aw my dear, you've sure got too much sense and book-learning to heed such tales," she said. "But when I was a girl my mother used to talk of them. Even now I scarce know what to make of such strange things."

"Oh, tell me of them," said Judith. "My father's just set on the wishing-wells and the lore of them. He was dictating to me of them all the morning."

"Eh, to think of that! Well, when I was a girl there were a many queer doings round the well. A maid would tell an old crone like Sally if she fancied a young man, and get some gabble to con over as she sipped the water. Or if a fellow had an ill-will toward another he'd consult a witch-woman and she'd write the name of his enemy for him, and bid him hide it in the well. And then, sure as eve or morning, tribulations drove fast on him, as long as his name bided there. His cows would go dry or his boat be wrecked or his children get deadly dwams or his wife break her marriage vows. Or he himself would pine and fail till he was scarce able to put foot to floor, and presently the bell would be tolling for him. Idle tales no doubt."

Judith had been drinking this in, eager as the thirsty earth drinks the rain after drought or as a starving man sets his teeth in food. Her mouth smiled, her blood beat high and strong, it was as if she was learning some news of good fortune which was hers by birthright. Just then there came a step in the passage and the door opened.

"Why, 'tis Steven," said Mrs. Penarth. "Come, lad, and pay your duty to Miss Judith, maybe she remembers you."

Tall as she was, he towered over her: he had a boy's face still, and the sea was in his eyes and the sun in his hair. And on the instant Judith knew that no magnet of man would avail to draw her from St. Gervase.

There was dictation again for her up till supper time, and when, after that, her father went back to his books, she strolled out, as she often did on hot nights like this, before going to bed. Never yet had she felt so strong an emotional excitement as that afternoon when Mrs. Penarth, talking of those old beliefs of her girlhood, had somehow revealed Judith to herself. All that narrative about the wishing-well was already familiar to some secret cell in her brain: she needed only to be reminded of it to make it her own. On the top of that had come Steven's entry, and her heart had leaped to him. Some mixed brew of these two was at ferment within her now; sometimes a bubble from one, sometimes from the other rose luminous to the surface. She felt restless and tingling with stored energy, and she paused for a moment at the gate of the garden uncertain how to spend it.

The night was thickly overcast, the road that led down to the village a riband of grey, scarcely visible, and as she stood there she heard a step brisk and active coming along it, and there swung into view, recognizable even in the deep dusk by his height and gait, the figure of Steven on his way to the village. Dearly would she have loved to call to him and walk with him, but that could not be: besides another desire tugged at her, and when he was past, she turned in at the lych-gate to the churchyard. The white tombstones glimmered faintly in the dusk, and she looked up beyond them towards the grave by which she had stood two days ago at the burying of old Sally. Then her breath caught in her throat for she could see the mound of new-turned earth gleaming whitely. She made her way to it: this dark earth was certainly luminous with some wavering light, and on the moment she was conscious that Sally herself, not the mere bag of bones that had been put away in the earth, was close to her. So vivid was this impression that she whispered "Sally! Are you here, Sally?" No audible response came, but the answer tingled in every nerve in her body, and she knew that Sally was here, no pale wandering spirit, but a power friendly and sisterly and altogether evil. It was trickling into her, growing warm in her veins, as by some transfusion of blood. She went to the wishing-well and kneeling on the kerb stone of it drank of its water from her cupped hands.

Something stirred beside her, and turning she saw at her side, illuminated by some pale gleam, a little bent figure shrouded in clean grave-clothes and the brown wizened face, which she had last beheld in the composure and dignity of death, now all alive with glee and with welcome. And her flesh was weak, for in a spasm of terror she sprang to her feet with arms flung out against the spectre, and lo, there was nothing there but the quiet churchyard with the headstones of those who slumbered there, and at her feet the black invisible water of which she had drunk. Despising herself for the fright, and yet winged with it, she ran stumbling from the place, not halting till she was back at the vicarage, where the light shining from the library window showed that her father was still pursuing his academic researches into the world of things occult and terrible of which the doors were now swinging open to admit her in very truth.

For some days the horror of that moment by the well was effective, and she threw herself into the normal ways of life which lured her with a new brightness. She often saw Steven, for it was he who brought the milk of a morning from the farm, and she would be out in the garden by the time of his early arrival cutting roses for her vases or more strenuously engaged in weeding the borders. At first she gave him just a nodded "good morning," but soon they would stand chatting there for five minutes. She knew she made a fine handsome figure; she saw he appreciated her healthy splendour, he looked at her with the involuntary tribute a man pays to a good-looking woman. Fond, wild notions took root in her mind, spreading their fibres beneath in the soil, and anchoring there . . . Another morning she heard him singing as he clattered down the road in the milk-cart, a big rough resonant voice, of high pitch for a man. Judith played the organ in church, conducting a choir-practice every Saturday for the singers, and next week Steven was sitting among the men while she took them through the canticles and hymns. Women and girls took alto and treble parts; the chief chorister was Nance Pascoe, a maid of twenty, and she was like a folded rose-bud just bursting into full flower. By some blind instinct Judith began to dislike her: she would stop in the middle of a verse to tell the trebles they were flat, which meant that Nance was the culprit. Again she would ask the tenors singly to sing some line over which they had bungled, and had a word of praise for Steven. Or she would go to the farm for a chat with Mrs. Penarth, and by some casual questions learn that Steven was hedge-clipping near by in the meadow. Then she would remember she wanted a chicken for next day, and go to tell him: it was but a step. In a hundred infinitesimal ways she betrayed herself.

Mixed with this growth of longing which had so firmly rooted itself was another of more poisonous breed. There was a power eager to help her, and like a frightened fool she had fled from its manifestation. But she knew she was making no way with Steven, and now she bethought herself again of it, and found that her terror had withered, and that her thirst for commerce with those dark enchantments was keen not only for the help they could give her, but for her own love of them. Once more in the evening, when her father was back at his books, she set out for the wishing-well.

Her step was noiseless on the grass of the churchyard, and she was close to the wishing-well, still screened by bushes that grew there, when she heard from behind them a ringing man's laugh, and a girl's voice joined in.

"Sure, she's terrible set on you, Steven. It makes me bubble within when she says at the choir-singing, 'Yes, very nice, Mr. Penarth,' and what the poor soul means is 'Aw, Steven, doo'ee come and give me a hug.'"

Steven laughed again.

"I'm fair scared of her," he said, "though mother laughs fit to burst when she's come up to the farm to see and order one egg or a sprig of mint. And every morning when I take the milk the old girl'll be weeding and hoeing, showing-off like, as if she was the strong man at the fair."

"Eh, I declare I'm sorry for her," said Nance, "for I know what it is to love you. Poor empty heart!"

"Nance, we must put our banns up," said he. "I'm scared, but give your lad a kiss to strengthen him, and I'll pluck up and ask Parson to read us out next Sunday."

There was silence.

"Eh, Steven, don't hug so tight," whispered Nance. "You'll get your fill of me ere long. Just a drink from the well for us both, and then I must get home."

Judith stole back along the grass and from behind the curtain in the parlour window saw the two, arm-entwined, pass down the road. No thought was there now in her mind of any love-philtre, no longer did she want the help of a friendly power to get Steven. He had mocked at her, he was scared of her, and soon he would have good reason for that. Of Nance she hardly thought: it was not for Nance that her heart was black as the water in the wishing-well . . . She felt no hysterical rage of longing for revenge; it was a hellish glee that fed her soul. Quaint and pleasant was it, she thought, as she wrote on a slip of paper the name of "Steven Penarth," that it should have been his mother who had taught her that. Mrs. Penarth had laughed "fit to burst" at her, so Mrs. Penarth must learn not to laugh so much.

She went forth with the inscribed slip. The power she courted was flooding into her, wave on wave. Now she was back at the well again, and there she knelt a moment drinking in like a thirsty field the dew of power with which the air was thick. She felt in the darkness for one of those fern-fringed niches in the wall, and deep among its fronds she hid the paper.

"Master of evil and of me," she muttered, "send sickness and death on him whom I here dedicate."

Something stirred beside her: she knew that the presence which had terrified her before was manifest again. She turned with hands of welcome, and there beside her was the shroud-wrapped figure and the wizened face, but now the shroud was white no longer but spotted with earth-mould, and the flesh was rotting from the face. Judith put her arms close round the spectre, and kissed the frayed lips fretted with decay, and she felt it melting into her. She shut her eyes in the ecstasy of that union: when she opened them she was clasping the empty air.

She was down early next morning, full of youthful fire and fitness, and presently the milk-cart clattered up to the gate. But it was not Steven who drove it, but Mrs. Penarth.

"'Tis I who've come with your milk to-day, Miss Judith," she said, "for Steven's got a terrible bad headache, and I bade him lie abed. But he charged me to ask Parson to put up his banns, come Sunday."

"Oh, is Mr. Steven to be married?" asked Judith. "Who's the maid?"

"Just Nance Pascoe whom he's played with since he was a lad."

"Then he's lucky," said Judith, "for she's pretty as a picture. I'll tell my father about the banns. And I'm so sorry Mr. Steven's not well. But he'll mend quick."

The days passed on, and soon it was seen that Steven lay stricken with some sore fever to which neither his mother's healing hands nor the doctor's potions brought relief. Every morning Judith learned from Mrs. Penarth that he was no better, and every morning she felt herself the object of some keen, silent scrutiny. She was not one who prinked before her glass, but one day after Mrs. Penarth had gone, she ran upstairs and questioned her face. It certainly had changed: it was sharper in outline, and that cast in her eye was surely more pronounced. But she liked that: it seemed an outward and visible sign of her power. Every night now she sat by the wishing-well concentrating on her desire. The news of Steven had been joyfully bad that day: his fever burned more fiercely, consuming the flesh on his bones and drinking up his strength. Twice now had his banns been called, but it was not likely that he would go to church next as a bridegroom.

The moon was soon to rise as Judith got up to go home: she fancied she heard something stir in the bushes by the well, and called "Sally, Sally," but no response came. Her limbs were light with joy, she danced along the strip of turf leaping high in the air for the very exuberance of her soul . . . As soon as she turned out of the lych-gate Mrs. Penarth stole out of the bushes. She had a dark lantern with her, and she searched the walls of the wishing-well. She spied the paper Judith had hidden there, and she drew it out and read it. She tore it in half, and on the blank piece she wrote another name, and put it back exactly where it had been. That night Steven slept well and long, and in the morning, even as Judith had surmised, he was "mending quick."

Judith was not in the garden at the milk-hour to hear the favourable report, and later in the day Dr. Addis was called in: he found her suffering from just such an attack of fever as he had been attending for the past fortnight. It puzzled him, but his treatment of his other patient was proving successful, and he assured her father there was no cause for alarm: fevers ran their course. And Judith's fever ran its course even more fiercely.

She was lying in her bed facing the window some ten days after she had been taken ill. She knew that the power she had absorbed into her when she embraced that spectral horror by the wishing-well was being drained out of her by some vaster potency, which, vampire-like, was drinking up her own vitality as well. She had been quite conscious all day, but often she had seen, waveringly, like the flame of a candle blown this way and that in the draught, the dim semblance of that shrouded figure round which she had cast her welcoming arms. It seemed to be still attached to her by some band of filmy whiteness and to be incomplete, but about the hour of sunset she saw that the spectre stood by her bed, fully formed and severed from her. The face was now deeply pitted by corruption, and it floated away from her and drifted out of the window. She was left here, human once more, but sick unto death.

She remembered how she had written Steven's name, and dedicated him to the power of the wishing-well. Yet what had come of that? For the last week now Steven had brought the morning's milk, hale and handsome, with enquiries about her from his mother.

Could it be, she questioned herself, that she had failed in some point of the damnable ritual, and that what she had written was active not for his doom but for hers? It would be wise to destroy that slip of paper, if she could only get to it, not because she had ceased to wish him evil, but from the fear that it was her vitality that was being drained from her on that fruitless purpose.

She got out of bed, giddy with weakness, and managed to get into a skirt and jersey, and slip her feet into her shoes. The house was quiet, and step by step she struggled downstairs and to the door. The wholesome wind off the sea put a little life into her, and she shuffled along the strip of turf down which she had danced and capered, and which lay between the lych-gate and the well. She passed round the screen of bushes and there on the stone bench, was Steven's mother. She rose as Judith appeared and curtsied.

"Aw, dear. Why you look poorly indeed, Miss Judith," she said. "Is it wise for you to come out? To the wishing-well, too: there have been strange doings here."

"Oh, I'll be mending soon," said Judith. "A drink from the wishing-well was what I fancied."

She knelt down on the kerb leaning one hand against the wall of the well, while with the other she felt among the ferns that fringed it. There was the slip of paper she had hidden, and she drew it forth.

"Take your drink then, Miss Judith," said Mrs. Penarth. "Why, whatever have you found? That's a queer thing to have gotten! A slip of paper in it? Open it, dear soul: maybe there's some good news in it."

Judith crushed it up in her hand; there was no need for her to look, and even as she knelt there, she felt a sweet lightening and cooling of her fever come over her.

Mrs. Penarth shot out her hand at her.

"Open it, you slut, you paltry witch," she screamed. "Do my bidding!"

Judith opened it, and read her own name written there.

She tried to rise to her feet; she swayed and staggered and she fell forward into the wishing-well. It was very deep, and the sides of it were slippery with slime and water-moss. Once she caught at the step on which she had knelt, but her fingers failed to grasp it, and she sank. Once after that she rose and then there came a roaring in her ears, and to her eyes a blackness, and down her throat there poured the cool water of the wishing-well.

THE BATH-CHAIR

Edmund Faraday, at the age of fifty, had every reason to be satisfied with life: he had got all he really wanted, and plenty of it. Health was among the chief causes of his content, and he often reflected that the medical profession would have a very thin time of it, if everyone was as fortunate as he. His appreciation of his good fortune was apt at times to be a little trying: he ate freely, he absorbed large (but in no way excessive) quantities of mixed alcoholic liquors, pleasantly alluding to his immunity from any disagreeable effects, and he let it be widely known that he had a cold bath in the morning, spent ten minutes before an open window doing jerks and flexings, and had a fine appetite for breakfast. Not quite so popular was his faint contempt for those who had to be careful of themselves. It was not expressed in contemptuous terms, indeed he was jovially sympathetic with men perhaps ten years younger than himself who found it more prudent to be abstemious. "Such a bore for you, old man," he would comment, "but I expect you're wise."

In addition to these physical advantages, he was master of a very considerable income, derived from shares in a very sound company of general stores, which he himself had founded, and of which he was chairman: this and his accumulated savings enabled him to live precisely as he pleased. He had a house near Ascot, where he spent most week-ends from Friday to Monday, playing golf all day, and another in Massington Square, conveniently close to his business. He might reasonably look forward to a robust and prosperous traverse of that table-land of life which with healthy men continues till well after they have passed their seventieth year. In London he was accustomed to have a couple of hours' bridge at his club before he went back to his bachelor home where his sister kept house for him, and from morning to night his life was spent in enjoying or providing for his own pleasures.

Alice Faraday was, in her own department, one of the clues of his prosperous existence, for it was she who ran his domestic affairs for him. He saw little of her, for he always breakfasted by himself, and encountered her in the morning only for a moment when he came downstairs to set out for his office, and told her whether there would be some of his friends to dinner, or whether he would be out; she would then interview the cook and telephone to the tradesmen, and make her tour of the house to see that all was tidy and speckless. At the end of the day again it was but seldom that they spent a domestic evening together: either he dined out leaving her alone, or three friends or perhaps seven were his guests and made up a table or two tables of bridge. On these occasions Alice was never of the party. She was no card player, she was rather deaf, she was silent and by no means decorative, and she was best represented by the admirable meal she had provided for him and his friends. At the house at Ascot she performed a similar role, finding her way there by train on Friday morning, so as to have the house ready for him when he motored down later in the day.

Sometimes he wondered whether he would not be more comfortable if he married and gave Alice a modest home of her own with an income to correspond, for, though he saw her but seldom, her presence was slightly repugnant to him. But marriage was something of a risk, especially for a man of his age who had kept out of it so long, and he might find himself with a wife who had a will of her own, and who did not understand, as Alice certainly did, that the whole reason of her existence was to make him comfortable. Again he wondered whether perfectly-trained servants like his would not run the house as efficiently as his sister, in which case she would be better away; he would, indefinably, be more at his ease if she were not under his roof. But then his cook might leave, or his housemaid do her work badly, and there would be bills to go through, and wages to be paid, and catering to be thought of. Alice did all that, and his only concern was to draw her a monthly cheque, with a grumble at the total. As for his occasional evenings with her, though it was a bore to dine with this rather deaf, this uncouth and bony creature, such evenings were rare, and when dinner was over, he retired to his own den, and spent a tolerable hour or two over a book or a crossword puzzle. What she did with herself he had no idea, nor did he care, provided she did not intrude on him. Probably she read those gruesome books about the subconscious mind and occult powers which interested her. For him the conscious mind was sufficient, and she had little place in it. A secret unsavoury woman:

it was odd that he, so spick and span and robust, should be of the same blood as she.

This regime, the most comfortable that he could devise for himself, had been practically forced on Alice. Up till her father's death she had kept house for him, and in his old age he had fallen on evil days. He had gambled away in stupid speculation on the Stock Exchange a very decent capital, and for the last five years of his life he had been entirely dependent on his son, who housed them both in a dingy little flat just around the corner from Massington Square. Then the old man had had a stroke and was partially paralysed, and Edmund, always contemptuous of the sick and the inefficient, had grudged every penny of the few hundred pounds which he annually allowed him. At the same time he admired the powers of management and economy that his sister manifested in contriving to make her father comfortable on his meagre pittance. For instance, she even got him a second-hand bath-chair, shabby and shiny with much usage, and on warm days she used to have him wheeled up and down the garden in Massington Square, or sit there reading to him. Certainly she had a good idea of how to use money, and so, on her father's death, since she had to be provided for somehow, he offered her a hundred pounds a year, with board and lodging, to come and keep house for him. If she did not accept this munificence she would have to look out for herself, and as she was otherwise penniless, it was not in her power to refuse. She brought the bath-chair with her, and it was stored away in a big shed in the garden behind her brother's house. It might come into use again some day.

Edmund Faraday was an exceedingly shrewd man, but he never guessed that there was any psychical reason, beyond the material necessity, why Alice so eagerly accepted his offer. Briefly, this reason was that his sister regarded him with a hatred that prospered and burned bright in his presence. She hugged it to her, she cherished and fed it, and for that she must be with him: otherwise it might die down and grow cold. To hear him come in of an evening thrilled her with the sense of his nearness, to sit with him in silence at their rare solitary meals, to watch him, to serve him was a feast to her. She had no definite personal desire to injure him, even if that had been possible, but she must be near him, waiting for some inconjecturable doom, which, long though it might tarry, would surely overtake him, provided only that she kept the dynamo of her hatred ceaselessly at work. All vivid emotion, she knew, was a force in the world, and sooner or later it worked out its fulfilment. In her solitary hours, when her housekeeping work was accomplished, she directed her mind on him like a searchlight, she studied books of magic and occult lore that revealed or hinted at the powers which concentration can give. Witches and sorcerers, in the old days, ignorant of the underlying cause, made spells and incantations, they fashioned images of wax to represent their victims, and bound and stabbed them with needles in order to induce physical illness and torturing pains, but all this was child's play, dealing with symbols: the driving force behind them, which was much better left alone to do its will in its own way without interference, was hate. And it was no use being impatient: it was patience that did its perfect work. Perhaps when the doom began to shape itself, a little assistance might be given: fears might be encouraged, despair might be helped to grow, but nothing more than that. Just the unwearied waiting, the still intense desire, the black unquenchable flame . . .

Often she felt that her father's spirit was in touch with her, for he, too, had loathed his son and when he lay paralysed, without power of speech, she used to make up stories about Edmund for his amusement, how he would lose all his money, how he would be detected in some gross dishonesty in his business, how his vaunted health would fail him, and how cancer or some crippling ailment would grip him; and then the old man's eyes would brighten with merriment, and he cackled wordlessly in his beard and twitched with pleasure. Since her father's death, Alice had no sense that he had gone from her, his spirit was near her, and its malevolence was undiminished. She made him partner of her thoughts: sometimes Edmund was late returning from his work, and as the minutes slipped by and still he did not come, it was as if she still made stories for her father, and told him that the telephone bell would soon ring, and she would find that she was being rung up from some hospital where Edmund had been carried after a street accident. But then she would check her thoughts; she must not allow herself to get too definite or even to suggest anything to the force that was brewing and working round him. And though at present all seemed well with him, and the passing months seemed but to endow him with new prosperities, she never doubted that fulfilment would fail, if she was patient and did her part in keeping the dynamo of hate at work.

Edmund Faraday had only lately moved into the house he now occupied. Previously he had lived in another in the same square, a dozen doors off, but he had always wanted this house: it was more spacious, and it had behind it a considerable plot of garden, lawn and flower-beds, with a high brick wall surrounding it. But the other house was still unlet, and the house agent's board on it was an eyesore to him: there was money unrealized while it stood empty. But to-night, as he approached it, walking briskly back from his office, he saw that there was a man standing on the balcony outside the drawing-room windows: evidently then there was someone seeing over it. As he drew nearer, the man turned, took a few steps towards the long open window and passed inside. Faraday noticed that he limped heavily, leaning on a stick and swaying his body forward as he advanced his left leg, as if the joint was locked. But that was no concern of his, and he was pleased to think that somebody had come to inspect his vacant property. Next morning on his way to business he looked in at the agent's, in whose hands was the disposal of the house, and asked who had been enquiring about it. The agent knew nothing of it: he had not given the keys to anyone.

"But I saw a man standing on the balcony last night," said Faraday. "He must have got hold of the keys."

But the keys were in their proper place, and the agent promised to send round at once to make sure that the house was duly locked up. Faraday took the trouble to call again on his way home, only to learn that all was in order, front door locked, and back door and area gate locked, nor was there any sign that the house had been burglariously entered.

Somehow this trumpery incident stuck in Faraday's mind, and more than once that week it was oddly recalled to him. One morning he saw in the street a little ahead of him a man who limped and leaned on his stick, and instantly he bethought himself of that visitor to the empty house for his build and his movement were the same, and he quickened his step to have a look at him. But the pavement was crowded, and before he could catch him up the man had stepped into the roadway, and dodged through the thick traffic, and Edmund lost sight of him. Once again, as he was coming up the Square to his own house, he was sure that he saw him walking in the opposite direction, down the other side of the Square, and now he turned back in order to come round the end of the garden and meet him face to face. But by the time he had got to the opposite pavement there was no sign of him. He looked up and down the street beyond; surely that limping crippled walk would have been visible a long way off. A big man, broad-shouldered and burly in make: it should have been easy to pick him out. Faraday felt certain he was not a householder in the Square, or surely he must have noticed him before. And what had he been doing in his locked house: and why, suddenly, should he himself now catch sight of him almost every day? Quite irrationally, he felt that this obtrusive and yet elusive stranger had got something to do with him.

He was going down to Ascot to-morrow, and to-night was one of those rare occasions when he dined alone with his sister. He had little appetite, he found fault with the food, and presently the usual silence descended. Suddenly she gave her little bleating laugh. "Oh, I forgot to tell you," she said. "There was a man who called to-day – didn't give any name – who wished to see you about the letting of the other house. I said it was in the agent's hands: I gave him the address. Was that right, Edmund?"

"What was he like?" he rapped out.

"I never saw his face clearly at all. He was standing in the hall with his back to the window, when I came down. But a big man, like you in build, but crippled. Very lame, leaning heavily on his stick."

"What time was this?"

"A few minutes only before you came in."

"And then?"

"Well, when I told him to apply to the agent, he turned and went out, and, as I say, I never saw his face. It was odd somehow. I watched him from the window, and he walked round the top of the Square and down the other side. A few minutes afterwards I heard you come in."

She watched him as she spoke, and saw trouble in his face.

"I can't make out who the fellow is," he said. "From your description he seems like a man I saw a week ago, standing on the balcony of the other house. Yet when I enquired at the agent's, no one had asked for the keys, and the house was locked up all right. I've seen him several times since, but never close. Why didn't you ask his name, or get his address?"

"I declare I never thought of it," she said.

"Don't forget, if he calls again. Now if you've finished you can be off. You'll go down to Ascot to-morrow morning, and let us have something fit to eat. Three men coming down for the week-end."

Faraday went out to his morning round of golf on Saturday in high good spirits: he had won largely at bridge the night before, and he felt brisk and clear-eyed. The morning was very hot, the sun blazed, but a bastion of black cloud coppery at the edges was pushing up the sky from the east, threatening a downpour, and it was annoying to have to wait at one of the short holes while the couple in front delved among the bunkers that guarded the green. Eventually they holed out, and Faraday waiting for them to quit saw that there was watching them a big man, leaning on a stick, and limping heavily as he moved. "That's he," he thought to himself, "so now I'll get a look at him." But when he arrived at the green the stranger had gone, and there was no sign of him anywhere. However, he knew the couple who were in front, and he could ask them when he got to the clubhouse who their friend was. Presently the rain began, short in duration but violent, and his partner went to change his clothes when they got in. Faraday scorned any such precaution: he never caught cold, and never yet in his life had he had a twinge of rheumatism, and while he waited for his less robust partner he made enquiries of the couple who had been playing in front of him as to who their lame companion was. But they knew nothing of him: neither of them had seen him.

Somehow this took the edge off his sense of well-being, for indeed it was a queer thing. But Sunday dawned, bright and sparkling, and waking early he jumped out of bed with the intention of a walk in the garden before his bath. But instantly he had to clutch at a chair to save himself a fall. His left leg had given way under his weight, and a stabbing pain shot through his hip-joint. Very annoying: perhaps he should have changed his wet clothes yesterday. He dressed with difficulty, and limped downstairs. Alice was there arranging fresh flowers for the table.

"Why, Edmund, what's the matter?" she asked.

"Touch of rheumatism," he said. "Moving about will put it right."

But moving about was not so easy: golf was out of the question, and he sat all day in the garden, cursing this unwonted affliction, and all day the thought of the lame man, in build like himself, scratched about underground in his brain, like a burrowing mole.

Arrived back in London Faraday saw a reliable doctor, who, learning of his cold baths and his undisciplined use of the pleasures of the cellar and the table, put him on a regime which was a bitter humiliation to him, for he had joined the contemptible army of the careful. "Moderation, my dear sir," said his adviser. "No more cold baths or port for you, and a curb on your admirable appetite. A little more quiet exercise, too, during the week, and a good deal less on your week-ends. Do your work and play your games and see your friends. But moderation, and we'll soon have you all right."

It was in accordance with this distasteful advice that Faraday took to walking home if he had been dining out in the neighbourhood, or, if at home, took a couple of turns round the Square before going to bed. Contrary to use, he was without guests several nights this week, and on the last of them, before going down into the country again, he limped out about eleven o'clock feeling ill at ease and strangely apprehensive of the future. Though the violence of his attack had abated, walking was painful and difficult, and his halting steps, he felt sure, must arrest a contemptuous compassion in all who knew what a brisk, strong mover he had been. The night was cloudy and sweltering hot, there was a tenseness and an oppression in the air that matched his mood. All pleasure had been sucked out of life for him by this indisposition, and he felt with some inward and quaking certainty that it was but the shadow of some more dire visitant who was drawing near. All this week, too, there had been something strange about Alice. She seemed to be expecting something, and that expectation filled her with a secret glee. She watched him, she took note, she was alert . . .

He had made the complete circuit of the Square, and now was on his second round, after which he would turn in. A hundred yards of pavement lay between him and his own house, and it and the road-way were absolutely empty. Then, as he neared his own door, he saw that a figure was advancing in his direction; like him it limped and leaned on a stick. But though a week ago he had wanted to meet this man face to face, something in his mind had shifted, and now the prospect of the encounter filled him with some quaking terror. A meeting, however, was not to be avoided, unless he turned back again, and the thought of being followed by him was even more intolerable than the encounter. Then, while he was still a dozen yards off, he saw that the other had paused opposite his door, as if waiting for him.

Faraday held his latchkey in his hand ready to let himself in. He would not look at the fellow at all, but pass him with averted head. When he was now within a foot or two of him, the other put out his hand with a detaining gesture, and involuntarily Faraday turned. The man was standing close to the street lamp, and his face was in vivid light. And that face was Faraday's own: it was as if he beheld his own image in a looking-glass. . . . With a gulping breath he let himself into his house, and banged the door. There was Alice standing close within, waiting for him surely.

"Edmund," she said – and just as surely her voice trembled with some secret suppressed glee – "I went to post a letter just now, and that man who called about the other house was loitering outside. So odd."

He wiped the cold dews from his forehead.

"Did you get a look at him?" he asked. "What was he like?"

She gave her bleating laugh, and her eyes were merry.

"A most extraordinary thing!" she said. "He was so like you that I actually spoke to him before I saw my mistake. His walk, his build, his face: everything. Most extraordinary! Well, I'll go up to bed now. It's late for me, but I thought you would like to know that he was about, in case you wanted to speak to him. I wonder who he is, and what he wants. Sleep well!"

In spite of her good wishes, Faraday slept far from well. According to his usual custom, he had thrown the windows wide before he got into bed, and he was just dozing off, when he heard from outside an uneven tread and the tap of a stick on the pavement, his own tread he would have thought, and the tap of his own stick. Up and down it went, in a short patrol, in front of his house. Sometimes it ceased for a while, but no sooner did sleep hover near him than it began again. Should he look out, he asked himself, and see if there was anyone there? He recoiled from that, for the thought of looking again on himself, his own face and figure, brought the sweat to his forehead. At last, unable to bear this haunted vigil any longer, he went to the window. From end to end, as far as he could see, the Square was empty, but for a policeman moving noiselessly on his rounds, and flashing his light into areas.

Dr. Inglis visited him next morning. Since seeing him last, he had examined the X-ray photograph of the troublesome joint, and he could give him good news about that. There was no sign of arthritis; a muscular rheumatism, which no doubt would yield to treatment and care, was all that ailed him. So off went Faraday to his work, and the doctor remained to have a talk to Alice, for, jovially and encouragingly, he had told him that he suspected he was not a very obedient patient, and must tell his sister that his instructions as to food and tabloids must be obeyed.

"Physically there's nothing much wrong with him, Miss Faraday," he said, "but I want to consult you. I found him very nervous and I am sure he was wanting to tell me something, but couldn't manage it. He ought to have thrown off his rheumatism days ago, but there's something on his mind, sapping his vitality. Have you any idea – strict confidence, of course – what it is?"

She gave her little bleat of laughter.

"Wrong of me to laugh, I know, Dr. Inglis," she said, "but it's such a relief to be told there's nothing really amiss with dear Edmund. Yes: he has something on his mind – dear me, it's so ridiculous that I can hardly speak of it."

"But I want to know."

"Well, it's a lame man, whom he has seen several times. I've seen him, too, and the odd thing is he is exactly like Edmund. Last night he met him just outside the house, and he came in, well, really looking like death."

"And when did he see him first? After this lameness came upon him, I'll be bound."

"No: before. We both saw him before. It was as if – such nonsense it sounds! – it was as if this sort of double of himself showed what was going to happen to him."

There was glee and gusto in her voice. And how slovenly and uncouth she was with that lock of grey hair loose across her forehead, and her uncared-for hands. Dr. Inglis felt a distaste for her: he wondered if she was quite right in the head.

She clasped one knee in her long bony fingers.

"That's what troubles him – oh, I understand him so well," she said. "Edmund's terrified of this man. He doesn't know *what* he is. Not *who* he is, but *what* he is."

"But what is there to be afraid about?" asked the doctor. "This lame fellow, so like him, is no disordered fancy of his own brain, since you've seen him too. He's an ordinary living human being."

She laughed again, she clapped her hands like a pleased child. "Why, of course, that must be so!" she said. "So there's nothing for him to be afraid of. That's splendid! I must tell Edmund that. What a relief! Now about the rules you've laid down for him, his food and all that. I will be very strict with him. I will see that he does what you tell him. I will be quite relentless."

For a week or two Faraday saw no more of this unwelcome visitor, but he did not forget him, and somewhere deep down in his brain there remained that little cold focus of fear. Then came an evening when he had been dining out with friends: the food and the wine were excellent, they chaffed him about his abstemiousness, and loosening his restrictions he made a jolly evening of it, like one of the old days. He seemed to himself to have escaped out of the shadow that had lain on him, and he walked home in high good humour, limping and leaning on his stick, but far more brisk than was his wont. He must be up betimes in the morning, for the annual general meeting of his company was soon coming on, and to-morrow he must finish writing his speech to the shareholders. He would be giving them a pleasant half-hour; twelve per cent free of tax and a five per cent bonus was what he had to tell them about Faraday's Stores.

He had taken a short cut through the dingy little thoroughfare where his father had lived during his last stricken years, and his thoughts flitted back, with the sense of a burden gone, to the last time he had seen him alive, sitting in his bathchair in the garden of the Square, with Alice reading to him. Edmund had stepped into the garden to have a word with him, but his father only looked at him malevolently from his sunken eyes, mumbling and muttering in his beard. He was like an old monkey, Edmund thought, toothless and angry and feeble, and then suddenly he had struck out at him with the hand that still had free movement. Edmund had given him the rough side of his tongue for that; told him he must behave more prettily unless he wanted his allowance cut down. A nice way to behave to a son who gave him every penny he had!

Thus pleasantly musing he came out of this mean alley, and crossed into the Square. There were people about to-night, motors were moving this way and that, and a taxi was standing at the house next his, obstructing any further view of the road. Passing it, he saw that directly under the lamp-post opposite his own door there was drawn up an empty bathchair. Just behind it, as if waiting to push it, when its occupant was ready, there was standing an old man with a straggling white beard. Peering at him Edmund saw his sunken eyes and his mumbling mouth, and instantly came recognition. His latchkey slipped from his hand, and without waiting to pick it up, he stumbled up the steps, and, in an access of uncontrollable panic, was plying bell and knocker and beating with his hands on the panel of his door. He heard a step within, and there was Alice, and he pushed by her collapsing on to a chair in the hall. Before she closed the door and came to him, she smiled and kissed her hand to someone outside.

It was with difficulty that they got him up to his bedroom, for though just now he had been so brisk, all power seemed to have left him, his thigh-bones would scarce stir in their sockets, and he went up the stairs crab-wise or corkscrew-wise sidling and twisting as he mounted each step. At his direction, Alice closed and bolted his windows and drew the curtains across them; not a word did he say about what he had seen, but indeed there was no need for that.

Then leaving him she went to her own room, alert and eager, for who knew what might happen before day? How wise she had been to leave the working out of this in other hands: she had but concentrated and thought, and, behold, her thoughts and the force that lay behind them were taking shape of their own in the material world. Fear, too, that great engine of destruction, had Edmund in its grip, he was caught in its invisible machinery, and was being drawn in among the relentless wheels. And still she must not interfere: she must go on hating him and wishing him ill. That had been a wonderful moment when he battered at the door in a frenzy of terror, and when, opening it, she saw outside the shabby old bath-chair and her father standing behind it. She scarcely slept that night, but lay happy and nourished and tense, wondering if at any moment now the force might gather itself up for some stroke that would end all. But the short summer night brightened into day, and she went about her domestic duties again, so that everything should be comfortable for Edmund.

Presently his servant came down with his master's orders to ring up Dr. Inglis. After the doctor had seen him, he again asked to speak to Alice. This repetition of his interview was lovely to her mind: it was like the re-entry of some musical motif in a symphony, and now it was decorated and amplified, for he took a much graver view of his patient. This sudden stiffening of his joints could not be accounted for by any physical cause, and there accompanied it a marked loss of power, which no bodily lesion explained. Certainly he had had some great shock, but of that he would not speak. Again the doctor asked her whether she knew anything of it, but all she could tell him was that he came in last night in a frightful state of terror and collapse. Then there was another thing. He was worrying himself over the speech he had to make at this general meeting. It was highly important that he should get some rest and sleep, and while that speech was on his mind, he evidently could not. He was therefore getting up, and would come down to his sitting-room where he had the necessary papers. With the help of his servant he could manage to get there, and when his job was done, he could rest quietly there, and

Dr. Inglis would come back during the afternoon to see him again: probably a week or two in a nursing home would be advisable. He told Alice to look in on him occasionally, and if anything alarmed her she must send for him. Soon he went upstairs again to help Edmund to come down, and there were the sounds of heavy treads, and the creaking of banisters, as if some dead weight was being moved. That brought back to Alice the memory of her father's funeral and the carrying of the coffin down the narrow stairs of the little house which his son's bounty had provided for him.

She went with her brother and the doctor into his sitting-room and established him at the table. The room looked out on to the high-walled garden at the back of the house, and a long French window, opening to the ground, communicated with it. A plane-tree in full summer foliage stood just outside, and on this sultry overcast morning the room was dim with the dusky green light that filters through a screen of leaves. His table was strewn with his papers, and he sat in a chair with its back to the window. In that curious and sombre light his face looked strangely colourless, and the movements of his hands among his papers seemed to falter and stumble.

Alice came back an hour later and there he sat still busy and without a word for her, and she turned on the electric light, for it had grown darker, and she closed the open window, for now rain fell heavily. As she fastened the bolts, she saw that the figure of her father was standing just outside, not a yard away. He smiled and nodded to her, he put his finger to his lips, as if enjoining silence; then he made a little gesture of dismissal to her, and she left the room, just looking back as she shut the door. Her brother was still busy with his work, and the figure outside had come close up to the window. She longed to stop, she longed to see with her own eyes what was coming, but it was best to obey that gesture and go. The hall outside was very dark, and she stood there a moment, listening intently. Then from the door which she had just shut there came, unmistakably, the click of a turned key, and again there was silence but for the drumming of the rain, and the splash of overflowing gutters. Something was imminent: would the silence be broken by some protest of mortal agony, or would the gutters continue to gurgle till all was over?

And then the silence within was shattered. There came the sound of Edmund's voice rising higher and more hoarse in some incoherent babble of entreaty, and suddenly, as it rose to a scream, it ceased as if a tap had been turned off. Inside there, something fell with a thump that shook the solid floor, and up the stairs from below came Edmund's servant.

"What was that, miss?" he said in a scared whisper, and he turned the handle of the door. "Why, the master's locked himself in."

"Yes, he's busy," said Alice, "perhaps he doesn't want to be disturbed. But I heard his voice, too, and then the sound of something falling. Tap at the door and see if he answers."

The man tapped and paused, and tapped again. Then from inside came the click of a turned key, and they entered.

The room was empty. The light still burned on his table but the chair where she had left him five minutes before was pushed back, and the window she had bolted was wide. Alice looked out into the garden, and that was as empty as the room. But the door of the shed where her father's bath-chair was kept stood open, and she ran out into the rain and looked in. Edmund was lying in it with head lolling over the side.

Monkeys

R. Hugh Morris, while still in the early thirties of his age, had justly earned for himself the reputation of being one of the most dexterous and daring surgeons in his profession, and both in his private practice and in his voluntary work at one of the great London hospitals his record of success as an operator was unparalleled among his colleagues. He believed that vivisection was the most fruitful means of progress in the science of surgery, holding, rightly or wrongly, that he was justified in causing suffering to animals, though sparing them all possible pain, if thereby he could reasonably hope to gain fresh knowledge about similar operations on human beings which would save life or mitigate suffering; the motive was good, and the gain already immense. But he had nothing but scorn for those who, for their own amusement, took out packs of hounds to run foxes to death, or matched two grey-hounds to see which would give the death-grip to a single terrified hare: that, to him, was wanton torture, utterly unjustifiable. Year in and year out, he took no holiday at all, and for the most part he occupied his leisure, when the day's work was over, in study.

He and his friend Jack Madden were dining together one warm October night at his house looking on to Regent's Park. The windows of his drawing-room on the ground-floor were open, and they sat smoking, when dinner was done, on the broad window-seat. Madden was starting next day for Egypt, where he was engaged in archæological work, and he had been vainly trying to persuade Morris to join him for a month up the Nile, where he would be engaged throughout the winter in the excavation of a newly-discovered cemetery across the river from Luxor, near Medinet Habu. But it was no good.

"When my eye begins to fail and my fingers to falter," said Morris, "it will be time for me to think of taking my ease. What do I want with a holiday? I should be pining to get back to my work all the time. I like work better than loafing. Purely selfish."

"Well, be unselfish for once," said Madden. "Besides, your work would benefit. It can't be good for a man never to relax. Surely freshness is worth something."

"Precious little if you're as strong as I am. I believe in continual concentration if one wants to make progress. One may be tired, but why not? I'm not tired when I'm actually engaged on a dangerous operation, which is what matters. And time's so short. Twenty years from now I shall be past my best, and I'll have my holiday then, and when my holiday is over, I shall fold my hands and go to sleep for ever and ever. Thank God, I've got no fear that there's an after-life. The spark of vitality that has animated us burns low and then goes out like a wind-blown candle, and as for my body, what do I care what happens to that when I have done with it? Nothing will survive of me except some small contribution I may have made to surgery, and in a few years' time that will be superseded. But for that I perish utterly."

Madden squirted some soda into his glass.

"Well, if you've quite settled that—" he began.

"I haven't settled it, science has," said Morris. "The body is transmuted into other forms, worms batten on it, it helps to feed the grass, and some animal consumes the grass. But as for the survival of the individual spirit of a man, show me one tittle of scientific evidence to support it. Besides, if it did survive, all the evil and malice in it must surely survive too. Why should the death of the body purge that away? It's a nightmare to contemplate such a thing, and oddly enough, unhinged people like spiritualists want to persuade us for our consolation that the nightmare is true. But odder still are those old Egyptians of yours, who thought that there was something sacred about their bodies, after they were quit of them. And didn't you tell me that they covered their coffins with curses on anyone who disturbed their bones?"

"Constantly," said Madden. "It's the general rule in fact. Marrowy curses written in hieroglyphics on the mummy-case or carved on the sarcophagus."

"But that's not going to deter you this winter from opening as many tombs as you can find, and rifling from them any objects of interest or value."

Madden laughed.

"Certainly it isn't," he said. "I take out of the tombs all objects of art, and I unwind the mummies to find and annex their scarabs and jewellery. But I make an absolute rule always to bury the bodies again. I don't say that I believe in the power of those curses, but anyhow a mummy in a museum is an indecent object."

"But if you found some mummied body with an interesting malformation, wouldn't you send it to some anatomical institute?" asked Morris.

"It has never happened to me yet," said Madden, "but I'm pretty sure I shouldn't."

"Then you're a superstitious Goth and an anti-educational Vandal," remarked Morris . . . "Hullo, what's that?" He leant out of the window as he spoke. The light from the room vividly illuminated the square of lawn outside, and across it was crawling the small twitching shape of some animal. Hugh Morris vaulted out of the window, and presently returned, carrying carefully in his spread hands a little grey monkey, evidently desperately injured. Its hind legs were stiff and outstretched as if it was partially paralysed.

Morris ran his soft deft fingers over it.

"What's the matter with the little beggar, I wonder," he said. "Paralysis of the lower limbs: it looks like some lesion of the spine."

The monkey lay quite still, looking at him with anguished appealing eyes as he continued his manipulation.

"Yes, I thought so," he said. "Fracture of one of the lumbar vertebræ. What luck for me! It's a rare injury, but I've often wondered . . . And perhaps luck for the monkey too, though that's not very probable. If he was a man and a patient of mine, I shouldn't dare to take the risk. But, as it is . . ."

Jack Madden started on his southward journey next day, and by the middle of November was at work on this newly-discovered cemetery. He and another Englishman were in charge of the excavation, under the control of the Antiquity Department of the Egyptian Government. In order to be close to their work and to avoid the daily ferrying across the Nile from Luxor, they hired a bare roomy native house in the adjoining village of Gurnah. A reef of low sandstone cliff ran northwards from here towards the temple and terraces of Deir-el-Bahari, and it was in the face of this and on the level below it that the ancient graveyard lay. There was much accumulation of sand to be cleared away before the actual exploration of the tombs could begin, but trenches cut below the foot of the sandstone ridge showed that there was an extensive area to investigate.

The more important sepulchres, they found, were hewn in the face of this small cliff: many of these had been rifled in ancient days, for the slabs forming the entrances into them had been split, and the mummies unwound, but now and then Madden unearthed some tomb that had escaped these marauders, and in one he found the sarcophagus of a priest of the nineteenth dynasty, and that alone repaid weeks of fruitless work. There were nearly a hundred *ushaptiu* figures of the finest blue glaze; there were four alabaster vessels in which had been placed the viscera of the dead man removed before embalming: there was a table of which the top was inlaid with squares of variously coloured glass, and the legs were of carved ivory and ebony: there were the priest's sandals adorned with exquisite silver filagree: there was his staff of office inlaid with a diaper-pattern of cornelian and gold, and on the head of it, forming the handle, was the figure of a squatting cat, carved in amethyst, and the mummy, when unwound, was found to be decked with a necklace of gold plaques and onyx beads. All these were sent down to the Gizeh Museum at Cairo, and Madden reinterred the mummy at the foot of the cliff below the tomb. He wrote to Hugh Morris describing this find, and laying stress on the unbroken splendour of these crystalline winter days, when from morning to night the sun cruised across the blue, and on the cool nights when the stars rose and set on the vapourless rim of the desert. If by chance Hugh should change his mind, there was ample room for him in this house at Gurnah, and he would be very welcome.

A fortnight later Madden received a telegram from his friend. It stated that he had been unwell and was starting at once by long sea to Port Said, and would come straight up to Luxor. In due course he announced his arrival at Cairo and Madden went across the river next day to meet him: it was reassuring to find him as vital and active as ever, the picture of bronzed health. The two were alone that night, for Madden's colleague had gone for a week's trip up the Nile, and they sat out, when dinner was done, in the enclosed courtyard adjoining the house. Till then Madden had shied off the subject of himself and his health.

"Now I may as well tell you what's been amiss with me," he said, "for I know I look a fearful fraud as an invalid, and physically I've never been better in my life. Every organ has been functioning perfectly except one, but something suddenly went wrong there just once. It was like this."

He paused a moment.

"After you left," he said, "I went on as usual for another month or so, very busy, very serene and, I may say, very successful. Then one morning I arrived at the hospital when there was one perfectly ordinary but major operation waiting for me. The patient, a man, was wheeled into the theatre anæsthetized, and I was just about to make the first incision into the abdomen, when I saw that there was sitting on his chest a little grey monkey. It was not looking at me, but at the fold of skin which I held between my thumb and finger. I knew, of course, that there was no monkey there, and that what I saw was a hallucination, and I think you'll agree that there was nothing much wrong with my nerves when I tell you that I went through the operation with clear eyes and an unshaking hand. I had to go on: there was no choice about the matter. I couldn't say: 'Please take that monkey away,' for I knew there was no monkey there. Nor could I say: 'Somebody else must do this, as I have a distressing hallucination that there is a monkey sitting on the patient's chest.' There would have been an end of me as a surgeon and no mistake. All the time I was at work it sat there absorbed for the most part in what I was doing and peering into the wound, but now and then it looked up at me, and chattered with rage. Once it fingered a spring-forceps which clipped a severed vein, and that was the worst moment of all . . . At the end it was carried out still balancing itself on the man's chest . . . I think I'll have a drink. Strongish, please . . . Thanks."

"A beastly experience," he said when he had drunk. "Then I went straight away from the hospital to consult my old friend Robert Angus, the alienist and nerve-specialist, and told him exactly what had happened to me. He made several tests, he examined my eyes, tried my reflexes, took my blood-pressure: there was nothing wrong with any of them. Then he asked me questions about my general health and manner of life, and among these questions was one which I am sure has already occurred to you, namely, had anything occurred to me lately, or even remotely, which was likely to make me visualize a a monkey. I told him that a few weeks ago a monkey with a broken lumbar vertebra had crawled on to my lawn, and that I had attempted an operation – binding the broken vertebra with wire – which had occurred to me before as a possibility. You remember the night, no doubt?"

"Perfectly," said Madden, "I started for Egypt next day. What happened to the monkey, by the way?"

"It lived for two days: I was pleased, because I had expected it would die under the anæsthetic, or immediately afterwards from shock. To get back to what I was telling you. When Angus had asked all his questions, he gave me a good wigging. He said that I had persistently overtaxed my brain for years, without giving it any rest or change of occupation, and that if I wanted to be of any further use in the world, I must drop my work at once for a couple of months. He told me that my brain was tired out and that I had persisted in stimulating it. A man like me, he said, was no better than a confirmed drunkard, and that, as a warning, I had had a touch of an appropriate delirium tremens. The cure was to drop work, just as a drunkard must drop drink. He laid it on hot and strong: he said I was on the verge of a breakdown, entirely owing to my own foolishness, but that I had wonderful physical health, and that if I did break down I should be a disgrace. Above all – and this seemed to me awfully sound advice – he told me not to attempt to avoid thinking about what had happened to me. If I kept my mind off it, I should be perhaps driving it into the subconscious, and then there might be bad trouble. 'Rub it in: think what a fool you've been,' he said. 'Face it, dwell on it, make yourself thoroughly ashamed of yourself.' Monkeys, too: I wasn't to avoid the thought of monkeys. In fact, he recommended me to go straight away to the Zoological Gardens, and spend an hour in the monkey-house."

"Odd treatment," interrupted Madden.

"Brilliant treatment. My brain, he explained, had rebelled against its slavery, and had hoisted a red flag with the device of a monkey on it. I must show it that I wasn't frightened at its bogus monkeys. I must retort on it by making myself look at dozens of real ones which could bite and maul you savagely, instead of one little sham monkey that had no existence at all. At the same time I must take the red flag seriously, recognize there was danger, and rest. And he promised me that sham monkeys wouldn't trouble me again. Are there any real ones in Egypt, by the way?"

"Not so far as I know," said Madden. "But there must have been once, for there are many images of them in tombs and temples."

"That's good. We'll keep their memory green and my brain cool. Well, there's my story. What do you think of it?"

"Terrifying," said Madden. "But you must have got nerves of iron to get through that operation with the monkey watching."

"A hellish hour. Out of some disordered slime in my brain there had crawled this unbidden thing, which showed itself, apparently substantial, to my eyes. It didn't come from outside: my eyes hadn't told my brain that there was a monkey sitting on the man's chest, but my brain had told my eyes so, making fools of them. I felt as if someone whom I absolutely trusted had played me false. Then again I have wondered whether some instinct in my subconscious mind revolted against vivisection. My reason says that it is justified, for it teaches us how pain can be relieved and death postponed for human beings. But what if my subconscious persuaded my brain to give me a good fright, and reproduce before my eyes the semblance of a monkey, just when I was putting into practice what I had learned from dealing out pain and death to animals?"

He got up suddenly.

"What about bed?" he said. "Five hours' sleep was enough for me when I was at work, but now I believe I could sleep the clock round every night."

Young Wilson, Madden's colleague in the excavations, returned next day and the work went steadily on. One of them was on the spot to start it soon after sunrise, and either one or both of them were superintending it, with an interval of a couple of hours at noon, until sunset. When the mere work of clearing the face of the sandstone cliff was in progress and of carting away the silted soil, the presence of one of them sufficed, for there was nothing to do but to see that the workmen shovelled industriously, and passed regularly with their baskets of earth and sand on their shoulders to the dumping-grounds, which stretched away from the area to be excavated, in lengthening peninsulas of trodden soil. But, as they advanced along the sandstone ridge, there would now and then appear a chiselled smoothness in the cliff and then both must be alert. There was great excitement to see if, when they exposed the hewn slab that formed the door into the tomb, it had escaped ancient marauders, and still stood in place and intact for the modern to explore. But now for many days they came upon no sepulchre that had not already been opened. The mummy, in these cases, had been unwound in the search for necklaces and scarabs, and its scattered bones lay about. Madden was always at pains to reinter these.

At first Hugh Morris was assiduous in watching the excavations, but as day after day went by without anything of interest turning up, his attendance grew less frequent: it was too much of a holiday to watch the day-long removal of sand from one place to another. He visited the Tomb of the Kings, he went across the river and saw the temples at Karnak, but his appetite for antiquities was small. On other days he rode in the desert, or spent the day with friends at one of the Luxor hotels. He came home from there one evening in rare good spirits, for he had played lawn-tennis with a woman on whom he had operated for malignant tumour six months before and she had skipped about the court like a two-year-old. "God, how I want to be at work again," he exclaimed. "I wonder whether I ought not to have stuck it out, and defied my brain to frighten me with bogies."

The weeks passed on, and now there were but two days left before his return to England, where he hoped to resume work at once: his tickets were taken and his berth booked. As he sat over breakfast that morning with Wilson, there came a workman from the excavation, with a note scribbled in hot haste by Madden, to say that they had just come upon a tomb which seemed to be unrifled, for the slab that closed it was in place and unbroken. To Wilson, the news was like the sight of a sail to a marooned mariner, and when, a quarter of an hour later, Morris followed him, he was just in time to see the slab prised away. There was no sarcophagus within, for the rock walls did duty for that, but there lay there, varnished and bright in hue as if painted yesterday, the mummy-case roughly following the outline of the human form. By it stood the alabaster vases containing the entrails of the dead, and at each corner of the sepulchre there were carved out of the sandstone rock, forming, as it were, pillars to support the roof, thick-set images of squatting apes. The mummy-case was hoisted out and carried away by workmen on a bier of boards into the courtyard of the excavators' house at Gurnah, for the opening of it and the unwrapping of the dead.

They got to work that evening directly they had fed: the face painted on the lid was that of a girl or young woman, and presently deciphering the hieroglyphic inscription, Madden read out that within lay the body of A-pen-ara, daughter of the overseer of the cattle of Senmut.

"Then follow the usual formulas," he said. "Yes, yes . . . ah, you'll be interested in this, Hugh, for you asked me once about it. A-pen-ara curses any who desecrates or meddles with her bones, and should anyone do so, the guardians of her sepulchre will see to him, and he shall die childless and in panic and agony; also the guardians of her sepulchre will tear the hair from his head and scoop his eyes from their sockets, and pluck the thumb from his right hand, as a man plucks the young blade of corn from its sheath."

Morris laughed.

"Very pretty little attentions," he said. "And who are the guardians of this sweet young lady's sepulchre? Those four great apes carved at the corners?"

"No doubt. But we won't trouble them, for to-morrow I shall bury Miss A-pen-ara's bones again with all decency in the trench at the foot of her tomb. They'll be safer there, for if we put them back where we found them, there would be pieces of her hawked about by half the donkey-boys in Luxor in a few days. 'Buy a mummy hand, lady? . . . Foot of a Gyppy Queen, only ten piastres, gentlemen' . . . Now for the unwinding."

It was dark by now, and Wilson fetched out a paraffin lamp, which burned unwaveringly in the still air. The lid of the mummy-case was easily detached, and within was the slim, swaddled body. The embalming had not been very thoroughly done, for all the skin and flesh had perished from the head, leaving only bones of the skull stained brown with bitumen. Round it was a mop of hair, which with the ingress of the air subsided like a belated *soufflé*, and crumbled into dust. The cloth that swathed the body was as brittle, but round the neck, still just holding together, was a collar of curious and rare workmanship: little ivory figures of squatting apes alternated with silver beads. But again a touch broke the thread that strung them together, and each had to be picked out singly. A bracelet of scarabs and cornelians still clasped one of the fleshless wrists, and then they turned the body over in order to get at the members of the necklace which lay beneath the nape. The rotted mummy-cloth fell away altogether from the back, disclosing the shoulder-blades and the spine down as far as the pelvis. Here the embalming had been better done, for the bones still held together with remnants of muscle and cartilage.

Hugh Morris suddenly sprang to his feet.

"My God, look there!" he cried, "one of the lumbar vertebræ, there at the base of the spine, has been broken and clamped together with a metal band. To hell with your antiquities: let me come and examine something much more modern than any of us!"

He pushed Jack Madden aside, and peered at this marvel of surgery.

"Put the lamp closer," he said, as if directing some nurse at an operation. "Yes: that vertebra has been broken right across and has been clamped together. No one has ever, as far as I know, attempted such an operation except myself, and I have only performed it on that little paralysed monkey that crept into my garden one night. But some Egyptian surgeon, more than three thousand years ago, performed it on a woman. And look, look! She lived afterwards, for the broken vertebra put out that bony efflorescence of healing which has encroached over the metal band. That's a slow process, and it must have taken place during her lifetime, for there is no such energy in a corpse. The woman lived long: probably she recovered completely. And my wretched little monkey only lived two days and was dying all the time."

Those questing hawk-visioned fingers of the surgeon perceived more finely than actual sight, and now he closed his eyes as the tip of them felt their way about the fracture in the broken vertebra and the clamping metal band.

"The band doesn't encircle the bone," he said, "and there are no studs attaching it. There must have been a spring in it, which, when it was clasped there, kept it tight. It has been clamped round the bone itself: the surgeon must have scraped the vertebra clean of flesh before he attached it. I would give two years of my life to have looked on, like a student, at that masterpiece of skill, and it was worth while giving up two months of my work only to have seen the result. And the injury itself is so rare, this breaking of a spinal vertebra. To be sure, the hangman does something of the sort, but there's no mending that! Good Lord, my holiday has not been a waste of time!"

Madden settled that it was not worth while to send the mummy-case to the museum at Gizeh, for it was of a very ordinary type, and when the examination was over they lifted the body back into it, for reinterment next day. It was now long after midnight and presently the house was dark.

Hugh Morris slept on the ground-floor in a room adjoining the yard where the mummy-case lay. He remained long awake marvelling at that astonishing piece of surgical skill performed, according to Madden, some thirty-five centuries ago. So occupied had his mind been with homage that not till now did he realize that the tangible proof and witness of the operation would to-morrow be buried again and lost to science. He must persuade Madden to let him detach at least three of the vertebræ, the mended one and those immediately above and below it, and take them back to England as demonstration of what could be done: he would lecture on his exhibit and present it to the Royal College of Surgeons for example and incitement. Other trained eyes beside his own must see what had been successfully achieved by some unknown operator in the nineteenth dynasty . . . But supposing Madden refused? He always made a point of scrupulously reburying these remains: it was a principle with him, and no doubt some superstition-complex – the hardest of all to combat with because of its sheer unreasonableness – was involved. Briefly, it was impossible to risk the chance of his refusal.

He got out of bed, listened for a moment by his door, and then softly went out into the yard. The moon had risen, for the brightness of the stars was paled, and though no direct rays shone into the walled enclosure, the dusk was dispersed by the toneless luminosity of the sky, and he had no need of a lamp. He drew the lid off the coffin, and folded back the tattered cerements which Madden had replaced over the body. He had thought that those lower vertebræ of which he was determined to possess himself would be easily detached, so far perished were the muscle and cartilage which held them together, but they cohered as if they had been clamped, and it required the utmost force of his powerful fingers to snap the spine, and as he did so the severed bones cracked as with the noise of a pistol-shot. But there was no sign that anyone in the house had heard it, there came no sound of steps, nor lights in the windows. One more fracture was needed, and then the relic was his. Before he replaced the ragged cloths he looked again at the stained fleshless bones. Shadow dwelt in the empty eye-sockets, as if black sunken eyes still lay there, fixedly regarding him, the lipless mouth snarled and grimaced. Even as he looked some change came over its aspect, and for one brief moment he fancied that there lay staring up at him the face of a great brown ape. But instantly that illusion vanished, and replacing the lid he went back to his room.

The mummy-case was reinterred next day, and two evenings after

Morris left Luxor by the night train for Cairo, to join a homeward-bound P. & O. at Port Said. There were some hours to spare before his ship sailed, and having deposited his luggage, including a locked leather despatch-case, on board he lunched at the Café Tewfik near the quay. There was a garden in front of it with palm trees and trellises gaily clad in bougainvillias: a low wooden rail separated it from the street, and Morris had a table close to this. As he ate he watched the polychromatic pageant of Eastern life passing by: there were Egyptian officials in broad-cloth frock coats and red fezzes; barefooted splay-toed fellahin in blue gabardines; veiled women in white making stealthy eyes at passers-by; half-naked gutter-snipe, one with a sprig of scarlet hibiscus behind his ear; travellers from India with solar topees and an air of aloof British superiority; dishevelled sons of the Prophet in green turbans; a stately sheik in a white *burnous*; French painted ladies of a professional class with lace-rimmed parasols and provocative glances; a wild-eyed dervish in an accordion-pleated skirt, chewing betel-nut and slightly foaming at the mouth. A Greek boot-black with box adorned with brass plaques tapped his brushes on it to encourage customers, an Egyptian girl squatted in the gutter beside a gramophone, steamers passing into the Canal hooted on their syrens.

Then at the edge of the pavement there sauntered by a young Italian harnessed to a barrel-organ: with one hand he ground out a popular air by Verdi, in the other he held out a tin can for the tributes of music-lovers: a small monkey in a yellow jacket, tethered to his wrist, sat on the top of his instrument. The musician had come opposite the table where Morris sat: Morris liked the gay tinkling tune, and feeling in his pocket for a piastre, he beckoned to him. The boy grinned and stepped up to the rail.

Then suddenly the melancholy-eyed monkey leaped from its place on the organ and sprang on to the table by which Morris sat. It alighted there, chattering with rage in a crash of broken glass. A flower-vase was upset, a plate clattered on to the floor. Morris's coffee-cup discharged its black contents on the tablecloth. Next moment the Italian had twitched the frenzied little beast back to him, and it fell head downwards on the pavement. A shrill hubbub arose, the waiter at Morris's table hurried up with voluble execrations, a policeman kicked out at the monkey as it lay on the ground, the barrel-organ tottered and crashed on the roadway. Then all subsided again, and the Italian boy picked up the little body from the pavement. He held it out in his hands to Morris.

"*E morto*," he said.

"Serve it right, too," retorted Morris. "Why did it fly at me like that?"

He travelled back to London by long sea, and day after day that tragic little incident, in which he had had no responsible part, began to make a sort of colouring matter in his mind during those hours of lazy leisure on ship-board, when a man gives about an equal inattention to the book he reads and to what passes round him. Sometimes if the shadow of a sea-gull overhead slid across the deck towards him, there leaped into his brain, before his eyes could reassure him, the ludicrous fancy that this shadow was a monkey springing at him. One day they ran into a gale from the west: there was a crash of glass at his elbow as a sudden lurch of the ship upset a laden steward, and Morris jumped from his seat thinking that a monkey had leaped on to his table again. There was a cinematograph show in the saloon one evening, in which some naturalist exhibited the films he had taken of wild life in Indian jungles: when he put on the screen the picture of a company of monkeys swinging their way through the trees Morris involuntarily clutched the sides of his chair in hideous panic that lasted but a fraction of a second, until he recalled to himself that he was only looking at a film in the saloon of a steamer passing up the coast of Portugal. He came sleepy into his cabin one night and saw some animal crouching by the locked leather despatch-case. His breath caught in his throat before he perceived that this was a friendly cat which rose with gleaming eyes and arched its back . . .

These fantastic unreasonable alarms were disquieting. He had as yet no repetition of the hallucination that he saw a monkey, but some deep-buried "idea," to cure which he had taken two months' holiday, was still unpurged from his mind. He must consult Robert Angus again when he got home, and seek further advice. Probably that incident at Port Said had rekindled the obscure trouble, and there was this added to it, that he knew he was now frightened of real monkeys: there was terror sprouting in the dark of his soul. But as for it having any connection with his pilfered treasure, so rank and childish a superstition deserved only the ridicule he gave it. Often he unlocked his leather case and sat poring over that miracle of surgery which made practical again long-forgotten dexterities.

But it was good to be back in England. For the last three days of the voyage no menace had flashed out on him from the unknown dusks, and surely he had been disquieting himself in vain. There was a light mist lying over Regent's Park on this warm March evening, and a drizzle of rain was falling. He made an appointment for the next morning with the specialist, he telephoned to the hospital that he had returned and hoped to resume work at once. He dined in very good spirits, talking to his manservant, and, as subsequently came out, he showed him his treasured bones, telling him that he had taken the relic from a mummy which he had seen unwrapped and that he meant to lecture on it. When he went up to bed he carried the leather case with him. Bed was comfortable after the ship's berth, and through his open window came the soft hissing of the rain on to the shrubs outside.

His servant slept in the room immediately over his. A little before dawn he woke with a start, roused by horrible cries from somewhere close at hand. Then came words yelled out in a voice that he knew:

"Help! Help!" it cried. "O my God, my God! Ah – h—" and it rose to a scream again.

The man hurried down and clicked on the light in his master's room as he entered. The cries had ceased: only a low moaning came from the bed. A huge ape with busy hands was bending over it; then taking up the body that lay there by the neck and the hips he bent it backwards and it cracked like a dry stick. Then it tore open the leather case that was on a table by the bedside, and with something that gleamed white in its dripping fingers it shambled to the window and disappeared.

A doctor arrived within half an hour, but too late. Handfuls of hair with flaps of skins attached had been torn from the head of the murdered man, both eyes were scooped out of their sockets, the right thumb had been plucked off the hand, and the back was broken across the lower vertebræ.

Nothing has since come to light which could rationally explain the tragedy. No large ape had escaped from the neighbouring Zoological Gardens, or, as far as could be ascertained, from elsewhere, nor was the monstrous visitor of that night ever seen again. Morris's servant had only had the briefest sight of it, and his description of it at the inquest did not tally with that of any known simian type. And the sequel was even more mysterious, for Madden, returning to England at the close of the season in Egypt, had asked Morris's servant exactly what it was that his master had shown him the evening before as having been taken by him from a mummy which he had seen unwrapped, and had got from him a sufficiently conclusive account of it. Next autumn he continued his excavations in the cemetery at Gurnah, and he disinterred once more the mummy-case of A-pen-ara and opened it. But the spinal vertebræ were all in place and complete: one had round it the silver clip which Morris had hailed as a unique achievement in surgery.

Christopher Comes Back

During five years of childless marriage Nellie Mostyn had lived in bondage to the fancied ailments and literary industry of her husband. For the last three of these Christopher had been engaged on a life and a definitive edition of the lyrics of the most obscure of Elizabethan poets – the little-known and less-read Francis Holder, – and morning after morning it had been Nellie's occupation to sit with her husband in his study, looking up references, copying out his notes, receiving his dictation, and rising at punctual intervals to fetch him his tonic, or his aspirin, or his glass of hot water. In the afternoon she took a drive with him, and was almost equally busy with putting one window of the car an inch up, or the other two inches down, with telling the chauffeur not to drive so fast or a shade faster, with adjusting the collar of Christopher's coat, or with shifting his hot-water bottle. Sometimes, if it was not too warm or too cold, he got out to walk for half a mile, and then she carried his woollen muffler, so that he could assume it again at a moment's notice if the breeze grew chilly or the sun went behind clouds. When he got back into the car he would say: "Well, we've had a famous walk to-day, Petsy," and then perhaps he would doze a little, with his large head nodding and lolling on that wrinkled neck, which was so like that of a plucked chicken. Or he had little tendernesses for her, of much the same nature as those that an elderly woman has for her lap-dog – little strokings and squeezes and pattings, with pet names and baby language. Her youth and vigour were always tonic to him, and he was eager to get home and set to work again.

It was so this afternoon, on this day of peerless spring weather, as they passed through woods tapestried with primrose and anemone, and more than once she had to use the speaking-tube to tell the chauffeur to go a shade faster, for Christopher would like two clear hours for dictation between tea-time and seven o'clock, when he always rested for half an hour. If he fell asleep it was Nellie's duty to give him five minutes' law and then wake him.

"And this evening, Petsy," he said, "it may be – though I promise nothing – that I shall have a little surprise for you. Ah! I think we will have the window quite up; the spring weather is often treacherous. Be quick, Nellikins, there is a considerable draught . . . A surprise, I was saying. How excited you will be when I tell you. Now you shan't get a word more out of me; don't tease me into telling you, my little rascal girl!"

They had left the woods seething with spring below them, and were mounting the flank of the hill where the village of Pole-Street stood on a shelf of the high downs. A couple of dozen shops lined the entrance to it, and after that came a circle of brick-built houses round the Green, antique and mellow, a survival of more spacious days, when land and leisure were not so dearly bought as now. It was at the farthest of these that their motor drew up; beyond it stood the church, the graveyard of which came up to the low garden wall, and below the ground fell rapidly away towards the woods through which they had passed. Tea was ready, and before five o'clock, Christopher, with his rug spread over his knees and his notes in front of him, had begun to dictate. They worked at the big table in his study, lined with books, and by the fireside was the rocking-chair in which he sat when Nellie read over to him some finished section. A pause occasionally broke the even flow of his voice when he sipped his hot water.

Nellie took down his words automatically; her hand had formed a habit of accurate transcription, and she could unleash her thoughts to wander where they willed. To-day they were alive with the sense of spring; they went dancing with the daffodils, coming back only now and then to supervise her manual employment. Her blood was alert with April, and here she sat day after day, so many of them, over her sapless employment, without lot or portion in the rights of her own spring-season, and in the briskness of her youth. Never did any of their neighbours, with one exception, cross the threshold of the joyless house, for after the morning's work Christopher could not contemplate the strain of a guest at lunch, who might linger unduly and curtail the hours of his motor drive. Tea was followed by work again, and after that he did not feel up to more than a quiet frugal dinner with a little reading aloud till bedtime. Nor could he accept hospitalities from others, if it was thus impossible to return them; besides, hostesses, ignorant of the sad plight of his digestion, might provide a dinner which would be just so many plates of poison to him, and Nellie, of course, could not go out and leave him alone. All this had long been fermenting within her, a perilous brew, and the sense of spring to-day had caused it to bubble afresh.

It may easily be conjectured who was the one person from outside who entered this hermitage. Dr. Bernard Eves paid a visit here regularly once a week to see that no disquieting symptoms were sprouting, to approve the continuance of the current dietary, or suggest some modification, and, in addition to this, he was usually summoned once or twice between his fixed visits to dispel chance alarms. He was a young man, lately come here, and Christopher had the highest opinion of his abilities. He was cheerful, he had a laughing eye, which became suitably grave when he tapped and pressed, and brightened up again as he congratulated his patient on his general soundness. When the examination was over he interviewed Nellie, and gave her the prescribed commissariat for the next week. Hardly a word, at present, of personal import had passed between them, but both knew that there was fire kindling.

She recalled herself to her work; opposite her sat her husband with his velvet skull-cap on his head, fingering the scanty greyish-brown beard that dripped from his chin. Though he was not yet fifty he appeared an old man; his mouth had a senile droop, his eyes an unfocused watery vagueness, his hands were creased with wrinkled skin. Fresh from her April thoughts, Nellie suddenly shuddered with a qualm of horror and repulsion at the sight of him . . .

His custom was to spread slips of paper with his notes written on them over the table in front of his oak arm-chair. His dictation was founded on these, and as each was finished with he tore it up. Now there was but one left, and he was beginning to tear it.

"For me," he said, "it will be sufficient reward to have rescued from oblivion one who, whatever his failings, we must consider to be one of the sweetest minor singers in the choir of English melody."

Nellie took down his words, and paused for the next. Then she understood.

"Oh, Christopher!" she said, "I see what your surprise is. The book's finished."

He rose with a chuckle of delight and a fondling hand.

"Clever Nellie!" he said. "But is it not wonderful? Little did I think, when three years ago I set myself this great task, that I should have strength to finish it. Tomorrow, Nellikins, we will have a holiday, and then we must buckle to again. You shall do the talking then, lazy girl, reading it all over to me from the beginning, just for verbal corrections, and then off it goes to be typed. Shall Christopher give Nellie 'ickle kiss for her cleverness in guessing? Such a bright little Petsy!"

The reading of the finished manuscript duly began after a day's holiday. Christopher found it less fatiguing to listen than to dictate, and an after-dinner session was added to the usual hours for work. Never was such progress made, until one evening when progress ceased altogether. Christopher was seized with an attack of severe pain which hot water failed to soothe. Dr. Eves was sent for. He recommended an examination by X-Ray. That left little doubt that his patient was suffering from malignant disease, and no doubt at all that an operation was impossible.

One morning some six months later Bernard Eves had paid his daily visit to the sick-room, and was now giving his report to Nellie.

"He has very little pain," he was saying; "because he's really only half-conscious. It's like an uneasy dream, probably, to him, not more than that. What's so astonishing is his vitality. A few months ago I should have said it was quite impossible that he should live through the summer."

Nellie's face was like a mask. For weeks now that hardness had been habitual to it.

"Tell me what you expect," she said.

"I don't know what to expect," he said. "All I can do is to keep him free from pain. Any recovery is absolutely out of the question, but his resistance amazes me."

Suddenly the mask dropped from her face; she got up quivering and shaking.

"Bernard, I can't bear it much longer," she said. "It's a daily horror, and something is giving way inside me under it. His eyes are like the eyes of a dead man, who is yet terribly alive. It's a miracle, you say, that he's alive at all; what if another miracle happens and he gets well? I simply couldn't go through more years of it."

"Nellie, darling, he can't get well," said Bernard. "You may take my word for that. Of course, for everybody's sake – his, yours, mine – one hopes it will be over soon."

She shook her head; she found no comfort there.

"And sometimes I think he knows how I shudder at him," she said, "and why I long for it to be over. He looks from me to you, and then back again. When people go on living on the brink of death like that, who knows but that the veil of material things wears thin, and they see the things of the spirit? I believe he knows."

He looked up at her sharply.

"Come, Nellie, you're talking nonsense," he said. "It's an awful strain on you, I know, but you can keep a hold on yourself, and you must. I wish you could go away till it's all over, but that's impossible. Remember that he's hardly conscious, and when he gives those long looks at you and then at me he is like someone half asleep, who sees figures by his bed. They are no more than dreams are to us. Besides, how could he know? Utterly impossible."

The nurse who attended Christopher went out for a couple of hours in the afternoon, leaving Nellie to sit in his room or in the dressing-room adjoining. Usually he lay in a drugged torpor, but she had instructions to give him a dose from an opiate mixture if he got restless or showed any signs of being in pain. This afternoon when she was with him he began muttering and turning in bed, and she went to the table where the bottle stood. There were three doses left in it, and she poured the whole into his glass and gave it to him. In a few minutes he was quiet again, and after some half-hour she told a servant to ring up Dr. Eves and bid him come at once. In ten minutes more he was with her, and she pointed to the empty bottle.

"Bernard, I gave him three doses of the opiate," she said.

He stared at her, incredulous.

"It's quite true," she said.

He rushed back to his surgery a hundred yards away, where he dispensed drugs, and brought back with him certain apparatus and a bottle unconnected with them. But his efforts to revive the patient were unavailing, and when the nurse came in from her walk Christopher Mostyn was dead, and in the bottle of opiate mixture were three doses.

"A sudden collapse," he said to her, "such as I have been expecting for many days."

The funeral was over, and Nellie came back to the house feeling that the last rim of the shadow of the eclipsed years had passed off, even as the blinded windows once more let in the day. She had no touch of remorse or regret for what she had done. Christopher had been doomed to death, and she had but freed him from further days of drugged discomfort. Since that afternoon she had not seen Bernard, for he had received news almost in the same hour of his mother's serious illness, and had gone off at once. Nor had she heard from him since, but nothing was more natural than that he should not write to her just yet. He knew everything, he had been prompt and wise in filling up the bottle to the level at which it had stood when the nurse went out, and she felt that by that action he had accepted what she had done. Before he left he had written the certificate of death, giving malignant disease followed by heart failure as the cause, and when he came back the past would be dead and done with. They would have to wait some months, she supposed, possibly a year, before they married.

The day was closing in, chilly, with flaws of rain that tapped against the windows. Otherwise the house was quite quiet; no muffled sounds came from the bedroom immediately above; nor would she presently hear the step of the nurse on the stairs coming down to give her news of the patient. Often about this hour he had grown restless and asked to see her, and then he would lie staring at her, but as Bernard had said, perhaps not knowing her. It was an infinite relief to sit here, secure from these ghastly errands, and listen to the rain on the darkening windows, and the soft flapping of the flame on the hearth.

Then there came to her ears the sound of an electric bell, and her heart leaped, for Bernard might have returned. She heard the step of a servant in the passage outside, but instead of turning the corner to the front door it went on towards Christopher's study. After a pause it returned, and the door opened.

"What was that bell?" she asked. "Not the front door?"

"No, ma'am. It was the bell from the study," said the maid. "I supposed you were there."

"You must have made a mistake," said Nellie. "See if it is not the front door."

The maid did not come back, so there could have been no one at the door, and Nellie rose and went to the study. It was nearly dark now, and as she turned on the switch for the light she thought she heard a creak from the oak rocking-chair where for so many mornings of work Christopher had sat over his notes. She looked, and saw that the chair was oscillating slightly as if someone had just got up from it.

For a moment she stared at it motionless and tense, for that familiar movement conveyed to her the sense of Christopher's presence in a manner terribly vivid; had he stood there visibly, reaching up for a book from the shelves, she could not have received a sharper impression of him. She glanced round the room, almost expecting to see him or hear his voice. But there was nothing; just the gleam of light on the big polished table, and lying there on his blotting-pad a duplicate of the printed proofs of his book, which had arrived only a week or two ago, when he was past all thought of them.

The movement of the rocking-chair died away, but the shock to her nerves remained, and, determined to control and master them, she moved about the room, and finally went to the window and looked out. The rain had ceased, and a splash of sullen red in the west showed that the sun had already set. Just outside lay the bounding-wall of the churchyard with its rows of headstones, and close at hand the mound of earth that marked the most recent of the graves. In this queer dim light the dark soil looked like a hole cut in the grass, as if the grave had never been filled in. She drew the blind, ran the curtains along their pole, and left the room, locking the door.

Her nervous perturbation passed off, and she settled down for a tranquil, undisturbed evening. Tomorrow, she thought, rain or fine, she would go for a long tramp on the downs, and by to-morrow night, perhaps, Bernard would be back, or she would at least have heard from him. If he was back he would be sure to let her know, and he must dine with her. She would tell him about that chair so strangely rocking, and he would laugh at her for imagining anything of the sort. Some germ of fear still lurked in her mind, for she wanted to be assured that it was but her eyes that had played her a trick, or her tread on a loose board that had caused that rocking movement . . . She dozed a little, she read a little, basking in the sense that no call could come for her; she told her parlour-maid that she need not sit up. By eleven o'clock she was ready for bed, and she went along the passage, quenching the lights, past Christopher's study to the stairs.

Opposite the door she paused; that germ of fear had fructified, and she must destroy its brood. So, with a summons to her courage, she unlocked the door and entered. But now there was no need to press the switch, for his green-shaded reading-lamp by the rocking-chair was burning, and on the table beside it lay the printed proofs of his book. And the rocking-chair was again oscillating to and fro, as if its invisible occupant had risen on her entry. Even as she stood there, feeling her hands grow cold and moist, that spectral light faded, and she was looking into the blackness of an unlit room. But something stirred there; she heard the faint thud of a footfall on the carpet, pacing there and pausing in the darkness.

She woke next morning to the radiance of a crisp October day, and, what was even better, to an indifference to that which last night had made her shake as with an ague. What did it matter, after all, if the spirit of Christopher or some astral semblance of it had survived the crumbling and perishing of his body, and haunted the scene of his earthly labours? It could not hurt her, it could not cramp and mummify, as he had done, the life which tingled within her, and which was now free of him. There was business to be got through in the morning, but she lunched early, and set off not for one of those "good walks" of a quarter of an hour, but for a long swinging circuit of the windy downs. Hour after hour she drank of the clear wine of the sun and open spaces, and it was not till dusk was gathering that she came back past the village green. But as she let herself into the house she felt that something was waiting for her return, and her vigour and briskness began to slip from her. There were letters on the hall table, but the one she looked for was still missing.

It seemed as if the presence which had manifested itself in Christopher's study last night was spreading like some chilly mist through the house. She went upstairs to change her walking attire, and on her way down again, as she passed the door of the room where he had died, she found that it was open. She could not imagine who had gone in there . . . or was it that someone had come out? She looked in; it was dark, but she heard coming from the place where the sheeted bed stood a sound as of moaning and muttering, very faint. She turned on the light, but the room was empty. Only on the table by the bed there stood a bottle, and she saw that it was the same which held three doses of the opiate mixture. She could have sworn that it had been removed with all the other appliances of the sick-room, and she advanced a step or two with the intention of taking it away. But some invincible horror seized her, and she left it standing there.

Downstairs her parlour-maid was bringing in her tea, and she noticed that the woman looked scared and white.

"What's the matter, Mary?" she said. "Anything . . . anything wrong?"

The woman looked at her with twitching lips.

"No, ma'am," she said.

Nellie was a good mistress; she was on friendly, confidential terms with her servants.

"Come, Mary," she said kindly, "something's upset you. Won't you tell me?"

"I was shutting up in here half an hour ago, ma'am," she said, "and I heard someone moving about in the master's room overhead. I thought perhaps it was you – that you had come in by the garden gate, and I went upstairs to see."

Nellie gave a little sigh of relief.

"Ah! And left the door of the room open," she said.

"No, ma'am, it was open, and I shut it," said Mary.

The woman went back to the servants' quarters, and again the house was quiet. But presently Nellie rose and went along the passage to Christopher's study. It was just because she feared going there that she had to do so; her fear was the force that pulled her. She unlocked the door, and once more there was no need to turn up the light, for the reading-lamp by the rocking-chair was burning, and in the chair, with his proofs in his hand, sat Christopher. He turned and looked at her, setting the chair in oscillation . . . and then she found herself staring into blackness.

She closed the door and stood leaning against the wall outside, bracing herself against this wave of terror, cold as the Arctic seas, which streamed over her, and though she had left him inside the room, yet he was here close beside her in the brightly lit passage. As she fought against this awful sense of his encompassing presence, she heard a bell ring somewhere in the house. Was he summoning her to come back and read his proofs to him? She fled from the place back to her sitting-room, and then there came steps in the passage, there was a hand on the door, and in panic she crouched in her chair. "No, no; don't come in. I can't bear it!" she whimpered.

And then the door opened, and Bernard stood there. She flew to him, hands outstretched.

"Oh, Bernard, you've come, you've come!" she cried. "How I've been longing for you! I've been terrified, but that's all past now that you're here. But I can't stop here—"

She looked at him, and her voice died away into silence.

"What is it?" she said at length. But she knew what it was.

He tried to speak, but could not. He put out his hands to her, and drew them back. She watched him, curiously detached and emotionless.

"I'll tell you then," she said. "You've come to say that you can't see me again, because I killed him."

She moved a step away towards the tea-table, and then suddenly her terror, stilled for the moment by Bernard's presence, and her love for him surged back on her together.

"Bernard, you can't leave me," she said. "You know what I did was merciful. Besides, we love each other . . . And there's more than that. Christopher has come back; he's in the house. He was in his study last night, though I did not see him, and his lamp was lit, and his chair rocking."

Her voice rose.

"This afternoon he was in the bedroom where he died," she said, "and just now I saw him visibly. He's getting more hold over me, his grip is tightening, and it's only you who can loosen it. He knows, and he's trying to keep us apart, so that he'll get possession of me again, and I shall be his. But I'm not his; I'm yours, and you must save me from him. He can't come between us if we are one. He mustn't . . ."

Her voice, which had risen to a scream, died away again, and the last words were but whispered. Her eyes were on Bernard no longer, but on some point in the air between them, and were focused intently on it. And he, watching her, saw what she was looking at.

A mist of filmy grey began to form there, twining and wreathing within itself, and growing swiftly more substantial, and taking the form and outline of a man. Features defined themselves on the face, blind-looking, watery eyes, and scanty beard, a bald head covered with a black skull-cap. From being transparent the spectre assumed a seeming solidity, the mouth twitched and mumbled as if trying to speak, the hands were held out as if to sever them. Then its solidity melted again; the weaving vapours out of which it had formed itself grew thin and vanished, and the two who were left were looking at each other, white and blanched with the helpless horror that stared from their answering eyes.

A couple of hours later the parlour-maid came in to tell Nellie that her dinner was ready. She was asleep, apparently, in her chair by the fire, and on the table by her stood the empty bottle which had held three doses of the opiate mixture.

The Sanctuary

Francis Elton was spending a fortnight's holiday one January in the Engadine, when he received the telegram announcing the death of his uncle, Horace Elton, and his own succession to a very agreeable property: the telegram added that the cremation of the remains was to take place that day, and it was therefore impossible for him to attend, and there was no reason for his hurrying home.

In the solicitor's letter that reached him two days later Mr. Angus gave fuller details: the estate consisted of sound securities to the value of about £80,000, and there was as well Mr. Elton's property just outside the small country town of Wedderburn in Hampshire. This consisted of a charming house and garden and a small acreage of building land. Everything had been left to Francis, but the estate was saddled with a charge of £500 a year in favour of the Reverend Owen Barton.

Francis knew very little of his uncle, who for a long time had been much of a recluse; indeed he had not seen him for nearly four years, when he had spent three days with him at this house at Wedderburn. He had vague but slightly uneasy memories of those days, and now on his journey home, as he lay in his berth in the rocking train, his brain, rummaging drowsily among its buried recollections, began to disinter these. There was nothing definite about them: they consisted of suggestions and side-lights and oblique impressions, things observed, so to speak, out of the corner of his eye, and never examined in direct focus.

He had only been a boy at the time, having just left school, and it was in the summer holidays, hot sultry weather of August, he remembered, that he had paid him this visit, before he went to a crammer's in London to learn French and German.

There was his Uncle Horace, first of all, and of him he had vivid images. A grey-haired man of middle age, large and extremely stout with a cushion of jowl overlapping his collar, but in spite of this obesity, he was nimble and light in movement, and with a merry blue eye that was equally alert, and seemed constantly to be watching him. Then there were two women there, a mother and daughter, and, as he recalled them, their names occurred to him, too: they were Mrs. Isabel Ray and Judith. Judith, he supposed, was a year or two older than himself, and on the first evening had taken him for a stroll in the garden after dinner. She had treated him at once as if they were old friends, had walked with her arm round his neck, had asked him many questions about his school, and whether there was any girl he was keen on. All very friendly, but rather embarrassing. When they came in from the garden, certainly some questioning signal had passed between the mother and the girl, and Judith had shrugged her shoulders in reply.

Then the mother had taken him in hand; she made him sit with her in the window-seat, and talked to him about the crammer's he was going to: he would have much more liberty, she supposed, than he had at school, and he looked the sort of boy who would make good use of it. She tried him in French and found he could speak it very decently, and told him that she had a book which she had just finished, which she would lend him. It was by that exquisite stylist Huysman and was called *Là-Bas*. She would not tell him what it was about: he must find out for himself. All the time those narrow grey eyes were fixed on him, and when she went to bed, she took him up to her room to give him the book. Judith was there, too: she had read it, and laughed at the memory of it. "Read it, darling Francis, she said, "and then go to sleep immediately, and you will tell me to-morrow what you dreamed about, unless it would shock me."

The vibrating rhythm of the train made Francis drowsy, but his mind went on disinterring these fragments. There had been another man there, his uncle's secretary, a young fellow, perhaps twenty-five years old, clean-shaven and slim and with just the same gaiety about him as the rest. Everyone treated him with an odd sort of deference, hard to define but easy to perceive. He sat next Francis at dinner that night, and kept filling his wine-glass for him whether he wanted it or not, and next morning he had come into his room in pyjamas, sat on his bed, looked at him with odd questioning eyes, had asked him how he got on with his book, and then taken him to bathe in the swimming-pool behind the belt of trees at the bottom of the garden . . . No bathing-costume, he said, was necessary, and they raced up and down the pool and lay basking in the sun afterwards. Then from the belt of trees emerged Judith and her mother, and Francis, much embarrassed, draped himself in a towel. How they all laughed at his delightful prudery . . . And what was the man's name? Why, of course, it was Owen Barton, the same who had been mentioned in Mr. Angus's letter as the Reverend Owen Barton. But why "reverend," Francis wondered. Perhaps he had taken orders afterwards.

All day they had flattered him for his good looks, and his swimming and his lawn-tennis: he had never been made so much of, and all their eyes were on him, inviting and beckoning. In the afternoon his uncle had claimed him: he must come upstairs with him and see some of his treasures. He took him into his bedroom, and opened a great wardrobe full of magnificent vestments. There were gold-embroidered copes, there were stoles and chasubles with panels of needlework enriched with pearls, and jewelled gloves, and the use of them was to make glorious the priests who offered prayer and praise to the Lord of all things visible and invisible. Then he brought out a scarlet cassock of thick shimmering silk, and a cotta of finest muslim trimmed round the neck and the lower hem with Irish lace of the sixteenth century. These were for the vesting of the boy who served at the Mass, and Francis, at his uncle's bidding, stripped off his coat and arrayed himself, and took off his shoes and put on the noiseless scarlet slippers which were called sanctuary shoes. Then Owen Barton entered, and Francis heard him whisper to his uncle, "God! What a server!" and then he put on one of those gorgeous copes and told him to kneel.

The boy had been utterly bewildered. What were they playing at, he wondered. Was it charades of some sort? There was Barton, his face solemn and eager, raising his left hand as if in blessing: more astonishing was his uncle, licking his lips and swallowing in his throat, as if his mouth watered. There was something below all this dressing-up, which meant nothing to him, but had some hidden significance for the two men. It was uncomfortable: it disquieted him, and he wouldn't kneel, but disrobed himself of the cotta and cassock. "I don't know what it's about," he said: and again, as between Judith and her mother, he saw question and answer pass between them. Somehow his lack of interest had disappointed them, but he felt no interest at all: just a vague repulsion.

The diversions of the day were renewed: there was more tennis and bathing, but they all seemed to have lost the edge of their keenness about him. That evening he was dressed rather earlier than the others, and was sitting in a deep window-seat of the drawing-room, reading the book Mrs. Ray had lent him. He was not getting on with it; it was puzzling, and the French was difficult: he thought he would return it to her, saying that it was beyond him. Just then she and his uncle entered: they were talking together, and did not perceive him.

"No, it's no use, Isabel," said his uncle. "He's got no curiosity, no leanings: it would only disgust him and put him off. That's not the way to win souls. Owen thinks so, too. And he's too innocent:

why when I was his age . . . Why, there's Francis. What's the boy reading? Ah, I see! What do you make of it?"

Francis closed the book.

"I give it up," he said. "I can't get on with it." Mrs. Ray laughed.

"I agree, too, Horace," she said. "But what a pity!"

Somehow Francis got the impression, he remembered, that they had been talking about him. But, if so, *what* was it for which he had no learnings?"

He had gone to bed rather early that night, encouraged, he thought, to do so, leaving the rest at a game of bridge. He soon slept, but awoke, thinking he heard the sound of chanting. Then came three strokes of a bell, and a pause and three more. He was too sleepy to care what it was about.

Such, as the train rushed through the night, was the sum of his impressions about his visit to the man whose substance he had now inherited, subject to the charge of £500 a year to the Reverend Owen Barton. He was astonished to find how vivid and how vaguely disquieting were these memories, which now for four years had been buried in his mind. As he sank into sounder sleep they faded again, and he thought little more of them in the morning.

He went to see Mr. Angus as soon as he got to London. Certain securities would have to be sold in order to pay death duties, but the administration of the estate was a simple matter. Francis wanted to know more about his benefactor, but Mr. Angus could tell him very little. Horace Elton had, for some years, lived an extremely sequestered life down at Wedderburn, and his only intimate associate was his secretary, this Mr. Owen Barton. Beyond him, there were two ladies who used often to stay with him for long periods. Their names? – and he paused, searching his memory.

"Mrs. Isabel Ray and her daughter Judith?" suggested Francis.

"Exactly. They were often there. And, not infrequently, a number of people used to arrive rather late in the evening, eleven o'clock or even later, stay for an hour or two and then be off again. A little mysterious. Only a week or so before Mr. Elton died, there had been quite a congregation of them, fifteen or twenty, I believe."

Francis was silent for a moment: it was as if pieces of jig-saw puzzle were calling for their due location. But their shapes were too fantastic . . .

"And about my uncle's illness and death," he said. "The cremation of his body was on the same day as that on which he died; at least so I understood from your telegram."

"Yes: that was so," said Mr. Angus.

"But why? I should instantly have come back to England in order to be present. Was it not unusual?"

"Yes, Mr. Elton, it was unusual. But there were reasons for it."

"I should like to hear them," he said. "I was his heir, and it would have been only proper that I should have been there. Why?"

Angus hesitated a moment.

"That is a reasonable question," he said, "and I feel bound to answer it. I must begin a little way back . . . Your Uncle was in excellent physical health apparently, till about a week before his death. Very stout, but very alert and active. Then the trouble began. It took the form at first of some grievous mental and spiritual disturbance. He thought for some reason that he was going to die very soon, and the idea of death produced in him an abnormal panic terror. He telegraphed for me, for he wanted to make some alteration in his will. I was away and could not get down till the next day, and by the time I arrived he was too desperately ill to give any sort of coherent instructions. But his intention, I think, was to cut Mr. Owen Barton out of it."

Again the lawyer paused.

"I found," he said, "that on the morning of the day I got down to Wedderburn, he had sent for the parson of his parish, and had made a confession to him. What that was I have not, of course, the slightest idea. Till then he had been in this panic fear of death, but was physically himself. Immediately afterwards some very horrible disease invaded him. Just that: invasion. The doctors who were summoned from London and Bournemouth had no idea what it was. Some unknown microbe, they supposed, which made the most swift and frightful havoc of skin and tissue and bone. It was like some putrefying internal corruption. It was as if he was dead already . . . Really, I don't know what good it will do to tell you this."

"I want to know," said Francis.

"Well: this corruption. Living organisms came out as from a dead body. His nurses used to be sick. And the room was always swarming with flies; great fat flies, crawling over the walls and the bed. He was quite conscious, and there persisted this frantic terror of death, when you would have thought that a man's soul would have been only too thankful to be quit of such a habitation."

"And was Mr. Owen Barton with him?" asked Francis.

"From the moment that Mr. Elton made his confession, he refused to see him. Once he came into the room, and there was a shocking scene. The dying man screamed and yelled with terror. Nor would he see the two ladies we have mentioned: why they continued to stop in the house I can't imagine. Then on the last morning of his life – he could not speak now – he traced a word or two on a piece of paper, and it seemed that he wanted to receive the Holy Communion. So the parson was sent for."

The old lawyer paused again: Francis saw that his hand was shaking.

"Then very dreadful things happened," he said.

"I was in the room, for he signed to me to be near him, and I saw them with my own eyes. The parson had poured the wine into the chalice and had put the bread on the paten, and was about to consecrate the elements, when a cloud of those flies, of which I have told you, came about him. They filled the chalice like a swarm of bees, they settled in their unclean thousands on the paten, and in a couple of minutes the chalice was dry and empty and they had devoured the bread. Then like drilled hosts, you may say, they swarmed on to your uncle's face, so that you could see nothing of it. He choked and he gasped: there was one writhing convulsion, and, thank God, it was all over."

"And then?" asked Francis.

"There were no flies. Nothing. But it was necessary to have the body cremated at once and the bedding with it. Very shocking indeed! I would not have told you, if you had not pressed me."

"And the ashes?" asked he.

"You will see that there is a clause in his will, directing that his remains should be buried at the foot of the Judas-tree beside the swimming pool in the garden at Wedderburn. That was done."

Francis was a very unimaginative young man, free from superstitious twitterings and unprofitable speculations, and this story, suggestive though it was, of ghastly sub-currents, did not take hold of his mind at all or lead to the fashioning of uneasy fancies. It was all very horrible, but it was over. He went down to Wedderburn for Easter with a widowed sister of his and her small boy, aged eleven, and they all fairly fell in love with the place. It was soon settled that Sybil Marsham should let her house in London for the summer months, and establish herself here. Dickie, who was a delicate boy, rather queer and elfin, would thus have the benefit of country air, and Francis the benefit of having the place run by his sister and occupied and in commission whenever he was able to get away from his work.

The house was of brick and timber, with accommodation for half a dozen folk, and stood on high ground above the little town. Francis made a tour of it, as soon as he arrived, rather astonished to find how the sight of it rubbed up to clearness in the minutest details his memory of it. There was the sitting-room with its tall bookcases and its deep window-seats overlooking the garden, where he had sat unobserved when his uncle and Mrs. Ray came in talking together.

Above was his uncle's panelled bedroom, which he proposed to occupy himself, with the big wardrobe containing vestments. He opened it: they were under their covering sheets of tissue paper, shimmering with scarlet and gold and finest lawn foamed with Irish lace: a faint smell of incense hung about them. Next that was his uncle's sitting-room, and beyond that the room which he had slept in before, and was now appropriated to Dickie. These rooms lay on the front of the house, looking westwards over the garden, and he went out to renew acquaintance with it. Flower-beds gay with spring blossoms ran below the windows: then came the lawn, and beyond the belt of trees that enclosed the swimming pool. He passed along the path that threaded it between tapestries of primrose and anemone, and came out into the clearing that surrounded the water. The bathing shed stood at the deep end of it by the sluice that splashed riotously into the channel below, for the stream that supplied the pool was running full with the rains of March. In front of the copse on the far side stood a Judas-tree decked gloriously with flowers, and the reflection of it was cast waveringly on the rippled surface of the water. Somewhere below those red-blossoming boughs, there was buried a casket of ashes. He strolled round the pool: it was quite sheltered here from the April breeze, and bees were busy in the red blossoms. Bees, and large fat flies, a quantity of them.

He and Sybil were sitting in the drawing-room with the deep window-seats as dusk began to fall. A servant came in to say that Mr. Owen Barton had called. Certainly they were at home, and he entered, and was introduced to Sybil.

"You will hardly remember me, Mr. Elton," he said, "but I was here when you paid a visit to your uncle: four years ago it must have been."

"But I remember you perfectly," he said. "We bathed together, we played tennis: you were very kind to a shy boy. And are you living here still?"

"Yes: I took a house in Wedderburn after your uncle's death. I spent six very happy years with him as his secretary, and I got much attached to the country. My house stands just outside your garden palings opposite the latched gate leading into the wood round the pool."

The door opened and Dickie came in. He caught sight of the stranger and stopped.

"Say 'how do you do' to Mr. Barton, Dickie," said his mother.

Dickie performed this duty with due politeness and stood regarding him. He was a shy boy usually; but, after this inspection, he advanced close to him, and laid his hands on his knees.

"I like you," he said confidently, and leant up against him.

"Don't bother Mr. Barton, Dickie," she said rather sharply.

"But indeed he's doing nothing of the kind," said Barton, and he drew the boy towards him so that he stood clipped between his knees.

Sybil got up.

"Come, Dick," she said. "We'll have a walk round the garden before it gets dark."

"Is he coming, too?" asked the boy.

"No: he's going to stop and talk to Uncle Francis."

When the two men were alone Barton said a word or two about Horace Elton, who had always been so generous a friend to him. The end, mercifully short, had been terrible, and terrible to him personally had been the dying man's refusal to see him during the last two days of his life.

"His mind, I think, must have been affected," he said, "by his awful sufferings. It happens like that sometimes: people turn against those with whom they have been most intimate. I have often mourned over that, and deeply regretted it . . . And I owe you certain word of explanation, Mr. Elton. No doubt you were puzzled to find in your uncle's will that I was entitled 'the Reverend.' It is quite true, though I do not call myself so. Certain spiritual doubts and difficulties caused me to give up my orders, but your uncle always held that if a man is once a priest he is always a priest. He was very strong about that, and no doubt he was right."

"I didn't know my uncle took any interest in ecclesiastical affairs," said Francis. "Ah, I had forgotten about his vestments. Perhaps that was only an artistic taste."

"By no means. He regarded them as sacred things, consecrated to holy uses. . . . And may I ask you what happened to his remains? I remember he once expressed a wish to be buried by the swimming pool."

"His body was cremated," said Francis, "and the ashes were buried there."

Barton stayed but little longer, and Sybil on her return was frankly relieved to find he had gone. Simply, she didn't like him. There was something queer, something sinister about him. Francis laughed at her: quite a good fellow, he thought.

Dreams, of course, are a mere hash-up of recent mental images and associations, and a very vivid dream that came to Francis that night could easily have arisen from such topics. He thought he was swimming in the bathing pool with Owen Barton, and that his uncle, stout and florid, was standing underneath the Judas-tree watching them. That seemed quite natural, as is the way of dreams: merely he was not dead at all. When they came out of the water, he looked for his clothes, but found that there was laid out for him a scarlet cassock and a white lace-trimmed cotta.

This again was quite natural; so, too, was the fact that Barton put on a gold cope.

His uncle, very merry and licking his lips, joined them, and each of them took an arm of his and they walked back to the house together singing a hymn. As they went the daylight died, and by the time they crossed the lawn it was black night, and the windows of the house were lit. They walked upstairs, still singing, into his uncle's bedroom which was now his own. There was an open door, which he had never noticed before opposite his bed, and there came a very bright light from it. Then the sense of nightmare began, for his two companions, gripping him tightly, pulled him along towards it, and he struggled with them knowing there was something terrible within. But step by step they dragged him, violently resisting, and now out of the door there came a swarm of large fat flies that buzzed and settled on him. Thicker and thicker they streamed out, covering his face, and crawling into his eyes, and entering his mouth as he panted for breath. The horror grew to breaking-point, and he woke sweating with a hammering heart. He switched on the light, and there was the quiet room and the dawn beginning to be luminous outside, and the birds just tuning up.

Francis's few days of holiday passed quickly. He went down to the village to see Barton's house, and found it a most pleasant little dwelling, and its owner an exceedingly pleasant fellow. Barton dined with them one evening, and Sybil went so far as to admit that her first judgment of him was hasty. He was charming with Dickie, too, and that disposed her in his favour, and the boy adored him. Soon it was necessary to find some tutor for him, and Barton readily agreed to undertake his education, and every morning Dickie trotted across the garden and through the wood where the swimming pool lay to Barton's house. His ill-health had made him rather backward in his studies, but he was now eager to learn and to please his instructor, and he got on quickly.

It was now that I first met Francis, and during the next few months in London we became close friends. He told me that he had lately inherited this place at Wedderburn from his uncle, but for the present I knew no more than that of the previous history which I have just recorded. Sometime during July he told me he was intending to spend the month of August there. His sister, who kept house for him, and her small boy would be away for the first week or two, for she had taken him off to the seaside. Would I then come and share his solitude, and get on there, uninterrupted, with some work I had on hand. That seemed a very attractive plan, and we motored down together one very hot afternoon early in August, that promised thunder. Owen Barton, he told me, who had been his uncle's secretary was coming to dine with us that night.

It wanted an hour or so yet to dinner-time when we arrived, and Francis directed me, if I cared for a dip, to the bathing pool among the trees beyond the lawn. He had various household businesses to look into himself, so I went off alone. It was an enchanting place, the water still and very clear, mirroring the sky and the full-foliaged trees, and I stripped and plunged in. I lay and floated in the cool water, I swam and dived again, and then I saw, walking close to the far bank of the pool, a man of something more than middle-age, and extremely stout. He was in dress clothes, dinner-jacket and black tie, and instantly it struck me that this must be Mr. Barton coming up from the village to dine with us. It must therefore be later than I thought, and I swam back to the shed where my clothes were. As I climbed out of the water, I glanced round. There was no one there.

It was a slight shock, but very slight. It was odd that he should have come so unexpectedly out of the wood and disappeared again so suddenly, but it did not concern me much. I hurried home, changed quickly and came down, expecting to find Francis and his guest in the drawing-room. But I need not have been in such haste for now my watch told me that there was still a quarter of an hour before dinner-time. As for the others, I supposed that Mr. Barton was upstairs with Francis in his sitting-room. So I picked up a chance book to beguile the time, and read for a while, but the room grew rather dark, and, rising to switch on the electric light, I saw standing outside the French window into the garden the figure of a man, outlined against the last of a stormy sunset, looking into the room.

There was no doubt whatever in my mind that he was the same person as I had seen when I was bathing, and the switching on of the light made this clear, for it shone full on his face. No doubt then Mr. Barton finding he was too early was strolling about the garden till the dinner-hour. But now I did not look forward at all to this evening: I had had a good look at him and there was something horrible about him. Was he human, was he earthly at all? Then he quietly moved away, and immediately afterwards there came a knock at the front door just outside the room, and I heard Francis coming downstairs. He went to the door himself: there was a word of greeting, and he came into the room accompanied by a tall, slim fellow whom he introduced to me.

We had a very pleasant evening: Barton talked fluently and agreeably, and more than once he spoke of his friend and pupil Dickie. About eleven he rose to go, and Francis suggested to him that he should walk back across the garden which gave him a short cut to his house. The threatening storm still held off, but it was very dark overhead, as we stood together outside the French window.

Barton was soon swallowed up in the blackness. Then there came a bright flash of lightning, and in that moment of illumination I saw that there was standing in the middle of the lawn, as if waiting for him, the figure I had seen twice already. "Who is that?" was on the tip of my tongue, but instantly I perceived that Francis had seen nothing of it, and so I was silent, for I knew now what I had already half-guessed that this was no living man of flesh and blood whom I had seen. A few heavy drops of rain plopped on the flagged walk, and, as we moved indoors, Francis called out "Good night, Barton!" and the cheery voice answered.

Before long we went up to bed, and he took me into his room as we passed, a big panelled chamber with a great wardrobe by the bed. Close to it hung an oil-portrait of kit-cat size.

"I'll show you what's in that wardrobe to-morrow," he said. "Rather wonderful things . . . That's a picture of my uncle."

I had seen that face before this evening.

For the next two or three days I had no further glimpse of that dreadful visitant, but never for a moment was I at ease, for I was aware that he was about. What instinct or what sense perceived that, I have no idea: perhaps it was merely the dread I had of seeing him again that gave rise to the conviction. I thought of telling Francis that I must get back to London; what prevented me from so doing was the desire to know more, and that made me fight this cold fear. Then very soon I perceived that Francis was no more at ease than I was. Sometimes as we sat together in the evening he was oddly alert: he would pause in the middle of a sentence as if some sound had attracted his attention, or he would look up from our game of bezique and focus his eyes for a second on some corner of the room or, more often, on the dark oblong of the open French window. Had he, I wondered, been seeing something invisible to me, and, like myself, feared to speak of it?

These impressions were momentary and infrequent, but they kept alive in me the feeling that there was something astir, and that something, coming out of the dark and the unknown, was growing in force. It had come into the house, and was present everywhere . . . And then one awoke again to a morning of heavenly brightness and sunshine, and surely one was disquieting oneself in vain.

I had been there about a week when something occurred which precipitated what followed. I slept in the room which Dickie usually occupied, and awoke one night feeling uncomfortably hot. I tugged at a blanket to remove it, but it was tucked very tightly in between the mattresses on the side of the bed next to the wall. Eventually I got it free, and as I did so I heard something drop with a flutter on to the floor. In the morning I remembered that, and found underneath the bed a little paper notebook. I opened it idly enough, and within were a dozen pages written over in a round childish handwriting, and these words struck my eye:

"Thursday, July 11th. I saw great-uncle Horace again this morning in the wood. He told me something about myself which I didn't understand, but he said I should like it when I got older. I mustn't tell anybody that he's here, nor what he told me, except Mr. Barton."

I did not care one jot whether I was reading a boy's private diary. That was no longer a consideration worth thinking about. I turned over the page and found another entry.

"Sunday, July 21st. I saw Uncle Horace again. I said I had told Mr. Barton what he had told me, and Mr. Barton had told me some more things, and that he was pleased, and said I was getting on and that he would take me to prayers some day soon."

I cannot describe the thrill of horror that these entries woke in me. They made the apparition which I had seen infinitely more real and more sinister. It was a spirit corrupt and malign and intent on corruption that haunted the place. But what was I to do? How could I, without any lead from Francis, tell him that the spirit of his uncle – of whom at present I knew nothing – had been seen not by me only, but by his nephew, and that he was at work on the boy's mind? Then there was the mention of Barton. Certainly that could not be left as it was. He was collaborating in that damnable task. A cult of corruption (or was I being too fantastic?) began to outline itself. Then what did that sentence about taking him to prayers mean? But Dickie was away, thank goodness, for the present, and there was time to think it over. As for that pitiful little notebook, I put it into a locked despatch case.

The day, as far as outward and visible signs were concerned, passed pleasantly. For me there was a morning's work, and for both of us an afternoon on the golf-links. But below there was something heavy; my knowledge of that diary kept intervening with mental telephone-calls asking "What are you going to *do*?" Francis, on his side, was troubled; there were sub-currents, and I did not know what they were. Silences fell, not the natural unobserved silences between those who are intimate, which are only a symbol of their intimacy, but the silences between those who have something on their minds of which they fear to speak. These had got more stringent all day: there was a growing tenseness: all common topics were banal, for they only cloaked a certain topic.

We sat out on the lawn before dinner on that sultry evening, and breaking one of these silent intervals, he pointed at the front of the house.

"There's an odd thing," he said. "Look! There are three rooms aren't there on the ground floor: dining-room, drawing-room, and the little study where you write. Now look above. There are three rooms there: your bedroom, my bedroom, and my sitting-room. I've measured them. There are twelve feet missing. Looks as if there was a sealed-up room somewhere."

Here, at any rate, was something to talk about.

"Exciting," I said. "Mayn't we explore?"

"We will. We'll explore as soon as we've dined. Then there's another thing: quite off the point. You remember those vestments I showed you the other day? I opened the wardrobe, where they are kept, an hour ago, and a lot of big fat flies came buzzing out. A row like a dozen aeroplanes overhead. Remote but loud, if you know what I mean. And then there weren't any."

Somehow I felt that what we had been silent about was coming out into the open. It might be ill to look upon . . .

He jumped from his chair.

"Let's have done with these silences," he cried. "He's here, my uncle, I mean. I haven't told you yet, but he died in a swarm of flies. He asked for the Sacrament, but before the wine was consecrated the chalice was choked with them. And I know he's here. It sounds damned rot, but he is."

"I know that, too," I said. "I've seen him."

"Why didn't you tell me?"

"Because I thought you would laugh at me."

"I should have a few days ago," said he. "But I don't now. Go on."

"The first evening I was here I saw him at the bathing pool. That same night, when we were seeing Owen Barton off, a flash of lightning came, and he was there again standing on the lawn."

"But how did you know it was he?" asked Francis.

"I knew it when you showed me the portrait of him in your bedroom that same night. Have you seen him?"

"No; but he's here. Anything more?"

This was the opportunity not only natural but inevitable.

"Yes, much more," I said. "Dickie has seen him too."

"That child? Impossible."

The door out of the drawing-room opened, and Francis's parlour-maid came out with the sherry on a tray. She put the decanter and glasses down on the wicker table between us, and I asked her to bring out the despatch case from my room. I took the paper notebook out of it.

"This slipped out from between my mattresses last night. It's Dickie's diary. Listen:" and I read him the first extract.

Francis gave one of those swift disconcerting glances over his shoulder.

"But we're dreaming," he said. "It's a nightmare. God, there's something awful here! And what about Dickie not telling anybody except Barton what he told him? Anything more?"

"Yes. 'Sunday, July 21st. I saw Uncle Horace again. I said I had told Mr. Barton what he told me, and Mr. Barton told me some more things, and that he was pleased and said I was getting on, and that he would take me to prayers some day soon.' I don't know what that means."

Francis sprang out of his chair.

"What?" he cried. "Take him to prayers? Wait a minute. Let me remember about my first visit here. I was a boy of nineteen, and frightfully, absurdly innocent for my age. A woman staying here gave me a book to read called *Là-Bas*. I didn't get far in it then, but I know what it's about now."

"Black Mass," said I. "Satan worshippers."

"Yes. Then one day my uncle dressed me up in a scarlet cassock, and Barton came in and put on a cope and said something about my being a server. He used to be a priest, did you know that? And one night I awoke and heard the sound of chanting and a bell rang. By the way, Barton's coming to dine tomorrow . . ."

"What are you going to do?"

"About him? I can't tell yet. But we've got something to do to-night. Horrors have happened here in this house. There must be some room where they held their Mass, a chapel. Why, there's that missing space I spoke of just now."

After dinner we set to work. Somewhere on the first floor on the garden front of the house there was this space unaccounted for by the dimensions of the rooms there. We turned on the electric light in all of them, and then going out into the garden we saw that the windows in Francis's bedroom and in his sitting-room next door were far more widely spaced than they should have been. Somewhere, then, between them lay the area to which there was no apparent access and we went upstairs. The wall of his sitting-room seemed solid, it was of brick and timber, and large beams ran through it at narrow intervals. But the wall of his bedroom was panelled, and when we tapped on it, no sound came through into the other room beyond.

We began to examine it.

The servants had gone to bed, and the house was silent, but as we moved about from garden to house and from one room to another there was some presence watching and following us. We had shut the door into his bedroom from the passage, but now as we peered and felt about the panelling, the door swung open and closed again, and something entered, brushing my shoulder as it passed.

"What's that?" I said. "Someone came in."

"Never mind that," he said. "Look what I've found."

In the border of one of the panels was a black stud like an ebony bell-push. He pressed it and pulled, and a section of the panelling slid sideways, disclosing a red curtain cloaking a doorway. He drew it aside with a clash of metal rings. It was dark within, and out of the darkness came a smell of stale incense. I felt with my hand along the frame of the doorway and found a switch, and the blackness was flooded with a dazzling light.

Within was a chapel. There was no window, and at the West end of it (not the East) there stood an altar. Above it was a picture, evidently of some early Italian school. It was on the lines of the Fra Angelico picture of the Annunciation. The Virgin sat in an open loggia, and on the flowery space outside the angel made his salutation. His spreading wings were the wings of a bat, and his black head and neck were those of a raven. He had his left hand, not his right, raised in blessing. The virgin's robe of thinnest red muslin was trimmed with revolting symbols, and her face was that of a panting dog with tongue protruding.

There were two niches at the East end, in which were marble statues of naked men, with the inscriptions "St. Judas" and "St. Gilles de Raies." One was picking up pieces of silver that lay at his feet, the other looked down leering and laughing at the prone figure of a mutilated boy. The place was lit by a chandelier from the ceiling: this was of the shape of a crown of thorns and electric bulbs nestled among the woven silver twigs. A bell hung from the roof, close beside the altar.

For the moment, as I looked on these obscene blasphemies, I felt that they were merely grotesque and no more to be regarded seriously than the dirty inscriptions written upon empty wall-spaces in the street. That indifference swiftly passed, and a horrified consciousness of the devotion of those who had fashioned and assembled these decorations took its place. Skilled painters and artificers had wrought them and they were here for the service of all that is evil; that spirit of adoration lived in them dynamic and active. And the place was throbbing with the exultant joy of those who had worshipped here.

"And look here!" called Francis. He pointed to a little table standing against the wall just outside the altar-rails.

There were photographs on it, one of a boy standing on the header-board at the bathing pool about to plunge.

"That's me," he said. "Barton took it. And what's written underneath it? 'Ora pro Francisco Elton.' And that's Mrs. Ray, and that's my uncle, and that's Barton in a cope. Pray for him, too, please. But it's childish!"

He suddenly burst into a shout of laughter. The roof of the chapel was vaulted and the echo that came from it was loud and surprising, the place rang with it. His laughter ceased, but not so the echo.

There was someone else laughing. But where? Who? Except for us the chapel was empty of all visible presences.

On and on the laughter went, and we stared at each other with panic stirring. The brilliant light from the chandelier began to fade, dusk gathered, and in the dusk there was brewing some hellish and deadly force. And through the dimness I saw, hanging in the air, and oscillating slightly as if in a draught the laughing face of Horace Elton. Francis saw it too.

"Fight it! Withstand it!" he cried as he pointed to it. "Desecrate all that it holds sanctified! God, do you smell the incense and the corruption?"

We tore the photographs, we smashed the table on which they stood. We plucked the frontal from the altar and spat on the accursed table: we tugged at it till it toppled over and the marble slab split in half. We hauled from the niches the two statues that stood there, and crash they went on to the paved floor. Then appalled at the riot of our iconoclasm we paused. The laughter had ceased and no oscillating face dangled in the dimness. Then we left the chapel and pulled across the doorway the panel that closed it.

Francis came to sleep in my room, and we talked long, laying our plans for next day. We had forgotten the picture over the altar in our destruction, but now it worked in with what we proposed to do. Then we slept, and the night passed without disturbance. At the least we had broken up the apparatus that was hallowed to unhallowed uses, and that was something. But there was grim work ahead yet, and the issue was unconjecturable.

Barton came to dine that next evening, and there hung on the wall opposite his place the picture from the chapel upstairs. He did not notice it at first, for the room was rather dark, but not dark enough yet to need artificial light. He was gay and lively as usual, spoke amusingly and wittily, and asked when his friend Dickie was to return. Towards the end of dinner the lights were switched on, and then he saw the picture. I was watching him, and the sweat started out on his face that had grown clay-coloured in a moment. Then he pulled himself together.

"That's a strange picture," he said. "Was it here before? Surely not."

"No: it was in a room upstairs," said Francis. "About Dickie? I don't know for certain when he'll come back. We have found his diary, and presently we must speak about that."

"Dickie's diary? Indeed!" said Barton, and he moistened his lips with his tongue.

I think he guessed then that there was something desperate ahead, and I pictured a man condemned to be hanged waiting in his cell with his warders for the imminent hour, as Barton waited then. He sat with an elbow on the table and his hand propping his forehead. Immediately almost the servant brought in our coffee and left us.

"Dickie's diary," said Francis quietly. "Your name figures in it. Also my uncle's. Dickie saw him more than once. But, of course, you know that."

Barton drank off his glass of brandy.

"Are you telling me a ghost story?" he said. "Pray go on."

"Yes, it's partly a ghost story, but not entirely. My uncle – his ghost if you like – told him certain stories and said he must keep them secret except from you. And you told him more. And you said he should come to prayers with you some day soon. Where was that to be? In the room just above us?"

The brandy had given the condemned man a momentary courage.

"A pack of lies, Mr. Elton," he said. "That boy has got a corrupt mind. He told me things that no boy of his age should know: he giggled and laughed at them. Perhaps I ought to have told his mother."

"It's too late to think of that now," said Francis. "The diary I spoke of will be in the hands of the police at ten o'clock to-morrow morning. They will also inspect the room upstairs where you have been in the habit of celebrating the Black Mass."

Barton leant forward towards him.

"No, no," he cried. "Don't do that! I beg and implore you! I will confess the truth to you. I will conceal nothing. My life has been a blasphemy. But I'm sorry: I repent. I abjure all those abominations from henceforth: I renounce them all in the name of Almighty God."

"Too late," said Francis.

And then the horror that haunts me still began to manifest itself. The wretched man threw himself back in his chair, and there dropped from his forehead on to his white shirt-front a long grey worm that lay and wriggled there. At that moment there came from overhead the sound of a bell, and he sprang to his feet.

"No!" he cried again. "I retract all I said. I abjure nothing. And my Lord is waiting for me in the sanctuary. I must be quick and make my humble confession to him."

With the movement of a slinking animal he slid from the room, and we heard his steps going swiftly upstairs.

"Did you see?" I whispered. "And what's to be done? Is the man sane?"

"It's beyond us now," said Francis.

There was a thump on the ceiling overhead as if someone had fallen, and without a word we ran upstairs into Francis's bedroom. The door of the wardrobe where the vestments were kept was open, some lay on the floor. The panel was open, too, but within it was dark. In terror at what might meet our eyes, I felt for the switch and turned the light on.

The bell which had sounded a few minutes ago was still swinging gently, though speaking no more. Barton, clad in the gold-embroidered cope, lay in front of the overturned altar, with his face twitching. Then that ceased, the rattle of death creaked in his throat, and his mouth fell open. Great flies, swarms of them, coming from nowhere, settled on it.

Thursday Evenings

With the death of Mrs. Georgiana Wallace, in 1920, a very notable link with certain artistic activities in the mid-Victorian era was severed. She had long passed her eightieth year, but her mental faculties were quite unclouded – the link, in fact, was unrusted and untarnished – and only a couple of days before she died she gave the last of her famous Thursday evenings. I was taken there by a friend, and that was the solitary occasion on which I saw Mrs. Wallace alive. She was tremendously vivacious that night in praise of past time and (with many little shakes of her pretty porcelain head and holdings-up of her hands loaded with mourning rings) in condemnation of the grotesque gods which the present age has enshrined in the Temple of Art. Her fairness of mind was shown in the fact that she considered that much in the Golden Age of Victorian Art was "sad rubbish." That "horrid old cynic," Mr. Thackeray, for instance, was one of her hottest aversions; Dickens, with his odious vulgar descriptions of low life, was another; the pre-Raphaelite movement was just "a piece of impertinence"; and when Mr. Swinburne was incautiously mentioned, she flushed a little and changed the subject.

Mrs. Wallace, then, did not regard any of these distinguished people as precious metal, and I found myself beginning to wonder where the lode lay. So far from these persons being pure gold, she did not consider them as being possessed of the smallest touch of gilding. But then her face lit up as she talked to us of that memorable evening when she heard the first performance of that famous song "The Lost Chord."

"That's what I mean by music," she said, "and where are you to find such music now? I went to a concert the other day at the Queen's Hall, but after sitting through an hour of it I had to come away. Such a caterwauling I never heard! There was an Overture by that dreadful Mr. Wagner, and there was a Symphony by Brahms – shocking stuff, and there was a piece by Debussy, which finished me: *Un après-midi d'un Faune*, they called it. I'm sure I wondered what he had had for lunch to give him such a nightmare afterwards. I stopped my ears, my dear, until it was over; and then I came home, and sang 'The Lost Chord' through twice, to put all those dreadful noises out of my head. Ah, I shall never forget the evening when it was sung for the first time at St. James's Hall. There wasn't a dry eye in the place. The words, too, by Miss Adelaide Anne Procter! A bit of lovely poetry!"

Then, with very little encouragement, after a sniff at her lavender salts, the old lady suffered herself to be led to "the instrument," as she called the piano, and sang the masterpiece again in a faint far-away voice which sounded as if it came from the next house but one.

She spoke of the tremendous excitement at the Private View of the Academy when the "Derby Day" appeared on its walls; and passing on to literature, she recounted how, soon after she was married, Mr. Wallace had read aloud to her Mr. Robert Montgomery's magnificent poem called "Satan," which he considered the finest thing which had appeared since Milton's *Paradise Lost*. He held the most advanced views on literary subjects, and she described how when *Adam Bede* burst like a bombshell into the placid circles of the novel-reading public, scaring and shocking so many, Mr. Wallace had always maintained that, though too daring in parts, and not fit to be read aloud, it was a fine book, and she shared his view. No doubt it was an extraordinary thing for a woman to touch such a theme, but if Miss Evans had accepted her invitation to any of the Thursday evenings, both she and Mr. Wallace would have given her a warm welcome in the name of Art.

She spoke, too, of the early years of these famous Thursdays, of which this was to prove the last. All the noblest in the realms of Art and Culture assembled in this very studio where we now sat, "and I assure you," said Mrs. Wallace, audaciously, "there were a great many gentlemen always present!" There was a dinner-party first in the dining-room next door, to which some twenty of the brightest and best were bidden, and the brilliance of the conversation was perfectly paralysing. After the crinolines had retired, the gentlemen would not sit long over their wine, for they were eager in those days to join the ladies. (This was said with great archness, and I wondered how many hearts Mrs. Wallace had seriously damaged in her time.) Moreover, the odious indulgence in tobacco was then quite unknown, even as it had remained in Mrs. Wallace's house to this day, and the gentlemen were quick on the ladies' heels. Soon the party began to arrive: artists, musicians, writers, actors (she gave us a catalogue of names which I cannot remember) poured in, and the wit and the recitations, the music and the singing, were the talk of the town next day. Mr. Wallace was Scotch, and the tartan-paper which streaked the walls to-night was then newly put up. We sat in the same stiff mahogany chairs; the same worsted-work curtains shut out the noises of London; the same antimacassars were spread on the backs of sofas; even the same "instrument," which had just now tinkled under Mrs. Wallace's fingers, stood in its old place; the same colza-oil lamps were reflected in the heavy mirrors and in the polished tables. Nothing in that shrine sanctified by the conversaziones of the Golden Age, had ever been altered.

Even as she spoke I seemed to get a glimpse of the toughness of the psychical bond which, while Mrs. Wallace lived, bound the Golden Age to ours. Week by week for all those mid-Victorian years the spirit of "The Lost Chord," and the "Derby Day," and Mr. Montgomery's poems had been pouring into the room, impregnating and haunting it, and it expressed itself not only in the mahogany and the colza-oil lamps, in the worsted curtains and the flowered carpet, but even more potently in the whole psychic environment. Drop by drop, from crinoline and conversation, sweet as lavender and remote as the stars, that essence, unrecapturable except through the mediumship, so to speak, of our venerable hostess, had soaked the spiritual atmosphere. She alone held it there; when she was no longer able to do that, the ancient volatile fragrance must surely fade, and be perceptible no longer to our modern bustling senses. So when, two days later, I saw in the paper the announcement of Mrs. Wallace's death, I felt that the Golden Age of Victoria, as loved and understood by her, had passed away for ever from the earth. It seemed to have fallen with a remote hissing sound (as when you drop a match into the river), down, down into the dark well of years, and to have been promptly quenched . . . Never in my life have I been so hopelessly and outrageously wrong.

There was a sale of the contents of the house, and, in spite of the extravagant prices then paid for furniture, those faded flowered carpets, those heavy mahogany chairs, those colza-oil lamps, failed to arouse the cupidity of purchasers, and it was melancholy to reflect how, but a few weeks ago, these objects had been the splendour and embellishment of a venerated sanctuary. Now that shrine was empty, and they were tumbled out undesired and unhallowed to freeze on the pavements outside second-hand furniture shops till their final dispersion into callous homes. There were engravings, too, "The

Monarch of the Glen," "Derby Day," "Queen Victoria Opening the Great Exhibition," which scarcely fetched the price of the gilding on their frames. Lot after lot was rapidly and contemptuously disposed of, and at the end of the day I found myself the possessor of a glass case of wax flowers and two pink vases, the hideousness of which was absolutely irresistible. With them in my hand I took one more look round the scene of the Thursday evenings, and for the moment I was alone there, as the auctioneer was finishing the disposal of the "boudoir" fittings. Just as I turned to leave I distinctly heard a voice at my elbow. It spoke very clearly, in a voice that I recognized at once.

"They may get rid of my things," it said, "but they don't get rid of me."

I was so startled that I dropped one of the pink vases, and, clutching my other possessions more tightly, I stole away on tiptoe.

Soon after came the sale of the house itself: the purchaser was Mr. Humphrey Lodge, the musical composer, whom the enlightened admire so greatly. His wife, as all the world knows, is the Cubist portrait-painter who sees the faces of her sitters as a series of planes separated from each other by coloured lines. In a few weeks the house was redecorated according to the most modern ideas, and resembled the setting of a Russian ballet gone mad, or, perhaps, a house so camouflaged that it ceased to be like a house at all. Electric light, of course, was introduced, and the lamp-shades were in the shape of large paper cauliflowers, bunches of carrots, and bundles of asparagus, painted by Mrs. Lodge. The walls of the studio were purple, with large green clouds sailing across them, out of which sprang flashes of magenta lightning, and dotted about among the clouds were some houses and steeples and a few faces. The room was extremely large, and there was plenty of space for Mrs. Lodge's easels in one half, and a big table for her husband in the other. Just now he was composing his twenty-third symphony for a small band: his siren-whistles, pieces of emery-paper rubbed together, watchmen's rattles, and penny whistles found places in the newer orchestra. Neither of them ever stopped smoking cigarettes, and neither was the least mad, but only modern.

One morning, as they worked together, she at a portrait of her husband, he at the slow movement of his Symphony, he scribbled the date across the page, and got up.

"That's finished," he said.

"Ah, you shall play it me in a moment, dear," said she. "Just sit still one minute more. I want to catch – yes, that's right."

She painted for a little while in silence, while he, reconsidering his last bars, put in a fortissimo semi-breve for the B flat rattle.

"And I've finished, too," she said, drawing a line of crimson across the plane of his nose. Then, putting back her head, she sniffed curiously at the thick air.

"It's odd," she said. "All the morning, while working, I thought I smelt that spiky thing that grows in gardens and among clothes."

"Lavender?" he asked.

"Yes, that's it. It must be my imagination if you can't smell it. Come and play me your slow movement."

He went across to the piano. This alone remained of Mrs. Wallace's furniture, for Humphrey Lodge had attended the sale, and, running his fingers over the antique keys, had discovered in them exactly that tinkly remote tone which he wanted for certain surprising orchestral effects, and had bought it on the spot. He spread the score on the music-rest, and picked up from the table half a dozen weird instruments.

"I can only give you the sketchiest idea of it," he said. "Yes, you take the two rattles and whirl them when I nod to you."

The crazy performance began. Humphrey was extremely agile with arpeggios for one hand, a few raps at the xylophone with the other, with hurried rubbings of the emery-paper and chromatic blasts on the siren which he held in his mouth. But, though Julia supplemented these activities with the rattles in E flat and B flat, he could but render a sketch, an adumbration of the score. With the musician's gift of internal audition, he could, as he followed his text, imagine the parts which want of fingers compelled him to omit, and the complete effect was as fully realized by him as if the omitted noises were all in full blast. Suddenly he stopped.

"There it is again," he said. "I've been hearing that at intervals all the morning."

"Hearing what?" asked Julia, checking the rattle.

"It's some kind of reedy sound which doesn't occur in my score at all." said he. "It's like an old lady singing in the next house, and it keeps interrupting me. Sometimes I catch a bar or two of a tune, some sort of hymn tune in G. This kind of thing:"

And with an exasperated finger he played a couple of lines of "The Lost Chord."

Julia listened; a dim recognition awoke in her fine eyes. "But that's a real tune," she said; "I've heard it before. Play it again, Humphrey; I shall remember what it is."

He repeated the ecclesiastical melody.

"I don't call it a tune," he said. "And, anyhow, there's nothing in my score that remotely resembles it. Why do I keep on hearing it?"

"I know what it is now," said Julia. "My mother used to sing it. It's called 'The Lost Chord,' 'Seated one day at the organ' – that's how the words began – and there's something about the crimson twilight and the sound of a great Amen."

She put out her hand, and touched the keys, attempting, rather unsuccessfully, to pick out the sound of the great Amen with one finger.

"I'm beginning to remember it," she said hopefully.

Humphrey jumped up with a start.

"But there it is again, correcting you," he cried. "Can't you hear it?"

For one second Julia Lodge certainly thought she heard a faint, flute-like voice crooning from somewhere behind her easel. Whether it was an illusion or not, the impression was only momentary; but once again, more vividly, she thought she smelt the odour of lavender.

"Yes, I thought I heard something," she said. "What is it?"

A little shudder of goose-flesh passed over her.

"It's all imagination," she said. "Let's get on with your lovely slow movement. Where are my rattles?"

From that morning a series of trivial but inexplicable incidents began to invade the domestic routine of the house; things trumpery in themselves, but inconvenient, like pebbles in shoes, and also arresting because no possible explanation could be found for them. Some of them suggested that a practical joker was exercising his despicable wit on the Lodges, for one morning there appeared on the hall table a package, addressed in a tall, slanting hand to Julia, which, when opened, proved to contain a wretched reproduction of "The Monarch of the Glen"; and on the same day, and in the same place, was found a similar package addressed to Humphrey, which contained a well-thumbed copy of one of Mr. Wetherby's songs. These packets had not passed through the post; but, even granting collusion with their servants, they could think of no one who would have thought it worth while to cut such childish capers. More inexplicable was the insertion in Humphrey's score of his new Overture of a passage for the tenor horn which proved to be the opening bars of an obsolete song called "Dresden China," by Mr. Molloy, whom he ascertained to have been an admired melodist of the nineteenth century. Of course, he indignantly erased it, and even while his knife was scratching at it, he thought he heard some noise, a mixture between a sob and a sniff, from the corner of the dusky studio. Again, one morning Julia found her cubist picture of her husband, which was still not yet dry, fallen face downwards on the floor, and much obliterated, because the wet paint had stuck to the carpet. This time there was no sob or sniff by way of comment, but a little noise, scarcely audible, which sounded to her much more like a cackle of laughter, followed up by an overwhelming whiff of lavender. Again, it was very odd that a copy of *Adam Bede*, a book of which neither of them had ever heard, well-worn, with passages heavily underlined, and pencilled in the margin with notes of approbation, should appear during lunch-time, on the lid of the piano. Curious noises were heard in the house – the tapping of shoes, the rustle of skirts, and once, when Julia and her husband were dining out, the servants in the kitchen, which lay below the studio, were amazed at the tinkle of the piano above their heads, and the parlour-maid came up with a tray of siphons and whisky, supposing that they had returned. She noticed a line of light under the studio door, clearly indicating that it was lit within. But on opening it she found herself staring into a darkness redolent with the smell of colza-oil. After a hysterical night she gave notice next morning, and Julia was obliged to sacrifice several days from her painting in order to find a new maid.

It was at this point that I had begun to form a certain intimacy with my new neighbours, and, meeting them one night at the theatre, they took me home for a half-hour of cigarettes and conversation. At present I knew nothing about these curious occurrences, but as we entered the studio I could not help observing that Humphrey cast a suspicious eye round the room, and Julia looked anxiously in the direction of her easel. They both seemed very *distraits*, and, as we sat down, a silence fell. Then suddenly Humphrey said:

"Let's tell him," and proceeded to enthral me with such details as I have already recorded. Instantly my own little experience in this room, which startled me into dropping one of my pink vases, flashed into my mind.

"I'm sure there's a ghost here," said Julia as he finished. "And I believe it's a woman, because it's much nicer to Humphrey than to me. There's lots you've left out, Humphrey. It's always leaving little nosegays of violets done up in mutton-cutlet frills on your dressing-room table. It—"

She gave a little gasp and pointed to the corner where her easel stood.

"Look!" she said, in a strange whisper.

I turned quickly, following her finger, and caught a glimpse of a green crinoline, of a low-cut bodice, of a lively but malicious little face with a chaplet of artificial rosebuds round its hair. The features were unmistakable, though fifty years of Thursday evenings had been peeled off them. There was no longer the slightest doubt in my mind that Mrs. Wallace, now a *Poltergeist* of infinite ingenuity, was at the bottom of all these strange happenings.

"That's Mrs. Wallace," I said firmly, and even as I spoke Julia's easel came rattling to the ground for the second time.

Julia rose.

"Well, it's very rude of her," she said. "She has no business here.

Humphrey bought the house; it's his. Why do you suppose she comes and haunts it? Has she done some atrocious crime in this room?"

Humphrey gave a scornful laugh.

"Julia, how can you be so ridiculous?" he said. "It's true that decades of atrocious crimes went on in this room, though. They talked Art here, the Art of 1860. They sang 'The Lost Chord' here. The room wallows in crime. But ghosts! There aren't any!"

There came a sudden crack from his music table; he went rather hurriedly across to it, and took up one of his orchestral instruments.

"And now she's broken my siren," he observed, greatly annoyed.

Julia, like a good wife, did not call attention to the singular inconsistency of this, but picked up her easel, and grew red with passion.

"She's spoiled it again," she said. "But we won't give in; we'll fight the odious old woman for all we're worth. She's a spiritual blackmailer; she wants to frighten us into some sort of surrender. It's monstrous that the next world should interfere with ours in this scandalous fashion."

Humphrey threw the fragments of the siren into the fireplace.

"Oh, bosh!" he exclaimed. "Bosh!" he repeated, as if to encourage himself.

I left them determined to keep the materialistic flag flying. But the next week witnessed a swift development in the power of the haunting presence. It – we may say "she" – began to materialize in the most convincing manner, and it was clear that this earthbound spirit was just as "arch" as she had been fifty years ago. She constantly appeared to Humphrey in simpering Victorian attitudes; she gave him little shy smiles, and seemed to be trying to propitiate him. Her attitude to Julia, on the other hand, had become far more aggressive: not content with casting her easel to the ground whenever she had made a peculiarly inspired cube on it, she visited her with the most atrocious nightmares, she broke her looking glass, she cloyed her palate with lavender. When Julia came into her black bathroom with the purple ceiling and the pink floor, she would hear the whisk of skirts behind the cistern; if she went into her bedroom to dress for dinner she would find the simulacrum of a green crinoline and a wreath of roses laid out on her bed. It was perfectly clear that Mrs. Wallace wanted to annoy the woman and wheedle the man into something that suited her ghostly will. And a week afterwards, sitting alone one evening, I received a telephone message that Mrs. Lodge would like me "to step round," if I was disengaged, on a matter of some importance.

They were both sadly changed. Humphrey wore a wild and hunted eye, Julia was full of jerky apprehensive movements. I was given a short and dismal account of these new experiences.

"Can you suggest anything that she would particularly like?" asked Julia humbly. "You say you met her once. What did she particularly value in her life in this house?"

"I should say her Thursday evenings," I answered.

"Bunkum!" said Humphrey, without conviction. "Besides, how are we to give her her Thursday evenings? We can't arrange evenings for the dead."

Julia had gone to her bureau by the window, and she took up an engagement-book, which she examined by the light of one of the cauliflower lampshades.

"To-morrow is Thursday," she said. "We're dining out."

There was silence. Here, at the top of the square, which is a cul-de-sac, there was no sound of traffic, and the silence began to sing in my ears. It began to sing a tune. Humphrey must have heard it, too, for he gave a loud squeal and clutched his hair.

"There it is again," he said. "I shall go crazy if this continues! I sat up till three last night, reading *Adam Bede*. I didn't want to, but I had to. I shall sit up again to-night, I know. Thank God, there are only fifty pages left."

"But she'll make you begin another book," said Julia. "It may be *The Wide, Wide World* next time."

"What do you want to do, then?" he asked.

"Darling, just to leave the studio empty to-morrow night," she said. "To lock the door and leave it. Then, if that succeeds, we might do the same thing the next Thursday. It's worth trying."

It was only a few evenings ago that I dined with the Lodges. It was, in fact, on Thursday. We sat rather long round the table, and Julia, looking at the clock, got up hurriedly.

"We won't sit in the studio to-night," she said. "It is pleasant upstairs."

We went upstairs, and I demanded news. Humphrey interspersed Julia's narrative with unconvinced expressions such as "Pish!" or "Rot!" She told me in brief how every Thursday afternoon she put bunches of lavender in the studio, and left some suitable pictures and books about. She also took out of the room her easel, and the score on which Humphrey was engaged, for fear of annoying "them." Since they had made these arrangements they hadn't been "bothered." . . . The clock struck ten, and, remembering that Mrs. Wallace's famous conversaziones always began at half-past nine, my curiosity rose.

"I have left my cigarettes in my coat pocket downstairs," I said. "I will go and fetch them."

Humphrey is not a fool; he did not say "There are plenty here." As for Julia, her eyes sparkled.

"Dare you?" she asked.

For some reason I kicked off my shoes when I got outside the drawing-room, and paddled noiselessly down to the floor below.

A short passage leads from the hall to the studio and dining-room; this was dark, but from below the studio door, at the end of it, there came a thin line of light. As I crept closer I heard the dim sound of many voices coming from it. Closer and closer I crept and my ear focused itself to the murmur.

"A fine book, in spite of its coarseness," I heard. "But one doesn't want to talk about it. Ah, Georgiana, here's Mr. Molloy asking if he may lead you to the instrument."

I heard the sound of the piano, less tinkly than when I heard it last, and then, unmistakably, the sound of a human voice. It was all thin and remote, as if borne from some great distance on the wind.

"And now," I said to myself, "I shall open the door and go in."

And then I did nothing of the kind. Poltroon and coward, I retraced my steps, looking fearfully behind me, in order to be sure that the studio door had not opened, and that from it some wraith of days long past was not spying on the impertinent future. I scurried upstairs, and with my shoes in my hand entered the drawing-room.

"Well?" said Humphrey and Julia, in one breath.

"There was a light under the studio door," I said. "There were voices, words, music."

"And you didn't go in?" asked Humphrey.

"Certainly not. If it comes to that, why don't you go in yourself? They are there."

He pondered a moment. "Bosh!" he said, with an effort.

The Psychical Mallards

Timothy Mallard was gifted from childhood with a variety of supernormal powers, which rendered him utterly different from all other children that his parents had ever come across, and his involuntary exercise of them extended back into his very earliest days. He was, in fact, hardly a month old when he first gave evidence of his peculiar endowments. One day he cried so long and loud (after being as "good as gold" throughout his four weeks of earthly pilgrimage) that his nurse took him out of his cradle and set him on her knee, where she proceeded to adopt the usual soothing process of rocking him violently to and fro and up and down with the pitching and rolling motion of a boat in a storm, in order to reduce him to the requisite state of dizzy quiescence. For some five minutes she persevered in this traditional treatment, but to no effect, and was just about to give it up in despair, and put him to bed again till nature was exhausted, when a large flake of the ceiling fell, crushing his cradle into a pancake of wicker and blanket. And as if a tap had been turned off his crying ceased . . .

That incident, naturally enough, was put to the credit of coincidence, and it was considered "very lucky" that his nurse had taken Master Tim out of the cradle just then, though it would have, perhaps, been "luckier" if there had been no such fall of lath and plaster. But from that time onwards the young years of Timothy Mallard were enveloped in a net of such curious phenomena, that it became impossible to attribute them all to coincidence, and his parents – healthy, normal people – were forced to the reluctant conclusion that there was something very odd about the child himself.

It was no use, for instance, making him put out his tongue, and then, with a bright smile, telling him that for a treat he was going to be given a spoonful of the most delicious red-currant jelly, because, without having tasted it, he announced that it was "powdery." But he tempered the obduracy of his refusal to indulge in red-currant jelly with a promise to "fink" his ache away. Tim then closed his eyes, gave a few little twitches, and seemed to relapse into unconsciousness. They had hardly begun to shake him when he came to himself, and it was quite apparent that he had thought away that troublesome ache, while his tongue, on re-examination, was discovered to be of the requisite rose-leaf description. Similarly, when his first visit to the dentist was planned, and he was told that he and nurse were going for a jolly walk in the High Street, he made the astounding announcement that he hadn't got toothache, and that he would bite any alien finger that intruded itself into his mouth. In this case (so the scientific student may observe) it was conceivable that he might, subconsciously, have overheard a conversation about dentists between his mother and his nurse, but such an explanation does not account for the fact that at the age of six he drew a detailed sketch of his own inside, showing with complete accuracy the position of the liver, pancreas, kidneys, and other interesting organs. The family doctor, to whom this artistic effort was submitted without hint as to authorship, said it was the work of a trained pathologist.

Dr. Farmer was interested in occult phenomena, and, when informed that this accurate and beautiful map was the work of Timothy, he told his disgusted parents that the boy was possessed of some supernormal power of lucidity or clairvoyance, which enabled him to perceive what was hidden from the ordinary vision. Other instances of this gift were shown in the fact that he could announce that his Aunt Anne was putting on her hat and cloak with the intention of calling on her sister-in-law, and that his father, who was up in town for the day, had missed his train at Charing Cross. So, though weird, this gift had its practical advantages, for his mother had time on the one hand to tell her parlour-maid that she was out, and on the other to put off dinner . . . Together with clairvoyance he developed a power of clair-audience, and by day and night heard voices which were quite inaudible to his elders and betters.

Apart from these little peculiarities Tim was normal enough, and at the age of thirteen presented the similitude of a big, merry boy, with large boots and tousled hair. His father determined to send him to Eton, where he had himself imbibed a love of cricket and a hatred of Greek, in the hopes that a sound classical education would speedily disperse those strange "clouds of glory" that the boy still trailed behind him. Roman history and hexameters and supines were powerful solvents of the unusual.

Mr. Mallard, puzzled though he was by these occult phenomena, still had a lurking feeling that the boy could curb them if he chose, and on the eve of his departure spoke to him kindly, but firmly, about it all.

"Remember, my dear Tim," he said, "that I am going to all this trouble and expense of sending you to Eton not merely that you should be able to write Latin verses and pass examinations with credit. You are growing up – boyhood passes very soon into manhood – and you must learn to behave as men behave. Those childish tricks, for instance—"

Tim, as is the custom of the new generation, treated his father like a child.

"But I've told you often and often," he said, "that I can't help it. I wish you would try to remember that. I don't want to see Aunt Anne in her bath, or know you are going to fall off your bicycle."

His father thumped the table.

"Now, I beg of you, Tim," he said, "not to argue like that. You can control those tricks perfectly well if you like. Dr. Farmer told me that they were of hysterico-ideo-exteriorizative origin—"

"What?" said Tim.

"The same as fidgets," said his father. "Occupy your mind with something else when you feel them coming on. You won't find yourself popular either with your teachers or your companions if you behave queerly. Queer! That's the word I wanted instead of Dr. Farmer's definition. There's nothing which wholesome English boys dislike so much as queerness. Get over your queerness, my dear, and do credit to the great middle class from which you come. I can let you enjoy an excellent education, and mix on equal terms with your superiors – never mind that – but you'll have to make your way in the world, and there's nothing that so goes against a man as queerness—"

He broke off suddenly and looked at Tim, who had shut his eyes and was twitching violently. He was naturally very much annoyed that the boy should give so small an attention to the remarks which he had so carefully prepared, and raised his voice.

"Tim, drop it!" he said. "Listen to me, Tim. *Tim*!"

Tim's twitching had ceased, and he lay back in his chair, breathing slowly and heavily. His father, irritated beyond endurance at this untimely exhibition of one of his tricks, was about to shake him violently by the shoulder, when his attention was attracted by a loud rattling noise behind him, and he observed his heavy knee-hole table advancing across the room without visible agency in the direction of the trance-stricken boy. He had barely time to skip out of the way of its ponderous march, when it came to a standstill, and he found himself with shaking knees and a dry throat staring at Tim across it. Dr. Farmer had already asked him whether Tim had shown any symptoms of teleo-kinesis, which (the obliging doctor explained) signified the movements of inanimate objects towards or from the boy, occurring without intervention of any visible agency, and, with a sinking of his heart, Mr. Mallard realized that here was a teleo-kinetic phenomenon . . . Then, without warning, this heavy table began to creak and groan again, and, retreating from Tim with the same swiftness with which it had advanced, came to rest in its usual position. So, even if Tim had pulled it towards him with a string in some inexplicable manner, he would have had to employ some strong and rigid rod to repel it again. Mr. Mallard's common sense rejected such a theory, and he was forced to suppose that his poor boy had suddenly developed teleo-kinetic power.

At this moment, while Tim still lay inert in his chair, there came a hurried step on the stair, and Mrs. Mallard, who had been sitting below, waddled into the room.

"I heard such a noise overhead," she said, "as if you were moving all the furniture instead of telling Tim about Eton. Why, what's the matter with him?"

"Teleo-kinesis," muttered Mr. Mallard. "My kneehole table has been behaving like a three-year-old."

Mrs. Mallard had the same wholesale dislike of occult phenomena as her husband.

"Oh, how tiresome!" she said. "But, thank goodness, the table has gone back. So upsetting for a housemaid to find all the furniture moved about. Dr. Farmer told me that we mustn't be surprised if something of the sort happened. He is a very naughty boy. He—"

Her voice froze in her throat, and she pointed a trembling finger at her only son. Mr. Mallard followed its faltering direction.

Tim was lying with closed eyes and crossed legs in his father's large arm-chair, and now began to rise out of it, not on to his feet, but into the air. It was as if some unseen arm-chair still supported him, for he rose in precisely the same position as that in which he had been lolling when he went into a trance, like a balloon gently leaving the ground. He was apparently without weight, for the draught from the door, which Mrs. Mallard had left wide, gently wafted him towards the open window, and, to his parents' horror, he floated out of it and lay suspended thirty feet above the pavement of the High Street. Then some opposing current took possession of him, and after he had bumped once or twice against the panes of the second window, Mr. Mallard had the good sense to open it, and Tim floated in again. He circled round the room as if in a slow eddy, and then came to rest on the top of the knee-hole table.

"Levitation, drat it!" moaned Mr. Mallard. "Dr. Farmer—"

Tim shook himself, upset an ink-bottle, and rubbed his eyes. "Oh, bother!" he said to his father. "What have I been doing now? Hallo, I'm sitting in a pool of ink! Why on earth didn't you stop me, one of you?"

Mr. Mallard did not feel himself bound to repeat these tiresome occurrences to Tim's house-master, for it was not fair that the boy should begin his school-life under a cloud, and Tim left for Eton (in a new pair of trousers) next day. For some weeks Mr. Mallard had reason to congratulate himself on his high opinion of classics and congenial companionship as a cure for psychical tendencies, for nothing unusual disturbed the scholastic serenity of that educational establishment. But often before the deplorable agencies that were responsible for occult phenomena had remained dormant for long periods, and Mr. Mallard, when he received a letter with the Eton postmark, never opened it without a qualm. The weeks, however, went on, and his apprehensions began to get drowsy, and when, eventually, on a Monday morning he took out of its envelope a letter from Tim's house-master, he had no premonition of disastrous news. But he turned white as he read it, and passed it over to his wife with a hollow groan.

"I feel bound to tell you," wrote Tim's housemaster, "that I am puzzled and pained by your son's conduct. Hitherto he has, beyond a few acts of boyish carelessness and disobedience, given me no cause for complaint. But this morning (Sunday), while attending chapel, some events occurred which it is impossible for me to pass over. He must have thrown his prayer-book at the chaplain (though no one actually saw him do it), for the book in question, with his name written in it by his mother, whose gift it was, certainly hit the reverend gentleman a severe blow in the eye, which completely incapacitated him from conducting divine service. He was led out of chapel, and the head master continued the office. What makes the offence more heinous is that your son then feigned complete unconsciousness. Had he owned up to throwing his prayer-book at the chaplain in some fit of boyish exasperation, I probably should not have troubled you with this serious report, and the head master would have dealt briefly with the whole question . . ."

Mrs. Mallard raised a blanched face from the perusal of this terrible letter.

"Poor darling," she said. "Teleo-kinesis."

"Read on," said Mr. Mallard, brokenly.

"I write," said Tim's house-master, "in a confusion of mind to which I am wholly unaccustomed. The Marquis of Essex and Moses Samuelson, two admirable and steady boys, both in my house, assisted your son out of chapel. They both aver, with the honesty that characterizes the English aristocracy and the ancient Semites, that when they came to the flight of steps leading from the chapel into the school-yard, your son, still unconscious, floated out of their hands ('Levitation,' sobbed Mrs. Mallard), and was wafted on to the railings of the statue of Henry VI, where he came to himself in considerable pain. I have just had a long talk with the head master, who, as you may know, is an enthusiastic member of the Society for Psychical Research, and he is inclined (in my judgment) to take an altogether too lenient view of your son's conduct. I told him, however, as I am now telling you, that if any further incidents of the sort occur, I shall be unable to keep T. Mallard in my house. You need be under no apprehension about his physical well-being, for the school doctor tells me that, beyond a few abrasions and punctures (owing to the railings), the boy is no worse for his adventure. But for myself I hold all psychical phenomena in contempt and abhorrence as being wholly un-English, and on any repetition of them I shall have to ask you to remove T. Mallard from my care."

It was no wonder that the news of this sensational Sunday morning soon got abroad, for every boy in the school wrote home to his parents saying how much he had enjoyed chapel that day, and Tim's parents were besieged with requests from various Occult and Psychical Societies to let the boy embrace the mediumistic profession. These they invariably refused, and appeals pointing out to them their obvious duty in allowing their son's young energies to be employed in the noble task of tearing away the veil between the seen and the unseen did not produce the smallest effect on them. Offers of considerable sums of money for séances given by Tim were even harder to resist, and it does the utmost credit to Mr. and Mrs. Mallard that neither avarice nor duty (according to occultists) made them swerve a hairbreadth from their resolve to give Tim every chance of growing up into a sensible and conventional man. Like decent parents they had their son's true welfare at heart, and they returned emphatic negatives to all the allurements of even the wealthiest Psychical Associations. As if to reward them, for a long time after this no further disturbance took place, and three happy years passed. Tim got his "Field" colours for football, he was likely to play at Lord's in the cricket team, and he developed an excellent repugnance for learning . . . Poor wretches! They had no idea how his psychical reservoir was filling.

Mr. Mallard, in Tim's last year but one at Eton, was the prey of financial anxieties, but as long as the Khamshot Oil Company continued to pay a dividend of thirty-five per cent, no wolf could come within reasonable distance of his doors. But one evening during the Christmas holidays Tim, while in the middle of an account of a football match, became cataleptic, and, with groanings and screams, had shouted out "Horrible Khamshot: sell, sell, sell!" It was very disappointing that after three years' immunity from nonsense he had suddenly become nonsensical again, and Khamshot was expected to pay a forty per cent dividend this year, so Mr. Mallard, intentionally defiant, sold out next day all that he was possessed of in other investments in order to put his entire fortune into Khamshots. The forty per cent dividend was duly declared, and Mr. Mallard very naturally said, "So much for poor Tim's clairvoyance."

But in spite of the affluence which the forty per cent dividend produced, those Christmas holidays were very trying to Tim's parents, for the boy was prey to continuous psychical invasions just when it might have been hoped that he was growing out of such irregularities. He constantly went into rigid and profound trances, during which the heaviest articles of furniture were wont to whirl about the room; levitations were of almost daily occurrence; and he developed a new and uncomfortable gift which Dr. Farmer told the parents was undoubtedly ideoplasticity. While in trance dreadful luminous spots used to appear on his waistcoat, from which exuded some wax-like substance that weaved itself into the semblance of human figures. These materializations took place in broad daylight, and since Dr. Farmer told Mr. Mallard that on no account must Tim be startled or violently awakened while these horrid simulacra were manifest (for a shock of any kind might derange his mind or even prove fatal), it was necessary to wait, with such patience as was possible, till these revolving exudations were absorbed again. Dinner on Christmas Day, for instance, was a very sorry banquet, for Tim had hardly begun on his turkey before he went into a profound trance, and plum pudding could not be served till nearly ten o'clock. He became markedly more clairvoyant, and what gave rise to profound uneasiness in his father, in view of the fact that Tim had so strongly urged him to sell Khamshot Oils, was that these visions invariably proved correct. He saw Aunt Anne writing her will afresh, and leaving her money to an orphan asylum instead of her brother; he saw himself holing a mashie shot at golf; he saw his mother sprain her ankle by slipping on a banana skin – all of which visions were promptly fulfilled. Aunt Anne died of pneumonia, and her will revealed this abominable codicil; Tim holed a topped mashie shot; and his mother was on the sofa for three days. But, with the obstinacy of a thoroughly sensible person, Mr. Mallard clung to his Khamshot Oils.

Tim still remembers with dreadful vividness the ensuing Ash Wednesday, when he was, of course, back at Eton. He had had a slight levitation that morning, but it had passed off unobserved, and his bureau had shown a tendency towards teleo-kinesis. But a keen game of fives had made him feel himself again, and he was on his way back to his house when he experienced a moment of terrible clairvoyance. Of its exact nature he never spoke, but the effect was that he rushed to the nearest telegraph office and sent off a wire to his mother, saying: "Don't let father get near razors." Ten minutes afterwards, passing a newsboard, his heart stood still, for he saw on it in large letters: "Stupendous

Earthquake at Khamshot." He went in and bought the paper, and read ruinous tidings. All the oil wells had been engulfed in an immense schism in the earth, and the island had nearly entirely disappeared under the sea. A few scattered reefs alone stuck out. This, of course, explained his clairvoyance about his father, and he could only pray that his telegram had arrived in time. Alas! it had not, for later in the day, his housemaster broke to him the terrible news that, in a fit of temporary insanity, caused by the loss of his entire fortune, his father had cut the throats of his cook, his wife, and his parlour-maid, and, subsequently, his own.

Youth is gifted with divine powers of recuperation, and after his first outburst of passionate grief was over, Tim resolutely faced the future. He was now quite alone in the world, his father's meagre balance at the bank was not more than sufficient to pay his school bills for this term, and it was clear that if he was to enjoy (as his poor father had wished) the full benefit of a Public School education, and spend another year at Eton, he must set himself to work to earn money in the holidays. With the full approval and consent of the head master, who, as has been already mentioned, was a serious student of the occult, he hired a couple of rooms in Sloane Street, neatly, but not expensively furnished, and announced in all the leading papers that Timothy Mallard, Esq. (the famous Eton medium) would give during the Easter Holidays a series of clairvoyant, teleo-kinetic, ideoplastic and other séances at his rooms in Sloane Street. He claimed no spiritualistic powers, professed to tell no fortunes, and invited the inspection of the police and other trained observers of the occult. References were permitted to the head master of Eton and his brother the Suffragan Bishop of Winchelsea.

Under such scholastic and ecclesiastical patronage the Eton medium spent a very busy and profitable Easter holiday. But, do what he would, he could not prevent enthusiastic spiritualists believing that he received and transmitted to them messages from the other side. It was no use Tim asserting that he only read their minds; they knew better than that, and insisted that they were in communication with all manner of defunct friends and relatives. Almost as popular were the materializations (ideo-plasticity), of which he could produce any quantity in broad daylight under the most searching test conditions, and the inexplicable movements of the largest pieces of furniture. Occasionally, the power failed altogether; but Tim, with a shrewdness that did credit to his classical education, never attempted to make good the temporary failure by fraud or conjuring tricks which, sooner or later, would be detected. The honest English boy refused to take the usual fees, and waited for the return of the power. But, though highly remunerative, the Easter holidays were very strenuous, and he was glad to get back to the quiet and leisure of the summer half.

He played cricket against Harrow that year at Lord's, and, naturally, as he walked out from the pavilion to bat, he made an experiment or two to see whether his occult powers were in working order. He tried to read the umpire's mind, but was disappointed to find that he could get no telepathic impression. But the teleo-kinetic gift was in full force, for without effort he caused one of the wicket-keeper's gloves to slip off his hand and trundle towards him along the ground. He felt, therefore, the utmost confidence in his batting powers, for he could apply the same treatment to the balls he received. The first was a yorker, but just before it touched his bat he exerted the full force of his mind, and, making a slogging gesture, caused it to soar away and break a window in the pavilion. This counted six runs, and, just to get his eye in, he repeated the feat with the remainder of the over. Then, to show he could play all round the wicket, he made some crisp cuts and pulled a few balls round to the boundary at mid-on. The power then completely failed, and he was bowled after just completing his century.

He had another year at Eton, and, by judicious mind-reading, won a scholarship at King's College, Cambridge. His holidays were spent in strenuous work, and before he took his degree he was not only living in the lap of luxury, but had taken a spacious house in Belgrave Square instead of the more modest quarters in Sloane Street, and had a thousand pounds to his credit at the bank. He was extremely industrious, and, finding that his power grew with practice, often spent an hour or two in trance without sitters, but with a stenographer to take down all that he said or did.

On one such evening he came to himself after a prolonged trance, bathed in perspiration, and feeling that his telepathic powers had projected his subconscious mind to some immense distance. He absently sipped a glass of Perrier Jouet (1894) as the stenographer arranged her notes.

"Well, what have I been saying?" he asked wearily.

She cleared her throat.

"Khamshot, Khamshot," she said. "Buy, buy, buy! Buy Khamshot! Fortune and opulence. Fresh earthquake and lakes of oil. Island emerged from sea again with enormous lake of oil constantly replenished by innumerable gushers."

"What?" said Tim.

She drew her finger down the page.

"Then you said, 'Buy!' nothing but 'Buy!' Mr. Mallard," said Miss Gray. "Then there's some more about the lake of oil. You talked about nothing else."

Tim put off his early sitters next morning, and went down to the city with a cheque in his pocket for a thousand and seventeen pounds, which represented his balance at Messrs Barclays. By an effort of cryptomnesia (or recalling what he had once known but completely forgotten) he remembered the name of his father's broker, and invested the whole of his savings in Khamshot Oils. The shares were to be had at the price of a few pence, and his money thus purchased (inclusive of brokerage) fifty-three thousand of them. He was already possessed of twenty thousand more, the only legacy which he had received from his poor father, so that he was now the holder of seventy-three thousand shares. Then he went back to Belgrave Square and resumed his séances ... The evening papers reported a prodigious earthquake among the reefs which had once been Khamshot Island.

This year a new medium took London by storm, and occult circles were evenly and acutely bisected as to whether she or Tim was the more remarkable repository of supernormal power. Her name was Miriam Starlight, a girl of not more than twenty and of extraordinary physical beauty. The two met at a psychical tea-party and instantly fell violently in love with each other. Nothing could have been more suitable, and the occult world of London was thrilled with the anticipation of what manifestations would result from their joint mediumship. Within a few weeks of their meeting they were engaged, and a few weeks more saw them married.

It was quite in the earlier days of their honeymoon, which they spent at Rye, that it became apparent that psychical London was doomed to experience a most terrible disappointment. Not wishing to let their blissful weeks slip by without some little practice in their life-work, they trifled with some easy feats in levitation, cryptomnesia, teleo-kinesis, and ideo-plasticity. Tim and Miriam in turn went off singly into trance, and the most amazing results followed. Each of them, singly, levitated with the greatest ease, and floated out of the window into the street or the garden; the furniture of the house (kindly lent them by the President of the Psychical Association) whirled round the room, and materializations followed each other in bewildering succession. Thus they knew that marriage had not spoiled their individual gifts, and with Tim's stenographer to note results, they began on the experiments which they hoped would add an entirely new chapter to the veracious history of mediumship, and composing themselves in two arm-chairs, went into trance together. Miss Gray, the stenographer, was quite accustomed to psychical phenomena, and as soon as she had satisfied herself (by pinching them) that they were completely unconscious, sharpened her pencils and adopted the procedure which she often followed when observing Tim.

"Teleo-kinesis, please," she said, in a business-like voice.

A large bureau instantly began to move towards Tim. But it had hardly started when it came to a standstill and began violently to quiver. It was exactly as if some opposing force had met it and refused to let it advance. There was an ominous creaking sound from somewhere inside it.

Clever Miss Gray grasped the situation instantly.

"Teleo-kinesis, Mr. Mallard alone, please," she said, and the bureau slid swiftly over the carpet.

"Teleo-kinesis, Mrs. Mallard alone, please," she said, and the bureau began to retreat again.

Miss Gray was a fearless observer, and this vastly interested her.

"Teleo-kinesis together," she said, retreating behind her arm-chair. "Full speed ahead."

The bureau, violently agitated, remained exactly where it was, and it was evident to her that the two high horse-power teleo-kinetic agencies were in opposition. Before she had time to realize what the result must inevitably be, it had burst into a thousand fragments. One dynamism, it was clear, attracted it, the other stubbornly repelled it.

Not wishing to risk the destruction of another Queen Anne piece, she changed her tactics.

"Levitation, please," she said, and on the instant the bodies of the lovers rose in the air. But instead of floating placidly out of the window which she had opened for the sake of the experiment, they kept colliding with hollow bumps. More than that, there seemed to be an active antagonism between them, for they drew back, while floating in the air, only to charge each other with augmented violence. She called off the levitation and awoke the lovers, who instantly clasped each other's hands.

"Darling, it was lovely," said Miriam. "Though quite unconscious, I knew I was marvellously at one with you! What did we do, Miss Gray? Oh, what are those splinters all over the room?"

Miss Gray diffidently explained the origin of the splinters, and the pronounced hostility of their levitated bodies. A bruise on Miriam's elbow, and the initial discolorations of a black eye for Tim, proved the truth of her depressing narrative.

Further experiments only confirmed the conclusion that was but too manifest, and the lovers returned to London madly devoted to each other, but in the deepest professional dejection. Their values, it seemed sadly certain, so far from being enhanced by conjunction, neatly cancelled each other; instead of the equation "x+x=2x," they must rate themselves "x−x=nothing at all." It was interesting for their sitters to observe the unparalleled violence with which chairs and tables flew into fragments, and many phenomena of that sort could be instantly obtained (their materializations, for instance, were extremely rude to each other), but psychical science made no further progress there. The two could not even hold separate séances simultaneously, for their bodies instantly levitated, escaped out of the windows, and had butting matches over the garden of Belgrave Square, at risk of doing each other serious injury. It was all very disappointing.

To make up for this, the most wonderful news came from Khamshot Island. The new earthquake had shouldered it out of the sea again, and when the water drained off, it was discovered to be a great crater full of oil renewed daily in prodigious quantities by gushers. An American company was formed, and the Khamshot one pound shares, of which Tim had bought so many thousand at the price of a few coppers, mounted to ten pounds. Even at that figure they paid twenty per cent, and Tim, when his wife was holding séances, and he himself was normal, tried to work out what percentage his thousand and seventeen pounds were bringing him in. Being a classical scholar he had no great grasp of mathematics, and his brain reeled in the computation of his dividends. But he dutifully put up beautiful tombstones, not only to his father and mother, but to the hapless cook and the murdered parlour-maid.

This curious and strictly historical narrative has now a strange sequel. Miriam bore one unique baby, who is close on four years old. Incompatible as were the magnetisms of his father and mother, Nature, by some reconciliatory process, seems to have united in him the psychical powers of each of his parents, and last night only I attended a séance given by this stupendous child. He recited in the original Hebrew the first chapter of the book of Genesis, and the Rabbi, Ben Habakkuk, who was present, confirmed the accuracy of every word (the child knowing no more of Hebrew than I do) and said that his pronunciation was of the purest Judaic inflection. He then gave the temperature at St. Moritz, accurately confirmed by this morning's "Times," and, pointing his baby-finger at me, said that

"that man" would live to the very advanced age of ninety-three. So if "that man" retains his memory then, he will record in his palsied handwriting the fulfilment of this remarkable prophecy. We must have patience . . .

The Recent "Witch-Burning" at Clonmel

The following essay clearly shows E. F. Benson's scholarly interest in the supernatural very early in his literary career.

The gruesome ritual murder known as the "Clonmel Witch Burning" was later described as the last burning of a witch in Western Europe. However this was not the traditional case of a solitary misunderstood old woman being persecuted by the local community. Bridget Cleary was a popular, attractive married woman aged twenty-six, leading a typical uneventful life in an isolated village, Ballyvadlea, near the small town of Clonmel in County Tipperary, southern Ireland.

Following a bout of mild illness and delirium, Bridget was systematically stabbed, burned and eventually murdered over a two-day period (14–15 March 1895) by a group of nine people consisting of her husband, father, close friends and neighbours. When police discovered her corpse a week later, not only the local community but the whole world was appalled by the hideousness of the crime. The nine accused were immediately arrested and remanded in prison, to be tried on the capital charge of wilfully murdering Bridget Cleary, and it was widely expected that most (if not all) would merit the death penalty.

It was then revealed to the press and general public that common widespread old beliefs in witchcraft and the supernatural were instrumental in causing this seemingly pointless and barbaric crime. All nine witnesses and participants, especially the main instigator Michael Cleary – Bridget's husband – respected and loved her dearly, and believed they were "saving her soul". They were all positive that an evil spirit or vampiric "changeling" had taken possession of Bridget's body, and their systematic torture and burning of the victim were specifically designed to evict this alien force and permit the young woman's banished soul to return.

Benson realised that the murderers' pagan beliefs were perfectly genuine, and identical to those of innumerable primitive tribes worldwide. He studied all the aspects of this crime very carefully in the weeks leading up to the trial; and published his final opinions in a learned article (now reprinted here for the first time) in the highly-esteemed and influential journal, The Nineteenth Century, *in June 1895.*

There seems to be no doubt, if we examine the motives which appear to have led to this crime, that the ten persons, nine of whom are to be tried on the capital charge of wilfully murdering Bridget Cleary, in the recent case of witch-burning at Clonmel, acted, if we may use such a word in connection with so ghastly a tragedy, honestly, and, as they undoubtedly appear to have believed, for the best.

This cruel and unnatural murder, as at first sight the crime seems to be, was committed deliberately, in cold blood, and throughout the preliminary examination no evidence, however slight, tended to indicate that either the woman's father, her husband, or any of those concerned in it were actuated by anger, malice, or motives of gain. The account given on all sides of the reasons for inflicting the tortures which eventually caused the death of this woman, with whom, apparently, all parties concerned were on the best of terms, are both too fantastic on the one hand, and, on the other, too authentically based on what was at one time a very widely spread superstition, to have been invented. That such a superstition should still be so deeply ingrained in the minds of these peasants as to lead in practice to so horrible a deed seems surprising enough on first sight, and becomes doubly surprising when we consider to how primitive a stratum of belief it belongs.

It appears from evidence given at the committal that Bridget Cleary, in consequence of certain nervous, excited symptoms which she had exhibited, was forced to swallow certain herbs, was beaten and burned, and was repeatedly asked the question, "In the name of God, are you Bridget Cleary?" During this treatment she received the injuries of which she died, but it is, I think, quite clear that the men neither wished nor meant to kill her. All the witnesses, who on important points entirely corroborated each other, agreed in saying that the object of this treatment was to drive out from her body the fairy which had taken possession of it, and which exhibited its presence by her nervous disorder. The woman's own soul would then be able to return.

This is not, then, a case of witch-burning at all. Bridget Cleary, they believed, was possessed, and they tried by violent means to make the invading spirit come out of her. But what is more convincing than the testimony of all the witnesses is the fact that they were acting strictly in accordance with a primitive and savage superstition.

However, the woman died, and we notice that after her death, which I hope to show was entirely unpremeditated and undesired, the prescription as it were having failed to act, these men fell back on another very common superstition. They do not seem ever to have been thoroughly convinced that they had succeeded in driving the spirit out of the woman's body, and when she died they still hoped that it was the possessing spirit they had killed, and believed that the real Bridget Cleary would return, sitting on a grey or white horse, the reins of which would have to be cut to enable her to come back. According to the latest accounts this is still believed, and men wait in the "fairy inhabitance" for the coming of the white horse that will bear Bridget Cleary.

Now, these two superstitions are quite distinct, and must be completely dissociated from one another. The second one only comes into notice after her death, when, being still unconvinced that they had driven the spirit out, the men concluded that she was body and soul a changeling. But while they were burning and beating her it is quite clear they did not think that she was a changeling, but that a fairy had taken possession of her body. This changeling idea is common enough among early superstitious beliefs – though it is somewhat rare for an adult to be changed, the victims being usually children – and is particularly common among Teutonic peoples. But it is that which possessed these men's minds (for truly it was they who were possessed, not she) as they were torturing her which I propose to examine, for it carries us back to a stratum of belief belonging altogether to a primitive and savage era. Also, as I have said, it can, I think, be made evident that this is not a case of witch-burning at all, and ought to be called manslaughter rather than murder.

Primitive man knows nothing about germs, microbes, nerves, or laws of nature, and when the simplest and most evident of natural phenomena, like disease, death, or storm, are brought before his notice, he forms an equally simple and natural theory about them when he refers them, as he invariably does, to the work of some malignant spirit. To the savage, and to primitive religion generally, the idea of a purely beneficent god is altogether foreign. To him life, health, and the supplies of the simpler means of life are the normal conditions of his consciousness; sickness, famine, and death the abnormal, the work of some external agency, obviously malignant. And we therefore find that the earliest conceptions which he forms about the forces over which he has no control represent them as entirely evil, interfering in the normal and beneficent course of events.

That the idea of external agencies being malignant should belong to the earliest stages of religious belief is natural enough, for evil is more readily referred to a cause than its opposite. The destruction of a crop by a thunderstorm, for instance, is easily traceable to the malignant spirit in the thunderstorm; whereas the slow ripening of wheat under the kindly influence of sun and rain is a more subtle phenomenon, because it is a less evident process, the workings of which are altogether hidden from him, and a more natural one, since, on the whole, wheat ripens more often than it fails to do so. Health, again, is naturally regarded as normal, and when disease attacks a town it is obviously due to a demon of disease, an evil hostile power, whereas health cannot be definitely referred to any one cause. Similarly, recovery and convalescence are but a reversion to normal conditions, due to the cessation of the action of the demon who sent the disease.

This theory accounts for the undeniable fact that a purely healing cult finds no place in any system of early religious belief. The primary function of the spirit who is concerned with such matters is, not to remove, but to send disease, though, in a secondary manner, he is regarded as being able to remove it, inasmuch as he can stop sending it. But by degrees, as spirits pass from being considered the enemies into becoming the friends of man, prayer and sacrifice begin to be offered to them, that they may confer directly prosperity and health, and remove evils not necessarily of their own sending. In other words, the secondary function of primitive gods becomes at a later stage their primary function. So, also, the sorcerer, who was the medium between man and the malignant spirit, and who induced him to send disease and death, while remaining his medium, becomes the priest of the god of health and life, and induces him to restore his suppliants to strength.

Now, the earlier of these two stages brings us back to the most primitive and elementary forms of belief, and it is to such a stage of belief that the death of Bridget Cleary is to be referred. Evil agencies are at work about mankind to injure, to destroy, and particularly to take possession, and they must be fought against in all their manifestations. The idea confronts us most prominently and immediately in the methods by which savages deal with disease, and in the functions exercised by their doctors. A few instances will suffice to illustrate this point.

The Patagonians regard all disease as possession by an evil spirit,[1] and in Australia illness used to be considered due to the agency of ghosts of dead men, who gnawed the livers of the living. Similarly, in Spain epilepsy was considered to be possession by a devil, who had to be exorcised;[2] and the same idea is found in the Gospels. Again, among the Veddahs of Ceylon medicine is never administered

[1] Denny's *Folklore of China*.
[2] Tylor, *Anthropology*, pp. 354, 355.

to sick men, but offerings are made to the demon who has sent the disease.[1]

In accordance with this idea, we find that in many savage tribes the priests or sorcerers are the only doctors. In Tonquin, the magicians, who were the medium between the malignant spirits and man, could also drive out disease.[2] In the Bodo and Dhimal tribes of North-east India the exorcists who can drive out disease are priests of the tormenting deity.[3] Again, among the Vancouver Indians the doctor used to pommel his patient in order to drive the spirit out, while all the family beat sticks together, in order to frighten it away.[4] So, too, in Western Australia, the doctor or sorcerer, here, as in so many places, identical, used to run round and round his patient, shouting as loud as he could, in order to frighten the possessing spirit away.[5] In other parts of Australia the idea of death by disease appears to have been incomprehensible. If not the result of violence, it was always attributed to the possession of a spirit, in most cases a demon called "Brewin," who is like the wind, and has to be exorcised. One of the Kurnai, for instance, who cures his father of colic, does so by calling "Brewin" opprobrious names until he quits his body.[6] Again, in Cambodia the Steins make a great noise day and night round the beds of their sick in order to drive the possessing spirit away, and the Dacotas rattle gourds and shout for the same purpose.[7] So, too, in Malabar, when a man was ill, the magicians, who were also the doctors, used to beat drums and basins round him, and blow on trumpets, in order to eject the tormenting spirit.[8] Again, the Hottentots of the Cape of Good Hope used to "shake, jolt, and pommel" a dying man in a final effort to drive the spirit of disease out of him.[9] But invariably, as time advances, these demons, originally malignant, and treated as enemies, to be got rid of by force and hostility, are found to be amenable to gentler means. In New Guinea, for instance, we find that the doctors used to paint their patient all over with bright colours, in order to please the spirit which possessed him, and induce him to come out.[10] He is still malignant, but can be approached in a friendly manner.

[1] *Transactions of Ethnological Society*, N. S., vol. ii. (Bailey).
[2] *Churchill's Voyages*, vol. v. pp. 28, 135, 366.
[3] Tylor, *Primitive Culture*, ii. p. 119.
[4] *Trans. Eth. Soc.*, N. S., vol. iv. p. 288.
[5] Lubbock, *Origin of Civilisation*, p. 25.
[6] Fison and Howitt, *Kamilaroi and Kurnai*, p. 250.
[7] Tylor, *Primitive Culture*, ii. p. 18.
[8] *Churchill's Voyages*, vol. vi. p. 160.
[9] *Sparman's Voyages*, vol. i. p. 310.
[10] Lubbock, *Origin of Civilisation*, p. 25.

A similar custom has been noticed among the Chippewa Indians, who, when an inmate of the lodge is sick, procure a sapling, and tie various coloured threads to it, which are deemed acceptable to the *manito*, who has sent the sickness as a mark of his displeasure.[1] This growing familiarity with spirits originally malignant, and their gradual change towards beneficence, has been traced on the Gold Coast. The natives there used to have a deity called Abroh-ku, a malicious god who lived in the sea-surf, and whose sole functions were to upset the canoes of his worshippers. But when they got to know him better he was found to be friendly, and now he raises the wave which carries them in safety to the shore.[2]

Now, all the details of the death of Bridget Cleary point to the earliest stage in such beliefs, when the possessing spirit was thought to be purely malignant, and had to be forcibly ejected. What caused these men to imagine that she had been taken possession of by a fairy was the exhibition of certain nervous and excited symptoms. This, again, is well paralleled from the folk-lore of other nations. To take a few instances: among the Zulus there are spirits, called *amatongo*, supposed to be the ghosts of ancestors. A man possessed by them exhibits hysterical symptoms, which are regarded as a sign of possession.[3] Among Siberian tribes, children liable to convulsions are looked upon as being possessed by the divining spirit.[4] So, too, the priestess at Delphi passed into an epileptic trance before the oracular spirit descended on her,[5] and the oracle of Trophonios produced hysterical laughter in those who consulted it.

A further confirmation of this theory as applied to this case is shown in the fact that the door was left open, in order that the ejected spirit might pass out. Had these men wished to murder the woman, the very last thing they would have done would be to leave the door open; but such a proceeding is entirely in accordance with the idea they had in their minds. Like the Hottentots, who "jolt and pommel" a dying man in order to drive the spirit of disease out, so they beat and burned this wretched victim of superstition in order to expel the spirit that possessed her. Far from wishing to murder her, they wished to bring her back into the land of the living, and it seems that the remorse with which her husband was seized after her death was perfectly genuine. It is inconceivable that, if they had wished to kill her, they would have left the door open, that they should have allowed their shouts to attract the neighbours, or that

1 Schoolcraft, *Thirty Years with Indian Tribes*, p. 101.
2 Ellis, *Tshi-speaking People of the Gold Coast*, p. 45.
3 Tylor, *Primitive Culture*, ii. 120.
4 *Ibid.* 121.
5 *Pind. Pyth.* iii. 2; *Eur. Iph. Taur.* 1250; *Hyginus Fab.* 53, &c.

ten persons should have been admitted to witness the deed. Terrible and ghastly as the case is, we cannot call it wilful murder.

After her death they were influenced by an entirely distinct and different superstition, one that is commoner to the country, less primitive, and more elaborate. They had been unable to completely satisfy themselves that the soul of the woman had returned to her body, and they fell back on the hope that they had killed, not Bridget Cleary, but a changeling which had been substituted for her. In neither case was murder present to their minds, for in the first stage their design was to bring her soul back to her body, and in the second they believed, and still seem to believe, that it was not she who was dead.

It seems, then, that whatever explanation we accept of the beliefs which led to Bridget Cleary's death, we cannot suppose that it was the purpose of these men to murder her. The account given of the matter by all the witnesses is too fantastic and too uniform not to be genuine. We cannot imagine that they, by pure chance, invented a course of reasoning to excuse their act which entirely tallies with a widely spread and primitive superstition, nor is there the smallest evidence to show that any of those motives which, for the most part, lead to murder were influencing, or had influenced, any of the actors. The story is too strange not to be true.

That such superstitions should still be believed in a Christian country, and by men who by religion are Christians, is appalling enough; but the remedy for such a state of things is not to be found in the hangman's noose, nor yet, perhaps, in the convict prison, and one cannot but feel that it would be in the spirit of that wise and merciful law which ordains that boys under a certain age may not be hanged for capital offences to spare these men, even if they are condemned; for children they are if, as can, I think, be proved, they have acted under the influence of such superstitious fears, as surely as the savage who fears his own shadow is a child. It is as impossible for educated and unsuperstitious people to appreciate the enormous force which such beliefs exercise on untutored minds as it is for a heathen to estimate the immense power of religion in determining the conduct of a man. But if, as this paper has tried to show, they killed, but not with intent to kill, still less should the extreme penalty be inflicted.

Postscript

Soon after Benson's article was published, the Crown Prosecutor withdrew the charge of "murder", and replaced it with "manslaughter". After the trial in July, Michael Cleary was found guilty of manslaughter and sentenced to twenty years penal servitude, and the others received surprisingly lenient much shorter sentences of penal servitude or imprisonment. (The tenth witness, a ten-year-old girl, was not charged.)

It is impossible to surmise how influential Benson's opinions were on the findings of the court, but the contents of his intriguing and fascinating article clearly display his deep interest in witchcraft and ancient lore, and also tell us much about the reasons behind the universal and random persecutions of innocent "witches", women and men, throughout the ages.